Warriors of the Continuum
Part One
ARRIVAL

Warriors of the Continuum

Part One

ARRIVAL

~~Roger P. Heath~~

Copyright © 2025 by Roger P. Heath

This is a work of fiction. Names, characters, places, and incidents either are the product of the author's imagination or are used fictitiously. Any resemblance to actual persons, living or dead, events, or locales is entirely coincidental.

All rights reserved. No part of this book may be reproduced or used in any manner without written permission of the copyright owner except for the use of quotations in a book review.

First Published in 2025 by LifWynn Books
welcome@lifwynnbooks.com
www.lifwynnbooks.com

ISBN 978-1-0684136-1-2

10 9 8 7 6 5 4 3 2 1

Cover design by Ken Dawson
Cover illustrations by Paola Andreatta

To Anne, my wife, who supported my desire to contribute to a world I've known since a child, when I was handed two strange books to read: *Stig of the Dump* and *The Weirdstone of Brisingamen*. And to my mother, who gave me those two books.

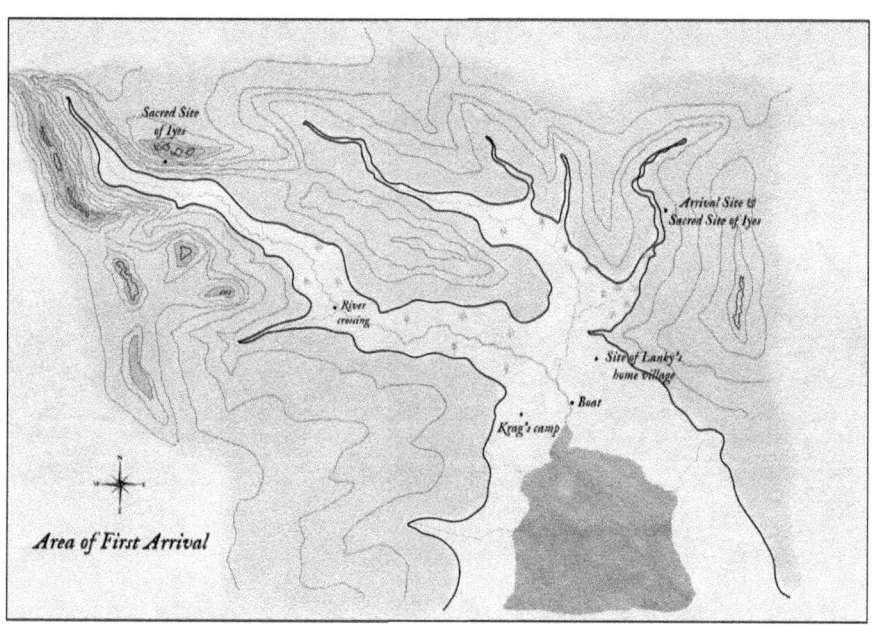

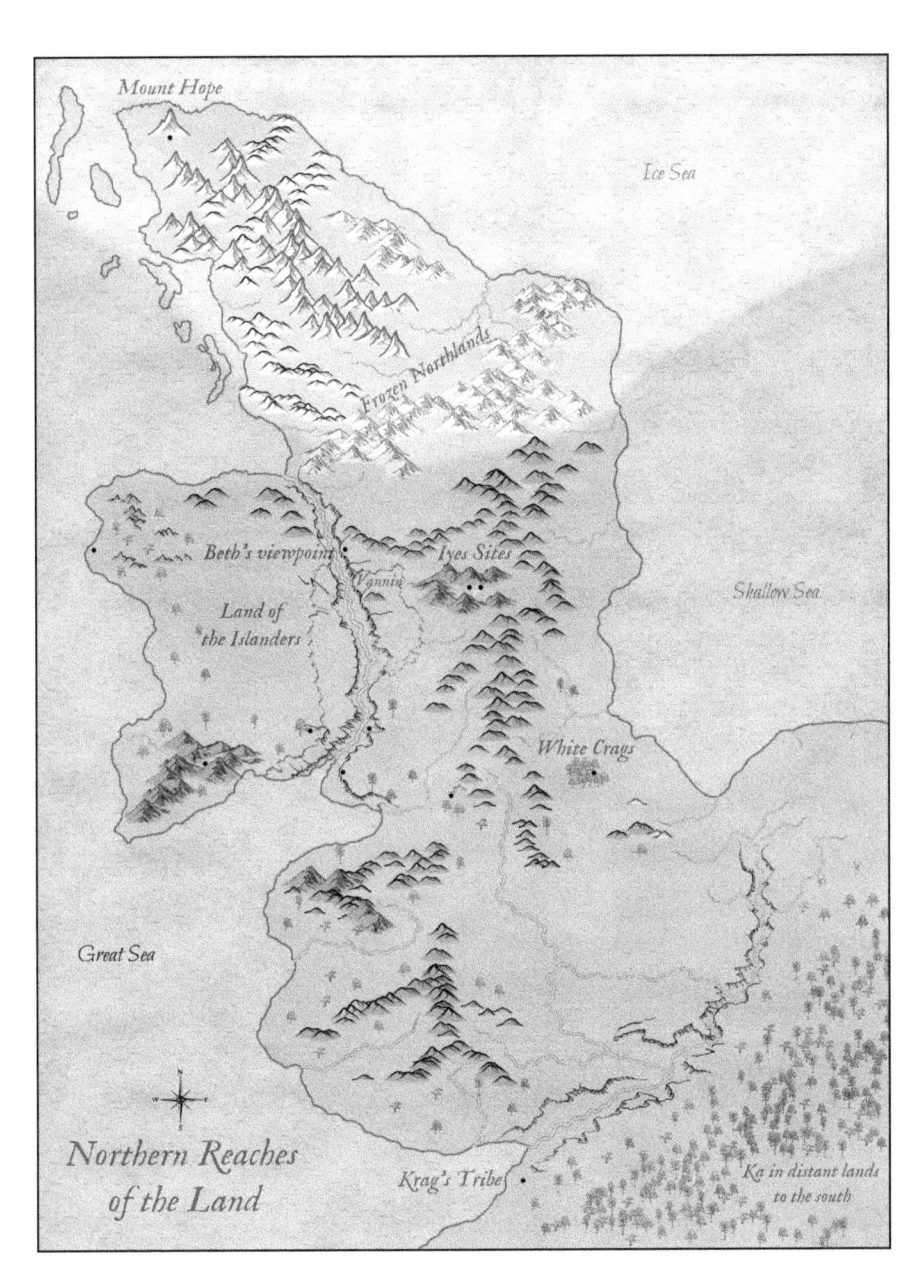

Dramatis Personae

THE TIME OF LANKY & JESSICA

Lanky, apprentice car mechanic, explorer, finder of the Staff
Jessica, trainee firefighter, twin sister of Eshe
Eshe, student, twin sister of Jessica
Beth, soldier, youngest lance corporal in her unit
Erin, college student
Tricia, aspiring artist
Mr. Robert Martin, bookseller, mentor, and family friend to Lanky
Fletcher, local police officer
Mrs. Rebecca Warhurst, Lanky's mum
The burnt man, unknown shaman of Jessica's nightmares
White-haired shaman, servant of the Dark
Alkazar, free-roaming daemon of the Dark, servant of Kaos

ANOTHER TIME OF THE CONTINUUM

Iyes tribe
Bear, leader of the Iyes
Naga, shaman, revered as Mother of the Iyes
River, hunter, sister of Sheba, adopted daughter of Bear
Sheba, skilled weapons maker, sister of River, adopted daughter of Bear
Amber, healer
Spider, scout, hunter
Knuckles, experienced hunter, fighter, Shield
Shorty, experienced hunter, fighter, maker
Svana, scout, hunter, twin sister of Rind
Dune, maker, twin brother of Scorpion
Scorpion, maker, twin brother of Dune
Eagle, hunter, scout

Freya, hunter, scout
Gravel, experienced hunter, fighter, Shield
Rind, leader of the White Crags camp, hunter, fighter
Darius, hunter, fighter

Ka and their allies
Shadow/Longhair, Disciple serving both the Ensi and the Shade
Sy, warrior monk allocated to Shadow
Krag/Bent-Nose, leader of his ragged northern tribe

Further players
Growl, shaman of unknown designs
Streak, black wolf, companion of Growl
Rakana, dragon, one of the Ancients deemed allies of the Ka
Stealth, servant of the Ancient
Cyrene, mage of the Islanders, serving the god Taran
Garrion, daemon in form of a black horse
Fen, daemon in form of a white wolf
Iolaire, daemon in form of an eagle
IY, god of the Iyes, of the Light
Kaos, god of the Ka, of the Dark
Taran, god of the Islanders

PROLOGUE

The shaman adjusted the hood of his jacket, pushing his long white hair, streaked with strands of black, back behind his ears and out of sight. Moving cautiously to the edge of the shadows, he peered through the driving rain to the glowing building beyond. Several groups hurried through the downpour and into the building, but not many were yet leaving. Not those he waited for.

He reached into a deep pocket inside his jacket, his long, bony fingers brushing the cold steel concealed within.

"Keep it simple," his master had said. "Do not alert them to your presence."

His gaunt face twisted into a grimace. Nothing was ever simple, and never when facing one with the power of the A'ven.

"Just a blade?" he had questioned.

"We must remain hidden," his master had snarled. "And the one you have found is weak, isolated. It will be enough."

Peering through the rain, he remembered the thrill of his discovery of a moon past. A chance passing encounter with a girl, a faint feeling of disquiet as he'd walked on, then a stunning recognition of what he'd discovered. He'd turned and followed the girl through the busy streets, until he was sure of what he'd sensed – the jarring aura of an enemy shaman.

"You move now," his master had instructed upon being told of the wondrous find. "Before she joins others."

And so he'd tracked his target and studied her, deciding the time and place to act.

And now here he was, a blade ready for a silent assassination. And the elimination of this shaman, weak or not, would be another lessening of the Light's power in the land. A shiver of excitement ran through him – and a stab of fear at the final words of his master: "Do not fail me."

The shaman licked his thin lips. No, he didn't want to fail. Not only would the rage of his master descend upon him, but also the eye of Kaos. This was a land of fine margins, but the Dark was descending. Gradually, inexorably, this world was moving towards a new world order. All helped by the Dark, pushed and prodded by the Dark. Allies of Kaos in key places, key positions. Allies striving to cleanse the world.

A world to be ruled by Kaos.

No, he didn't want to fail. He wanted his place in that new world as a trusted servant of his god. *Concentrate. Focus.* Slipping back a fraction into the shadows, he watched and waited.

*

Jessica watched Eshe weave a path through the crowd to join her by the foyer entrance. The girl was easy to spot, already standing a head taller than the other kids around her. *Except me.*

"Who chose that movie?" Eshe grumbled as she approached her smiling twin. "It was terrible."

"I thought it was great," Jessica said, her striking brown eyes flickering with amusement. "That assassin kicked ass."

"He had a nice ass," Beth murmured as she joined them.

Eshe glanced at their friend. "And that's your take on the film? He had a nice ass?"

Beth furrowed her brow, pursing her lips. "Mmm … No, not just that. Like Jess said, he was a cool fighter."

Eshe shook her head. "What is it with you two and fighting?" A mischievous glint in her eye, she glanced at Beth. "Why do I need to ask that? You and your army cadet stuff. And you," she continued, turning to her sister, "with your karate. You'd like any old rubbish if it had the slightest hint of a fight. Well, I say this film was boring and predictable. Boy meets girl. Boy is kidnapped. Girl searches for him, killing everybody she meets, and then just as she finds him, boy is killed."

Jessica laughed, playing to her sister's mock irritation. "What's predictable about that?" She tilted her head slightly. "Well, apart from boy meets girl …"

"I'd like a girl to find a boy …" Eshe caught Jessica's eye. "Or a girl that she can ride off into the sunset with. A girl who can carve a path through her future with the one she loves by her side. I'd like—"

Beth laughed. "Sounds like you shouldn't be coming to the movies with us then – you should try to find this boy of yours." She scanned the melee of people leaving the cinema. "Maybe him? Or him? Or – ow!" She held her shoulder where Eshe had punched her. "That hurt."

A wry smile touched Eshe's lips. "I thought you army cadets were tough girls. Seems they take anyone these days."

"Come to my school next week and say that to the others," Beth said with a grin. "They'll be pleased to show you how weak they are."

Laughing, Eshe turned and looked out through the glass entranceway. She groaned. "It's still pouring down out there."

Jessica came to her side. "We've no choice, sis. We've got to catch the next bus, else we'll be sleeping here tonight."

"And I've got to get mine," Beth said behind them. "We better get going. Any plans for next week?"

Eshe turned to Jessica. "You said Tricia and Erin could make it."

"Yep, the full gang will be back. And I'll have passed my test. We can drive out to the beach."

Eshe punched her sister lightly on the shoulder. "Don't count your chickens yet, Jess. The best fail the first time around."

"It's in the bag, sis." She faced Beth. "Sound like a plan?"

"Good for me," Beth said, grinning. "Give me a call when you've passed. We'll sort out a time then."

Moments later, the three passed through the entranceway and out into the rainswept evening darkness.

"See you," Beth called as she hurried off across the car park.

"See you," Eshe and Jessica called in unison.

Tightening the hoods of their jackets, the two sisters left the car park and made their way towards the rainswept road leading to their bus stop.

"It really was a terrible movie," Eshe muttered.

*

He watched as a large crowd exited the building, most turning away from him towards the car park of the cinema, others towards the taxi and bus ranks. His narrowed eyes scanned those few figures walking his way—

He saw his target.

Two tall figures walked towards him. Two girls – two sisters – he recognised even from a distance. Both tall with long dark hair and the same strong features. *Not easy to tell apart,* he thought casually to himself. But if you studied them, yes: a slightly wider nose on that one, a slightly narrower chin on the other.

The shaman smiled. Yes, he knew which would die tonight.

He watched the two girls step over a low fence and into the quiet road beyond. The bright yellow jacket of the target glowed in the streetlight as they walked out of sight to his left. He slipped into a narrow alleyway, then turned right into a poorly lit lane. He walked along at an even pace, keeping to the shadows. The rain grew heavier.

Good.

As he neared the end of the narrow lane, the two girls appeared on the quiet road ahead, heads bowed against the deluge. The shaman strode out into the gloomy light and gradually picked up his pace behind them.

*

Eshe pulled the hood of her bright yellow jacket tighter around her face and picked up the pace. "It's getting heavier."

"No kidding," Jessica muttered, cold drops streaming down her face. "The rain gods have it in for us tonight."

"Gods? You struggle to believe in just one."

"Because why would someone choose to inflict you on me?" Jessica said, a smile playing on her lips. "You gate-crashed my arrival into this world."

"That depends on your point of view, sis. I'd say I was your guardian angel."

Jessica's smile slipped at the haunting memory of being pulled, half drowned, from the sea by Eshe. Tired limbs and an unseen riptide had almost taken her life. *If it hadn't been for Eshe's quick wits.* "Okay, you have me there."

"And who paid for the tickets tonight? Me, your caring sis, the one who has a job at weekends to pay for the other, who disowns her."

"Hmm, maybe you do have your uses."

Eshe laughed, the raindrops bouncing off her hood in the gloom. "I do indeed. And next time, I'll pick the movie."

A warm glow filled Jessica's heart, and she glanced across at her sister, who jumped across a larger puddle on the pavement. *I don't tell her enough how much I love her*, she thought as she caught up with Eshe. *She's my rock. My best friend. She …*

A glacial chill suddenly ran down her spine.

Her chest tightening, she slowed, sickening dread sweeping over her.

What's happening? she thought, struggling to breathe.

A stride ahead in the driving rain, Eshe half turned towards her. "Come on. We—"

"I have you!" growled a triumphant voice behind them.

Jessica screamed and spun around.

A hooded figure slammed into her, his fist driving into her face. Stunned by the savage blow, she stumbled and fell. As she hit the hard ground, a horrific scream rent the air. Chilled to the core, she rolled and sprang to her feet, spinning around to face their assailant. Abject terror froze her as she saw her sister fall to the wet ground, convulsing, a long-handled knife jutting out of her neck.

A hooded figure strode away.

"No!" Jessica cried out, rushing to her sister and dropping to her side. "Eshe!"

Blood rushed from the jagged wound.

Jessica looked up, wild eyes blindly searching the evening gloom. "Help," she rasped, her voice weak with horror. "Please, help."

Her words drowned in the streaming rain.

Limbs ice cold, her mind numb, she staggered to her feet. "Help! Help me! My sister's hurt!"

But no one came.

"Jess," came a gargled sound from the ground behind her.

Jessica stumbled back to her sister, and dropped to her side, desperately scrambling for her phone.

Eshe's hand shot out and grasped her tightly by the arm. "Jess ... no time ... listen ..."

Shaking uncontrollably, Jessica stared wide-eyed at Eshe.

Her sister's eyes seemed to gleam in the darkness. "You ... It needs to be you ..."

"Eshe," Jessica whispered. "Stay still. Please. I need—"

"Save life ... All trapped ... You ..."

A rasping breath left her sister's mouth, then her head slumped to the side.

Anguish tore through Jessica, raw and lashing. "No," she stammered, fumbling with the phone in her hand. "I'll get someone, Eshe. Someone will come."

Her body shook, and as if trapped in a merciless waking nightmare, she somehow made the call. She spoke, but her words were as not her own. Someone responded to her. Help would come, they promised. She ended the call.

As rivulets of rain and tears streamed down her cheeks, she dropped the phone from her shaking hand and stared, unbelieving, at the still face of her sister. "Someone will come," she whispered in a voice barely heard. "They have to come."

She slumped onto Eshe's chest, her whole body wracked with crippling pain. *Don't leave me, Eshe. You can't leave me.*

But cloying tentacles of dread closed around her soul as a brutal truth hammered into her. *I can't save her. I can't save my sister.*

She couldn't breathe.

I've lost my sister.

Raw, convulsive grief ripped through her.

I've lost my beautiful sister.

<--->

The desert wind blowing from the east swept over the moonlit cliff and down into the verdant river valley, where it swirled through the deserted encampment. Did it consider itself a wind of the past, of a long-gone age of the Continuum? No. Because it was also a wind of the future to some. And the wind of the present to those who felt its soft caress.

The warrior, known by his people for his strength and guile, shivered. Eyes narrowed, he scanned the silent camp before turning to Dye-face, the tattooed captain who had stepped to the entrance to the leader's hut. "Where is everybody?"

"Sent away. Now keep quiet and wait," the powerful woman commanded.

The faintest flicker of fear ran through the young warrior. A rare sensation, and one he disliked. *What is going on here?* He glanced at Dye-face, whose eyes locked onto him as though a lion on prey. No point pushing that one. Steadying himself, he forced a smile. "Then I will wait."

He walked away to a broad canopied acacia tree, where he sat, leaned back against the curved trunk, and closed his eyes.

He was awoken to a sharp dig in his ribs. "Up," Dye-face ordered. "Now."

He scrambled to his feet to see the leader himself striding towards him.

"You have served us well," came his leader's soft voice as he approached. "Were it my choice in this matter, I would retain you in service to the tribe. But it seems you are destined for another path. Another wishes your service."

There was silence as the leader paused. "Will you accept another's offer of service?"

A big question, the young warrior thought, his mind racing, *given I've no idea what's happening*. But you didn't ignore your leader's question. "Who is this other, who would have me serve?"

Dye-face gasped and took a step back.

The warrior glanced to his leader. Had his question been too bold?

'I would!' hammered a voice in his head.

Startled, the warrior turned, the voice ringing in his ears—

He froze as he stared into the fiery eye of a tremendous beast. His head and heart were telling him to run – run and never look back – but his legs refused to move.

'I would,' repeated the voice, much quieter this time. *'And still your fears. I am a friend.'*

"What are you?" the warrior whispered.

'A friend,' repeated the beast. *'And someone who needs your aid.'*

The warrior stared at the beast, disbelieving. *This needs my help?* His hands shaking, he turned back to the leader. "You want me to go with that?"

The leader inclined his head. "This is our ally, a supporter of Kaos, and one I support if I am able. But when a request such as this is made, it must be freely accepted by the person chosen."

"And if I say no?"

"Then the ice dragon will leave, and you will stay. But you must choose now."

The warrior's heart hammered in his chest. "Why me?"

"I do not know."

"How long am I needed? One sun-cycle? Five? My lifetime?"

"I do not know."

Frustrated, the warrior faced the dragon. "What aid can I give you?"

'You will be surprised.'

"For how long do you need my service?"

'As long as you prefer.'

The warrior took his chance. "Then one sun-cycle only? No, less, maybe—"

'Done. We leave now.'

"Hold on! I didn't—"

'Follow me.' The dragon swung its massive bulk around and walked away, heading out of the camp.

Shaking, the warrior turned back to his leader, who acknowledged him with a nod of his head, then he too turned and walked away.

"Hold on," the man said, stepping forward. "I need—"

Dye-face moved silently and quickly, blocking access to the leader.

His blade hand instinctively tensed ... *Calm yourself,* he told himself, his heart thumping. *Your leader has spoken.* He gave a short bow and stepped away.

'Come,' thundered the voice of the dragon in his head. *'We leave now.'*

The young warrior stared after the beast, which was entering a clearing to the west of the camp. "What has just happened?" he whispered. "What have I just done?"

You've done nothing yet, a part of him answered. *You don't have to go.*

He stood, fighting a sudden, acute urge to turn and run. He clenched his fists. *No. I can't disgrace myself by fleeing. I can't shame my ancestors.* Steadying his mind and his body, he saw a truth emerging. His leader had been instructed in this. A higher force was in play.

Kaos wished it.

I can't refuse my god.

With a grim acceptance of his duty to his tribe and his god, he found himself walking towards the clearing with the beast. *I will serve. I will serve for the one sun-cycle I offered.*

One cycle ... *Why did I not offer less?*

He sighed and walked on.

<--->

"Are we ready, Mother?" the bear of a man asked.

"No, but the Request must be made," answered the old woman sitting beside him.

The man licked his lips. "Do you think it will work?"

The old woman touched the bracelet on her wrist. *If you answered honestly, what would you say?* She hesitated. *I cannot disappoint him.* "Maybe."

The man shifted uncomfortably yet hope shined in his eyes. "We need them."

"And they will need us – this will not be easy." The old woman settled herself, relaxing her mind. "It is time. Protect me. Nothing should cross the boundary until they appear."

"It shall be so," the man said, then with one final glance back at the shaman, he walked out of the ring.

The shaman sat cross-legged, her hand on the bracelet, feeling for the Land's energy. It was here. It was now. Their Story was about to come alive.

'I am ready,' she pulsed to her god, IY.

I. ARRIVAL

CHAPTER ONE

Was an opportunity missed from the very start? Even now, I cannot answer.

Darkness enveloped her. She could see nothing. But she knew they were coming for her.

This is a dream. You know it's a dream. Wake up!

But as with all the worst nightmares, you can never wake up before the terror arrives.

"What can I do?" Jessica pleaded. "Why are you doing this?"

"You are the Guardian," came a quiet, silky voice. "You know what to do."

"I don't!" she cried, engulfed by a cold dread of what was to come.

"Well," came the voice, "then you know what happens next."

Faint howls drifted in from the fetid gloom.

It's them. They're here.

She turned and ran, but her feet sank into thick, swampy ground and she stumbled. "No!" she cried, desperately trying to pull her feet free from the cloying mud. "I can't let them catch me again!"

"Then tell me where the Staff is," came the voice. "I can aid you."

"I don't know anything about a Staff!" she cried, still fighting to pull free. "Help me! Don't let them catch me!"

Her heart froze as she heard wild, discordant shrieks from the approaching masses. "Please, you must help," she cried, fighting with all her strength to escape.

"Call the Warriors. Let them aid you."

A wave of despair swept through her. *I'm not going to get out of here.* "I don't know these Warriors! Why do you keep asking me this? I don't know—"

"You are the Guardian. You know all."

As she continued her frantic struggles, an indistinct shape appeared before her, slowly growing in size and morphing until a single yellow eye hung in the blackness before her.

A malevolent eye that seemed to burn into her soul.

"No! Why do this? What do you want from me!"

"Just the Staff, Guardian, and then you will be free."

Through the crushing despair, a wave of anger flooded through Jessica. "How many times do I need to say this?" she spat. "I don't have it!"

She recoiled in sheer horror as the other appeared before her. The burnt man. The man with a ravaged, scorched face, strips of rotten flesh hanging loose down his cheeks, eyes burning with white fire, and his chest torn apart, a black haze floating in the gaping hole.

"Then, we shall meet again tomorrow night. But first, die again …"

In the sallow light of the yellow eye, the seething morass of ghostly creatures of the Dark arrived, and she screamed as they flowed around her, over her, raking at her body, tearing at her mind. As the seething, clawing horde tore into her, her whole body exploded with mind-numbing pain. She tried to scream …

But her throat was ripped apart.

Wake up! Please wake up!

"Jess! Wake up!" came a distant voice.

As the yellow eye disappeared behind the cocoon of death, she felt herself drowning in a sea of blood. *Help me! Please help me!*

A sharp pain ripped across her cheek.

Gasping, she snapped open her eyes.

Light flooded in.

"Thank God," a voice said beside her.

Beth!

Jessica lay on the floor, sucking in deep lungfuls of air.

"You okay, Jess?" Beth said, putting her hand on her shoulder.

"No," she panted.

Beth gently squeezed her shoulder. "Sorry I hit you, but that was some nightmare. Thought you needed to break out of it."

Breathing hard, Jessica lifted her throbbing head and slowly pulled herself to her feet to perch on the edge of her bed. "Sorry," she panted, looking across at her friend. "Didn't mean to scare you."

"Don't sorry me, girl," Beth said, rubbing a bleary eye. "That didn't look pleasant. The same nightmare?"

Fighting to steady her breathing, Jessica nodded.

Beth pushed a strand of tangled dark hair from her face. "You sure you're okay?"

"Give me a moment ... I'll be fine."

As her breathing settled, her terror slowly ebbed. *That wasn't nice. Not nice at all.*

Beth sat on her haunches, tilting her head as she studied her friend's face. "The same nightmare as last night?"

Jessica's sigh was pained. "Pretty much."

Beth frowned, absently rubbing the small scar on her cheek. "Much as I hate doctors, maybe you should head into town later. See if there's someone available to help you with something to ... you know, to sleep better?"

"Maybe," Jessica said, licking her dry lips. "But right now, I need a drink – and maybe something for my splitting headache."

Beth slowly climbed to her feet. "Wait there, I'll fetch you something."

As she walked to the door, Jessica spoke in a quiet voice after her. "Don't tell the others, Beth. I don't want them to worry about this now."

Beth glanced back. "Might be better if we did."

"And tell them I'm dreaming of monsters trying to kill me? No, I can imagine where Trish would go with that. Leave it for now. I don't want to mess up their holiday too."

Beth studied her for a moment, then nodded. "Okay, be back in a minute." She walked out of the room.

Jessica leaned forward and put her head in her hands. *These hellish nightmares.* Why now? On their annual get-together. *When I should be relaxing with my best friends.* And where had it come from? What had triggered such a foul dream?

She sat quietly, holding her head until Beth returned with a glass of water and a pill.

"Here you go. The others aren't up yet." Beth gave a wry smile. "And I guess I wasn't planning to be either after last night."

Jessica grimaced. It had been a late night again, as always on their first few nights back together, before the collective wisdom kicked in to remind them that some sleep was quite useful. *Sleep. Now that* would *be nice.*

She took a drink of water, then looked at the pill. She sighed. A walk in the fresh air would be a better idea. She placed the pill on her bedside table.

"You want to talk about it?" Beth asked, sitting on the edge of her bed.

Jessica sighed "No use. It was the same as last night – and the nights before."

"Some dude asking you about a staff before killing you?"

"That's about it – it's not pleasant."

Beth pursed her lips. "I used to dream about axes."

Jessica arched a brow. "That's slightly random."

Beth shrugged.

"Axes," Jessica muttered, forcing a smile. "Well, that suits you down to the ground, Corporal."

"Lance Corporal still," Beth corrected her.

"Whatever," Jessica said, still trying to shake the gruesome visions from her mind. "I guess you and your army folk all dream about your shiny weapons."

Beth laughed. "Not if I can help it. I prefer my other dreams." Jessica raised her eyebrow. "And anyway," Beth continued, "we don't get issued stone axes these days."

"Why were you dreaming of stone axes?"

"Why are you dreaming of a guy trying to buy a staff off you?"

"He's not … ahh." Jessica grabbed a pillow and threw it at Beth.

Grinning, Beth caught it.

As a silence fell, Beth's smile slipped. "You sure you're okay, Jess?" she said softly. "Is it …" She fell silent.

Jessica's stomach lurched. "My sister?" she said, her voice hushed. "Maybe …"

An image flashed into her mind – her sister's blood-soaked body on the ground, a knife in her neck, and a hooded man striding away.

And a memory of her own screams.

I screamed, but I didn't help her. I froze. I moved too late.

No one knew why it had happened, or who had done it. The killer was never found.

Eshe had been murdered. Executed on a dark winter's evening. Gone from her life forever. *And I wish I'd listened to her. I wish I understood what she wanted to tell me.* She fought to stem the rising panic, to push back the horrors of that night. *Three years now, but it still feels as yesterday.* She forced herself to draw deep, steady breaths. *Remember how she lived. Remember the joy, the laughter, her wonderful spirit. We were as one. We are still as one.*

"Jess?" came Beth's quiet voice.

Jessica looked up. "I miss her so much, Beth, and there isn't a day I don't wish I could turn back time and change something, stop that godforsaken killer in his tracks. But I know she lives on. Somewhere, my beautiful sister lives on."

Beth leaned over and wrapped her arms around her.

Jessica hugged her back, feeling the love and warmth of her friend's embrace.

She held her for a moment, then pulled back. "It hurts. It really hurts. But these nightmares …" She shook her head. "I don't know … I don't think it's because of that."

Beth's regard was touched with compassion. "I've seen what you've been through, Jess, what your family's been through. I've seen the pain. We've all felt the pain. She was part of us. One of the gang." She drew a quiet breath, then put her hand on her shoulder. "These nightmares … I don't know, Jess, but I think you should speak to someone about them. Just in case."

In case they're because I blame myself for not saving my sister. Not calling for help faster. "I will. If they continue, I will." She saw Beth's eyes narrow slightly. "I promise."

Beth squeezed her shoulder. "Good." She studied Jessica's face. "You want to rest awhile?"

"Think I'll head out for a walk to clear my head." Jessica forced a smile. "Need to play back those wondrous dreams."

"You sure?"

"I'm sure. Better than popping pills. You want to come?"

"Tell you what," Beth said, climbing to her feet. "You go clear your head, and I'll rouse the others and get a hearty breakfast on the go. How's that sound?"

"Sounds good." Jessica stood, reached for her clothes, then paused. "And don't tell the others. I'll be fine. I promise."

Beth held her gaze. "Fine. But don't hold anything from me, okay? I'm here to help."

"I know. I couldn't have got here without you." *I wouldn't be here without you.*

Beth smiled. "Okay. Go enjoy your walk and get ready for a 'Beth breakfast' feast."

*

Jessica headed up the trail from their cottage and into the hills, the sun just rising above the eastern range into the blue sky of the warm summer morning. It was a quiet spot, reached by a narrow road up from the village centre. It offered a perfect base for their annual catch-up, their third since they'd finished school. After three days of hiking and canoeing, they'd planned a quieter day today. And after last night's poor sleep, she needed it.

She strode up the track, no other folk visible at this early hour. A few tourists used the trail as a circular route into the hills and back to the village, but most stayed close to town, sticking to their creature comforts. *Their loss. Keeps it quieter for those who like to explore.*

Or to clear their head.

As she walked on, drawing in deep lungfuls of the cool morning air, the foggy memories of her nightmare drifted away, leaving swirling thoughts of her wonderful sister caressing her mind. *We were always there for each other.* Always there through the ups and downs, always there to encourage the other to reach for their dreams. *And each encouraging the other to beat the boys.* She smiled. *We always won, sis. We kicked their asses.*

She looked up to the trail ahead. "Look through my eyes, sis," she whispered. "Let's go on a walk together."

Jessica strode on easily, the sounds of the water rushing through the depths of the steep ravine to her left. Recent rains had flooded the gorge, and she could imagine the white water in the rapids below. Entering a sun-dappled wood, she walked on, listening to the birds chattering in the trees and scrub as they foraged for their morning breakfast, until at last, the trail reached the crumbling stone bridge over the river.

She paused to look at the water as it bounced around the rocks on its way to the first of the falls, where it tumbled in a glittering spray to the pool below. She could hear the noise from the next fall below as it knifed its way into the gorge. But this was an insignificant pimple in the greater landscape around her, itself forged from the erosive power of water, and, more impressively, from ice. Her geology teacher, Mr. Acke, had brought them here on school trips, describing the ice sheets that had come and gone over thousands of years as the ice ages carved out their legacy. *A tremendous power to have created this,* she thought as she looked up at the crags around her.

She took a last look around, then began the walk back down to the cottage. As she reentered the woods, she saw glimpses of old mine-workings on the slope to her left. How many people had once worked here? *How many —*

A tremendous crashing sound exploded on the slope above. She jumped and spun around to see a dishevelled man launch himself out of the bushes, shouting aggressively as he rushed towards her. As the attacker reached her, her years of training with her sensei kicked in. She crouched, then thrust upwards, twisting, using the man's momentum to throw him off the trail and down the slope. She watched, stunned, as he tumbled twice before disappearing off the edge of the cliff into the gorge below.

A flock of startled birds swept up from beyond the cliff edge, their urgent, piercing calls mimicking her own shock. *What the hell just happened?* She stood, shaking, staring at the space where the man had disappeared. *He attacked me, that's what happened.*

Nerves stripped raw, Jessica reached for her phone, and with shaking fingers dialled for help.

A calm voice soon answered. "What service do you require?"

"Err, police, I think. I've just been attacked."

"And is the attacker still there?"

"No, I pushed him off a cliff."

"Could you repeat that, please?"

"Yes, I've pushed him off a cliff."

There was a moment of silence, then: "Please tell me your location."

"I'm on the path up to Low Bridge, just outside the village. But I don't want to stay here. I don't feel safe. I'll head back to my cottage at Hows End – you know, the old one at the end of the lane."

After answering another couple of questions, she gave the number of the cottage and hung up. Her hands still trembled as she looked across to the edge of the ravine where the man had disappeared. Where *her attacker* had disappeared.

The sidling doubt touched the edge of her mind. *He did attack me … didn't he?*

She glanced back to the trail. *I should go.*

But she didn't move. She looked back to the cliff edge. *I can't just walk away.*

Girding herself, she slowly walked back to the point she'd seen the man drop. As she cautiously neared the edge, she heard a voice.

"Yes, the bloody maniac attacked me on the path and threw me over the edge! She must be mad! It was lucky I landed in this tree, but as I told you, now I'm stuck."

There was a pause in speaking, and then: "Yes, halfway to Low Bridge. She's mad."

Jessica grimaced. *I'm mad? It was you who attacked me.*

The flicker of doubt grew.

"I'm going to try to get up," the young man continued, "but I don't think I can. Can't reach the top ledge. I'm going to call John. He'll bring a rope."

Good, Jessica thought, her breathing finally slowing. *We need help.*

"Yes, I bloody do want this followed up!"

A silence fell.

She stared at the cliff edge. What had appeared to be a madman didn't now sound like a madman.

But he had come charging out of the bushes at her.
Hadn't he?
Or had it been more of a stumbling charge?
She took a cautious step to the edge. "Hello?"
Silence.
She peered over the edge.

A severe face topped with tousled hair stared back at her. A young man, maybe just younger than her. Was a boy a better description? When did a boy become a man? Either way, he sat within a tangle of branches of a stubby tree growing out from the cliffside.

"Hello," she said.

Dark clouds gathered in his face.

"Are you okay?"

He scowled. "Do I look like I'm okay?"

"Why did you attack me?"

He looked up at her, open-mouthed. "Attack you?" he finally spluttered. "Why the hell did you attack *me* and throw me off the cliff? I'm supposed to be at work in five minutes. John will go mad. You're mad!"

She bristled. "You appeared out of nowhere, screaming at me – what the hell were *you* doing?"

"I bloody fell over and only just stayed on my feet until you decided to pick me up and throw me here. I could have been killed!"

Jessica glared at him, then the truth of his words filtered through her anger. A cold shiver ran down her spine. *He could have been killed.* "Okay, maybe I've made a mistake here, but you were a goddamned fool to come barging into the path like that. How did you expect me to react?"

"To not throw me down here for a start!" he exclaimed, scowling up at her. He shook his head. "Look, I wasn't doing anything apart from trying to get to my work and … well, falling over, okay? Can you please get help? I don't fancy learning to fly."

A loud creaking noise broke across them. The tree he sat in dropped a foot. "Crap!" they both shouted out in unison.

"Can you move?" Jessica breathed, her heart pounding.

The young man clung tightly to a branch of the tree. "No, I don't think that would be smart right now. Fetch help."

Yes … Help … "Hold on," she said, her voice wavering. "I'll be back as quick as I can."

She scrambled to her feet and raced towards the trail.

Racing down the track to the cottage, she lengthened her stride, her long legs covering the ground effortlessly. Running was a thing she did very well. Admitting to others she was wrong was much harder. And in this case, she may have got this one slightly wrong.

Maybe, she answered to herself, *but what* had *he been doing?* You didn't just charge out at people unannounced. He was a bloody fool.

And you? You almost killed him. And he's still not safe.

A few breathless minutes later, she arrived back at the cottage and rushed in through the front door …

And collided with Tricia.

"What the …" Tricia exclaimed, "Where have you been?"

"A slight problem," Jessica wheezed. "Do we have rope?"

Tricia frowned. "Yes, we have rope. Beth was climbing yesterday, remember?"

Yes, of course, we've got rope – stay calm.

"What's happened, Jess?"

"Lad fell over cliff. Or sort of … pushed over. But don't have time to explain – get the rope. And get Beth!"

As Tricia rushed to the back of the cottage, Jessica grabbed a pair of gloves. Tricia returned quickly with Beth, each carrying a set of ropes.

"Come on!" Jessica shouted. "Let's go!"

"I'm still in my pj's!" Beth exclaimed. "What the heck is going on?"

"A lad on the trail … I bumped into him, and he fell. He's stuck in a tree and it's moving. We have to get him out."

"What!" Beth exclaimed. "Well, at least let me get my boots on."

The three left the cottage just as a bleary-eyed Erin appeared downstairs. "What's going on?" she said to an empty house.

*

Within minutes, they were heading back up the trail. Slowed by the weight of rope, it took ten minutes to reach the fall site. As Jessica hurried to the edge, she heard a voice. No, she heard the dulcet tones of someone quietly singing. Badly. She couldn't catch the tune. She reached the cliff edge and looked over. The now familiar face glanced up at her, ceasing his dissonant crooning.

He scowled. "You took your time."

She bristled. "Well, we can wait for your mate John and the police to arrive, or we can drop this rope down to you?"

"Just drop the rope."

"Do you know how to tie it off?"

"I'll figure it out, just drop me the rope."

Shaking her head, Jessica turned to her friends. "Let's just get him up."

Beth found a robust-looking tree and looped one end of the rope around its trunk and secured it. They fed the other end down to the stranded man. "You sure you know what you're doing with the rope?"

Silence greeted them as the young man quickly wrapped the rope around his waist, tying it off with a sliding knot before climbing to a standing position. "Okay. Pull me—"

He cried out as the tree unzipped itself from the cliff face and careered down towards the rushing water.

Jessica froze, her heart in her mouth, as the man fell towards the river. The rope jerked as it snapped tight, and she winced as he swung into the cliff face, catching his face and leg on a jutting rock. She waited for the snap of the rope and the terrible cry from the lad as he fell into the raging torrent below.

But the rope held.

"Are you alright?" she called down, her heart hammering in her chest.

"What do you think?" came the rasped reply.

"We'll pull you up!"

Tricia glanced at her, fear in her eyes. "I'm not sure we can," she whispered.

"We have to bloody well try," Jessica grated.

Standing a few feet from the edge, she pulled on her gloves, then took up the strain. Tricia and Beth took position behind her, each grasping a section of rope.

"Gloves," Beth muttered, noticing her friend's bright yellow pair. "Thanks for bringing ours."

"We're about to start pulling you up," Jessica shouted, leaning back to ready herself. "Do you understand?"

A clear yes came back. They all took the strain and began to haul.

"He's heavy," Tricia groaned as the rope began to move.

Jessica grunted as she hauled in a foot of rope. She was strong – stronger than the other two – but Tricia was right, it was a fair weight to pull, and to hold. *But we have to get him up.* "Another. One, two, three, pull!"

Another step and another exclamation from Tricia.

"One, two, three, pull! We'll need another five or six to get him to the top."

The rough, gravelly growl of a motorbike came from down the trail.

"Help's coming. Keep going. One, two, three, pull!" Jessica's arms burned as she hauled on the rope. *I won't let this go. Just hold—*

The rope suddenly stuck fast.

He's reached the edge!

The rope jerked. The sound of crashing rocks echoed off the cliff.

"What are you doing?" she shouted. "Hold still, you fool!" Leaning further back, she called out to Trish and Beth. "Don't you dare let this rope slip."

"Is he trying to get us to drop him?" Tricia yelled.

As the rattling growl of the motorbike echoed into the clearing, the rope twisted again. Jessica breathed a sigh of relief as she saw two people arriving on a sleek red bike. The bike stopped, and the man at the back, clearly a police officer, jumped off. "Thanks for the ride, John," the officer called as he ran towards them. "Saved me a long climb."

"You can buy me a beer later," the other man called back, climbing off the bike.

"I think we've got him to the edge," Jessica panted as the officer arrived. "But I can't hold on any longer."

The officer, a young man sporting a goatee, ran behind her and grabbed the rope. She felt him take the strain. "Thank God," she gasped, stepping away.

"Take a look at what's on the end, John," the police officer instructed.

The stouter man, John, came into view and walked to the edge, carefully peering over. Her arms burning, Jessica joined him.

"That's a fine mess you've got yourself into," John said. "You okay?"

"Fine, it's just that …" The lad seemed distracted.

"It's just what? That you're dangling over a thirty-foot drop and polluting the river with your bleeding flesh? Or that you're hanging there wondering what's for tea? Give me your hand."

The man reached down for the young lad's arm.

Jessica watched as the lad – Lanky, she'd heard him called – hesitated, his gaze seemingly fixed on the rock face. *What the hell is he doing?*

"There's some tired women here holding your sorry arse out of trouble," John muttered. "Give me your arm."

Lanky sighed and looked up. He smiled at John. It transformed his face.

An easy face to look at, some might say, Jessica thought. Not the face of a madman.

"Sorry, John," Lanky said lightly, reaching up and grabbing John's wrist. "Think I'll be late for work today." He was quickly hauled up and over the lip of the rock face.

As Jessica breathed a huge sigh of relief, Tricia and Erin collapsed to the ground, breathless.

Moments later, the police officer came to her side. "Not sure how this came about," he said, "but reckon we'll have plenty of time to talk about it back at the station. Take a breather for now." He walked over to Lanky. "You okay?"

"Yeah. Seems I'm in still one piece." The lad glanced over to her and scowled. "No thanks to the crazy woman over there."

"Guess I'll find out a little more soon enough," Fletcher, the police officer, said, rubbing his short goatee. "You'll need to visit the clinic first to check on those cuts." He turned to John. "Could you take our wounded warrior down to see Hazel at the clinic?"

John grunted. "As long as he's quick. There's work to be done." He gestured to Lanky. "Let's get moving. Time is money."

Jessica watched as they walked across to the bike and quickly mounted. Within moments, the bike headed down the trail.

"A story to be told here, I think," said a voice to her side. She turned and looked into the sharp eyes of the sergeant. "I suggest we walk down to your place and have a natter along the way. I think I'll be ready for a cup of tea when we get there. That sound good to you?"

Knowing that this wasn't really a question, she nodded. The police officer smiled, then walked away, stopping by the edge of the cliff and pulling out a small notebook.

Her jaw tightened. *Well, this day has started well.* She glanced at the steep slope where this stranger Lanky had so suddenly appeared. Just what had he been doing up there? Nothing good, she suspected.

But you almost killed him.

She stood alone with her thoughts for a while, still trying to understand what had happened.

"You okay?" Beth murmured by her side.

"Seems to be the question of the day," she muttered.

"The sergeant's ready to head down with us. You good to go?"

Jessica sighed, then nodded. They walked over to the waiting sergeant.

As they all walked off down the trail, Jessica glanced back towards the cliff edge. *Why did he hesitate down there? What was he looking at?* She exhaled softly. *Don't go there.* The guy was obviously deranged. *Best that we never meet him again.*

CHAPTER TWO

No one knows but I, who wrote this here and why.

Clinging onto John as they drove down the trail through the woods, Lanky berated himself for choosing to head out earlier that morning. *Why did I decide to do it? You said yesterday was going to be the last time.* But he'd been unable to ignore the persuasive call of the dawn's clear sky. A good hunting day, he had told himself as he picked up his logbook and headed out into the mild summer morning. *Just one last time.* Around halfway up to Low Bridge, he had swung off the track, heading off into thicker woodland upslope. Then, taking out his logbook and noting the time, he'd begun exploring.

But after another long, tiring search, he'd realised it was yet another fruitless mission.

And realised he'd be late for work. Again. His boss was a good man, but a hard taskmaster. Arriving late for the second time in two weeks would mean trouble.

And I found trouble.

He winced at the memory. He'd been scribbling notes in his logbook as headed back down the hill, when, scrambling through heavy undergrowth and scrub, he'd tripped on a low branch. Crying out in surprise, he'd been propelled into the open trail, and unable to stop himself, he'd collided with a young woman on the trail. Before he knew it, the woman had attacked him, flipping him into the air, sending him rolling down the slope and tumbling over the cliff edge, his stomach lurching as he fell.

The tree had saved him.

Just.

Sitting on the bike now, it was finally sinking in how close to a fatal fall he'd come. What had that woman been playing at? *She was mad. Crazy.*

The bike slowed and rumbled as it crossed a cattle grid. Looking up, he saw them pass the 'new' cottage on their left – new around here being anything less than around forty years old. It was built from a local stone, a hardened volcanic ash, a remnant from an ancient time in this landscape's intricate history … Despite the lingering shock of his fall, he gave a wry smile at his wandering thoughts. *Seems Robert's teachings are deeply ingrained in me.*

Robert. A friend of his family. The one responsible for getting him hooked into this obsession. *Which you quite happily took on and ran with, remember?* That was true, but see where it had led. *To problems for me and for those around me. Like mum …*

He checked his watch – and grimaced. His mum would be up. Which was a blessing, of course, the worst of her illness now behind her, but he didn't want to worry her with talk of his narrow escape. *Get yourself fixed up and get to work.* He could then treat it as just a normal day when he got home.

Except …

His heart beat a little faster.

Except, despite the horror of the fall, there'd been something else. As he'd been hauled up the cliff face, a piece of rock under his hand had come loose, triggering a small avalanche of rocks. Reaching out to steady himself, he'd spied a glint from a patch of brighter rock, and glancing over, he'd seen the writing – carved letters in the rock face, just below the edge of the cliff. When he'd brushed away a layer of moss from the smooth, fine-grained patch of rock, a strange inscription had appeared:

No one knows but

i

Who wrote this here and

y

The style of the lettering appeared relatively modern and the carving very good – whoever'd done it was a skilled sculptor. But there'd been no time to make sense of what he was seeing before John had shouted down to him. Reluctantly, he'd allowed himself to be lifted free.

What had he found? Not the rough graffiti of kids. Someone with talent had carved it. But who? Some visiting artist leaving their mark, happy that only they knew it was there? Or someone who'd somehow fixed it to the cliff face as some form of token or memorial? He sighed. It was likely he'd never know. And even if he did, what was its importance to him? *It's probably like all I've ever found – nothing of any value.*

His mood darkened. He needed to give this up. Because he couldn't ignore what had just happened; his obsession had almost cost him his life.

And the dreams, the voices? *No, don't go there. Enough.*

He touched the graze on his face. *Fix yourself up and get back to work. Ignore everything else.*

He looked up as the bike picked up speed and entered the village. *But that writing ...*

*

Humming along to the track playing in one ear, Lanky gave a quarter turn on the bolt and completed what he hoped was his last job of the day. It had been a long day. A very long day. He had told his boss, John, he would work later to cover the time he'd lost earlier; it was Friday, and there were cars to be collected in the morning. His escapades couldn't ruin John's promises to his customers. *And you don't get money for nothing.*

He walked out from under the car and hit the button to lower the vehicle to the ground.

"You done?" John growled from the spartan office to the side.

Lanky pulled his earphone free from his left ear. "Yep. That one was a breeze."

"Lucky for you, son," John said as he stood and walked out towards him. "Means you may get some sleep tonight."

The words he'd been waiting for; he could finally head home. And although it was late, he knew he'd escaped lightly. "You still more to do?" he asked John, wiping his hands on a clean rag.

"Always more to do," his boss said. "But I'll be out of here soon." John opened the door of the car and climbed inside. A moment later the engine fired up, revving loudly. Just as quickly, John shut it off and climbed back out. "Good job," he said, clapping Lanky on the back. "Mrs. Tryell will be pleased."

Lanky smiled. "Then I'll be off."

After packing away his tools, he walked over to a chair and grabbed his bag. "Have a good weekend and see you Monday. On time," he added with a smile.

"I'm sure you will."

Lanky made to turn away, but John's hand stopped him. "I know you like your search for buried treasures, lad, but don't let it get in the way of my business. You're a good, honest lad – it would be a shame to lose you." He left enough of a pause to let the message sink in, then his expression lightened. "After all, who would make our tea?"

Lanky smiled. "Don't worry. Tea boy here will be on time from now on. Somebody needs to get you from behind your desk from time to time."

"Get out of here," John said, waving his hand. He walked back towards his office. "And say thanks to your mum for the cake. Went down a treat with my cuppa."

Lanky grinned and walked out of the garage; his mum would be pleased.

Tired, but relieved, he walked out into the dark of the late evening, a light rain spattering his face. No damage had been done to John's promises to his customers. He felt the throbbing cuts on his face. And no stitches needed to patch him up. *This day could have been a lot worse.* He walked on up the narrow lane, the guitar riff of the last track playing in his head.

But as he walked on up the low incline to the centre of the village, slowly, inexorably, his thoughts began to drift. He enjoyed the work at John's, but that was not the end game for him. The draw of college was growing stronger, and with his mum now back to health, it had become a real possibility. But should he do it?

Probably, because that question had become more and more insistent.

'But what about the axes?' came the calm, ethereal voice in his head.

He immediately slowed, then came to a stop. He waited, wondering if he would hear anything else – but nothing. He glanced around, suddenly self-conscious. Did anyone see him standing alone, listening out for voices? But he saw only the pooled shimmering of the streetlights reflected off the wet pavement, and on the opposite side of the lane, a couple of people, hurrying on their unknown journeys before the heavier rain came and forced them inside. He shook his head. It seemed the more he tried to delay the decision, the more the stress grew. *And the more I talk to myself. Or hear voices ...*

"Then make the decision," he muttered with sudden frustration.

He drew a deep breath, trying to calm himself down. *You know, Lanky. You know what you should do.* Because how many days in the cold and the rain had he spent out and about in these hills, searching, endlessly striving to find these axes of power?

Which, he now realised, didn't exist.

'They do. You know they do.'

"I don't know anything, damn you!" he instinctively muttered. He quickly looked around again, fearing that someone would be standing accusingly before him. "I'm not crazy," he breathed as if they were.

He waited, half expecting that the voice would reply.

Silence.

He sighed. He was tired. Tired of the search. And his mind wouldn't rest. *This search has gone on long enough. Move on.*

He started up the hill, searching for a tune to match his mood. But it seemed his mood wasn't interested. As he reached the crest of the hill and the junction with the high street, his eyes caught the glow of the village bookshop, its warm light breaking the shadows cast by the worn canopy above.

The bookshop where it had all begun.

His thoughts drifted back ten years, to a time before the obsession had overcome him.

*

On this particular day ten years ago, Lanky had walked, whistling badly, into the shop to return a book he'd borrowed only two days before. Telling a story about a boy wizard, it had proved impossible to put down until he'd read the last chapter three times. He had been surprised to hear one lady on television arguing that it poisoned young kids' minds to give them stories on magic and fantastical creatures, and that nothing good would ever come of it. He thought she was wrong; he'd heard of an ancient, epic poem for adults, written over a thousand years ago by some long-forgotten storyteller, which told tales of heroic deeds, monsters, dragons, and the like. It was still remembered, still told, today – but who would remember that lady on the TV?

Lanky scanned around the quirky shop. Although it was known as a bookshop, the ground floor was crammed with antiques and bric-a-brac, and Mr. Martin was most often tucked away at his desk in the corner, where he could both work and serve customers without blocking them from wandering around the tall, improbably stacked shelves.

On this day, Mr. Martin couldn't be found downstairs, so Lanky climbed the winding metal stairwell to the upper floor of the shop, where he caught sight of the top of Mr. Martin's head between the shelves of books. He decided not to call out, as Mr. Martin often balanced precariously on the lower shelves to place high-up books. He walked to the end of the aisle where he would be seen.

"Oh, hi there, Sam. Hold on a second and I'll be right with you."

Sam. Only Lanky's mum and Mr. Martin still called him Sam. Although his father was long gone, the nickname he'd fondly bestowed on his son continued to be worn by Lanky as a badge of pride. His father had left the family, but not Lanky's heart.

Lanky glanced at the haphazardly stacked row of books next to him, a handwritten sign scribbled on the shelf: *Old Books*. He never came here. Stepping along the row, he stopped at a book showing a man on top of a hill with an axe in his hand. "The Axe Factories of the Long Valley" read the cover.

"An interesting book that one," Mr. Martin said behind him, "for one willing and patient enough to read it."

Lanky glanced up to see the bespectacled face of the grey-haired bookseller smiling at him, then looked back at the book. "I've heard of the axeheads of the Long Valley. Our teacher told us about them. Stone Age man, wasn't it, building them? Think folk have found some pieces – seen them in the museum. Does this tell you where to find them?"

"Not exactly. But it's no secret an axe workshop existed here back then. 'Stone Age' is a little too simplistic a label for that time, but I agree it was an age of stone. The book does its job that it set out to do – borrow it if you like."

Lanky hesitated. "Actually, I wondered if the next wizard book was out. I liked the first." He offered Mr. Martin the book clasped in his hand. "Here it is, and no damage."

Mr. Martin smiled, accepting the book. Then he pulled his hand out from behind his back. "I happen to remember that it's your birthday today, Sam. Here's a small gift for you."

"Wow, thanks, Mr. Martin," Lanky said, taking the parcel gingerly. His hands shook with excitement. "Shall I open it now?"

"On you go," Mr. Martin said, grinning.

Lanky ripped open the paper. "That's great!" he beamed, seeing the title. "Brilliant. Thanks, Mr. Martin."

"Hope you enjoy it."

"I will, for sure," Lanky replied, holding the book tightly in his hand.

"You can take the other one, too," Mr. Martin said, pointing at the *Axe Factories* book. "I knew the author. We did a lot of work together."

Lanky reluctantly put down his present, then lifted the *Axe Factories* book from the shelf. He flicked through the first few pages. "I don't see your name here," he murmured, half to himself.

"Well, I said we worked together, I didn't say we wrote the book together. We had a ... hmm, a difference of opinion on how to write it – and what to include. I had different ideas back then, some might say radical."

"On what?" he said, looking up at the bookseller.

Mr. Martin hesitated. "Well, you may laugh now, Sam," he said, adjusting his glasses, "but I thought I knew where to find, ahem, magical axes."

Lanky's eyes widened. "Magical axes! Are you joking?"

Mr. Martin shook his head slowly. "No, Sam. I'm not."

"But why?" he asked, his new book forgotten. "Why would you think that?"

"You really want to know?" Mr. Martin said, his bright eyes peering over his glasses at Lanky.

Lanky nodded.

Mr. Martin scratched his ear, then walked over to a well-worn stool in the narrow aisle. He sat down and picked up a mug of tea from the floor, then looked across at Lanky. "I'll keep it brief," he said, smiling. "If I let myself wander, we'll be here for the rest of the week."

He took a sip of the tea, then began. "Well, you know of my interest in the history of this area. It came from my parents, you see, both archaeologists. And good ones at that. Most worked in Fryka: Misr, Enya, places like that."

Lanky wondered when they would get to the magical axes.

"Well, some of that work led them here," the bookseller continued, placing his mug back to the floor. "To the Long Valley. They thought there was a link between the peoples and cultures here and those of the other places they had studied. They were clearly excited about what they'd found and spent months out in these hills."

"What had they found?"

"Well," Mr Martin said slowly, "there is the problem. They didn't give much away about their work here, even to me. It was frustrating, of course. Remember, I had travelled for years with them, been on many of their digs, but once here, I wasn't allowed into the inner circle. But after two years studying, they were most definitely excited about something." He glanced away. "But then they had to leave."

Lanky frowned. "Where did they go?"

Mr. Martin turned back. "A long way away. I had to live here by myself. For quite a while."

Lanky was shocked. His own father had left, but he hadn't been left alone. He had his mum. "Do you see them now?"

Mr. Martin smiled. "That's another story, Sam. But in *this* story, there's more to tell. Before my parents left, I'd overheard them one morning. 'Do you think we'll be able to open it today?' I heard my mother say. 'We can only try,' my father replied."

"What were they talking about?"

"Well, I tried to find out. Much of their work remained in their study when they left. It was a mess, or seemed that way to me at first, but as I looked at the first few pieces of paper on the desk, I saw my mother's handwriting. Even when she wrote quick notes, they seemed pieces of art to me – the flowing lines curved and crossed each other with a flamboyance that flew from the page. You'd expect them to march off the paper and onto the table, instructing the rest of my father's dowdy text to sort itself out and do better for the next inspection. I was nosy, so I sat and read them, each and every one I could see."

"What did you find?"

Mr. Martin tilted his head, studying Lanky as if uncertain how to continue. Or whether to continue.

Lanky waited.

"Well, now here we are," Mr. Martin said slowly. He leaned forward. "My parents believed, from all their work, that long-lost artefacts lay undiscovered in this area that ... well, that reportedly had mystical powers."

"Mystical powers," Lanky breathed. "Like what?"

"Axes," he murmured. "Axes that could endow the carrier with immense strength. Axes that could draw a power from the very land itself and defend the world against an enemy seeking to destroy it."

Lanky's wide eyes were fixed on the bookseller.

Mr. Martin smiled. "Embellished stories, of course, but of the existence of axes revered by an ancient people, *that* I believed." His gaze seemed to drift elsewhere. "And maybe, just maybe, I believed in axes carrying some mysterious purpose. A concealed power." He refocussed on Lanky. "Maybe there are things left in this world that we don't fully understand."

"You believed these axes existed?" Lanky whispered. "You believed they might have had some hidden power?"

"For a long time, I did, and when my friend wrote that book, I tried to get him to include some of my ideas. But of course, he wouldn't." He sighed. "But now I don't. That's why I need your promise not to tell anyone what I've told you. And I'm rather glad my friend didn't publish my ideas in that book."

"But how could you have believed? And why did your parents think that? Things like that only exist in stories." He glanced at the new book in his hand. *Like this one.*

"Well, one answer to part of your question would be another question. Where do the stories come from? But putting that aside, why believe it? Because of what I read in their notes, their sketches. And from all my own work over the following years. All providing hints of axes with mystical powers hidden somewhere near here."

"But ... but ..." Lanky spluttered. "I don't understand. Why believe it, and then not believe it?"

Mr. Martin shrugged. "Because I searched, and I didn't find them," he said simply. "I found nothing to support those written words."

Lanky saw a glimmer of sadness in the man's eyes. "So, you don't believe it now?"

"I'm afraid I don't. I think there have been some great storytellers through history, and they can describe and weave a compelling view of the world, one that many of us would like to be true – well, most of the time." He smiled. "I guess none of us really want to see Dracula in our bedrooms." He shook his head. "I think this is what these writings were – stories to entertain. I don't regret trying – I've grown my passion for books and writings through it – but no, I don't believe in mystical axes anymore."

He stood. "However, I do believe there may well be some beautiful axes waiting to be found, and I think my parents were onto something there. But for me, the search ended ten years ago, and I'm happy with my life here as it is." He walked up to Lanky. "And on that note, I really think you should head home."

Lanky nodded, yet his mind was already restless with half-formed questions.

"And you can tell your mum this," Mr. Martin added as he ushered Lanky to the staircase. "Rebecca knows this story."

"Mum knows?"

"She does."

Another surprise for the evening. One he'd need to follow up. "Well, it's certainly a tale," Lanky said, heading down the stairs. "And I definitely won't blab to anyone else."

Mr. Martin chuckled. "Good. I wouldn't want people thinking me deranged."

Books in hand, Lanky reached the ground floor, and after a final farewell, he made his way out of the bookshop. He heard Mr. Martin's voice behind him.

"Enjoy your book, Sam. Enjoy both your books."

*

That innocuous chance encounter had fired his imagination, providing a faint yet rich aroma from a distant past of something more tantalising but as yet unknown. Robert's simple words had sparked a fire that had driven him to discover more of those ancient times and forgotten peoples. It had begun a quest to find one of those mysterious axes with their hidden purpose, their supposed mystical power, and hold it in his hand.

It had triggered an overwhelming obsession.

He now stood by the bookshop window. It was softly lit by a rope-strung lamp casting light and shadow over the jumble of books and antiques in the window. The *Closed* sign hung in the door. He gazed into the window, remembering that day as if it were yesterday. He'd certainly enjoyed the book. Both books.

Turning to go, he froze, catching movement inside the shop.

A thief?

He ran to the door and peered inside. He jumped as he saw Robert's shadowy face looking back at him. Catching his breath, Lanky waved sheepishly, as though caught seeing something he shouldn't have. Robert walked towards the door and opened it.

"Hi," Lanky said, seeing a strained look on Robert's face. "I thought someone had broken in."

Robert smiled. "Always things to do, Sam. You want to come in? I've just put the kettle on."

Lanky hesitated. He was tired and hungry, yet Robert was a good friend. "Okay, but just for a few minutes. I've not been home since …" He was about to say, since his morning's fall, but for some reason stopped himself. "Since we had to work so late." He followed Robert inside.

A few minutes later, they sat upstairs at a small mahogany desk in the children's books aisle, steaming-hot mugs of tea before them. "Working late?" Lanky asked, eying a pile of papers on the desk, which currently blocked most of the aisle – it had clearly been carried up from the jumble below.

"Bills. Always bills to pay," Robert murmured, taking his glasses from his nose and rubbing an eye.

"You look as though you should get to your bed – these bills will still be here tomorrow. And why are you doing this here and not at home?"

"Good advice about the bed," Robert replied as he replaced the glasses on his nose. "I could say the same to you. And seems you had an adventure up by the bridge today. Nice scar."

So, avoiding the question about why you're not at home. He saw the strain in Robert's face. Not something to pry about now. "You heard about my fall?"

"Nothing stays quiet here, Sam, you know that. Anything else interesting today?"

'Say nothing of the writing,' came the calm, ethereal voice.

Lanky flinched. *No. Not again.*

Robert frowned. "Are you okay?"

"I … my leg," he lied, praying the voice had gone. "It hurts when I get it in the wrong position." *Why am I lying?*

'Because you need to.'

Lanky looked down at his mug of tea, trying to hide his rising panic. *This makes no sense. What am I saying?*

"Ah," Robert said, sounding concerned. "I didn't realise you'd been injured. I shouldn't—"

"No, no," Lanky said, desperately trying to clear his thoughts. He looked up and forced a smile. "It's not too bad. Just a twinge, that's all. Just been working on it all day and it's stiffened up." He took a sip of his tea, trying to ignore the ache of fear inside. *These voices … I need to get home and get some rest.*

"Must have been quite a scary moment."

"It was quite a shock, that's for sure," Lanky said, forcing himself to concentrate on what Robert was saying. "Not every day you get thrown off a cliff."

"I can imagine. Seems this woman thought you were attacking her."

"What!" Lanky exclaimed, his sudden anger genuine. "Who told you that?"

"Fletcher was around here, checking if I knew what you were doing up there this morning."

Lanky's anger flared. "He thinks I was to blame?"

"He thinks nothing – and he thinks everything," Robert said calmly. "He's just doing his job. He knows you, Sam. He just needs to be thorough. As always."

Lanky shook his head, the voices momentarily forgotten. *What's she being saying about me?* "She attacked *me*! She threw me off the cliff!"

Robert took a drink of his tea but said nothing.

Lanky bowed his head and rubbed the back of his neck. *She said I attacked her? That's madness.* He gritted his teeth. *That's it. I've had enough of all this. Where's all this getting me?* "I'm going to give it up," he muttered.

"Your job?"

He looked up. "That as well. But I meant the search for these bloody axes, these artefacts or whatever they really are. Today was the straw that broke my back." He let out a heartfelt sigh. "It's been an adventure, a fun time." He gave a wry smile. "Most of the time. And with all that material you gave me, I was sure I'd find something. Especially those axes. But if there are mystical objects hidden around here, I don't know where they are. Copper coins, yes. Even gold coins, yes. But mystical axes …?" He sat back in his chair. "No, it's time to move on."

Robert pushed back his chair, stood, then walked absently down the aisle. He stopped, his back to Lanky. "You have done the memory of my parents proud, Sam. For that, I am grateful."

His parents? Lanky hadn't heard Robert mention his parents since those very early days. Robert didn't want to talk about them, and no one ever asked him to.

"My parents were onto something here, you know," continued Robert softly. "They saw the patterns in those old scraps of paper, in the ramblings of madmen and heretics. They believed. As you believed." He hesitated, then turned to face Lanky. "They never told me they were leaving, you know. I heard them that morning, talking excitedly about a new chamber they wanted to open. Then they left, and just never came home. Ever."

Lanky stifled a gasp. He knew Robert's parents had left, but not that he'd never seen them again. *He's never spoken about this.* "I … I didn't know. Are they …" *Still alive?*

"They've never been found," Robert answered.

Lanky could think of nothing to say.

"I searched hard," Robert said, walking back to the desk. "As hard as you. I searched for them. I searched for their magical axes. But nothing. The pain grew too much and so I chose not to believe. I placed them and their memories into a bottle and placed it close to my heart. Once in a while, I open it, and remember their warm embrace." He slowly sat back down. "So, when you showed an interest, well, they came alive again, through you."

And now I'm stopping. "I'm sorry."

"Don't be. As I said, you have done them proud, and I've been pleased to help you as I could. You couldn't have done more."

Lanky smiled. But he had seen it. Hadn't he?

The briefest flash of anger in Robert's eyes?

But why? Why anger?

"Look," Robert said, his face brightening. "I shouldn't have ended your evening on a note like this. Stop listening to the ramblings of an old man and get yourself home."

Lanky forced a laugh. "Old? Hardly. You've the edge on folk half your age." His mind frazzled, he had nothing left to say. He wanted to get home.

Robert smiled. "Well, I like to think so, that's true enough." He climbed to his feet. "But come on, you need to get on. If you pop around tomorrow, you can tell me what you plan to do next. But tonight … well, we are both past our best, shall we say?"

Lanky laughed. "That sums it up nicely."

A short while later, Lanky walked down the road towards his house. He sucked in the late-evening air, the rain cooling his brow. Could this day throw any more at him?

As he arrived back at his house, he breathed a sigh of relief. *The gods have stopped playing with me for today.*

But what did they have planned for tomorrow?

CHAPTER THREE

How precisely it would happen wasn't known, but the pull of the Staff was too great for them to ignore.

"Wakey, wakey, sleepyhead!"

Jessica grunted, pulling the sheet over her head.

"Oh no, you don't," came Beth's firm voice then the sound of the curtains being opened. "Seems you had a better night's sleep last night, hey? That's good, 'cos we need to be out by ten to get cracking on our walk."

"What walk?" Jessica muttered, sticking her head further under the covers.

The cover was rudely pulled away, and she shielded her eyes from the blaze of morning light.

"You've got time for a shower, breakfast, and sorting out your kit for the day. Move it!"

"This isn't the army, Beth!" Jessica shouted as she heard her friend leaving the room. Rubbing her bleary eyes, she yawned. Had they really agreed on a walk this early? Unfortunately, it seemed they had. She ran her fingers through her tangled hair. *Well, there goes my lie-in.*

She climbed out of bed and stood, stretching, her fingers brushing the low-hanging ceiling of the old cottage. Her arms complained, still sore after the previous day's tug-of-war with the lad from the village, but she held the stretch, easing the tightness. The face of the tousle-haired lad flashed into her mind. *Idiot. What was he doing?* Relaxing her arms, she pushed the thought away and walked across to the chair where she'd draped her towel. *Forget it. It's gone. Try and enjoy the rest of the vacation.*

She glanced out of the wood-framed window, seeing a clear blue sky above the distant hills. Her head slowly clearing, she realised Beth was right. She *had* slept better. No hellish nightmares, no waking in sweat-drenched terror. *Thank God for that.* The last nights had been draining – and worrying – but maybe those dread dreams would be now gone for good. *Was it because I spoke with Beth about them ... or because I talked about Eshe?* Either way, they'd gone, and for now, that was all that mattered.

She left the bedroom and walked down the corridor to the bathroom. As she reached the bathroom door, it suddenly opened, and Tricia rushed out, her hair an explosion of just-washed, frizzy black curls. "Morning, Jess," she said brightly as she pushed her way past. "Still in your pj's? We're out at ten, remember. See you at breakfast." And on she marched to her and Erin's room.

Jessica wandered into the bathroom, closing the door behind her. She stepped into the shower and within moments enjoyed the calming sensation of the cascading water's gentle massage.

Someone hammered on the door. "Whoever is in there, I need to get in! There's only one toilet, and I need to pee!"

"Just come in, Erin, the door's open."

"I'm not coming in when you're in there, that's gross."

"Gross will be you peeing in your pants when you can't hold it any longer. I'm not moving."

The door flew open, and Jess saw blurred movement through the steamy shower door.

"You can be a real pain sometimes," Erin scolded.

"Is there a party in here?" came Tricia's voice at the door. "Are we all invited?"

"No," Erin shouted. "Get out!"

"If you two want to enjoy yourselves in the bathroom, I suggest you keep the door shut. See you at breakfast." The door closed.

"It's like living with children," Erin exclaimed. Jessica heard the toilet flush, the taps run, and a moment later Erin leaving.

She smiled. Erin liked to get things done but liked them done the right way. *Guess we need her to keep the rest of us in line.* She reached for her shampoo and squeezed some onto her hands. The gloves she'd worn yesterday had saved her hands, unlike the other two, who had messy burns. She worked the shampoo through her hair. Lying just past her shoulders, it was long enough to tie up when needed, but not so long it became a hassle to deal with in the morning. In fact, none of the four of them were 'hair-bears'. *Just nice, tidy, 'do something fancy occasionally' type hair.*

As she stepped out of the cubicle, she glanced at herself in the mirror. She flexed her arms and smiled as her biceps appeared. Her and Eshe's cousin had always liked showing off the size of his biceps ... until the point theirs overtook his. *Us girls can be tough too, hey, Eshe?*

Still smiling, she walked out of the bathroom.

Straight into Erin.

"What ...! Put some clothes on!" Erin exclaimed, jumping out of the way.

"Ah, sorry, forgot I wasn't at home." She shifted her towel.

"You two definitely are enjoying this morning," Tricia said as she came around the corner from the stairs, her curly hair now held high with a yellow bandana. "Is there something you'd like to tell us?"

"Take a hike," Erin retorted, glaring at Tricia. "She just came out."

"Came out? Are you coming out too? This is certainly news for the day. I'll go tell Beth."

Erin walked off, muttering.

Jessica watched them stride away. *No, no news today, girls. Maybe another day.*

*

"Get me a large cold beer and keep it cold until I get there," Tricia called, a few yards behind the accelerating Beth.

Jessica watched as Beth pulled away up the Struggle. She could have matched her friend's pace but was happy to take it easy. Let the warrior get her exercise. And let her deal with the hassle of securing a table at the busy pub.

"Looking forward to that drink," Erin said, the sweat dripping off her forehead and glistening on her neck below her blonde, short-cut hair. "That was some climb to the peak. The path went just one way – up!"

Jessica smiled. "And you found the quickest way down," she said, recalling Erin's fall.

"Ouch, yeah, that was sore."

"Did you have anything to do with that, Jess?" came Tricia's laboured voice behind them.

Jessica's smile faded. "Not this time."

"I still can't believe you threw that lad over the cliff," Erin panted as they hit a steeper section.

Jessica felt a sting of irritation. "Can't we drop it now? It happened, but that's yesterday's news."

"It does seem you were unlucky, Jess. Right place, wrong time."

"Which isn't so unusual as far as Jess is concerned," Erin quipped, turning her icy blue eyes to Tricia. "What about the time we only just escaped from a war zone in that pub when mild-mannered cool cat here hit the biggest guy in there? Or the time we had to strip and swim across the bay because she bet four blokes we could beat them."

"Well …" started Jessica.

"Or the time at the local shop when—"

"Okay, okay, we get the idea," Jessica said, holding up her hands as she walked. "Move on."

"Maybe that company that's hired her as a trainee firefighter," Tricia panted behind them, "didn't know that she can be a competitively stubborn pain in the neck at times."

"I am here, you know."

Tricia stopped behind them. "Quick rest," she wheezed, dropping to her haunches.

Jessica and Erin turned and waited for Tricia to catch her breath.

Eventually, Tricia glanced up at Erin and continued as if she'd never stopped. "We also know Jess has no mean bone in her body. Whatever this guy was doing, he sounds as though he would have scared anyone coming down that path. The difference is we'd have hightailed it back here as fast as our arses could pump us, and not jujitsu'd him over a cliff."

Jessica scowled. "It wasn't jujitsu, it was Wado-Ryu."

"And there's the difference between you and us, Jess. I guess they don't teach Erin the finer points of martial arts in genetics, and I may be an aspiring artist, but not of the martial variety. Anyway, we know you didn't mean to throw him over that cliff." She hesitated. "Did you?"

"Of course not," Jessica said quickly. "Not over the cliff anyway …"

Tricia laughed. "Come on," she said, standing, "a cool beer is waiting. That will wash away our worries."

They walked on.

*

"Morning, Mum," Lanky said brightly as he walked into the kitchen. "Is that bacon I can smell?"

"Morning?" His mum looked up at the clock. "Guess it's still morning. Just. And yes, it was bacon, and it was delicious." She gestured to the fridge. "There's a couple of slices left if you want to fry them."

He grinned. "Great."

Within a few minutes, he was sitting at the table, tucking into a tasty sandwich, a mug of steaming tea by his side. He felt so much better today. A great night's sleep. *And no bloody voices.* He took another bite of his sandwich. *And that's because you've made the decision.*

He took a sip of his tea, then: "Mum, I've been thinking …"

"That can be dangerous," his mum said, looking up from her paper.

He smiled. "Well, I won't make a habit of it. But seriously, I've been thinking about what I do next."

"Ah, so it could be dangerous."

He laughed. "No, I don't think college would be that."

His mum peered at him over the rim of her glasses. "College?" She removed her glasses and sat back, her face lighting up. "You've decided to do it?"

He nodded. "I wanted to wait until you'd definitely turned the corner. I know you told me this time it was different, but I had to be sure. And now I can see it. You are so much better." He grinned. "And it's amazing."

His mum smiled. "And I think so too."

Lanky laughed again.

His mum sat forward. "Well, you know already I think it's a wonderful idea. I'd have pushed you harder but knew you wouldn't listen. You can be quite stubborn at times."

"I wonder who I got that from?"

She regarded him, her expression warm, yet edged with quiet determination. "You've been a wonderful help to me these last few years, Sam, and I'm not sure what I could have done without you." She sat a little taller. "But I am through it all now, and it's time you got on with your own life."

"I have been," Lanky said quickly. "I've—"

"Oh, I know you've enjoyed the work at John's, but I also know you've always wanted to try something different." She cocked her head. "To be an engineer?"

He smiled, then nodded. "And I think I'll be able to afford college with the money I've made from the apprenticeship." He paused, looking down at his mug of tea. "It's only these last few days I've been thinking about it seriously." He looked up. "You sure you'd be okay with it?"

"Okay? I'm delighted," his mum said, her bright eyes shining. "You're a smart boy, Sam, and you've been a wonderful son. I really couldn't have gotten by without your help. But it's time to spread those wings of yours." She took another sip of her tea. "College. Yes, it's a wonderful idea. And it will get you off this folly that Robert started you on."

Folly? It was the first time he'd heard her refer to his exploring as that. *How long has she thought that?* He sighed. Well, he *had* come to the same conclusion. "Well, I guess it's up to me now to see how this could work."

"It will work. And I'll be fine. A mother has to see her son leave the home at some point – or kick them out!"

Lanky laughed. Pushing back his chair, he climbed to his feet, then walked around to his mum. He leaned down to give her a hug. "Thanks, Mum. Gives me confidence that it's the right next step."

She hugged him back. "Just remember me when you're rich and famous."

He laughed again.

A short time later, he left the kitchen and bounded up the stairs to his room. As usual, all lay in organised chaos. Shelves covered every available wall space, each stacked with books, maps, notepads, computer disks – anything that didn't fit elsewhere. Even below his bed, tattered ends of rolled paper peeked out, evidence of further hoards. He walked over to his small desk by the window. Littered with paper and pens and illuminated by a tired, sprung lamp, this had been the nerve centre for his exploration.

Reaching over, he flicked the switch on his old stereo and let the music play from where he'd last left it. The quirky, drawling voice of the dead singer filled the room with its irresistible shuffle and hook. "Old garbage," said his friends. But these were the sounds of his earliest childhood, memories of his dad. *And I like it.*

Humming softly, Lanky picked up his logbook and started flicking through the pages, watching years of his scribblings flash past. Years of enthusiastic and determined efforts which had turned the hobby into an obsession. Had he enjoyed it? *Mostly,* he admitted, *but what has it gained me?*

He stopped on a random page. A list of coordinates stared back at him – coordinates that defined the locations of just a few of the many places he'd searched over the years. He drew a slow breath. How many locations had he visited? Too many to remember. And he'd searched them all. *But I found nothing ...*

He studied the writing on the page. These particular locations were from the archives of Robert's parents, the result of years of their own detailed research. He remembered the bone-tingling thrill when Robert had first handed the work to him. This was it! Success was inevitable! One of the locations would be hiding an artefact of power! An axe of power!

Or so he'd naively believed.

But over time, he had thoroughly explored them all, and location after location proved disappointing, yielding nothing. Suspecting the locations were disguised or coded in some way, he even attempted corrections and adjustments to the coordinates, diligently searching each new area they pointed to.

But nothing. Every day, nothing. At least not what he was looking for.

And yet still he had continued. *I foolishly believed.*

A thin smile crossed his lips. And was that so bad? *It kept me out of trouble.*

And it wasted a good chunk of your life.

Sighing, he forced those thoughts away. This was a new day. This was the start of a new chapter in his life. He flicked through the rest of the book until he came to the final page, yesterday's, the entry not yet closed out. He sat back in his chair, the memory vivid. "The carving," he murmured, recalling the writing on the cliff face. "What *was* that?" It was quirky, sure, but probably the work of some satirical artist. Certainly not an artefact he'd been searching for.

But what if ...?

His brow furrowed. It wouldn't take long. Just head back up, record the details, and close the journal. *Close that chapter of my life and move on.* His gaze lingered on the incomplete journal entry. *But do I really want to head back there?*

His gaze switched to the other item on the floor. His map. His prized possession. He unfurled the crinkled, browned paper, then rolled it out onto his bedroom floor. It was adorned with his tiny writing and sketches, all drawn from the scant evidence teased out of the various documents and scraps of paper in his possession. He glanced at two vivid red stars marked on the map, two locations that Robert's parents seemed to have consistently targeted. Offset from the two stars were many fainter pencil marks, each testament to his persistent efforts. He studied them closely. Had he really tested that many coordinate shifts for ways the actual locations may have been disguised, shifted from their true location? He couldn't deny what lay before him. He'd tried and tried hard.

But still I found nothing.

And yet, still he'd gone back, a dogged persistence driving him on through the seasons. In the background, the insistent singer's refrain and guitar riff reminded him of his deep winter's outings in the hills. *Yes, even out in the cold.*

His brow furrowed. *What about that writing I saw yesterday?* He grabbed a pencil from his desk and knelt beside the map. Quickly scanning its well-worn surface, he found the place where he'd fallen from the cliff and seen the carving. He made a pencil mark, adding an entry to the map legend. So, where was the closest red star from there? *There, only three kilometres to the north,* he noted. So, a simple shift of three kilometres to the south matched that red star to the location of the carving.

He looked at the second red star on the map, over in the Long Valley. He measured three kilometres south of that star and made a new pencil mark, scribbling its reference in the map key. He squinted at the new mark; it was an area he'd studied in detail many times. He looked back at the 'fall' location. *But I've been around this area many times too, and never found this carving.*

He sat back and looked at a smaller inset map of a northern area of the country he'd pasted onto the corner of the larger map. *So what about the third red star over there?* He leaned across and measured the offset. *So that moves down to here? To Mount Hope.* He marked the point and scribbled a final reference in the key.

He climbed back to his feet and gazed down at the map. And as the music played, he suddenly knew what he was going to do. *I can't ignore it.* It was in his blood now. *I'm an idiot, but at least it will close out this entry.*

And then he was finished. He had enjoyed it for years, but now it was time to move on, and like Robert, leave the idea of mystical artefacts well behind him.

*

Rested and refreshed, the girls left the pub and joined the trail west, working their way slowly up the side of the scree-covered slope, heading up to the ridge encircling the corrie. Beth and Jessica soon pulled ahead.

"Seems Erin is having a tough time," Beth said in a low voice. "I knew she'd split from Paul, but her job? I didn't realise she hated it so much."

"She holds stuff like that in. But it's good she's talking it through with Trish." She scowled. "Her boss sounds like an ignorant pig."

"A sexist pig, you mean," Beth said, anger in her voice. "If that bloke had called *me* emotional, he'd have been thinking about my answer flat on his back with a bloodied nose. Erin's too nice."

Jessica glanced at Beth and saw the familiar flare of her friend's eyebrows, a sharper intensity to her dark eyes. It was a face with the intent of a prowling tiger – determined with a quiet ferocity.

And one she thought beautiful. *The face of one I love, one I wish could be closer to me.*

She suppressed a sigh. But that wasn't to be. The one – the only one – who had caught her heart looked elsewhere for love. A soft regret swept over her at the memory of that moment, a year ago now, of that awkward, fumbling conversation when she'd opened up to Beth. The hurt still lingered. Not from any mistakes she'd made, any mis-said words, any unspoken words, but from that moment when she'd seen the answer in Beth's eyes. Her friend had not been surprised, seemingly having sensed something hidden in warm words, casual gestures, moments of subtle hesitancy … *and yet my love could only reach so far.* And now, friendship remained, a most precious friendship, but a part of her heart remained sundered. *Will I ever find one who comes close to her?*

Glancing sidelong at Beth and seeing the smouldering fire in her friend's eyes as she walked on, she pushed the painful thoughts away. *My best friend is here, beside me. A friend for life.* Veering closer to her, she held her voice light. "You would, wouldn't you? Thump him, I mean."

Beth smiled, her face softening. "There's a time and a place to follow the rules …" She held up her fist, mischief in her eyes. "And there's a time to thump a sexist pig on the nose."

Jessica cast her a sceptical gaze. "I doubt even in the army you can do that."

"Depends who's looking," Beth countered, a roguish smile on her lips. She walked on, whistling.

Jessica shook her head. "And how about you, Beth? All okay?"

"All good with me, Jess. And long may it continue."

"Where did you say you were being posted next?"

"I didn't."

"Ah, okay, one of those 'I'd have to shoot you if I told you' situations?"

"Or given I don't have a rifle with me, push you off this ridge."

"You think so? They don't teach you all the moves in the army, you know."

"Enough to get you off this ledge before you realised it. No charging out of bushes yelling at you, giving you all the time in the world to get ready – you'd be arse over tit, skydiving before you could twitch a finger."

"Yeah, right, try it!"

Beth laughed.

They pushed on, slowly climbing the next steep section of the ridge trail until it flattened off beside a steep rock-strewn slope plunging into the valley below. Beth stopped and pointed back to Tricia and Erin. "Should we wait for them?"

Jessica turned to look back—

She felt a tap on the back. "Whack – bye-bye," came Beth's satisfied voice.

Jessica laughed. "Very funny, smart-arse. You had to win this one, didn't you?"

Beth swung her pack off her back. "I'll give you a slug of my coffee to make you feel better." She gestured to a boulder off the trail. "We can sit there and wait for them to catch up. Aunty Trish may have worked her magic on Erin by now."

A short while later, coffee in hand, they watched Tricia and Erin slowly winding their way up the trail.

Jessica felt Beth's eyes on her. "Seems you had a clear night last night," her friend said.

"Yes, thank God." She glanced at Beth. "Those nightmares have been so real – just like me talking to you here."

"Except I'm not some evil dude threatening to kill you."

Jessica raised an eyebrow. "No, just an evil dude pretending to throw me off this ridge."

A thin smile crossed Beth's lips. "Well, I hope I'm not quite as scary?"

A sudden shiver ran down Jessica's spine at the memory of the burnt man of her nightmare. "Not by a long way."

Beth reached out and held her hand. "Any idea what triggered it?"

Jessica considered for a moment. "I don't think it has to do with Sis. Why a nightmare like this? And why now, just as we arrived here?" She released a shuddering sigh. "I'm just glad it didn't come back. He said …" She fell silent.

"He?"

Jessica looked away. *He said it would be worse next time. He said …* She pulled her thoughts back from that descent into darkness. *It was a dream. A bad dream. And now it's gone.* "They *were* a terrible few nights, Beth, but those nightmares seem to have broken." She squeezed Beth's hand. "All's good now."

Beth frowned. "I know you too well to fully believe that."

Jessica smiled. "And that's why you're my friend." She held Beth's eyes. "Look, if they come back, I'll tell you, okay? I promise."

Beth's concerned gaze lingered, then she sighed and nodded.

They sat in silence for a while. "And your love life?" Beth said eventually, a slight hesitation in her voice. "Any movement there?"

A lover by my side? Not the one that I want. "That's a place I don't want to go today, Beth." *And why? Because deep down, I'm scared I won't find that special someone to walk by my side.*

Beth gave an imperceptible nod. Then she smiled, put down her coffee, and leaned over, wrapping her arms around Jessica. "There's someone out there for you, Jess. And you'll find her – or she'll find you."

"Hey!" came Tricia's voice from down the trail. "Now I *am* feeling left out!"

Beth groaned. "Great timing, Trish," she muttered.

Despite the ache in her heart, Jessica laughed. "That's Trish. Always keeping us on our toes."

Beth glanced down the hillside. "Maybe. But she's certainly not on her own toes right now."

*

As Tricia dropped to her haunches, breathing heavily, Erin glanced up to the top of the ridge where Beth and Jessica sat waiting. "You think she's okay?"

Tricia looked up, a sheen on her rounded face, her yellow bandana drenched in sweat. "Me? No. Someone forgot to install the escalators." She glanced up to the ridge. "But I guess you meant Jess?"

Erin nodded. "She seems better today, but these last few days she's not been herself. Don't think she's been sleeping well."

Tricia slowly climbed to her feet, then pulled off her bandana, locks of her curly black hair springing free. "Yeah, think we all noticed." She pulled a tissue from her pocket and wiped her brow. "I think she's said something to Beth, 'cos when I asked her about it, she clammed up." She shoved the tissue and bandana into a side pocket of her pack. "The loss of Eshe still hurts her – hurts us all. We're here if she needs to talk, but there's no point pushing it." She sighed and glanced up to the ridge. "But, yes, we'll need to keep an eye on her."

Erin looked up the trail, the warm breeze blowing strands of her hair across the side of her slender face. "I miss Eshe," she whispered. "She should be here with us."

Tricia came to her side. "She was a wonderful soul. Yet she's not lost to me. I feel she still walks beside me."

It was the only way. To recognise that Eshe's spirit walked by their side. *Still one of the gang.* She glanced at Tricia. "How long have we all known each other?"

Tricia's face took on a mock pained expression. "Too long. Should never have spoken to you all those years ago in the school playground. Especially you ... Knew you were trouble from your weird accent."

Erin smiled at the memory. Her family moving south from a remote northern isle to a bustling city had been challenging for her. *Not least the slow drawl of these southerners.* "Guess we were about twelve back then. So, eight years ..." *Eight years of forging deep bonds with three fantastic girls.* She sighed. *And with Eshe ...*

"Didn't like you at first," Tricia said matter-of-factly as she studied the ridgeline above. "You were too boring."

Erin's blue eyes twinkled. "So you've said before. But turns out you didn't get on with many kids back then."

"They were boring too. Except Jess and Eshe. And sometimes Beth."

"As I understand it, Jess was one of the few kids who'd speak to you. And that was only because she lived on the same street as you. And Beth was Jess's best friend at school, and Eshe was Jess's sister ... So they kind of *had* to speak to you too."

Tricia shrugged. "They were drawn to my wit and talent. As were you ... eventually. And you turned out okay in the end."

"Glad to hear it."

Tricia was silent for a moment, then: "Is it really eight years that I've been stuck with you lot? Seems like a lifetime."

"You're still only twenty, Trish." Erin glanced up to the ridge where Jessica and Beth sat waiting for them. "But it's been a good journey so far." The face of Jessica's sister drifted into her mind. "And as you say, Eshe still walks with us."

For a short while, they both stood alone with their thoughts.

Then Tricia sighed and gestured ahead. "I guess we should push on."

Erin nodded, then smiled at her friend. "This is the last stretch, then we're there."

Tricia scowled and scanned the rocky path ahead. "You said that an hour ago. This ridge seems to move further and further away."

Erin put her arm around her friend's shoulder. "Well, this time it's true. And past this ridge, it's downhill all the way. Last push now."

Tricia grunted. "Fine." She walked back onto the trail, muttering. "Guess there'll be no cold beer waiting up there."

Still smiling, Erin watched her trudge up the steep, rocky trail. Tricia would complain all day, but she would cover the same ground as them all, and then be ready to go again the next day. She followed after her friend, enjoying the warmth of the sun on her face ...

But as she stepped back onto the trail, a sudden sense of unease swept through her. She slowed, then stopped, glancing around in a dazed confusion. As her eyes scanned the ridge where Beth and Jessica sat watching them, the unease deepened to a frightening sense of loss—

"You coming?" came Tricia's voice. "You know this is the last bit, right?"

Her friend's words shattered the fell sense of foreboding.

Steadying her shaking hands, she drew a deep lungful of air, then breathed out slowly, releasing the tension that had gripped her. *What the hell was that?* She stood for a moment, allowing the irrational panic to ebb away.

"Erin?"

She looked up to see Tricia staring down at her from the trail.

"You okay?"

Forcing a smile, Erin nodded. "Coming."

But am I okay?

Unsettled, unwelcome memories of her break-up with Paul returned. Maybe that painful period had been tougher on her than she'd realised. Maybe—

Her hand immediately clenched to a fist. *Come on, Erin. You're in a beautiful part of the world. You're with your friends. Don't waste your time and energy on that cheating snake.* Her expression tightening, she cast aside the painful – the worthless – memories, mentally brushing herself down. *Focus on what's in front of you. Move on.*

She drew herself up, then walked on with a purpose up the trail towards her waiting friends.

Yet faint remnants of unease lingered …

*

Lanky glanced over the grassy fringe of the clifftop, and saw the stubby tree trapped in the base of the narrow ravine far below. *Well, I guess I was pretty lucky.* Noticing the scar left by the rock fall he'd triggered, he moved along a few paces, then dropped to his knees, then his front, to better examine the cliff face. He gingerly crawled forward and peered over the edge …

And there it was, the peculiar section of rock face he'd seen yesterday.

And the inscription!

As he'd noticed before, the inscription was sharp and cleanly cut, appearing as though only recently carved. But now he saw that the area around the carving was smooth, almost polished, quite different from the rough, weathered surrounding rock. It was as though that section had been embedded somehow into the cliff face. He frowned. Why would anyone go to the effort of placing that here, on a cliff face that no one would see?

His attention shifted to the inscription. It was certainly an intriguing statement, but why write the single 'i' in lower case, when whoever did this clearly had the means to write capital letters. And why write 'why' as 'y'? Again, he ran his fingers over the letters, deeply carved and intricately done, but with a slight roughness. *So, done by hand.* If so, it was an impressive feat; the stone appeared particularly hard and not easy to work.

Stretching his hand out to separate his thumb and forefinger, he measured the length of the polished rock section, working his hand from one end to the other. It was around thirty inches, with about half of that taken by the writing. He guessed around fifteen inches for the height. *But let's see.*

He measured the first hand-span, which took him from the top of the rectangle down to the letter 'i'. On his second hand-span, his thumb sat on the 'i', and as he reached down with his finger, he landed on the 'y'—

A loud crack rent the air, and he cried out as a vicious shock lanced up his arm. Yanking his hand away, he managed to steady himself to avoid slipping over the edge. There was the crash of falling rocks and then silence.

He drew a ragged breath. *What the hell was that?*

He waited, and when all remained still, he peered over the edge. The polished rock surface was gone. "What just happened?" he whispered.

Looking closer, he could see a gaping hole where the rock surface had been. A shiver of excitement running through him, he pulled himself as far over the edge as he could and saw the same strange polished rock forming the inside of the newly created cavity. He reached down and put his shaking hand inside.

His fingers brushed an object.

His heart racing, he ran his fingers around it – it seemed rounded, with several indentations. *Damn. What is this?* Hand still shaking, he grasped the object, then pulled – it moved easily. A nervous excitement built. *Whatever this is, I can get it out!* Taking care not to rush, he pulled gently, slowly easing the object out of the hole.

He gasped as a sleek wooden rod came into view, an elongate purple crystal seamlessly set into the warm golden-coloured wood. He stared at it, stunned. *This can't be happening. Is this real?* A surge of swirling emotions swept through him: elation, shock, disbelief. After years and years of scouring the hillsides, nothing ... *And now this!*

Trying to steady his hands, he eased the object out until, with around three feet of the rod in view, the weight balance began to change. *So, maybe six or seven feet long? Some form of staff?* He slowly eased the staff further out, rotating it up towards him until the end swung free of the opening.

Relief flooded through him. *It's out! I have it!*

He lay trembling, his arm stretched out, holding the staff in the air. *I have it. Whatever it is, I have it.*

*

"That's Low Bridge, isn't it?" Tricia said as they rounded a bend in the trail. Through the trees ahead lay a stone bridge crossing the river to their right. She grinned. "We're on the last stretch now, girls. Not far to our cottage now."

Beth came alongside Jessica. "Wonder if that lad will try to attack you again today, Jess?"

Jessica roused herself from her thoughts and looked up. "Well, at least there are four of us to tackle him."

"Don't think you need our help, given yesterday's performance."

"Wonder what he's up to now?"

"Probably scaring old ladies in town by jumping out from behind lampposts," Tricia said, passing around the trunk of a tree. "Or jumping out of bushes in the park. Yaahhh!" she cried, leaping out from behind the tree.

Beth reached for her water bottle. "I don't care what the imbecile is up to, but I doubt we need to worry about him again."

"Well, that's good," Tricia said, rejoining them. "I'm too tired for a fight." She groaned. "Blimey, my legs know they've been walking today. Glad it's not my turn to cook. And I'm grabbing the first shower, then chilling in my pj's, and you lot can serve me." She wiped her brow. "Who *is* cooking tonight?"

Erin swore softly. "Me," she muttered, unscrewing the cap of the bottle. "How about we go out for a change?"

"I don't have the energy to go out," Tricia groaned. "Once I'm in, I'm not moving. Unless you carry me."

"How about you two?" Erin said. She took a swig of water.

Beth shrugged. "Either's fine by me."

"Think I'm with the stay-in crowd tonight," Jessica said. "My legs are well walked-in today."

"Yeah, way to go, sis!" Tricia shouted. "Good, sorted! Ahh, bring it on. What you cooking, Erin?"

"I don't know," Erin grunted, replacing the stopper and slotting the bottle back in the side of her bag. "I was dreaming about the great food in the restaurant in the village."

They laughed.

As they walked on down the hill, Erin and Tricia veered over to the bridge. "Just going to take a couple of pictures," Tricia said. "We'll catch you up."

Beth and Jessica walked on into the woods.

Walking into the dappled shade, Jessica felt the day's hike in her legs. But it was a good ache, the ache of a day well spent. Approaching a corner in the trail, she glanced ahead … and grimaced as she recognised the familiar surroundings. She glanced upslope. *That lad ran out of the bushes up there.* Her gaze drifted downslope towards the cliff's edge. *And I threw him down—*

She came to a sudden stop, eyes widening as she saw a figure through the trees sitting on the grass by the cliff edge. Grasping Beth's arm, she pulled her friend back. "It's the lad again," she said in a whisper, gesturing towards the ravine.

"What!" Beth hissed. "What's the fool doing now?" She peered through the trees. "He's got something in his hand," she whispered. "A big stick, or a staff of some sort."

Jessica started. *A staff?*

*

Lanky lay on his back, trying to get his head around what he'd just found: an artefact deliberately hidden in an obscure place and secreted inside an exotic, bespoke container, protected by … by what? By something that had given him a bloody painful shock, that's what. And whoever had hidden it had thought to inscribe a short rhyme, carving with a great degree of skill. But why? *To mystify me, that's why.*

He sat up, facing the cliff edge, then picked up the staff, laying it across his lap. It was a dense wood, but well balanced and light enough to be easily carried. *A weapon?* Maybe. However, the crystal adornment suggested it was likely an ornamental piece, or possibly ceremonial?

He took a closer look at the crystal. Translucent, veined with shades of purple through to black and white, it had been carved into a sleek elongate shape with polished, unblemished facets. And it was set very cleverly within two slender strands of wood, each skilfully twisted to form the interlocking coils of two upright snakes. He ran his hand along the golden-hued shaft, noting the fine writings and figures covering its surface, his fingers slipping smoothly over the delicate carvings.

Climbing to his feet, he hefted the staff. Although smooth, the staff undulated in thickness along its length, with slight swells and dips in places. His hand found a natural grip in one of the depressions. Rotating the staff, he noticed a finely carved symbol below the crystal. It displayed two circles, one enclosing the other, between which lay complex markings with no obvious meaning. In the centre of the inner circle lay a carving of two coiled snakes, tightly interlocked as though one.

Lanky reached up and touched the symbol—

A scream cut through the air.

His heart lurching in his chest, he spun around. He stared in utter disbelief as he saw two of the women from the day before.

And the one who'd thrown him over the cliff edge lay on the ground, groaning.

*

Beth dropped to her friend's side, fear in her eyes. "Jess, what's wrong?"

Jessica groaned. "My head feels as though it's about to explode."

"Damn it, Jess. I said you needed to see a doctor, and now look at you. Do you think you can get down to town?"

Waves of nausea swept over Jessica. She turned her head to the side and threw up.

"What's happened?" came a concerned voice.

"My friend," Beth said, glancing up at Lanky. "She needs help. She needs a doctor."

"No," Jessica said quickly, the cramp in her stomach settling. She wiped her mouth. "Just give me a minute."

"Jess, this is serious. I'm calling for help."

"No," Jessica said firmly, turning around and pulling herself up to a seated position. She fought back another wave of pain and looked up. "I'll be okay in a moment."

The lad, Lanky, studied her, concern clear in his face. "You don't look well. Your friend is right – we should get someone here."

Jessica caught movement further up the trail. Erin and Tricia were running down the path towards them. "Help me up," she said quickly. *I don't want to make this a big scene.*

She'd been talking to Beth, but Lanky bent down, offering his free hand. She hesitated, then reached across to take it.

As she did so, her hand caught the staff—

She screamed as every inch of her body convulsed, seemingly on fire. The pain was intense and relentless, leaving no capacity for thought or action. It was a state of pure and simple agony. Through terror-widened eyes she saw nothing but cloying darkness. It enveloped her, subsumed her, all sense of the world gone. Only the void remained.

The Void.

Numbed with horror, a part of her screamed for release. Release from the crippling pain; release from the suffocating sense of threat surrounding her. But the darkness deepened, and her waking nightmare descended into hell as shadowy, alien creatures swarmed over her body, raking at her mind. Screaming, she desperately, instinctively, fought them, somehow keeping them from reaching her soul. And yet on they came in furious swarms, each contact a burning lance of pain, each incursion a violation of her being—

The darkness, the pain, suddenly vanished as quickly as it had appeared.

With a harsh ringing in her head, she collapsed to the ground, shaking, ghostly visions of unknown terrors still fouling her mind.

Wild cries and gut-wrenching screams exploded around her.

Wide-eyed and gasping for breath, she saw Beth and the lad lying next to her, both crouched low, cowering from the insanity around them.

A fierce cry sounded to her left, and in a daze she spun around.

Glacial fear engulfed her as she saw a brute of a man standing beside her and beyond, two terrifying figures running towards her, their faces painted, their teeth bared, and carrying spears in their hands.

She tried to move, but dread paralyzed her limbs. *We're going to die. I don't want to die.*

As a hand grabbed hers, she heard herself scream.

CHAPTER FOUR

All were unprepared. The Warriors. The Iyes.
Even the Ka made mistakes.

Time seemed to stop for Lanky as a savage onslaught of noise thundered into him, a mind-numbing assault on his senses so severe he couldn't move. It was as though another had possessed his body but with no idea how to use it. His eyes were open, but nothing made sense.

Only a darkness existed, a haze of seething hatred.

He felt himself falling …

He cried out as he hit the ground.

Groaning, he fought to clear the thick fog clouding his mind – then froze as spine-chilling screams of pain cut into his consciousness.

Primal fear rose. *What the hell is happening?*

Lifting his head, he looked up … and flinched as the looming figure of a powerful man stepped over him. The man picked up speed, sprinting away towards other armed men heading their way. Eyes widening in horror, Lanky saw he lay in the midst of a brutal fight, a fight in which several lay bloodied on the ground.

Trembling, he forced himself to move. *I need to get out of here.*

Pushing himself to a low crouch, he readied himself to run. But as he searched for a way out, he saw the mad woman who'd flung him off the cliff lying beside him. *I can't leave her here.* He grabbed her hand, but she screamed and pulled away. "We have to run," he hissed, and grasped her hand again. This time, she held it, blindly staring at him, despair written deep in her eyes. His heart pounding, he took a quick glance around. Seeing a gap behind them, he readied himself. "Get up and follow me!" he commanded. "Now!"

As the terrified woman scrambled to her feet, Lanky jumped up and ran. Hearing harsh shouting behind him, he glanced back. The woman was following, but to his horror, an armed man was running after them. "Run!" he yelled. "Run hard!"

Something whistled past his ear. The hairs on his nape stiffened as he realised it had been an axe. He ran on as hard as he could, praying that she was still following.

*

Disorientated and scared, and feeling as though her whole body had been hit by a train, Beth stared, unbelieving, at the vicious fight around her. What ghastly madness was this? People were dying. Her stomach churned at the sight of the grisly wounds of those lying, moaning on the leaf-strewn ground. She forced the nausea away, desperately trying to see a way out, but the sounds of vicious fighting surrounded her. There was no easy escape from this. And the sounds of battle – the grunts, the bloodthirsty cries, the screams of the injured – continued unabated. Horrific sounds she had once heard before when a routine patrol of her unit was ambushed. Sounds that told of a deadly fight with many formidable combatants.

Including these two heading my way.

As she spied the crude yet brutal hand weapons they carried, a cold acceptance settled on her. There was no choice here. She had to fight to stay alive.

Drawing a deep, slow breath, she tensed to rise …

But was immediately pushed back to the ground by forceful hands.

A bear of a man, armed with a spear and wearing a white fur jacket, stepped over her, then ran purposefully towards the two attackers. He knew what he was doing. The first assailant took the spear in his stomach, and as the second swung his axe, the bear of a man leapt into his chest, taking them both to the ground. Wrenching the attacker's axe from his hand, the powerful man sprang to his feet, then swung the axe in a vicious arc, cleaving his opponent's head.

"Run!" came a cry from behind.

Beth turned to see Jessica out in a stand of trees beyond the core of the battlefield, sprinting away with the lad, Lanky, who still held the staff. She pulled herself up to follow but was hit from behind and knocked to the ground. A heavy foot stood on her back and a guttural voice spoke words she couldn't understand. She tried to get up – the foot pushed down more firmly. Frustrated, Beth scanned the woods for Jessica. Her friend and Lanky had broken away from the fighting, but to her horror she saw they were being chased by a stocky figure, his axe primed to throw.

"No!" Beth cried out. "Run, Jess! Run hard!"

A lithe figure sprang in front of Beth, launching a spear at Jessica's attacker. As the axeman hurled his weapon, the spear hammered into his back, knocking him to the ground. The thrown axe flew narrowly wide of Jessica's head. The spear-thrower sprinted on towards the stricken man, a knife in his hand.

Beth looked away.

Still pinned to the ground, she glanced towards the continuing hand-to-hand fighting. *What in God's name is happening? And how did we get here?*

Nothing made sense.

Except one thing. *I need to get out of here.*

But it still wasn't clear how she could do that.

She tried to calm her thoughts. The one holding her down hadn't killed her. *And he could have by now.* Could she take him out? No, she couldn't yet. She had no idea what weapon the man had trained on her. And while she'd been in tricky positions before, this was bad. This was not a time to act blindly.

Wait for your chance.

She drew a slow breath. While part of her waited for a spear in the back, another continually assessed the situation. *It's getting quieter. There's less fighting.*

The foot lifted from her back.

Beth instinctively tensed, readying herself to run if the opportunity came …

A knee pressed into her back, then a man's face appeared beside hers, thickset, heavily scarred, with a prominent brow. The man growled words of an unknown tongue. Then his hand appeared, holding a spearpoint – her mind registered that it was flint. The flint pressed against her neck, and the hand gestured to where Jessica and Lanky had fled. The flint pushed harder against her neck, then was released. The man spoke again, quietly yet firmly.

Beth got the message. If she tried to run like the others, she'd get a spear in her back. *Keep your head down for now, girl, and figure how to get out of here.* She nodded to the scar-faced man. "Guess I'll be good for now."

The man's fierce eyes studied her for a moment, then he gestured to a spear-carrying, leather-clad woman close by, who quickly ran to them. After a few brief words, the scar-faced man hurried away towards the ongoing fighting. The woman, heavy-set and strong-featured, stood over Beth, her spear angled towards her chest.

Sudden, wretched tiredness flooded over Beth. She settled her head on the ground and closed her eyes. *What's just happened? Who are these people?*

She found no answers.

Only more questions.

*

Through a fog of terror, Jessica had heard Lanky's frantic cry to run and had scrambled to her feet, then sprinted hard after the fleeing man. She heard nothing and saw nothing, only the fleeing figure ahead as they both bounded over the rough ground, branches whipping into her face as they careered through thickets of vegetation. Her fear drove her on, her only thought in the moment to leave that brutal savagery far, far behind. But as they fled, her fearful glances behind brought a sickening realisation – her friends were not with them! In the frenzied panic of her escape, she hadn't noticed.

But now she saw the truth. *I ran away and left my friends!*

She almost collided with Lanky, who had abruptly stopped.

"We need to rest," he panted. He gestured to a jumbled stack of boulders surrounding a crooked tree. "We can hide in there."

Anguish gripping her at the thought of her abandoned friends, Jessica followed him to the moss-covered rocks, where they slipped between a narrow gap to a shaded space behind. Lanky slumped to the ground, his back against the arched tree trunk, his face pained. Breathing agonised breaths, she dropped to the ground opposite him, her head in her hands.

Silence fell, save for the alarmed chirping of birds in the trees around them.

"What's happening?" Jessica whispered as her breathing eased. "And where are my friends?"

She heard no answer.

She looked up and saw Lanky sitting as she'd been, with his head in his hands. "I don't know," he muttered. "I really don't know. And I only saw one of your friends up there. The one who was with you when I met you on the trail."

Beth ... I abandoned her ... "And Erin and Tricia?" she whispered to herself.

"If those are the names of your other friends," Lanky said, his head still in his hands, "they weren't there."

Jessica's gut twisted. *Then where are they?* She glanced through the gap between the boulders. "We have to get to the village and fetch help ... find Beth and the others." She looked back at Lanky. "Are those men still chasing us?"

Lanky looked up, his tousled hair echoing his distress. "I don't know. Maybe. I didn't see anyone. I was too busy trying to find which way to go, but I couldn't find the path. It's all different."

Different? Fractured images of their panicked flight flooded back. In the terror of the moment, she hadn't really noticed. But ... "What do you mean different?"

"It just isn't the same place. No paths, different wood." He paused. "And we should be at the edge of the village by now."

"What do you mean? Are we lost?"

Lanky's brow creased. "I don't know. It doesn't make any sense."

"Damn you," Jessica hissed in frustration. "This is all your fault. Where are we?" She suddenly remembered her phone. She pulled it out of her pocket and unlocked it – then glowered. "No bloody signal." She slipped it back in her pocket and climbed to her feet. "I'm going to see where we are."

"No! Don't go back out there yet. They may still be chasing us."

Ignoring him, Jessica slipped out through the narrow gap in the rocks, then stood with her back to the boulders and looked around. She stood on a sloping hillside at the fringes of birch tree woods. Turning slightly to look out through the trees, she saw a rugged, valleyed land beyond. Tall, swaying grasses covered most of the hillsides, interspersed by scattered thickets of juniper bushes and shimmering-leaved birch tree stands. Occasional boulder screes ran down the hills from steep, stark ridges above. There was no sign of paths, fences, or walls anywhere. *What is this place? How did I get here?*

She turned back in confusion. The young lad stood in silence, watching her.

She froze as a shocking thought struck. This was the one who had attacked her, the one who had been waiting for them with that staff he carried. "You're involved in this, aren't you? Are these people your friends? You trying to scare us because of what happened yesterday?" She took a step towards him, her anger flaring. "That's it, isn't it? You've set us up! Well, well done. Yes, it scared the crap out of me, and I hope you feel great – but you won't be pleased when you're explaining this to the police."

Angry, confused, scared, she started walking back to the north. *Get away from him. Get back to my friends.*

"Don't be an idiot," she heard the lad hiss. "Those people up there are dangerous, and the best way we can help your friends is to find help. We can't tackle people like that ourselves."

"Go home," she shouted. "I'm going to find my friends. Goodbye."

And she started to run.

*

Lanky stood in the shadows of his refuge, watching Jessica run up the hill until she disappeared into a thicker stand of trees. He cursed. It was utter insanity to go back up there. Those had been a brutal set of people, with bad stuff happening. *It looked as though people were killed.* Grimacing, he glanced blindly around. None of this made sense. One minute he was sitting by the cliff edge, the next he was …

A nameless dread engulfed him. *I was what? Tell me what happened.*

But he was unwilling to chase that thought, unwilling to face half-heard answers whispering at the edges of his mind. Whatever had happened, he needed to get away from those madmen and bring help. He glanced up the hill. And heading back into danger wasn't an option.

Glancing around and seeing no one, he walked fully out into the open. He scanned the land beyond the trees. It seemed a remote area, but he was sure there must be a settlement somewhere. If he headed downhill, surely he'd hit a road?

But the damn fool Jessica had gone the other way.

Get help. That's the only way to help.

Shaking off a pang of unease – or guilt? – he started walking south, keeping low, constantly looking around. He felt the weight of the staff in his hand and gripped it more tightly. It was his only form of defence, and while unlikely to help him against those thugs up there, it gave him some small comfort.

And what about her? What defence does she have? And what does she think she can achieve by going back? It could make things worse.

Forget it. Let her go. There's no way I could stop her anyway, so stop thinking about it and just get out of here.

He walked on.

What can she hope to do against them? She's crazy.

She's worried about a friend, that's what.

Just forget her.

He walked a few paces more … then blew a sigh of frustration. *Damn it. I can't just leave her.*

He turned and started walking north. And then he ran. She had a head start, but maybe he could catch her.

And he hadn't gone far when he saw her in the distance, sitting on a rock beside a lone tree. Her head was in her hands, her long dark hair covering her face. He ran on towards her.

"I don't know which way we came," she whispered as he approached, her head still bowed. "There's no path, I don't know where my friends are, and this bloody phone still won't work."

Hearing the terrible despair in the young woman's voice – a despair echoing his own gut-deep dread – Lanky reached out and placed a hand on her shoulder. He said nothing.

Eventually she looked up. "Why did you come after me?"

Because I don't really know what to do. Because I'm scared. Terrified. Because ... "I'm not really sure. All I know is that I couldn't let you go back up there by yourself. Best we stick together for now."

She studied him, fear flickering in her eyes. She had a sculpted face, a strong jawline, a slightly flared nose. *And striking brown eyes,* he thought as she continued to stare up at him. *Brown with a hint of green.* It was not the face of one he'd think would frighten easily. He suppressed a shiver. *But who wouldn't be scared by what we've seen?*

"You're not responsible for what happened up there, are you?"

He shook his head.

"And yesterday?"

"I was just out ... exploring and didn't know you were there on the path. I stumbled. I fell." He shrugged.

"And today?"

"Today I was ... exploring again," he said, sheepishly. "And I found this." He held up the staff.

"Seems you like exploring."

Lanky inwardly winced. *Once I did. But now ...* He said nothing.

She held his gaze for a moment, then said in a quiet voice, "I'm sorry I shouted at you. And ignore what I said. You couldn't have set this up." She held out her hand. "My name's Jessica. And I'm scared."

Lanky reached out and took it. He forced a smile. "Pleased to meet you, Jessica. I'm Lanky. And I'm scared too."

She gave a weak smile. "Lanky. Yes, I heard your name at the gorge." She hesitated. "And I'm sorry for throwing you over that cliff." Her eyes flicked down to his body. "You must be lighter than you look."

"It's why my dad called me Lanky. Tall and nothing to me." He tilted his head. "Guess you're tall too. But not light."

Jessica raised her eyebrows.

Lanky's eyes widened a touch. "I don't mean you're fat – not that there's anything wrong with being fat – or thin. I just mean you ... err

...." He trailed off as her eyes narrowed. "Guess I was trying to make small talk. Not my specialty."

"No, that seems to be exploring." She raised an eyebrow. "Exploring what exactly? Why—"

A sudden crashing sound exploded behind them.

Turning, Lanky stared wide-eyed as a massive stag bounded out of a thicket towards them. "Down!" he hissed.

They both dropped to the ground, panicked eyes on the beast as the fearsome animal leapt over them, its sweeping antlers seeming as dark frozen fire reaching for the sky. He watched, transfixed, as the prodigious beast hurtled up the slope to the north.

He sat up—

And immediately dropped again as a herd of deer crashed through the thicket towards them. Almost as huge as the first, these veered around them as they bounded off in the direction of the stag.

"Unbelievable," Lanky said as the herd vanished from sight. "Did you see how big those things were?"

"Where did they come from?" Jessica whispered, gazing after them.

Lanky frowned, then glanced to the south, suddenly tense. "They may have been scared by something. Quick. Follow me and stay low."

With Jessica following, he made his way quickly to the thicker vegetation, where he dropped down into a crouch. "Stay quiet," he whispered.

It wasn't long before they heard voices.

Holding stock still as the voices drew closer, he feared his beating heart would be heard across the valley. *We can't show ourselves. We can't take that risk until we know who they are.* He heard the unknown figures pass close by before moving quickly away to the north. Releasing a slow breath, he risked a peep above the long grass. He saw three heads moving into the distant trees, but it was too far to make out any detail before they disappeared from view.

"Who were they?" Jessica whispered.

"Couldn't tell," Lanky breathed, still staring after the men. "Friend or foe? No idea."

A silence fell, the tension biting.

Nervous heartbeats later, Lanky ran his hand through his thick, unruly hair. "Okay, here's my thoughts." He gestured to the north. "There's some really bad stuff happening that way. What was happening, and why, I've no damn idea, but that was a nightmare we don't want to enter again." He saw the anguished uncertainty in Jessica's eyes. "I know your friend may still be up there, but I still think we should move south and get to the closest path, road, or whatever we can find to get help. It's the best way to help your friend. What do you think?"

*

Jessica studied the young man's strained face. She'd been a fool. She'd lashed out at him because she'd been scared and confused. Terrified. And guilt-ridden at leaving her friends.

She glanced to the north. *Beth is up there.* Her stomach twisted. And Erin and Trish? Where were they? *I have to find them. I have to find them all.* She looked back at Lanky. But he was right. There was nothing the two of them could do alone against those they'd seen.

She nodded. "We need to fetch help."

Lanky's face set in a grim resolve. "Then let's get moving."

As they warily raised their heads above the tall grasses, she peered around the scattered trees around them, then scanned the rugged terrain beyond. She saw nothing moving, no obvious threat. Lanky gestured for them to move and she followed him to the fringes of the tall grasses. Seeing all still clear, they headed out into the more open ground, then cautiously made their way downhill.

Keeping themselves low and continually scanning for danger, they moved as quickly as they could through the low grasses of the sparse woodland. As quiet as they thought they were, skittish birds scattered from hiding, the larger scooting off through the grassy undergrowth, the smaller taking to the air in alarm. *I pray that anyone hearing this thinks it's just deer moving,* Jessica thought as another flock scattered above them.

Her mouth dry, she ran on beside Lanky, searching for signs of a path, road, house, even the pervasive stone walls of the fells in which they'd hiked these last days. But she saw nothing, no evidence of people, anywhere.

Her fear deepened. *Where the hell are we?*

Reaching the fringes of the sparse woodland, she heard the rippling sounds of a river, and moments later caught glimpses of its sparkling waters angling towards them from the right. She caught up with Lanky and signalled for him to slow. They stopped near a lone, bowed tree, a low rocky ridge to their left. The river ran on, then swung around to the left, curving behind the flank of the ridge.

She glanced to the crest of the rise. "We should head up there and figure out which way to go."

Lanky nodded, and they quickly headed to the base of the ridge, then scrambled up the rocky slope. Slowing near the top, Jessica lay down, then peeked her head over the crest.

The river lay below them, curving first to the left and then around to the right, where it merged first with a tributary from the north, then with a larger tributary from the west. Swollen with their waters, the river meandered on through the broad valley before flowing into the head of a dark-watered lake. An open plain, teeming with animals, lay to the left of the lake, abutting a rising hillside.

Her breath caught as she gazed at the plain. Where she may have expected flocks of fells sheep, instead scattered herds of massive deer, similar to those they had seen earlier, grazed the land. And interspersed between them, horses, their multihued coats and long, flowing manes unlike anything she'd seen.

"Look over there," Lanky whispered. "Are those spotted horses? And there" – he pointed to a group of imposing beasts with ornate, sweeping antlers – "they look like elk."

"It's incredible," she whispered. "Incredible, but wrong. What are they doing here?"

Lanky had no answer for her.

They lay for a while longer, then she shivered. "It's cold. How is it so cold all of a sudden?"

"I noticed it before. It's seemed colder since ..." He hesitated. "Since we arrived here." He gestured to the west. "But more importantly, do you see the smoke over there?"

She looked to her right, and in the distance, across the river on slightly higher ground, she saw a faint tendril of smoke reaching into the sky. She couldn't see a fire, but now her eyes were focussed on that area, she could see movement. "I think I see someone over there."

"I see them too," he said, gazing to the distance. He seemed to consider for a moment. "Problem is, they could be part of that gang up there. Maybe that's their camp?" His gaze shifted back to the valley plain below. "Do you see any tracks or roads or houses anywhere?"

"Nothing." She pulled out her phone and checked it again. "Aah! What's wrong with this thing? Why's there no signal?"

She glanced up at Lanky to see him scanning intently around the landscape. "It makes no sense," he murmured as if to himself.

"What makes no sense?"

He looked out into the valley, seemingly reluctant to answer. "I feel as though I'm going mad. But look, forget the lack of houses and roads, just look at what we can see." He gestured to the black waters of the lake. "Down there is the lake. In the distance is the High Ridge. And over in the distance are the peaks of the Long Valley. Okay, I admit it's not exactly the same, but it's damn close to the land I know." Ignoring her look of utter disbelief, he gestured to their left. "Down there should be the ruins of that ancient fort. And down there," he said, pointing to the empty valley below, "should be my village."

Jessica stared at him, stunned at what he was suggesting. She glanced back to the vista before them. She saw a vague familiarity to the scene ... *But to remove a whole town?* "You realise how crazy you sound?"

Lanky let out a slow breath. "Crazy?" He wiped his brow. "It ain't necessarily so," he whispered.

She frowned.

He glanced at her. "Sorry, did I say that out loud? A dumb game I used to play."

Her brow furrowed. *A game? Who plays a game at a time like this?*

Lanky looked out to the low-lying plain nestled in its cradle of fells. "Maybe I am crazy," he whispered. He sighed. "Let's go back down and figure out a plan." He pushed back from the crest, then climbed to his feet and headed down the rise.

Her troubled gaze followed him. *Maybe we're both crazy.* She shook her head. *Just keep moving, and fetch help.*

Joining him at the bottom of the ridge, she shivered again. The cold was eating into her, as was the fear. Real fear. Not the adrenaline-fuelled fear of earlier, but the cold, stark, brutal fear of assessing a situation and seeing no way out. "I'm scared," she stated simply.

"Me too. This has not been one of the better days of my life."

"Do you think we head over to the people with the fire?"

"I guess that's the big question. We either head over to see who they are and see if we think they'd help us, or we—"

A man leapt out of the grasses, swinging a club. Jessica tried to duck, but the last thing she felt was a tremendous pain – and then darkness.

CHAPTER FIVE

The shaman did well – it was the quickest way.

The sounds of battle had slowly faded, replaced with the quiet murmuring of subdued voices, interspersed with low groans of the injured. The woman guarding Beth gestured for her to sit. Cautiously pulling herself up and settling into a nonthreatening, seated position, Beth nervously watched a small group of robust-featured men and women, dressed in a variety of leather and fur clothing, quietly move around the battlefield, stripping the dead of their weapons. A disturbing collection of spears, stone axes, and bows gradually accumulated beside the bodies of the dead. The bear of a man in the bloodstained white fur jacket seemed to be their leader.

Whatever else was happening here, it was clear she was a captive of unknown hostiles, and with numerous armed people surrounding her, escape was impossible. That said, no one had yet directly threatened her, other than the clear command to stay put by the one she'd named Scar. She pushed a strand of her sweat-drenched hair from her cheek. *Go with it for now, Beth, and take the opportunity when it comes.*

Like Jess.

An intense flood of relief rushed through her. At least her friend had managed to escape, together with the lad carrying the staff. That took one great worry off her shoulders. *And Trish and Erin?* She slammed a hold on the thought. They weren't here. She had to hope they hadn't been caught up in ... *in whatever this is.*

As a grim-faced group led by Scar carried away the bloodstained bodies, Beth glanced around the sparse woodland, struggling to understand what had happened to her. One minute she'd been helping Jess, the next a pain beyond comprehension had ripped through her head, and she'd blacked out.

And woken up here. Wherever here is.

How? Had they been attacked? But with what, and by who? Who were these brutal warring factions? And where had they come from? *And why dressed like this? A cult?*

No answers came, and soon the area was cleared of the dead.

His grisly task complete, Scar dropped to his knees beside a gurgling stream, then washed his hands before scooping up a mouthful of water. Beth licked her lips; she hadn't realised how thirsty she'd become.

At that moment, the powerful man in the white fur jacket strode past. *Definitely the leader of this group,* she thought, seeing the confidence of the man's gait. She watched him climb the hill from the stream, then disappear from sight behind a moss-covered boulder. He quickly reappeared and called down to the group, gesturing for them to follow. Scar climbed to his feet and walked over to her. Taking her arm, he nodded towards the hill.

She tensed. *Where are we going now?* She glanced around, looking again for an opportunity to run. As if reading her mind, Scar tightened his grip on her arm. A second man, carrying a spear, walked up behind her. She silently cursed. *I can't risk it.* Scar pulled on her arm. She forced a hold on her fear. *You've no choice. Go with them. Look for your chance.*

Heart thudding heavily in her chest, she followed Scar up the hill towards the large boulder. As he rounded the boulder and vanished from sight, she cautiously followed – she found herself facing a shadowy entranceway into the hillside. *A cave?* Her fear flared. *No. I don't fancy that.* She half turned—

A hand pressed on her back, urging her onwards.

"Damn it!" she hissed. "Stop pushing me."

But a firmer push from behind forced her to stumble on, and she ducked and entered. Staring into the deepening gloom, she licked her dry lips. *What do they want from me?* The terrifying question echoed unanswered as the insistent hand pushed her further into the ever-darkening passageway.

After only a few steps, she halted as she reached a narrow crevice. The hand gently pushed her forward. "Wait," she grunted, peering into the darkness. "I've no idea where to put my feet."

The hand pushed more firmly.

Cursing, Beth held out both hands and ran them along the walls of the tight opening. If that stocky leader of theirs had made it through, so could she. *Not that any sane person would want to.* With the persistent pressure on her back, she slipped through the opening and entered the narrow passageway beyond. Having no other option, she continued on.

Despite her stumbling on the uneven, sloping ground, she was not allowed to pause. Even in those places where she was forced to crouch beneath low-hanging rock, the unyielding hand on her back gave no respite. "Lucky I'm not claustrophobic," she muttered to herself. On and on, they walked, her eyes playing tricks, telling her it was growing lighter. Eventually, she realised that the gloom was indeed lessening, and the shadowy, rough-hewn tunnel walls slowly became visible. Light was entering from somewhere below.

She walked onwards, following the passageway as it took a sharp turn to the right. The light grew noticeably brighter. Squeezing around another corner, she found herself at the top of rough-cut steps. She heard voices below. A push from behind forced her on, and she descended the steps – and walked out into a large torchlit cavern, where a group of fur-clad men and women, maybe eight to ten, sat or stood, scattered around the cavern.

Fighting to calm her breathing, Beth quickly scanned the chamber, making a mental note of what she saw. To her left against the rugged wall of the chamber lay a cache of crude weapons – axes, spears, bows. Against the wall to her right lay a neatly piled collection of furs and hides. *Clothing?* At the far side of the cavern lay a stash of other items, but she couldn't make them out. On the far wall yawned a small opening. *A possible exit?* And on the walls were various drawings and sketches, some painted.

Her gaze returned to the people. Some stood in silence, appearing as if caught midsentence; some sat, or lay, on scattered rugs, their faces etched with the pain of recent battle; all were dressed in a similar style to those she'd seen outside – slim-fitting leather and fur clothing. *Well made,* she noted absently. And she could smell cooked food and the rich yet faintly acrid odour of a recent wood fire. *They've been living in here.* This was clearly a base of some sort, but beyond that, she struggled to make sense of what she was seeing. *A base for what? And why here?*

She saw most of the eyes in the room were on her. The bear of a man she thought of as their leader was talking to an old woman. Both were also looking at her.

The old woman caught her eye and gestured for her to come forward.

Beth glanced at the entrance. Two men stood by it. *Guards. Not that way then.* She looked back at the old lady. *Okay,* she thought, girding herself. *Let's try this.* She walked over to them with a confident stride and held out a hand to the old woman. "Hello. I'm Beth."

The woman regarded her with a penetrating gaze, then took her hand. Beth gripped the woman's hand firmly – it was as though she held a leather shoe. The old lady said something Beth didn't understand, then gestured for her to sit. Beth acknowledged her with a curt nod, then sat down on a white fur. The old woman spoke briefly with the bear of a man beside her, then sat down opposite Beth. As the reflection of a torch opposite flickered in the old woman's deep-set eyes, her rugged, weathered face creased into a smile.

Okay, maybe I'm still not toast yet. And this doesn't seem to be a lady who is about to hit me with an axe. But who knows today?

They sat studying one another until the leader returned with a bowl carried in each hand. He handed one to the old woman, and the other to Beth, who took it, cradling it in her fingers. The bark container held a clear liquid of some kind. The old lady took a sip from her bowl, then gestured to Beth. *She wants me to drink too.* She licked her lips again, then took a sip. *Water.* She took a long, refreshing draught, then offered it to the leader. He gently pushed it back to her. *Okay, it's mine, I guess.* She placed it beside her.

As the old lady and the leader spoke in a hushed voice, Beth glanced back to those in the cavern. They seemed to have lost interest in her, and a quiet chatter had replaced the silence. She noticed Scar had taken off his upper garments, and a red-haired woman smothered a dark substance over the various cuts on his arm and neck. Another younger man she recognised from the fight outside lay on the ground, already snoring. Another appeared through the entrance, carrying an armful of clothes. *From the attackers, I guess.* She shook her head. *Who are these people? What—*

A loud voice sounded at the chamber's entrance, and Beth turned to see a girl appear in the cavern, her face like thunder. Dressed as the men in a variety of close-fitting leather garments and carrying a bow and a container of arrows on her back, the girl stopped in the centre of the chamber and glared at Beth.

Beth tensed. *She looks younger than me. And unpredictable. This could change things.*

Moving quickly towards them, the girl approached Beth, glared down at her, then spat at her feet. Her eyes afire, the girl turned to the leader and the old lady, speaking aggressively while gesticulating at Beth. A hard look in his eyes, the leader held up his hand, then spoke sharply and firmly to the girl. The girl stared daggers at him, then strode away to the other side of the cave, where she remonstrated with Scar.

"I don't think she likes me," Beth said softly to herself as she eyed the girl, a knot forming in her stomach. And that was a problem; she could end up with an arrow in her head.

She glanced at the entrance. One of the guards had walked over to the angry girl. The other watched him. She immediately tensed. *This might be the only chance I get. Time to try to get out of here.* With no further thought, she leapt up and raced for the exit. As the guard turned in surprise, she lashed out, kicking him hard in the groin. As the man bent in pain, she kicked at his head, knocking him to the ground. Jumping over the prone man, she sprinted ahead—

A man appeared out of the shadows of the passageway, blocking her exit as he ran towards her. She grabbed his arm, and using his momentum, she twisted her body, flinging him easily over her shoulder. She sprinted towards—

A stabbing pain lanced through her right arm. Looking down, she saw a bloodied gash on the side of her upper arm. Spinning around, she saw the girl reach for another arrow. Beth roared and charged towards the girl, slamming into her just as she notched the second arrow. As they fell to the ground, Beth rolled and swung her fist, connecting violently with the girl's head. *Ow, that hurt.*

The girl went down, concussed.

Sucking in air, Beth looked up …

Four men stood in a semicircle around her. Behind them, the leader looked at her and shook his head. He pointed at the white rug.

Beth held up her hands. "Okay," she panted. "Okay." *Not this time.* Her chest tightening, she took a step towards the white rug …

Sudden dizziness swept over her, and the figures ahead blurred. She took another step but staggered. *That drink …*

The leader took her arm and helped her back to the rug. She was aware of something being wrapped tightly around her injured arm. The old lady talked to her, but it made no sense to Beth's drifting mind.

After a time, someone pulled her upright, encouraging her to walk. In a moment of lucidity, she was aware of passing through the exit at the back of the cave. Dazed, she walked on through a gloomy passageway and into a small cavern beyond.

Her world began to spin.

And the paintings on the cavern's wall shimmered and flowed.

The paintings seemed alive.

Alive with ghostly animals.

Beth watched, mesmerised, as the animals detached from the painted walls, their fluid forms streaming into the warmth of the chamber. A silver-coated reindeer veered towards her, its majestic antlers sweeping to the sky; a glistening, black-coated horse with a flowing black mane and white diamond-shaped marking on its forehead galloped beside her; and a wolf pack on the hunt howled in the distance, a single massive white-furred male peeling off the pack and joining the chase—

A blaze of blinding light exploded around her, and staggering, she fell to her knees.

Her head spinning, her mind floating, she looked up to see a swirling array of scintillating colours streaming around her. The dreamlike animals raced into the fringes of the magical display, dancing in and out of the kaleidoscopic river with hypnotic harmony.

A hand gently pushed her head down …

Shimmering, wraithlike forms swam on the ground before her. She could make no sense of what they were. The beautiful horse she'd seen before swept into view and swirled around one of the objects.

Beth reached down and grasped it.

As an ear-shattering crack of thunder rocked the chamber, a streak of searing pain ripped up her arm and through her body. She tried to open her hand, but her fingers gripped tighter.

She heard and felt a deep laughter.

Then a voice.

'Welcome back, Bethusa.'

CHAPTER SIX

Shadow failed to recognise all that was before him this day. At the conclusion of all that follows, we might return to this moment and ask, "What might have happened if he had understood who he held?"

*H*is head pounding, Lanky groaned and slowly opened his eyes to see the ground moving beneath him. Tight bindings cut into his body as he rocked to and fro, suspended from a rough pole that dug into his back. Moving his head, wincing against the pain in his stiff neck, he saw the legs of two figures, fore and aft, who were carrying him.

A chill of foreboding brought a cold terror sweeping through him. Who were they? What did they want with him? *Where are they taking me?*

Calm down! a part of his mind instantly commanded. *Figure out what's happening.*

Forcing several deep, silent breaths, he felt the tremors in his body slowly ease.

That's it, came a thought from deep inside. *Understand.*

Ignoring the lancing pain in his head, Lanky glanced to the side. He saw Jessica strapped to a pole – or rather a rough-hewn tree branch – carried on the shoulders of two bulky men. Her head lolled about; she was clearly unconscious. The menacing figures carrying Jessica were dressed in a mix of rough-looking brown leathers and furs, like those he'd seen at the earlier brutal fight. Ahead of them all walked another man. *Not much older than me.* Somehow, he looked different to the others; a very short, sculpted beard, long black hair swept behind his head and tied into a short ponytail, and clothing that looked … *more tailored.*

As if feeling Lanky's eyes on him, the long-haired man glanced towards him. The man immediately raised his hand. The people carrying Lanky stopped moving, and he heard voices – an alien language – then he was dropped.

"Aargh!" he exclaimed as his head hit the ground.

Rustling footsteps sounded around him, then rough hands raked the backs of his calves and thighs. Moments later, the bindings fell from his legs. He cried out as someone roughly pulled the pole from his back, the jagged bark scraping and tearing his skin. Someone grabbed his bound arms and pulled him up to his feet. His head swimming, blood dripping from his nose, he took a step to steady himself.

He grunted at a sharp blow to his arm.

Wincing, he looked around. A stocky, bent-nosed man stood beside him, a crude wooden club in his hand. The man lifted his free hand to a necklace around his neck, then gestured to Lanky and smiled. Pain-racked, Lanky glanced to the object the man held in his fingers. A wave of nausea ripped through his stomach as he saw what the man wore. A necklace strung with teeth. He dropped to his knees and retched. He heard laughter from the bent-nosed man beside him and then felt another blow on the arm. A commanding shout came from the front, and the bent-nosed man walked away, laughing.

A moment later, a hand grasped Lanky's arm and pulled him up. He straightened to see the man with the ponytail facing him. The man raised a vicious-looking harpoon and held the point to Lanky's neck. The man said something unintelligible, then increased the pressure on the harpoon, just enough to nick the skin.

"I'll cause no trouble," Lanky said instantly, quickly recognising that the man had saved him from a beating. "I promise."

Pushing Lanky in front of him, the long-haired man switched the harpoon to press into his back. The man spoke briefly, and one of the other men moved off ahead of the group. Two others hauled Jessica's pole back onto their shoulders and followed. A push in the back with the harpoon signalled Lanky to follow. Stumbling forward, he wiped his mouth with the back of one of his bound hands. *Those teeth … They couldn't be …* His stomach twisted. *Don't go there.*

As feeling returned to his recently bound legs, he fell into a dazed stride behind the men ahead. Who were these animals? What were they doing here? Whoever they were, they were dangerous, especially the guy with the club. He needed to stay clear of him. But the long-haired guy … *He seems to be the boss – and he helped me.* He wiped his bloodied nose on his arm. He just needed to do what they said for now, and hope the long-haired guy realised they were no threat. *Else we need to look for a chance to run.*

He looked up and saw a column of smoke rising just ahead of them; they'd crossed the river while he was unconscious. It was clear now that the smoke they'd seen was from their captors' camp, and that's where they were heading. *From the frying pan, into the fire.*

*

Jessica had come to early but decided to stay quiet, trying to control her head movements as much as possible whilst not giving away she was awake. As they had travelled, she'd risked brief peeks to see where they were going, and had seen them cross the river. Later, she'd heard the call from Lanky alerting their captors he'd awakened, then heard his cries as one of the men assaulted him. She was glad of her decision to stay quiet.

And now they approached the fire they'd seen. Her gut twisted. *This can't be real. This is a nightmare—*

Without warning they dropped her, and she cried out as she hit the ground.

"Are you okay?" came Lanky's worried voice.

She turned her head and found him crouching next to her. "Sore and scared. Very scared." She tried to move but her body remained bound. "Can you shift this pole from my back?"

"Don't think so. My hands are still tied. And they may not like me trying either."

"What can you see?" she asked, struggling to see what was happening.

"Six people, all men. One is standing here – a scrawny man, seems he's our guard. Two others are behind the fire, and three are arguing between them. The nasty guy with the bent nose is the loud one. I don't see anyone else."

"And my friends?"

"Not that I can see."

Relief flooded through her.

Relief that was short-lived. "Are these the ones from that hellish fight?"

"I think so. They're definitely dressed the same way. And that Bent-Nose seems a real dangerous character." His voice lowered to a barely heard whisper. "I've no idea what's happening, but we have to be very careful here. Keep your movements slow and respond only if they want you to do something. The only thing going for us now is that the long-haired guy seems to have some say in what's going on. And he protected me … Hold on, that guy is coming over."

"Which one?" Jessica whispered.

"Longhair."

"Thank God."

She managed to turn her head slightly and saw two men approaching: Longhair and a second man, whose head was shaved at the top and the sides, and whose remaining black hair was bound at the back of his neck like Longhair's. Longhair stopped beside them and spoke briefly with the scrawny guard. The guard then stepped to her and undid the cords binding her to the rugged pole. He gently removed the pole from her back.

Twisting herself around into a sitting position, she rubbed her legs with her still-bound hands. Feeling the blood flowing, she sat back and glanced at the guard. "Can I have some water?" she asked, gesturing a drinking motion with her bound hands. The scrawny man glanced at Longhair, who stood silently watching them. Longhair nodded and the guard walked away.

Longhair's gaze shifted to Lanky. He held up Lanky's staff and spoke, gesturing to it with his other hand.

Lanky frowned. "I've no idea what you're saying."

The man lowered the staff, then reached out and gripped Lanky's chin, pulling his head left and then right, studying it intently. He spoke again.

Lanky knocked the man's hand away. "I've already told you," he rasped. "I don't know what you're saying."

"Stay calm, Lanky," Jessica hissed. "Remember what you just told me?"

Longhair's attention switched to her, and he stepped over to where she sat. He held up the staff and spoke again.

She looked up. "I can't understand you. I don't know what you want."

Longhair reached down and grasped her face in his hands, then turned her head, left and right as he'd done with Lanky, as though examining an antique vase. He angled her face towards him and leaned closer, staring into her eyes. He spoke quietly, his bright eyes searching hers.

"I don't understand," she said, her voice shaking.

Longhair studied her for a moment longer, then released her face and scanned down her body to her feet. Bending down, he examined her boots, then looked up at her shorts. She tensed as he pulled at the fabric before running his hands over the fabric of her t-shirt. His face unreadable, he stood, then walked over to join his colleague, where he spoke, voice muted, all the while casually watching her and Lanky.

Shaking, she turned to Lanky. "What did he want?"

"I've no idea. But it's as though he hasn't seen clothes like this before. Or people like us."

Jessica's lips thinned. "I've felt prejudice before." She glanced to Longhair and his friend, and then to the others beside Bent-Nose, who were still arguing loudly. "But it's those three over there that scare me the most."

"Don't stare at them, Jess. We don't want to provoke them."

As she flicked her eyes away from the three, she saw their guard return. Longhair waved him on. The guard stepped towards her and held out a leather container. It was wide at the base, narrowing to a small neck at the top. She took it in her bound hands, and tipping it slightly, saw a clear liquid spill out. *Looks okay.* She put the spout to her lips and took a sip. It tasted of … nothing. It was delicious. She took a long draught, then the guard snatched it from her and passed it to Lanky. He took several swigs before the guard grabbed the bottle and took it back.

Longhair gestured for them to stand. He pointed towards the camp.

Lanky stepped to her side. "Let's do everything he says, and hope that this Longhair realises we aren't any part of whatever is going on here. Maybe then he can help us." He took her bound hand in his, and she gripped tightly as they moved into the men's camp.

*

Walking towards the fire, Lanky noticed how sparse the camp was. Several weathered leather packs lay at one side of the fire, but no evidence of a tent or hut. It didn't seem these people had been here long. Harsh laughter sounded to his left, and looking around, he saw Bent-Nose and two others pointing at them. Lanky looked away, but not before he saw one of the men – a big brute of a man – stand and walk towards them.

The big man sauntered across to him – and then punched him hard in the stomach.

Lanky doubled over in pain.

Then he heard Jessica scream.

Gasping for breath, he looked up. The same brute of a man had grabbed Jessica and was hauling her towards Bent-Nose. Ignoring the pain in his stomach, Lanky scrambled to his feet, then launched into the side of the unsuspecting man, knocking him to the ground. The man roared in anger, then quickly regaining his feet, he strode over to

Lanky and struck him savagely on the side of the head. Lanky staggered, then fell to his knees. His head ringing, he looked up. *I'm in trouble now.*

Someone shouted – a loud and clear command.

Silence fell.

Lanky clambered to his feet, rubbing his head. With a sigh of relief, he saw Longhair standing between the big man and Jessica. The big man raged at Longhair, who simply stood calmly, head turned slightly, arms by his side. *He's not scared of the brute*, Lanky thought, noting for the first time Longhair's well-toned, lean body. *The brute may be big, but this Longhair looks tough.*

Longhair spoke in a low voice to the big man, gesturing to where Bent-Nose quietly watched. The man glared at Longhair, then spat on the ground before walking away.

Longhair turned—

The big man spun around and lunged towards Longhair—

Without turning, Longhair rolled to his side and the brute stumbled through empty space. Completing the roll, Longhair sprang easily back to his feet, crouching low and facing the raging man. As the brute charged, Longhair launched forward, hammering his right hand upwards to strike under the brute's chin. The big man screamed, but his momentum carried him on, and they both fell, the big man pinning Longhair to the ground.

Bent-Nose and his friend stood up, smiling.

The big man rolled away.

And lay still.

Longhair climbed to his feet, brushing himself down. A dagger point protruded from the top of the big man's head. Longhair reached down and pulled the bloody object from under the man's chin.

Lanky bent over and retched.

His stomach churning and a desperate horror chilling his soul, Lanky wiped his mouth. *He killed him. He slaughtered him.* He fought back another wave of nausea. *Who are these people?* His bound hands shaking, he glanced to Longhair. The man was slowly cleaning his stone dagger and speaking to a now grim-faced Bent-Nose. Cold realisation cut through his torment. *This Longhair is a killer – but without him we may already be dead.* He saw the stocky Bent-Nose nod in response to Longhair's words, then gesture to one of his rough-looking henchmen. Bent-Nose and his crony crossed to the dead man's body, hauled it up, then carried it away from the camp.

Lanky immediately rushed across to Jessica and knelt by her side. "You hurt?" he asked, voice wavering.

She shook her head. "What happens now?" she whispered, her gaze unfocussed.

I don't know. He looked up to see Longhair watching them. Then the killer sauntered back to the other side of the fire, where he spoke with his companion, who had stood by in silence during all that had happened. *His companion doesn't seem to speak,* crept an absent thought into the midst of Lanky's fraught mind. *It looks like he's signing.*

The thought vanished as Longhair looked over and gestured him over. Despite the man's horrific act, he knew they needed his protection from the foul Bent-Nose. *The lesser of two evils ...* "Longhair wants us to follow him," he said, reaching for Jessica's hand.

"When will this nightmare end?" she whispered as she took his bound hands in hers.

Lanky helped her up, then they cautiously walked around the fire to join Longhair, who gestured for them to sit. As they dropped to the ground, he saw they'd been positioned on the far side of the fire from Bent-Nose and his cronies. Their scrawny guard hurried over to them, then sat down between them and the fire. Lanky glanced at Longhair, who continued his conversation with his companion. *He continues to protect us. But why? And for how long?*

The two men conferred a while longer, then Longhair's companion walked across to a pack lying beside the fire. Grasping the spear resting against the pack, he strode away, the shaven side of his head gleaming in the firelight. The man walked on out of camp, heading towards the lake. For the briefest moment, Lanky wondered where the man was going ... but what did he know of anything here? Trying to still his shaking hands, he glanced over at Longhair. The man had lain down on a fur next to the fire and closed his eyes. He stared at the man, incredulous. He'd just killed a man – how could he sleep now? *Because he's done it before,* came his cold, stark thought.

Nerves wrung raw, Lanky turned to Jessica, who sat on the ground with tear-filled eyes. He dropped to her side and placed his bound hands on hers. He could think of nothing to say.

Wiping her eyes, Jessica looked up. "What hell have we landed in?"

He shook his head. He couldn't answer. He'd raked his mind but found that nothing made sense.

Except maybe—

"The staff," Jessica murmured, hesitant as though reluctant to follow her thoughts.

A ripple of fear ran through him. *It's as though she read my mind.*

"My nightmares," Jessica whispered as if to herself. "Someone asking for a staff." He felt her shiver. "Am I still dreaming?"

He shook his head. "This is no dream." He regarded her with an uneasy gaze, fearful of where his own crazed thoughts were heading. "You mentioned nightmares ..."

She shivered again. "I don't want to talk about it." She pressed closer to him. "I'm cold."

As they huddled closer together – for warmth and for comfort – Lanky's mind raced. *Nightmares? About the staff?* His thoughts leapt back to his long years of futile searching. *It couldn't be ... could it?* After all that time searching for artefacts from the past, searching for artefacts that scattered fragments of ancient writings said held a hidden power, could this staff be such a thing? *Have I found what was concealed within those maniacal scrawls of ancient madmen?* Where once an elated excitement would have coursed in his veins now trembled a terrible dread. *If this is such a thing, what has it done?* His troubled eyes flicked around camp, lingering on the exotic faces, the primitive clothing, and beyond, the unknown – *yet strangely familiar* – landscape.

It just can't be ...

Can it?

CHAPTER SEVEN

The Warrior and Bethusa were so alike, she failed to see her influence until much later.

Beth gasped as a surge of vibrant energy rushed through her, instantly banishing the fog in her mind. Alert and attuned to her surroundings, she spun around to face the old lady and white-jacketed leader. The leader took a step back, his eyes widening, but the old lady gave a gentle smile and held out her hands, palms up. "You can relax, Warrior. You are amongst friends."

Beth's eyes narrowed on the woman. So they spoke her language after all. What mad, dangerous game were they playing? "Forget the 'friends' crap," she rasped. "You poisoned me."

The old lady studied her. "I think it will take time to fully understand all you say, but I understand your concern. You are a Warrior who has only just arrived. You—"

"Warrior? What the hell are you talking about?"

"Look to yourself," the woman said quietly.

Frowning, Beth glanced around her without letting the old lady or the seemingly wary leader drift from her sight. They stood in a small rounded chamber, the leader in the centre, his head almost reaching the concave roof that arched over them before dropping to form the walls of the chamber. Abstract animal paintings, most fragmented images but in places complete forms, adorned the rough-hewn ceiling and walls.

And on the floor lay three gleaming green-stone axes.

It was then Beth became aware of her stance. She was crouching, her left hand held out in front of her and her right bent, relaxed, but primed. And holding a razor-edged, green-headed axe.

What? What am I doing?

But she didn't move.

She was angry, but in control. She knew she would use the axe if needed.

No, I'm not going to use it.

But if needed, I will, came her own calm rebuttal.

She shook her head. *Stop talking to yourself and figure out what to do.*

She tightened her grip on the haft of the axe. *I know what to do. Find Jess.* She glared at the two ahead of her. "I don't know what game you're playing, but it ends here. Move aside, I'm leaving."

The leader flicked a nervous glance at the old lady, but she placed her hand on his arm. "Stay, Bear," the woman murmured. She held Beth's eyes. "We will stand aside, and you will be free to go wherever you wish, but please first hear what I have to say."

Beth shook her head. "No. Move aside."

The old lady's face betrayed a sudden stirring of fear. "Please listen. It will help your friends."

Beth's gaze sharpened. "What do you know of my friends? Where are they?"

The old lady held Beth's hostile glare. "I will tell, but please relax. We mean you no harm."

Beth snorted. "No harm? You poisoned me."

The old lady flinched. "It was needed," she said, a flicker of pain in her eyes. "I am sorry … but I can explain. Please listen. I can help you and your friends."

Beth stood, suddenly uncertain. Did they truly know something about her friends? Or was she merely stepping into more trouble? She scanned their faces. The one the old lady called Bear seemed on edge, which was strange because she'd seen him in action – he was a fearless fighter. Why was he afraid of her? The old woman seemed calm on the outside, but beads of sweat glistened on her forehead. Beth's brow furrowed. *So, she's nervous too. Why?*

As she studied the two before her, she realised she was standing just a foot away from the old lady, axe ready to strike. *What are you doing?* she thought, licking her lips. *Are you actually going to strike her?* She took a short step back and relaxed her stance. But only a little.

The old lady drew a quiet breath, the slightest tension easing from her face. "We mean you no harm," the woman said again. "I swear on the heart of IY."

Beth held her stance. *Her words feel true but look at what they've just done to me – I can't trust them.*

But she used IY's name, came an unbidden thought.

So bloody what! Who the hell is that?

'*Someone you can trust,*' came a voice.

A familiar voice?

A name flashed through her mind. *Garrion.*

Feeling a cold sweat on her forehead, she strove to steady herself. What had these drugs done to her? *Focus! Focus on your friends.* "You sit here," she rasped, gesturing to the old lady, and pointing to a spot just to the right of her. "And you," she continued, turning to Bear, "sit by the wall over there, away from the entrance."

The powerfully built man glanced at the old lady, who nodded. They moved as instructed.

Beth dropped to her haunches within striking range of the old lady, keeping Bear and the entrance within view. "I'll give you a moment to talk and answer my questions, but when we're finished, this is what will happen. You," she said, gesturing at Bear, "will stay here. Then you and I," she said to the old lady, "will walk out of here with my axe at your back. Any wrong step and you die. We'll walk out to that other chamber, and you'll tell everyone to stay back and let me leave. Then you and I will leave, and when I'm back out into the open, I'll release you. Is that understood?"

"It is," the old woman answered calmly.

She turned to the seated leader. "And you?"

Bear's deep-set eyes showed disquiet, but he nodded.

Beth glared at the old lady. "Who are you? Talk."

The old lady, sitting with her legs folded under her and one hand turning a stone bracelet on her wrist, tilted her head a fraction. "I am Naga, and I will help you as I can." She glanced at the axe in Beth's hand. "But could you lay that aside while we talk?"

Beth shook her head. "Why would I do that?"

"It is difficult to talk when faced with the threat of death. I don't ask you to abandon it, just place it on the floor next to you."

Beth saw the tension in the woman's face. "Fine," she muttered, placing the axe on the ground. "Now talk."

Naga held Beth's gaze. "You are still holding it."

Beth glanced down. The axe was still in her hand. *But I put it down.*

She reached to drop it to the floor – but she didn't want to let it go. Not because she was scared. She wasn't scared. She was angry, but not scared. It was just calming to hold it. *This belongs to me. This is my axe ... my Axe.* "Just talk," she growled, trying to shake off the disturbing thoughts.

The old woman considered her for a moment. "I will keep this as simple as I can. First, we only understand what you say now because you are speaking our language."

Beth grunted a harsh laugh. "Very funny."

"It is true," Naga insisted. A slight frown crossed her face. "Though while you may understand all I say, some of your words do not translate easily. Your language is more complex."

Beth scowled. "Do you take me for a fool?"

'She speaks the truth,' came the voice. *'Listen to what she has to say.'*

Beth clenched her fist around the haft of the Axe. *This is madness. Or am I mad?* She tilted her head, studying Naga's face. Maybe so, but a part deep within her wished to hear what the woman had to say. She adjusted her grip on the Axe. "Just tell me who you are."

The old lady gave the faintest of nods, then spoke. "As I said, my name is Naga, and the people you have seen here are part of my tribe." She gestured to a thickset man sitting by the wall. "And Bear is the leader of the tribe. We are the Iyes, and though we are small in number, we are long-lived – and we carry a formidable burden." A fierce intensity lit in her eyes. "We have carried this burden through countless sun-cycles, passing it from mother to child, from father to child, from sun-cycle to sun-cycle. Most of those who lived this way died without the need for action, but a brave few, those who lived in the most horrific of times, were forced to draw on sacred knowledge preserved within our tribe – within our Story." She sat straighter, her face hardening. "This is such a time, and in such times, we may call on the Warriors to aid us. We—"

"Hold on," Beth stammered as a flurry of bewildering images and emotions seared through her mind: images of a darkness, a void – *the Void* – with blinding streaks of white and black lightning slicing the air; remembered feelings of merciless joy as she destroyed the hateful denizens of the Dark streaming into the Gate; memories of her standing shoulder to shoulder with another, every fibre of her being straining to prevent the bestial hordes of the Void passing her and her beloved …

She gasped as an overwhelming sense of loss flooded through her. The horror of one being ripped from her side.

"No," she breathed, scrambling to her feet. *No, these are not my thoughts, my memories. What is happening to me?* Her heart aching as though from some unknown anguish, she forced the fragmented memories away. Far, far away.

Hands shaking, her gaze levelled on Naga. *What did they do to me?*

"Hear our Story, Warrior," Naga pressed. "Then, you—"

"No," Beth grated. *This isn't right. Get to Jess and the others. Ignore all else.*

Her Axe firmly clasped in hand, she climbed to her feet. "Enough. Where are my friends?"

The flicker of fear returned to Naga's eyes. "Please. A moment longer. Believe me, it will help you understand."

"Where are my friends?" Beth said in a cold voice, a surge of energy rippling within her.

"I see I must simplify what I must say. For now, believe me when I say that my tribe is important. Important on a scale that is difficult for you to understand. There are others who seek to stop us. These are the people you saw today, the people who tried to capture you. These are the people who have captured your friends."

Beth scowled and took a step forward. "Show me where they are. Right now!"

Naga held up her hands. "Please understand. We have the same interest as you in recovering your friends. Maybe more so," she finished quietly.

"Tell me where they are!" Beth commanded, her voice changing pitch.

The old woman half climbed to her feet, then stopped. Beads of sweat appeared on her forehead. She clasped her hand around the bracelet on her wrist and instantly relaxed, settling back down to her haunches. "You have strength," she murmured, regaining her composure.

Beth glared at the old lady.

"We know where your friends are. They are close. But they have a person of some strength with them – it will take a careful effort to recover them. One of our best scouts is there, and I also keep my eyes on your friends."

"You're not doing a good job of watching them from here."

Naga closed her eyes and placed her hand back on the bracelet on her wrist. "At this moment, your two friends are sitting next to each other beside a fire. Both are safe. For now."

Beth's eyes widened. "How do you know that?"

Naga opened her eyes and smiled. "A simple skill I learnt as a child from my mother. But I think you might not believe me right now if I explained it."

Beth grunted. "And you'd be right." *Yet she said both are safe.* She studied Naga, considering her words. "Just two of my friends?"

Naga frowned. "Should there be more?"

Erin and Trish ... Maybe they did escape this hell. "Only two?" Beth repeated.

Naga's dark eyes scanned Beth's face as if seeking to understand her question. "Only two," she answered.

The slightest tension eased from Beth's frame. *Then maybe one less thing to worry about.*

Naga's questioning gaze lingered. She leaned imperceptibly closer. "Would you let me touch the Axe?"

"No!" Beth replied instantly.

Naga held out her arm. "In that case, would you touch my bracelet?"

"Put your arm down, lady, I want no more tricks from you." Her lips thinned. *No more talking. I need to move.* She gestured to the old lady. "Up you get. And you, Bear, stay here."

Naga's face creased with regret. With a resigned sigh, she slowly climbed to her feet. "Do as she says, Bear."

Stepping behind Naga, Beth raised the Axe to the old lady's neck. "Move."

As they walked out of the chamber, Naga spoke, her quiet words drifting on the cool air of the passageway beyond. "I believe you have strength, Warrior, but you do not yet know your powers. You need time and training. Please believe me."

"Quiet. Just walk."

They walked in silence up to the larger chamber, where they were greeted by an array of armed people.

"Stop!" Beth recognised the voice of the angry girl. "Drop your weapon," the girl commanded.

"I don't think so. Lady, tell all your people to drop their weapons."

Naga calmly looked around the cavern. "It is okay. Please put down your weapons."

"No!" the angry girl shouted, stepping towards them. "She will die!"

Naga shook her head. "River, it is *I* who would die first. I would rather that not happen today. Put down your weapons."

All in the cavern dropped their weapons …

Except the girl, River. She held her bow, arrow drawn, aimed at Beth's head. "She's not quick enough, Mother. She will die."

The girl released the arrow.

Beth saw the arrow fly and blinked.

And for her, time slowed.

She watched as the arrow eased its way through the air towards her.

And then watched as her Axe deflected the arrow harmlessly to one side.

She blinked again, and time resumed its flow.

Anger flared – anger and cold pleasure. "That was very stupid," she growled. Gripping the haft of the Axe tightly, she swung it at the old woman's neck.

Time slowed once more as the Axe swept in a smooth arc to its target.

Halfway through the swing, a commanding voice thundered in her mind: *'No! She cannot die.'*

Reacting in an instant, Beth's muscles and tendons clenched, slowing the deadly strike …

The Axe stopped, its edge drawing a thin line of blood from Naga's neck.

Beth turned and glared at the wide-eyed, shaking girl. "Do not do that again," she said, the rage falling away as abruptly as it had flared. She glanced around the chamber. "Any of you."

She felt her hand trembling and a bead of sweat on her forehead. Sudden cold reality struck. She had almost killed the old woman.

Me? An icy grip clenched around her heart. *It felt like another.*

A clatter broke into the silence of the chamber as River's bow dropped to the ground. "Mother, I am sorry …"

Beth heard the terrible anguish in the girl's voice.

Naga's eyes hardened. "You must learn, River, and learn quickly. If not, we will all fail."

Beth fought to clear a fog in her mind. What was happening to her? She looked around. All eyes were on her. *Keep moving. Save your friends.* She turned to Naga. "We're leaving. Move."

Naga didn't move. "I will not prevent you from leaving as we agreed, Warrior, but believe me, if you try to rescue the others now, they will die. Are you ready to taint your hands with innocent blood? It is difficult to clean and stains your life for a long time."

'Too late for that,' came a ruthless voice from deep within Beth. A voice different from the other.

Damn it! Stay out of my head!

Silence.

Breathing hard, the muscles of her jaw tightened. *Ignore the voices. It's the drugs talking. Focus!* She glared at Naga. "If I do nothing, then regret may stay longer. We're going. Move."

"Then please take someone with you. As a guide. You do not know the ways here."

"Fine. You can come."

"You have seen me, Warrior. If you would like to arrive when the sun next rises, then take me. If sooner, then take River. She will move as fast as you."

"And have an arrow in my back. No thanks."

"She will go with you unarmed, and in this I trust that she does not get an axe in the back."

They try to delay me. "She is not—"

'She will be useful,' came the calm voice. *'Naga is right, you don't know where you are going.'*

Beth's eyes narrowed. *'Who are you?'*

'One who can help you.'

'Who are you?' she repeated, feeling a faint, distant memory of … of what?

There was no answer.

She cursed silently and looked up. Naga was staring intently at her. Beth cursed again. *This was her doing. She drugged me.* Her jaw tensed. But in this moment, she had to ignore that. *Because I don't know where I am. Or where the others are.* She needed help.

Her fierce gaze fell on the distraught girl. *Maybe this is the one to take – she will not risk an attack again.* "You. River. You come with me. Lady, you stay with us until we get to the exit from the cave."

River glanced at Naga, uncertainty written on her strained face. "Are you certain of this?"

"We must help her," Naga replied. She turned to Beth. "You should not leave yet, but I have to prove that we are not against you." She turned back to River. "Please remove your blades."

River's eyes flashed, but she reached into her tunic pocket and pulled out a serrated stone blade. And then bent and retrieved a blade from her leggings.

"And the third blade," Naga murmured.

River's eyebrows rose in surprise. She pulled a third blade from a strap concealed inside her tunic.

"Now a jacket."

The girl glanced at Beth, checking her size. Their eyes met and Beth saw a fire still burning deep within. River broke the contact and crossed to the stack of garments by the wall. After quickly rummaging through them, she returned with a dark-grey leather jacket. She thrust it towards Beth, who took it and slipped it on, feeling the warmth of the fur lining.

"Let's move" she said, and they exited the chamber.

*

Frustrated with the Warrior, Naga forced herself to stay calm. It had been the old Mother who had told her to always expect the unexpected, the old Mother who had revealed Naga's destiny. Distant memories, undimmed by the passage of time, came flooding back.

As a young girl, she had learnt together with the other children of the tribe, enjoying the telling and playing of scenes from their Story. They heard about the time of the Warriors when their saviours would arrive to save the Land from the great Enemy. She smiled. That had been a precious time of joyous play enjoyed between the many days of relentless, hard work surviving in difficult lands. She had most enjoyed playing the Warrior who held IY's Staff, using it to defeat enemy tribes, or as protection from attack by mountain lions or hyenas.

She sighed. *How quickly those times passed.* Her learning quickly became more focussed and serious, only she taken for lessons with the Mother, the shaman, the one whose life had been long, the longest any could remember from the generations before. It was the Mother who had revealed Naga's destiny, and, in time, released the role of shaman to her.

It was she who had said: "Naga, our tribe has seen countless sun-cycles, and all has been well. But still we have not forgotten what our forefathers and foremothers saw, nor what they told us. And now I believe the signs are here and a Land entombed in ice is returning. You should prepare. You may need to make the Request for the Warriors in your lifetime."

"But if I am wrong and call at the wrong time?"

"Then you will die," the Mother had said, "and we would lose much."

Only when she had come to accept the role as Mother and shaman, only in the transfer from the old Mother to the new, had she truly understood what the Mother had told her. If this vast chain of knowledge, passed from one living Mother to another, was broken, how long would it take to rebuild? Even with the aid of IY, the tribe would wait many generations for another with the strength, knowledge, and power to Request.

The Request ... In that, I didn't fail.

The Request had been made, and the Warriors were here.

But the Arrival ...

The Arrival had been a disaster.

Two Warriors lost, and the Staff taken.

Naga tried to curb fraught nerves as they approached the cave entrance. How had the Ka known? The answer to that was clear. *The enemy shaman has a deadlier reach than we realised.* And now the Warriors were in danger. *We did not prepare them, and they do not know who they are.* The Warriors were vulnerable.

Will they survive? Adapt?

"Be prepared. Then adapt," the Mother before her had told her. But she had been talking about the Iyes tribe, not the Warriors. "The only certainty is that it will not be as you expect; it will not be as you have prepared for. And do not force yourself on them; if you alienate them, you could lose them. I pray you have wisdom when they arrive."

Naga grimaced. They had misplaced this wisdom. *I cannot afford to fail again.*

And yet she was allowing this Warrior to leave.

Allowing? No. We are unable to stop her.

And not because of the Warrior's physical strength. Yes, this slender young woman moved lithely as a fighter, with a predator's fire in her eyes. But aside from a small nick to her face, the Warrior looked unscarred by previous battles, untested by the allies of the Dark. *Without access to the energy of the Land, several of the fighters in our tribe would best her in battle.* But with the Land's energy, with what lay hidden from most, none of the Iyes could stand against her. *This one hides a great power within, one far surpassing my own.*

She ground the remnants of her teeth. But there was a problem. The Warrior hadn't fully awoken. *We haven't prepared her.*

So try harder to persuade her not to leave.

Naga shook her head in the gloom. That was not the way. *We are not Warriors. We are not the chosen of IY.* The Warriors had their own journeys to make, their own destinies lying ahead of them. Support them, yes, but make their decisions for them? No. That could not be. *The Warriors must ultimately choose the path to take to defeat our Enemy. To defeat Kaos.*

They soon reached the entranceway, now darkened by the evening gloom. "Freya," Naga whispered. "I know you can hear me. Come out where we can see you."

A shape detached from the bushes, and a short, hooded figure approached, halting a short distance away.

"Who's that?" the Warrior demanded.

"Simply a guard. And please keep your voice low. You're as loud as an avalanche and will be heard on the other side of the valley."

The Warrior scowled but remained silent. *Good. At least she hears me.* "Freya. Come closer."

As the woman moved closer, Naga saw Freya's young face under her hood, curls of her thick hair brushing her cheek. Her face was strained.

"Relax, all is well," Naga said calmly. "Tell the others that River and our Warrior are moving and heading to the Southerners' camp. They are not to be followed." She flicked her veiled fingers. "Is that understood?"

"Yes, Mother, I understand." Freya dropped back and disappeared into the shadows.

"River will lead you from here," Naga said to the Warrior. "If I were younger, I would accompany you, but although my mind is willing, my legs are not. I will trust you not to endanger either your friends or my people by your action. May IY travel with you."

The Warrior gestured to River. "We waste time. Lead on."

River glanced at Naga. Naga smiled and nodded.

River hesitated only a heartbeat. "Follow," she said, glaring at the Warrior. "We travel quickly."

Naga watched as the two set off down the hillside, angling towards the distant river – towards the distant camp of the enemy. She watched until they disappeared into the gloom, then walked back to the cave entrance. "Wait a few moments, Bear," she said in a low voice, looking at the figure standing in the shadows, "and then follow them. But take no action unless you think the Warriors are in danger. Freya will tell Spider to join you."

The shadowy figure nodded.

Naga glanced towards the darkening sky beyond. The Arrival was not as expected. Not at all. *Yet you were told to expect the unexpected.* Her hand reached for the comfort of her bracelet. *I must trust in them. I must trust in the Warriors.* She drew a deep breath. *For they are our salvation.*

CHAPTER EIGHT

*The Ka's knowledge of the Iyes's lands was poor.
Their choice of ally in this region was poorer still.*

Jessica awoke to find her head resting on Lanky's shoulder. She heard a faint, discordant murmuring. *Is he singing to himself?* Lifting her head, she groaned at an aching stiffness in her neck. Rubbing it, she saw the evening twilight had descended around the camp. "Sorry, seems I drifted off." Her brow furrowed. "What was that song you were murdering?"

He frowned. "Song? Was I singing? I do hum when I'm nervous. Maybe I sing when I'm terrified."

"Many would argue against that noise being singing."

Staring across the camp, Lanky ignored her jibe. "Been keeping my eye on Bent-Nose over there."

Jessica's stomach lurched. She looked across the camp and saw that the two men who'd left with the body of the man killed by Longhair had returned. "When did they get back?"

"I'd say about an hour ago." She heard the fear in his voice. "They're trouble. When night falls, let's see if we can get out of here."

Looking up at the clear evening sky, she saw it wouldn't be long before the light faded. Would they have a chance to escape under the cover of darkness? Where would they go? And who else might be out there?

She caught movement beside them. Their guard had climbed to his feet and was looking to the south of camp, tension in his stance. A low voice sounded from the gloom, and the guard instantly relaxed. The scrawny man dropped back to his haunches and took up his quiet vigil.

Some moments later, Longhair's companion walked into the light of the camp, laden with something draped over his shoulder. He walked to within a few yards of the fire, then dropped his burden. She recognised the body of a small deer.

Within minutes, Bent-Nose and his friend began to work on the carcass. She noticed they used blades made of stone to skilfully skin and dismember the animal. As they worked, they dropped chunks of meat into a large bowl seemingly crafted from bark. After adding water and other unknown ingredients, they placed the bowl on a glowing offshoot of the fire, leaving it to cook. "You notice they're not using any metal? None – anywhere. Not in their cooking, not in weapons, not in clothing. None."

"I did," Lanky said, his voice subdued.

It was as though they'd been transported to a different place. A different time.

A terrifying place and time. A place of nightmares.

She glanced around the camp, her gaze resting on Longhair. *Only he keeps us safe.* And yet what did he want from them? He'd visited them a second time and repeated his questioning of them in a language neither of them understood. *But he wants to know about that staff, I'm sure of it.*

A memory replayed. Of Lanky with the staff by the cliff edge.

She shifted her gaze to him. "Where did you find that staff?"

He was silent for a moment, then: "By the trail. Where you threw me off."

"How did you know it was there?"

"When you were pulling me up on the rope, I saw writing on the rocks. I didn't have time to look closely then, so that's why I went back."

"What did the writing say?"

"'No one knows but I who wrote this here and why' – why spelled just 'y'."

"And what does that mean?"

Lanky shook his head. "I don't know. When I looked at it more closely, part of the cliff broke off and revealed that opening – revealed the staff. I'd just managed to get it out when I heard you scream." He cast her a questioning glance. "What *had* happened to you?"

She winced. "Pain. Terrible pain, as though my head was on fire. And when I grabbed your hand, more pain …" *And horrific images of alien creatures swarming over me. Like my nightmare.*

He studied her, his expression troubled. "When I tried to help you up, something happened to me. I seemed to black out for a while. And the noises …" His gaze seemed to drift to another place. "Could it be?" he whispered as though to himself. "All that searching …"

Jessica jumped as a figure appeared beside them. The guard, with two bowls.

"Think they want us to eat," Lanky said, looking up and sitting straighter. "And we need it. Get us warmed up."

She suddenly felt very hungry. There was more to understand about this lad, Lanky, but for now he was right. They needed to eat.

Lanky held up his bound hands to the guard. "May have a problem eating like this."

The guard glanced at his hands, then after a brief hesitation, shouted over to Longhair. Jessica didn't hear the response, but the guard pulled out a stone dagger from his belt and quickly cut the reeds binding their hands.

Lanky quickly took the bowls and handed one to Jessica. Made of woven strips of bark, liquid seeped through the bottom of the bowls into her hands. She examined the contents and was pleasantly surprised. It looked and smelled like a regular meat stew. Grabbing a piece of meat, she took a bite. It was surprisingly good, and it didn't take long before her bowl lay empty.

Beside her, Lanky tipped the remaining juices from his bowl into his mouth. Then, finally finished, he dropped the bowl to the ground, and wiped his mouth on the back of his hand. "I guess if they're feeding us, they plan to keep us around for a while."

"Maybe, but I don't feel any safer with that guy around." She glanced around. The men were all eating, and no one seemed to be watching them.

She reached down to her pocket. Her heart fell. "It's gone," she whispered. Lanky looked at her. "My phone. It's gone. Must have dropped somewhere when they carried us here."

"I'm not sure it would have helped," he said in a low voice. "Would have been good to check, but ..."

"But what?"

"I mean that we can't rely on someone helping us. We need to make a run for it."

She fought a rising panic. "Do you think we can?"

"It will be dark soon. If we see a chance before they tie us up again, I think we should take it."

"We'd have to be sure we'd make it. I don't want to give that guy a chance to get hold of us on the run."

"We don't do anything unless we both agree. Hold on, Longhair's coming."

Despite her fear, Jessica bristled. "Why's he doing this?" she hissed. "Doesn't he see that we have no clue what he's talking about? Does he think we're hiding something?"

"Maybe, but I think this time it's different. We must be moving from here. Look."

Longhair approached, fully dressed, bags strapped across his back, his similarly attired colleague walking beside him. Longhair stepped in front of her, holding the staff loosely in his hand. Gazing intently at her, he spoke.

Her anger flared. "This is crazy. We've no idea what you're saying." As Longhair studied her, she heard Bent-Nose's harsh laughter from the far side of camp.

Longhair raised the staff and spoke again.

"Not this again. I've already told you it's not ours!" she said, exasperated.

"Stay calm," Lanky whispered. "We don't want to rile these people."

Realising the danger of losing control, she calmed herself as Longhair delivered his speech to Lanky. Lanky calmly repeated himself, trying different gestures to explain himself. Nothing worked.

Longhair lowered the staff to his side, then turned to his colleague. He spoke only a few words, and then the two of them walked away, heading out of the camp.

She suddenly realised what was happening. *No!* They couldn't leave them here. Not with these vile men. She jumped to her feet, caution forgotten. "No! Come back! You have to take us with you!"

She started forward, but the guard stepped in her path.

"Get out of my way!" she yelled, striking high with her foot, catching the scrawny man in the chin. The guard howled and fell backwards. Her panicked eyes found Longhair and she ran towards him—

Someone hammered into her side, and she stumbled and fell, hitting the ground hard. Ignoring the flare of pain in her side, she hit out with her hands and feet, driving the heavy man off her. She leapt to her feet, readying herself for a fight.

"Jessica! Don't!"

Hearing the tension in Lanky's voice, she turned to see him kneeling with a knife at his neck. A knife in the hands of Bent-Nose.

Beyond the fire, Longhair and his companion melted into the gloom beyond the firelight.

Glacial terror ripped through Jessica's body and mind. *No! This can't be happening!*

Harsh, bestial laughter drifted across the camp, slicing into her soul.

She collapsed to her knees, struggling to breathe. *They've left us in hell. We're going to die.*

*

The Axe comfortably strapped to her back, Beth ran on. In the fading twilight, River glided over the rough ground as though it were simply a racetrack, but twice Beth had hissed at the girl to slow down. *Else I'll break my ankle.* As they ran, the old lady's warning echoed in her mind. Was this a mistake to head to this camp herself? What was she going to do when she arrived there? Her jaw clenched. *Focus. This is the most important mission of your life. Get Jess out of there.*

She studied the darkening landscape ahead. Grasses, birch trees, and scattered juniper thickets dominated the slopes of the valley. The old lady had said that she wouldn't know her way around here, and now Beth could see why. She didn't recognise this place. Although—

She almost ran into River.

"What is it?" she whispered, staring at the girl, who was holding her hand up to Beth.

"Be silent. Listen."

Beth froze … and heard the faint sound of movement off to their right. "Someone's there," she whispered.

River held up a finger to her mouth, glaring at Beth.

A low growl came from the woods and then the quiet rustling of something moving away.

"Just a wolf," River whispered. And on she moved.

Beth's eyes narrowed. *Okay, girl, let's go with wolf for now.*

They ran on, maintaining an even pace, weaving their way down the valley until the ground slowly flattened out, the view opening up to the distant peaks on the horizon. Beth stopped for a moment, scanning the twilight-lit landscape. She frowned as the distant ridges formed themselves into a pattern in her mind – a pattern she'd seen before on the map they'd used for their hikes. But it couldn't be the same place. *Because right now, I'd be standing on the western edge of town!*

"Look!" River's hushed voice cut across her thoughts. Beth followed River's gaze and saw tendrils of smoke rising in the distance. "Your friends are there."

It didn't seem far, but Beth noted one problem – the river. "How do we cross that?"

"There is a way." River sprinted away.

They ran over flatter, easier ground, and although River was pulling ahead, she left a clear trail through the tall grasses covering these lower reaches of the opening valley. But aside from the evidence of animal trails, Beth saw no defined walking trails. And no roads or dirt tracks, no fences or walls, no evidence of the presence of people. *None of this makes sense,* she thought, yet again. Gritting her teeth, she ran on. *Get Jess, then figure this out.*

A short while later, she approached the slow-flowing river.

Where there was no sign of River.

Damn. Where is she?

"Hey," came a hushed call from the water. A small coracle appeared from long grasses overhanging the near bank. Using a gnarled wooden oar to manoeuvre the boat, River drifted around to Beth and gestured for her to climb in. Once she was on board, River pushed off, and they headed for the far bank.

"Someone has used it recently," River said. "If they're still here, then they'll have heard us – you move like a cow."

Ignoring River's barb, Beth glanced back at the bank they had just left.

She saw nothing. And yet …

She looked further to the right …

The hairs on the back of her neck stood on end. She could see nothing, but a calm part of her said: *Yes, he's there.*

"Someone's watching us," she whispered.

River scanned the bank. "I see nothing."

"Even so, he's there. I think we were lucky."

Scanning the dimly lit bank, Beth knew the watcher had pulled back into the shadows … but somehow, she still sensed he was there. It was an experience she'd had a few times during her army service, and her unit had grown to trust their young colleague's 'sixth sense'. But this feeling was much stronger. She knew the man was watching them, and a picture of him had formed in her head – not an image of his face, but a recognition of a calm yet deadly individual.

"Is he still there?" River whispered.

As Beth made to answer, the sense of the other vanished. "Maybe," she murmured, suddenly unsure. *Or maybe he's somehow veiled himself.*

"We should move on," River hissed. "Here is not safe."

Beth crouched in the boat, staring at the far bank, a lingering echo of the man's presence in her mind. *Who was he?*

And who am I?

And what is this Axe?

My Axe.

She shuddered at the disturbing thoughts. What had happened to them? To her, to Jessica, to the lad who found the staff? And where were they? This was not the place they'd been this morning. These were not people who had been here this morning.

The boat thudded to a stop. They had reached the far bank.

River jumped out and scrambled through the reeds to the firmer ground beyond.

"Stop!" Beth commanded, her thoughts wild with confusion as she climbed out of the boat.

River turned, frowning.

Pushing through disturbed vegetation, Beth strove to tame her thoughts. She needed to focus. *One thing at a time. Like this girl. Is this my enemy?* The man she'd sensed just now, that man was an enemy, a recognisable, clear danger to her. Rationally, she had no idea how she knew that, but it *was* true. And yet in the time she was in the cave, she'd had no similar reaction to the people around her. *I felt fear, anger, and the need for action – but didn't have the triggers I felt just now.*

She halted before the girl, who stood watching her from the corner of her eye. She sensed no innate danger in the girl. So, a friend? No, this one hated her. *But why?* "Look at me," she said.

The girl scowled but levelled her gaze directly on Beth.

"Do you want to kill me?"

The girl glared at her but said nothing.

"Do you?" she repeated.

Silence.

Beth pulled out a stone blade from inside her coat pocket. She'd felt it immediately when she had put on the coat; these people had weapons concealed everywhere. She turned it hilt first to the girl. "Take this."

The girl hesitated.

"Take it."

River glared at her ... but she silently took the blade.

"My weapon is on my back. You have a chance now to do what you wanted back in the cave. Go ahead."

River held Beth's gaze. "I believe I could kill you right now. A Warrior or not, you can't reach your Axe in time to stop—"

The girl's hand struck at blistering speed and the blade drove forward – and stopped, its tip touching Beth's neck.

Beth's head had not moved an inch.

River's expression was contemptuous. "I don't believe you are a Warrior. Somehow you tricked my tribe. But I have my instruction from Mother. My reputation would die instantly if I took your life." She pulled back her blade. "And I told you that you'd be too slow."

Beth smiled – and moved her hand a millimetre.

River's eyes widened as Beth's blade pushed against her stomach. "Correct," Beth murmured. "Too slow for the Axe."

*

River stood, frozen, looking down at the blade. She was stunned; she hadn't seen the woman move. And the woman clearly hadn't reacted fully to her attack. In fact, she had done very little to protect herself, as if knowing that she wouldn't be struck. *If she'd reacted in anger, I'd be dead.*

The stranger, still smiling, withdrew her blade.

Dazed, River took a step back, her eyes flicking over the young woman before her. *Could it be? Could this be a Warrior?* She flicked the thought away. This simple woman before her, a Warrior? No. A skilled fighter, maybe, but a saviour foretold by their Story? A saviour to aid her people to defeat the Ka, to defeat Kaos? No. That couldn't be.

Then who was she? Who were these strangers?

A stab of frustration ran through her. She hadn't seen herself what had happened at the Arrival site, as she hadn't been there, too busy tracking two enemy fighters that Shorty and Knuckles had let slip past. She'd only realised too late that those enemies had been decoys to draw defenders away from the Arrival site. *We made mistakes. Too many mistakes.*

And I didn't see where these strangers arrived from. Her fear resurfaced. Could they be in league with the Ka? *But two were captured by the enemy.* Subterfuge? A way to infiltrate the Iyes tribe? *I have to see the enemy camp myself. I have to see the truth of what is happening there.* "Are you ready to move on?" she said, holding her voice steady.

The stranger's fierce eyes locked onto hers. "Who are these people who have taken my friends?"

"How much did Mother tell you?" River said, unsure how to answer.

"Let's just say I wasn't interested in her version of what was happening. You tell me."

River held the woman's intense gaze. *I need to give an answer.* But what? What could she say to this woman she didn't trust? "There is a group called the Ka who oppose our tribe's beliefs, and who seek to erase my people from this Land. They discovered our location and attacked us – you were there and saw the attack. The camp we are heading to is a camp of these people."

"A camp of these people you call Ka?"

River hesitated. "Yes, but it seems only two are from the Ka tribe itself. The others are allies, seemingly with knowledge of this area."

She watched the stranger closely. "The Ka fighters are skilled and dangerous. Mother warned you that you place your friends' lives in danger by your actions."

Her expression pensive, the woman absently brushed a strand of her dark hair behind her ear. Then she nodded. "Then we should take care and be ready." She gestured to the blade in River's hand. "Keep the blade."

River slipped the blade into her tunic. "I will help you recover your friends, but there will be a reckoning between us." *I will find the truth.*

A grim smile crossed the stranger's lips. "First, my friends."

River turned away, scanning the darkening shadows between the trees. Then she motioned for Beth to follow.

As the moon edged above the hills, they flitted from cover to cover, pausing to listen for movement ahead before moving on. River hoped that only she heard the faintest of sounds from the two of her tribe tracking them – two who must have swum across the river at another point. Back at the cave, she'd seen Naga's shielded hand signing to Freya, and then recognised her father's wolf's signal as they'd travelled to the river. Knowing they were close was reassuring. It would—

A distant scream cut through the evening air.

Before River could react, the woman beside her raced ahead, Axe in hand. *This one has no fear,* River thought, pushing back her own dread. Girding herself, she sprinted after her. *There are answers ahead, I'm sure. And then we will see.*

She ran on.

*

Hidden in the thick vegetation, Shadow watched the two women leave the riverbank and head cautiously towards the camp he'd just left – Krag's camp. His eyes narrowed. What he'd seen altered his plan. One of the women had known he was there – she'd sensed him. This was unexpected. So unexpected that he'd neglected to shield his mind. *Because I saw nothing from the prisoners.*

Certain that the women were out of sight, he climbed to his feet, then reached behind his neck and adjusted the binding of his long black hair. Satisfied, he turned to Sy. "We need to go back," he signed. "We have to follow this one." *We have to find out who she is.*

Frowning, Sy signed: "Are you sure? The Ancient will arrive soon. We must deliver the Staff."

"This one seems different from the others. I need to be sure."

Sy, the shaven sides of his head catching the last of the evening's twilight, flicked his fingers. "Be quick."

"You better get the boat then. That water's too cold for me."

Sy shook his head but began to strip. He was a good friend.

As Sy removed the last of his clothing and headed down the bank, Shadow looked again at the Staff. The great prize. The one that would allow his people to gain the aid of the Ancient. *And I hold it in my hands.*

But it might not have been. The idiot, Krag, had come close to destroying their entire mission with the shambolic raid on the Arrival site. They had followed none of Shadow's plan – none – leading to the loss of Trek, a skilled Ka fighter, and the escape of the travellers. Shadow scowled. Most of Krag's people had proven pathetic in battle, wiped out in a blink of an eye. True, these Iyes had shown themselves to be fearsome fighters, his intelligence on that proving correct, but he'd expected more of Krag and his people.

Did you? Did you, really?

No, he answered ruefully. *I didn't.*

He sighed. He would never have willingly chosen to work with one such as Krag, but they'd needed his knowledge of this northerly region, an area rarely visited but thought to be a refuge of the Iyes, those known to some as the Hidden. And over the last days, Krag's people had navigated with little error. Scouts and pathfinders, yes; fighters, no.

Shadow shook his head. At least he'd recovered the situation, seeing at the battle scene what others had not – two of the travellers had fled, and one with the Staff. Hastily signalling to Sy, the two of them had withdrawn, followed quickly by Krag and two others, and together they'd hunted down and captured their prize. Returning to the makeshift camp, he knew the Iyes wouldn't risk an immediate direct attack, fearing for the safety of their precious arrivals. That allowed him valuable time to see what else he could learn.

Which turned out to be very little.

He grimaced. His mission was to capture the Staff and return with it. Beyond that, it hadn't been certain what else he might learn. "The travellers with the Staff may prove useful, or they may not," his leader had told him. "Stay with them as long as you can, but you must be ready by the full moon, when the Ancient will come to you." The travellers hadn't arrived until this day, and the full moon shone this very night. The Ice Rider was coming.

I learnt nothing from them, he thought in disgust. *In that, I failed.*

Three times he had asked from where they'd brought the Staff and who had sent them, and three times they had answered in a language he couldn't understand. But he'd seen clearly in their eyes that there was no pretence, no games; they did not understand him. And more than that, he'd seen no fire in their eyes, no yearning to retrieve the Staff.

"Do not touch them, nor let them touch the Staff whilst you hold it," his leader had warned him. "You may not survive it." He'd let Krag deal with their capture and had kept the Staff apart from the strangers. A precaution he now saw as unwarranted. *They were no threat.*

He was strangely disappointed. Disappointed he'd learnt nothing more from them, but more so that after sun-cycles of honing his skills for this day, he couldn't test them against the enemy's supposedly fearsome Warriors. The travellers, with their strange features and exotic dress, clearly did not hail from his land, but neither were they the ravening destroyers foretold in his people's stories. No, these travellers were weak and ignorant.

He drew a deep breath and shook his head. From the terror he'd seen in their faces, they were most likely ignorant carriers caught in a game they neither understood nor wanted to play. When he'd walked out of the camp and heard Krag's sadistic laughter, he'd felt the faintest pang of sorrow that they would die. *I saw the torment of the innocence in their eyes.* But they had been holding the Staff, the weapon of his enemy, and in war, there were sides, and they'd landed on the wrong one.

He glanced to the far bank, where the unknown woman had stood. Here was a mystery. *She sensed me, and she didn't appear scared like the others.* Who was this one? What was her story? His eyes shimmered in the twilight with sudden anticipation. *Let us go and see.*

He heard a gentle splash and saw Sy pulling the boat partway onto the bank. The Ka shaman had said the boat would be here, and he'd been right. *Again.* The man had a long reach.

Shadow strode down the bank and climbed into the boat. "Grab your things. You can dry when you get me to the other side. And give me your staff. You can keep this one safe with you." He placed the captured Staff into the boat. "Hurry! Time is against us."

Sy scowled at him as he strode up the bank towards his dry clothes and pack. His fingers flashed.

"Okay. I know you've been telling me all day that time is short. I just wanted a chance to tell you for a change."

Reaching for his pack and clothes, Sy ignored him.

Moments later, they were heading across the river.

Time. Time was always short. But it was precious. He didn't understand those people who wasted their days dreaming or complaining or arguing. Didn't they understand they were losing the only time they'd been gifted in their land? Most believed they would meet their family and ancestors after death, and that would be their true life. He did not. He respected the gods, but thought they had enough work to do with the living, both animals and people, without being bothered by the hordes of the dead.

And even if he was wrong, and his ancestors were indeed waiting for him, what would he want to tell these past people of his own life? That he had complained about the rain, or cold, or poor hunting, or any of the countless other moans people had? That he had closed his eyes to the wonders of life around him and to the joys of listening to the lives and experiences of others?

No! He wanted to live. He wanted to do great things. And this was a wondrous task that had been set. How many others had been prepared over the generations? Many, many others. But it was during his lifetime that the task had fallen.

And I was chosen.

He would not fail.

"Row harder, Sy," he signed, facing the warrior monk. "They'll be way ahead of us now."

Sy scowled. But rowed harder.

*

Krag couldn't quite believe the Ka had left. Walking over to the edge of the camp, he sat for a while and watched and waited in the dying twilight of the evening as the firelight slowly spread its influence further away from the camp. But he'd heard nothing but birds and wolves calling in the distance. No sight nor sound of the Ka.

As the full moon edged above the hills, the truth became clear. The Ka *had* left. His scarred lip curved into a smile. This was an unexpected but most welcome gift from his god. *We're rid of the cursed Ka. I'm rid of the rock on my back.* He knew Shadow didn't like him, and knew he'd been close to pushing the Ka too far. *But you have to enjoy yourself when you can,* he thought, smiling. He enjoyed pushing people – he liked a fight.

Now finally sure the Ka had left, he stood, stretched, then turned back to camp. This had unfolded much better than he'd hoped. He was now back in control. It was time to enjoy his evening with the prisoner, then return home to his own tribe and await the rewards from the Ka for his service to them.

I hate them, but I need them.

"It seems we'll have a good night tonight, Root," Krag growled as he walked into camp, looking to the thickset man standing over the captive woman. "But no thanks to Mouse over there," he continued, scowling at the scrawny man holding a spear against the neck of the other, now naked, prisoner. Krag ground his teeth. The useless piece of dung had almost let the woman escape, but luckily Root had reacted quickly, catching her before she could flee the camp. Krag spat to the ground. He wished he hadn't needed the useless runt, but Mouse was the only one of the tribe who knew something of this part of the land. *And the one who'd reported sightings of people.* They hadn't known it was the Hidden at the time, but it had proved good intelligence. Intelligence that was helping him get what he needed from the Ka.

Krag scowled. *The cursed Ka.* Ever since a child when his father had used them as a deterrent to his and his brothers' wild behaviour – "The Ka will slit your throat in the night" – the Ka had loomed as an ever-increasing threat over his people as they expanded from their homeland in the south. When the time had finally come for him to take his rightful place as leader of his people – when he'd *grasped* his rightful place – he had pushed his tribe further north, retreating from the Ka, readying – hardening – his tribe for the battle that would surely come.

And yet his god had seen a different path for him and his people.

During the last moon, three travellers from the Ka had come, and he, Krag, met with them. "We search for a tribe," the Ka had said. "We search for the Iyes, for those known to some as the Hidden." What a wondrous gift from his god this had been.

"We can help you," Krag had said, standing tall and imperious. "But this is what I need in return."

A fire lit inside him at the memory. The Ka had agreed to his demand, and now he would get what he'd so desperately wanted: the weapon technology of the Ka, access to better stone, and more women for him and his men. His small tribe could finally grow and expand, pushing outward into new lands, becoming the dominant tribe. *We will dominate the land.* He smiled. *And maybe in time we'll pay the Ka a visit.*

Feeling a surge of elation, he glanced to the prone woman lying at Root's feet. *But first we can celebrate our success.* He gestured to Root. "Kill the man, then we will spend some time with this one."

Root flexed his arms, a blade held in each hand. "He has a thin neck. It will be quick."

"Wait!" came Mouse's wavering voice as Root approached. "Take care! Killing him might send his god against us."

Krag walked up to Mouse and struck him across the face. "Quiet, scum! His gods have provided little protection for him today, and I fear no god but my own."

"But think, Krag," Mouse whimpered, holding his hand to his face. "Why didn't the Ka kill him? He failed to answer their questions, yet they didn't kill him. They walked out and left no orders."

"I don't need orders, you fool! I give the orders! Something you seem to have forgotten."

Krag hit Mouse again with the back of his hand, then grabbed Mouse's spear from his hand.

Before the prisoner could react, Krag plunged the spear into the man's body.

The woman screamed.

The naked man fell to his knees, eyes wide as he looked down at the embedded spear in his side, rivulets of blood streaming from the vicious wound.

The man slumped and fell on his side, his head striking the ground.

The woman cried out once more.

Smiling, Krag sauntered across to her. *This one I may keep for a while. I will enjoy—*

Her fist hammered into his face, rocking his head backwards. Then he cried out as her foot slammed into his chin, knocking him to the ground. Grimacing with pain, he rolled and sprang back to his feet, staring at the woman in disbelief. Testing his jaw, he steadied himself. Sensing no lasting damage, he slowly ran his eyes down the woman's body. She was strong. His scarred lips curled into a smile. He would enjoy this evening. He stepped forward and swung his fist towards the side of her head …

It missed and he grunted as her foot slammed into his chest.

Rocked backwards, his smirk vanished. Growling, he steadied himself, then ignoring all else, he rushed at her, hurling into her with all his might. She slammed her foot hard into his chest, but she was no match for his weight, and he careered into her, locking his arms around her as they fell. He quickly pinned her neck with his arm, then pulled out a blade, holding it to her eye. "Time to have some fun."

"I don't think so," came a menacing voice behind him.

*

Beth strode into the firelight, her long shadow dancing behind her. The bent-nosed man pinning Jessica to the ground looked up, his blade held to her friend's face. The thickset man beside him stepped towards her, a blade in each hand.

"Put down your weapons," Beth grated.

The bent-nosed man holding Jessica stared at Beth, his brow furrowing in surprise. And then he laughed. "So, you do speak our language. A good act from your friends. Please join us. We've a nice evening planned."

"I will only tell you once more. Put down your weapons."

Anger flashed in the bent-nosed man's eyes. "I need only this one, Root. Take her!"

The thickset man with the two blades moved confidently towards her.

Beth waited, noting each flex of the man's muscles, each twitch of his eye—

The man launched himself towards her.

Time slowed.

Beth saw his left hand come high, heading over her Axe arm, and his right slicing low, aiming for her gut. She swayed backwards, swinging her Axe in a rapid arc under his right arm—

His blades shaved past her body.

Her Axe cleaved into his side, slicing cleanly through half his body.

Time resumed its regular pace, and she watched the man crumple to the ground.

Without pause, she reversed the path of the Axe and released it with force.

*

His blade held above his captive's eye, Krag looked on, aghast, as Root fell to the ground, his guts spilling out. His rage exploded. *I will kill them both!*

But as he tensed to drive home his blade, an intense pain seared across his throat and neck. He put his hand to his throat – and felt liquid streaming through his fingers.

No, he tried to say – but nothing came out, just bubbles in his fingers. His vision swam, and he dropped to his knees.

Get up! he silently screamed. But his body didn't respond. *Get up! I must lead my people. I am Krag!*

He fell, his head slamming into the ground. *Help me! Someone please help me!*

He lay, despairing, until the darkness finally swallowed him.

*

Recovering her Axe, Beth moved to the third man, intending to kill him. She wanted to clear the camp of these vermin, then she could focus on helping Jess. She reached the scrawny man, who knelt, groaning, an arrow in his leg. River had been at work.

She hefted her Axe.

"Beth! No!"

As Jessica's voice rang out, Beth froze. Her muscles straining to deliver the killing blow, she glared at the whimpering man, suddenly uncertain.

"Beth, don't! That one didn't hurt us. You can't kill him, Beth."

Beth turned to Jessica, her eyes afire. "I can."

Jessica rushed forward, and pushing the Axe to the side, she grabbed Beth in a fierce hug. "Thank God you're here," she whispered. "I'm so sorry for leaving you. What happened to you?" She hugged Beth even tighter. "But you're here … That's all that matters now."

Held in the warm embrace of her friend, the ruthless determination that had driven Beth to the camp fled, replaced by a bone-deep exhaustion. She drew a deep lungful of air as her friend cried against her. "You're safe, Jess," she breathed, relaxing the Axe to her side. *Thank God, you're safe.*

They hugged for a moment longer, then Jessica broke away, tears streaming down her face. "They killed him," she sobbed. "They killed Lanky." She stumbled across to his bloodied body. "Why did they do this?"

Following her friend, Beth looked down at the young lad. His face was pale, his chest unmoving.

Her breath caught. *But he isn't dead!* "River! We need help. Bring the others who've been tracking us."

A flicker of movement in the shadows, then River emerged into the light of the fire, quickly followed by the sturdy frame of her father – Bear, as Naga had called him. Bear ran up to them, then knelt down beside Lanky. "He lives," he said, an intense relief in his voice. He looked up at Jessica. "We must keep him warm. Find clothes and see what else we might use."

Jessica, eyes wide with fear, stared blankly at him.

A cold shiver ran down Beth's spine as she realised Jessica didn't understand him. *So, the old woman was right.* She grasped her friend's arm. "Lanky's alive. We need something to keep him warm."

Jessica gasped. "Not dead?"

"Clothes, Jess," Beth said firmly. "Did you see any?"

Her hand trembling, Jessica gestured to a dark shadow in the gloom. "Over there," she whispered.

Beth relayed that to River, who quickly moved off.

"Spider!" Bear called out.

A tall young man emerged out of the shadows, his matted hair pushed back behind his ears.

"Head back to Naga," Bear said as Spider approached. "Tell her to move the tribe to the western cave, where we will be safer. We will travel on this side of the river and use the northern crossing. But bring Amber as soon as you can to aid the Warrior."

His face grim, Spider glanced briefly towards River, then hurried away.

Bear looked back down at the injured man. "He is in bad shape. Removing the spear will be difficult. We'll treat him as best we can until our healer arrives."

Beth nodded. She turned to Jessica ...

Her friend was staring at her in astonishment. "You talk with them. In their language. How?"

Beth drew a slow breath. *Yes, how? An old woman ... An Axe ...*

I don't know ...

She placed her hand on her friend's shoulder. "We need to talk, Jess."

Jessica glanced down at the injured man, then nodded. She climbed to her feet and followed Beth away from the fire.

"What's happening, Beth?" Jessica asked as they stopped at the edge of the fire's light.

She hesitated. "That's difficult to answer."

"I know that!" Jessica grated, her voice rising as she wiped her eyes. "But what's easy to answer is that people are getting killed. They almost killed Lanky." Her face twisted in pained confusion. "And you ... That axe ... Those men ..."

"It's not the first time," Beth said in a quiet voice.

"Maybe. But like this?"

She'd been caught in a terrifying battle before ... *But, no, not like this.* She said nothing.

Fraught moments stretched on, then Jessica spoke. "Where are we?"

Beth looked back to the camp, where Bear and River knelt beside Lanky, tending his wound. "I know this is going to sound crazy, but haven't you noticed how familiar this landscape is?"

"What! Not you as well."

Beth turned to her friend. "What do you mean?"

"Lanky said the same thing earlier. But that's insane. A village can't just disappear."

"Yet it's not there. No town, no roads, nothing." Beth held Jessica's eyes. "Remember when you fell ill on the trail, when Lanky came over to help? What happened next?"

Jessica flinched. "Shock, pain ... disorientation. And then that fight ..."

"And no time passed or was missing?"

Jessica hesitated, then in a quiet whisper: "No."

Beth glanced around the camp, scanning the bodies, the weapons, the packs ... "I don't understand it, but whatever's happened must be linked to that staff Lanky found. And it's happened to all three of us." She felt the weight of the Axe in her hand. *My Axe.* A shudder of unease raked through her. *And what's happened to me?*

"And Erin?" Jessica said. "And Trish?"

Beth felt the wretched burden she was carrying– a burden uncalled for and unwanted – momentarily ease. "They're not here. I think they escaped this hell." *Whatever this hell is. Or whenever this hell is.*

There was silence, save for the crackling of the fire behind them.

"My nightmares," Jessica said in a whisper, her face flickering in the light of the flames. Beth saw the fear in her friend's eyes. "I dreamt someone was asking me for a staff. I dreamt that some evil wanted that staff. And now it feels as though I'm living that nightmare."

A nightmare that we have to understand. Beth glanced towards the fire, the memory of her fraught meeting with Naga returning. "The old lady tried to tell me."

"Old lady?"

"One of these people. But I didn't want to listen." *Because she drugged me.* She looked back at Jessica. "With all that's happened, we desperately need help. Lanky needs help. I wouldn't listen to them before, but whether we trust them or not, for now, we should accept their help."

Jessica hesitated, then nodded weakly.

Beth noticed her friend trembling. *She's in shock.* She gently took her arm. "Let's get you to the fire."

"I'm sorry," Jessica said as they walked back into the warmth of the fire. "I'm tired. And cold. I ... I just can't think straight."

"That's okay, Jess. Get some rest. It can't have been easy for you in this camp."

As Jessica settled by the fire, Beth laid another fur over her friend's shoulders. *I'm so used to a resilient Jess, but this nightmare would scar anybody.* She glanced across at Lanky. *He will know what happened. He had the staff.*

'You know,' came the voice inside.

Beth winced and pushed the voice back, fearing its eager embrace.

Glancing around the camp, she saw Bear examining one of the two dead bodies. "I'll be back in a moment."

Seeing Jessica's almost imperceptible nod, she walked across to Bear.

"I know this one," Bear said, gesturing to one of the dead as she approached. "His name is Krag. A particularly despicable man with a tribe to the south. I didn't know he had aligned with the Ka."

"What do we do with their bodies?"

"I will deal with them."

"And that one?" she said, pointing at the scrawny figure holding his wounded leg.

"We will keep him here for now. I want to question him." He turned to her. "And well done. There was no margin for error in your attack on the camp – and you made no error."

He turned back to examine the second body.

No error? No, that wasn't right. Lanky was badly hurt. She'd arrived too late.

But you saved Jess.

The pang of guilt was quick. *Yes, and in doing so, killed two people.*

Her face hardened. *Our lives were in danger.* Those people had been trying to kill her and had already tried to kill Jessica and Lanky. She'd seen the opportunity to immobilise them and taken it. And the actions she had taken had been performed flawlessly. It had helped that the two men had been slow to react, but even so, they stood no chance against her. *They were weak. They deserved what came to them. They —*

She shuddered. *Stop. What are you thinking?*

She fought to steady her swirling thoughts. *Jess is safe, that's all that matters right now.* She glanced to the others by the fire. *I need to figure out who these people are, what they know, and why we are here.* And once they knew that, they needed to get out of here. *Because something's happening to me, and whatever it is, I don't like it.*

Feeling a sudden coldness in the air, she left Bear and walked back towards the fire. Realising she still carried the Axe in her hand, she hefted it and swung it easily into the harness on her back. She shivered as an unbidden thought swept through her mind: *It's back where it belongs.*

CHAPTER NINE

The Ancient once again executed its grand plan with ease – until the speed of the Warrior surprised it. Nothing was lost, however. No, much was gained.

Jessica glanced across to the still body of Lanky. How close had he been to being killed by the brutal Bent-Nose? And how close was he to dying now? She saw the one called River pull a pelt across Lanky's legs, then sit back on her haunches, watching her blade heat in the fire. Once the wound was cleansed, this girl would attempt to remove the spear from Lanky's side. It was madness. It was hell. And yet I need to let her do it. We have to do something to help him.

With the cold evening air seeping into her bones, Jessica pulled the fur closer around her, then edged closer to the fire, shuffling forward until the heat on her face grew too fierce. She gazed into the flames and gradually withdrew from the cruel world around her.

The fire was entrancing, hypnotic, drawing her into a remembered past.

As a child, she had wild camped with her family and friends, and recalled the joy of a campfire by night, when the adults gossiped with drinks in their hands and left her and her friends the freedom to play as they liked. They would poke the fire with broken twigs, excitedly watching the sparks leap up from the hot, crackling wood. Later, as the flames died back, with sleep finally creeping up on her, she would gaze into the fire, entranced by the pulsating, shape-shifting glow of the red-hot embers, appearing to her as alien, living beings. Occasionally, she would blow gently on the coals, and the flames would return and dance merrily for a while, until they eventually flickered out, leaving the heart of the embers to beat again.

She gazed into the fire in front of her now, and saw pockets of this strange, pulsating life below the flames, shifting patterns constantly painted and repainted in the shimmering core of the fire. It was beautiful to behold. Allowing herself to be drawn into the comfort of the glimmering display, she gently rocked herself to and fro, a motion both hypnotising and soothing, emptying her mind of the horrors of the day.

The world around her ceased to be.

The exotic patterns shimmered with fiery hues, constantly morphing from one shape to another, pulsing in a rhythm to match her rocking – brighter, dimmer, sharper; now blurring, now faster, now slower. As she watched, mesmerised, ethereal yet recognisable forms emerged from the heart of the fire: a horse with a flowing mane; a wolf with sleek white fur; a mountain lion rippling through the flames. The animals flowed around the fire in a fiery dance, occasionally peeling off to pass in front of her face, their sharp eyes catching hers for the briefest of moments before the animals swept back around the fire.

And then the ethereal animals began to dim and fade as another shape emerged within the centre of the fire. This shape did not pulse but grew brighter as the others faded …

Glacial terror flooded her veins as she suddenly saw what had come before her. She screamed as the malevolent, yellow eye locked onto her. She tried to pull away, to tear her eyes from the baleful gaze, but she was trapped. She couldn't breathe.

"I see you!" crowed a triumphant voice, and a crushing pressure enveloped her mind.

Jessica froze, the familiar, hateful voice echoing with a terrifying sense of malice. *The burnt man! He's here!*

A ghostly hand appeared, reaching out for her—

A blaze of white light exploded around her, and a searing heat blasted from the fire. She screamed and threw herself away, collapsing to the ground. The blazing light vanished.

"Jess!" came Beth's panicked cry. "What's happened?"

Jessica lay, gasping, unable to speak. But the cloying pressure had gone. The burnt man had gone.

Beth appeared at her side. "Jess! Are you alright? What happened?"

The burnt man was here. The devil.

"Are you hurt?"

Drawing deep lungfuls of air, Jessica pushed herself up, then sat, shaking, head in hands. "Give me a minute," she managed, striving to push the nightmare from her mind. *Just a nightmare?* Her skin prickled as if brushed by phantom wings of fear.

After a short while, she looked up, hands trembling, to see Beth's worried face looking back at her. "I must have fallen asleep," she whispered, glancing around to see the bear of a man standing beside them. "I was dreaming ... A nightmare ..." She wiped her damp brow. "It seemed so very real."

"Describe it," came the voice of the bear-like man.

Her voice hushed, Jessica described the terror of her dream.

"I fear the work of the Enemy," the man said as she finished, his rugged face flickering in the light of the fire. "We must get to the western cave and speak with Naga. Until we do, take care. Protect your dreams."

Protect my dreams? "How do I do that? I—"

"Hold on, Jess," Beth interrupted. "How did you understand what Bear said?"

Jessica stared at Beth, confused. Then her eyes widened.

"You understood him, Jess. A moment ago, you didn't."

"It seems you have connected with this Land," Bear murmured.

They both turned to him.

"Our Story talks of this. That the Warriors must first connect with the Land, with the source of their power. You did this in the chamber of the Spirits," he said to Beth. He turned to Jessica. "And now you seem to have connected with the Land's energy." His penetrating eyes searched her face. "It may have been you who forced back this attack of the Enemy ..."

Jessica's mind spun. "No ... I ... I did nothing."

"You are a Warrior," he said simply. "You are all Warriors."

Jessica turned to Beth. "Do you know what's going on?"

A flash of unease crossed Beth's face. Her gaze shifted to Bear. "Why do you call us Warriors?"

"You answered the call."

"That doesn't help me," Beth said, an edge to her voice.

Bear tilted his head a fraction. "Then are you now ready to hear me? Mother tried, but you were not willing to listen."

"I had more important things on my mind. Like saving my friend. I'm listening now."

Bear searched her face for a moment. Then he nodded and spoke. "As Mother told you, we are of the tribe Iyes. Our tribe is long-lived, surviving on the edges of humankind to protect our Story. But whilst others may call us the Hidden, we ally with many tribes, sustaining our knowledge and developing our skills. And protecting our shaman."

"The old lady?"

"Yes. Naga is the keeper of our knowledge, the continuity with the past." He hesitated. "Only the shaman knows what she knows, but from it emerges our Story, one telling of the Warriors, the saviours in our time of need. And that time is now. You are the Warriors."

Jessica's fractured mind rejected what she was hearing. "No. We're no saviours, no Warriors."

"And yet, you answered our shaman's Request. You are here."

She stared despairingly at Bear. What was he saying? This made no sense.

"If we are Warriors, why are we here?" Beth said, her dark eyes glimmering in the firelight.

Bear's gaze was searching. "You truly do not know? You who stand here with an Axe?"

Beth didn't answer.

Jessica glanced at her friend – who was staring at Bear, her eyes afire. She reached over and touched her shoulder. "Beth?" For a moment, she thought she hadn't heard her. Then Beth blinked, and the anger in her eyes vanished. Gut-deep unease stirred. What was happening to her friend? *She holds that Axe as though it were her own. She stands here as though she's always been here.*

"What?" Beth said, her eyes flicking between Jessica and Bear, who both looked at her in silence.

"*Do* you know why we're here?" Jessica said.

Beth frowned. "I just asked that." She faced Bear. "Answer the question."

His expression thoughtful, Bear continued. "An enemy tribe lies to the south. The Ka. The one you named Longhair – and his companion – are of this tribe. These are callous people with a powerful shaman led with draconian force by one known as the Ensi. And above them all, a corrupt god, Kaos, and his agents of the Dark. Together we name them the Enemy."

Jessica's chest tightened. The eye of her nightmare, the burnt man – was this Kaos? She tried to still the thought. *It was a nightmare only.* And yet deep beneath her tangled fear, a part of her knew that wasn't true. *It was no nightmare. Something attacked me. Something tried to kill me.*

"Into the unknown mists of time, we have fought this Enemy, halted the ice, protected the Land. We—"

"Ice?" Beth said with a frown.

"When the power of the Enemy grows, the ice comes. It comes from the north and kills our Land. And the Ka kill our people. To halt the Ka, to defeat Kaos, we must call upon the Warriors to aid us." Bear studied them in turn. "And the ice is returning. The battle with the Enemy is here. And so, you have returned. Our saviours. Our Warriors. Only you have the strength to defeat Kaos. Only you have the power to defeat the one who wishes to wipe out the people of this Land – defeat the one who wishes to destroy the Iyes and our goddess, IY."

Jessica saw the passion in Bear's eyes. *He speaks as though his god stands beside him.* A whisper of dread curled around her mind. *He truly believes this Enemy of his seeks to destroy his god. He truly believes we are his saviours!*

Beth studied Bear with a penetrating gaze. "But these ages of ice you speak of last for immense periods of time."

A grimace crossed Bear's face. "It is an immense struggle."

Beth slowly shook her head. "A war that is not easy to win, it seems."

Bear hesitated, then agreed. "In more ways than one, that appears to be true. Our Story tells that the Warriors save both our people and the Land …" Another pause. "And yet our Enemy is never completely destroyed. Why, I don't know."

As a silence descended, Jessica felt completely and utterly lost, as though wandering a vast, barren desert with no way of knowing where to go or what to do. *Just how did we get here?* An inescapable truth arrived with cold certainty. *The staff. The answer lies with that staff.*

She glanced across to Lanky, where River tended him, ever vigilant. "He knows what happened," she whispered. "He knows, I'm sure." She turned to her friend. "What do we do? What *can* we do?"

Beth's answer was firm. "Before anything else, we have to get that lad more help." She turned to Bear—

Then froze, staring intently into the gloom beyond the fire. "Someone's watching us!"

Jessica spun around but saw nothing but darkness beyond the light of the fire.

"The man from the river!" Beth exclaimed, hoisting her Axe from its holster.

Before anyone else could react, she was racing out of the camp.

*

Shadow was impressed. Hiding in the shadows beyond the light of the fire, he'd watched the formidable axewoman dispatch Krag and Root with a simplicity he could admire. This was a fighter showing a strength and a courage lacking in those they'd captured. It seemed they'd captured the wrong travellers. With Krag and Root lying dead, he'd continued to observe the camp, waiting to see whether any other travellers would appear, waiting to see what else they may have missed.

And it was as he had patiently watched that he sensed a ripple of energy emanate from the camp. His eyes had flicked to the fire, where one of the travellers sat, rocking to and fro. *A shaman? Was the woman a shaman?* He had stilled his breathing, waiting to see what would develop.

Not a moment later, a surge of energy had erupted by the fire, then an intense flash of light had blinded him. As he heard the woman scream, pain had exploded in his mind, and he'd dropped to the ground, holding his pounding head.

Now, his head finally clearing, he tried to understand what had happened. At least one other shaman had briefly entered the camp, but who and why, he didn't know. He'd sensed no presence of the Ka's shaman, but whoever had briefly entered here had been as powerful a figure. Confused, he slowly pulled himself up to his knees to see what was happening. He looked back to camp—

Directly into the gaze of the axewoman, who was staring directly at him.

Then she started running – straight for him.

"Kef!" he muttered under his breath. *Time to go!*

Gripping Sy's fighting staff, he turned and ran, drawing the defences over his mind – defences that he'd let slip, distracted by the blast of light. *You defend your mind now, but it's too late,* he scolded himself. *Again.*

Despite the full moon rising above the hills, its light was yet to fully illuminate the land, and in the gloom, he struggled to keep a great pace. He heard the woman closing in behind him – and he'd seen her in action. *This is not good. I could get an axe in my back.* He pulled a Ka obsidian blade from his tunic. *Change of plan required.*

He suddenly stopped, then spun around and leapt into an attack, the staff in his left hand, the blade in his right. The lightning slash of his blade would have sliced the body of any regular fighter, but the woman swayed to one side and let the blade flash harmlessly by – and swung her axe in a vicious strike towards the back of his head. His years of training saved him – his reflexive twist of his body arced him out of the path of the blade.

He faced her, crouched and ready. She faced him, crouched and ready.

"You move well, my lady," he offered.

"You move like a slug."

He laughed and they circled. "I know that now might not seem the time, but I have two questions for you—"

"Here is your answer!"

The woman swung the axe in a wide arc from his left. He raised his staff to block, but then saw her concealed left hand appear low below him. He dropped, kicking out with his right leg as he fell. His foot connected with her hand and the blade spilled out. As he hit the ground, the axe whistled over his head. He rolled and leapt to his feet to see the axe swinging for him again – he blocked with the staff. Her left leg caught his right hand, and he lost grip of his blade. Instinctively, he dived to his right and felt the axe clip his left shoulder. Still falling to the ground, he swung low with the staff, catching her leg, unbalancing her. He grabbed his fallen blade and rolled into a crouching stance.

Breathing hard, he saw her facing him once again, her eyes bright and fearless. *I can take no chances with this one.* "Impressive," he murmured, slowly dropping his blade hand to his leg harness. He smiled and glanced to her right. "But can you face my friend at the same time?"

A flick of her eyes was all he needed. Releasing the blade he held, he grasped the weapon in the leg harness and sprang forward. She moved, and moved fast, and he missed her chest – but the blade embedded in her arm. Sweeping past her, he caught his balance, then spun back to face her.

She faced him, the shock quickly clearing from her eyes.

Yes, she is dangerous. This had to be done. "The blade is poisoned," he said quietly. "You will die." He lowered his staff a fraction. "I can save you," he lied. "Tell me who sent you. Tell me who gave you the Staff. For this, you may be forgiven its theft and live."

The woman bared her teeth. "No. And I don't believe this blade is poisoned." She pulled it free and hurled it to the ground.

He felt a sting of regret. *Poison is a coward's choice, even in war.* "Forgive me, but it is. I can save you, but you must surrender to me now, and tell me of the Staff."

"Even if I knew what you're talking about, I wouldn't tell you. Burn in hell."

An owl screeched in the distance. *Sy.*

Shadow's keen gaze lingered on her, seeing the easy poise of her stance and the fierce determination in her eyes. *One who would make a good Ka. But one who will give me nothing more.* He gave a short bow. "I wish we could have met under different circumstances—"

The woman leapt for him, but anticipating, he rolled to the side, regained his feet, then sprinted away. For a short while, he heard her determined efforts to catch him, but the sounds of her pursuit soon faded. *The poison will act quickly.*

Settling into an easy jog, he realised how close she had come to landing a crippling strike during this most brief encounter. As he'd seen at the camp, she had been fast, skilful, and audacious, a deadly combination seen in only the best of the Ka. So who was she? What was she? A tantalising thought crystallised. Had he finally met a Warrior? Had he now killed a Warrior? He dismissed the idea instantly. A skilled fighter, yes, maybe even a shamanic fighter, but a destroyer of his people? *No, not this one.*

He heard Sy's owl call, closer this time.

He lengthened his stride, a calm settling on him. Whatever they were, it was clear these travellers were no threat to his people. Some parts of the tales of old had been proven wrong. *Now, the Staff. Concentrate on getting the Staff to the Ancient.*

As he ran on, a nagging thought crept to the edge of his mind. *Would I have beaten her without the poison …?*

*

Arriving at the river, he saw Sy waiting impatiently in the boat. Sy glared at him, then pointed to the sky, his fingers flashing a message. So, the Ancient One had arrived and already made two passes overhead. The next pass would be the last.

Shadow jumped into the boat. Taking an oar, he helped row them across to the far bank. This would be close. If they didn't make this rendezvous, it would have consequences. In many ways. His leader, the Ensi, had made it clear that this was not a meeting to be missed. *And I know it. Our people's lives depend on it. My life depends on it.*

Yet despite the fearsome burden he carried, this was an encounter he had dreamt of since first hearing of the dragon from his teacher. Only a handful of Ka knew that the legend of dragons' existence was indeed no myth: the Ensi, the four Disciples, and now Sy, the warrior monk assigned to him for this mission. Yes, there had been others before him who would have been told, others of the Ka long gone, but most had died knowing only a story. *But I will see the story come alive. I will meet this Ancient.*

Immediately, he cautioned himself. *Don't feel so special, Shadow. Don't believe you are the sole confidant of the Ensi.* Because the Disciples were only one part of the Ensi's complex web. A shrouded web. *And Sy constantly warns me to stop prying.* He smiled. *But I am a curious soul.*

They reached the far bank, and both climbed out. Shadow took back the stolen Staff from a sodden Sy. "You're wet, Sy – you been swimming?"

Sy signed to Shadow.

"Yes, I saw their scout leave the camp. So, he took the boat over and you had to swim back over for it. Not the night or temperature for this much swimming, Sy."

Sy flashed a finger at him.

"That's not a nice thing to say."

Sy ignored him and picked up his axe. He swung it and smashed through the bottom of the boat.

"That make you feel better?"

Continuing to ignore him, Sy pushed the stricken boat out into the river. As the boat floated away, slowly sinking, Sy clambered up the bank. He swept his arm in an arc from the northern sky to the south, then gesturing for Shadow to follow, he headed off towards the more open ground behind them. Shadow glanced to the north. *So, the Ancient made its flypasts here.* His eyes widened as he caught a glint of reflected moonlight in the distant sky. *And there it is.*

He hurried after Sy, his pace hampered by the rough ground. *We can't miss this pass. We need the support of the Ancients.* And that was not a given. The Ancients were said to be a proud race, here long before the Ka and answering to no man. *But our stories tell that they have always allied with us. I can't let my people down.* Ahead, Sy had stopped in the open area and was waving one hand frantically and pointing with the other to something behind Shadow. Reaching Sy, Shadow spun around.

The silver beast was almost upon them!

Shadow thrust the Staff in the air and a white light blazed into the sky.

The Ancient's head instantly turned, its left wing twisting high in the sky as it banked sharply towards them. As it approached, both wings angled steeply, slowing it dramatically before its soft landing a short spear throw away – an unnaturally quiet landing for such a massive beast. *Yet what do I know of such beasts?*

His heart thumping in his chest, he and Sy slowly approached the enormous dragon, which had settled back between the twin cowls of its folded wings. As the radiated heat from the Ancient's jaws grew too great to bear, Shadow halted, and as told by his master, he bowed deeply, holding the Staff high in front of him, its fierce light casting sharp shadows around them. He then straightened and cleared his throat. "On behalf of the Ensi, I present you with the Staff. My leader is thankful for your aid and hopes that this will be our last request."

The sleek head of the dragon swung towards him, and as it did so, its scales – ornate platelets sheathing its body and wings – shimmered with an intense silver sheen, a multitude of rippling colours seeking to break out through the surface. Flowing back from the Ancient's nostrils and jaw, long, sculpted ridges curved backwards and outwards towards its thick plated neck. And within the deep, shadowed whorls of those sculpted ridges, the Ancient's eyes glowed with fiery yellow light.

One fearsome eye stared at him now.

Shadow's mouth felt as dry as desert sand.

A rumble sounded deep within the dragon, and as its head swung closer, an acrid, fetid stench swept over him. Shadow's gut wrenched with primeval fear, yet he forced himself to stand proud. *Do not show any weakness. I am a Ka.* In answer, another part of him grunted an imagined wry warning from Sy. *Yes, maybe. But don't do anything foolish. I don't want to die tonight.*

The Ancient opened its great jaws a fraction, and a searing heat slammed into Shadow. Face aglow, he held his stance, unsure of what to say or do. There didn't seem to be anything else sensible he could say. The words of his obdurate old teacher echoed in his mind: *Better to be silent and thought a fool, than speak further and prove it.*

'Accepted,' came a voice in his head in answer to his seemingly long-ago offer – a female voice, it seemed to him, but how was he to know with such a beast?

He sighed with exultant relief. They had done it. The Ancient had accepted the Staff. *We have a most formidable ally on our side.*

As the dragon swung her head away, the Staff's light snapped out. The beast lowered herself to the ground, one leg angled to the side. *'Climb and find purchase. We leave now.'*

Sy immediately moved.

Hesitating for only a few euphoric heartbeats, Shadow followed Sy, and they clambered up the Ancient's scaled leg, avoiding the runnels of dirt trickling down the creases and joins on the creature's body before settling into the dip between the fall of the beast's neck and the rise to her ridged back, where three rows of larger plates continued towards her tail. Sy sat in front, holding on to the edges of plates on either side of the beast's neck. Shadow sat immediately behind with one hand around Sy's waist. Ferocious exhilaration coursed through him. What glorious yet terrifying wonder to be seated on such a beast.

We are the first Ka of these times to travel with an Ancient. The first of millennia!

Rocked sideways as the Ancient rose from the ground, both men strengthened their hold on the beast. Behind them, the Ancient's wings lifted, and Shadow sensed the immense strength – and power – being deployed as they rose higher into the sky. Nervously glancing sideways, he felt a shift in the dragon's body and saw the wing angles change. They began to pick up speed. *Now we head into unknown territory.* He didn't know – he'd never been told – where the Ancients lived. He guessed in the frozen north. *Maybe the Ensi knows.*

As they picked up height, he spotted the fire of their temporary camp. He tensed. The dragon seemed to be heading straight for it – and at great speed.

*

Jessica stared into the growing darkness beyond the camp, despairing of Beth's actions. Despite an almost crippling fear, she'd moved to follow her friend, but Bear had held her back, worried it was a ploy by the Ka to separate them, leaving Lanky vulnerable. And she knew he'd been right to stop her. *What could I have done?* An icy dread laced through her veins. *And what does Beth think she can do?* That was a frightening question, for she was seeing a side to Beth that was terrifying.

Even so, searching the shadows beyond the light of the fire, restless frustration grew. *This is my friend out there. What are you doing to help her?* Although the petrified part of her wished she would wake up and end this waking nightmare, another part – a growing part – understood that wasn't going to happen.

This was real. Somehow, this was very real.

Come on, Jess, you're stronger than this. Find a way to deal with this hell. You have to engage. She glanced at Lanky, who lay on a makeshift stretcher enduring a fevered sleep. The girl – River, Bear had called her – mopped his brow. *He deserves your strength. Remember, he gave you a chance to escape.*

Her gaze shifted to River. The girl had done what she could for him, working with tremendous skill to cut the blade free from his side, then treating the deep wound as best she could with what she had to hand. *Which is virtually nothing.* At least now they had the stretcher to carry him, quickly fashioned from the branches that had carried her and Lanky to this hateful camp. She turned to Bear, who was still standing beside her, scanning the perimeter of the camp for sign of the returning Beth. "When will your healer arrive?"

"Soon, I hope."

"Is she a good healer?"

Bear considered for a moment. "I have seen from your clothes that you hold skills that we do not. But we will do what we can to save the Warrior."

"So, there are no others like us here?"

"All people are different, so, no, there is no one like you here."

"A clever answer."

"A true answer."

"Will you help us get home?"

Bear hesitated. "If that is what you wish, then I will help you."

Jessica studied his face, seeing an imposing strength in his deep-set eyes. *He means it. He believes it. And I need to accept that for now.* "Thank you. And my name is Jessica," she added with a faint smile.

Bear acknowledged her with a slight nod. He reached out and placed his hand on her shoulder. "Warrior – Jessica – I know you are not of this place and will find it difficult to accept what you see and hear. I believe you when you say you have been pulled here against your will – not something I expected, nor understand. But whether you accept you are a Warrior or not, you must accept that you are here in this moment – and that enemies are close by. We must prepare for further attack and be ready to help your friend."

She pushed back a stab of fear. "What can I do to help?"

Bear stood back and glanced around the firelit camp. "Here we are exposed. Until your friend returns, we should move into the cover of the trees." He walked off towards River, gesturing for her to follow.

Jessica walked after him, his words cutting deep. *If Longhair or the other returns, then Beth would be … No! Just deal with what's in front of you, Jess.*

"We need to move," Bear said as they joined River, who knelt by Lanky's side.

River climbed to her feet. "At last. I don't want a spear in my back."

Working as quickly and carefully as they could, they manoeuvred Lanky onto the makeshift stretcher. He groaned but didn't waken.

"We will move over there," Bear said, gesturing towards a moonlit clump of trees to the north of the camp.

"What about him?" River asked, nodding towards the injured guard.

"We'll return for him. First, let us move the Warrior."

With Bear taking the front of the stretcher, and Jessica and River the rear, they made their way towards the cover of the trees. They'd barely left the flickering light of the fire when River froze. "Something's coming! There, in the sky!"

"The ice lizard!" Bear hissed, staring wide-eyed to the darkening sky. "Get down now! And stay quiet!"

*

Beth was slowing. And nauseous. *That knife. That devil told the truth.* She peered once more through the gloom and could now see the glow of the fire at the camp ahead. *Not far ...*

She pushed on.

The man had been too fast. She had avoided the final killing strike from his blade, but taken a bad cut to the arm. *A wound that may yet kill me.*

Ignore the pain! Push on!

Poison, the man had said. She hadn't believed him. *Could he have saved me?*

Her scattered thoughts were broken by a deep humming sound behind her. Dropping to the ground, she turned to see a glistening shadow in the night sky. As it hurtled towards her, she realised it was huge. *What the hell is that?* Lying flat to the ground, she watched in astonishment as a sleek silver shape cruised overhead, its enormous wings shining in the growing moonlight and two figures on its back. *What! A dragon?* Her heart pounded as she tried to make sense of what she was seeing. *This is impossible!*

No, possible, said the voice inside her. *Get moving. Your friend is in danger.*

A surge of energy coursed through her, sweeping aside the pain and nausea. *Jess is in trouble!* She clambered to her feet and raced towards the camp. As she pushed herself hard over the rough ground, a huge flare lit up the night sky ahead, and she heard someone screaming. Drawing on the surging energy within, she lengthened her stride, the distance to the camp shortening fast. Another huge flare streamed down from the sky, and this time, she saw the silver beast banking hard as it completed its attack before veering upwards and away. Unbidden, the thought came: *It's swinging around for another attack. It will come from there.* She ran on into the camp, then halted, readying her Axe as she faced its expected line of attack. Several tense heartbeats, then she saw a silver flash in the distance as the beast turned and headed towards her.

She stood and waited.

The beast grew in the sky as it cruised towards them.

"Beth! Run!"

She cursed as she caught sight of Jessica running towards her. *Ignore her. Focus.*

The dragon banked slightly and arrowed in on its new target.

Beth hefted her Axe and steadied her breathing. *Calm. You have one shot.*

She watched as the dragon swept down to near ground level, bearing down on her friend—

Now!

She hurled the Axe.

It flew straight and true, glinting in the firelight as it sliced through the air before hammering into the neck of the dragon. An ear-shattering cry rent the night air, and the beast flailed wildly in the sky. But as she watched, the Axe fell from the beast's neck and the dragon quickly regained control. It banked sharply, climbing steeply into the night sky. Picking up speed, it arrowed away from camp, heading north.

*

Shadow clung on to Sy as they continued climbing, the camp dwindling behind them. The dragon was agile, quick, and had been in aggressive attack mode, not conducive to an easy and secure ride on her back. And with each rumble beneath them, the sky had lit up into a fiery blaze, followed by a searing wall of heat sweeping over them. It was not an experience he wanted to repeat.

The attack stopped abruptly with a shriek from the dragon, then Shadow fought desperately to hang on as the beast flailed uncontrollably. After what seemed an eternity, the ride settled, and they swept northward.

"What happened?" Shadow hissed, glancing down into the shadowy, moonlit land below.

Sy lifted one hand, putting his forefinger down and thumb out to the side.

"An axe?"

Sy nodded.

His hands firmly grasping onto Sy's tunic, Shadow shook his head. "The axewoman. Well, well. I underestimated her strength." He glanced back and caught a glimpse of the now distant camp, flickering figures seen in the light of the dwindling campfire. "A pity she wasn't a Ka," he murmured, feeling a strange empathy with this unknown fighter. He sighed. "But she wasn't, and now the poison will do its work."

'Don't be so sure, human,' came the Ancient's voice. 'The Axe has power, and the Warrior can use it. Knowing this, I cannot risk the Staff. We travel.'

Shadow gasped. "You call this one a Warrior? Why?"

'Because that is what she is, fool. Hold steady. We travel fast.'

Incredulous, he struggled to accept what he was hearing. *A Warrior? No, that was no destroyer I faced – she was merely a fighter, a shamanic fighter ...*

But those thoughts now sounded hollow.

And if she was a Warrior? "I didn't slay her, Sy. I didn't kill her when she stood before me."

"The Ancient is right," Sy signed. "You are a fool."

The vision of his poisoned blade slicing across the woman's arm flashed into his mind. *The poison* must *surely kill her*, he told himself. *It always kills.* Yet in this moment, even that assertion felt under threat. *Kef! We should make sure she dies.* He risked the question. "Ancient One, shouldn't we continue the attack? They seem weak. Maybe now is our chance?"

'Did the Axe cut you, human? I think not. A slight wound only, but it was as a blade through my heart. We travel. And prepare.'

Shadow heard the finality in the beast's words. He looked back towards the site of battle, but all was now lost in the distant gloom. *I had no choice*, he told himself. *I ran out of time. I had to meet with the Ancient One.* He frowned. *And so, I gave this Warrior a chance she shouldn't have had.*

He shook his head and glanced ahead. To the north. To wherever this beast was carrying them and the Staff. He sighed, accepting his mistake. What was done, was done. And if the poisoned blade somehow failed to deliver death? *Then in time we'll meet again – and I won't fail twice.*

*

Shaking, Jessica tracked the silvery beast's flight to the north. Glistening in the moonlight, it didn't deviate from its path and was soon lost from view. *What was that ... thing?*

You know what it is, she found herself answering. *And you know you're not in your own land anymore.* Because the reality of their plight had been seared into her mind by the sight of that fearsome beast in the sky. *That fantastical beast.* No, this wasn't her own land she walked in ... *but where are we?*

Turning back, she looked out into the gloom. Beth had retrieved her Axe and was walking back towards her.

"You bloody idiot," she grated, her fear morphing to anger as Beth joined her. "What were you thinking of?"

"Good to see you too," Beth said with a smile as they walked back towards the light of the camp. "And I might ask the same of you."

Remembering her panicked rush to help Beth – *though what could I have done?* – Jessica winced. "I thought I could help … I had to do something."

"It was brave," Bear said as he came out to meet them. "It gave your friend a better chance to strike the dragon."

Beth's face hardened. "It did. But it was also foolish."

Walking on to the camp, Jessica glanced at her friend. "I can't stand back any longer, Beth. We're in this together."

Beth took a moment to answer, then she sighed. "That's certainly true."

They fell silent until they reached the flickering fire-cast shadows at the edge of camp.

"What was that thing?" Jessica said, glancing north.

"Something I truly believed I would never see," Bear answered to her side. "It was an ice dragon, a creature that serves the Enemy. The Story tells us it can appear in times such as these, but some things are hard to believe until you see them."

A dragon. A creature of childhood stories. *Yet moments ago, one almost killed us.* "Will it return?" Jessica asked as River joined them.

"The dragon was clearly hurt. It will be wary. That should give us time to move from here."

"Did you notice the people on its back?" Beth asked quietly.

"Yes. Ka. Their alliance with the Ancient is forged, it seems."

"On its last attack, I saw the face of the Ka I fought. He left me a present." She held up her arm.

"Hell, Beth!" Jessica exclaimed, only now in the light of the fire seeing the sliced and bloodied tunic on Beth's arm. "That looks bad."

"A flesh wound," Beth said, weariness in her voice. She glanced at Bear. "Except maybe more."

"That wound was from a Ka?"

Beth nodded. "I only just survived the encounter. He let me go but said I would die."

Bear's eyes dulled with dismay. "If that was a Ka blade coated with poison, then I am surprised you are still alive."

Jessica gasped.

"I admit, I'm not feeling too good," Beth said, her face becoming more drawn by the second. "Do you have an antidote?"

Bear shook his head. "We do not."

Jessica stared at Bear in disbelief. This couldn't be happening.

Bear studied them, his thickset features strained. "The fact that you are still standing provides hope. It is possible that the bleeding may have removed some poison, but our wish must be that the Ka made a mistake on the blade, and it was not effective." He hesitated. "Failing that, we pray to IY for help."

Jessica struggled to stem a growing despair. *Stay strong. Beth needs you to be strong.* "What can we do?" she said, holding her voice steady.

"Move," Bear said, surety returning to his voice. "If the Ka and the Ancient return, then we die. You are not yet ready to fight them."

"Speak for yourself," Beth growled.

"Bear is right," Jessica admonished. "You're in no shape to fight anybody, let alone that beast."

Beth seemed about to argue, then her shoulders slumped. "You're right ... not today, anyway."

"We should move now," Bear said. "We will follow the river north to a crossing point upstream where the healer will be waiting. They should have mobilised by now." He turned to Jessica. "Where did you hide the Staff?"

A shiver ran down Jessica's spine. "What Staff?" she said in a hushed voice.

"The Staff of IY. The one the man here was carrying when you arrived."

The Staff ... Her nightmares, their captors ... *They wanted the Staff ...*

She found she couldn't speak.

Bear regarded her with sudden piercing intensity. "Did you not use it to get here? This is what we have been taught. Is it wrong?"

Jessica's mind reeled. *What have we lost?* "The Ka took it from us ..." she managed, her stomach churning. "When we were captured ... He walked away with it when he left."

Bear's eyes widened. "The Ka took it?" he exclaimed, grabbing her arm. "Why didn't you tell me? No! Tell me this is not true."

"What is it?" she stammered. "Why is it important?"

He stared at her, aghast. "You don't know? How is it you don't know?"

It was in my nightmares. But I knew nothing.

"What is this Staff, Bear?" Beth asked firmly. "And let go of my friend's arm."

Bear released Jessica's arm, then slowly shook his head. "Together with the Axes, it is one of the most important objects the Warriors hold. It is our salvation. And it was your way home."

CHAPTER TEN

The memory of the night long ago, when the two babies and two toddlers were abandoned in the Iyes camp, never left Naga. Grown into young adults, those four had become a wonderful boon to the tribe. But their origins remained a mystery; and that confusion would prove most useful in times to come.

Watching the dying flames in the moonlit plain below, Spider took another nervous swig of water, then looked again to the north. All remained quiet. The dragon had not returned. *River will be okay,* he told himself yet again. *She's smart. She'll have found refuge from the beast.*

"So, the Ancient lives," Eagle said behind him.

Spider turned to his fellow scout and pathfinder, who sat beside Amber on the bowed trunk of a fallen tree. Both looked to the clear night sky, their moonlit faces etched with apprehension.

"In this, our Story again proves true," Spider said, struggling to believe his own words.

"And if it returns, we're exposed here," Amber said quietly.

That is also true. After leaving the safety of the cave, they'd made good progress in their effort to reach the river crossing before Bear and his group – until the dragon had been seen. Now they were vulnerable in the sparse tree cover on this side of the valley.

"But the silver beast headed north," Eagle said, turning to Amber. "We may still have a chance."

"Did *they* have a chance?" Amber murmured, staring at the scattered fires glowing on the plain.

Spider's stomach churned. Had Bear and the group survived the attack? Had River survived? He pushed the fear away. "Naga will tell us soon," he said, glancing over to the rocky bank of the stream where Naga sat, eyes closed, far-seeking. "But Bear is no fool. They *will* be safe."

Amber turned to him. "Yes. I believe that too. And that means we still have an injured Warrior to treat. We can't delay much longer."

Spider glanced to the northern end of the plain, where the river swung west to the crossing point. "We're making good progress," he said, passing the water skin to Eagle. "Once we get the all-clear, we'll reach them soon enough."

"Even so, I hope that River managed to remove the blade before the redness damaged the Warrior's spirit."

"I'm sure she will do what she can," Eagle said, forcing a smile. "You're a good teacher."

Amber reached out and took Eagle's hand. "I hope so." She squeezed his hand, then climbed to her feet. "I'll check on Gravel. He doesn't complain, but I can see he's still hurting."

Spider saw it too. Gravel was a tough fighter – a tough man – but it had been a hard and vicious defence of the Arrival site; many carried wounds from the battle.

Amber bent down to Eagle, saying a few words that Spider didn't catch before giving him a gentle kiss and stepping away. Eagle watched her go.

"So, Eagle," Spider said, smiling with genuine warmth. "Does Amber now have you captured and trapped like a fly? You two will make a fine pair. Does Firuz know about this?"

Eagle took a swig of water and then wiped his short beard, which was carefully sculpted each turn of the moon. "Yes. And no. Yes, Amber and I will seek Mother's approval to pair. And no, Firuz has not yet returned, and so doesn't know. But he will know soon – and just have to accept it. Amber and I have declared for each other."

Spider clapped Eagle on the back. "Congratulations!"

"Quiet, you fool," Eagle hissed, nervously scanning the sky.

"These things have to be celebrated," Spider said. His smile quickly faded. "But yes, unfortunately, far too briefly."

They fell silent.

"What did the Ka look like?" Eagle asked after a while.

Spider shook his head. "I didn't see them. And I'm glad I didn't. A single man facing them alone? No, I'd be dead in a heartbeat."

"Then how can they be defeated? This enemy who has the might of dragons with them."

"They bleed. So, they can die."

Eagle looked away, his tired eyes scanning the night sky. "Why do they seek to destroy us?"

"The Ka, or the Ancient?"

"Both."

Spider shrugged. "You know our Story. They are raised to destroy us. They live and die to destroy us. All guided by the twisted influence of their god of the Dark, Kaos."

"Yet, still," Eagle said, shaking his head. "What threat do we pose to them?"

"You ask what every Iyes asks. Our Story—"

"Spider," Gravel growled behind them. "Mother wishes to speak with us."

Spider glanced around, but Gravel had already moved away. He shook his head. "Talkative as ever," he muttered. He turned back to Eagle. "All we can do is protect ourselves. And protect the Warriors until they're ready to protect our Land." He placed his hand on Eagle's shoulders. "Stay strong, my friend. And fight for the ones you love."

Eagle looked up, sudden fire in his eyes. "That I can easily do."

Spider smiled. An image of River formed in his mind. *Yes, it was easy to fight for those you loved.* He turned to leave. "Okay, let me find out what's happened out there." *And I pray that she is safe.*

*

Naga watched as the three men walked over to her. Spider, already the best tracker in the tribe, but also a gifted strategist, was being tested for future leadership under the stewardship of Bear. Too young? Maybe. Gifted? Definitely. The other two, the tribe's Shields, poles apart in character, but both steeped in experience and respected by the groups they led. It was these three who had rediscovered the Sacred Site earlier this sun-cycle. *And just in time.* It had allowed them to make the preparations for the arrival of the Warriors.

But the Ka ...

She had not expected the Ka to find them so quickly. They had all underestimated the Ka's knowledge and skill, allowing their hated enemy to infiltrate unseen. The consequences had been severe, and now they would need all her tribe's skill and cunning to recover the situation. Especially as the Ka had use of the ice dragon. They had all seen the flash of silver in the sky, and the ferocious, demoniacal fire raking the plain. She fingered her bracelet. *And I saw the attack on the camp.*

Her rugged brow furrowed. She had struggled to accept this part of the tribe's Story, believing it a misunderstanding of a long-past event, warped and twisted by the vast passage of time. But she could not doubt what she had seen in her far-seeking. The dragons were real.

But the group survived, thank IY. Thanks to the Warrior.

And now Bear, River, and the Warriors were heading towards the river crossing and would likely reach it before them. *I could move there now.* She fingered the bracelet again. But that would drain her. *No, it is not yet so desperate.*

She looked up at the three men she had summoned. "An ice dragon has attacked the camp," she began. She held up her hands as Spider immediately started to talk. Gravel frowned, his deeply scarred face showing his displeasure at Spider's impatience. Knuckles, a head shorter than Gravel but as stout of heart as his fellow Shield, waited patiently for her to continue. "The Warrior defended them, and no one was hurt in its attack." She saw the tension ease from Spider's face. "But we now know that one of the Ancients is abroad. Our Story speaks true – it serves the Enemy."

Knuckles shook his head. Gravel's scowl deepened.

"Bear is moving to the river crossing – and quickly. We will leave now to get aid to the wounded Warrior. Knuckles, Spider, take Amber and Shorty and travel ahead. Gravel, you will lead our group." She looked at each of them in turn. "Be wary of the Ancient and may IY travel with you."

"And with you," they answered. They gave a respectful nod, then hurried away.

Her gaze lingered on them. She had chosen not to reveal that the Staff had been lost. They would cross that stream when they had taken the Warriors to safety.

She turned to a young woman readying her pack close by. "Sheba."

Sheba looked up, pushing a strand of her jet-black hair from her face. "A moment, Mother."

She watched as Sheba readied herself, setting one pack over one shoulder before strapping one of the Warrior Axes over another. Seeing the young woman now, few would believe she was with child, but Naga had noticed the slowing of her movements. She smiled, thinking of her own stiffening limbs. *There is slow, and there is* slow. *The advantages of youth.*

Youth? What age was Sheba now? She thought back to the strange night when the babies had been found. *Sixteen sun-cycles ago? Maybe seventeen.* The two babies and two toddlers, all found in the midst of their camp. And no one seen, no one heard. Until the babies cried.

It had happened before, some mother's unwanted child abandoned. Naga's eyes narrowed. *But four in one night?*

And ...

And what? she challenged herself. *You think you felt something, smelled something?* Whatever she had thought, it was now a long time ago. And now Sheba, one of those two abandoned babies, was herself with child, and the two toddlers, most clearly blood sisters, had grown into two of the most respected young women in the tribe. She smiled as the familiar faces of Rind and her older sister, Svana, drifted through her mind.

She sighed. *Time passes so quickly.*

Sheba strode towards her, grimacing. "These packs seem to be getting heavier."

"I doubt that, Sheba," Naga said, smiling. "I suspect that it might be you who is getting heavier. Your sister will soon be able to outrun you."

Sheba smiled. "Hah, maybe. That just shows how slow River really is."

Naga smiled. Competitive the two certainly were, but they were also very close, and often partners-in-crime on some prank or other. *Not helped by their father.* Her smile faded. It was no surprise that Bear turned a blind eye to some of their escapades. Losing their adopted mother early had not been easy on any of them. Their family bond had been – and still was – strong. A credit to Bear and Ravine's love and nurturing after agreeing to take the abandoned babies as their own. Whether the babies had been sisters by birth, she didn't know ... *But they are as sisters now.*

And yet neither Sheba nor River knew of the truth of their beginnings. *It never needed to be said. Their lives restarted with us.* And now Bear was Sheba's loving father.

Naga's shoulders tensed. *What else do I hide?* All knew Sheba was with child, but not what she carried. None knew but her that in these most terrible times, the Light had chosen the one to continue the line of Mothers of the Iyes. *River will follow me, then this child of Sheba.* And she had already sensed the burgeoning strength within that unborn child. This would be a Mother to rival the strongest their tribe had seen. Maybe the strongest. *I must continue to watch over Sheba and the future Mother she carries.*

She hid a pang of frustration. Sheba, and all those within the tribe, needed more than her protection now. *We need the Warriors.* It was now in the hands of their saviours to help preserve the Land, not just for the future Mother of the Iyes, but for all life of the Land. *They need to understand who they are. They need to act.*

"Mother?"

Naga pulled herself out of her reverie and forced a smile. "Come, Sheba. Let us join Gravel. It's time to move on."

A short while later, with Spider and his group of four disappearing from view, Naga, Sheba, and six others moved quietly through the moonlit landscape. They moved in pairs, each taking a slightly different route, with Naga and Sheba staying in the centre. From time to time, Eagle would signal his position out in front, guiding their path with a low owl's hoot. And strapped on the backs of three of the tribe hung the Warrior Axes. *Axes that should have been with the Warriors by now.* It was not supposed to have happened like this. The Warriors were vulnerable. *They must complete the bonding at the western Sacred Site.*

Naga heard Sheba stumble. "How is the little one doing?"

"She's moving. She must know we're about to travel."

Naga smiled. "And she's letting you know all is well."

Sheba was quiet for a moment, then: "I agree, Mother, but I'm worried we're now at the time of the Warriors. Had she been born more than ten sun-cycles ago, she would have developed the skills to engage with our fight. But now?" Naga heard the tension – the fear – in the girl's voice. "Do we really know how to defeat the Enemy? I'm scared, Mother."

With the moonlight aiding their path to the river crossing, Naga drew closer to Sheba. "I think we are all scared as to what will happen. But what will come, will come. As our tribe has ever done, we will do our best for those around us. Especially for your new life. We will support you, have no doubt." *The future of the Iyes must be preserved.*

Sheba smiled. "I don't doubt you, Mother."

"And we will support the Warriors. That is our path to defeat this Enemy – and to keep our children safe."

As they continued in silence, the weight on Naga's shoulders grew. *This is a dangerous time for us all.* And a challenging time. They would need all their strength, resilience, and cunning to navigate a way through.

And not all of us will make it.

She felt a sudden pain in the certainty of those words. The words of the shaman. The realism of the shaman. *Our Story never tells of this – the sacrifices that must be made.* The core of the tribe numbered thirty-four: eight travelling in her group, six others close by, including those with Bear and Spider, and twenty to the south, including the children. It was a healthy-sized tribe, with allies to call on. They were in good shape to support the Warriors.

But how many will be left by the end?

For there would be a cost – but they couldn't fail their ancestors.

*

Bear led them at a gruelling pace, and although he could see the wounded Warrior Beth was struggling, he had not slowed even over the rougher ground. He was angry. How could they not understand the importance of the Staff? He had known the ones who answered the Request would need help, but not like this. Only one Warrior had shown any skill. The others seemed no different from those in his tribe. Weaker even. *These were Warriors?* It made no sense. And they knew nothing of the power of the Staff. That it was this Staff that allowed them to travel to this age. That it was this Staff that their Story told was needed to defeat the Enemy.

Pushing the group on, he knew his anger rose from a cutting sense of injustice. For sun-cycle after sun-cycle, he and others had maintained the knowledge and readiness for the re-emergence of the Enemy. And before them had toiled generation after generation, all dedicated to keeping the tribe at the forefront of knowledge and skills – all with a readiness to support the Warriors in the war ahead. *And for these?*

"I need to rest," came the wounded Warrior's voice.

"We keep moving," Bear replied stubbornly.

The stretcher pole was almost yanked from his grasp as Beth stopped walking. "No, we stop."

He tried to walk on—

"Father! Stop! Now!" River commanded.

With a scowl, Bear halted. "We cannot waste time. The beast may still be searching for us."

"We *will* stop," River said firmly. "We've seen no sign of the beast, and we need to rest. She's wounded, remember?"

Bear glared at River in the darkness. She was right, of course, but it didn't lessen his mood. He looked ahead and could see the moonlit glint of the river through the trees. They were at the crossing. "We can rest here a while," he growled.

They lowered the stretcher to the ground, and then Bear walked a short distance away, anger simmering. He reached for his water skin, took out the wooden stopper, and took a drink. Their progress had been good, but the stretcher was cumbersome and heavy. They were all tiring.

River walked up beside him. He saw the strain in her face. "This stretcher is no good," she said. "We won't get much further like this."

He nodded.

"And those clouds are thickening," she continued. "We'll lose light soon. I think we should stay here for a while. We can make a better carrier for him."

She speaks like her mother. Clearheaded and decisive. His anger cooled. "You're right," he said, his voice softening. "We will rest awhile."

A short while later, a small ember fire glowed in the clearing. To one side of the fire, Beth and Jessica spoke in low voices beside the supine form of Lanky, who remained in a restless sleep. To the other side, River sat down beside her father.

"You need to be patient," she said in a low voice.

"I expected ... more," he murmured, sitting hunched, feeling lost.

"I understand," she said softly, "but we cannot know the thinking of IY." She glanced at Beth, who had now lain down. "I have always doubted the Story, but that one ... I can't doubt what I see. She is not of this Land."

Bear stared at his daughter. *She believes.*

River looked back at him and placed her hand on his shoulder. "Do not waver at the start, Father. They need you. The tribe also needs you."

His heart warmed, Bear smiled. He reached up and placed his hand on hers. "Thank you. And you are right – I do not know the ways of IY. Our task is harder than it might have been, but I cannot abandon hope before we have even begun." He straightened and then climbed to his feet. "Warriors – a moment."

The two women looked over at him.

"Forgive me. Losing the Staff was a shock. A great shock. But my behaviour has been like a child. For that, I am sorry."

"It's forgotten," Jessica answered. "We're all stressed. We—"

Beth sat up, then clambered unsteadily to her feet. "Someone approaches," she said, lifting her Axe from its holster, her wounded arm held limply to her side.

River quickly stepped to her side. "How many?"

"Four. They move like cows."

River glanced at her ... and smiled.

An owl sounded to their right.

"Amber!" River exclaimed. She put her hands to her mouth and echoed the call.

Moments later, four figures materialised out of the gloom of the trees. River rushed to Amber, greeting her with a hug.

"Meet members of my tribe," Bear said, stepping forward. "Spider you met earlier. This is Amber, our healer. And these two are Shorty and Knuckles."

He saw the Warrior quickly assessing the newcomers. After a moment, she lowered her Axe, a strain returning to her face. He frowned. *I was wrong to push her so hard. She is a Warrior, to me that is clear, but she fights the Ka poison. She needs to rest.*

"I hope you can help him, Amber," Beth murmured, then she sat back down, her head bowed.

Shorty and Knuckles looked at each other but said nothing.

Jessica walked forward. "I'm Jessica," she said, halting in front of the newcomers.

Bear glanced at the tall woman, relief coursing through him. She was engaging at last.

"You must be Shorty," Jessica said, looking at a clean-shaven shorter man, who stood beside a tall man with a black bushy beard.

"No. I'm Knuckles." The short man gestured to the one beside him. "This is Shorty."

"I apologise, Shorty." She took in the taller man. "My mistake. So," she continued, turning to the tall woman beside them. "You are Amber. Is that right?"

Amber smiled. Her hair cast a deep, fiery red in the light of the flames. "I am." Her smile faded. "Can I see the injured Warrior?"

"Which one?" Jessica muttered, a flash of pain in her eyes as she glanced over at Beth. She gestured to Amber. "Please. This way." She led Amber to the fevered Lanky.

Bear watched Amber examine the Warrior's wound, then his gaze shifted to the lean man standing silently beside him. A man whose keen dark eyes searched the shadows around them. The eyes of a scout never rested. "You made good time, Spider."

The scout turned, his lean, youthful face now catching the flickering light of the fire. "We did," he said, pushing a lank strand of his matted hair behind his ear, "driven by the fear of what we'd find. We saw the Ancient's attack from afar."

Bear grimaced. "It was the Warrior over there who saved us. Drove it away with her Axe."

"Then it seems it can be hurt. Have you seen sight of it since?"

"Thank IY, no. And for that I'm grateful."

"What was the Ancient One like?" Knuckles asked, stepping closer. "Always good to know your enemy."

Bear turned, seeing the rugged, weathered face of the experienced Shield looking intently at him. A face he was glad to see. Despite his constant bickering with Shorty, this was a man the whole tribe respected. *Though they'd never admit that to his face.* "It is a creature that I hoped I would never see. Our stories tell us of many things, but always you have doubts – this dragon was my doubt." Yet all scepticism had vanished within a heartbeat. "It is a fearsome beast. Much larger than a crocodile or horse. And fast, attacking from the air with fire as we have heard in our stories. We can only be thankful it does not show itself other than at these times."

"A forbidding adversary indeed," Knuckles said, running his scarred hand through his short, thick hair. "But as my grandfather said, there's always a way to defeat a living being, either by strength or trickery. We'll find which is needed with this one."

"The way is with the Warriors," Bear said, his face hardening. "That one is not for us."

"Where is it from?" Jessica said, coming up behind him.

"The Story tells us it is one of the Ancients, creatures that have been here longer than the people of this Land. Many existed, but only this race, the ice lizard – a creature of the northern ice lands – was seen by the ancestors. Our Enemy appears to hold an ability to call them, but it is told the Ancient Ones trouble themselves little with the battles of the tribes – even during times such as these." And yet it was here, now. "It is said that the ice dragon covets the Staff. This might explain its presence at this time." *And now the Ancient has it.*

His eyes sharpened on Jessica. "Our Story tells that you must hold the Staff for our Request for Warriors to succeed. *Did* the Staff bring you here?"

Jessica hesitated … then nodded. "I think it must have."

He frowned. "Yet only three of you are here. Our Story tells of—"

"Bear!" Shorty shouted. "The Warrior! She's collapsed."

Bear spun around and saw the Axe Warrior lying flat on her back, twitching.

"Beth!" Jessica cried, running to the Warrior's side.

Bear's urgent gaze sought out Spider. "We need Naga! Go! Tell her what's happening."

Spider immediately turned to leave.

"Rest, Spider," came a clear voice from the trees. "I am here."

Naga walked into the clearing.

*

Naga examined the crude circle, then frowned and walked over to an Axe on the circle perimeter. She made a slight adjustment, then stepped back. *Three Axes and two of the relics. That should be sufficient. And the Warrior has the fourth Axe beside her.*

She turned to the watching group. "Do not cross the threshold," she said firmly. "Inside is a safe place for the Spirits and their daemons. Let it remain so." She turned back to the circle, then stepped inside to join the supine bodies of the two Warriors. Bringing her hand to her bracelet, she reached for its latent power. She prayed that sufficient energy remained. For when she'd heard Bear's cry, she had acted instantly, drawing power from her bracelet to connect with a Cord and move. But it grew harder to activate the Cord. Each time, she needed more and more energy. *I grow old. The time for the new shaman is near.*

Settling her thoughts, she brushed her fingers on the smooth stones of her bracelet and pulled in the energy of the Light – IY's gift to her, to the shamans of the Iyes. Breathing gently, she raised her hand and weaved the energy around the circle, the bands of energy snapping to the Axes and relics, before rising upwards to form a barrier around them. A barrier to those of the Dark who might seek to enter. A safe place for the Spirits' daemons to aid the Warriors.

She breathed a sigh of relief as the barrier locked into place. Though this was a skill unique to her, one that had shocked the old Mother on her first attempt at weaving such a safe place, the effort was great, and success not guaranteed. A forgotten guilt swirled at the edge of her mind. *That calm, ephemeral voice showed me the way.* Heard only once as a young woman, she'd never revealed that source of this skill. *He was of the Light, I am sure. And he swore me to secrecy.* In the naivety of youth, she'd accepted the gift – and maintained her silence. She pushed that pang of guilt away. *In times such as these, I am grateful.*

Naga looked down at the exotic faces of the Warriors. The Warrior Lanky lay in a trancelike state, only the occasional twitches of his fingers showing the presence of life. Beside him, the Warrior Beth's strained face and shivering body was of far more concern.

The Warriors needed help. They needed to be in the Sacred Site.

But we are not. We are here.

And I have done what I can. The Spirits will now aid as they are able. They …

She frowned. Something was wrong. She could sense no Spirits. Why? She quickly scanned her shield. It was strong. It was—

Fear surged as she sensed a minute warping of the shield, the slightest of flaws that shouldn't have been there. *Something has tunnelled through! An enemy is within!* She frantically reached for the remaining energy of the bracelet and prepared to defend the Warriors.

*

Beth sensed the poison that had entered her blood with the slash of the Ka's blade attacking her body and fatiguing her mind. As she drifted into a fitful sleep, vivid scenes from her fight with the Ka replayed.

Again, and again, she watched the man move with such speed that she couldn't evade the attack, the blade plunging into her arm, delivering its deadly venom. *Tell me of the Staff,* he repeatedly asked before then bizarrely apologising for poisoning her – a perverse form of chivalry from a hated enemy of the Iyes. Who was he and who really were the Ka?

As she drifted into a deeper sleep, thoughts of the Ka – and of the dragon and the brutal events that had befallen them – floated away and she entered calmer waters.

She looked around. She was standing, surrounded by a translucent mist gently flowing and ebbing around her. Ahead, the mist parted in a rippling wave to form a path winding up to a warming light on a distant hill. Peace settled on her, and she walked towards the light with no other thought than it was right to reach the safety of its welcoming glow. It was a long walk, but she moved easily, with the joyful anticipation of reaching those waiting for her on that hill.

She increased her pace.

The mist on the side of the path began to swirl as though disturbed by something moving out of sight. *I must keep walking.*

The disturbance grew, and a sense of a great evil swept over her soul.

She started to run.

'Beth! Turn back! The way ahead is your doom!'

She ran faster – she knew she had to reach the light. And her goal was much clearer now: a smooth marble tower topped by three angular crystals, each emitting a broad beam of light. *A lighthouse for those in need,* she thought.

'Beth! This is the work of the Enemy. If you reach the light, the poison will kill you. Listen to me! You have to stop and turn away!'

But safety lay in reaching that light, she knew. 'Go away! I will reach the light.'

She sprinted to the base of the hill—

A section of the mist wall blew inwards across the path, and a glistening, black-coated horse galloped into view. She stumbled to a stop as the horse wheeled around to face her, its flowing black mane like a wind-blown wave. She saw a diamond-shaped mark on its forehead, shining a brilliant white. It was the horse from her dream at the cave.

A voice came out of the mist. 'Get on the horse, Beth. It will take you away from this.'

'Who are you?'

'It's me, Lanky.'

'You're injured at the camp. This can't be you.'

'Well, I could say the same. Aren't you injured, lying by the fire? Believe me. You have to get out of here.'

Beth's desire to reach the light faltered. She studied the horse – the daemon. 'I know you …'

'And I know you,' came a voice in her mind. 'I can aid you. Touch the white diamond.'

Beth hesitated, fearing deception. *Yet I know this daemon.* She moved closer to the black horse, which silently watched her approach before lowering its head towards her. Reaching out, she touched the white diamond on its forehead—

She staggered as a blaze of images swept past her eyes. Of her standing beside another, fighting against an unseen enemy. Of her rescuing a child from a swirling, swollen river. Of her standing on a mountainside, a blazing white fire streaming from her Axe to a vast rent in the sky.

She stood before the black horse, stunned. 'Garrion,' came the daemon's name from a place deep inside.

'Welcome back, Bethusa,' came the reply in her mind.

She looked up at the tower on the hill – it rippled, then split asunder, and a black oily morass streamed down the hill towards her.

'Go!' Garrion cried.

Beth leapt onto Garrion's back, and the horse galloped away from the evil chasing them. The winding path had vanished, and they galloped, apparently blindly, within the shadows of the misty cloak.

A black beast leapt up from the horse's right flank, and with no conscious thought, Beth swung her Axe in a savage arc. The beast vanished. Two more attacked from the front, but Garrion thundered on, trampling one underfoot, and Beth's Axe smashed into the other as they swept past.

'Keep fighting, Beth!' Lanky urged. 'It's the only way to destroy the poison!'

They rode for what seemed like hours, and she grew desperately tired. 'I don't think I can keep this up.'

'You must,' Lanky insisted. 'You have to destroy it all.'

'Can't you help?' Beth pleaded, dispatching yet another beast.

'I can't. Keep fighting!'

Another hour passed. Wrung by exhaustion, Beth struggled to hold the Axe. 'Stop, Garrion. I have to rest.'

Garrion halted, and Beth slumped off the horse into a heap on the ground. 'I can't do this anymore.'

Garrion's head pushed against her. *'Is this the Bethusa I have fought alongside for aeons?'* came the voice in her head. *'The Bethusa who has fought for life against darkness and despair? Stand up and fight! How dare you submit!'*

The words sliced through Beth, and a boiling anger erupted. She climbed back to her feet, exhausted yet fiercely defiant. *'Do your worst, devils! I will spend from now to eternity fighting you!'* She howled at the mist, hurling her Axe into its thickest and darkest centre—

A blaze of white light erupted, and a shock wave exploded outwards, spinning off a multitude of vast eddies until a whirlwind raged around them—

The mist vanished.

She blinked and looked around her. She stood, her Axe glinting in the fire's light, with Naga standing wide-eyed beside her.

*

Jessica and Beth knelt beside the sleeping Lanky. Amber had been quick to prevent him getting up, forcing him to lie back down to rest on the stretcher. He'd quickly fallen into a deep and peaceful sleep, surrounded by the Axes that Naga had insisted stay beside him.

Beth reached over and stroked his face. "Thanks, my friend. I owe you one."

Jessica spoke. "What happened?"

Beth looked up, her drawn face catching the dwindling light of the small fire beside them. "It seems their Enemy tried to kill me." She described what had happened.

"The Enemy's strength grows," Bear said, approaching behind them. "It somehow passed Naga's defences." He sat down by the fire, a weariness to his face. "When Mother has rested, we will travel to the Sacred Site. There we will be safe."

Jessica looked over to Naga, who was curled up beside a younger woman, her head in the shadows. "Is she okay?"

"She will recover," he said slowly. "She also fought the Enemy and is drained. Her power …" He hesitated.

"What about her power?"

"Best not discussed here. You have already seen the reach of the Enemy."

Jessica's gaze remained fixed on him, as though challenging him to offer more. Then she sighed and turned to Beth. "How are you feeling? I thought you were dying. But now …" She shook her head. "You look tired, but very alive."

Alive, but confused, Beth thought, a vibrancy to her senses, a tingling across her skin. It had been a dream, and yet she knew somehow it was real. Lanky had helped her. A daemon had helped her. *And yet what is a daemon?* She smiled at Jessica. "I am better. Not great, but better. The Ka poison has gone."

"It is clear you have access to the Land's energy," Bear said, studying Beth's face. "But you need help to harness your powers and to strengthen your defences." His gaze sharpened. "Although it seems you have knowledge of them already."

Beth shook her head. "I've no idea what I did. I was stuck in a dream – a nightmare – and then the horse appeared." *Calling me Bethusa.* "And Lanky ... Well, you know the rest."

"The horse you saw is the manifestation of the daemon helping you. Did you see it at the cave?"

"I saw many animals, but this one guided me to this Axe." *The one named Garrion.* "What are these daemons?"

Bear gazed into the fire. "When the Axes were created by our tribe's first leader, IY supported him to imbue them with great power. But our leader also needed the support of our Spirits – our ancestors and those allies of IY whose kind roam this Land beside us: the wolf, the eagle, the lion ... the vast array of wondrous life that exists far beyond us." He looked up at Beth. "But the Spirits do not allow any outsiders to connect with them. They do not trust them."

"Even the Warriors?"

"Even them. Power corrupts. Even the strongest minds can succumb if not prepared over many sun-cycles. Our Spirits do not take that risk. Only those of the Iyes tribe who have been readied for the task may connect with them. And we are trusted," he said, the pride clear in his voice. "But, to answer IY's call, they allow chosen daemons to support the Warriors in their time of need. Powerful entities, each of whom agree to bind with a Warrior and support that Warrior in their battles to come. Even so, to connect you must hold true intent in your heart and be in a place in our Land where the daemons do not feel threatened. You have been in one such place."

Beth scowled. "Yes. Against my will."

"The attempt was needed. Without a full connection, you are vulnerable ... as you have just found out."

"That is no—"

"Please, let me finish," Bear said quickly. "We come to the core of our problem. How does a Warrior make contact? Or more accurately, how does a Warrior allow a daemon to contact them? For you do not choose – no, it is not possible for any of humanity to choose a daemon.

They choose you, if they desire it. But for you and the daemon to meet, your mind must be ready, prepared. Even in our sacred places, many sun-cycles of worship are needed to achieve the mind state to connect with our Spirits – and to understand what they say. It may be easier with the daemons, who are eager to connect with the physical realm, yet still it is not simple."

"And so, you drugged me," Beth snapped.

"As I said, it was needed, else you may not have survived long in this Land."

Beth glared at him but said nothing.

"So, Naga tried to create a safe place here," Jessica said, fighting to follow what Bear was telling them.

"Yes, a Glade, a place those with access to the Land's energy can create and enter. A place protected by the Spirits and used by the daemons. There you can converse with others or travel a distance from your body to see things afar. They are safe spaces for you."

"It didn't seem that safe to me," Beth muttered.

Bear's thick brow furrowed. "It may be the attack on you had already started. Even so, the Glade's defences allowed you time with your daemon to protect yourself. And time for Lanky to aid you." He looked over at the sleeping young man. "Which suggests he already connects with a daemon." His gaze returned to Jessica. "And you? Have you seen IY's daemons?"

*

Jessica saw the hope in the man's eyes. *He hopes I understand what I've seen.* She shuddered. But what had she seen? A dragon, a dream of ghostly animals swirling around her … *and the eye.* What could she understand of these hellish things from childhood nightmares?

Nightmares …

Her stomach churned at the thought of those horrific dreams.

She glanced at Bear, whose deep-set eyes studied her intently. "I had nightmares before I came here. Something, someone, wanted the Staff. But I didn't know … anything."

"This is a danger you face accessing the Land's energy in such an uncontrolled way. It is why we carefully planned your Arrival. To prepare you." Regret swept across his face. "But the Ka …" A pained sigh escaped him. "I cannot change what has happened, but you now have a chance. You—"

"Bear. Naga needs you," came a voice from behind them.

Bear glanced to a young man with a sculpted beard. "I'm coming now, Eagle."

He climbed to his feet, then looked down at Jessica, his face calm, yet edged with a ruthless will. "We are where we are. But do not delay your connection, Warrior. It leaves you, and us, vulnerable."

As Jessica watched him walk away past the sleeping Lanky towards the huddle around Naga, she suddenly felt utterly drained. And lost. How could a person survive an ordeal like this?

She turned to Beth. "Where are we, Beth? Why are we here?"

"I don't know," she said, her face drawn. "But I know this is not our world. At least, not our time." She looked up to the night sky. "A real power permeates this place. I sense it ... I feel its strength. It's a power that makes me alive, elated even. It makes me ... invincible." She glanced back at Jessica. "And that worries me, Jess, because I think to leave this place, we have to engage with it. We must use it."

Beth's words swirled in her mind. *Not our time ...* She glanced over to Lanky. "It's that Staff he found. Wherever we are, it was that Staff that brought us here."

Beth followed her gaze. "He's more to tell us, I think."

Yes, what does he know? He'd told her he'd been exploring for artefacts near his home village, but what exactly had he been exploring for? What ...

She frowned as she saw a snarl on the young man's lips. She leaned forward ...

Lanky's body jerked.

Jessica scrambled to her feet. "Beth! Something's happening to Lanky! Bear! Amber!"

Lanky's eyes shot open—

And he howled.

CHAPTER ELEVEN

'Touch the diamond.' How hard Fen tried ...

*P*anky grew more and more frustrated. And angry. He thought he'd found a safe place away from the pain – and the voices – but the damned wolf kept finding a way past the shield he'd erected. Only the Axe kept the fearsome beast at bay.

How did it keep finding him?

Nervously humming to himself, he drew back into the shadows of his mind, pushing back the pain.

The pain ... In the aftermath of his stabbing, the pain had been intense, and he'd drifted between states of semiconsciousness to storms of wild nightmares, frenzied visions of hell fracturing his mind; sordid images of a world of chaos, a world ruled by chaos.

He'd been dying.

But beneath the morass of hate and pain sweeping through his body, a part of him had stood unbowed and defiant. *It's not my time to die. Not here. Not now.* A feeble flame had sparked into being, its paltry light swamped by the malevolent darkness surrounding it.

But its nascent light was enough. It was a place of respite. It was a place of hope.

Slowly – how long, he knew not – the single pitiful flame had strengthened, burning ever brighter and forcing back the clinging, cloying shadows. He didn't know how, but somehow, he was fighting off the attack on his body. Terrible pain remained, but the shackles had dropped from his bound consciousness, and he sensed shadows of the outside world around him: Jessica and Beth, the Iyes – *and the dragon!*

But it was as though he watched an antique, flip-card, picture movie, where the cards were sticking, entire sections missed. Those scenes he did see were badly drawn: a streak of fire in the dark sky above, Jessica's concerned face peering down at him, the moon dancing through the branches of trees. And he heard voices, sometimes gentle, sometimes angry, and other times violent cries or anguished screams.

And then the ghostly animals had appeared, harassing him, streaming around him, darting this way and that. Sometimes coming in close, sometimes disappearing from view.

And always the white wolf. A savage beast, it harried him constantly. Each time it sprang close, he drew an imaginary Axe, sweeping it at the wolf, holding it at bay.

He liked the Axe. He would hold on to this Axe.

Intertwined with these torments came fragments of overheard conversations between Beth and Jessica. Meaningless chatter heard in isolation, but once pulled together by his disturbed brain, it allowed a semblance of understanding. And out of this fragmented view of the world, together with memories of his past with the bookseller, Robert, had emerged a single staggering thought. *The staff I found – the Staff – has brought us to another place. Another time.*

His tortured mind had tried to lock onto this thought, to understand it. *I feel an energy in this land – in this Land – and the Staff is part of it.* Drawn further, deeper, he'd entered terrifying waters of his mind. *The Warriors are part of it. I am part of it.* And in those dark, murky pools, other distant images – memories? – pulsing at the very edges of his fevered awareness. Of an Enemy, of a darkness. *The Dark.* Drawn by unknown instinct, he'd striven to reach those memories. To understand. But they had eluded him, then faded away.

About to pursue them, all thoughts shattered as a wash of distress had borne down on him. Not his fear, but the desperate fear of Beth. He'd acted with no conscious thought as a surge of energy had flooded into him, and he'd travelled to her as though in a dream. He held blurred memories of aiding her, of helping her fight off her attacker … *The Enemy. The Dark.*

Yet how do I know that?

As Beth had fought free, the Enemy's eye had snapped onto him. Knowing he couldn't fight – wasn't ready to fight – he'd fled. He'd escaped to a place far away from that malign threat to a distant refuge hidden from the world outside.

He was safe in the Glade.

He grimaced. *What's a damned Glade?*

To that he had no answer, but he knew it was a safe place to be – no pain, no nightmares, a sanctuary from all that sought to harm him.

But the damned wolf had found him.

It would suddenly appear, darting in towards him, snarling, then fleeing swiftly as soon as he swung his Axe. Time and time again, the dance repeated. A flash of white, a sweep of the blade. As the wolf continued its harrying, his initial alarm turned to frustration, his frustration to anger. *Just one wrong move, wolf, and I will have you!*

But it was Lanky who made the wrong move. In his growing tiredness, he missed the wolf's silent approach from behind. Too late, he spun around, swinging his Axe, but the wolf had already pounced. A growling fury of muscle, fur, and razor-sharp teeth leapt at him, knocking the Axe out of his hand, hurling him backwards onto the floor. A curled lip and fang-filled jaw thrust forward. Hot and putrid breath poured over his face.

Lanky froze, death staring him in the face.

The wolf let out a low growl. "Dysam," the wolf snarled. "You make this hard. Very hard."

Lanky stared at the wolf, waited for the killing strike.

The wolf let out another low growl. "Why does it always start this way? Garrion seems to have it easy. That said, it is strangely pleasing to see you in this state, Dysam. A treat to see you stumble as a child until you return to us." The wolf bared its fangs. "However, we don't have time. Touch the black diamond."

The wolf's words penetrated the cloak of dread shrouding him – yet they made no sense.

"Touch the black diamond," the wolf snarled, angling its head downwards.

Lanky saw a sharp-edged black diamond of fur on the wolf's forehead. "Why would I want to do that?" he said, somehow forcing the fear from his voice.

"Because you need my help," the wolf growled. "As always."

"You want to help me?" Lanky said in utter disbelief.

"Complete the bond, Dysam. You will know then I speak the truth."

'He speaks a truth,' came a calm, ethereal voice.

Lanky started. The voice had returned! The voice he'd heard back home. *'Who are you?'*

Silence answered him.

But he was certain of what he'd heard. It was the voice that had haunted him back home, quiet whispers testing his sanity. Staring at the great wolf hovering above him, his sense of dread deepened. Who were these who thrust themselves upon him?

'You know,' came the wolf's voice in his mind.

Anger flared. "Stay out of my head," he snapped.

The belligerent beast let out a low growl, then fell silent, watching him, waiting.

Waiting ... Within the maelstrom of his emotions, a glimmer of hope rose. *Maybe this really isn't my time to die.* Girding himself, he forced himself to a sitting position. "Who are you?" he said as steadily as he could manage.

If a wolf could sigh, this wolf did so. "Do we have to go through this?"

Lanky forced a strength into his voice. "Tell me."

He flinched as the wolf swung its massive head closer to him, lips curling back, showing once more its razor-sharp fangs. "I have the misfortune of working with you, Warrior."

His mouth suddenly dry, Lanky held the wolf's merciless glare. "You have a name?"

"Fen," the beast snarled.

"And you can help me?"

"If you touch the diamond."

Lanky stared at the wolf, his thoughts a storm of confusion. What truly was this apparition? Could it help him leave this darkness? Could he trust it? Could—

"You are pathetic," the wolf growled. "Do you truly not see what you are?"

Lanky's anger flared ...

And in some detached part of his consciousness, a stunning chain of awareness dragged him into the light. He could sense the power in the beast. He could sense the power in this Land. He could sense shapeless energy swirling just beyond his grasp.

And the Staff brought us here.

The Staff he had found.

The realisation was terrifying yet laced with an incredible elation. *We were right.* After all those years studying the shadows of a forgotten history – those warped ramblings of ancient madmen, those fragments of long-forgotten stories – *Robert, his parents, and me, we were right.* The truth was clear. He'd stumbled upon an artefact with incredible power, one that had brought them to an age brimming with rich, vibrant energy.

An energy I can wield, he thought with sudden certainty.

A sense of familiarity rose, the scent of a path walked before. It was time for another to come to the fore. It was time for the Warrior to—

He froze, cold terror gripping his soul. *Time for another to come to the fore?* "No," he hissed, clenching his fist, and forcing the chilling thought from his mind. "I am Lanky, no one else."

Fen growled. "We don't have time for this. Touch the diamond."

Shivers of terror remained, edges not yet dulled. The power of this age was potent, intoxicating – and it was a power he didn't understand. And how close had he come to relinquishing it to another? *Relinquishing it, or relinquishing me?*

A low snarl from the wolf brought his focus back on the beast. *I don't trust you.* And the black diamond? "No, I don't think I'll do that."

Hackles rising, the wolf leaned closer, its massive head hovering over Lanky's face. "Then you will fail."

Clamping a hold on his fear, Lanky glared back at the wolf. "Then help me."

Its monstrous jaws hovering over him, the wolf bared its fangs, drops of foul liquid dripping onto his face. The wolf snarled, then raised its head and howled.

All of Lanky's barriers simply exploded.

Raw, unbridled energy coursed through his veins as the Glade vanished, and his eyes shot open. He instantly rolled, saw *his* Axe, and grabbing it, leapt to his feet, readying himself. Panting, he quickly assessed the threat around him.

"Remember where you are, Lanky," a voice said behind him. "And remember who you are."

Lanky spun around, growling. He sniffed the air, glaring at the woman who had spoken.

"Stay calm. It's Beth. You helped me, remember?" She slowly and cautiously held out her hands, palms up. "There's no threat here."

Lanky growled at her, but Beth held her ground.

"It's just me – Beth," she repeated. "And Jessica is here too."

Another woman slowly stepped forward, her hand outstretched. "You know who I am, Lanky. I'm a friend."

As she reached him, he sniffed her hand and then looked up at her face. "Jessica?" Shaking his head, he blinked—

He was crouching with an Axe in his right hand, ready to strike. *What am I doing?*

Licking his dry lips, he looked around, an unnerving, otherworldly haze clearing from his mind. Scattered memories flooded back. *They'd moved me. From Bent-Nose's camp.* With echoes of tortured dreams reverberating, a deep tiredness swept over him. He slumped to the ground, dropping the Axe to his side. "What the hell just happened?"

He heard sighs of relief from those surrounding him.

Beth walked up to him and knelt beside him. "You okay?"

Drawing deep lungfuls of wondrous fresh air, he allowed the last remnants of a strangely intoxicating rage to slip away. "I think so."

Beth laid her hand on his shoulder. "You've made a connection to this Land ... and I don't need to ask to what. It seems your wolf friend is pretty aggressive."

A stark vision of glistening fangs snapped into focus. "Aggressive? It scared the life out of me."

"Scary?" she murmured. "Maybe. But you sense something of this Land? Of what it can offer?"

Lanky glanced at her. Her face held a mix of concern and ... and what? Excitement? Hunger? *And at times in that tortured place, that's what I felt.* But in the midst of that sudden and visceral sense of belonging had been that terrifying moment when another had striven to push to the fore. *And that damn wolf Fen ...* "I sensed the energy of this Land," he answered her. "But of what else I felt? Of what I was offered?" His jaw clenched. "I'm not bonding with some unknown beast with unknown purpose. That's not going to happen."

Her penetrating gaze searched his face, then she nodded. "It's your choice," she murmured.

It is. And so it will remain until I figure this out.

"How are you feeling?" Jessica asked, coming to his side.

"I've felt better," he muttered. He reached down to his injured side. "And this hurts like hell." He raised his bloodied hand. "And needs fixing up again." His eyes narrowed. "But considering what happened to me, someone, or something, is helping me." He glanced at Beth. "Helping us."

"Yes," came a woman's firm voice, one he recognised from his fitful dreams. He turned to see the healer, Amber, walking towards him. "I'm helping you. Now, lie down and rest. Warrior or not, you have to give yourself a chance to heal."

"That's fine by me." His dry lips cracked as he spoke. "Is there something to drink?"

"Here," Amber said, passing him a water skin. "Not too much."

He drank sparingly, then she took the skin from him. "Thank you. And thanks for treating me."

Amber frowned. "I'll thank you if you lie still on the rest of our journey. You have to let the wound heal."

The throbbing pain in his side added credence to her words. "I will. I promise."

"Only make promises you may keep, Warrior. Let me get my pack, your bandage needs to be changed."

As she walked away, another stepped forward. "Welcome, Warrior. I am Bear, and I thank you for coming to our aid."

Another voice from his dreams. *But coming to your aid? That remains to be seen.* He acknowledged Bear with a nod, then glanced at Beth and Jessica. "I know some of what has been said, but not all. And I believe I know where we are, but not why." He looked back at Bear. "And I hear you call us Warriors, yet I don't know what a Warrior is."

"Patience, Warrior. Let us first arrive at the Sacred Site. There we will be safe for a while." Bear glanced up through the trees. "The sky is clearing, the moon returns. We should move now, while we have the light. Prepare yourselves," he said to Beth and Jessica as he strode away.

Lanky watched him walk away. *This Bear seems calm and in control. We need that.* He turned to the others. "So are you two going to carry me?" he said, the hint of a smile on his lips.

Beth snorted. "Hah. I'm also injured, remember."

"Don't worry, Warrior," came the gruff voice of a tall man with a bushy beard walking towards him holding one end of a stretcher. "We'll be carrying you."

"You're not carrying anyone, Shorty," said a short man holding the other end of the stretcher. "You're too tall – the Warrior would just slide off the back."

"At least I can lift it off the ground, Knuckles – we don't want the Warrior's head bouncing its way to the safe cave."

As the two men dropped the stretcher beside him, Lanky turned to Jessica and Beth. "You sure you two can't do it?"

"Relax," Jessica replied. "Shorty and I are carrying you."

"You get all the good jobs, Shorty," Knuckles said, thumping his friend on the arm.

"Let's get moving," came Bear's firm voice behind them. "Knuckles, call in Spider and then lead on. Usual set up to the river crossing."

"Don't get lost, Shorty," Knuckles quipped as he moved away. "And don't drop the Warrior."

*

As the group moved on to the river, Bear saw Spider approaching out of the gloom. "We should reach the Sacred Site in good time," he said as Spider joined him. "And so far, all remains clear. But the Enemy knows where we are, and it seems it can attack the Warriors from afar. We enter difficult times."

"It seems so," Spider agreed, his keen eyes glancing to the Warriors ahead.

"But the Warriors are here. They have arrived. Best now that you head south to meet with Rind at the White Crag's camp and tell what has been happening here. Ask Rind to prepare our safe place and be ready to receive the tribe and the Warriors. I know not whether we will all travel, but they should expect to see some of us before this moon ends."

He paused, tension in his stance. "If none appear by that time," he said, his voice lowered, "then Rind is to take leadership of the tribe. Send a party back here to find out why we did not return – and then act on that knowledge, and the knowledge of our history."

Spider nodded, his face grim.

"But no one should move or act before that time unless a threat is upon them. Is that clear?"

"Clear." Spider hesitated. "I'd like to say goodbye to River before leaving."

Bear relaxed and smiled. "I thought you might. Have you had that conversation yet?"

"Not yet. I've not found the right time. And I think she sees me as a friend only."

Bear chuckled. "I think you need to be more direct." His smile faded. "But, unfortunately, again, this is not the time. See her only, then leave directly." He held out his arm, and Spider took his wrist and gripped it. "Safe travel, my friend."

"And may IY travel with you." Spider turned away and disappeared into night's dark cloak.

A good man, Bear thought, holding his gaze to empty darkness. *Am I right to allow him to leave us?* He squared his shoulders as if facing an oncoming storm. This was no time for doubt or regret. *We are only just beginning. These are child steps compared to the giant strides that will be needed.*

*

Spider took a wide route around Jessica and Shorty, who were carrying the stretcher, and jogged ahead to join River. He couldn't see Knuckles or Amber but knew they wouldn't be far ahead.

"At least it has quieted down," he said in a soft voice as he came alongside River. "It keeps Knuckles and Shorty separated for a while."

"They know what they're doing, those two. When they focus, they could sit next to a deer without it realising they'd approached." She raised a brow. "Aren't you supposed to be scouting?"

"I've a new task now."

"Oh, and what's that?"

"I'm heading down south to Rind's camp to let them know what's been happening. I'm off now."

"That's a bit tough on you, but if Bear thinks you need to do it, then it has to be done."

Spider could sense her concern, but the tribe looked out for each other all the time, so it was not unusual. "I think it will take me four days to reach them. If I can find food easily. Should be fairly straightforward."

But they both knew that travelling alone for a few days was always a risk and generally avoided.

"Do the others know?" River asked.

"No – and Bear wants to keep this quiet, so leave it to him to tell the others."

"So why did Bear want you to tell me?"

Spider hadn't thought this bit through. "Ah – he thought the Warriors wouldn't notice, but that you might – so best I told you."

"So, you will tell Knuckles and Shorty?"

He thought he sensed her smiling but was obviously mistaken. "Ah – we thought best not to distract them."

"Is that so?"

They walked on, and he couldn't think of anything else to say. "Well. I better get going. Bear was insistent I leave now."

"So, no more details?"

"No – I don't think so."

"Nothing else to say?"

"No. I think we've covered it."

She snorted.

"Are you okay?" he asked.

She didn't reply but seemed to have a small cough.

"Are you sure you're okay?"

She took a moment to answer. "Yes, Spider, I'm fine. You travel safely. Bear has chosen wisely in this." She reached into her pocket and drew out something unseen. "Take this," she murmured, holding out her hand. "It's my lucky charm for travelling. Make sure you bring it back."

Lucky charm. No, it couldn't be. His hand shaking, he reached out, and she placed the object in his palm. As soon as his fingers brushed the polished bone, he knew it was indeed her most precious possession.

Her horse carving. *She never parts with this.*

A lump formed in his throat. "This is a truly great gift. I'll see it safely back in your hands."

"I know. Travel safely, Spider."

"And may IY travel with you, River."

Turning away, he caught the beautiful profile of her face and a glimpse of her wondrous eyes sparkling in a thin beam of moonlight cast through the trees. His heart pounding, he stole into the night.

Travelling easily and silently through the sparse wood, snatches of conversation played in his head. *What did I say? Did I thank her properly for it?* He berated himself for not saying more. But gently stroking his thumb over the smooth bone carving, he knew that Bear had been right, this moment wasn't the time to explain how he felt. *But when we next meet, I will tell her.* Slipping the carving into his pocket, he jogged on in the darkness, already thinking through what he would say.

*

Unseen in the gloom, River smiled at Spider's stumbling effort to tell her what was on his mind. *As if I don't know.* Should she have played it differently, helped him settle his nerves so he could explain his feelings for her? Her smile faded. *Yet what do I feel? Truly feel?*

Her thoughts wandered, memories of the scout's past returning. Although they were the same age and had grown up together, he wasn't originally part of the tribe. He'd been found as a young boy hiding on a trail to the south – the remains of his father had lain further down the trail. The tribe had discovered from the boy that he and his father had been attacked by an unknown group and his father killed. The boy had been told to run by his father, who had seen the attackers approaching. The boy had hidden, but watched, terrified, as his father was struck down. The tribe had scouted the area for some time but been unable to find the attackers. It remained a mystery who they had been, and why they had targeted the boy's father.

We gave that boy a new home, a new family.

Yet we are cautious.

Cautious at accepting newcomers into the tribe given the great burden of protecting their Story and ensuring it was preserved through the generations. Even a young child could be a threat if the Enemy had carefully prepared them. But neither Naga nor Bear had sensed any threat within the boy. He was certainly well trained, as he'd survived for at least one turn of the moon, judging by the remains of the father, and had only been spotted by Knuckles, even then one of the best trackers in the tribe. Knuckles had watched the boy from afar, seeing him evade detection by the main tribe as it passed. "He was as quiet as a spider," he had said. The name stuck.

Spider had been placed with her, Sheba, and Amber, and the four of them seemed destined to be together, having the same energy, inquisitiveness, and curiosity. *And the same knack for landing in trouble!* As they'd grown older, she, Sheba, and Spider had joined the hunts and scouting trips, while Amber spent more time with Naga, being shown the skills of a healer. But however long they spent apart, they'd all remained great friends.

And Spider and I grew close on our many missions together.

And he is still a great friend.

And more?

She had seen his attention to her change. He was obviously attracted to her. *And I to him.* But, in this period of change, should she take it further? Her smile returned as she thought once again of his hesitant approach. *Maybe I should wait for him to tell me how he feels – and that will give me the time I need to decide how I will respond.*

She felt a sudden warmth in her heart. *You've already responded; you gave him your most cherished carving. May it and IY protect him.*

*

"We are almost there," Bear said as Beth scanned the rugged hills around her, their jagged peaks slicing into the starry night sky. The moon had dropped to the western ridge line, the way ahead partially shadowed from its cool light. "That peak is our destination," he said, pointing to the tallest to their right.

"I know this place," Beth murmured.

Bear regarded her in the darkness but remained silent.

Jessica and Shorty stopped beside them, then lowered the stretcher and the sleeping Lanky gently to the ground.

"I know it too," Jessica said quietly. "We walked here two days ago. Different, and yet the same."

"I think it was a little longer than two days," Beth said, staring into the sky.

"What do you mean?"

"It's an impressive sight, isn't it?" she said, seeming to ignore Jessica's question. "Even with the last light of the moon I can see a myriad of stars." She glanced at Bear. "Which of these stars is the star that stays fixed in the night sky?"

Bear looked up and pointed. "That is IY's Sentinel. IY told the Sentinel to guard our Land at night. That is where he sits, never moving through the night."

Beth moved in closer. "Which one?"

He took her arm, and looking down it, moved it into position. "That one."

"That's incredible," Beth whispered.

Jessica came over. "What is it?"

"Bear says that's the North Star. And that star is called Vega."

"Hold on, Beth. The North Star is Polaris, which is … Now, where is it?" She hunted around the night sky. The Milky Way appeared as an ethereal band across the sky, and she found it difficult to recognise some constellations because of the sheer number of stars visible.

"You can't see it, can you?"

Jessica frowned. "Cassiopeia and Ursa Major should be there, but it looks as though they're down there below the hills. It makes no sense."

Beth was silent for a moment. "It makes sense in one scenario, Jess."

"The planet's precession," came Lanky's voice from the stretcher.

Beth looked down at the shadowy figure of Lanky. "Yep. Like those old spinning tops, wobbling as well as spinning. And, if I remember correctly, our planet completes that wobble once every twenty-six thousand years, meaning its axis points to a different part of the sky over time. We don't notice it in our day-to-day lives. We see Polaris as our North Star. But over time …"

"Over time we'll get another North Star."

"And I know that Vega is that North Star about halfway around the wobble."

Both women looked up again at the night sky.

"If Vega really is the North Star …" Jessica murmured.

"Then we've shifted back in time," Lanky said.

"At least thirteen thousand years," Beth said.

They looked to the heavens in silence, trying to take in the enormity of what they were seeing.

*

River stood beside Amber, listening to the two women speak. She failed to understand all they said but understood the concept of time. Her tribe knew their history, knew that lives had come and gone over countless sun-cycles. There were ancestor names that would always be remembered because of their great deeds or ideas – she wished they could bring some of them back to help in this time of dire need.

But their time had gone, and it was the responsibility of the new generation to build on their achievements and improve the life of the Land; to improve the Land for themselves, and for others; to show the ancestors their efforts had not been in vain. She dreamt of going back to visit them but knew they would stay in her dreams.

For the Warriors, it seemed different.

The tribe's Story told of previous Warriors, of how they travelled from a different time – or place – from their own, as these two women now believed.

How could this be?

Her ancestors had lived and imprinted themselves into the fabric of IY's Land. It was a past that had happened. She had memories from her ancestors and in dreams could visit them. But to imagine an age ahead? How could you do that? No one knew what they would do next. Not even IY. IY had been clear in her teachings that she would support and protect them if they followed her principles but would not *force* them to follow her. IY did not control their lives.

And so, I can't say what will happen tomorrow, or the next day.

Then how could you move ahead to a time that had not yet been? A time which hadn't yet seen the life energy of people? She could see nothing to move to. Even in dreams, it was impossible to recall stories of events that had not yet happened.

No, she didn't believe it possible to move to a time ahead, and so could not believe the Warriors had moved from a time ahead to here. For her, the time ahead was unmapped, holding a myriad of possibilities depending on the individual choices of people or events that befell them: the accidental trip that might break an arm and prevent hunting; a yearlong drought that might starve animals and plants. There were countless, unknowable happenings that might change what happened next sun-cycle, let alone over multiple sun-cycles.

To believe that the Warriors had come from a time ahead would mean believing that every step, from now to then, was mapped out and would happen exactly as needed to arrive at the Warrior's time, that all the Warrior's ancestors had lived in a certain way to ensure the Warriors were born at their right time and place.

She couldn't believe this. It would mean their lives were fixed before birth. And that couldn't be. *No, our lives are free.*

And yet ...

And yet, these two women were talking about this possibility.

"Okay. Let's move on," she heard Bear say.

River looked back to the stars. There was so much here that was unknown. Their tribe's Story held part of the answer, but it also seemed their Story was incomplete.

Did Mother know more than she had told?

The thought was troubling. The Land was becoming bigger than River had ever imagined it to be.

CHAPTER TWELVE

Though in very different ways, the Ancient One and the Ka loyally served their cause. They both did what was needed.

Shadow was chilled to the core. They had been flying over an increasingly rugged terrain, snow and ice slowly blanketing greater and greater areas, until now all he could see below him was a glistening white landscape punctuated by tall mountain peaks. It was an unknown land to him, a desolation becoming colder with each soft beat of the dragon's wings.

He wasn't dressed for this.

Seemingly aware of the real danger of him and Sy arriving at their destination as frozen corpses, the Ancient had released a steady stream of wonderfully warm air from its mouth and nostrils ... but even this was insufficient to encourage him to poke his face out of his furs for too long. He did, however, have the advantage over Sy sitting ahead, who faced the full brunt of the chill wind, albeit moderated by the trickle of warm air. Shadow thought the beast must have some limit to the amount of heat it could afford to generate for them; but what did he know of such a creature?

He snuggled into the back of Sy's coat and drifted into a light, restless sleep.

Dreams quickly followed.

He was flying on broad, expansive wings, soaring on warm evening thermals over a rich savanna teeming with life. Everywhere he looked, the land was alive with exotic creatures, each alert to the movements of others around them, each seeking even the smallest opportunity for themselves and their families. The lion hoped for an injured prey for an easy kill; the hyena followed in its wake, wishing for a tasty prize to be scavenged; and the zebra watched them both, wishing it could survive another day.

And over there, an unknown group of humans gathered by a fire in their travelling camp. Each member of that band wished the same as the animals. And with tools and skills the other animals could never imagine – if those animals could imagine at all – those humans were confident their tribe would prosper. And with the technological advances made over the generations, who would doubt them? Fire, of course; blades for hunting and processing animals; needles for sewing, sealing wounds, making nets, repairing boats; dyes for decoration, painting, camouflage. On and on, humanity advanced, leaving their fellow animals in their evolutionary wake.

Shadow's dreaming mind thought of his own people. *But even with the tools we have, there are limits to what we can achieve.* More progress was needed to provide better and safer times for the Ka. *And with the help of the Ancient, we can achieve this.*

An anger flared. But always the threat from the destroyers, the so-called Warriors. Using their powers to attempt to destroy his homeland. Forcing the rains away and scorching the ground. Killing his land, whilst making the lands of the Hidden richer. It was a time of droughts and famines, pushing his people to the brink of extinction.

Only the Ensi's people stopped them.

Only we stop them. We, the Ka.

And now it was *his* turn to ready a place next to his greatest ancestors – by helping Kaos defeat the enemy.

In his dream, he saw an enemy Warrior on the ground far below him. He furled his wings and dived to attack—

But his dive was steeper than he'd planned, and he felt himself sliding—

Something hit him hard in the side.

"Kef!" he exclaimed as he awoke with a start to find himself slipping off the dragon's back – only a hand from Sy kept him from falling further.

They were in a steep dive.

With a panicked grunt, he somehow managed to right himself, and then gripped tightly onto Sy, gulping in the cold air. *Sleeping on a dragon! What were you thinking of!* The wrong things, clearly.

Below, several jagged peaks jutted out from the moonlit, icy realm below, and as they arrowed through the clear night sky, he saw they were heading towards the furthest mountain peak, beyond which lay an unbroken, desolate expanse of ice as far as he could see. Closer and closer they sped to this tallest of peaks, descending towards a terraced plateau at the mountain's base.

He was unable to judge their height against the pure white of the snow, but at a certain point, the Ancient angled her wings, slowing her speed until she hovered just above the ground.

Then she gently landed.

For a moment, there was absolute silence. The awe-inspiring quiet of pure wilderness.

Which was broken by a deep rumble from the dragon as she lowered a flank to the ground. *'Dismount and follow,'* the Ancient ordered.

Following Sy, Shadow slid down the side of the dragon to land in soft snow, where he stumbled before catching his balance. Immediately, the Ancient rose, and then with mighty strides, her massive feet punching through the snow and ice, she strode ahead towards a steep wall of ice at the rear of the plateau.

Stretching to relieve the stress in his knotted and strained muscles, Shadow shivered as the icy cold drove deeper into his bones. "I guess we need to follow," he said, rubbing his frozen hand as he turned to Sy … who was already striding after the dragon. He shook his head. "Always in such a rush," he muttered to himself as he strode after Sy and the dragon.

They were heading towards a deep shadow on the ice wall, and as they drew closer, he realised it was a gaping opening into the ice. Walking into the breach, the dragon opened her viciously fanged jaws, casting fiery light into the tunnel beyond. The smooth icy walls glistened as the Ancient passed. He and Sy strode down the gently inclining slope, heading deeper into the thick ice sheet.

Doubt cast a shadow on his thoughts. Was this his fate? A frozen entombment like the ancient mammoth they had stumbled upon during a training mission in distant mountains? Released by a melting glacier, the creature had looked as though it had only died that day, for though the spirits of those frozen creatures were displaced by the cold, their bodies were preserved. *Who would find me? And what would they make of me?*

He shrugged and continued walking, the gradient steadily increasing. As they dropped deeper into the ice, he caught the occasional sharp crack from the shifting ice. *Fine, so long as it breaks somewhere else.*

Deeper and deeper, they travelled until the dragon's light revealed a wall of solid rock blocking the tunnel ahead. To the left appeared to be another passageway heading along the rock face, but as they approached, he saw it was merely a deep indentation in the ice tunnel wall. Facing the rock wall, the Ancient spoke, her voice sounding clearly in his mind. The words had no meaning for him but obviously held a power and purpose, for the rock face silently parted. A section slowly swung free before slotting into the embayment to the left. *Impressive. I wish we had these makers back home.*

They walked through the opening and entered a rocky passage. *So, not ice. Maybe an entombment in stone instead?*

As they walked on, Shadow's mind raced. How would this play out? Although the Staff was to be handed to the Ancient – in return for great gifts of knowledge and power for the Ka – there had been no instruction beyond its delivery by the full moon. *As I've now done.* But for the first time in that service, doubts were surfacing. Yes, he had dedicated much of his life to serve the Ensi's will, remaining honest and true to his leader's cause – and to himself and his ancestors – but was that service now complete? *Does it end here?* He gave an imperceptible shake of the head. A pointless question. No one knew the mind of the Ensi. *Even so, I hope my time is not yet done. I have much I wish to do.*

Laughter sounded in his head. 'Don't worry, young Ka. You have more yet to give. Whether you are strong enough remains to be seen. Now I leave you for a while. You may enter the area to your right, where you will find food and a place to rest. Remain there until summoned.'

The dragon moved on along the main passageway. Shadow watched until her massive frame disappeared from view. He turned to Sy. "Appears we are on our own for a while."

Sy shrugged, then walked towards a flickering torch on the wall. Lifting it off its cradle, he headed off towards a dark passageway to the right.

"Warmth, food, and a place to sleep, that's what I need now," Shadow murmured to himself as he set off after Sy and the precious light. He was cold to the bones. That was not a journey to be quickly repeated. *Although we need to get out of here. I need to get home.*

Travelling further down the passageway, they explored several side tunnels, finding a variety of low-roofed chambers containing stores of wood, clothing, and weapons. It was clear to Shadow that humans had visited this place before. From one of the chambers, they each grabbed a thick, fur-lined jacket and moved on. In a wider part of the passageway, two large and freshly killed white-feathered birds lay on a small bed of leaves on the ground, a glowing ember fire beside it. *Not the work of the Ancient. So, who else is here?*

Sy immediately went to work, and within a short while, the skinned birds were cooking gently on the fire, a little smoke rising and drifting upwards then out along the passageway, pushed along by a gentle draft.

"I wonder how long we'll be here," Shadow mused, listening to the delicious sounds of sizzling meat.

Sy shrugged.

"You are a man of few words, Sy."

Sy shrugged again.

Shadow smiled. Though unable to vocalise his thoughts, when he wanted, Sy could communicate with others as well if not better than many people Shadow had met. But Sy was a man who didn't like to guess, or postulate, or stray too far from what he saw in front of him. If he had nothing to add, he wouldn't try. And Shadow liked that in his partner. It made them a good pairing.

And, unlike me, Sy doesn't ask dangerous questions that could get him killed.

But this was another reason they made a good pairing; Sy had an annoying but probably lifesaving habit of preventing him from further exploring the answers to his questions. *Well, usually ...*

Soon the meat was cooked, and they ate quickly and greedily. Though lacking any greens, nuts, seeds – *what do they find in this icy wilderness?* – the meal was welcome, nonetheless. After only a short while, only a pile of cleaned bones remained. Washing his hands with a little water, he pulled his jacket around him, then lay on a fur next to the fire. "It's been a long day, Sy. I need sleep."

He closed his eyes, escaping the duties of his mission, if only for a while.

*

Rubbing his eyes, Shadow sat up and glanced around the gloomy chamber. He sensed it was early morning, but this deep below the surface, there was not much chance of seeing the daylight to prove it. Whatever the time, he was now awake and well rested, his body warm and refreshed.

Sy leaned over the glowing remains of their ember fire and handed him the skin of water. Shadow drank deeply.

"Not too cold down here," he said, passing the bottle back. "Not like the icy hell above." He glanced to the shadowed passageway outside the entrance to the chamber. "Anything else of interest down here?"

"No," Sy replied, flicking his fingers. "The passage continues on a little further, but then narrows to an impassable crack."

So, a nice little prison. "I wonder how long we'll be here."

Sy shrugged.

"Well, we kept our part of the bargain. The Ancient has what she wanted. What I want now is help out of here. I'm not trudging for days through that snow out there to get back south. We don't know the area, we aren't kitted out for it, and there are only two of us. We wouldn't get very far."

Sy nodded.

"And now I'm rested and warmed up, I have a question. And that question is, why are we here?"

"We brought the Staff."

"I know that," Shadow said with a hint of frustration. "But couldn't our flying friend have carried that here herself? Yes, not easy for the ones lacking our nimble digits, but it could have been done."

Sy shrugged and flicked back: "But we are here."

"Yes," Shadow muttered. "That's not the point." His brow furrowed. "Unless, for some reason, she can't touch it."

'Well done,' came a booming voice in his head.

Shadow jumped. "Kef! Don't do that!"

'Return to the top of your passageway. Someone will meet you there.'

Sy stood and reached for his pack.

Shadow looked up at him. "You heard it too?"

Sy nodded. "Get a move on," he signed.

"Always in a rush," Shadow grumbled, climbing to his feet.

A few moments later, they were walking back up through the passageway to see who awaited them.

"She said someone will meet us up here. That implies it won't be her."

Sy shrugged and continued walking.

"I wonder if it will be another dragon. Do you think there's more than one?"

Sy walked steadfastly onwards.

"Maybe I should ask for a different partner."

Sy shrugged.

And then, ahead at the exit of the passageway, Shadow saw a figure awaiting them: an older, slightly stooped man with a short white beard and shoulder-length grey hair. The man looked dead on his feet.

Shadow smiled as he approached the man. "You look as though you've been waiting here a long time, my friend."

"A fair while," the man replied. "But this morning, only a few heartbeats."

Well, that's good, Shadow thought, holding out his hand. He didn't think the man could last many heartbeats longer. "My name is Shadow. And this is Sy."

The man considered Shadow's hand. "I know your names. And I feel no need to hold your hand. I think you'll be able to follow me without it." The man walked – no, shuffled – away into the mouth of a tall, wide tunnel – a dragon-sized tunnel.

"I think you may get on with this man," Shadow muttered to Sy. He turned to see the old man shuffling off. "I guess the plan is to follow him. We should give him a head start, as I don't think I can walk that slowly."

It took an eternity to walk along endless passageways – at least it felt that way to Shadow. "We'll be dead by the time we arrive," he signed to Sy. Sy ignored him. Shadow changed tack. *'Hello! Ancient One,'* he thought. *'If you're listening, could you just direct us which way to go? It will be much quicker, and we'll then still be alive when we meet.'*

Silence answered him.

And so, on they trudged, following the path of the shuffling man until they eventually reached a pair of enormous stone doors quite different to those they had seen at the mountain entrance the night before. These were of a smooth, polished white marble, on each a seemingly identical carving. Shadow considered each carving in turn, but they were unrecognisable to him. "Any idea what these symbols are?" he signed to Sy, who was studying each intently.

"No," Sy signed. "But it's strange. I feel that I should recognise them – but I can't. Why I should feel this, I don't know. I will think on it."

Shadow glanced at Sy. If this was something Sy should think about, then it was definitely something that Shadow needed to think about. Standing by the side of one of the doors, the old man held his hand to the wall ... Shadow watched in wonder as the doors slowly opened. *Now that's impressive. What makers constructed this?* As the doors fully opened, a wall of heat washed out over them.

The old man shuffled on through the doors, waving them to follow.

Enough following. Shadow strode forward, passing the shuffling man ... But almost immediately halted as he saw the stunning sight before him.

He'd entered a massive arched chamber, the polished white stone of its gleaming walls and ceiling dancing with yellow and red light. In the centre of the chamber stood a raised platform on which lay the sleek silver dragon that had carried them to the mountain, her head held proudly high, one baleful eye fixed on Shadow. Trying to ignore the intense glare of the Ancient's gaze, Shadow scanned the wider chamber. Spaced around the foot of the walls lay many tall stone pots, some emitting a bright white light, others burning with a bloodred flame. Ranged behind the platform stood three intricately carved pillars. Through these Shadow could see a mountain of gleaming yellow. Curious, he walked towards the carved pillars, nodding respectfully – he hoped – to the dragon as he passed. Passing between two of the pillars, he approached the hoard. He could now see it consisted of thousands of individual irregular-shaped pieces, varying in size from a small berry to items larger than his head. "That's an interesting collection. I've seen pieces like this in riverbeds. This must have taken quite a while to amass. Why do you collect it?"

Something hit him on the back – hard.

Shadow spun around, crouching low with a blade already in his hand …

The old man stood before him, holding a slender fighting staff.

Shadow relaxed and straightened—

Moving with lightning speed, the old man struck low with the staff, taking Shadow's legs from under him. As Shadow dropped to his knees, the old man glowered at him. "You do not walk in here unannounced. You do not just walk wherever you please. And you do not speak to the Ancient without being asked."

"Those are a lot of rules," Shadow said in a quiet voice as he climbed to his feet. "And I don't appreciate being hit without being asked." He sprang forward, aiming to snatch the old man's staff …

Only to find himself sprawling on the ground again after taking a hit to the head.

"Enough!" a voice boomed out into the cavern, and Shadow winced as the voice reverberated around the chamber – and around his aching head. As the echoes died, he slowly climbed to his feet, rubbing his head, feeling a bump where the man had hit him. He glanced at Sy – who was smiling.

"I think it best that you do whatever the Ancient says," Sy signed. "Otherwise, the old man will have you on the ground again."

Shadow looked sidelong at his grey-haired assailant, who was now standing, half stooped, looking as though he would die on the spot. *What game does this one play?*

He blew out a long sigh. *Forget him. Focus on what is needed now.*

Passing back between the pillars, he trudged into the main chamber and approached the dragon's dais. *'Permission to speak,'* he thought at her.

The dragon inclined her head slightly. "Proceed," she said into the chamber.

"Well," Shadow began, "ignoring some interesting questions about this place, I think we can agree that we've fulfilled our errand for you on behalf of my leader, and that you could now help us get back home ... please."

The dragon tilted her head at Shadow. "Always in a hurry, you humans. Do you not like it here?"

Shadow scanned the chamber before looking back at the Ancient One. "It's true there are things here I wish we had time to study fully, but the Ensi was clear; we were to attempt to deliver the Staff to you by this full moon – which we've done – and then return with any message, which I hope would include confirmation of your valued support for my leader's efforts."

A rumble sounded within the Ancient, and a waft of hot, putrid air washed over him. "I am sure your Ensi would be pleased if you could stay awhile longer, human. To better build our relationship and understanding of each other. I am sure Stealth here would be pleased by your company – we have few visitors here."

Stealth. So that was the man's name. But Shadow doubted that the man would be pleased at all by spending another single moment with him. And the feeling was mutual. "Whilst I do appreciate the offer—"

"Good. It is settled. Stealth will be your guide. I will call for you when my response is ready."

"But—" Shadow stuttered.

A forceful hand pulled him away, guiding him towards the doors. Stealth! The man's grip was immense, and Shadow had no choice but to walk with him.

"You can let go now," Shadow said through gritted teeth as they left the chamber. "I heard her. And it seems we have the pleasure of your company for a short time. Maybe we should reintroduce ourselves."

"I don't think so," Stealth said dismissively. But he released Shadow's arm. "Follow me." The grey-haired man strode from the chamber.

Shadow glared after him. "Well, this will be enjoyable."

As they returned to the point in the passageway where they'd first met, Stealth faced them. "You know your way from here," he said. He turned to leave.

"Now hold on," Shadow growled, stepping in front of Stealth. "I'm not going to walk back down into that prison and just sit and wait until she deigns to call me."

"Get out of my way," Stealth ordered.

Shadow could see Sy signing behind Stealth's back – but he ignored him. He glared at Stealth. "You heard what she said – you're our guide."

"And to here, I have guided you. Now out of my way."

"No."

Stealth moved blindingly fast, swinging his staff towards Shadow's body. But Shadow – not to be fooled by the 'old man' trick again – was ready for him. Anticipating Stealth's dummy swing with the staff, he struck his arm down, blocking Stealth's left hand thrust to his stomach. He returned with a straight punch to Stealth's face—

Which missed.

Without slowing, Stealth struck at Shadow's head, while aiming a kick at his chest. Shadow rolled fluidly, twisting and arching his back, and both of the old man's attempted blows flew narrowly wide. Shadow immediately retaliated with a jumping high-kick to the side of Stealth's head. Stealth blocked it with ease, grabbing at Shadow's leg as it dropped. Twisting rapidly, Shadow yanked his leg out of Stealth's grasp, and continuing his rotation, brought his other leg around to strike at the back of the old man's head. He caught him a glancing blow. Following up with a fluid stream of alternating attacks with his arms and legs, Shadow slowly pushed back the old man – who was now working hard to avoid the onslaught.

He's slowing, Shadow thought, breathing hard. *At his age he can't—*

In this moment of distracted thought, the blow to his head stunned him.

Fool! You've fallen for it again.

His ears ringing, Shadow fought desperately to defend against an incredible sequence of moves from Stealth, utilising all his skill to avoid being hit. A surge of anger coursed through him. *Right – enough of this!* Ignoring all his wealth of training, he lowered his head and charged at the old man. Taking several hard hits, he thundered into Stealth, and they both tumbled to the ground. Taking his chance, he head-butted Stealth on the nose before rolling away and leaping back to his feet. He prepared to launch another attack but felt Sy's hand on his shoulder, tapping the recognisable signal of the Ka to indicate submission during mock battle. His friend was telling him to stop.

Breathing heavily, muscles and tendons tensed, Shadow watched Stealth slowly stand, blood streaming from his nose. Through the haze of battle-fuelled adrenaline, an uneasy thought crossed his mind. *Not the best first meeting with our long-coveted ally. I wonder what the Ancient will make of this.*

And then the old man grunted a laugh.

Shadow frowned.

"That was good," Stealth wheezed. "I haven't had the chance of a decent fight in many sun-cycles." His short white beard stained with flecks of red, the old man wiped the blood from his nose, then slowly walked up to Shadow with his hand held out.

Staring at him in disbelief, Shadow warily grasped the man's wrist.

Stealth clasped his hand around Shadow's wrist, then reached out and grasped his shoulder. "You fight well," he panted, his grey eyes bright, vibrant energy in his sweat-drenched face.

"You're not too bad yourself," Shadow said, still not quite believing what the man had done. "So, your welcome was a way to get me into a fight?"

"I wanted to test myself again. You wouldn't have fought the same way unless I made it real."

Shadow studied the man for a moment, then gave a wry smile. "Well, you certainly did that." He felt the burning pain in the muscles of his legs and arms. "I hope I'll be as tough as you at your age."

"Tough, maybe, but I misread you. You were controlling your anger well – I didn't expect a berserker charge, the move of an angry man. Small mistakes that I once never made." He caught his breath, then grinned. "But enjoyable, nonetheless." Walking off towards the cavernous tunnel, he gestured for them to follow. "We'll head to my quarters, where we can talk some more. I'm sure you have a few questions for me."

"One or two," Shadow said, glancing at Sy as they walked back into the deeper cave network. "Like, when we will get on our way," he signed silently to Sy.

"Patience," Sy signed. "Let's see what we can learn here."

Shadow grunted, knowing the warrior monk was right. Again. "Fine, but I'm not waiting long." For he knew he needed to get back. An empty Disciple chair could be quickly filled if the incumbent spent too long away from the Ka homeland. *Especially with that devious snake, Cobra, around.*

He looked ahead to Stealth, who was turning into a narrow side passage. *But this man's story interests me. One night then.* Relaxing, he followed Stealth and Sy into the narrow tunnel. *And maybe he's a better cook than Sy.* Shadow walked on easily. *Learn what you can, then head back home to continue the fight.*

CHAPTER THIRTEEN

The shamans of the Iyes knew only a part of the whole. Should more have been shared with them? Maybe ... but probably not. Some things remained safer for the Guardian to discover – if she proved to be the one.

Jessica walked out from the shadow of the cave entrance, and squinting against the morning glare, she made her way carefully across the glistening rocks to the edge of the ridge. Shading her eyes, she looked down the plunging scree-laden slope into the green valley below. Occasional movement betrayed the presence of life – at least one she could see was human. She glanced to the sky. A dark ridge of clouds moved north, taking the rain with it as the sun broke through in its wake – a welcome warmth given the chill in the air.

A tall figure detached from the shadow of a large boulder. "Greetings, Warrior," said the young guard, Eagle, his sharp, sculpted beard in stark contrast to the unkempt appearance of the barbarous men who'd captured her and Lanky the day before. "Greetings, Shield."

As Knuckles, her minder for the day, acknowledged Eagle, Jessica considered the guard's words. *He calls me a Warrior. They call us all Warriors.* Scattered images flashed through her mind. Of Beth storming into camp to rescue them. Of Beth launching her Axe at the beast in the sky. The tangle of fear that had eased overnight tightened once more. They'd arrived in a place she didn't understand, a place where people called them saviours ... *Warriors.*

And that terrified her. *I know nothing of Warriors. I am Jess.*

She glanced to the clearing sky. But what she feared most in this moment was the sense of something in the air just beyond her reach. Something sweet and vibrant calling to her as if a drifting memory of some wondrous time from her childhood, something she should be able to reach out and grasp, drawing it within to gift to her soul. But what was it? And what consequence of tasting its delights?

Unnerved by the disquieting thoughts, she drew deep lungfuls of the cold, fresh air. *Whatever this place is, don't get sucked in, Jess. We just need to find a way home. And quickly.*

She turned to Knuckles, who was watching her closely. The short man's thick, light-brown hair was cut far shorter than the other men she'd seen, but in the crisp light of the morning, it was his clothing that caught her eye. His leather tunic and trousers were close-fitting, cleanly cut and sewn, and his inner garment of a well-woven thread. *Thread? Fibres maybe.* Around his wrists were leather bracelets, each intricately patterned with coloured beads and interlaced thread. And around his neck a pendant of a twine-held polished stone. *No, a polished fossil, an ammonite,* she recognised. These were refinements not noticed in the terror of the previous day; whoever these people truly were, they were skilled artisans. "Eagle calls you Shield," she said, making a tentative step into his world.

Knuckles's strong, weathered face relaxed into an easy grin. "I'm responsible for a motley group of these men in our tribe," he said, his eyes twinkling. "Gravel also has that dubious honour."

"Too many names," she said, wracking her brain to recall Gravel.

"You've seen him around – the handsome one with all the scars."

"Ah, that one," she said, remembering the hard eyes of the scar-faced man. "Beth pointed him out – it was the first face she saw here." The first face of this unknown land.

Knuckles laughed. "Pity her." He glanced at Eagle. "But, yes, IY help us, I was unfortunate enough to be named Shield. To help, to advise, to hit around the ears now and then. And to keep them out of harm's way. Not that I think this one is worth the trouble."

Eagle grinned. "We've had the scout reports in this morning – no threats seen. But I guess you know that anyway," he added, seeing Knuckles's wry smile.

Knuckles patted the young man on the shoulder. "Keep your eyes peeled, son." He turned to Jessica. "You have a particular place you want to go?"

Home. I want us all to get back home. But she knew that wouldn't be. Not today. Not tomorrow. Her stomach twisted. Would they get back home? Would they find a way out of this nightmare? She pulled back from those dread thoughts. They needed to talk with Naga, this old lady of the Iyes who supposedly had the answers. She glanced to the cave entrance. But when would she awaken?

She loosed a resigned sigh. For now, she would take the chance to see the landscape in the cold light of day. *Look, and see for yourself what Lanky thinks he saw.* She glanced up the slope and was surprised to see that they were not far off the summit. "Can we head up there?"

"We can. Best we head over to the right. We'll gain a better view down the valley."

"Okay." She took a few steps, then glanced back. "Wait here and give me a moment to water the plants."

"Ah. I will. Don't go too far. There's a steep drop over there."

After a short climb, and nature's call, Jessica scrambled on up the slope. She soon reached a sheltered plateau bordered by three discrete summits. She could see what Knuckles had meant; the summit furthest to the south would afford the best view over the valley below.

"Hi there!" came a familiar voice from below.

She looked back down the slope to see the tousled hair of a young man, who was gingerly climbing towards her, Knuckles by his side. "Lanky! Shouldn't you be resting? You're in no fit state to be on your feet, let alone clambering around here."

"Wise words," Knuckles called up. "But maybe he knows better?"

"I will. I promise," Lanky answered, a faint smile on his strained face. "But I wanted to see where we are. And then I found out you were up here. Be good to see it together."

"Well, on your head be it," Jessica muttered. There was no way he should be up and about after what he had suffered yesterday, but she *was* pleased to see him. They'd all been exhausted when they'd finally arrived at this so-called Sacred Site late last night – or was that early this morning? – and only spoken briefly before sleep had taken them. Now, at least, they could see what Lanky had to say about what had happened to them. *And figure out what to do next.*

She waited until the two men joined her, and then they made their way to the base of the southern summit. From there it was an easy climb to the top – for her. Lanky took his time, not helped by the Axe he was carrying. *Another one carrying a bloody Axe.*

Reaching the crest, Jessica looked to the south at the wide sunlit vista before her. The summit she stood on plunged steeply, merging with the steep valley wall, which arced off to the east and west, forming the northern edge to the U-shaped valley. To the right, the valley curved away and was lost behind the tallest of the three peaks. And to the east the valley ran into the distance before opening out ...

And there was the lake. *The lake beside the town that isn't there.*

Lanky, supported by Knuckles, joined her. He was breathing hard.

"So, you still think coming up here was a good idea?"

"I'm fine," he panted. He stood and looked out over the valley. "It's incredible, isn't it?"

Incredible? It's beyond belief. Seeing the landscape now unveiled from the horror of the previous day's flight, she recognised the terrain they had walked in only days before. But how could this be real? The same place, but thirteen thousand years in the past. How was that possible?

Because you brought us here.

She almost gasped aloud at the unbidden thought which had arrived with a keen edge of certainty. *Me? I did nothing.* Hardly daring to breathe, she waited, fearing – expecting even – a dismissive challenge to her denial. But nothing came. She felt a cold sweat on the palms of her hands. Was she losing a hold on her mind? Was she losing hold on reality?

She drew a deep breath. *Get a grip, Jess. You're stronger than this.*

She looked over at Lanky. He was real. This all was real. She drew her gaze back to the valley, locking onto the reality before her. *Focus on what's in front of you, Jess. Deal with what's in front of you.* "In this light, it looks brighter somehow. Sharper edges to the valleys, the cliffs …"

"Sculpted by ice over thousands of years," Lanky said quietly. "It's close to the landscape we know, but not quite … finished." He gestured to the valley walls. "As you say, the rock faces are fresher and brighter, and much of the rubble left by the ice has not been washed away – clearly, the ice has only just left."

The reality was stunning. "So, we're still in an ice age?" she whispered. "But isn't it too warm for that?"

"But cold for summer, yes?" Lanky gestured to the distant hills. "And to finish sculpting this? Definitely more ice to come." He rubbed his chin. "It must be one of the short warmer periods within the ice age itself – before the final ice sheets return." He turned to her. "We've travelled back thirteen thousand years …"

She shuddered. *Don't go there again. Not yet.*

"We can't ignore what's before us. One way or another, we are here." A wry smile crossed his lips. "One way or another …"

Jessica's eyes narrowed. "This game of yours again?"

Lanky shrugged. "Can't help it." His smile faded. "But the more important question is, why are we here?"

Two sharp whistles sounded below them.

"We're needed," Knuckles said. "It may be Naga is awake."

As Knuckles moved off, Lanky turned to her. "I hope she's awake. Maybe then we'll get the answers we need. And then find a way to return home."

I hope we get answers too, Jessica thought as she followed Lanky back down the mountainside. *But will we like those we hear?*

*

Feeling the calming breath of the Spirits, Naga left the Sacred Chamber and considered again how lucky she was to be alive. *Its attack almost breached my defences. The Enemy grows more deadly, its reach frightening.* She met Bear in the torchlit passageway.

"Did they help you?" he asked gently.

"I am recovered," she said, avoiding his eyes. "In that, the Spirits aided me."

Bear eyes narrowed. "And what are you not telling me?"

Naga smiled. "It seems I can never keep my thoughts from you." Her smile faded and she ran a finger over her bracelet. "It has been damaged, the daemon driven from it. I am limited in what I may do." Bear's face fell. She gently touched his arm. "Do not despair. We have brought the Warriors to safety. Now we have hope."

"If they can engage with their powers."

"It will come. And we will aid them until they have adjusted – until they have become true Warriors."

"And we can do nothing more to quicken their learning? What else can our Story tell us?"

Naga felt the weight of his question. *I hold the knowledge of all those before. And yet ...* She glanced back to the Sacred Chamber. "Some things remain hidden, knowledge not shared with the Iyes's shamans."

"That makes no sense. We need to know all, else how can we fully aid the Warriors?"

"No," she said firmly, turning back to face him. "*We* are not Warriors. *We* are not the chosen of IY. We—"

"We are better prepared than these children," Bear snapped. "These who know nothing of our Land. Nothing of the teachings of IY."

She could understand his frustration, his anger. *But ...* "We know what we know," she said firmly, "and that must be enough. We should be patient and trust in IY."

Bear's anger simmered, then his shoulders sagged. He walked a few paces away, head bowed. "This is not what I imagined," he said, his voice subdued.

Naga waited.

Bear sighed and drew himself up. "Forgive me, Mother. Ignore my words. I am ... frustrated."

Naga walked to him and placed her hand on his shoulder. "I need you to remain strong, Bear. As you have always been. We will aid the

Warriors, but it must be they who take control. I repeat, we are not the Warriors."

He nodded. "I understand."

You accept my words, but none of us truly understand. We just have faith. Faith in IY. "Come," she said. "We will talk with the Warriors. I expect now they will be willing to engage with me."

A few moments later, they walked together into the main chamber to see the three Warriors seated together beside Knuckles and River. Two of the Warriors stood as she approached, Beth choosing to remain seated, polishing her Axe. *I think I may have bridges to build there.*

"Stay seated, my friends," she said. "I will sit here."

She sat, legs folded beneath her, and looked across at the three Warriors. Tired faces, but impressively resolute given what they had been through. *There is hope.* She turned to Lanky, seeing the strain in his face. *Yet after that injury he suffered, it is truly incredible he sits here before me.* "How is your wound?"

"It would stand a chance of getting better if he rested it," Jessica muttered. "Instead, he thinks it far better to go rock climbing."

Lanky smiled, yet she still saw his concealed pain. "She's right, but I got to see what I wanted to see."

"And what was that?"

"Confirmation that we've travelled back in time – around thirteen thousand sun-cycles is my guess. Same place, different time."

"And you all accept this," Naga said, scanning Jessica's and Beth's faces.

Jessica nodded. Beth continued to polish her Axe.

"And you, Beth? How is your injury?"

"Feels as though I only scratched it," she said, not looking up. "I guess I'm getting some help from somewhere. Or from someone."

Naga's dark eyes beneath her heavy brow studied the Warrior. For a Warrior this one was. Of that, Naga had no doubt. She had rapidly adapted to their Land, and from River's descriptions, had already shown impressive battle skills. But this war would not be won by physical strength alone. It would take those who could wield the Land's energy to confront those who were coming. *And I feel the Land's energy buffeting around this one. I sense the power beyond any shaman I've met.* A surge of elation flooded through her. The Request had most definitely brought Warriors to their aid.

She leaned forward. "Two Warriors connected with their Axes, and two feeling far better than they should, a day after almost fatal injuries. I would say, yes, you are receiving some help." She turned to Jessica. *This one is afraid of stepping in too far. But we need her to fully engage.* "And you? I hear you also have made a connection with the Land. Are you ready to receive your Axe?"

Jessica glanced at Beth, then looked back at Naga. The Warrior's eyes revealed her suppressed fear ... and yet also a glimmer of an untapped strength. "Maybe these Axes are helping Beth and Lanky heal, and if so, great, but unless they'll help us get back home, I won't be taking one."

Naga caught the fleeting disquiet cross Bear's face. Jessica was in a dangerous time and place and needed to be ready for what was to come. And quickly. *She needs the aid from her Axe.* But she saw the steadfast expression of the Warrior. *Move on for now. But she must take an Axe.* Her gaze flicked across them. "None could have predicted exactly how we would gather, but after a difficult beginning, we are finally together. We—"

"Difficult?" Beth said, scowling. "There's an understatement."

Naga hid her own regrets on how the Arrival had unfolded. It had been a near disaster. "We have our Warriors together," she continued, holding her voice steady. "Two of them hold their Axes, and all recognise a power exists in our Land, a power hidden from most. For this, we can be thankful."

"And thankful to IY," Bear murmured.

"But, yes, this has not been an easy introduction."

"You can say that again," Lanky muttered.

"It has not been easy for us to talk safely," Naga continued. "In this place we can." She looked around the group. "This is a chance to better understand each other, to ask the questions that are foremost in our thinking. Then we can agree on what should be done next."

"Questions?" Lanky grumbled. "Where do we start with that one? Maybe how did we get here? Why do you think we are Warriors? What did you expect us to do? Why—"

"You are here because we made the Request to IY," Naga said, her eyes locking onto his, "the Request for Warriors. The Staff brought you here, and you are here to help us defeat our Enemy, one who seeks to destroy our Land. Destroy your lands."

Jessica shook her head. "Somehow you may have brought us to this place, but Warriors? No, we're not Warriors."

Lanky grunted a laugh. "Warriors? I guess there are plenty of warriors on our planet in our time, but what are we? I'm a car mechanic with an unhealthy interest in history – or the other way around. And these two are – well, actually I don't know what they are, other than tourists – both present and future."

Bear's expression was puzzled. "There is a part of that I don't follow. But you say there *are* other Warriors in your time?"

"What Lanky is trying to say," Jessica said, glaring at Lanky, "is that there are many people in our time. Many, many people. But out of all the people I know, only Beth here is actually what you may call a warrior."

"And yet you all came when we called. You came with the Staff of IY." Bear's deep eyes studied them. "And what do I see? I see three who hold fear, yes, but I also see three remarkably in control given what has happened. Three who do not seek to flee, but who search for answers, who seek to understand."

Unease flittered across Jessica's face. "That may well be, but what I can say is that none of us were expecting to be here. Not now. Not ever. We knew nothing about this place until we arrived here."

Lanky put his hand up. Naga, Bear, and River looked at him, bemused.

Jessica kicked him. "Just talk. But sensibly."

"I always think I'm talking sensibly."

Jessica punched him.

"Ow. That hurt. I'm an invalid, remember?"

"You'll be further 'invalided' in a moment. Talk."

"Well," he said, rubbing the stubble on his chin. "I was just going to point out that it's not strictly true what you just said."

"Which part?"

"That we knew nothing about this."

"Get to the point, Lanky, or I'll help Jess," Beth said, scowling.

"Well, when I say I had an interest in history ..." He grimaced. "It was pretty full on – it got quite out of hand for a time."

"And?"

"And ... well, I'd seen references to artefacts – including axes – supposedly with special powers."

"What!" Jessica and Beth exclaimed together.

"Bit of a long story. Got a tip-off from a bookseller."

"You have to be kidding me," Jessica exclaimed. "I thought you knew something about that Staff ... but these Axes too?"

"A long story. What I had were only snippets, scattered fragments, remnants of ancient texts and carvings. Each on their own were discarded by scholars as trash, but when pieced together, they could be read as referring to ancient artefacts lying hidden in this part of the land." He shrugged. "I found nothing for years, and then ... well, then you came along and knocked me off the cliff. Years of hard work and then a moment of sheer luck."

"I suggest it was not luck that led you to the Staff," Naga said, staring intently at Lanky.

Lanky's brow furrowed. "Maybe. But all I know is that I wouldn't have found it if I hadn't been flung off that cliff."

Jessica's wide eyes betrayed her incredulity. "I still can't believe you knew about these Axes. Why didn't you say something earlier?"

Lanky snorted. "When? When I was being hunted by killers, or when I was being skewered with a spear?"

"No need to be funny," Beth said sharply.

"I'm not being funny. And anyway, there's quite a difference between dreaming about finding magical axes and being thrust thousands of years into the past with people trying to kill you. That messes with anybody's head. I'm amazed we're still sane!"

"You are being helped," Naga said softly.

"By who?" Lanky said, scowling. "By the daemons? I'm not sure I want to be helped by the one who has visited me."

Another surge of hope rose within Naga. *This one is sceptical but accepts their presence.* She held his challenging glare. "Helped by the daemons, yes. And likely by IY herself."

"IY? This god of yours? Who exactly is this IY?"

She turned to River. "You know our Story. What does it say about this?"

River looked at her in surprise. Naga waved her to continue.

River gave a brief nod, then faced the Warriors. "IY is the goddess of the Iyes. It was in this very place, in aeons past, that IY came to Tinashe, the original Ancestor, and brought a message that a great threat was emerging for his people. An evil was rising, fuelled by a god of the Dark, Kaos, one that would destroy not only Tinashe's people but all people of the Land, all life of the Land.

"IY told Tinashe that Kaos could be stopped, but that she would need his help to defeat him."

"Why?" jumped in Lanky. "Why couldn't this great goddess stop the evil herself?"

River's eyes flashed in anger. "You will not speak of her in this way. Show us that much respect."

Lanky flinched. Then he held up his hand. "I'm sorry," he murmured.

River's eyes bore down on the Warrior, but tension eased from her shoulders. "IY is nothing without life. Life is nothing without IY. IY, the Spirits, life – these are all one. Together they are formidable. Together they could defeat Kaos."

River shifted her gaze to the other Warriors. "Under the guidance of IY, Tinashe fashioned the Axes of Power. Crafted out of a sacred green stone found only in this area, it is said he worked for three sun-cycles to fashion these Axes, imbuing each with the ability to connect daemons to chosen Warriors, forming a link between IY, the Spirits, and life. Once completed, IY revealed the entrance to this cave, instructing Tinashe to take the Axes to the deepest chamber – to leave them there, awaiting the Warriors to come."

River paused, but seeing no questions, continued. "IY told Tinashe that he must educate his people and ready them to preserve their knowledge for generations and generations to come. Tinashe brought his small tribe to the cave to witness his creations, and for them to hear directly from IY herself. And so, the Iyes tribe, and their destiny, was formed.

"With IY's guidance, Tinashe toiled for many sun-cycles, developing the skills and knowledge of the tribe. But most importantly he chose the first Iyes shaman. A Keeper who would hold the Story."

River glanced briefly at Naga, who merely sat in silence, looking down at her hands. River looked back at the Warriors. "IY saw all this and was pleased. She saw the tribe was ready. Once again, taking Tinashe away from the tribe, she guided him in creating a Staff. A Staff that would connect with the Warriors and bring them to our aid in the Land's time of need."

She turned to Lanky. "This was the Staff that brought you here, in response to our Request. And this was the Staff you lost."

Lanky shifted uncomfortably.

"And so, the beginnings of our Story were born," Naga said softly. "A Story kept alive in the minds of the shamans of the tribe, preserved and protected by those Keepers from the ravages of time." She sighed. "Preserved as well as such a thing can be after journeying through a vast span of generations." She glanced at Lanky. "And it seems some remnant of the Story was seen by you."

"Yes," Jessica said, her eyes narrowing. "Just how did you – or this bookseller – know of this?"

"His parents were archaeologists. They were the ones who unearthed the references – fragments really – in ancient texts, in the ramblings of madmen, that sort of thing."

"Not from a Story?" Naga said, her heart beating fast.

Lanky hesitated. "Not in the way I think you mean." He glanced to the Axe he held. "But maybe something once existed …" He fell silent.

Naga noticed that Jessica was staring at Bear. "You have another question?"

Jessica glanced at her, seemingly uncertain.

She is scared of being drawn further into our Land, Naga thought, waiting. *But she must.*

As if hearing her, Jessica turned to Bear. "Yesterday, you asked me if we used the Staff to get here. You said it was part of your Story, but that there was a difference?"

Bear's thick brow furrowed as if recalling the conversation. Then he nodded. "Yes. You used the Staff to get here, but our Story talks of four Warriors arriving after the Request is made."

"And there are four Axes?"

He nodded. "Were there more Warriors than you three? If so, why did you all not travel?"

Naga caught Beth's quick glance to Jessica. Her eyes narrowed at the memory of her previous meeting with Beth. "Just two of my friends?" the Warrior had asked when Naga had used her bracelet's power to far-seek the enemy's camp. Naga leaned forward. "There were more besides you three, I think."

Jessica glanced again at Beth, then turned back to Naga. "Two of our friends were close. They were heading towards us when we … left. It seems they didn't arrive here with us."

Bear frowned. "Are we certain those others are not in the Land? The Request was made."

Naga glanced at Bear. "The Request was made, and these three came to the Arrival site. We must assume that those others remained in their own land."

"And are safe," Jessica said quickly.

Naga's fingers brushed her bracelet. *Maybe safe. Maybe not. And whether one of those others should have also travelled here is not clear. But in time, IY will deliver the four Warriors we requested.*

She said nothing.

"Whether you expected three or four, only three of us are here," Beth said, her eyes glinting in the torchlight. "Which brings us to the next question. Warriors or not, what did you expect us to do for you? What, in fact, can we do?"

"That's two questions," Lanky muttered.

"Shut up!" Beth and Jessica said together.

Then Naga felt all eyes on her.

A bead of sweat forming on her forehead, she clasped her hands together and looked back at Beth, whose sharp eyes sought answers. They were arriving at a key moment, her key admission. "In answer to your first question, you must defeat the god of the Dark. You must defeat Kaos."

Her gaze unwavering, Beth waited.

Naga felt her mouth go dry. "In answer to your second question ..." She paused, then forced herself to answer. "I don't know how you can do it."

"What!" Jessica exclaimed. "What do you mean, you don't know!"

Naga found she couldn't respond.

Anger flared on Jessica's face. "We didn't choose to be here, remember. You summoned us. And now you say you don't know why?"

The tension in the chamber grew, and fear trickled down Naga's spine. *They could abandon us.*

"You need to explain yourself, shaman," Lanky said, his face hardening.

At his words, River stepped forward, bristling. Naga held up her hand to halt the girl. Bear took River by the shoulder and pulled her back. River glowered but held her silence.

Naga's gaze returned to Lanky. "Let me answer as best I can," she said, striving to settle frayed nerves. She ran her fingers over her bracelet. *But no help there.* "What I know is this. We know one of our Enemy well, the Ka. This tribe's home is in a southern land, a dry land across a sea, beside a desert. A harsh place to survive for the unwary, but many tribes *do* live there, scattered along a fertile river valley, offering them a rich environment to thrive. These tribes are mainly good people whose only wish is to live in peace. But the Ka ..." Her eyes grew hard. "These are an aggressive, ambitious people preying on the weaker tribes, seeking out the greedy, turning those weak souls with promises of fabulous rewards. Many resist the influence of the Ka, but often at a terrible cost."

"That I can believe," Lanky muttered. "Most people, in most countries, are good people, wanting a decent and safe life for their families. It's the idiots at the top that cause the problems. Once those idiots are in place with their cronies ..." He shook her head. "It can be impossible to shift them."

"And the Ka are indeed expanding, embedding themselves, pushing their corrupt tentacles far into others' lands. All driven by their Ensi, their leader, who in turn is driven by the god of the Dark."

"The one you called Kaos?" Jessica asked quietly.

Naga heard the agitation in the young woman's voice. *Bear said an enemy came to her in a dream. The Warrior fears it is Kaos.* She suppressed a shiver. *And so do I.* "Kaos lurks in the shadows behind all acts of terror, behind all the foul schemes of his agents of the Dark – the Ka, his shades, and his daemons. I, and the Spirits, sense their growing strength and reach. Already, we discern the first breaths of the dread cold, the harbinger of a returning age of winter."

"Ice ages," Lanky murmured.

Naga's eyes narrowed. "Ages of ice, yes. Our Story tells that when the Ka begin to expand, the ice returns, driving our people south into the very jaws of the Ka. But we – the Iyes and the people of this Land – cannot fight this darkness alone; already it has grown too strong. Only the Warriors have the strength to defeat these agents of the Dark. Only you."

She looked at each of them in turn, studying their eyes. *The eyes tell all.* She saw fear and confusion, but also questions. *Despite all that has happened to them, they wish to learn.* And that preserved hope. *And yet, we come again to the gap in our Story.* "But how do you defeat the Dark?" A small sigh escaped her. "That is not known to me, not told in our Story."

Lanky climbed to his feet and stepped a few paces away, rubbing his temple. "You speak with a certainty that we are these Warriors of your Story. But look at me, do I look like someone who can defeat a god?"

It will be the mind I cannot yet see that will answer that question, Naga thought, holding his gaze. She said nothing.

"Okay, then what about this? Surely the past Warriors you speak of told you – told your ancestors – how they defeated this Enemy?"

And this is it, Naga thought, clamping a hold on a raking pang of unease. The glaring rent in their Story.

She caught Beth staring at her with an intense gaze. "No one spoke with the Warriors afterwards, did they?" Beth said in a low voice. "And that's because they weren't there to speak to."

You must tell of what you know. And of what you don't. "Our Story tells that the Warriors left to battle the Ka and the hidden darkness of Kaos. And that soon the ice retreated, and our ancestors returned to the Land. But nothing is told of what those Warriors did. And of our Enemy's secrets, nothing."

Lanky scowled. "So, after defeating this Enemy, the Warriors are not seen again?"

Naga looked up at him. "This is true."

Lanky stared at her, disbelief etched on his face. "And you want us to be these Warriors? You want us to fight some deranged god with no knowledge of how to defeat him?"

I do. You must. She left that unsaid.

Lanky muttered something unintelligible, then walked away, shaking his head.

"So where do they go?" came Beth's subdued voice. "What happens to them?"

"Well," came Lanky's gruff voice as he paced seemingly aimlessly. "How about killed? Captured?"

"Could be," Beth murmured.

Lanky glanced at her with a scowl.

Beth's eyes sharpened on Naga. "The ages of ice, the winters you mention, you believe your adversary causes this?"

"We believe it so."

Beth pursed her lips. "And yet you say these Warriors reversed this. I'm no expert on ice ages, but I remember they lasted for thousands of years. Just how long were these Warriors fighting their war? It's not my plan to stick around for that long ... If at all."

Naga sighed. "I cannot answer. I only know they succeeded."

"Succeeded for a time – but you say your Enemy has returned once more."

Lanky ceased his pacing. "That's a good point." He glanced at Bear and Naga. "They seem to keep reappearing. How? And why exactly are they seeking to exterminate you, seeking to destroy these lands?"

Beside Naga, River's eyes blazed. "Because we, the Iyes, stand opposed to their tyranny! Opposed to their wish to rule over all peoples of this Land! Opposed to their wish to destroy all those who stand against them, all who would remain free!"

"But it doesn't make sense. Why destroy your Land with ice? That can't be good for a tribe wishing to expand—"

"They bring the ice to destroy us," River spat. "And they make their lands in the south richer." She glared at him, fury held beneath her voice. "You don't believe?"

As Lanky hesitated, Naga saw a flurry of emotions cross his face. Frustration, anger, suspicion, confusion ... and desire. *Beyond the fear, he seeks the truth.*

Lanky ran his hand through his tousled hair. "What do I believe? That isn't easy to answer." Drawing a deep breath, he turned to Naga. "I believe the Staff I found brought us here. I believe an enemy stands against you, one who has already attacked me, Beth, and Jessica. I believe you think we can help you in your fight. But what I haven't heard is how you think we can help you." He glanced at Beth and Jessica. "Or how we get home."

"I know how you can help!" River said fiercely. "You fight! We know where the Ka are. We use the power of the Axes to take the fight to them and destroy them forever."

"It's not clear that is the right way to go, River," Naga said softly. "The Ka have grown in number, and the Enemy's strength is growing with each turning of the moon."

"It's *very* clear," Beth muttered. "I am not here to go around slaying hordes of people. I—"

"Why not?" River said hotly. "The Enemy is trying to destroy *all* peoples."

"You are forgetting an important point," came Bear's calm voice. "We don't have the Staff."

As silence fell, Naga felt the biting impact of his words. What would happen if they couldn't retrieve the Staff? *There lies an unknown.*

Jessica leaned forward. "I know this Staff is important to us – you say we need it to get home – but why is it important to you?"

Naga glanced at her. *It's as though she read my mind.* She studied the tall woman's face, seeing her striking brown eyes locked onto hers. Brown eyes, but with the faintest flicker of green. And yes, these eyes showed fear, but a fear belying the strength beneath. These were eyes with depth and purpose, eyes that glimmered with something unseen, unreachable … *Maybe this one is the strongest of the three. Maybe.*

"Our Story says that to defeat the Dark, the Warriors must hold the Staff, that the Staff provides control and balance for the Axe wielders. But how is unclear." *And control of what?* She now realised that while the ancestor's Story aided them greatly, there were vast chasms running through it. *We call the Warriors. We connect them with their Axes.* Beyond this? *We expected the Warriors to know so much more, yet they seem to know nothing.*

"Well, that's useful," Beth rasped. "The Warriors hold the Staff. And do what? Magic this god of the Dark away?"

Naga saw the Warrior's anger and frustration. "I can only tell you what I know," she said, realising that – although true – these words were scant comfort.

"Control and balance," Lanky said, echoing her words. "That would imply that someone – or something – could get out of control without it."

A dangerous place to have stepped into, Naga thought. The Spirits cautioned that the daemons were forceful, independent beings, and allies through choice. Did the Staff provide control of the daemons? That she did not know. But it would serve no purpose to push the Warriors away from the daemons they needed. *And it is not my place to do so.* "We have nothing to tell us this happened," Naga said carefully. "But it *is* told that the Warriors always carry the Staff. That they need the Staff."

"So, who holds the Staff?" Lanky said. "And who controls the holder of the Staff?"

"Our belief is that IY ensures the holder of the Staff is skilled enough to wield it. And to choose the right paths."

"Hmm, that's a big belief in many ways."

"But we don't have the Staff," Jessica interjected, looking at Naga. "'Control and balance' you said. And without it?"

"At this moment, you have each other, as witnessed in the help Lanky gave to Beth. And you, Jessica, can aid the other Warriors by taking your own Axe. Our greatest chance of success lies with all Warriors together."

"I agree, Mother," Bear said, "but Jessica is right. The Staff is lost. Maybe the Ancient One did take it north, but where? That we don't know."

"I think I do," Lanky said, sitting himself back down between River and Jessica.

All eyes turned to him.

*

Lanky fought to control the conflicting emotions battling within him. In one part of his mind stalked a cold foreboding, wrought by all that remained unknown about the place they had landed in. Warriors? Kaos? The Dark? What were these to him? What was expected of him? Too much, too fast, too little understood.

And yet, set against this, burning intensely in a deep, detached part of his mind, lay an awestricken wonder at what he was seeing and hearing – and feeling – in this fantastical new world. His planet, but an alien people, with a preternatural, pervasive energy steeped in its core; an untold power he could instantly tap into with the aid of the daemon in his Axe. And this part of his mind screamed out to him: *This is real. You are here. Engage.*

Thoughts which twisted his gut with icy dread.

He inwardly grimaced as a truth reared vivid and clear. *You wanted to find these Axes, remember? You searched for years to find them!*

But I didn't know. I didn't know anything.

He shuddered. But now he knew something. He had arrived in a world where these people believed them Warriors. He had arrived in a world where he, Beth, and Jessica were expected to fight. And he had connected with a daemon – or a daemon had connected with him.

But not fully, it seemed. *Touch the diamond,* the wolf continually insisted. No, that wasn't going to happen anytime soon. Especially after Naga's worrying words about the Staff? "It controls the Axe wielders," she'd said. Well, he wasn't in any hurry to cement a deeper bond with an aggressive beast that might need to be controlled.

He sighed. And yet, here he was – here they were – supposed saviours for this people. *Saviours* ... A distant memory pushed again at the edge of his consciousness ...

"Lanky!"

He started, his thoughts scattered. "What?"

Beth glared at him. "You said you know where to look."

He pulled himself back to the moment. "Yes, I think I do."

"Well?" Jessica and Beth said together.

Lanky rubbed his chin, wondering where to begin. "I have a map," he said, picturing the prized possession he'd spent those many years working on, "which I believe shows the location of the two Iyes caves in this area."

"What?" Jessica exclaimed. "How?"

"From the same sources as everything else. But I didn't know what they were. It's only now I'm making the connection."

Jessica flicked a wide-eyed glance at Beth, then looked back at him. She started to say something, then seemed to change her mind. "Okay. You have a map. How does that help with the Staff?"

"I have more sites marked on other maps." He noticed the look between Bear and Naga. "I guess those may be similar places to these caves."

Beth turned to Naga. "Is that true? Are there are other places like these?"

Naga nodded. "We have several that the tribe has used for generations. Many others are lost to our memory, and many others are no longer accessible."

"And how far north do these sites exist?" Lanky asked.

"This is the farthest north in this western part of the Land," Bear said. "Our tribe has travelled further north at times when conditions allow, but it is not a place to tarry."

"Again, how does this help with the Staff?" Jessica urged.

"Well," Lanky said, "on one of my maps is another location, one targeted by my bookseller's parents. And it lies to the north. Given the two sites here actually exist, an obvious question is, what's at the site to the north?"

Everyone was looking at him.

Lanky glanced at Beth. "You said the beast flew north with the Staff. It's a long shot, but maybe there's a connection between this other site on my map and this beast."

"One hell of a long shot," Beth grunted.

"Do you know where this site is?" Naga said.

"About three hundred miles north of here."

"What distance is that?" River asked.

"Well," Lanky said, calculating, "I walked a long-distance trail to the south of that peak in five days, and that's one hundred miles. But north of where I finished, the walking would get tougher. So … Well, I'm not sure. Maybe twenty days away. But it was good weather, and I made good progress."

"That's a long way to travel on the chance that we can find a concealed cave unknown by this tribe for millennia!" Jessica exclaimed. "And I don't suppose you've a satnav handy to help find this place, and a description of how to search out a cave entrance? You couldn't even find the ones under your nose."

Lanky winced and rubbed his chin again. "Yes, Jess, I know, but I didn't know exactly what I was looking for before. Now I do."

"That's not true. You have a mark on a map. You don't actually know if there's anything there at all. If there is, then what's the likelihood it's this dragon's hideout? It could be anything."

"'Anything' is a bit broad." He sighed. "But I agree, we won't know … unless we find it."

"So, you say twenty days' walk?" Bear said. "And in good weather?"

Lanky nodded.

"Well, north of here, after maybe ten days, you encounter the first of the snow. North of that is generally snowbound. So, depending on where it is, and which route is taken, your twenty days could turn into twenty-five to thirty. And was your hunting good on your twenty-day journey? Accessing food in the north is a problem."

"Ah. Hunting … Well …"

"Hold on," Jessica said. "Let's back up a second. Is there anything else that can pin down where that dragon may have taken it? What do you and Naga know of this dragon's lair?"

"To that we have no answer," Bear said. "But we have known it as the ice dragon, a creature of the north."

"Then it could be the dragon's lair," Lanky said, flicking a glare at Jessica.

'I would agree.'

Lanky jumped as the gruff voice of the daemon sounded in his head.

'A little jumpy, aren't we, Dysam?'

'What do you mean by "I would agree"?' Lanky grated, ignoring the wolf's barb.

'I mean that the Ancient is indeed a creature of the north. The Staff will lie at the place you discovered.'

Lanky's heart hammered in his chest. *I found a dragon's lair?* His eyes narrowed. 'What do you know of such a place?'

'Enough. And I know a Warrior should travel to retrieve it.' A low growl sounded in his mind. *'But you are not yet recovered, and one is not yet ready. The choice is made for you. Bethusa should travel now.'*

Bethusa? A question for another time. 'I ask again, how do you know of this place?'

Silence answered him.

'Wolf?'

More silence.

Damn wolf!

He frowned. Despite his irritation, it seemed his wolf friend held knowledge of the dragon. How? And could he trust him?

'If you complete the bond, Dysam,' came the wolf's voice once more, *'then you will know.'*

'How do you know of this place?' Lanky said quickly.

'Complete the bond.'

'I'm not completing any bond. Just answer the question.'

Silence.

Damn!

"Lanky!" came Jessica's voice, making him jump again.

"I wish people would stop doing that."

Jessica looked at him more closely. "Bear was talking, and you just sat there, ignoring us. What's going on?"

He glanced around the group, calming his thoughts. "My wolf friend was telling me he agrees with me. He says the Staff will be at this place in the north." His face scrunched to a frown. "But how he knows …"

Bear's attention sharpened. "It appears you have a valuable ally. This is good." He leaned forward. "So, we may know where the lair of the Ancient One lies, but what else do you know of these creatures, these dragons? What knowledge of these do you hold in your time?"

"Knowledge? We have many stories of dragons, but that's all they are – stories made for entertainment." He paused, his brow furrowing. "But it seems that somewhere in these stories are forgotten grains of truths …"

"But you have no tribe preserving the Story?"

Lanky heard an undercurrent of hope in his voice. "Maybe there is a tribe somewhere that preserves an ancient knowledge, but no tribe that we know of. In our world and in our time, people struggle to remember their grandfather's life, let alone generations of ancestors. But it's a big world, and some peoples and tribes are better than others at preserving their past. It's possible your Story survives somewhere."

"So, hope remains," Naga murmured. "That is good." Fleeting pain crossed her face. "We strive to keep our Story alive, but this is a time of exploration and discovery, with new peoples entering old lands. Peoples intolerant of others, with very different views on how their tribes should live. Unfortunately, my ancestors bore the brunt of these changes, and very few of us survive to this day. But there lies another tale. The question for us now is, what next?"

What next? For Lanky, this was clear. He glanced at Jessica and Beth. "What do you think?"

"We have to find the Staff," Jessica said immediately. "Whatever else it may be, it seems it's our way home."

He couldn't help himself. "You took the words right out of my mouth."

Jessica cast him a searching look, then shook her head. "We have to find the Staff," she repeated, "but it's still not clear how we do it."

"It is clear," Beth said, sudden fire in her eyes. "I need to travel north to find this Staff."

Jessica's intake of breath was sharp. "You?"

Lanky studied Beth's face, seeing a hard, unyielding intent. *It is her and yet it is as though another regards me.* "And why do you think that?" he said in an even voice.

"Because you're not the only one who speaks with an ally."

An ally? He felt a tremor of unease. *She speaks of that daemon, Garrion.* "Take care, Beth. We don't know who these daemons truly are. Don't get too close."

"True, but in this they're right. We need that Staff back, and you," she said, gesturing to his bandaged wound, "are not ready for such a journey." She turned to Jessica. "And you're not ready to connect to the energy of this Land."

"And you are? What do you really know of this place, Beth? What do you really know of what you might face?"

"I know we need to get that Staff back."

And there it was. The simple unavoidable reality. *The Staff brought us here. We need it to get home.*

"The Warrior would not travel alone," Naga said quietly. "She would travel with my most trusted people." She gestured to the stalwart man by her side. "Including the leader of our tribe."

Bear nodded. "We can leave within two days."

Lanky saw the sudden tension in Jessica's face. *Which echoes what I feel.* His gaze shifted to the purposeful face of Beth. *She sees a way to help get us out of this mess. But at what cost?* He tensed, digging his fingers into his temple. How violently they'd all been thrust into this alien land, with no warning, no portent of what was to come. *But that's not true, is it? What about that voice you heard? And what was it you searched for over all those years? Axes with magical powers. Guess what? You found them.* He glanced down at the Axe in his hand. *But not this. Not in my wildest dreams would I have expected this.*

"Lanky," came Jessica's insistent voice.

He looked up.

"What do we do?"

His stomach twisted, but through the fog of his fear, he knew what needed to be done. "Beth travels north."

CHAPTER FOURTEEN

The traitor was unseen. Unseen? No, unknown.

Jessica glanced up at Naga, who sat cross-legged on a white pelt in the middle of her tent. Why am I here? she thought, trying to still jagged nerves. What do I want here?

You want to help Beth, she answered herself. *You want to travel with her to recover the Staff.*

And so you need to act now.

She drew a deep breath. Bear wished to travel north with Beth now, saying the weather would only grow colder as autumn approached and that four out of the five autumns past had been the coldest their tribe had known.

So they were leaving in the morning. Things were moving fast.

And I need to move with them.

She tried to steady her shaking hands. "We know so little of this place. And these Axes …" She shuddered. "How is it possible to acknowledge they hold a power when only yesterday I knew nothing?" She paused. "Except …"

Naga calmly watched her, waiting …

"Except those dreams, those nightmares." *The burnt man.*

Her gnarled fingers stroking her bracelet, Naga scanned Jessica's face, her deep-set eyes burning with fierce intelligence. "You have a strength, a power, that you do not yet understand. Abilities beyond your imagining. And until you take your Axe, this remains a danger to yourself and to others. I do not know this burnt man you describe, but clearly, he has knowledge we should be rightly fearful of, knowledge imparted by Kaos." She paused, thoughtful. "And this place in which you find him is undoubtably a Glade."

"But that can't be. I know nothing of these Glades."

"You know. You are who you are. But," she continued, seeing Jessica about to protest, "it is true you lack control of this power within you. In your dreams you drift unknowingly into an unprotected Glade, exposing yourself to great risk."

Jessica tensed at a sudden prickling fear. A fear of something watching her, waiting. Of something that abhorred her. Of something that wished she was dead.

The Dark ...

"I don't know what to do," she whispered. "I'm not ready."

Naga reached out and placed a hand on Jessica's knee. She smiled. "In this moment you may think that, but we hold a tremendous capacity to adapt. One day I was a carefree young girl spending time with my friends as we carried out our tasks for the tribe; the next I was led into the introspective existence of a shaman. Another day I am listening to my father's wondrous tales, the twinkle in his eyes betraying his more fantastical embellishments; the next I am burying him."

Her smile faded. "Life can be hard, but we adapt. And if we embrace the change – with the pain, joy, and worry it can bring – we grow stronger and wiser, bringing a greater benefit to ourselves, our family, our friends, our tribe. But if we do not, then there lies the path we do not want, nor need, to tread. That path leads our tribe to barren lands."

She studied Jessica's face for a moment, then continued. "You are Warriors. Whether or not you like it, whether or not you want it, you must embrace it. You say you know little of this place? Well, learn. Talk to our tribe. Watch our tribe. Walk out into our Land and truly see it." She smiled. "And embrace your destiny. Embrace your Axe."

Jessica hesitated. "It scares me."

"And this pleases me. It is right to be cautious when faced with an unknown. It is right to be scared when faced with such great power. What will you do with it? How will you respond? With great power comes great choices – and great temptations." She reached out and covered Jessica's hand with hers. "You are strong, Jessica. I can see it. And your heart is strong. But there may be – will be – times where you will need to harden your heart to choose which path to take. Those choices will not be made lightly nor easily, but even when fear threatens to overwhelm you, they must be taken."

"And if it's the wrong decision?"

"You will have tried. You will have chosen a path, being true to yourself and others. Your ancestors will bear witness and be proud, and you can join them with your head held high."

My ancestors ... My family ...
My sister.

Eshe's face suddenly flashed into her mind. *I didn't save her. I failed her.*

The familiar stab of pain swept through her ... but with it came a flash of anger. *I will not fail again. I will not fail Beth.*

Naga leaned forward, her eyes seeming to drift to another place. Her voice when she spoke seemed ethereal. "I see little of what is to come, but I know you must prepare yourself. I think you will not finally understand what must be done until you have truly touched the darkness." The old woman drew a sharp breath, then sat back, thick brow creased as though momentarily confused.

Touch the darkness? All I see is darkness.

Naga seemed suddenly tired. Her gaze flicked to Jessica. "You know where the Axe lies," she said softly. "If that is the path you wish to take."

Jessica nodded, steely determination growing.

Naga straightened, stiffened limbs clearly resisting. "But now, my child, if you would forgive an old woman, I think I will rest for a while."

"Of course." Jessica climbed to her feet.

Naga glanced up at her. "The curse of age. The mind is willing, but the body is not. You, on the other hand, have a willing mind and a formidable resilience. Use this strength wisely. Use it to aid your friends. Use it to aid my people."

Jessica forced a smile. "I will see what I can do."

The old woman nodded. "And keep your smile. You have a smile that lightens our souls and pleases the Spirits."

A warmth came into Jessica's smile. "Rest well, Naga."

"I will indeed. It is one of life's pleasures."

Leaving the tent, Jessica walked a few paces, then paused in the warming rays of the sun. She looked up from the valley floor to the heights above.

To the hidden cave.

To the place she had to go to engage with the power of the Land.

*

"It's incredible how much better I feel today," Beth said, scooping up a handful of clear, icy water from the gurgling stream. She slurped a mouthful, then glanced at Lanky, who was washing his face, softly humming. "Amber can't believe how quickly the wound healed, and I sense the poison gone. What else is possible here?"

Lanky looked up, water dripping from his lean face. "I don't know, Beth, but take care. We've agreed to engage as we can to get the Staff back, but all this is way out of our comfort zone – well, mine anyway. We're not indestructible, and you don't want to go around getting stabbed every day."

"Don't worry. That's not high on my list today." She glanced at the rippling waters, then back at Lanky. "Even so, I sense an energy here, a vibrancy. And look at us, each about to head out into this Land, each agreeing to tackle this challenge before us. How are we so calm? Why aren't we distressed nervous wrecks?"

"I might not look it, but inside, I am."

"But still you prepare." *Still we try to learn about this age we've been thrust into.* She tasted again the subtle sweetness of a faint energy around her. *Still we step cautiously into the unknown.* "We hold a strength within us that wasn't there before. It fortifies us. It prevents us from running to the hills."

Lanky brushed the water off his face, then regarded her with troubled eyes. "Did you sense anything before?" he said in a hushed voice. "Before we came here?"

The remembered panicked state of Jessica after her nightmares flashed back. "I had dreams, random dreams … of an Axe. But nothing that worried me, nothing that scared me. Not like Jess. Yet even Jess's nightmares … who could have imagined this?"

Lanky fell silent, his attention seeming elsewhere. Then: "I heard voices. I thought it was because I was tired, stressed, but now …" His gaze fixed on her once more. "What do the daemons call you?"

They call me Bethusa.

But I don't want to be Bethusa.

A cold shiver ran down the back of her neck. *Why? Who is Bethusa?*

Disturbed by the thoughts, she absently pushed a strand of hair behind her ear. "Bethusa," she whispered. "They call me Bethusa."

"And they call me Dysam. Why?"

She shook her head. *I don't want to know.*

Fear flashed in Lanky's eyes. "Have we been here before?" he said in a low voice. "Do they know us by a different name?"

Here before? Could that be true? Could … Her fingers curled tightly into her palm, the sharp pain of her nails banishing the thought. *No! I am Beth! No one else.* "I've never been to this place," she said more sharply than she'd intended. "I know that for sure."

Lanky's gaze was searching, as if seeking hard answers to quell his doubts. Then he sighed. "No, I guess that's something we wouldn't forget in a hurry."

A voice cut across them. "Hurry, you two," Knuckles called. "There's work to be done."

The disquiet in Lanky's eyes was replaced by a sudden forceful resolve. "They can call us what they like," he grated. "But I'm Lanky, and you're Beth. Whatever happens here, we have to remember that."

And I am Beth. As Lanky stood, she turned back to the stream and scooped up a final draught of water. Her thirst slaked, she climbed to her feet. *I am Beth, and I have to recover the Staff.*

Lanky glanced to the sky. "We better get moving. The sun's climbing above the trees already, and Bear's packed a lot into today."

Refocussing on the morning ahead, she made her way with Lanky towards the temporary camp where Shorty and Knuckles were preparing the day's training. *Preparing us on how to survive in the lands beyond this camp.* And that would take far more than a single day – she knew she would have to learn and adapt as they travelled. *But learn what you can now.*

Approaching the camp, she saw Knuckles and Shorty laying down a long, slender branch, adding it to a stack of others. *Poles for the huts we'll make,* she guessed. A tall, dark-haired woman they hadn't met before stood beside them. *So, who's this?*

Knuckles and Shorty broke off from their task and walked over to meet them. "Let me introduce Svana," Knuckles said. "She'll be the pathfinder for our group of six heading north."

"Only Spider is a better scout," whispered Shorty, who had stepped to Beth's side. "But I'd never tell her that."

She's a confident person, Beth thought immediately, watching the lithe woman approach, her sharp eyes scanning them both.

"Hello, Warrior," Svana said, holding out her hand to Lanky.

Lanky grabbed her wrist behind the hand. "Pleased to meet you, Svana. And Lanky is the name."

Svana dipped her head in acknowledgement, the curls of her hair brushing her shoulder.

Beth held out her hand to Svana. "Beth."

Svana reached out to grab her wrist – and Beth deftly caught her hand and grasped it. "Pleased to meet you, Svana," she said, tightening her grip.

Svana smiled. "Hi, Beth," she said, gently increasing the pressure of her hand. "I've heard much about you already, Warrior."

Yes, confident, Beth thought, *and not at all fazed by 'Warriors'. Good.* She released her grip, and Svana immediately released hers.

"So, we travel north," Svana said, a slight lilt to her voice.

"Some of us," Beth said. "Lanky here is heading south with Jessica."

"And where is she?"

Meeting Naga. Figuring out what she will do. "She may join us later."

Svana's gaze levelled on Lanky. "I heard you will go south to our main camp. To show Rind and the allies that the Warriors are real. To mobilise them."

Lanky shuffled his feet. "I hope the scout, Spider, has already done that. Rousing the troops is not my speciality."

Smiling, the pathfinder said, "Then you will need to practice. They won't be impressed by Spider alone." She turned back to Beth. "This mountain, the Mountain of Hope that your friend tells is our goal, Bear said you visited this place before. In … your time."

"I did. With my family. As a child."

"And you would remember this place? Recognise it when you saw it?"

Would I? I remember the open view to the north, looking across the plain into the sea loch on the coast. "Possibly. We approached from the north, and it's a clear feature from there – at the head of the range. From a southern approach? Not sure. And remember, this is in my time …"

"For sure, it will be different," Lanky said. "But my guess is it should be even more prominent – before thirteen thousand years of erosion have hammered away at it."

"Then I hope I'll recognise it."

"Or it'll be a road to nowhere," Lanky murmured as if to himself.

Beth cast him a questioning glance.

Knuckles cleared his throat. "So which route will we take, oh great pathfinder?"

"Along the coast," Svana answered, ignoring his jibe. "Inland is shorter, but already snow and ice cover much of that northern land and many valleys will be impassable. So west to the coast from here, and then north, keeping to the lower lands as much as possible."

"Better chance of food that way," Shorty said. "Gives us access to the sea."

"When we reach the northern land's end," Svana continued, "we turn east until the Warrior recognises this Mountain of Hope." She shrugged as though dismissing the journey's difficulty. "It can be done if we avoid problems with the weather. Or unprepared companions."

"Hey!" Knuckles said sharply. "This Warrior learns fast. And has a long memory."

"My apologies," Svana said, dipping her head. "My choice of words is sometimes lacking." As Svana looked up, Beth caught a faint smile on the woman's lips and a glint in her eye. "But I wasn't talking about the Warrior, Knuckles …"

"Hey!" Knuckles exclaimed again. "That makes it even worse." His eyes narrowed. "You meant Shorty, right?"

The tall, bearded man next to Knuckles thumped him on the shoulder.

Beth laughed. "Whoever you meant, Svana, I can say for sure that Lanky, Jessica, and I *are* unprepared. We had these Warrior roles thrust on us, neither asked for nor wanted. So, we will need help ... and advice. I look forward to working with you."

Smiling, Knuckles caught her eye and winked.

"I'll certainly do my best, Warrior," Svana answered, tilting her head slightly.

Knuckles clapped his hands. "Right, so that's the introductions done. And since you're here, Svana, you can help me and Shorty teach our Warriors how not to get themselves killed. We don't want them starving to death nor freezing to death in a storm, do we?"

Svana rolled her eyes. "Then it's a good job I'm here."

"Right," Knuckles repeated, a sparkle in his eyes. "Where do we start ...?"

*

"Think we're just about done," Knuckles said, placing the last bundle of grasses on the edge of the hut's domed roof.

Lanky looked across at the other hut, where Svana was watching Beth tie off the final cords on their roof. "It looks like they're almost finished, too."

"Let's get this last one tied down, and then we're done for the day. The sun's almost down, it's cold, and I'm starving."

"You're always looking after your stomach," Svana called from the other hut, "that's why you're so close to the ground."

Shorty, who'd been helping Beth, let out a roar of laughter.

"I just burn it fast," Knuckles said, grinning. "My mother said I had hollow legs. But I checked – I don't. I just burn it faster than you lot."

"I think it's your mouth – it doesn't stop working. Food in, garbage out."

Shorty laughed again.

"That's because I've lots of interesting things to say."

"Well, we never hear them," Svana said, moving her pack into one side of the hut. "And no, I don't want to hear them now either."

Knuckles grinned as he looped a cord around the frame of the hut and over the bundle of grasses. "Okay. I'll tell you while we're eating."

"How did you check you don't have hollow legs?" Lanky asked, winking at Shorty.

"Did you have to ask him that?" Svana muttered. "I'm going, before I have to listen to any more of his rantings." She walked off towards the crowd of people sitting around the low fire.

Knuckles chuckled. "Svana's wonderful. I just need to get her to see the brighter side of life."

Shorty smiled. "What, like you, do you mean?"

"Well, there's no question I like her, and who knows, her liking of me might grow a little on this trip."

"That implies that you're starting from a position of some liking. You're a little further down the scale – maybe into dislike? Anyway, you're too old for her."

"Ah, but I'm a positive thinker. That gives me an edge. Always stay positive and life is all the brighter."

"That's probably true in your head, but maybe the life of this Land isn't quite seeing it the same way."

"Now, that's an interesting thought, my friend. Did you know—"

"Oh, no. What have I done?" Shorty grumbled, bundling his pack into the completed hut.

"The Land is neither happy nor sad," Knuckles continued, pulling the final cord tight. "Not joyous nor angry. It just is. It is—"

"I know," cut in Shorty, opening his arms out wide, mimicking Knuckles's voice. "It is us – and these birds and animals around us – that decide whether they're happy or sad, whether to shout angry words at each other or to seek warmth in each other's company, not the Land."

"Very true, my friend," Knuckles said, tying off the last corner. "You've been listening after all. Yes, it's our choice. Us, not the Land around us."

The sound of Svana's slow handclapping drifted towards them. "You could, of course, decide to mock your better's great words." Knuckles stepped away from the hut and turned to Lanky. "Well, I think that's us done."

Lanky examined his now completed hut – their sleeping quarters for the night. A low domelike structure formed of a framework of arched, stripped branches, covered with a patchwork of leafier branches and grasses. He reckoned it was around six feet wide and four feet tall. Enough to sleep three or four. *Enough to keep three of four alive through days of bad weather.*

"We're finished too," Beth said, walking towards them with Shorty.

"You happy you know how these are built?" Shorty said. "If not, we can work on another."

"No, I can see how it's done."

"Remember, adapt depending on what's on hand. In this place, we hold a stock of wood and hides, lasting us for several seasons. Travelling, you use what you can, even if it's what you wear or carry. So long as you stay warm and dry, you'll be okay. Cold is the big killer."

"And there's my next question," Beth said. "How are we going to deal with the snow and freezing temperatures further north? And what do we eat?"

"Not enough for Knuckles," Shorty answered, laughing.

Knuckles grunted in agreement. "Tramping about in the white stuff isn't anyone's idea of a good day. We need to be there and back as quick as we can. Food? Hunting while moving fast isn't easy – and as you say, it will be colder in the north – but at this time, we'll still be okay. Inland, we'll find reindeer and hare, and on the coast, fish and shellfish."

"We'll also carry what dry foods we can," Shorty added. "For those days we need it."

Knuckles grinned and patted his stomach. "And some of us hold our own reserves of summer energy." He glanced at Beth. "And so, my Warrior, do not fear, we shall try to keep you warm and fed. And the warmest will be in my b—"

"Don't go there, Knuckles," cut in Bear, who had walked up behind them. "Let's eat, and then we can ready ourselves. We need a good start in the morning."

"Food," Knuckles said, his eyes gleaming. "Always best to fill your stomach before a trip like this." He walked off towards the fire.

As they followed Knuckles, Lanky studied the short Warrior. Short, yes, but lean and toned as most of the tribe. He smiled. *Seems he does have hollow legs.*

By the fire, they picked up wooden bowls and spoons, then ladled out servings of the hot stew from the scorched birch container sitting within the adjacent ember pit. His bowl full, Lanky took a place beside Amber and Beth by the fire, and a silence fell as they tucked into their steaming food.

"How are the injuries?" Amber asked after a while, strands of her fiery hair aglow in the last rays of the sun.

"It's incredible," Lanky answered through a mouthful of food. "Aside from the throbbing pain, from the outside you'd think it a minor cut."

Beth nodded. "Same – and it seems I could eat my way through that entire pot of stew."

"You'll have to move fast to beat Knuckles," Amber quipped. She shuffled closer to Beth. "But really," she said in a low voice, "are you sure you're ready to make this trip now? Those were dreadful injuries you both suffered – Bear will delay if you're not ready."

Beth ate a few more mouthfuls, then smiled at the healer. "I'm ready. I may not be fully healed, but my strength returns hour by hour." She glanced at Lanky, her smile fading. "I feel as though I draw a healing energy from elsewhere – from the land, from the air, from that which surrounds me. I draw this energy and feel a capacity to accept more. And while a part of me is worried by what's happening, another is intrigued, stimulated even."

Lanky put down his bowl. "I don't have a worry side, I have a 'suspicious as hell' side, and that's keeping some things at bay. And while I understand what you say about this energy and its healing power, until I understand more, anything else has to be on my say-so." *You hear that, wolf?*

The leader of the Iyes cleared his throat and glanced across to Lanky. "That aside, are you ready for your task in the south?"

To mobilise the Iyes. To mobilise the allies. To mobilise those I know nothing of. "I will be, I suppose. I guess I have to be." *To give us time. To give Beth time to find the Staff.* "But I still don't understand why you have no army ready and waiting to meet these Ka."

"To maintain our Story in readiness of the Warriors' arrival requires a faith, a belief. And a longevity of belief, one kept alive by the will of our tribe over generation after generation. To expect others to do this? No, that is not possible. Only when the time is here, when we can show the proof of our Story, can we ask all tribes to fight alongside us. This is your task, yours and Jessica's. Only on seeing you will people believe."

Believe me? Of that, he wasn't so sure.

"And the talk of armies is misleading," Bear continued. "The Enemy cannot be defeated this way. Yes, we can protect our people for a time, but it is the Warriors who must ultimately find the way to defeat them. To defeat Kaos."

"A way which, at the moment, we don't know," Beth murmured.

"Even more important that we mobilise support, to give you the time you need."

But need for what? Lanky thought. *To recover the Staff, yes. But beyond that, there I'm still blind.*

He grunted and climbed to his feet. "What I need time for right now is another bowl of this delicious stew."

"It's that lanky body of his – full of holes," came Knuckles's voice.

As Lanky walked towards the fire, he looked around. "Is Jessica not back yet?"

Amber looked up. "I saw her talking with Naga earlier."

Lanky frowned and glanced towards Naga's hut. "That was a while ago. Think I'll find her. She needs to eat."

"She'd better be quick," Knuckles said as Lanky walked away.

As he walked towards Naga's hut, a sense of unease crept through his body.

He lengthened his stride.

*

River reached for her water skin and took a long draught. Her pack was almost ready to go. She smiled. *Always be prepared.* A trait that she and Sheba shared. *No surprise there.* Her father was not the most patient when he was ready to move. They had learned from a young age to be ready.

Most of the tribe were assembled in the valley below, but she had wanted to ensure nothing had been left here in the cave, and that all was safely stowed for their return. *Whenever that may be.* As she attached the water skin to her pack, she heard a slight sound at the far side of the cave. She turned to see a figure exiting through the rear passageway.

Jessica?

She sat and gazed at the now empty space. *She passed silently by. No acknowledgement. Why?*

She climbed to her feet, uncertain what to do. The Warrior clearly didn't want to be disturbed. *But what is she doing?*

She hesitated. Should she fetch Naga? *And tell her what?*

She wavered only a moment longer. *Be honest, you want to know what she's doing.*

Walking to the passageway, she headed inside.

*

Shadows flickered across the walls as Jessica made her way across the small chamber, two Axes glistening in the fiery light from the torches. She was calm, much calmer than she'd expected.

For she'd felt a warming energy as she entered the chamber.

Felt? Maybe 'aware' was a better word. An awareness of the presence of … of what exactly? That she couldn't easily put into words. Simple words created boundaries, constraining that being described to what you knew – and these days had been far beyond anything she had experienced or believed. All she could say was that she was simply aware. Aware of something beyond the visible. Not a threat as her calmness testified, yet something still not known or understood.

And was she truly calm? Or was this calmness imposed by her own mind? *Or by others?* A barrier imposed around her to keep her sane. But such questions were meaningless right now. *Just keep moving,* she told herself. Ignore all the doubts, terrors, and fears. She had been thrown into a game, the game of her life – a game *for* her life – and one where she knew few of the rules.

But for her, the aim was clear ... *Return home.*

She looked at the two Axes lying on the ground. Lanky and Beth had both taken an Axe, allowing them access to a veiled power, and committing them in some way to this strange land from her past. Was one of these truly hers? Naga's words replayed: "You have a strength, a power, that you do not yet understand ... until you take your Axe, this remains a danger to yourself and to others."

She forced a cold grip on her thoughts. While her future steps were uncertain, her meeting with Naga had convinced her of what she should do now.

Lowering herself to the ground, she sat cross-legged before the two weapons and closed her eyes. She breathed slowly in and out through her nose, filling herself with the calming chamber's energy. Relaxing her body, she focussed on her breathing, observing the thoughts entering her mind, then allowing them to drift on by. Almost immediately, she sensed the quiet presence of others approaching the boundaries of the chamber.

The daemons come.

A patch of grey mist drifted in from the right of her dream vision, slowly coalescing into the form of a great white wolf. Fully formed, the wolf sauntered into the centre of her view, then stopped. Thicker mist swirled in from the left, splitting as it approached, one swirl emerging as a glistening black horse, fine tendrils trailing from its wild mane, and the second as an eagle flying high. The eagle swooped down, settling on the branch of a tree. Then, beneath her feet, below the shimmering surface of the deep-blue sea, she saw the enormous form of a whale appear, dwarfing the company above.

The daemons settled and became still.

But not completely.

She could see the chest of the horse expand and contract as it breathed; the eagle extended the talons on its right claw; the whale flexed its tail imperceptibly. Only the wolf appeared to be perfectly still, but its eyes bored into hers, a piercing stare with frightening intensity.

The sudden tang of fear was bitter on her tongue.

"Hold your worries, companion of Jalu," came a rich, lilting woman's voice. "These four cannot harm you – will not harm you."

Jalu? Who is Jalu? She scanned the four before her. *The voice had not been from them. Then who?* In the shadows of that question lurked a disquieting gloom. *Keep moving.* "I'm here to present myself before you," she said, holding her voice steady. "You," she said, gesturing to the wolf, "have a bond with Lanky. You are aiding Beth," she continued, glancing at the horse. "And so, I believe we should talk," she finished, addressing the whale and eagle.

The daemons regarded her in silence.

"It is not that simple," came the unknown voice.

She hesitated, thrown. "What do you mean? I agree to take an Axe, as have Beth and Lanky. Show me what to do."

The daemons continued their silent regard of her.

All sense of calmness shattered. "Don't play games! What do I need to do?"

Still no answer.

She saw a haze form in the centre of the daemons and fought a rising panic. *Someone – something – else comes.*

The haze dissipated, and visceral dread flooded her veins as she saw an eye forming. A yellow eye. *No! It can't be. Naga said this place was protected.* Trembling, she reached out and grasped an Axe.

"No! Don't!"

She hefted the Axe and swung forward to strike the centre of the ring—

The daemons vanished.

She was left standing alone, complete darkness around her, no visible walls, ceiling, floor. She was standing, yes, but in a space completely void of features, no visual guide of where she was or where to go. She tottered, lost her balance, and fell.

"You have lost, Guardian," came a deadly, familiar voice behind her.

Fear ripped through her. *The burnt man!*

She spun around in horror.

Limned in midnight black, a foreboding figure loomed in the shadows.

"No! This can't be!"

"I am your executioner," the shadowy figure snarled, stepping towards her. "And now you die."

"No!" Jessica screamed, terror engulfing her. *Get out! Get out of here! I need to get home!*

An arm enveloped her …
And then a savage blackness descended.

*

Silently entering the Sacred Chamber, River observed Jessica seated cross-legged in front of the Axes, her eyes closed and her body still. Feeling suddenly as though an intruder into Jessica's space, River halted, questioning her decision to follow the Warrior. But there were forces at work here that these Warriors hadn't encountered before. Forces that went beyond the Warriors' experiences, but which she and her tribe had been aware of for millennia. While Jessica appeared in control, there were potent energies present in this place that had to be approached with care.

She sat at the side of the chamber and waited.

And it wasn't long before she heard Jessica's breathing become shorter and sharper, mumbled words spilling out as though she spoke with someone unseen. As the Warrior grew more and more agitated, River sprang to her feet. *I have to get help!* But as she turned to go, Jessica grasped an Axe, then swiftly stood, striking out aggressively.

Frozen, River watched as Jessica lost her balance and slumped to the ground. Forcing herself to move, she rushed forward and knelt beside the Warrior, wrapping an arm around her, and grasping for the Axe for support.

Her hand closed around the haft—

River cried out as an agonising pain ripped through her body. As darkness enveloped her, she heard a voice.

'*Revri! Stay strong! One will aid you!*'

Blackness swallowed her.

CHAPTER FIFTEEN

Dysam was held at bay. Thank the Light for that.

"They can't just have vanished," Beth growled, standing within the Sacred Chamber, staring at a single Axe on the ground. "Someone must have seen them leave."

"We've questioned everybody," Bear said, his face drawn. "They were not seen leaving this cave."

Beth's eyes blazed. "Well, somebody missed something. They're clearly not here."

Lanky's troubled gaze flicked between the two. Beth was right. And Bear was right. River and Jessica were gone, and an Axe was gone. But no one had seen them leave. It made little sense. Why would Jessica take off without talking to them? And why leave with River?

His stomach twisted. He hadn't known these women long, but already a close connection had formed. *We're in this together. We must survive this together.* The fear in his gut deepened. *So where are you, Jess?*

He turned to Bear. "You sure they couldn't have slipped out some other way?"

"There is no other way out," Bear said firmly. "And we have eyes on the entrance at all times. No one could enter or leave without us knowing."

"Well, that clearly isn't the case," Beth retorted.

"I understand your frustration, Warrior, and would wish to ease it, but I can only state what my people are saying. No one saw them leave."

"Well, someone wasn't doing their job then."

Lanky saw the big man's discomfort, but Bear accepted the admonishment in silence.

Amber came to Lanky's side. "Was anything said last night that might indicate why Jessica might leave?" she asked, scanning around Jessica's sleeping area.

"I can think of a million reasons she might want to leave," Lanky muttered. "But leave without us like this? No. No way."

Beth glared at Bear. "I agree."

"I asked her to take the Axe," came Naga's quiet voice behind him.

Beth spun around. "What!" She took a step towards the old woman. "What have you done?"

Naga held up her hands. "Nothing such as you are imagining, Warrior. You know she came to me freely."

Beth scowled. "Even so, what did you do?"

Naga sighed. "Jessica was concerned with how little she knew. She was struggling to reconcile what she had been with what she was being asked to be."

"So, you drugged her and brought her down here?"

"I encouraged her to embrace her Axe, that was all." Naga straightened. "The Warriors have assembled. A great challenge lies ahead. You need the aid of the Axes, of the daemons." She held Beth's eyes. "You have engaged with your Axe daemon and must know the truth of my words. Jessica also needed to hear this."

"Maybe she didn't need to hear that right now. Maybe she didn't like what was being asked of her. Maybe—"

"Warrior, this is not a conflict to stand and watch from afar," Naga said as firmly as Lanky had heard her. The shaman's steely eyes fixed first on Beth and then on him. "Would we stand on faraway mountains, casually observing the ravaging of our Land, the destruction of our peoples, our loved ones destroyed before our eyes?" Her eyes blazed with anger. "What then? We would be left standing there on our grand mountain, tears streaming down our faces, asking how could this happen? What could I have done? Many useless questions asked by those who do not take part, who do not put themselves in the stream of history. Bystanders hoping that others will guide their future for them."

Naga took a step forward, shaking her head. "No, our Land needs those few brave people who will step out of their safe places and come to life's aid, else there will be no safe, faraway hill to stand on."

She's right, Lanky thought. *Can't argue with that.* A slow clapping reverberated around the chamber. *Well, maybe someone can. That's taken the life out of the message.*

"Nice words, Naga," Beth said, her voice dripping with sarcasm. "And so how does that help us find Jessica?"

Sudden tiredness swept across the old woman's face. "Engage with your daemons," she said simply, holding Beth's glare. "Visit a Glade, as you have done before. I can aid you."

Lanky saw the earnest belief in her eyes. He walked over to Beth. "Much as I hate to agree," he said in a low voice, "she's right. We need to speak with them." *Speak with the damn wolf.*

Eyes still on Naga, Beth's jaw tensed. "Fine. Let's do it now."

*

With Naga and Bear sitting to one side, Lanky glanced at Beth, who was seated cross-legged in front of him, her Axe lying across her lap. "You ready?" Seeing Beth nod, Lanky reached out and held her hand. As Naga had described to him, he closed his eyes, settling his thoughts, and allowing his mind to sense the chamber around him, the sounds, the taste ... the energy.

A rich vibrancy flooded him, bringing a crispness to his thoughts, a sharpness to his senses. *This is my world*, he found himself thinking as he scanned the energy around him. He smiled as he saw a particular vibration, a subtle change in the energy's colour. *A Cord. A path to a Glade.*

'Here,' he said to Beth.

He felt her mind move with his—

He blinked.

He stood next to Beth atop a rocky crag bathed in a soft light. Beyond the limits of the dimly lit crag lay a deep darkness.

"Well, you know how to treat a girl," she said dryly.

Lanky glanced around the confines of the narrow crag. A Glade. A refuge from those of the Dark. Reached by a Cord.

Unease whispered its way through his soul. *I know this.*

But how?

"I saw what you did to get here," came Beth's calm voice beside him. "And as I watched, it seemed I'd always known what to do."

Lanky turned to her, seeing her dark eyes glimmering in the faint glow of the Glade. "In that moment, I just acted on instinct." *I knew how to connect with the Land's energy, how to wield it.* He glanced out into the gloom beyond the crag. "I spent years searching for Axes with a hidden power, but this?" He shook his head. "Nothing can prepare you for this. It feels like a dream."

Beth's face hardened. "It's real. Very real. And to find Jess, to get ourselves home, we have to engage."

Home. Lanky's gut wrenched as an image of his mum flashed into his mind. *She must be hurting. I just vanished from her life. I have to get back.*

"There's a familiarity here," Beth continued, "as though we've been here before. But we both know we haven't. So how do we know how to do these things we do?"

"Naga said that the daemons help us. Maybe this is their way?"

"They aid us, yes. Garrion has shown that. But beyond that?" She looked down at the glowing Axe in her hand, a steely look in her eyes. "It's us who somehow wield the energy of the Land. We need to figure out how to use what we've been given. Then we have to use it to do what needs to be done."

Lanky's disquiet deepened. *To do what needs to be done.* "Take care, Beth. Don't step too far before we understand more." *Before we understand more of these daemons. Of that damned wolf!*

And be careful of Bethusa, he almost said.

He felt an icy finger run down his back. *Why?*

Beth looked up, a fire burning deep in her eyes as they locked onto his. "We have no choice. We have to engage. How else do we get home? And while I can't fully trust Naga's actions, I believe much of what she says. I sense a threat to this Iyes tribe. I sense a threat to this Land." She hefted her Axe. "But while I believe we are Warriors, I agree, exactly what we do next isn't clear." Her eyebrows drew sharply together. "Aside from first finding Jess and recovering the Staff."

Lanky glanced at the Axe in his hand. Warriors? Saviours of this Land? A whisper of fear ran through him. Yet a subdued fear, a dampened fear. *You know she's right,* came a reluctant thought. *We are Warriors.* He pushed against it. *Maybe. Maybe not.* He felt a tingle in the haft of his Axe. *My Axe?* An unnerving certainty rippled through his mind. *Yes, my Axe.*

He grimaced. All was moving too fast. The Staff, the vicious wrenching from their own time, the Iyes, their capture by the Ka, the dragon, the daemons … *This energy rippling around me.* How could anyone stay sane under such an onslaught?

Hand clasped tightly around the Axe, he strove to calm his restless thoughts. *Focus.* Whatever else was happening, whatever Beth believed them to be, Jess was missing. They needed to find her. *Focus on that.*

His gaze settled back on Beth. "I know we have to engage. Just be careful."

"I'm always careful."

His eyes narrowed. "Of that, I'm not so sure."

A faint smile crossed her lips.

Girding himself, he looked out into the ether. "Okay, wolf," he growled. "Let's talk."

Beth frowned. "You really think that's the best way to start this?"

He shrugged. "How do you talk to a daemon? A foul, aggressive daemon?"

Beth shook her head in disgust. "Garrion," she called, her voice calm yet insistent. "We must speak with you. We need your help."

Lanky watched as Beth searched in vain in the surrounding darkness. "Ah, I see, so that's how you do it. Very good, I wish—" A shadowy hand came up and slapped him hard across his face. "Ow! That bloody hurt."

"A splendid effort, Warrior," chuckled a voice to the side.

Lanky turned to see the great white wolf staring at him.

"He deserved it," Beth muttered. "And this is no laughing matter."

"True, quite true, yet a little well-placed humour can serve useful at times. Especially when a great Warrior disappears."

"Good of you to turn up," Lanky grunted, rubbing his cheek. *How did she do that?* "And, since you clearly know that Jessica has gone, maybe you could tell us where she is."

"I could. But not yet."

"And why not?"

"To achieve what needs to be done, we must fully connect. Touch the diamond, Dysam."

Lanky scowled at the wolf. "Not bloody likely." *I don't trust you an inch, wolf.* He needed more time to figure out what he could do by himself, without getting caught in this beast's jaws. "Call Garrion again," he said to Beth. "It seems the wolf here is playing games."

"What do you think I've been doing? She's not answering."

"Ah," the wolf murmured. "That may be because I am blocking her arrival."

"What!" Lanky and Beth exclaimed together.

"Why would you do that?" Beth shouted.

"Because he's a devious bastard, that's why," Lanky said, glaring at the wolf. "So, you really are going to play this card? Force me to connect with you, else you won't talk?"

The wolf sauntered towards him, floating upwards as he did so, until his muzzle almost touched Lanky's face. His lips curled back, revealing razor-sharp fangs.

Lanky steeled himself and stood his ground. Then he bared his own teeth and leaned into the wolf. "Back off," he snarled. "Now."

The two glared at each other—

Lanky struck the wolf – hard. The result shocked him. The blow sent the wolf tumbling across the narrow ridge before coming to rest at the edge of the crag.

The wolf slowly stood, shaking himself. "I see you have progressed further than I imagined, Dysam. For that, I am glad. But our situation is unchanged. We cannot progress until you connect. Touch the diamond."

Scowling, Lanky strode towards the wolf.

"Lanky!"

He continued on.

"Lanky! You will hear me now!" Beth commanded, her voice echoing around the Glade.

He halted and slowly turned towards her.

"Let's talk," she said in a gentler voice – he suddenly found himself standing beside her. "And you stay there," she grated, turning to the wolf, who watched them from the far edge of the ridge.

Lanky eased his grip on the Axe. "Seems you've already got the hang of this place."

Beth frowned. "When I figure out how I'm doing this, I'll let you know." She glanced across at the wolf. "I know you don't trust him, but don't fight him. We need his help."

Lanky felt the hackles on the back of his neck rising. "I can't help it," he muttered. "He's an irritating bastard."

"But we need his help."

And there was another harsh reality. "I know," he muttered, "but whichever way we play this, I won't be consummating this relationship anytime soon."

"You need me, Dysam," the wolf snarled. "Touch the—"

"Stop calling me Dysam!" Lanky growled, anger surging. He stepped forward, brushing off Beth's restraining hand. "Who is this Dysam? Who is Bethusa?"

The massive white wolf raised his head, baring his fangs. "Ancient Warriors that you must release to do what must be done. They are needed here, not you. Touch the diamond!"

Formless dread rose. "What do you mean, ancient Warriors?"

The great wolf lowered his head and stalked towards him. "Release those who know what to do here, those who have lived and fought in this Land long before you. Release Dysam and allow him to the fore. Touch the diamond."

Lanky's chest tightened as his thoughts whirled around a cold knot of fear. Warriors from the past? Warriors within them? "No," he whispered. "That can't be."

The wolf stopped before him, fangs glistening with drool, fierce topaz eyes boring into his. "You are not needed. Release Dysam."

The beast's words exploded in his mind, and he staggered, blinded by a searing white light. As the blazing light faded, hazy, fractured images were left glowing in the darkness. Broken images of a savage battle on a windswept beach, of a marble temple lying on the fringes of a vast desert, of a …

"No!"

With ferocious anger sweeping through him, he spied a fiery Axe in his mind's eye. Grasping it, he swung it through the array of shimmering images – the vision shattered, scattering to the furthest reaches of his mind …

He found himself staring at Beth's strained face.

"Are you okay?" she said, reaching out and gently holding his shoulder. "What happened?"

"This beast plays games," he rasped. He brushed off her hand and stepped to the wolf. "Whoever, whatever, this Dysam is, that is not me. That will not be me. I am Lanky, no one else." He turned to Beth, his eyes burning. "And you are Beth."

She studied him for a moment. Then she nodded. "I am Beth."

The wolf let out a low growl. "You will fail. Touch the—"

Eyes wide, nostrils flared, and steam rising from her back, Garrion appeared. The great horse, a sheen of sweat glistening on her powerful black body, reared up in front of the wolf, then stamped down, narrowly avoiding crushing the daemon's head. "Impede me again, warg, and I will crush you to a pulp!" Garrion roared.

The wolf swung his massive head to the daemon. "A momentary delay only, my friend. I needed to speak with my Warrior alone."

"And as usual, warg," Garrion thundered, "you have the skills of a skunk in dealing with others."

"I—"

"Quiet!"

The wolf swung around and stalked off before dropping to his haunches a short distance away.

Lanky glanced at the wolf. *Warg? Yes, that suits this beast well.*

Garrion turned to Lanky, wildness in her eyes. "You have work ahead of you. Fen is impatient, but he has the same aim as us all – to defeat our Enemy."

His shoulders tense, Lanky gaze lingered on Fen, echoes of the stark visions he'd seen reverberating at the edges of his awareness. Maybe the warg had the same aim … *But maybe also others unseen.*

"And he is right," Garrion continued, wisps of steam swirling from her back. "To develop your strength, your skills, you and he must bond. But I see the trust is not yet there. Find a way to build it. We need you."

"Well, the warg's doing a great job so far," Lanky growled, casting a truculent glance to the wolf. Hardening his mind, he forced a brutal clarity to his thoughts. *Forget the warg, forget ancient Warriors. I am Lanky, no one else.*

Beth moved to his side. "Where's Jessica?" she said, looking up at Garrion.

A wave of distressed confusion swept over Lanky. The distress of Garrion. "What's happened?" he demanded.

Garrion's deep brown eyes flicked between them. "She spoke with Naga and chose to act, chose to fully connect with the Land. She entered the Sacred Chamber and called for us to attend. For this meeting, IY herself wished to attend. We daemons arrived first to prepare the way and make contact. But then ..." Garrion flicked her tail.

"Then what?" Beth grated.

"Then the Enemy broke through."

Beth gasped. "What! I thought the Sacred Site was protected!"

A deep growl came from Fen. "It was."

"Then how?"

"That is not clear," Fen grated, padding towards them.

Lanky quickly glanced at the massive wolf. Had there been an undertone to the warg's voice, or had he imagined it? "What happened to Jessica?" he demanded.

"She picked up an Axe and tried to attack us," Garrion replied. "Then she fled."

Lanky saw the wolf's eyes slide briefly to Garrion, then the wolf's louring gaze fell on him. The sense of something untold was raw. *This warg knows more than he's saying. What's going on here?*

"So, where did she go?" Beth said, a bite to her voice.

"It would seem she has travelled beyond our realm," Garrion answered. "Where to? That we cannot sense. I fear she has travelled far from this time."

"What!" Beth exclaimed.

"How did that happen?" Lanky rasped.

"Because you fail to do what is needed," the wolf growled. "You have to do better. Time is our enemy."

"Ignore him," Garrion said, moving closer. "I will tell you what we know ... and what we don't."

"Then talk," Lanky snapped.

A flare of true annoyance briefly flashed in Garrion's deep brown eyes, then was gone. "The Request made by the Mother of the Iyes calls four Warriors, each to be connected to the most powerful daemons of the day. And beyond this, unknown to any in the Land, the Request calls a fifth, the Staff Holder – the Guardian – one who is linked to IY herself."

"What!" Beth exclaimed. "That's some pretty valuable information there. A Guardian? And a link to your ancient god?"

"Our ancient god?" Fen muttered. "Fools."

"The Guardian holds the Staff," Garrion continued, "the Staff that has been lost."

Lanky spun around to face the daemon, a sudden connection hammering into his mind. "IY was arriving to meet Jess. IY was arriving to meet the Staff Holder."

"That is true. Your friend is the Guardian."

Beth gasped.

"She holds the Staff, she wields the Staff. It is she who brought you here."

Lanky glanced at Beth, who looked back at him in stark disbelief. He turned back to the daemon. "But how? How did she do that?"

"Because she is the Guardian," Fen growled.

"What the hell is the Guardian?" Lanky snapped.

"The one who walks the Continuum," Garrion said. "But in this moment, it is enough to know she wields the power of the Staff. She will be needed for what is to come. And she will be needed to get you home."

Lanky stared at the daemons, utterly bewildered. Jessica was this Guardian? "Does she know?"

"Of course not, you fool," Fen growled. "Do you not listen? She vanished before IY arrived. Ignorant children."

Scowling, Lanky stepped towards the wolf.

A rough hand pulled him back. "Where is she now?" Beth rasped by his side. "I thought we needed the Staff to travel out of here, and Jess didn't have it." Her thin brows knitted, and she glanced at the Axe in her hand. "Jess took an Axe. Is that how she did it?"

Neither Fen nor Garrion answered.

"Okay, smart-arse warg, where's your answer now?" Lanky growled, glaring at Fen.

"I can answer this in two ways," Garrion said, stepping between Lanky and Fen. "The first is to say the Axes do not allow travel from this realm. This is not their purpose. They serve to connect you with the daemons, enhancing your strength and skills in battle." Garrion paused, then: "How the Guardian travelled from here remains unknown." Lanky snorted. "But my belief is that she found her way back to her land and time."

"Your belief?" Lanky muttered. "I thought you were the all-mighty, all-knowing daemons? Where did that go?"

Fen let out a low growl.

"We live in our time," Garrion murmured, "and so cannot be all-knowing. We know what we know, and there remains much we don't." The daemon's sleek black head swung to Beth. "And the second answer I have for you is that you are mistaken in who took the Axe. The Axe was taken not by the Guardian, but by Revri, the one you know as River."

Lanky gaped at Garrion. *Revri? River?* "Why would River need an Axe?" But as soon as the words were spoken, he knew what the answer would be.

"She is my Warrior," came a new voice.

Lanky glanced around. He saw nothing beside them, but a movement above caught his eye. Glancing up, he saw a bird circling high above them, too distant to determine its size or type. "Who's that?"

"You'd see it for yourself, if you had my eyes," the wolf snarled.

Lanky scowled. Concentrating on the bird, he imagined flying beside it. The bird blurred, then snapped into focus, and he gazed upon a majestic eagle, its hooked yellow beak glowing against the dark ether as it soared effortlessly on wide-spanned wings, tipped out with rippling feather fingers.

"Greetings, Warrior," came a melodious voice. "I am Iolaire."

"River is a Warrior?" Beth said incredulously, staring up at Iolaire. "Why did no one tell us?"

"Did you ask?" Fen growled, his voice dripping with sarcasm.

"Did she know?" Lanky asked, pulling back from the soaring eagle.

"Did you?" Fen shot back. "Before you came here."

The memories of his home village flooded back. His mother, his friends, his simple life before being thrust to this place, this age. *I knew nothing of this.* His breath caught. *Except those voices …*

"I dreamt of these Axes," Beth said quietly. "Back in my time. Just dreams, I thought, but now …"

So not just me …

"No," Garrion said, swishing her tail, "you could not have seen this before. Not before your arrival. Not before you became Warriors. To preserve their safety, no Warrior is revealed – or made aware themselves – until such time they are needed. They remain hidden, out of sight of the Enemy, out of sight of us."

Lanky saw Beth glance at him. *There was something. We both experienced something connected to this world.* He looked back at the daemon. *But this one says that shouldn't have been possible.* The tension within him grew. *Too much, too fast.*

"Revri has been chosen," Garrion continued, "but there was no time to say her name. She will not—"

"Not true," came the voice of the eagle. "Revri touched the Axe. I spoke her name."

"Ah. Then there is a chance!"

"A chance indeed," Fen said, staring intently at Lanky.

Lanky caught again an undercurrent in the warg's voice. There was something else going on here. Something the warg held back unsaid.

"One Staff Holder, four Axes," Beth said by his side. "Then where is the fourth Warrior?"

"We have already explained, we do not know this until they are revealed. That is yet to be known by us all."

Garrion suddenly looked up. "We must leave now. We will consider what has happened here tonight."

"Hold on," Lanky hissed. "What about Jess? How do we find her? What do we need to do now?"

As the daemons faded, the barely audible voice of the warg drifted to Lanky. "Need my help, do you? You know what is needed, Dysam. Get started."

*

Naga waited while the Warriors regained awareness of their surroundings, then quickly moved to Beth's side. "Did you learn anything?" she asked, fearful of the answer.

"We learnt a lot – and we learnt nothing," Beth spat. "Did you know that River was a Warrior?"

Naga stifled a gasp. *A Warrior!*

"According to our daemon friends, River has now been chosen as a Warrior. Which unfortunately helps no one, as she's disappeared."

Naga thought furiously. Was this true? There were no stories of Warriors from the people of this Land. None. She sought to calm herself. Think. It was unexpected, but there was no reason this couldn't be so. Somehow holding her gaze steady, she turned to Lanky. "Did you hear the same?"

"We both heard the same. An eagle flies for her."

Iolaire, Naga breathed to herself. *One who is told to be steadfast and true.* She silently thanked IY – if River was truly a Warrior, a calm-headed influence was at her side.

"It might be good news for you to know another Warrior exists," Beth growled, "but we still don't know for sure where Jess and River went. Nor how they left here."

"The daemons did not know?"

"They think they travelled back to our land and time – but they don't know that for sure."

"Who was present at the gathering?"

"Daemons of the horse, eagle, and wolf spirits," Beth answered, glancing at Lanky.

She is wise to hold back their names. Rightly cautious. She rubbed the bracelet on her wrist, uneasy. These daemons they spoke of were formidable allies of IY, but while the Warriors could travel the pathways of the vast Continuum, she suspected the daemons could not – if Jessica and River had left the Land, none could truly know where they had gone.

Bear shifted from his position by the wall, where he'd been quietly listening. He spoke, his voice grave. "There's no hiding from the difficulty we face, Mother. Four warriors revealed, yet two now displaced. And the Staff out of our hands. We—"

"More difficult than that," Lanky said with a scowl. "River is a Warrior but may not realise it, and these daemons say Jessica isn't a Warrior holding an Axe, but the Guardian, the Staff Holder. But she doesn't know that either."

For the second time during their telling, Naga struggled to hold the shock from her face. A Guardian? What was this? This was something she had never heard.

With an immense force of will – the will of the Mother of the Iyes – she calmed herself, quickly searching for the truth behind this new knowledge. *A Guardian ... One holding the Staff ... Our Story tells of the Staff providing control.* Quiet hope eased into her heart. *This Guardian could be the one to provide that control.* If so, the Light had chosen well in Jessica.

And yet her nascent hope was tempered by frustration. *Why does our Story not tell of this Guardian?* This seemed another gap in their knowledge. Had it been lost over the millennia, or was it never told? *Or has it been kept from me?* Feeling the eyes of the Warriors on her, she cast the disturbing worries aside. *IY will tell each of us what we need to know and hide what should be hidden.* She settled herself, choosing her words carefully. "It is good to know," she said evenly. "IY has chosen wisely."

Lanky ran his hand through his tousled hair. "So how will Jessica get back? That's if she wants to come back," he added in worried tone. "She wasn't particularly taken with this place."

"While we're here, she will want to get back," Beth said fiercely. "And return with River. No matter how terrifying this is to her."

"Beneath her fear lies a powerful woman," Naga said. "She will strive to return."

"If she can," Lanky said, scratching his head and walking a few paces away.

Which brings me to a question I dared not ask before. "Were you in contact with daemons in your own world?"

Lanky frowned. "We knew nothing before we arrived here. Daemons? Many people have their beliefs and their gods – and their daemons – but, for better, or for worse, we didn't."

And now a most important question. "Do animals of the daemons exist in your world?"

Lanky considered for a moment. "Horses, wolves, eagles … I guess there will be many differences, but yes, they are there."

And so, their spirits and daemons should remain. "Which of your tribes converse with the daemons?"

Lanky glanced at Beth, clearly looking for her to answer.

Beth shrugged. "In our day-to-day lives, few. Some cultures revere the animal world, but I guess for many, they link their religion to human prophets or sages – not animal ones."

"Hmm, interesting that, if you stop to think about it," Lanky said wryly. "Maybe because humans talk with other humans and generally not, day-to-day, with animals? Humans set the tone, the narrative – the influence. Animals? So long as they're cuddly and cute, taste good, or fit nicely in a zoo, then we'll accept them. The rest, forget it, got more important things to be doing, like chopping down some more forest. That author was right, some are more equal—"

"And this is all very well and good," Beth interrupted, glaring at him, "but this is helping us how?"

"Well," began Naga, "what we cannot deny is that a power exists in your time. The Staff of IY was in your land. Warriors were chosen and sent here." Her fingers caressed her bracelet. "You may not have been aware of it, but the fact you could leave your land tells us that IY's power must still be present. Do you agree?"

She saw the Warriors glance at each other, and then Lanky nodded. "It tells us some power could move us here, I agree."

"Then if the daemons are right that Jessica and River left for your time, we can hope they will be aided in their efforts to return."

Lanky rubbed his chin. "You argue that there's still a power in our time, but maybe it's all contained in this artefact, the Staff. And that's here. There may be no link left back to this age."

"But Jessica travelled back home," Beth said, frowning. "Surely that shows something – some power – exists on the other side?"

"Not necessarily. What if … what if, with the Staff lost, its pull on us is gone, and we each end up heading back where we started? Possible, yes?" No one answered. "And remember, we don't actually know where she's gone – she may not be home at all."

As a silence fell, Naga knew she could not allow it to linger. *Else insidious doubts may blind them to what must be done.* "We must leave the daemons to find a way to locate Jessica. And we must trust in Jessica. If she is this Guardian chosen by IY, then she *will* find a way to return." She considered them in turn. "It is a desperate situation, but the daemons are correct; we had already decided what to do – go north to recover the Staff. Two Warriors remain, and willing, able people from the tribe. For us, and for you, recovery of the Staff is of utmost importance, and I do not believe we should change from this path."

Lanky stood and paced across the chamber. "And if Jessica returns while we're travelling?"

"Then I'd be thrilled," Beth said without hesitating. "But I agree that we can't hang about here waiting. From what I've seen, this Enemy of the Iyes is moving fast. And outsmarting us. That has to stop. We must move."

Lanky's eyes narrowed. "As I keep saying, take care, Beth. One step at a time."

"And the first step is to retrieve that Staff."

He studied her for a moment – then nodded.

Naga's eyes lingered on Beth. *She said the Enemy is outsmarting 'us'. She draws closer to our cause.* She glanced across at Bear and gave a slight nod of her head.

Bear stepped forward. "We should return to the upper chamber. We can begin our planning now." Joined by Amber, the two walked out into the passageway.

Lanky crossed to Beth's side, and they spoke briefly in quiet tones before they too left the chamber.

Alone, Naga's gaze settled on the sole remaining Axe. River, a Warrior? This was unexpected – and troubling. Not because IY had chosen a skilled Iyes like River – though young and unprepared, in some ways she had an advantage over the others from another time, as she understood the Land and the threat to it and its people. No, what was now unknown were the ramifications that may come from a transfer of life from this world to that of the Warriors. For, unlike the Warriors, who knew what lay ahead, that future world was unknown to River. *She will see her future. She will see what is to be.* And if she returned – when she returned – would her path be changed by what she experienced there? And if so, how would that impact the Continuum? What might happen to that future beyond their time? This was one more task added to their burden. On River's return, they would have to assess her intentions quickly.

Her gaze refocussed on the remaining unclaimed Axe. *If Jessica doesn't hold an Axe, then one Warrior remains to be revealed.* Pulling her thoughts from that unknown, she made her way out of the chamber. *Keep a focus on what's in front of us, and hope these Warriors prove worthy.*

II. TREACHERY

CHAPTER SIXTEEN

Ereboz grew in strength, yet still the Shade resisted;
but it was a solitary battle, one unwitnessed by most.

Spider was enjoying his dream, delighting in the soft and intriguing caresses from River as she lay beside him. She snaked her fingers along his upper arm and face, smiling seductively as she leaned in closer to his face. Her mouth reached his ear, and he felt the soft brush of her breath and then her whispering: "Wake up, you fool, it's a snake!"

His eyes shot open, but he remained stock-still.

The cold, slow slithering of a snake brushed the side of his face, its triangular head rising up and to the right. *Keep still*, he thought. *That's easy for you to say*, he answered himself. The snake's head swung around, and one of its beady eyes seemed to look straight through him. He could see the zigzag pattern further down its back. A rare snake this far north. But rare or not, it was here. And deadly.

He focussed on his breathing – slowly in, slowly out. The snake turned away, and its body rippled across his face. *That's it, keep moving that way – nothing to eat here.* The unnerving weight of the snake diminished as it slipped onto the ground. He waited several anxious heartbeats, then slowly lifted his head; the snake had disappeared from view. Carefully, he manoeuvred himself onto his side and saw it slithering away into the undergrowth. Blowing a sigh of relief, he pulled himself up to sit on his haunches. Not a wake-up he'd wished for. *But it was a pleasant dream!*

Looking around, he realised that the sun was already above the horizon. *Looks as though I slept a little longer than planned.* After the excellent progress he'd made so far on his journey south to meet Rind at the main camp, he wanted to keep up the pace. Rind needed to know of the Warriors' arrival.

He stood and stretched and looked again at the surrounding landscape. In the distance, gently rolling hills swept down to the wide river valley before him. His gaze followed the valley to the west, where it opened out into a vast, wide plain. A day beyond lay the western Canyon and then the plateau land before the Great Sea. The land of their great allies, the Islanders. The land of his father. *I remember his stories.*

And the Islanders. It was said the plateau had once been an island, in a time when the ice lay further north. *But not today.* Today only a deep canyon remained, separating the Islanders' land from that of the Iyes's.

He looked longingly to the west. It had been over five sun-cycles since the tribe had visited the western coast and its great people. A warm and engaging people to their friends, but an unyielding and savage people to their enemies. He had cherished memories of the times the Iyes had spent there – a beautiful time of his youth when, unaware of the growing concerns of the elders, he was able to play, hunt, and study with few worries. He hoped with all his heart to travel that way again.

And with River at my side.

He sighed. But that was for another day. He turned back to the southeast and picked out the northern peak of the far hills. His goal for the day.

*

Spider had eaten and now sat with his back against the gentle curve of a lichen-covered boulder, humming to himself as he took a moment to enjoy the evening sky, richly painted by the last light of the sun as it descended below the horizon. The temperature was dropping fast, but the glowing fire by his side warmed him. Several horses grazed in the distance, and he could hear squirrels scampering in the trees behind him, where also a bird refused to cease her evening song as though she could hold the sun in the sky a heartbeat longer.

The bird's song gave him comfort – she had seen no threats. And he had seen no evidence of predators here. Although wolves were a constant presence, they kept their distance from humans – and from fire. Cave bears were unlikely to roam in this area and preferred their own green diet to him. And he hadn't seen a cave lion for a long time and was unlikely to do so, as they would have retreated further north.

His fire would keep all but the most desperate away, and he'd cooked no meat, so offered no alluring smells to attract unwanted attention.

Unwanted. Now there was a conundrum. Both the lion and the bear were unwanted by many, but both were beautiful creatures, grown and nurtured by the land, perfectly in tune with their environment, perfectly adapted to the colder climes of their hunting territory.

And both precious parts of IY's realm.

A memory of his first hunting trip drifted into his mind. It had been winter, and a strong northerly had been blowing. Travelling from the south along a ridge, the lead hunter, a young Bear, had signalled a halt – and for silence. Bear had then gestured to Spider, signalling him forward. Creeping slowly along the ridge, he'd reached Bear, then, eyes moist with the biting wind, he'd peered ahead. Only a spear's throw away were two powerfully built animals with pale fur and faint stripes along their backs. Approaching against the wind, the cave lions had not detected them. One stood proudly, looking to the west as though surveying its land in the valley below; the other, leaner and sharper-faced, lay at its side, cleaning its tufted tail.

The larger lion had then turned and looked directly at Spider, who froze, trapped in the animal's icy gaze. The leaner lion stood, nuzzling into its partner, who lifted its head and emitted a low growl. Both animals then turned and sauntered away, disappearing from view to the right.

"You can release my arm now, Spider," Bear had said. He'd released his tight grip and taken a deep breath. "Remember this sight," Bear had continued. "You won't get many sights of this animal – and soon it's likely no one ever will."

Sitting here now, Spider understood Bear's words more clearly. The peoples of the Land were continually growing in numbers and expanding their territories. *Bad news for those who get in our way.* Including some humans. Naga's ancestors had almost been wiped out by a degree of intolerance, mistrust, and misunderstanding that was difficult to comprehend. *By our own kind!* Could people not see that they shared an ancestor who must weep at her legacy? What were her sons and daughters doing to themselves?

But he did understand.

Detested it but understood.

He understood the myriad of individual thoughts, pains, stresses, hungers, and joys that drove people into very different choices. Choices that were driven by survival for them and their children. Choices made understanding little of the consequences but driven by the necessity of the moment. Each incremental step having little local impact, no apparent immediate consequence; each step benefiting the individual and his tribe; each step continued by generations with growing benefit to the tribe and his people.

But over time, and when made by many? Well, then a growing litany of victims – forgotten victims – never to be remembered, discarded by the wayside by the relentless onward march of people.

His face taut with the tension of his thoughts, he forced himself to relax. *Break out of it, Spider. You said you weren't a worrier. It's not all bad.*

That was true. His tribe, and many others, taught their young well. There were many great and smart people who would work to prevent humans making these mistakes in the future, and to teach others to live sensibly together with all peoples. *Understanding each other would be a good start.*

He sighed. *Focus on what you can control right now.*

Like River?

Yes. Sleep with dreams of River was what was needed right now. He yawned. He would sleep well tonight—

He froze.

He listened.

Yes, there it was again. A voice.

Rising, he reached for his spear, then glided into the cover of a stand of trees – shrouded in darkness but keeping the fire in sight. The voice drifted across to him, sometimes seeming loud, sometimes very quiet.

And now some snippets of sense – of a sort.

"Definitely a fire we could see from afar. Making it up, you said. But see – there is the smoke. Most definitely a fire." Incoherent mutterings followed. *Two people or more?* The voice slowly became louder. "There. We told you. There it is. No smoke without a fire. What did we say? But no fire without people. Not that fire. No, no. So where are the people?"

A man carrying a pack and holding a spear slowly walked into Spider's view. He was dressed in close-fitting, multicoloured garments, the jacket a patchwork assortment of pelts, and his light leg-coverings bound in places with leather ties. His silvery-grey hair was drawn back and tied behind his head, a neatness matching the trim of his grey beard. As the man came closer, Spider saw that he looked a fair age.

The man walked right up to the fire.

"Recently lit is that fire. Particularly appetizing on this cold evening. It would be good to stay here for the night – if you would have me, my friend," the man said, turning to look directly at Spider.

Very good eyesight for an old man, Spider thought, stepping out from the shadows, his spear in hand. He approached the figure cautiously, scanning the area for others. He stopped and studied the man, noting his relaxed posture, but also the keen intelligence in the man's eyes. *What do we have here?* "Good evening to you," he said, keeping his voice light. "Where are your companions?"

"Companions? We have no companions. No. No. No companions. Just us."

Spider looked into the man's face. It was a face that had seen many sun-cycles and looked like the leather on his boots. It didn't seem an unfriendly face, but in these times, enemies could take many forms. "I thought I heard you talking to others – I may, of course, be mistaken?"

The old man smiled. "A simple set of words. But was it a statement or a question? Or maybe a challenge? What do we think?" He tilted his head. "We think it depends on how the receiver receives it. We think it was a statement, and you were indeed mistaken. Maybe we are correct?"

"Maybe you are indeed," Spider replied, eyeing the man cautiously. What *did* he have here? At the very least a distraction. But what else? He tightened the grip on his spear. "Where are you heading?" he asked in an even voice.

"Many questions he has, hasn't he? And before we have even been introduced. A cautious man. He doesn't seem a threatening man, does he?" The old man glanced at Spider's spear. "Are you a threatening man, my friend?"

"I try not to be," Spider said. "But on occasion it has, unfortunately, been known."

"Oh dear. We wouldn't want that, would we? No, no. Maybe we should ask him a question. Maybe: Where are you going? It would seem fair to some, given he asked it of us. But maybe this would not be wise. No, I think this is the best." And the man whistled.

Spider heard a noise behind him and whirled around, cocking his spear.

"Steady, my friend. It is only Streak. Not a companion. No, no. The answer was honest. No, Streak is a loyal friend."

Spider's heart hammered in his chest as he watched an enormous black wolf pad around him, then cross to the old man, who received it on bended knee and outstretched arms. "Streak likes us, and we like Streak," the old man said, hugging the wolf's head.

But Spider doesn't like Streak, Spider thought with growing unease as he lowered his spear. *This could be tricky to get out of.*

The man looked up. "We hope you see that we mean you no harm. No harm at all. No, no. We wouldn't want to harm you. Or anybody." He slowly climbed to his feet. "But you can see, we hope, that if harm was meant – and we don't, no we don't – you wouldn't have seen the harm coming?"

Seen it? I'd no idea that the beast was there. "I saw it," he lied, glancing at the massive wolf, whose deep yellow eyes were now trained on him. "I wanted to see what your next move would be."

"Hmm, an interesting man we have. He appears a very trustworthy man, one we think would always speak truths. Yes. We don't believe this to be a man who would ever lie to us."

Spider inwardly squirmed.

"I think we will answer his question. We are seeking the tribe of IY. Do you know of it?"

Spider felt a sudden compulsion to answer the man's question. "I believe that tribe lies to the south of us," he said. "In fact, I seek that tribe myself." He suppressed a gasp as the words left his mouth. *What are you saying? Don't say any more.*

The old man's eyes narrowed slightly. "Do you indeed? Do you? Well, this is a fortuitous encounter. Who would have thought, in a land this great, we would meet another on the same mission as us? Extraordinary. We wonder why you would want to seek this tribe yourself."

This time, Spider heard the subtle change in the man's tone and became acutely aware of the wolf's eyes boring into him. *This man is a shaman. A most clever shaman.* He focussed his mind, closing his thoughts as Naga had taught him. "It won't prevent a shaman entering your mind," she had said, "but it will make it more obvious if they do." He forced a smile he didn't feel. *Tell him nothing more.* "So here we are again, at an exchange of questions."

"Will he ask us the same question? Will he, we wonder?"

"Why not?" Spider said, smiling. "What interest do you have with this tribe?"

"He did. He did," the man said, grinning gleefully. "He asked us the same question." He tilted his head. "Maybe we both agree not to answer. Would that be best, we wonder?" The old man glanced to the fire. "Could we rest awhile? Streak may not be weary, but we are."

That was not a question, Spider thought grimly. *What choice, but to play along for now?* He forced another smile. "I think it's best that we both sit and have a drink. That might give us both a chance to talk a little more. My name is Fly."

"Fly. Fly. Don't let the spider catch the Fly," the old man said, sitting down. "We thank you, Fly, for your generosity in sharing your fire. And our name is Growl. It is a good name. An easy name for Streak to remember. And we most look forward to our drink."

You might, Spider thought, walking across to his pack, then reaching for his water skin. *But not me.* Licking his dry lips, he took a short draught of water, then glanced to the man, Growl, who had squatted and sat cross-legged by the fire, his wolf at his side. Who was this man – this shaman – who searched for the Iyes? Friend or foe? Neither trusted the other, so that might not be easy to find out. *Best I move on as soon as I can.* Fear stirred. *If I can …*

*

A while later, Spider sat, his thoughts miserable. He had shared a drink and a little of his food with the man, and endured his constant wittering, but Growl showed no signs of leaving.

"You are most kind. The kindest of flies we have known. Oh yes. The kindest fly."

Spider glanced up. "You're welcome," he said, keeping his tone neutral.

"And we feel welcome, we do," Growl said jovially, gently stroking the wolf's head. "Not everywhere are we welcomed. We wonder whether it is the gentle old man or the terrifying wolf that keeps the welcome at bay?"

My guess is both. You would talk yourself out of any welcome you received. "I wouldn't know," Spider replied evenly.

Growl laughed. "We think you would if you were a spider – the spider usually outwits the fly, you know. Skill and patience can catch the most energetic of flies. Oh yes. An intelligence of sorts."

What game is he playing? "Yes," Spider replied, cautiously, "I think I was well-named Fly, as I am easily outwitted. But I've often found those thought to be intelligent look quite the same when waiting to be buried."

The old man laughed again. "Yes. So true! Dead, we are all suddenly brought down to the same height – except those with the bigger bellies. Maybe it is the lovers of food, whose great stomachs tower over their prone colleagues, who have finally reached the greatest heights? Could this be a new religion? We could become the priest of the stoutness religion, leading our followers in orgies of feasting, all offerings to the gods diverted and eaten by us to appease the Tubby God! The High Priest position taken by the widest girth." He sniggered. "We think it would force us to lead a counterreligion bowing to the Skinny God. Yes, and we would be High Stick, leading our followers in pursuit of absolute thinness. Most easy to bury too."

I have to lose this madman as soon as possible.

Growl's voice lowered, and his brow creased. "But in our poor travels, we have seen many religions and cults, and it has been difficult to see their benefit to the mothers, fathers, and children to whom they preach. Little in common with our own simple ideas, oh no, rather much to the High Grandness and their council. Little else. The last thing I would want is to create a new burden for the people."

What was that? A slip? A slight dropping of a mask? Or something else? The man had a rambling style and referred to himself in the plural, a habit Spider wouldn't raise to this unpredictable madman. *But he used 'I' there.* He glanced up at the old man, who was now staring ahead, whistling to himself. "I'm sorry," Spider said in an easy voice. "I'm moving early in the morning and was about to sleep when you arrived. I hope you don't mind," *and I don't care if you do,* "but I'll ready myself now."

"No. No," he exclaimed. "Prepare away. Prepare yourself all you need and want." He patted the wolf. "In fact, we were going to prepare ourselves too. Yes, we were."

Spider gritted his teeth in the shadowy darkness. *He's not going to move on. Sleep and nighttime exit, I think.* "That's good," Spider said, his voice calm. "I'll move to the side of the fire by the trees, and you're welcome to sleep where you are."

"That is most kind of you. Most kind. We are light sleepers and will keep this fire tended as we can."

I think I'll be a light sleeper tonight too. "Well, goodnight," Spider said, starting to rise.

"Yes, yes … and, tomorrow, it seems, we are travelling together to the same destination."

Spider froze. *I'm heading there. You don't know where it is.*

"At least, you are heading there," Growl said, his piercing eyes locking onto Spider, "and given we don't know the way, we would like to accompany you."

Spider sat back down, his worst fears realised. *He knows I know the way.* Cold resolve rose, born of the visceral need to protect his tribe, his family. *Accompany me? No. That's not going to happen.* The flickering light of the fading fire caught the man's sharp eyes. *What is his game?* "You didn't say why you wanted to find this tribe?" he said, an edge to his voice.

"And we are quite sure we didn't hear this from you. Did we miss this part somewhere?"

"And so, it appears our drinks didn't loosen our tongues."

Growl smiled. "It seems not."

Spider's patience was worn thin. *Forget this nonsense. Leave him tonight.* He smiled. "It seems that we both respect each other's privacy, and you've been an ... intriguing guest for the evening. Let us travel together tomorrow and test each other's company. If we are still agreeable tomorrow evening, we shall continue. If not, then I can provide directions for you, and we shall continue as we were." *But I will be long gone by then.*

"Delightful!" Growl replied. "You see, Streak. We told you this was an honourable man."

Spider stood and brushed himself down.

"And Streak," the old man said, "make sure you guard this man's camp during the night. We don't want anyone moving around in the dead of night, do we? Oh no, we don't need that." The man looked up at Spider, smiling. "Streak here could spot a fly at a thousand paces. You can sleep well, my friend. Sleep well."

*

Feigning sleep, Spider tensed as he heard the soft rustle of a leaf as someone moved quietly towards him. So, his guest was making his move. Eyes still closed, he reached for his blade—

"Awaken, my fly," came Growl's urgent whisper. "We have new visitors."

Opening his eyes, Spider peered up into Growl's shadowy face and blinked, trying to clear his thick head. "Where?" he whispered, sitting up and looking around the firelit glade.

"Over there. Very close. They are here to kill. We must hide, and then strike." Growl pulled away and dashed out of the light of the fire, disappearing into the shadows.

Spider silently pulled himself up into a crouch and listened. He heard nothing.

He cursed under his breath. Could he believe this troubling stranger?

And then he heard it, the softest brush of feet through the depths of the wood. *Cautious traveller or silent enemy?* A stark memory flashed back. Of a game he'd played as a child: friend or foe? He grimaced. It was a game he should play now to flush out the truth. He crept out of the gloom of the trees and made his way cautiously to the edge of the firelight. Then he stood and waited, his back to the approaching visitors.

As he had as a child.

The adult would approach with stealth from behind. But approaching with a bowl of food, or carrying a rock, or a weapon?

Therein lay the game. Were the movements of a friend or foe? A slow or quick approach? Soft steps or confident, heavy steps? A natural gait, or too slow or too fast? Any evidence from breathing? Over time, no one could fool him – only Bear.

He shook off the thoughts. *Forget the past. Focus!*

Moments later, he heard footsteps approaching the clearing.

Cold calmness swept over him.

Soft footsteps continued into the clearing.

Cold beads of sweat formed on his brow.

The man behind paused, then Spider heard the faintest whisper of movement—

He dived to the ground, and as he fell, he heard the whistling of a projectile overhead, then a thud as it hit a tree. Rolling, he sprang up and sprinted back into the cover of the trees. A scream came from behind him, and he curved his run to the right, arcing back around towards the source of the anguished cry.

He slowed, then dropped, crouching low behind a tree as the screams continued ahead. Calming his breathing, he waited. The intruder's entry into camp had been slow and cautious – but *too* cautious. They had continued their approach beyond the point a simple traveller would have stopped, either turning away because they disliked the look of the person by the fire or stopping and hailing him to avoid triggering an unwanted reaction. He'd moved just in time. *But if that had been Bear, I'd now be dead.*

The screaming stopped and only the sound of sporadic gurgling could be heard. Tensed against all movement, he held his position. He heard the gurgling die down ... and then it fell quiet.

He waited.

And waited.

Then, over to his left, he made out the smallest of movements. Someone – or maybe more than one – was slowly working their way towards him. *Krez! Have they seen me?* He tried to calm already afire nerves. If he stayed where he was, he might catch a spear in his neck before he could move. *Think! It's my move again.* Catching glimpses of movement nearby, he made his decision. He needed to flush them out.

Hesitating only a heartbeat, he lay on the ground, then readied himself to play the next deadly charade. *No time to waste. Just do it!* He drew a steadying breath, then: "No!" he cried out. "Please no. You've killed my friend. What do you want with me? Don't kill me."

He heard a rustling, then saw a shape moving towards him. "Excellent work, Brag," the shape said as it came closer.

"No! Please no!" Spider shouted as the shape approached.

"Brag?"

All the muscles in Spider's body tensed.

A shadowy figure came into view, a spear cocked and ready to strike. "What the—"

Spider was already moving, rolling and springing to his feet, his own spear thrusting towards the man—

A snarling beast sprang out of the shadows, hammering into the unknown attacker, sending him sprawling to the ground. Streak pounced on the stricken man, biting for his throat. But the man was clearly strong; he heaved the wolf off him and scrambled to his feet, facing the animal.

I hate doing this. Spider leapt forward and hammered the spear into the side of the man's neck. The man screamed and dropped to the ground.

Streak moved in.

I don't need to see this.

He staggered back through the trees towards the fire. The old man appeared to his right from the shadows. Ignoring him, Spider grabbed his water skin in a shaking hand, then drank deeply. The old man walked across to his sleeping area beside the fire, then sat down without saying a word. *At least he's quiet for once,* Spider thought, attempting to restopper his skin with trembling hands. Once done, he sat, head in hands, shivering despite the heat of the fire.

The sickening sounds in the trees slowly died, and a deep silence fell.

After a while, with a warmth returning to his body, if not his soul, Spider glanced over at the old man. Growl. The one who had saved them. "How did you know they were coming?" he breathed. *Because he's a shaman,* he answered silently.

"We didn't know," Growl answered. "But Streak, he knew. Oh yes, nothing can creep up on old Streak."

"Then how did he know?"

"Old Streak has many eyes, don't you, my friend," Growl said, patting the dripping fur of the enormous beast, who had just loped back into camp. It seemed the beast had washed himself in a nearby stream, as there were no remnants visible from his grisly work.

Cool numbness settled on him. Taking a life was never easy. *It's why I'm a scout, I guess, and not a fighter.* Some might say that made him a coward, but he was past any guilt on this, and knew he was valued for his role in the tribe. *But I can't escape the realities of life.* The reality was that there were people who wished to prey on other people, to dominate, subjugate, and enslave. *Like the Ka, and those tribes that choose to fight for them.* And for him, the taking of someone's freedom was the worst crime that one could commit and needed to be resisted immediately. With force. These people didn't engage in parlay, and if they did, it was mostly subterfuge to strengthen their hand before their next brutal move. They had to be met by uncompromising resistance; failure to do so would allow a continued expansion of a despot's rule. *And yet ...* The last sounds of the dying man came back into his mind. *And yet this will never get easier.*

He glanced at Growl. "Who are they?"

"For that, we will need to examine their bodies. But from their movements, we believe they are scouts attached to the Kutr."

The Kutr. A tribe he knew, and one under the influence of the Enemy. But if these were indeed scouts of that tribe, they'd worked extremely well to have progressed so far without his own tribe's network picking them up. *Like those Ka who attacked the Arrival site*, he thought, recalling the terror of their ancient enemy's appearance. "Are these the only ones seen?"

"It appears so ..." The old man studied Spider for a moment. "But we believe these two had you in their sights, yes, indeed."

The night air seemed suddenly colder. "And why do you think that?"

"We think that, because he thinks that," Growl replied, pointing at the wolf drying by the fire. "His friends tracked these men for several days. Only over the last day did they meet another and then deviate this way. We did not know this was their destination for sure. But now we do."

Spider regarded the man in silence, seeing a strain on the man's face. Here was a conundrum. *Do I believe this man?* If so, then the Enemy had pushed far more fighters north than had been known, including skilled hunters. Or had the man in his midst now become a very dangerous part of the threat?

"If we were you," Growl continued, "a great suspicion would now be upon us. But please remember, we alerted you to this threat, and aided you in dealing with it. These men might have killed us all, were it not for Streak."

Maybe. But you know more of them than you've told. "Why were Streak's friends tracking them? And how did Streak find out about these men?"

The old man glanced at the massive wolf. Streak growled, holding the man's gaze for a few moments. Growl turned his attention back to Spider. "It seems Streak places a trust in you. Even so, we cannot fully answer you. Our words are for the tribe of IY and must only be heard by them."

Then while you say your wolf trusts me, my trust is not so easily gained.

Growl seemed to wait for a response, but when nothing came, he shrugged. "If it is to remain this way, my fly, so it shall remain. But as our furred friend here respects the fly, we will offer an answer in part. Distance is no barrier to my friend here, and the wondrous realm of wolves is wide. They travel far, travel well, and they travel silently. Streak carries a deep respect within his cadre of friends, and so they help him wherever and whenever they can. Report interesting movements, shall we say." Growl smiled. "We did say it, and so it is said. This was one such movement and report."

Spider glanced across at the wolf. Was this possible? They accepted within their tribe that Naga had an ability to seek afar, bringing early news of distant events. But the ability of this wolf? This would be something new to him and would indicate a daemon presence.

His gaze shifted to Growl's weathered face. *So what to believe?* On the face of it, Growl had indeed saved their lives. But trust him? No. That couldn't be. But he now had a problem. "Someone has been tracking my movement – or yours. We can't stay here, and I can't sleep anyway. We need to move."

Streak growled.

Growl smiled. "It seems that particular problem has been solved. The tracker will track no more."

"Streak's friends?"

Growl nodded. "It seems we can move unhindered for now. But given it is a while before the sun rises from her sleep, might we suggest we remain here and rest? It would be a shame to waste this fire. And you may not need sleep, but we feel most weary, yes, we do. Rest would be welcome."

Spider looked over at the wolf, now lying beside the fire, eyes closed. "The bodies will attract other unwanted guests here."

"Don't worry, our friend dragged them to the stream. Nature will deal with them from there."

Spider grunted.

"And rest assured, my fine fly, Streak is not one to let visitors arrive unchallenged. He combines his rest with a striking awareness of the potential for mischief. We are safe … for now."

Spider held Growl's gaze, and inwardly cursed. A shaman and a wolf. Not company he needed, but there was no easy way out. These two would be by his side whether he left or stayed. He wrapped a hold on his fear. He'd felt no further pressure on his mind from the old man, and it didn't seem they were planning his immediate demise. His thoughts focussed onto his only option. Daylight would bring a chance to examine the bodies, to understand who was tracking them. *And to understand more of who I have here.*

He sighed. "Fine. You rest. I'll take the watch until dawn, and then we move." He stood and walked over to his pack, grasping the spear which lay beside it. Moving over to the far side of the fire, he muttered to himself, "And this dawn can't come fast enough."

CHAPTER SEVENTEEN

The Continuum. Am I surprised the Iyes retained this in their Story when its immense reality lay beyond them? No. IY taught them well.

"Well, that's you set." Shorty tightened the shoulder strap of Beth's pack. "We're good to go, Bear," he shouted, turning away to put on his own bulkier pack.

"Excellent," Bear said, strapping a jacket to his own pack. He stood, wiping his brow despite the coolness of the dawn air. "Okay, say your goodbyes. Let's get some distance today while the weather is good."

Lanky walked over to Beth and smiled. "You look fully loaded there. You sure you don't need a little more to carry?"

She grimaced. "Don't go there. Compared with some, I'm carrying nothing. It doesn't seem fair." She looked over his shoulder. "But I guess I'd struggle with the weight of those other packs right now."

Lanky glanced across to where Knuckles stood beside two tall, lithe men, their long, dark hair waving in the light breeze. He recognised the twins, Dune and Scorpion. On the ground beside them lay two bulging packs. "Yeah, those look heavy. What's in them?"

"Mix of extra supplies they want to take. Dried foods mainly, but also rope, some extra tools – things like that." Beth touched the pack on her back. "We're carrying our own weapons and basic kit, like the light fishing net and dried food, but given where we're heading, they want to take the extra rations."

Lanky saw that strapped to the side of the packs were glistening bone- or antler-handled blades of various designs, a hunting bow, and at least one green-stone spear-thrower. *Things I've only seen in a museum – but weapons that are vital for their survival.*

He watched as the twins spoke a few unheard words before embracing then parting with warm smiles – yet with clear tension in their frames. Scorpion and Knuckles hefted their packs onto their backs, set their straps, then walked over to join Bear. Dune's gaze lingered on his brother for a moment, then he made his way to the group beside Naga. Lanky's gut twisted. *This is now real for us all. This is happening.*

He turned back to Beth. Despite the tension in the air, he smiled. "Axe over your shoulder, spear in one hand, daggers on the belt – a knife in your mouth, and you'd be truly armed to the teeth."

"Always be prepared," Beth said, brushing a strand of hair behind her ear.

He believed that she always was. "Do you still have the sketch of Mount Hope we drew?"

She tapped the upper part of her tunic. "It's in here." He saw stitches on the outside of the tunic, sealed with some form of wax where the pocket must be sewn. Beth half smiled. "And if we somehow manage to find it, I'll need to pickpocket the lair of a dragon."

Lanky couldn't help himself. "You little thief."

She tilted her head, brow furrowing. "Still this mindless game of yours?"

He shrugged. "Nervous. Can't help it." He glanced around, seeing the others ready to move out. He looked back to Beth. "I just hope the call to head up the western route is the right one. From what I remember, it can get pretty rugged along there."

"It is, but Bear says its advantage is food supply versus the inland route. I bow to his wisdom."

"They understand this place much better than us." His face darkened. "They're aiding us, more than can be said for our other friends. Have you made contact?"

She shook her head.

"Damn these daemons," he muttered, shaking his head.

"Watch your tongue, Warrior," Bear growled, standing beside Naga. He held up his hand as Lanky protested. "Take care with your language. You are now connected to power in this Land, and neither you nor I know what consequence could be borne from such words you utter." He turned back to converse with Naga.

"I—"

Beth grabbed his arm. "He's right, Lanky. There's an energy here that we know very little about – but it's there. Let's not sabotage this mission ourselves."

He bristled. *Yes, there is. But I thought these daemons were here to help us. So why the silence?* But he said nothing.

"So," Beth continued more quietly, "when are you leaving?"

Pushing back his frustration, he said, "As soon as you're on your way. We'll close the camp here and then move out. We should meet up with Rind and the rest of the IY tribe within a few days, and then we'll react as we need to, based on their intelligence."

"And if they're stupid?"

"What? Ha, ha, very funny," he said, seeing her grin. "We hope the reports from their scouts will let us know what movements have been seen in the south. And I guess if they've seen any stray dragons. After that, I'm not—"

"Okay, let's move out, people," Bear called.

Lanky's stomach churned. "I guess this is it."

"It is," she said, her grin fading. "And it has to be done. We need that Staff."

He forced a smile and held out his hand. "Good luck, Beth. I—"

"Come on," she murmured, moving in and wrapping her arms around his waist and broad shoulders. "We need a bit more than that to say cheerio." She hugged him tightly. "Look after yourself."

He hugged her back. "And you look after yourself too. And good luck." He stepped back. "And I know Garrion said we should travel silently, but we should aim to talk soon – just to be sure all is well before we get too far into this."

"We'll talk in a Glade in a day or so." She placed her hand on his arm and flashed him a smile. "And you take care." She gestured to the Axe strapped on his back. "Remember, you'll need the daemon's help, so don't block him out completely. Good luck," she finished, with a gentle hit on his shoulder.

"And to you," he said, returning the gesture. "Enjoy your vacation."

Beth half smiled, then walked away to join Bear.

He watched her acknowledge the farewells of other tribe members – all wishing to pass on best wishes – before she joined the other five members of her travelling party, who were waiting for her beside Naga. *A strong group,* he thought, his gaze shifting from one to the other: Beth, Bear, Knuckles, Shorty, Svana, and Scorpion. Despite the fear they each must be carrying, he saw a quiet determination in their eyes. *They will bring back the Staff, I'm sure of it.*

Naga stepped forward to face the travelling group. "I will be brief, my family," she said with a strength that carried her voice to the watching tribe. "While such a trek north is not to be taken lightly, this mission is well within your means; you have the skills and experience with you, and we can hope this fine weather holds. We pray to IY for that." She glanced at Bear. "I trust the first few days will be at a pace that allows Warrior Beth to continue her recovery."

Bear nodded in acknowledgement.

Naga scanned the faces of the attentive travellers. "We don't know, but we have to hope and expect that the Staff will be held at the place found by Warrior Lanky. Thus, we expect you will face your severest challenge at your trail's end. A most severe challenge indeed."

There was silence amongst all watching and listening.

Naga turned to face the rest of the tribe standing with Lanky by the fire. "The Warriors have aided our peoples over vast spans of time. We are told how victory looks and feels to us, but the Warriors' fate – and some of their allies – that we do not know."

She looked around at the faces in front of her. "This is now a time when all of us will be tested, each in different ways, and each at different times. But whatever the outcome of these trials, we must stay resolute, trusting we are on the right path – and proud of the actions of our people."

Lanky sensed those beside him stand a little taller.

Naga turned back to the readied travellers. "We all hope, and expect, to see you again, and we look forward to that day. But, if, for some reason, our paths do not again cross, then know that you have the love and respect from your family and friends, and that we will not forget you. May IY travel with you on your journey."

And with those last words fading into the dawn's cold air, Bear gave the briefest of nods. He gestured to his group, then together with Svana, Knuckles, Beth, Shorty, and Scorpion, they walked away, taking the first few steps on a journey to recover the Staff.

Lanky found himself quietly humming to himself as he watched the group disappear from view along a faint animal trail through the trees. He turned and gazed into the dying flames of the fire. *With all my heart, I wish you well, Beth. And I don't know you, IY, but I'm with the rest on this one – may you be with them on their journey.*

*

They headed west for most of the day, travelling first out of the deep arcuate valley system where they'd left camp, then up and over a steep, rugged hill range, winding their way through the rock-strewn ravines and gullies of its heights before dropping into another series of interlinked river valleys. *That's undoubtedly Vaten Lake,* Beth thought as they had marched along the banks of a narrow, dark-watered lake lying in the shadows of a foreboding, scree-laden ridge. *Or at least a version of the lake. And right where it should be.*

She took another mental note to mark their route on the back of Lanky's map. For whatever they found at their destination in the north, they also needed to find their way back to the Iyes camp. And maybe quickly, with a dragon on their tail. A fell shadow crossed her face as another reality hammered home. *And maybe not all will return.* She needed to know the route back herself. *I have to get the Staff to safety.*

You do. And then you need to engage the Enemy.

She quailed at the unbidden thought. And yet it was a thought that, with each hour she spent in this ancient land, she knew deep down was true. They had arrived – been called – for a reason. *We are needed.* But the way ahead lay cloaked in thick, swirling mist. After retrieving the Staff, what then? *Where is this Kaos who threatens the Land? Who is—*

'Release me!' came a strident cry from a fearsome presence surging within. 'I know this Land! You are not needed!'

Gripped by sudden panic, Beth instinctively slammed the rogue presence back down deep inside, weaving ironlike threads of energy to restrain it.

The ferocious attack on her mind vanished.

Heart pounding, she quickly scanned the terrain for threats. But this wasn't an attack from an unknown enemy. *This Warrior within me seeks to break free. This Bethusa.* For she believed Fen's words. Ancient Warriors lay within them. *And Fen wishes them to come to the fore.* And that was terrifying. *Because what happens to me?*

"Are you okay, Warrior?" came Svana's voice from behind.

Nerves raw, Beth took a moment to answer, tensed against another onslaught. But the alien presence inside lay silent, imprisoned by the intuitively wrought bindings. "Fine," she panted eventually. "I'm okay." Glancing ahead, she saw Bear and Scorpion walking on along an animal trail in the distance. Knuckles had stopped and stood on a flat-topped boulder, looking back at them. Lanky's words came back to her. "As I keep saying," he had said, "take care, Beth. One step at a time." She clenched her hand more tightly around the haft of her Axe. *One step at a time. But as Beth, not as this Bethusa.*

Girding herself, she gestured to Knuckles to continue and forced herself to walk on. *And, yes, take care, Beth. Watch for the enemy outwith, but also this one within.*

As they travelled onwards through the undulating terrain – with little talk and few rest breaks – the tension inside eased as the inner voice remained silent. And as the sun dropped in the sky, the stress in her mind was replaced by a growing strain in her legs as they maintained their determined pace westward. The group made use of the numerous animal trails where they could, but much of the way lay over newly broken ground. And they had already covered a significant distance – *maybe close to twenty-five kilometres?*

Shielding her eyes from the low sun, she squinted ahead. From what she remembered of this land in her time, they would soon hit the coast. But scanning the horizon, she couldn't make out the sea. Her legs burning, she increased her pace and caught up with Knuckles. "How soon until we hit the sea?" she asked as she came alongside him.

"The big water? Not for many days."

Beth raised an eyebrow. If they were where she thought they were, the sea should have been close by. "Then we don't continue to the west?"

"No. Tomorrow, we swing north. We'll make camp at the escarpment, not far from here."

"We've slowed. Is this pace too fast for you?" Svana asked from behind.

Yes, my back and shoulders are aching and the knife wound throbs. "Fine," Beth answered. "Just getting started."

"Liar," Knuckles whispered softly. "We'll be stopping soon. Not far now."

Beth knew she shouldn't be doing it but didn't want to show any weakness in front of Svana. Jessica's imagined voice immediately scolded her: *'You're an idiot.'* She sighed. And Jess would be right. The last thing they needed was a casualty of their own making. She glanced at Knuckles. "Okay," she muttered. "You're right. Just don't tell her."

Knuckles laughed.

"What's so funny?" Svana asked.

"Private joke," Knuckles shouted.

"Hah. The only joke is *your* privates."

"And how do you know that?" Knuckles replied with a chuckle. "Would you like me to tell you a joke tonight?"

"If you try, I doubt your private jokes would remain yours – I'd display them around camp on a stick."

"In that case, I'll refrain from any more private hilarity. It seems only a few recognise my talent."

"Hah," came the dismissive reply.

Still chuckling, Knuckles walked on, Beth following behind.

They continued in silence, walking ever westward, the sun cruising towards the horizon. Zoning out of anything except keeping herself moving, Beth trudged on, eyes on the ground, the landscape passing by unseen.

She almost walked into the back of Knuckles before she realised he'd stopped. Looking up, she saw that they were standing beside Bear, who was looking ahead.

"It's always a magnificent view from here," Knuckles murmured.

She took stock of her surroundings. They stood on a shallow escarpment, which ran to the south and the north of them, steepening dramatically in places to form rugged cliffs where seabirds soared on the rising winds. Following Bear's gaze to the west, she saw that the expansive grassland ahead sloped gently away from them, flattening to form a low plain cut by numerous interweaving streams. This lowland continued to the far horizon, broken only by an isolated, elongate hill range in the distance.

A quite extraordinary map of the land took shape in her head.

Turning to face the route they'd just travelled, she studied the profile of the hills they'd crossed ... *The hills of the Western Ranges.* "It's incredible," she whispered, turning back to the isolated hill rising from the plain ahead. "Truly incredible." Any remaining doubts that she stood in a different age had just been blown away in a gale.

"Let's set camp down there to the right," Bear said to the group now assembled. "In the lee of the escarpment."

Knuckles, who had been watching Beth, waited until the others moved away. "What do you see?" he asked quietly.

She pointed west across the unbroken terrain to the prominent range rising in the distance. "That's the Isle of Vannin. Or it will be." She stared in wonder at the hill rising out of the dry plain: lowlands that would be inundated by the rising sea over the next few thousand years; an incredible, almost unbelievable snapshot of the ever-changing planet they lived on. The surrounding landscape had a familiarity bred from her recent travels around this countryside. Starker featured, not yet rounded by many thousand more years of erosion – but a place she could navigate from memory.

Only no houses, roads, tractors, nor planes in the sky. And the staggering realisation that this was true for the whole planet. An entire planet as yet unscarred by humans' later technological advances.

Advances – or an onslaught?

"I don't know about you, Warrior," Knuckles said, breaking her reverie, "but my stomach tells me it's time to make the fire."

Beth nodded, but she stood a moment longer, trying to get her head around the stunning truth. But an entirely pristine planet was a vast concept to digest.

*

Shorty sighed, hands on his belly. "Well, that has set us up nicely for tomorrow's march. A tribe marches on its stomach, as they say."

"Ah, please. No talk of marching right now, my tall friend," Knuckles groaned. "You'll give us indigestion, isn't that right, Svana?"

"More likely give us pains in the neck, I think – two of them."

Laughter came from the area behind them, where Scorpion was burying the dregs of the meal.

"Now then, Scorpion," Shorty said. "Don't be encouraging such hurtful attacks – we'll feel picked on, won't we, Knuckles?"

"Too right. We'd have to make a complaint to our chief, and that takes time and effort, that does. It—"

"Well, the chief won't be hearing that complaint anytime soon then," cut in Svana. "I don't think we've ever seen much effort from you two."

"Oh, that hurts," Shorty said in an injured tone. "Cuts to the bone, that does. See now how we're being picked on, Scorpion? How cruel she is to us?"

"It doesn't sound too far from the mark to me," Scorpion said, pushing his long hair behind his ear as he walked back towards them.

Knuckles feigned a scowl. "You see, Warrior, how they bully us? How they push us out of the warm embrace of the tribe?"

"Warm embrace?" Beth said, warming her feet by the fire. "I can figure what kind of warm embrace you two are hoping for. But you'll have to work on your chat-up lines."

Appreciative clapping came from Svana's direction.

"See how people so misjudge us, Shorty – it stabs at my heart."

"Don't give me ideas," Svana muttered.

Beth jumped at a loud rustling off to their left.

"Just a skittish critter," Knuckles said, seeing her start. "Probably a fox. We wouldn't hear the big ones."

"Well, that's reassuring," she said, scanning the deep shadows beyond their fire.

Knuckles laughed. "They rarely approach the fire. Only if they're really hungry – and there's plenty of food around these parts."

"What else is out there?"

"The predators? Around here, wolf and brown bear mostly, cave lions where we're heading."

She frowned. "That sounds nice."

"No," Knuckles replied, "I wouldn't say they're nice, and it's best we don't meet them. But they rarely attack groups." He shifted his gaze to the fire. "Rarely."

"You've had to deal with them before?"

He was slow to answer. "I have," he murmured eventually, staring into the fire.

The camp fell quiet.

"It was not long after we found Spider and brought him into the tribe. We were out on an early-winter hunting trip led by my grandfather and had taken Spider with us to teach him our skills. My grandfather was a skilled hunter, and Spider was with him up ahead, tracking an injured deer through a light snow. We didn't see the lion until it was upon them."

He paused, clearing his throat. "I still don't know why it attacked us – it isn't usual for a single lion to attack a group. Regardless, it was there and had targeted the youngster. My grandfather was the quickest to react and leapt in front of the boy, thrusting his spear into the shoulder of the lion. But it was a huge beast – it simply crashed into him, wrenching him to the ground. I reached them in seconds and went to help my grandfather. But he shouted for me to get the boy away."

Knuckles cleared his throat a second time. "I reacted and obeyed – it's how he'd taught me. I grabbed the boy and carried him away to safety. It took only a few heartbeats, but felt like a lifetime. By the time I got back to the scene, our whole group was battling the lion. I saw my grandfather on the snow – in the bright red snow – a chunk missing from the back of his neck. He didn't move again."

He coughed and wiped his eye. "He was a great man. And he saved a young life that day. But I lost a grandfather." He glanced at Beth. "I speak to him each night and know he has earned his place with our ancestors – but I still wish I could have said goodbye to him that day. That is the hardest …"

Blinking through her own tears, Beth watched him turn back to the fire. He shrugged. "But we move on. We strive to make our ancestors proud of us, so we can look them in the eye when we meet them beyond the Horizon."

He sat in silence for a time, then turned back to her. "So yes, I prefer to avoid these beasts where we can." A small smile returned to his face. "But I don't think they'd want to meet me."

They all remained silent for a while, each to their own thoughts.

"Would you permit me a question, Warrior?" Shorty asked after a while.

Beth nodded.

"You seem uncertain of these predators. I'm unclear why. Are they unknown to you?"

Beth cleared her thoughts. "Unknown? No. I know of the wolf, bear, and lion, and many other animals." She paused, then added, "When I say know, I mean I've read about them. Or maybe seen them – in a zoo, say. But I guess I've never seen one in the wild. They—"

"Wild? Zoo? What do you mean by this?"

Beth inwardly cursed. *Okay, so how do I explain a zoo?* "I mean, I've only seen them when they've been captured and kept safe so people can see them."

"You catch them and hold them? You mean, alive?" came Scorpion's surprised voice as he stepped into the fire's light. "Why would you want to do that?"

You've dug a hole for yourself here, she thought. "I guess so that people can see them and understand more about them. If you understand them, you can do more to protect them."

"Protect them? From what?"

Hesitating, she wondered how far down this path she needed to go. "There are many, many people in our time," she said carefully, "and as we step further into the animals' realm, this can cause conflict." *Animals displaced or killed is more accurate.* "As people and animals share less and less of the same space, people see fewer animals. Hence the ... trapping. It allows people to see that other life shares the land, and that maybe it's a good thing to protect it."

"I guess I can see part of what you're saying, Warrior," Shorty said, slipping his blade into his tunic. "It's happening here – animals hunted to extinction as the number of tribes grow, their spirits lost forever. These tribes see only the need for food and supplies, not realising they destroy that very resource. And the expanding influence of the Ka doesn't help us."

His words had a worrying resonance. Was it humanity's curse to repeat history's mistakes? Because how many species were being wiped out in her time? And driven by what? Greed? Ignorance?

"Beth?"

She glanced up and realised that Scorpion was trying to get her attention. "You said something before," he said. "You 'read about them', I think you said. What do you mean?"

Beth jumped as something large detached from a rock to her right.

"I think you meant your cave paintings, didn't you, Warrior?"

Beth had forgotten that Bear was there. And he seemed to have made a pointed intervention. She chose her next words carefully. "Yes, Scorpion. There are many talented artists, and their creations reveal much about our land's animals and plants."

"Those must be marvels to see," Scorpion said, his eyes shining in the firelight. "What dyes do they use? How detailed are the paintings?"

"There talks our budding artist," Knuckles said, reaching for his pack. "He'll not let this go now."

Beth smiled at Scorpion. "No, it's a fair question, but I'm afraid that I really don't know what they use. And I couldn't do it. They capture a lot of detail. Enough for me to visualise them as though they were real." *How do you explain things like television, films, internet in a world like this?*

The looming figure of Bear drew closer. "Imagination would bring them alive, I'm sure. Now I know you could question the Warrior all night, but I need to discuss some aspects of our journey with her. Then, we should let her rest and recover strength for tomorrow's trek."

"No problem," Knuckles said, grinning as he reached inside his pack. "This means time for a game, Shorty. I've got the knuckles; you go find some suitable stones from over there. I'll prepare the ground."

"Oh, here we go," came Svana's voice. "The two brains of the party going head-to-head with a stone-throwing contest. Why don't you just hit each other with sticks? It's much simpler."

"It doesn't sound that she understands the complexities of the game, Knuckles."

"Sounds a good reason to get her to play. I might win something. Who knows, even—"

"Don't go there," Svana growled.

*

Walking out beyond the flickering light of the fire, Beth followed Bear as they climbed back up to the crest of the escarpment. The moon was rising to the east into a clear sky filled with a myriad of stars, more appearing as her eyes adjusted to the darkness.

"You say that in your time the sea reached here," Bear said as she came to his side.

"It did. It does."

"As we understand from our ancestors, when the ice comes, the sea leaves, only returning when the ice retreats. You live in a warmer time with no ice – and you say the sea is here. It is good to hear another part of our Story proved true."

"That seems to be the case. Though, I wouldn't say no ice. We still have ice on higher mountains, and of course at the poles."

"The poles?"

Ah. How much knowledge of this planet did these people have? "In my time, ice extends to the extreme north of our lands – and to the extreme south. We call these regions the poles."

"This I do not know. It is impossible for us to travel to the far north – nothing can survive there. Much is told through our Story, but I know this can be just a fraction of all that could be known." She saw him look up, his solid frame silhouetted against the sky. "Things such as the stars above. These are beyond IY's realm and are unknowable. Are they holes in the rotating disk above our Land, hinting at another place beyond? Are they other lands, or suns like ours, suspended far, far away? Naga believes they are from the original creator and that we are all made from stars, that, ultimately, we will return to them. I prefer the notion of other lands, but this, I think, will remain unknown. Wherever the truth lies, the stars remain entwined with our Land, aligned with our seasons, guiding our journeys."

Beth was astonished. There were insights here she wouldn't have believed possible for this age. These were not simple people. *Not a simple 'stone age' people. These were a curious and intelligent people. They are the people who led to the creation of the future world. My world.*

A sudden stunning realisation struck. *Somewhere – right now – my ancestors walk this Land. A mother, a father, a child … My ancient family are here … somewhere.*

As the staggering thought swirled in her mind, Bear spoke. "There are many questions I would like to ask you. What is it that you know that could help our lives here? What ideas do your people have, ideas we may never have considered but are staring at us in plain sight? I believe we could spend many days sharing this between us." He looked up at the sky again. "But Naga has warned us against this. Warned that she sees disaster for us if we take this path. Although, as you have just heard, people remain curious; you handled the questions well."

She dragged her attention to Bear's words. "Disastrous in what way?"

"I do not know all, nor fully understand all; this is something that Naga the shaman knows, not Naga the Mother of the tribe."

"There's a difference?"

"Possibly. I think I understand her well enough as the Mother, but who can fully know the mind of the shaman? They speak to those who do not speak to me."

Beth could believe that. With Naga, there were more questions than answers.

"No," Bear continued, "I do not know the full mind of the shaman, but there are parts I know. And parts that a Warrior should know."

Ah, so we come to the reason for this evening stroll. "And what do I need to hear?"

Bear walked a few paces away, as though considering his answer. "Of what I will tell is something I first heard from Naga a long time ago. Of course, back then, I was not ready to receive such … thinking. It is difficult to comprehend, to follow. It is of the link between the past and the future. It is something Naga wishes you to understand."

She tilted her head, waiting.

Bear looked down to the fire below. "What if the past, the present, and the future are naturally entwined? Each constantly in flux, but each smoothly flowing together as one; synchronised, compatible, and aligned; a past/future Continuum. And changes made in any part of this Continuum reacted to and adjusted. Unseen and undetectable, but adjusted, nonetheless. Whatever happens in this Continuum, happens. The Continuum doesn't care. It has no grand plan. It just evolves, responding to the life within it. It just is."

Beth stared at him in astonishment. Was this the same man she had been travelling with this day? She cleared her throat, uncertain how to respond. "So, in this … Continuum, any changes made here, would result in … adjustments. But undetected?"

"You speak, you act, you live. And what happens, happens. If the Continuum needs to adjust, it adjusts, either the past, present, or future. Whatever – wherever – is needed to restore alignment. To restore continuity. But we live in the moment, unable to see what is happening in another time. If our actions require an adjustment, we might never know. And those changes may be good, beneficial. But those changes could also have catastrophic consequences for the future – for you, for others, and for the Land." He swept his hand over the night sky. "Maybe for everything." He sighed. "This was Naga's fear."

"That our actions here might change the future? Well, if such a Continuum exists, we all should be afraid." She drew a deep breath. "But right now, I still feel like me. I remember my … land, my friends—"

"And likely true, but right now, you stand here, in this age. You cannot observe the future 'you'. Does that future 'you' even exist? Does your land still exist? And if you *had* changed, well, in this seamless Continuum, would you ever know?"

"Well, the 'me' here is getting a sore head," Beth said, forcing a laugh. But inside lay a cold dread. What effect could their actions have on that future world?

"The answer is, we don't know," Bear said.

He answers his own question ... and my fears. She forced a grip on her thoughts. Naga had wanted Bear to share this with her. *So what more do I need to understand?* "Let me play a scenario," she said, warily probing. "If I die here – not a pleasing thought, but one that's clearly crossed my mind – then I wouldn't be able to return to my time. What happens then? Do people there still remember me?"

"It might depend."

"Okay, on what?"

"If you do not disturb its alignment, then in the eyes of the Continuum, you may simply be another casualty, along with ..." He pointed to the stars. "That many others. You will be dead here and missing in your time – but remembered by your friends."

"And if I do disturb it?"

"Then the Continuum may adjust in a way that leaves your land a very different place to the one you left. A land where you – and maybe your friends – might not have existed. A land where all has been aligned across the ages." She felt Bear's gaze on her. "And if the disturbance was great, then maybe many peoples of your age would no longer exist. Maybe even the land itself would be destroyed. This would be our fate if the Enemy is not defeated. The future uncertain, maybe even lost. And you – as you are – would not exist."

"But right now, since I still remember ..."

"Then it is likely that all is as it should be. Right now, *you* still exist in the Continuum. *You* exist as you were – nothing yet has changed the state of the Continuum. All is there. All that has happened. And all that is to happen, should happen."

Beth frowned. "Then this Continuum of yours seems to preordain my life, mapping it out in minute detail. I have no free will."

"Not true," Bear countered forcefully. "It is we – the life here – that define the Continuum. Not the other way around. The Continuum simply reflects how we have acted. You are free to act in any way you choose."

Beth grunted. "If it was that simple, I should go back and warn the future me and Jessica not to go out for a walk that day." She saw Bear shaking his head. "Okay, what's wrong with that?"

"You cannot cross your own path – that is not possible. If you return to that particular point in time of which you speak, then you will not be as you were. The Continuum adjusts to ensure alignment. To preserve a consistency. Paradoxes such as you suggest simply cannot occur. Ever. None could predict how it might be done, but the Continuum would adjust to preserve continuity, consistency."

If that were so, then ... "That would make it quite important to get back to the right time," she murmured. "How do we manage that?"

Bear didn't answer.

"Ah," she said slowly. "I can see the neatest solution for the Continuum there – that we don't get back. Right?"

"You look at it the wrong way around. The Continuum understands no right or wrong. Whatever you do, however you act, whatever your fate, it merely adjusts, synchronises. I doubt that dealing with you alone, either way, would trouble it."

Beth laughed. He was either attempting a joke or deadly serious ... *Either way, it's funny.* "No, I guess little old me is less than an atom's worth of stuff to deal with in all this," she said, sweeping her hand across the night sky.

She saw a tension in Bear's stance. "I have passed on what Naga wished, but of what must be done, that I cannot answer. You are the Warriors, not I. It is for you to understand how to act. And the Continuum? If it is truly as we are told, it will simply adjust, align."

Beth fell silent, gathering the threads of Bear's breathtaking concept. It was one she'd have dismissed as utterly insane before seeing – feeling – what she'd experienced here. She glanced at Bear, sensing his eyes still on her. So, Naga wished her to know this. *To know that I could change this Continuum.* She looked up at the stars. But how? What could she do to change all this?

Her mind seemed caught in a sudden gale, thoughts whipping in the gusts. *You could say the wrong thing. You could take the wrong action. You could kill the wrong person. You could—*

Stop!

She drove back the shocking thoughts. *I don't want to kill anyone.*

As the eddies of the storm passed, she felt the familiar ripple of unease. Were these the thoughts of her stressed mind? Or thoughts of Bethusa?

"Warrior?"

She drew a deep breath and focussed on Bear. "Just trying to understand all you've told me." But how could anyone understand this? "I'll need to sleep on it. I know you wanted to talk about the journey ahead, but maybe we do that tomorrow?"

He nodded. "I just had to get you away, to share this with you."

"Well, you've definitely done that." She sighed. "Let's get back down to the fire – I hadn't realised how cold I was getting."

She walked back down the slope to the camp, her thoughts restless. *The Continuum. Warriors. The Enemy. Bethusa.* What mad world had they entered? And how far into the murky darkness should they step? She gritted her teeth. *Retrieve the Staff. Find a way out of here. And then decide.*

"Ah, just in time to join the game. Sit yourself there, next to Scorpion."

Forcing a smile, she joined Knuckles and the others.

Knuckles grinned. "Now let me explain …"

CHAPTER EIGHTEEN

What might have happened if she'd chosen to stay? Or if they hadn't believed her? Maybe another question: If this had happened to you, would your friends have believed you?

*G*roaning, Jessica rolled onto her side, waves of nausea sweeping through her, sharp pains ripping through her head. Hazy images of a terrifying nightmare loomed at the edges of her mind: rabid, alien creatures seeking to destroy her as she'd travelled through the darkness of a void; the stench of a malign evil clawing for her soul. *What hell haunts my mind?* She curled into a ball, hands clasping her temples, then lay for a while until the pain finally eased.

With a quiet moan, she opened her eyes. To darkness.

Stark memories flooded back.

Where is the burnt man? Where are the daemons?

Another bout of sickness pulsed through her. Gritting her teeth, she waited, squirming, until the nausea passed.

She looked again into the darkness but saw nothing. Sensed nothing.

Her heart leapt. *I escaped the eye! I escaped the burnt man.*

She lay still, waiting for her fogged mind to clear, then placed her hand to the floor to push herself up …

And froze.

Her fingers brushed neither the hard rock of the cave floor nor the smooth softness of a fur pelt. *Carpet?* She stilled her breathing. In the background droned a faint humming sound … and wafted the scent of a subtle floral perfume. *I recognise that!*

Her aching head forgotten, she clambered to her feet and peered into the darkness. She saw the faintest, vertical crack of dim light. Her hands trembled. *Can it really be?* Stepping forward, she held out her right hand, searching ...

She found the handle of the door.

Her heart hammering in her chest, she turned the handle ... and a gloomy light flooded into the room as the door opened onto the narrow corridor of their holiday cottage.

Jessica stood, gaping, stunned by the startling realisation. *I'm back ... I'm back in my own time.* Her mouth dry, she glanced back, seeing her belongings scattered around the room – tidier than when she'd left, but most definitely hers. *How? How did I get back here?* She turned back to the door, the reality sweeping all doubts away. Whatever had happened, she *was* back. Somehow, she had escaped the madness of that other age. As though in a dream, she stepped into the corridor. *This may be a dream, but I've escaped a nightmare.*

She saw a familiar door ahead. Heart thumping against her chest, she rushed forward and flung open the door. "Trish! I'm back. Trish!"

"Aaahhh!" a voice screamed. "Aaahhh!"

There was a flurry of activity in the dimly lit room, and a figure flew off the bed, slamming into her, knocking her to the ground.

"Erin! Erin! Help! Call the police!"

"No! Trish! It's me, Jess."

A fist lashed out, hitting her in the face. "You picked the wrong girl to rob tonight."

As Jessica fended off another attack, she realised Tricia wouldn't stop. She twisted, lifting her knee, and heaved her friend off her. Rolling with Tricia, she straddled her, pinning her down. "Trish! Stop! Look at me. It's Jessica."

Tricia froze. "Jess?" her friend gasped, stunned disbelief in her voice. "It can't be ... You're ... lost."

Releasing her hold on Tricia, Jessica clambered to her feet. Rubbing her jaw, she walked back to the door and flicked on the bedroom light. She turned back to see Tricia sitting up, staring at her wide-eyed, her frizzy hair a wild explosion.

"Jess ... is it really you?"

Jessica blinked to clear her eyes. "It's me, Trish. I—"

A light danced around the room, then a familiar voice called from the stairs. "Trish. What's happening? I've called the police."

Jessica flinched. *The police! No. Not yet.*

Tricia climbed to her feet. "It is you, isn't it?" Tricia whispered, ignoring Erin as she arrived at the door, breathless, torch in shaking hand.

Suddenly unable to speak, Jessica nodded.

Tricia rushed forward and grabbed Jessica around the neck, hugging her tightly. "What happened to you? Where've you been? And what are you wearing? Ahh! You smell!"

Jessica slumped against Trish and sobbed.

"Who are you?" Erin cried out.

"It's Jess," Tricia whispered.

"Not her. Her!"

Her stomach lurching, Jessica pulled away from Tricia and spun around.

She stared in horror at the frightened girl standing in the corridor behind Erin. "No … It can't be … River …"

*

Jessica heard the car start up, and then the grate of the gravel as the wheels took hold. The noise from the engine slowly faded as the car wended down the lane from the cottage. She breathed a sigh of relief. The police officer had gone.

"Okay," she said to River, who sat beside her on the bed. "We can talk now."

"What is this place?" River whispered, eyes flitting around Jessica's room.

Jessica saw the fear on the girl's face. She needed to calm her before they went downstairs to meet Tricia and Erin. *And who will calm me?* She pushed that aside. *Help River.*

"River," she said in a low voice. "You're safe. You and me, right now, are safe. Do you understand that?" River didn't respond. *She's shaking like a leaf.* "Okay. You need to listen to me – and I need to know that you've heard me. You're safe. Do you understand?"

River glanced at her, her hands trembling. She nodded.

The tension gripping Jessica eased. "I know this place and I know these people. You won't be left alone here. Understand?"

"Yes," River answered, her voice wavering.

"Okay. That's good." Jessica glanced around her room. *And how alien this must appear.* "We're in my house – well, not quite my house, but a place that we're using for now. Nothing here will hurt you, but just to be safe, touch nothing."

River looked around, then back at Jessica. "How did we get here?" she whispered.

Familiar dread returned. *Yes, how did we get here?* "I met the daemons. To take an Axe." She looked down at the Axe by her side. "I thought this was the way to help my friends. To help them find the

Staff ..." Remembered words spoken with Naga returned. *And I thought I should understand more of what was asked of us.*

"What happened?"

The burnt man from my nightmares appeared. "A devil came for me." She looked up at River. "One that has visited me before."

River's eyes widened. "Kaos?"

"Maybe. I don't know. But what I know is that devil found me again. I just needed to escape." She glanced at River. "You must have been there."

River pursed her lips. "I followed you down to the chamber," she said, her eyes fixed in the past, "and found you sitting there, alone. You were restful for a while, then you stood and started shouting. When you fell, I ran to you and held you – held the Axe. And then ... and then, I woke up here."

The horror of that moment was raw. *I just wanted to escape the devil. I just wanted to get home.* She frowned. "How did we get here? I thought we needed the Staff to travel. This makes no sense."

"I don't know, Warrior. And I don't know how the Enemy reached you in our Sacred Chamber. That just cannot be. The Spirits and the daemons protect it."

"Well, somehow it wasn't. That devil broke through. Something failed. Or someone failed."

She glanced around the room, seeing familiar and comforting belongings scattered haphazardly about on the set of drawers, beside the bed, around her travel bags. *Home ...* With the frenzied panic of their arrival waning, a dawning realisation was waxing in its place. *I'm back! I can stay here!* A surge of utter relief flooded through her.

"What do we do?" River said, her soft words an echo of her inner turmoil. "What will your friends do? What will my tribe do?"

Jessica's elation shattered in an instant. *What will your friends do? Beth!*

The smiling face of her wonderful friend seared into her mind. And those glorious memories of just a few days before. Of four friends enjoying their precious time together, four friends revelling in each other's company.

And then this. This hellish living nightmare.

She leaned forward and put her head in her hands. *This isn't fair. Why did this happen to us? Why?* Her chest tightened at the stark reality. *I can't leave Beth. And I can't leave Lanky. I have to go back.*

A chill ran down her spine. *But the burnt man ...*

She forced herself to stand against the rising tide of fear. *I must go back.*

She felt River's hand on her shoulder. "I will help as I can, Jessica. We can help each other."

She heard the genuine warmth in River's voice. She looked up to see the girl's resolute face looking down on her. Resolute, yet clearly holding back her own terrible fear. She nodded. "This is hard, River. Hard on us both." *And hard on my friends.* "But you're right. We have to help each other." She reached up and squeezed River's hand. "I will get you home. I will return to my friends."

And we need the Staff, came a voice from deep within her. *You are needed.*

Jessica recoiled at the unbidden voice. Voice or thought? Hers or another's? What could she be sure of in this moment? *You are needed ...* The thread of this thought wove another cloak of uncertainty. The Iyes believed them saviours from the threat of a lurking evil. *From the threat of this Kaos.* And after speaking with Naga, she'd known – for the sake of her friends, *for the sake of my sanity* – that she had to learn more of what they'd been thrust into. But now all seemed unclear. What could she, Lanky, and Beth do against what they'd seen, what they'd felt?

She drew herself up, cursing at the futility of her thoughts. For now, she needed to forget all else and figure out how to get back to Beth and Lanky. And to do that, they needed help. Help from someone who wouldn't think her mad.

And she had an idea who. *The bookseller. The one who Lanky spoke of.*

She turned to River. "There is someone here that may help us. Someone Lanky knows. But first, we'll speak with the others here."

"No," River said quickly. "I heard those people attack you." A flicker of guilt crossed her face. "I was too scared to help."

"This," Jessica said, touching the bruise on jaw, "was a mistake. They are my friends." She squeezed River's hand, forcing strength into her voice. "And don't be ashamed of being afraid. Do you remember what I did when I arrived in your world? I ran. I ran as fast as I could to escape the chaos engulfing me. A great Warrior? No, a frightened woman with no clue what was happening around her." Smiling, she touched River's cheek. "You will see how quickly you'll lose that fear. I will help you. Is that good or bad?"

A smile touched the corner of River's mouth. "Good."

Jessica smiled. "Okay. Then we should go and meet them now."

The frightened look appeared again in River's eyes. "Has the enemy gone?"

Still smiling, Jessica climbed to her feet. "The police? That was not an enemy. They are a ... tribe. They help with problems you have." *Like help to find someone who disappeared a few days ago.* Her smile faded.

"Only my story wouldn't be believed. Not their fault – I doubt anyone on this planet would believe me." Well, maybe there were a few, but those would also be deemed crazy. "No. We can't discuss this with anyone, else that will give us even more problems. We have to find a way back to your time ourselves."

"And your friends?"

Now there was a question. She sighed. "Let's find out." She picked up the Axe and placed it under her bed. *This will remain hidden for now. One step at a time.*

*

While Erin perched on a pedestal chair at the breakfast bar, and Jessica continued to talk to the stranger sitting next to her at the table, Tricia filled the kettle. "Nothing beats a nice cup of tea in a time of crisis," she said, the brightness of her voice belying a tension beneath. She placed the kettle on its holder and flicked the switch. Leaning back on to the edge of the kitchen countertop, she flicked her gaze over the two seated women.

Jessica had removed the leather jacket and boots she'd been wearing, revealing the same clothes she had been dressed in many days ago. Dirty, torn, and smelly – but the same clothes. And now a bruised face. *My bad.* The newcomer – clean looking, curly dark hair pulled back and tied in a ponytail, and a strong-featured face – was dressed in an assemblage of close-fitting leather garments. She looked petrified but was alert and watching their every move. She also looked lean and toned; it would be a struggle to stop her leaving if she wanted to get out of here.

And Tricia didn't understand a word they were saying to each other.

She pushed herself from the countertop and girded herself. *Time to figure out what's been going on.* "Sorry I hit you, Jess," she said, walking up to a pedestal chair next to Erin and climbing on to it. "Didn't recognise you in that." She pointed to the rough leather jacket on the floor.

Jessica said something to the girl next to her, then turned to Tricia, her face drawn. "Not your everyday occurrence," she said, a faint smile appearing on her lips. "You're forgiven."

"You look a state. And she doesn't look much better. What's her name?"

"River. A friend."

Tricia glanced at the terrified girl who spoke an unknown language. She was staying very close to Jessica, as if that was the only place she felt safe. *As if she's known Jess for years. Yet I know nothing about her. What the hell is happening?* She drew a deep breath. "Okay, Jess. We played it your way with that officer, Fletcher. We told him I had a nightmare, and that Erin thought I was being attacked. He wasn't happy, but at least he's gone." Her sharp eyes locked onto Jessica. "What's going on? Why did we have to lie to the police?"

"That's difficult to explain," Jessica said, her brow furrowed. "And even harder to understand."

"It's not been easy here, either, Jess," Erin said, fidgeting with a pencil on the table. "Explaining things to the police about your disappearance. Worrying about what had happened, where you were. We were worried sick."

"I'm sorry," Jessica said quietly. "I know it must have been tough." She studied them for a moment. "That day I ... left. What did you see?"

Erin glanced at Tricia, as if wanting her to answer.

Tricia tensed. *I don't believe what I saw.* "That's also difficult to explain. We saw you on the trail below us, and then ..." She couldn't say it.

"And then you were gone," Erin said quietly. "You, Beth, and the lad from the village."

Jessica flinched.

Erin flicked the pencil away. "You're listed as missing persons – you were missing – but now you suddenly reappear with a stranger, speaking a strange language. Just what happened to you, Jess?"

Tricia saw the hesitation – and the fear – on Jessica's face. *Fear of what?* "We're your friends, Jess. Whatever has happened, we can help. Are you in danger? Is Beth in danger?"

The kettle rattled and hissed behind them. The stranger quickly stood, staring at the rising steam and whispering in urgent tones to Jessica. Jessica made a calming gesture, speaking softly. The kettle clicked off and the noise quickly subsided. Jessica spoke again, and the girl reluctantly sat back down – but her anxious eyes continued to scan the kitchen.

She's scared, Tricia thought. *Not necessarily of us but scared of being here. Like a trapped animal. What—*

"When you say we were gone," Jessica said, looking first at Tricia and then Erin, "what do you mean? What did you really see?"

A haunting vision twisted Tricia's gut. *I don't believe what I saw. I don't know what I saw.*

"I saw you vanish," Erin said in a whisper.

The room went quiet.

I don't know what I saw, Tricia told herself again. *It made no sense.*

Jessica's penetrating gaze searched Erin's face, then she sat forward in her chair. "We *did* vanish. And this is what happened …"

*

Tricia opened the fridge and took out a small bottle. *Light on the tonic tonight, I think.* There was a satisfying fizz as the tonic splashed into the glass, which already contained more than enough gin. She took a drink. A long one.

"That's not the best option right now, Trish," Erin said, frowning at her friend. "We need clear heads."

"And you don't drink gin," Jessica added.

Tricia ignored them. Tonight, she drank gin. This was the only way to deal with a friend telling you that they'd travelled back in time and discovered a land with magical Axes. You drank and hoped your brain could adapt to a fantastical story. "You're both right, but sometimes you must swim against the current of righteousness to avoid becoming trapped in the norm." Somehow, this didn't feel to be the norm. "I suggest you grab one yourself – at least then our heads will be as one."

She took another swig.

With a disapproving glance at Tricia, Erin turned to Jessica. "It's unbelievable. If I hadn't seen …" She hesitated, then turned back to Tricia. "I told you that's what we saw. I said they just vanished."

"You did," Tricia murmured. *And I may well have seen the same. And yet, travelling in time with a mystical Staff?* She could see Jessica believed what she was saying. A cold shiver ran down her spine. *But what can I believe?* "Are Beth and the lad, Lanky, safe?"

"They're as safe as they can be at the moment," Jessica said, her hands clasped together tightly on the table. "But I have to get back to them. And quickly."

Quickly. And so, a threat remained to them. Just how much of this story was untold? Tricia studied her friend, seeing the fraught emotions on her face. Confusion, pain, fear, yet a restless urgency beneath. Wherever Beth and this Lanky were, Jessica desperately wanted to get them back.

She shifted her attention to the girl, River. *And get this one back.* Her gaze lingering, she saw a strong, weathered face, younger than her, but beyond this, neither the hue of her skin nor the cast of her features, or any other obvious measure one might find, differentiated her greatly from another who might have walked in the door. *Yet still I can see she's not from this time. And she's scared. She looks to Jess for support every second that passes.* This was a girl who would rather be anywhere else, other than here.

But a girl that Jess had named friend.

Tricia turned to Jessica. *And this is also my friend.* "You truly believe this happened?" she said in a hushed voice.

"I do."

Tricia held her friend's eyes. "And you're not being coerced into this, Jess? You're not being threatened to do something against your will?"

She saw Jessica wince. "Not in the way you're thinking. But my hand is forced. I have to get Beth and Lanky back."

"And the police can't help?"

"They'd think I was deranged. And might lock me up. What chance then to get Beth back? I have to try my way first."

Tricia saw the certainty etched in her friend's face. Whatever was happening here, Jessica was making the call to act, no one else. *But I still can't understand how this can be happening.* She glanced down at the glass clasped in her hand. *And yet, do I need to understand? This is Jess. This is my friend.*

She drew back from her doubts and looked up. "There's no way we can understand what you've been through, Jess. No way on earth. And neither can we comprehend all you've told us. But we can clearly see you need help." *And I will help.* "What do you want us to do?"

Jessica's sigh was heartfelt. "Thank you."

Tricia forced a smile. "You haven't told us what you want us to do yet."

"The bookseller," Jessica said quickly. "He knows Lanky. He knows about these Axes. I need to speak with him."

"That won't be easy," Erin said. "The police – everybody – has your pictures."

Then we can't go to him. "We'll have to get him here," Tricia said, taking a swig from her glass. "Leave that to me."

Jessica nodded.

"Talking of the police," Erin said. "That village sergeant who came tonight. Fletcher. I don't think he bought our story. He's been suspicious of us since that day you left. He'll be back, I'm sure."

Jessica's face hardened. "Then we need to move quickly. First thing in the morning."

"You hear that, Trish," Erin said, turning to her friend. "Ditch the drink and get to bed. You've volunteered to see this bookseller. You better be up and ready to go first thing."

"Okay, okay," Tricia said, draining her glass. "Let's call it quits for tonight." She climbed off her stool and stood, rather unsteadily. "I'll say goodnight to our new guest first."

She walked around to the table where Jessica and River sat and stood before the stranger. She held out her hand. "Good night, River."

Jessica spoke to the girl and immediately River held out her hand. Tricia took it in hers, feeling the tough, rough skin of her hands. *This is no office worker.* She smiled at the girl. "I'm sure we'll get you back, River. Not sure how, but we'll find a way. Or the bookseller will."

The girl stared back at her in confusion.

"I guess I'm not helping," Tricia said, releasing the girl's hand.

Crushing weariness swept over her. "You two need rest," she said to Jessica. "We all need rest. Lots to do tomorrow."

Jessica spoke hushed words to the girl, and they both stood. "Thanks again, you two," Jessica said quietly, glancing at Erin then Tricia. "This means a lot."

"It's what friends are for," Tricia murmured. "Although, even in my wildest dreams, I couldn't have envisaged this."

"Maybe I could have," Jessica replied. "In *my* wildest dreams." She stepped up to Tricia and reached for her hand. "Believe me that with all my heart, I wish this wasn't true and that this nightmare had never happened. But it has, and now I have to get Beth and Lanky back and return River to where she belongs. So, I'm digging deep. Really deep."

Tricia leaned in and hugged her. "I can see that, Jess. But remember, we're with you on this." She smiled as she stood back. "Whether you like it or not."

"Thanks, Trish. It means a lot, it really does."

Tricia nodded. "Okay, now it's sleep time. Then, tomorrow, we see if we can get this book man to help us. I somehow think we need it."

*

River spent a fitful night on the floor of the chamber, waking several times in a sweat, a mix of nightmares and the fact that the place was so warm, even without the discarded blankets and tunic. Each time she awoke, she looked across in the strange light to check Jessica was there before lying still and drifting off into another disturbed sleep. The final time she awoke, she had given up on sleep and sat mesmerised by the torch next to Jessica's bed. It was quite unlike any fire she'd seen. No flicker, no smoke, just a constant and steady glow. *And the chamber ...* This was filled with a treasure trove of objects, their shapes and materials unlike any she had ever seen.

Finally, Jessica had awoken, and they were now walking down the stairway to the lower level. *So smooth,* River thought as she reached out, letting her fingers brush the carved wood running along the side of the stairs to her side. Reaching the ground below, they entered through a doorway. She blinked to adjust her eyes against the light flooding in through a wide opening on the left. Looking around, she recognised the same chamber as last night – and the same women. She sat down next to Jessica at a wooden table, and the women began speaking together in subdued voices.

Feeling the hard, cold, smooth floor beneath her feet, she looked down and saw they constructed it with a regular pattern of square stones, a stone she had seen before, but never cut and polished in such a way. Looking at the chair she sat on, she ran her hands along the wooden seat, noting its precise, straight cuts and fine edges. She looked up and scanned the chamber, and realised most of the many items within it, large and small, were cut with the same very regular and smooth finish.

And the chamber was so well lit. She looked across at the wide opening to her left and could see green bushes outside swaying in a light wind. But the view was strange, in part a view of the bushes, and in part a reflection of the chamber she was in. She moved her head and realised that the reflection came from a transparent material in the opening. She frowned. *What is that?*

And the smells. A familiar smell drifted across the chamber – from the sizzling meat on a fire – but there were other unfamiliar scents in the air, including an unpleasant odour that prickled her nose.

"River," came an insistent voice.

She realised that Jessica, seated on her right, had been trying to talk to her. "Yes?"

"Trish is going to find the friend of Lanky's that we spoke about. And then – well, that will depend on what she finds." She grimaced. "And the man's reaction."

"Do you think this man will help us?"

"I hope so. We need it."

River looked around the chamber. "I don't belong here. This is not my land."

Jessica shifted on her seat. "I understand," she said slowly. "But this *is* your land, River. Your people's blood remains."

River was not so sure of that. *It may be so, but—*

"But that said," Jessica continued. "I will get you back to your time. Somehow, I will get you back."

River saw the intensity in her eyes. "I believe you, Jessica. But remember, the people of my time also need you."

Jessica nodded, but River saw a flicker of uncertainty creep into the Warrior's eyes. *So, doubt still remains.*

'*She will aid us,*' came a voice.

A voice or a thought?

The moment passed as Jessica spoke. "Let's see what the bookseller can offer us. Pray to your gods."

Yes, River thought. *If you are still in this land, IY, please help us. In whatever way you can. Help me – and Jessica – return. There are things to be done.*

'Indeed,' a calm, ethereal voice said.

CHAPTER NINETEEN

His planning was quite meticulous. And ruthless.
He was a credit to his master.

At daybreak, Spider joined Growl by the stream, examining the ravaged bodies of the two men who had attacked their camp, their torn and shredded remains now washed gently by the icy waters. A grisly job, but needed. The men had obviously been daunting fighters in life, well-built, lithe, and well-armed – difficult to believe in their present state.

Growl lifted the arm of one man and pointed to a symbol on its inner side. "The Kutr," he confirmed. "A tribe of a great lineage but subverted by the Ka, and now dancing to their tune." He pointed to the mark – a simple, circular scar. "A mark of the Ka's most favoured subjugated, part of a fantasy told to those people that they grow closer to the Eye and hence will ascend to join the Ka and their god." He dropped the arm and looked down on the bodies. "This is the reality."

A search of their bloodied clothing produced a selection of spare arrowheads and a well-crafted second axe. The stone of the weapons was of a black obsidian, a finish that Spider had seen before, sourced from a dormant volcano far to the southeast. The workings on the stone were particularly fine.

"A style much to the taste of the Ka," Growl said, "and whilst we like not the taste of Ka, their taste of stone has to be admired."

They searched the wider area, finding another two spears, armed with the same patterned obsidian. Taking a moment alone, Spider studied the black arrowhead he'd stripped from a spear. Clearly these men had been well-prepared, skilled hunters who had evaded the Iyes tribe's network of scouts. But what had been their goal? Not assassins. No, these would stand little chance against the Iyes fighters. He glanced towards the stream, where Growl was washing his hands. Then hunting the old man? Unlikely, because his wolf would be a formidable opponent. *Then most likely scouts, searching for our tribe.*

He glanced to the south, where the Iyes's White Crags camp lay a few days trek away through this northern wilderness of their Land. He needed to reach Rind soon and tell what they knew: that the Warriors had arrived, but the Ka were abroad in the Land. *We must ensure the Warriors have a safe place to prepare for their battles to come.* He glanced towards the stream. *I just have to lose this old man somewhere along the way.* He placed the obsidian arrowhead into his pack and readied himself to leave.

A short while later, he strode out of the broken camp with an easy but resolute stride, Growl following in his wake, and the great wolf ranging out to their flank. As they walked on through the low, rolling terrain, the sun rose higher, finally adding a little warmth to the side of Spider's face. They covered the ground at a steady pace, helped by their decision to stay out in clear ground, not attempting to stay hidden. No one but a large group would attempt to attack them with the beast at their side, and according to Growl, the wolf had confirmed the path ahead was clear.

For now. And if this old man and his wolf are to be trusted ...

But despite the strange company, the tension in Spider eased, his head slowly clearing of the night's stresses. *And at least we've had some silence this morning.*

"Good progress, and a good morning," piped up Growl. "We think we have been remiss this morning by neglecting you, my friend. Do your legs tire yet? Maybe a rest when we crest the next hill?"

Spider groaned.

"From the sounds you make, maybe rest is needed now?"

"No, I'm fine. Let's keep moving, especially since your companion senses no problems ahead."

"No problems. Hmm. Well, we don't believe that. No, not at all. Many problems ahead, we believe. But maybe you talk of the here and the now?" Growl made a show of studying the surrounding terrain. "Then indeed, yes – no problems for us, right now. And that is good. Most fine indeed. Life should be enjoyed, when those problems are away, else we should worry, and worry, and worry forever. Waiting for the next problem. No, that should never be. Not a fruitful life that way, don't you agree?"

Spider sighed again. But the old man had a point. Life was not for worrying.

A legacy from my father. A message passed on in such a short time together.

A short time, but wonderful memories. And great teachings, rich teachings, grown out of his parents' epic migration from the east; a mixture of need, curiosity, and hope driving two young people to explore new areas, unknown lands; two skilled craftspeople journeying together with like-minded travellers; explorers. Two people developing a myriad of experiences that they could eventually pass to their son.

But teachings eventually passed on only by his father …

She died giving me life. But she is richly painted and still alive in my thoughts.

A memory returned of a conversation as his father lay wounded from a hunt, sick with a fever.

"You look worried, Tei," his father had said. Tei said nothing.

"What is wrong, son? Out with it."

Tei cast his eyes down. "I am worried you will die."

His father laughed. "What is there to worry about there? We all die. All living beings in this Land die. It makes no sense to worry about the inevitable. You have a life. Why waste it worrying that you will die, then die having just wasted your life! Does that make any sense?"

His father had reached over and placed a hand on his son's shoulder. "You are given this wonderful chance to live … to live and to enjoy being alive. There should be no time to worry. Move forward, always look forward. Yes, learn from the past, Tei, but do not live in the past. And if I die, so be it. I will have lived as I wanted to live; the future is for others to have their chance of living. Remember me, yes. But do not mourn for me. I am happy."

One sun-cycle on from that conversation, he'd watched his father being killed. And of course, for all his father's noble words, he had been shocked, devastated. *This is not how you should have died!* He thought it then, and he still believed it to this day. But the greater part of his father's teachings had acted as the rock to stem the tide of despair.

He had moved forward.

Day by day, moon by moon, he'd survived in the land near his father's broken body, keeping it safe under a cairn of rocks, surviving using the skills taught by his father and friends.

Waiting.

Waiting for what? He had not known, but it had felt right to stay in that area, protecting his father's body from scavengers, and as he did so, he remembered his father as the great man he was. And remembered stories of his mother, the tales of their life.

And then, one fine day, the tribe of IY had appeared, a collection of people who approached him with care and enveloped him with their kind embrace. A tribe who honoured his father, sending him on his way to his ancestors. From that point onward, Tei was remembered – but Spider moved on.

As they walked on now, Spider looked across at the old man and belatedly answered him. "Yes, no point worrying ... and yes, let's stop for a short break at the top of the rise."

Spider girded himself as Growl took up another rambling story, the start of what he expected would be a long day of the old man's contorted nattering. He sighed. *Remember to enjoy life ... even this!*

*

After a day travelling ever south across the low, undulating terrain, they'd spent an uneventful night on the bank of a narrow river, sourced from the valleys of the hill range ahead of them. Surprisingly, Spider had slept well and uninterrupted. During their light breakfast, Growl had said it had been unnecessary to wake him, as he and Streak were quite alert to any dangers to their camp. But though a part of him recognised no immediate danger from this shaman, Spider couldn't shake his feeling of unease. *I can't bring myself to trust him.*

Even so, fully rested, they journeyed on towards the hills ahead, and to Spider's pleasant surprise, Growl remained quiet. He now wondered whether the old man had picked up on his irritation with his constant chattering. *Maybe I'll even converse with him today? Well, maybe later—*

"Another fine day, don't you think? Fair progress shall be made again today. Oh yes, we think so."

Spider cast a furtive glance at the old man. *I felt nothing, but does he read my mind? Or is it coincidence?* "I was thinking just the same. You must be reading my mind."

"Now that would be quite a skill, wouldn't you think? A fair skill indeed. We don't know many who claim to see into others. And not a skill we would claim ourselves. No, not at all."

Hmm, you might not claim it, but I've already seen – and felt – some of your shamanic tricks. "You claim the ability to speak with your wolf," Spider pressed. "If true, then why not my mind, or another's?"

"Our wolf? No, not *our* wolf. No, no one can own the free creatures of the land. No, nor should they." He scowled. "People try. Oh, they try. We know of peoples in the south who tried to control animals, to keep them fixed to their own lands. But they fail. Always fail." His leathery brow furrowed. "Will they succeed? We think they will. But at what cost? Would you like to be owned, controlled by another? To be nurtured, to be grown, only to be butchered? We think that would not be a nice place to be. Streak here is a friend, an ally – not *our* wolf."

You didn't answer my question, Spider thought, glancing at the man striding easily beside him. *Are you listening to me now? Will you answer?* Growl whistled a quiet tune and strode on. "Why Growl?" Spider asked, switching tacks.

"Why Growl?" the man echoed, interrupting his whistling. "That seems quite a wide question and may need an even wider answer."

Me and my stupid mouth.

"Let's see, where should we start on this one? Maybe here, maybe—"

"Let me make my question a little easier. Why were you given the name Growl?"

"Ah. Then this narrows the answer a little. Of course, we may still consider it wide – do I answer it from our perspective or from that of the giver of the name? Let me see—"

"Let me help you again," cut in Spider. "Let's try in stages, shall we? Who gave you the name Growl? And please consider it a very narrow question."

"Ah … Archea."

"Archea?"

"Yes."

"And who is Archea?"

"Was."

"Was?"

"Yes."

"Do I glean from this that Archea is deceased?"

"Yes."

"Okay. And who was Archea?"

"She was the Mother of the pack."

"Your mother? Or of your tribe?"

"No."

"No to mother, or no to your tribe?"

"Both."

Spider replayed the conversation. Pack. That was what he had actually said. "Let me make an educated guess – was Archea the mother of a pack of wolves?"

Growl clapped. "We like this game. Continue."

Spider swore under his breath. "The rules have changed. Just tell me how a wolf gave you the name."

"Can't we continue as we were? It is an excellent game."

"No. Just answer. Please."

"Ah, it is such a long time since we have played games. Streak sees no pleasure in games – only winning." He glanced over at Spider. "Indeed, you do seem set to end the game. A pity." Gaze returning to the land ahead, Growl strode on. "Archea found me after they left me to die as a baby, and she adopted me into her pack. I was raised for many sun-cycles until she finally drove me out – but with a wolf of her pack at my side, as friend and guardian."

"That can't have been Streak."

"Oh no, Streak came later … much later. That first guardian of mine was Diamond – she had a hard streak when needed. But was a great friend. When Diamond eventually died, the next day Crow appeared and sat by my fire. Crow became my next trusted friend and ally, staying for many sun-cycles until his untimely death – an injury taken defending me from a pack of hyenas. A new friend appeared the next day. And so, it continued, and continues to this day with Streak."

"And the name Growl?"

"Ah yes," Growl said, continuing to stride ahead. "Of course, the first people I met feared me … well, Diamond." He smiled. "She was not friendly to strangers. Not at all. But Crow, he kept his distance, and they ignored us. Mostly. Some would throw rocks at us – or worse. Then I met a tribe who allowed me to follow them. I tried to talk with them, but all they heard was growling." He shrugged. "Growl became my name."

Raised by wolves. Spider had heard of this before in stories but had not believed it to be true. And what else about this tale was nagging him? *'I', 'me'* … "You were talking of yourself there, Growl, as—"

Suddenly, Growl stopped and held his hand up as though for silence. Spider tensed, not sure what he was about to do. Unmoving, Growl's gaze seemed elsewhere.

"Growl?"

Growl's gestured again for silence.

Spider waited … and then fidgeted.

"Enemy ahead," Growl said, lowering his arm and looking at Spider. "Five individuals travelling fast towards us."

"How far?" Spider said immediately.

"Less than half the day. They will intercept us before nightfall."

Krez! Their intelligence on our movements is exceptionally good. And this even with a cordon of Streak's friends around them. *So not from scouts on the ground then.*

It seemed the Enemy had a long reach.

Spider glanced skywards. Birds constantly flew to and fro. If the Enemy's power was as strong as Naga said, could they be using these as eyes? Or maybe one of the birds of prey circling high above their heads? He glanced at Growl, who was staring back at him. Could he have this conversation with this man?

He tensed. He couldn't. Not yet. These were perilous times, and he couldn't risk letting this man he still knew very little about closer to him yet. "I guess we should get ready for a fight then. How about I take four and leave you and Streak the other?"

Growl smiled.

*

They decided that, given these men seemed to know where they were located, it was pointless to hide or try to spring a surprise ambush. "Straight for the jugular then," Spider said, and they agreed on a simple plan of attack. Now they just needed to wait for Streak to send a signal.

Spider fixed his eyes on Growl, who stood by a lone tree far to his left, but cast the occasional glance to the top of the rise. *Who are these people and just how are they tracking me?* He was certain it was another ally of the Ka. But why target him? And were they actually tracking him? *Or are they tracking Growl? If they are tracking us this well, then should I continue on to Rind, possibly compromising the camp there?* Now there was a big question.

He silently cursed. It was the waiting that was the worst. Too much time to think.

At that very moment, Growl held up his arm and pointed ahead. The signal!

Spider held up his arm to acknowledge, then strode forward.

Both men covered the ground at an easy pace, soon climbing the grassy rise. The timing of the signal had been perfect. As they reached the top of the rise, they saw the enemy group heading up towards them from the other side. One man clearly saw them, and the enemy group halted. Without hesitating, both he and Growl strode on.

Animated chatter drifted up from the men below, who were clearly uncertain how to deal with their sudden and direct action. Someone shouted orders, and Spider watched as the group split and fanned out ahead of them. *And so here we go,* he thought, girding himself for what was to come.

He jogged onward, stepping easily over the light vegetation, aiming for the figure to the right of centre. As he closed, there was a commotion at either end of the line of attackers, and a man screamed.

He ignored it, remaining focussed on his target, who had glanced briefly to his left, distracted by the shouting there. *You shouldn't have looked,* he thought as he hurled his spear at the man's chest. The man looked back towards him – but too late. The spear hammered into the man's chest, knocking him backwards with the impact. Spider was immediately upon him, driving a hand blade deep into the man's throat. He pulled the blade free and rolled away. He heard the man on the ground beside him screaming in agony. *He's out of this fight.*

As he stood, Spider caught a movement to his right, and on instinct, he dropped and rolled away to his left – but not before a glancing blow caught his right shoulder. *Krez! That hurt!* Scrambling to his knees, he saw a man bearing down on him, already swinging an enormous axe for a second blow. He rolled again, just clearing the axehead before it thumped into the ground. As the man pulled the axe out of the ground, Spider leapt up and readied himself – the element of surprise had gone, it was face-to-face combat now.

He could hear fighting to his far left and another struggle away to his right.

Focus!

The man facing him was massive and armed with a fearsome battle-axe.

Okay, this is going to be slightly tricky—

The huge man sprang forward with alarming speed, whipping the deadly axe around towards Spider's head. He ducked, feeling the axe brush past the hairs on his head. Heart thumping furiously, he twisted around and saw the axe already making a reverse sweep towards him – he ducked again, taking a step back. Without slowing, the attacker brought the axe back around a third time, keeping it low, aiming for his ankles. Spider leapt into the air, and the axe swept beneath the soles of his moccasins. Landing in a crouch, he tensed to strike with his blade – but his assailant's axe swept around once more, and he was forced to leap backwards, the edge of the huge man's axe-blade nicking his tunic as it passed.

Breaths coming in urgent gasps and his hand clenched tightly around his blade, Spider desperately sought an opportunity to strike, but his opponent's relentless onslaught drove him ever backwards. *At some point, he's going to figure out he can just charge me and take me out by simple brute force.*

As he continued to evade the man's frenzied attack, he felt a growing ache in his right shoulder. *That blow did more damage than I thought.* Instinctively, he switched his blade to his left hand. *Now that might have been a mistake,* he thought as the big man paused and grinned.

"Hurt, little man?" the huge man said in thickly accented words. "Prepare to die."

His fear drove him to act. *It's now or never!* As the enemy leapt at him, Spider dived forward, dropping to the ground. As the big man adjusted his axe swing in response, Spider twisted in his dive, his back slamming into the ground between the man's legs. At the same time, he grasped the man's right leg in his right hand and, ignoring the sharp pain in his shoulder, used the leverage to swing his left hand as hard as he could towards the man's crotch—

The sharp blade penetrated easily through leather – and more. Howling, the man stamped down on him – he grunted in pain as he felt a rib break.

But the damage was done.

As his assailant staggered away, the blade tugged out of Spider's hands, too deeply buried to easily withdraw. The crippled man sank to his knees, his hands between his legs, moaning. A rush of blood spilled to the ground as he pulled the blade free. Sickened, Spider looked away, but could not block out the man's whimpering. Forcing himself to his feet, he scanned the area, avoiding the sight of the dying man. Growl was making his way over to him, tailed by the wolf, Streak.

"All accounted for," Growl said as he approached. "And all dead, save this one." Growl walked over to the mortally wounded man. "And I see this one soon will be."

"Finish me," Spider heard the dying man say. "Please."

Growl pulled out his blade and put it to the throat of the man. "Who sent you?"

"I'm not the boss," the man groaned. "That was him over there."

"What tribe?"

"Azgoths."

"And the boss?"

"Same man."

"Why?"

The man's face contorted in pain. "Who knows what the Ka want?" he managed.

So, the Ka are indeed reaching far into our lands, Spider thought, fighting a growing dizziness. *I need to get to Rind.*

The fatally wounded man groaned and doubled over. "So much pain. Finish it. Please …"

"Last question, my friend," Growl said softly. "Where are the Ka now?"

"Everywhere … Please … It hurts …"

"Go rest with your ancestors, my friend." Growl made a sharp movement with his hand. He slowly lowered the man to the ground, and then turned and studied Spider. "What have you done to annoy the Ka, my friend?"

Spider's head spun. "It takes nothing to annoy those fiends," he breathed, holding his shoulder.

"You are hurt."

Spider shook his head. "Just a scratch." But as he turned to scan around them, he staggered, then fell to his knees, terrible nausea twisting his gut. He bent over and retched.

"We think you have travelled as far as you are able today, my friend," came Growl's calm voice. "We will rest down by that stand of trees for the day – and maybe the night. Unless you insist that we travel on."

Lifting his head to answer, Spider cringed as a stabbing pain shot down to his gut. He leaned over and threw up again.

"We take that as a no," came Growl's quiet, wry voice. "Camp here it is."

As another wave of nausea cut through him, Spider groaned. *Here. Yes, here. But please, don't speak. Leave me in peace. Please.*

Growl helped him to his feet, then guided him down the rise.

The shaman didn't say a word.

CHAPTER TWENTY

Throughout the great span of the Continuum, many tribes, many empires, have come and gone. So, what of the Ka? What was their place in the Continuum? What was their place in history?

"Now that is a very interesting drink," Shadow said, downing the contents of his smooth wooden bowl and handing the cup over to Stealth. "I'll gladly take another."

"You are more than welcome, my friend. It has been a while since I had the pleasure of drinking with company." The grey-haired man waved the cup at Sy. "And you?"

The warrior monk gave an imperceptible shake of the head, then took a sip from his still-full cup.

"I'm intrigued by your wine-making skills, old man," Shadow said as Stealth crossed to a carved stone basin by the glowing ember fire. "This has a fair bite, and several of these cups would loosen the tongue. A drink that may stab you in the back in the morning."

"Backstabber indeed," Stealth said, sliding back the wooden cover on the stone basin. "Created with help from the land's smaller creatures, but who were none too pleased when I raided their hive." He dunked each cup into the pool of liquid within. "This seems a good night to take full measure of its character … and ours."

Drops of rich, deep-red liquid spilling to the ground, Stealth returned with the two newly filled cups. He passed one to Shadow, then raised his own. "Health and strength to you both," he declared, then took a deep draught.

Shadow watched as the old man sat back down into a quite wondrous chair. Constructed using expertly curved pieces of sleek, carved wood to form its frame, a taut leather hide cleverly strung between two of the main struts served as the seat. *A most comfortable place to sit. It seems this Stealth is a skilled maker.* Shadow raised his cup. "And health to you, old man – not that it seems you've been short of it."

Savouring the delicious wine, Shadow felt the tension ease from his mind. This was proving a most welcome – and unexpected – relief from the stresses of the last days. Days that had included furtive scouting and readying for battle in the company of that fool, Krag. Preparations that had culminated in a near disaster with the failed attack on the Iyes tribe. *We were lucky to retrieve the Staff.* He blew out a low sigh. And lucky the supposed Warriors had failed to materialise.

Save one.

Yes, save one. The woman he had sliced with his poisoned blade. The woman who should now be dead. He swirled the glistening contents of his cup. *Should be dead, but the Ancient One was unsure that it would be so …* He muttered a curse under his breath. *I had the chance, and I may have missed it.*

He took a good swig from his cup. *Let it go for now.* He glanced across at Stealth, who sat in silence in his most comfortable chair. *Learn what you can here, then return home and report to the Ensi – and then prepare for war.*

He took another gulp of wine, then leaned forward, switching his attention to his intriguing host. "So how does one obtain a role serving a dragon?" he said brightly. "And how does one survive such a task?"

Stealth laughed. "This task was offered and accepted in but a fleeting moment of madness when the Ancient One – until then a fantastical myth of our storytellers – arrived in my homeland, seeking a new servant. My leader volunteered me, and I foolishly agreed. And to survive? Jump when my master says jump. Very simple."

"Even if off a cliff?"

"If commanded, then yes, I'd have to take the plunge and hope for the best. Luckily for me, that request has not been forthcoming – and I don't worry my master by asking about it."

Sy's fingers flashed.

"My friend, slowly savouring his drink over there, wonders how long you've lived here."

Stealth glanced over at Sy, who sat cross-legged opposite him. "You follow my conversation? You read my mouth?"

Sy's fingers flashed.

"Oh, he can hear you fine," Shadow said, ignoring Sy's answer.

Stealth looked surprised. "But you sign to him all the time."

"Yes. Annoying, isn't it?" Shadow saw the confusion on Stealth's face. "He insists I do it, because he has to do it. Keeps me in tune with him, he says. Keeps me skilled in the art, he says." Shadow gave a wry smile. "A real pain, I say."

Stealth smiled and stroked his short white beard. "Well, in part answer to your friend's question, it seems I've lived here but a moment, yet it must be many, many sun-cycles since I first arrived." He glanced across at Sy. "Long ago, I stopped measuring the passage of time, and so I have the dilemma of being unable to answer your question directly." He smiled. "I must be doing something right, because she retains my services."

Sy's fingers flashed, and Shadow spoke. "Does 'she' have a name?"

"Yes. Master."

"That's not particularly friendly, but I expect being a feared predator doesn't lend itself to making many friends." Shadow swirled the remaining liquid in his cup before draining it.

"I expect she prefers it this way."

"Not my way of living. What is life if you can't enjoy it with friends? And with a drink in your hand. Speaking of which, I'll refill once again. No, stay on your throne, I'll help myself. And help you to another if you wish?"

"My cup suffices for now, but I see your thirst is greater than mine." Stealth gestured to the stone basin. "Please, relax. Enjoy."

Needing no further prompting, Shadow rose from the squat fur-covered log he sat on, then wandered over to the stone vessel, where he dipped his cup into the inviting pool. "So just a half-moon ago you made this, you said. Honey, you mentioned. Also, a red berry, I presume. What else is in here?"

"Ah, I need to keep some secrets for now. But I'll give you one of the berries. Hawthorn."

"Not a plant you find around here," Shadow observed, returning to his seat. "Nor indeed a plant bearing berries at this time."

"Indeed. A bonus from a brief trip south last sun-cycle. Stored safely in ice on the mountain here to use when needed for my ... concoctions."

Shadow kept his voice even. "A quick trip alone?"

"In that case, no. I travelled just as you arrived here."

"So, these are regular trips you make with your master to collect berries, or do you occasionally branch out into other ventures?"

"I'm at my master's service, Shadow. I simply do her bidding."

"And Sy and I can understand that." Shadow swilled the rich liquid around his cup. "We too are faithful servants to our Ensi." He took another drink. "And so, you can see our frustration by the offer of an extended stay here – one it seems I was in no position to refuse. And I don't mean to be ungrateful, for I am pleased to make your acquaintance, but our leader was keen for our early return; we have urgent work to attend to."

Stealth smiled, sitting back in his chair. "'Urgent' is a word that my master pays little heed to." He took a sip of his wine. "And in fact, she may be right – I suspect many things are falsely claimed to be such."

Shadow glanced at Sy's flicking fingers. He shook his head.

"Your friend has a view on this?" Stealth asked, raising an eyebrow.

Shadow smiled. "Sy always has a view. Even as a young boy, he was the most talkative amongst us – not with his voice, of course; that was not a skill deemed needed for him." He grinned at his friend. "But you didn't need a voice to pester your friends constantly, did you, Sy? Or to get your friends into constant trouble and then be the first to disappear."

Sy tilted his head and signed back. Shadow laughed. "Yes, it's true, the rest of us were just too slow and lazy." He turned to Stealth. "What about you? I can't see you being slow and lazy as a child."

"No, I don't believe I was. I was never given time to be so, even though I tried. A big stick will make most children move eventually."

Shadow smiled. "Although maybe not the best way to build trust and loyalty – they can turn on the big stick when you least expect it."

"Very true." Stealth took a sip of his wine. "I expect you are very aware of this risk – in the Ka tribe …"

Shadow savoured another mouthful of his drink. "That statement could be taken in many ways, my friend, but as your guest, I take it as not meant to criticise." He glanced to the ember fire. "It's true the Ka live a disciplined life, one true to the teachings of Kaos. But it is needed. There are those who would help destroy this land, despoilers who are skilled and determined about their task, devils constantly striving to infiltrate tribes and infect them with their lies, twisting them to their goal."

Stealth gazed at him over his cup. "You have someone in mind?"

Shadow frowned. "You need to ask this question? You, a servant of the Ancient?"

Stealth smiled. "And yet I ask."

"The cursed Iyes, of course. Who else?"

"Who else indeed," Stealth murmured, taking a sip of his wine.

"The cursed Iyes," Shadow repeated. "Liars and spreaders of hate against our people. Killers of our people." He took a deep draught of wine. "But Kaos saw this, saw we needed a disciplined and regimented approach to defend against them and to ultimately defeat them."

"The origin of your first Ensi, I believe."

"The first Ensi," Shadow echoed in agreement. "The greatest man of his time, the one commanded by Kaos to create the Ka. He aided this man to become our first true leader, helped him shape that embryonic tribe into a fearsome defence against the growing evil of the Iyes." He sighed. "So, a big stick? Yes, and more. To keep a discipline. To keep an enduring guard against the destructive lies of the Iyes."

Stealth tilted his head a fraction. "Not that I want to question this doctrine – I agree discipline weaves worthy bonds within a tribe – but to the extreme practiced by the Ka?"

"It must be this way. We grow in numbers, both from within the tribe and from those brought in from outside, those brought in to contribute and help develop the tribe. We must maintain a discipline and a culture. Those who progress with us understand why it is this way and what it does for them – making them better people; better skilled and educated; better prepared; and yes, ultimately more loyal to our cause and to the Ensi. Those who reach the required level have a hard but rewarding life."

"And those that don't?"

"They leave. They must leave. It's unfortunate, but we can retain only the best. And for those leaving, it's the best for them too." Shadow shrugged. "I bear no animosity to those who leave, they simply were unable, or unwilling, to dedicate their lives to us or to aid us in our fight against the Iyes and their vengeful god. I pity those that leave, but, in the end, they too will benefit from the actions of a brave few."

Shadow looked into his cup. "This is one of life's lessons – a brave few take us forward to a better life, new opportunities. The many? They accept what they have, wishing no change, no discomfort, until they and their tribe fester and stagnate, swept into oblivion by others who have moved on."

"I'd have thought it better if the progressive tribe could move on and leave the others to their way of living. Wouldn't that seem fairer?"

"Ha!" Shadow exclaimed with a scowl. "Fairer? Of course, it would be fairer. But have you seen it out there? New tribes, new peoples, expanding across all lands with no regard for those before them, all driven on by the foul talk of the Iyes." His distaste gave a sharp edge to his voice. "And within those masses of peoples are particular scum, the most cruel and unjust you could ever have the misfortune to cross, leading tribes that are the most savage you could meet. Try having a conversation on fairness with them with an axe in your forehead. It might not end well." He glared at Stealth. "Tribes must defend themselves against that tyranny. They must stay one step ahead of those looking to destroy them. Then it may be possible for us all to move on."

"Move on to where, my friend?"

"To stop the slaughter of innocents!" Shadow shouted, throwing his cup across the chamber. He stood and walked over to stare into the soft glow of the fire. "To stop the endless killing," he whispered.

*

Stealth watched the man standing, head bowed, in front of the glowing embers. *That one hurts inside.* That was clear. Yet recognising someone's pain was different from understanding it. *My master said this one was different, but I am yet to see it.* He glanced over at Shadow's companion, still seated on the ground to his right. *Sy.* The name of an owl found far to the east, a particularly aggressive hunter of the night, known to attack humans if threatened. The man certainly moved with a fluidity and grace that suggested a much tougher proposition to fight than Shadow. But aggressive? He didn't appear naturally so – but neither did the owl on first sight. No, aggressive was not the right description for this man. Deadly, maybe. Smart, definitely. Very difficult to read, absolutely. *A man who keeps his emotions in check, but who undoubtably follows a mission with a passion.*

And a man who observed everything around him whilst appearing to see nothing.

"I'm sorry," Shadow said in a low voice. "It seems this drink does indeed release the tongue."

Stealth glanced back to the Disciple of the Ensi, who remained standing by the fire. "Nothing to apologise for, my friend. Passion creates a far richer conversation than those who would merely nod and smile at their partner's dreary monologue. And being brutally honest, I accept any form of dialogue these days."

Shadow turned, a thin smile on his lips. "Well, that removes any pressure to entertain you this night."

Stealth took a sip from his cup. "My first impression of you – if I may be so bold – suggests you don't suffer under that pressure at all. I doubt any consider you poor company."

"Only to myself, I think," Shadow replied, loping back from the fire. "And those conversations you don't want to hear."

Sy's hands flashed.

Shadow grunted a laugh as he sat. "Sy believes I'm generally dire company, and you've only now seen the better side of me – my back."

Stealth smiled. The two men had a good bond between them. "Who taught you both this hand language?" he asked, moving the conversation away from the Ka's enmity with the Iyes, a subject that had darkened his guest's mood.

Shadow's eyes brightened. "Ah yes, a most fortuitous encounter." He leaned forward, his malaise slipping away. "In one of our remote empire tribes lived a woman who'd been helping her son communicate with her. The son had stolen from another but lied about his crime when confronted. In keeping with the required Ka punishment, they cut out the man's tongue. They allowed him to stay in that tribe but restricted to camp work only. His mother developed a way for him to use his hands to talk to her, and the signing was observed by the Ka overseer, who noticed a complexity he hadn't seen before. The information found its way to the right place. They realised it could be adapted to other situations, such as aiding Sy here."

And for your fighters, Stealth thought. The Ka wouldn't miss a silent means of complex communication. "A strict punishment. What did he steal?"

"That matters not," Shadow said, shaking his head. "He stole and then lied. If he'd admitted his wrong, his punishment would have been less. He was a fool." His eyes flicked to Stealth as if reading his thoughts. "Yes, it's strict, but all tribes of the empire must hold to the Ka values; they must be aligned to fight against those who seek to destroy our lands." He took a slug from his cup, then shrugged. "Unfortunately, our enemy isn't visible day-to-day, and so some of our allies relax their guard."

"And maybe don't appreciate the strict regime imposed on them?"

"We return to the big stick. A discipline has to be maintained so that we're ready."

"I can see you have your own discipline, my friend. But …"

"But?"

Stealth took a sip of his prized wine. *My best yet, I would say. And perfect for my special guest.* He glanced at Shadow, eyes twinkling in glowing firelight. "But I don't see a strict, regimented person before me, someone who wishes his life to be constrained by the discipline he so easily talks of. Rather, I see one who would rather be free from the shackles of conformity and order, one who accepts authority yet refuses to embrace it. This doesn't seem compatible with the attributes your leader might choose."

Out of the corner of his eye, Stealth saw Sy change his position ever so slightly, and knew the man's keen eyes were on him.

Shadow laughed. "You judge my character so quickly? But how accurately, you wonder?" The Ka turned back to the fire. "And it would seem a risk to hold such a man close, would it not?" He drew a long draught of wine, then tilted his head. "What would I think if such a man stood by my side? I would think that maybe this man, if he were brave enough, might tell me what he really thought. Maybe he would even disagree with me to my face. And maybe this man may prove a most valuable source of contrary views and opinions, slicing through the stale diatribes of the rest of the kowtowing crowd." Shadow flicked a glance to Stealth. "A dangerous role to take on, for sure, but potentially rewarding if done well." He smiled. "I could see the value in that."

With these words, memories flooded back to Stealth. Of when he'd been younger. Of when he'd spoken words such as these. The first stirring of genuine warmth for the Ka rose within him.

Shadow downed the last of his cup. "But enough of these musings. I see in you a skilled storyteller, and while I refill our cups, we should hear the tale of the dragon and his companion. A tale that should be told before we drain the last drop."

*

Sipping from his refilled cup, Stealth stroked his short beard. "I was the best fighter in my tribe. The best of any fighters I knew. Better than you, as you are now."

"Ha," Shadow said, shaking his head. "That isn't easily proven."

"No matter," Stealth continued. "When our tribe came under the control and influence of another, they assigned me to a special unit, which sought new tribes for assimilation – or for destruction. We were very good. I was very good. After one sun-cycle, our unit leader was killed – unexpectedly – and they asked me to take over command."

Shadow raised an eyebrow. "Unexpectedly?"

"And so, I led this unit for another sun-cycle," Stealth continued, ignoring Shadow's accusatory question. "And then for many more. During that time, we'd occasionally cross the paths of those previously conquered tribes – and it was as though we'd never been. They'd abandoned all we'd taught them. Yes, they knew that each sun-cycle they should send one, or two, of their best people to my tribe's home base, but this—"

"Home base? Your tribe must have been a large tribe. What was its name?"

"But this was only to keep us away," Stealth continued, again ignoring the interruption, "and to ensure they could continue their life unchanged." He took another sip. "In my view, this was wrong. What was the point of educating these tribes, when as soon as we left, they reverted to their primitive ways? At some point, they would stop sending people, and then we'd have to search for them again and punish them to remind them of their obligation."

"Well, did you have a better idea?"

"Embed someone in their tribes. Someone to teach them our ways, our ways of working, healing, manufacturing, to build supply chains for those materials we needed – or desired."

Shadow raised his cup. "A grand idea, my friend. So, who did you present this great idea to?"

"I went to the top. I found out the time of the next council meeting, and I invited myself to it."

"Hah!" Shadow exclaimed jovially, the contents of his cup swirling dangerously close to the edge as he waved his hand. "A wondrous idea. And you obviously survived such an invitation."

"I did," Stealth said, stroking his beard. "Just. I was insistent that I speak. A blade held to a council member's back was enough to encourage him to introduce me to the council and invite me to speak. I'd just started to present my thoughts when a council member thought it strange for another member to be standing beside me. He instructed the man to join them. Of course, I couldn't prevent this – as soon as the man was a stride away, he ran, shouting that I was an assassin come to kill the leader."

"Ah," Shadow murmured, nodding sagely. "Now, undoubtably, this would be a foul position to find oneself in."

Stealth smiled. "I quickly hid the blade, then threw my hands in the air, pleading my innocence, explaining I only wanted to share important information that the council would want to hear."

"Well, important to you – and I can see even more so now, given your predicament."

"By now, guards surrounded me. The council members instructed them to take me away to be punished later. It was at that moment the leader spoke. His was a quiet voice, but one that instantly silenced all present.

"He asked me a few questions, and then told me to proceed with my submission. With a confident voice born of the unshakeable belief in my words, I relayed what I'd seen, and what I thought. He listened but said nothing throughout. When I finished, he spoke with a woman on his left; her face was dyed a striking red-and-black design. This dye-faced woman bowed, then spoke with a guard. The guard saluted, then walked with a purpose to me, bidding me follow him. I admit, my heart sank. Fearing the worst, I prepared to fight my way out—"

"Fight your way out of your own tribe? Where is the loyalty there?"

"I had – and still have – an overwhelming urge for self-preservation. Anyway, I was mistaken. The guard guided me to a tented shelter, instructing me to wait for further instruction. The presence of two armed men by the entrance of the tent encouraged me to bide my time. As I awaited my fate, I noticed a table laden with fruits and berries, and so I passed the time quite easily. Then the dye-faced woman returned. 'From tomorrow, you will be based here,' she told me, 'and you will implement your ideas.' She clicked her fingers, and another woman appeared. 'Show this man the camp layout and begin his instruction.' The woman bowed almost to her feet. Then, as Dye-face left, she instructed me to report back at the turn of the moon."

"Did this Dye-face have a name?"

"My liege."

Shadow grinned. "Did she at least accept you had a name?"

"She called me ... anything she wanted."

Shadow laughed.

"And so, I studied, I reported, and then for the next two sun-cycles, I implemented my plan." Stealth smiled. "It was a success. Within another sun-cycle, I was sitting on the leader's right hand as his special advisor."

"Impressive ... *hick* ... very impressive," Shadow said, following it up with a loud burp. "Ah, better out than in." He shifted position, swaying slightly. "So, you found your way to the top. But where did the dragon come in? We need to hear more on this."

"Just as soon as I've replenished my cup," Stealth said, climbing to his feet.

Shadow held out his own cup. "Excellent idea! I was thinking just the same."

"*Our* cups it will be," Stealth said, taking the proffered vessel.

"Thank you, my good friend," Shadow drawled. "Full it fill ... Or something like that ... And then onto dragons ..."

*

Stealth leaned back, his story complete. "And that is how I met my master. A request for me to serve, yes, but it seemed the deal was already done. I had been chosen." He shook his head and smiled. "And to think I agreed to but a single sun-cycle. But here I still am ..."

"Indeed, here you are," Shadow said, his bright eyes beginning to glaze. "Drinking wine with two wondrous companions, your life's ambition finally met! Let's drink to that." And Shadow downed his cup.

Stealth lifted his own, saluted Shadow, and drank. "Well," he said, standing, "I wish you two men a pleasant remaining evening, but I must rise early on the morrow." He glanced at his empty cup. "And I fear that won't be easy."

"But the story is unfinished," Shadow protested. "You tarried here much longer than your promised single sun-cycle. What changed? Why stay so long? And I would hear of your master's work. Where—"

"Questions – and answers – for another time. I would request that you allow your host to retire for this night. But don't let me stop you both. Please enjoy what's left of the wine."

Shadow struggled to his feet, then stood, rather unsteadily, gripping his cup tightly as though fearing Stealth might steal it away. "I think I'll have one more with Sy here – just to ensure we've fairly treated your wine and hospitality." Sy frowned. "And on this evening," Shadow continued, "I wouldn't wish to hurt my host's feelings by saying I wish instead I'd been heading home. And so, I won't. Instead, I'll thank him for his company and for his tale, then wish him a pleasant night."

He held out his hand, and as Stealth grasped his wrist, Shadow pulled him into an embrace. "Good health, my friend," he slurred.

"Good health," Shadow replied.

Stealth pulled away, then made his way across the chamber to the exit. He paused and glanced back. "Oh, and my old tribe?" he said quietly. "The Ka." He turned and walked out of the chamber.

CHAPTER TWENTY-ONE

One sought help. The other grasped his opportunity.

Walking past the old coaching inn into the heart of a lakeside village already bustling with the morning's tourists, Tricia, her mouth dry as desert sand, turned down the hill to the bookshop. How was she going to open this conversation? She had an opening gambit in mind, but how would the chess game unfold after that? There was no set Sicilian Defence or Ruy-Lopez to follow. This was like making the first move, knocking all the pieces off the board, and then waiting to see how the opponent responded.

Why on earth was she thinking of chess at a time like this?

I'm bloody good at it, that's why.

That's still no reason to bring it in right now, her sensible half replied. *It's not relevant – you're just stressed.*

Go to hell, her irrational side replied. *I don't need you right now.*

Tricia sighed. In this, she needed irrational, even slightly unhinged. Because what of any of this seemed sensible, especially now in the cold – and sober – light of day?

But you saw them on the trail. You saw them vanish right before your eyes.

She winced. For days, she'd pushed that fantastical memory away, driven it deep in the darkest recesses of her mind. And she'd told Erin to do the same: "All we know for sure is that they walked ahead of us, we caught glimpses of that lad, Lanky, and then we lost sight of them." This was the story for the police. And it was true. *Except you left out the vanishing bit.*

Because they would have been locked up if they had told that part.

And, anyway, I didn't believe what my eyes had seen ...

Until Jess came back.

Tricia grimaced. Until her friend returned with a tale of vanishing from this age, then landing in another. And with a girl in tow who was … different. Which was no problem in itself; she liked different. It was to be celebrated and embraced. But she recognised different when she saw it. River wouldn't be out-of-place on the streets of most towns, far from it, but her actions and behaviours were of a caged animal trapped in a threatening environment and aching for release.

A girl who could well have come from another time and place. There, I said it. Happy now?

She looked up and saw she was approaching the bookshop. The one with the antiques in the window, Jessica had said. She passed the closed door, then stopped at the window, pretending to browse the books on display. *I should just go in.* But how would the bookseller react? He knew Lanky – who was now a missing person. *If I mention his name, will he think I'm involved in his disappearance? Will he simply go straight to the police?*

She drew a deep breath. They needed the bookseller to meet Jessica. *So stop stalling.*

She scanned the shop for customers, which was difficult to do given the number of antique objects and books on display in the window. And of course, there was an upstairs out of sight. But she saw no one inside. *Then move.* Steeling herself, she turned back to the front door, pushed it open, then entered the shop.

"Good morning," came a welcoming voice. A man she guessed to be in his late fifties sat at a small desk, peering at her above his steel-rimmed glasses.

"Good morning," Tricia replied, her words pushing past the fear in her throat.

The man smiled. "Let me know if I can help you with anything. I'll be right here."

She smiled back. "Thank you, I—"

The door opened behind her, and she turned to see a family of four enter. "Thank you," she stammered at the bookseller. "I'm just going to browse for now." She walked away to the nearest bookshelf.

The family seemed to have no particular book in mind, and happily browsed the antiques before heading upstairs. *Heck. Do I wait for them to come down?* She glanced across at the bookseller, who was now reading a morning newspaper. *What if someone else comes in?* She listened to the group chatting upstairs. *Do it. Now!*

Forcing herself to walk over to the desk, she rubbed her hands, suddenly cold and clammy, on her trousers leg.

The bookseller looked up as she approached. "Found something?"

"Not yet," she said, fighting an overwhelming desire to turn and run. "There's a particular book I'm looking for. I tried the antique book section over there, but unfortunately, I didn't find it."

"And what were you looking for?"

Here goes. "Well, a friend of mine intrigued me with tales of the Long Valley. In particular, on the tales of the Axes of Power."

It was only slight, but Tricia caught the sharpening of interest in the man's eyes. "Axes of Power? Is that the name of the book?"

"I don't know the name of any specific book, only that these Axes seemed of particular interest to my friend – he told some fantastic tales about them. I thought this would be a good place to see if I could find out more about them."

The bookseller studied her for a moment, then shook his head. "It sounds as though your friend is a good storyteller, to have captured your interest so," he said, holding his engaging smile. "Unfortunately, I don't know of any such books. It seems on this occasion, I am of little help. But please look around – maybe there is something hidden away that may enlighten us both."

Tricia felt a sinking feeling in her stomach. *He's not biting.* She glanced to the staircase. The family was still upstairs. She looked back at the bookseller, who held his pleasant smile. Yet his eyes didn't smile. *He doesn't trust me. He doesn't know me.* She thought furiously. *But he knows the lad.* "That's a pity," she said, playing her queen to attack his king. "My friend, Lanky, will be disappointed."

The man stiffened, his smile evaporating. "Lanky? Not a common name around here."

"No, he's the only Lanky I know here. I believe you know him."

His eyes hardened. "Who are you?" he whispered. "How—"

"… yes, and if we get three of them, we can get a deal," came a woman's voice floating down the stairs.

"But will you read all three? We've only a day left of the holiday," said the man, who Tricia guessed to be her partner, "and you don't read at all back home."

"Well, if not, I can save for next year's holiday, can't I? How much for these three?" asked the woman, dressed in attire ready for the next Artic blizzard, as she and her family approached the till.

Tricia stood aside to let the family through to the till. The woman brought out her wallet to pay, then noticed Tricia as if for the first time. "Oh, I'm sorry. Were you here first? Oh well," she continued, without waiting for a response, "I'll be gone shortly, and then you can be served. I do apologise."

Holding her tongue, she waited for the lady to finish paying, then watched her exit the shop with her family.

"How do you know Lanky?" the bookseller asked sharply, looking far less friendly than he had a moment ago.

Yes, how do I know the lad who vanished from this village? Her hands shaking, she held the man's glare. "I was there when he disappeared," she said, sacrificing her queen to attempt to save the game. "And we need your help. I don't understand all that's going on, but maybe you will."

The man gaped. "Just who are you? What—"

The door opened behind them, and in wandered a very familiar, and very unwelcome, face – the local police officer. Tricia's mind worked fast. "Yes. Thank you so much for your help, it's kind of you to deliver. I really can't thank you enough. And just to confirm again – it's the cottage at Hows End. Anytime really – but, of course, the sooner the better – even by lunchtime would be great. Ha, ha. Joke." *Stop talking!*

The bookseller's hesitation was barely noticeable. He smiled. "I will try my best."

Tricia smiled back. "Good. Well, thank you again." She turned and, knowing she couldn't simply ignore him, walked up to the officer. "Ah, Sergeant," she said, lowering her voice. "How are you? Any news?"

The police officer acknowledged her with a respectful nod. "Nothing more in this moment, Ms. Williams. But if there is, I will let you know."

Tricia nodded. *Just leave it at that.* "Thank you, Sergeant. Let's hope we hear something soon." She smiled at him, then made her way out of the shop, desperately holding herself back from sprinting away up the street. Halfway along the road, she forced herself to breathe. *I tried. Now we wait and see.*

*

Fletcher watched as the young lady left the shop, and then turned to Robert. "Doing deliveries now? That's a new one for you, isn't it?"

"You're right," Robert said, moving some items on the desk. "Seem to be going soft. The truth of it is, I must have climbed out of bed on the wrong side this morning. Forgot to bring in the card machine. I'll have to close up the shop for a short while to get back home and fetch it."

Robert crouched behind his desk, then Fletcher heard the fumbling clink of keys as he locked a drawer or cupboard. Reappearing, Robert walked around his desk and out to meet Fletcher. "Best I do it now before I risk losing more business. But forgive me, Fletcher. What was it you wanted? Not really a big book man, are you? Or have I finally converted you?"

The young officer smiled. "Afraid not yet. I was just doing my daily check around town to see if anyone had seen or heard anything – anything out of the ordinary."

Robert shook his head. "Unfortunately, nothing. And I guess that means you have nothing new? Not even your people from out of town?"

"You know the score, Robert. I can't go into much about the wider investigations – all for good reasons. But, no, we still have a missing persons investigation going on, and that tells you the state of play. How's Lanky's mum doing?"

Robert's face fell. "Still devastated, of course. She's grateful for the support you've been giving her, but it has hit her hard. I hope we get something soon."

Fletcher sighed. "We all do. This isn't a pleasant situation for anyone."

A silence fell, each briefly alone with their thoughts. Then Robert glanced around the shop. "It's why I keep doing this. Keeps me busy. Keeps the mind off what-ifs."

"I can understand that. People deal with events like this in different ways … people like that young woman who was just in here."

"Oh?"

"It was one of her friends who disappeared at the same time as Lanky."

"Ah yes. Hows End cottage, she said. Two of them up there, I think I've heard?"

Fletcher nodded. "She's held it together very well – seems a positive character at heart."

"She's friendly. But it must hurt."

"Yes, it must." He paused, then: "Would you buy books at a time like this?"

Robert held his gaze and smiled. He gestured at a bookshelf. "Books are my livelihood. And for many, they are solace in times of need."

"Of course." Fletcher reached over and half pulled a book from the shelf. "Did she mention anything of particular interest?"

Robert's brow furrowed. "No, nothing I can immediately think of. I spent most of my time dealing with another family."

Fletcher nodded. He pushed the book back into place. "Okay, I should keep on with my rounds," he said, making his way to the door.

"I know I don't need to remind you, but anything you see or hear that might be of relevance, just give me a call."

"Of course, Fletcher. Of course."

Fletcher opened the door to leave. "Oh," he said, pausing and glancing back. "Did I ask what books she ordered?"

"No, I don't think you did." Robert rubbed his cheek. "Hmm ... five books ... I think three were fantasy/sci-fi books, and the other two were ... hmm ... related to this area. You know, its history, the geology ... I've the ticket if you want to see it?"

Fletcher held up a hand. "No, no, that's fine. Just my natural interest to know stuff, I guess." He laughed. "'Nosiness' it could be called in a different profession." He turned to the door. "Well, I'll be off. And you better get off on your errand quickly. I can see this gent wants to get in. See you later."

"Ah yes. See you later, Fletcher." There was the briefest of pauses, then Robert's words to his customer, "I'm extremely sorry ..."

Nothing new offered by that visit, Fletcher thought, stroking his short goatee as he ambled slowly around the corner and on towards his next stop.

No, nothing offered, but possibly something gleaned.

Because something wasn't right here. No, not at all. He'd seen Ms. Williams from his vantage point across the road – a lucky coincidence as he'd just been stopped by old Mrs. Whitcombe with a complaint about potholes on the pavement – and observed the young woman enter the bookshop with a caution not usually displayed by your casual shopper. And then the slightly odd – *strained?* – reaction from both her and Robert to his appearance. A connection between her and Robert? It seemed the most unlikely connection he would have made, but one he could not, and would not, ignore.

As he walked on past the post office, his eyes narrowed. Ever since Lanky's and the two women's disappearance up in the valley, his thoughts had repeatedly returned to the two friends remaining at the cottage. He was certain they knew more than they were telling. But if they did know something more, why hide it when it might help locate their friends? That he didn't know. *Which is why we'll hold them here for a while longer, to see what else we can find.*

Maybe he was reading too much into what he'd seen ... and maybe not.

An interesting start to the day. Let's see what else it offers.

*

"Just one more coffee, then my brain might engage." Tricia took a sip from her mug, then placed it on the breakfast bar.

"You said that about the last one," Erin muttered from the kitchen table.

"And the one before that," Jessica added, sitting beside River across from Erin. She ran her brush through a last tangled strand of her drying hair. Despite the harrowing strain on them all, a shower had been a necessity she just couldn't ignore.

"That shows you how much I need it," Tricia murmured, glancing again to the window.

Jessica placed her brush on the table and looked over at her friend. "We've waited long enough, Trish. I can't risk staying any longer. The police officer you saw will be even more suspicious after seeing you with the bookseller."

Pursing her lips, Tricia glanced at Jessica. "Suspicious of what? Me being in a bookshop? Given we've been told to stay in the area for a while, I don't see the problem with buying books to help relieve the stress about my missing friends." Tricia held a finger to her chin. "Mmm, except now you're not missing. Hey, maybe I should cancel that order I gave the guy."

Jessica shook her head. When stressed, Tricia used humour as her defence. *Attempted humour.* But that was of no use to them right now. "And even if he saw nothing wrong with you being there," she said firmly, "my guess is he'll still be thinking of his visit to the cottage last night ..." She glanced at Erin. "Thinking of your panicked call about an intruder in the house. I know I would."

"Sorry. But there *were* intruders in the house. Two of you."

Tricia took another sip of her coffee. "Well, if he comes for another visit, you can skedaddle upstairs with your friend, and Erin and I will have coffee with him. We've plenty to serve him."

"And my final point," Jessica said, glaring at Trish, "is that we've no way of knowing whether the bookseller is going to turn up. It didn't sound like your meeting went that well. We could waste a full day, getting nowhere. Or worse, finding ourselves arrested."

"I hope he turns up. I ordered books."

Ignoring Tricia's lame joke, Jessica continued. "I can't wait any longer. I need to go and find him because he's the only one who may be able to help us." The now familiar nausea twisted her gut. "And we need help now, else ..." *Else Beth and Lanky may be trapped within the nightmare of that ancient land.*

Tricia made to say something, then seemed to change her mind. She took a sip from her mug, her face suddenly serious. "He reacted, Jess.

I know we didn't have long to speak, but I saw the shock in his eyes when I mentioned those … those Axes." She picked up her mug and walked over to the table and sat beside Erin. "And as I said, he didn't spill all to that police officer. He kind of played along with what I said."

"What you ranted, you mean," Erin muttered. She flicked her sharp, blue eyes to Jessica. "We don't know what the bookseller said after Trish left, but after hearing what happened, I reckon that sergeant's probably suspicious as hell. You can't stay here."

Dark thoughts lingering on Beth and Lanky, Jessica forced herself to the present. *Focus on the bookseller. Find him, see his reaction, then decide what to do next.* She turned to River … who was screwing up her nose. She placed her hand on the girl's shoulder. "You okay?"

"I just smell strange. I think it's that liquid I put in my hair."

Despite herself, Jessica smiled. "Well, we're both cleaner, and I for one needed that shower."

It had been quite an effort persuading River to get into the shower cubicle, even though they'd set everything up and left the water running. They ended up leaving the cubicle door open and living with a very wet bathroom. But when they eventually had to head outside, the last thing they needed was to draw attention to themselves, appearing as bedraggled as they had. She gently squeezed River's shoulder. "I know how different all this is for you, but you're doing really well."

River glanced around. "There is just so much of … everything. You must have great makers to create all this," she said, gesturing around the room. "Everything is crafted, yet all so smooth, so precise. And crafted of such strange materials." She picked up a fork from the table. "Like this. What is this made from?"

"It's a metal," Jessica replied, seeing the wonder on River's face as the girl ran her fingers down the handle of the fork. A metal that wouldn't appear until millennia past River's time.

"I don't know this word, but I see this … metal everywhere here." River glanced up, peering at the window. "And that opening over there, filled with a clear material like the crystals you find in rocks. Like quartz. How is it crafted in this way?"

Jessica turned to the kitchen window, seeing the ceiling lights reflected in the pane. "Yes, another specialist … maker."

"The same as this?" River said, pointing at a glass of water on the table.

"The same."

River took hold of the glass, turning it around in her hand. "It is so thin, but so strong – incredible."

"Take care. It's not as strong as you think – and sharp as hell if you break it."

River carefully placed the glass back down on the table. "How do you have access to such a place, Jessica? Is this a house of Warriors?"

Warriors? Jessica suppressed a shiver. *The Iyes truly believe in these Warriors.*

Because they are real, came a thought from the depths of her being. A flurry of images swept across her mind's eye. Beth's Axe streaking through the moonlit sky to strike the fearsome dragon. Lanky howling like a wolf after seemingly aiding Beth to destroy the Ka poison within her. Of her, Jessica, sitting in a Sacred Chamber, daemons of the Iyes appearing before her ... *Before the burnt man came.*

All these vivid recollections of events she could never have imagined happening.

And yet it all happened.

Her mouth suddenly felt so very dry. Warriors. Could it really be true? *Are we truly these Warriors of their Story?*

"Jessica?" came River's voice.

Jessica snapped out of her reverie. "A house of Warriors?" she repeated slowly as she refocussed. "No, River. Not a house of Warriors. Just a dwelling for normal people." *Normal people like me.*

River glanced around the room. "Incredible," she whispered. "Truly incredible."

Struggling to understand her own place in this unfolding nightmare, Jessica suddenly understood the full scale of the change for this girl from a distant past. The shock of her own arrival into River's world had been horrendous, but that had been a particularly brutal entry with a violent conflict raging around her. The landscape itself – the hills and the valleys of that ancient land – held all the elements Jessica recognised. The natural world, as she would call it. *I had seen its like before.* But for River to arrive to this modern world, when all she had ever known was that raw 'natural world', well, it was almost impossible to truly imagine River's shock and awe at this new 'man-made' world. *The changes from then to now are just so massive, so dramatic ... We've forever changed our planet.*

And all River had seen was inside one unassuming cottage. What about the world outside? Okay, outside was no big city, just a small village in the countryside, but it was a well-visited village with lots of tourists. *And not just the people.* The buildings, the lights, the cars, the noise ... all of it. How did you handle a situation like this?

She realised River was still watching her. "What I mean is, the people who have lived in this area built many places like this. Many. And they all look similar to this."

"So, this is the land of Warriors?"

"No, it is just the land for normal people like you and your tribe. But you're right, the people here have access to skilled makers and technologies that you'll never have seen."

River fell silent. Her look of fascination slowly turned to one of disquiet. "It is incredible, and my head is crowded with questions. Many questions. But I keep coming back to one – how can I get home?" She gestured towards Tricia. "But it seems her mission failed. The man who may have aided us has not arrived."

"No. Nothing has failed yet. I'll go soon to meet this man. But you're right, we can't stay here." She turned to Tricia. "Trish. We need to talk. We—"

The doorbell rang.

*

Robert studied the two young women sitting across the table from him. The one called Erin was biting her lip; the other, Tricia, the one who had come to his shop, was adjusting her bandana. Both were clearly nervous … but also afraid.

But afraid of what?

His gaze lingered on Tricia, a woman of whom he knew nothing, but a woman whose words had raised hackles at the back of his neck. She had mentioned Lanky. She had mentioned the Axes of Power. *And that's the only reason I chose to learn more of the words of a stranger.* Maintaining his challenging gaze, he saw the glistening beads of sweat on her forehead. But stressed she may be, this Tricia was smart. The book ruse had been quick thinking – she couldn't have known Fletcher was going to come in. *Yes, smart, but how does she know Lanky?*

And why did I lie to Fletcher?

He wiped a clammy hand on his trouser leg. *You know why.*

He forced his attention back to the two women. How did they know about the Axes? Was this the work of Lanky? Some elaborate hoax, planned and executed with their aid? His own answer came immediately. *Not a chance.* Lanky's mother was in pieces, and there was not enough money on the planet to get him to do that.

It hasn't stopped you.

Once more, he pushed the errant thought away. *I do what I need to do.*

He leaned forward. "Okay, what's your story?"

Without hesitation, Tricia spoke: "Last night a visitor arrived unannounced. Well, two visitors …"

During the next few minutes, Robert sat in stunned silence as Tricia told of the miraculous return of her friend, Jessica, and the fantastical tale she had told. His nascent questions were simply discarded, half-formed, his mind working furiously to comprehend the startling events from another age. But as Tricia brought her tale to the present, including her visit to the bookshop, elements of the story were already slotting into place, lighting up an existing framework formed many years before.

It was stunning. Really quite stunning. *They found the Staff!*

His heart hammered in his chest. After all the years searching, could it really be so?

"And that's it," Tricia said, her tightly clasped hands resting on the table in front of her. "You now know as much as we do."

"A quite fantastical tale," he said in a hushed voice.

He saw a flash of anguish on the faces of the two women. "It's difficult to believe," Tricia said, her face drawn. "I know that. But please—"

Robert held up his hand to forestall her. "You misunderstand me. It is a strange and wonderful tale, but that doesn't make it untrue. In fact, Tricia" – he broke into a gentle smile – "I believe you have witnessed something quite extraordinary and quite real."

Tears welled in Tricia's eyes. "You mean you don't think Jessica is crazy? We're not crazy?"

"Not crazy in the slightest. And I now understand why you approached me."

Watching relief flood over their faces, he fought to control his own surging emotions. *A chance remains. I may yet get them back.*

But first, he needed to know more. "Where are Jessica and her friend right now?"

Tricia wiped her eye. "Upstairs. Hiding in the closet." She smiled. "They like it there, it's warm."

*

The closet door opened, and light flooded in.

"It's okay, Jess, you guys can come out now," came Tricia's breathless voice. "And the bookseller's still here."

Jessica scrambled out of the closet. "He believed you?" she said, stretching out her cramped legs. "Will he help us?"

Tricia nodded.

Sweeping elation surged through Jessica. "He will help," she said fiercely to River. "We're not alone."

River's eyes lit up. "When do we leave?"

"Soon, I hope." Jessica turned to Tricia. "Let's meet him."

As they headed downstairs, Jessica listened as her friend briefly explained what had happened. Entering the kitchen, she smiled at Erin, who offered a strained smile in return, then she glanced across to the middle-aged man seated at the table. "Hello," she said, making her way to him and offering her hand. "I'm Jessica."

The bookseller climbed out of his seat and took her hand. "Robert."

"And this is River," Jessica said, standing to one side.

"Hello, River," Robert said warmly, holding out his hand.

River glanced at Jessica, who gave a slight tilt of the head towards Robert. River turned back to the bookseller, then slowly walked up to him. Copying Jessica's movements, she grasped Robert's hand.

"So wonderful to meet you," Robert said, his voice wavering.

They stood, hands clasped, but as moments stretched on, River glanced to Jessica.

"You can let go now," Jessica said, seeing the wonder in the man's eyes.

Robert held on for a few beats longer, then released River's hand. His marvelling eyes never left the girl as she walked back to Jessica's side. "Incredible," he murmured under his breath.

"And I'm sure she thinks you're great too," Tricia said, "but we're not here to admire each other. We have to figure out what to do now."

Robert turned to Jessica. "Quite incredible," he repeated.

"It is. But Tricia's right. Now you've heard our story, I'd like to hear your thoughts." She gestured to the table. "Please. Take a seat."

With the bookseller seated, she walked to the head of the table. "So, what do you think?"

Robert removed his glasses, wiped an eye, then replaced the glasses high on his nose. "I didn't know that Lanky had found this Staff. In fact, I was sure he was close to abandoning his quest." He looked back at River. "It seems he was not quite finished – as you now know." He turned back to Jessica. "And you believe it was this Staff that allowed you to leave this place – to visit her time?"

Jessica nodded. "It took a while to believe it."

"Can I see it?"

She hesitated. Parts of her tale she had chosen not to tell. Why? Because it hadn't felt right to talk of the daemons and the dragon. But the fate of the Staff … "No. It was lost."

"Lost!" Robert exclaimed, half standing.

Jessica's eyes sharpened in sudden surprise. *He reacts as though it was his. What is this Staff to him?*

Robert sat back down, rubbing his hand on his chin. "Sorry." He took a quick drink of water, then looked up at her. "As Lanky may have told you, I invested a lot of my own time and effort to search for these ancient artefacts. But to no avail. To hear just now that you found this Staff and then as quickly to hear you lost it … Well, it hurts me as much as it hurts you."

Jessica saw genuine distress in the man's eyes – a distress which explained his reaction. *But though it hurts you, it cannot match that felt by me or River. Or Beth. Or Lanky.*

Robert took another drink, then leaned forward. "If the Staff is lost, then how does Lanky get back? In fact, how did you get here?"

"That, I wish I knew."

"How was it lost?" he asked, his sharp eyes locking onto hers.

It was stolen by a dragon. But dragons were for a later telling. "Someone stole it," she said evenly.

"Do you know who? Or where they went?"

"Enemies of River's people. We believe they went north. And Lanky had an idea where – related to places he'd marked on a map."

Robert's eyes lit up. "The map …" He looked at her intently. "And where was this place?"

"A place named Mount Hope. Precisely where on that mountain, I don't know, but from what Lanky told me, it will be on his map."

"Was this map with him?"

"No. The way he spoke, I assumed it was here – in his home."

Robert's excitement grew. "He kept the map in his room. It's where he did all his work."

Then the map may still be there! The map providing the vital link to Lanky – to his thoughts, his ideas. *To this place in the north.* "Can you get us to it?"

"In theory, yes." His expression became troubled. "But you are a missing person, someone who can't simply stroll through the village to someone else's house. It may be better if I can bring the map here."

"No. I don't want to stay in the cottage any longer." Jessica straightened. "We'll come with you in your car. Can you do it now?"

"Not now. I have to get back to the shop to avoid rousing suspicion." He held up his hand as she made to protest. "But occasionally, I close early, so I'll do that today. I'll come back here, and we can leave together. But you won't be able to come in the house with me. Lanky's mother lives there."

"Ahh. So, he does have family here?"

"Yes – and she's devastated." A flicker of pain crossed his face. "This will be hard. I won't be able to tell her the whole truth of my visit. I won't be able to tell her that her son is alive."

"Does she know what Lanky was researching?"

"Oh, she knows all of that, but that's very different to explaining that her son has left – that he has travelled to another age."

"Almost impossible to explain to any sane person," Tricia muttered. "So, what does that make us?"

Jessica ran her hand through her hair. "Okay, I agree. I can't meet her – or anyone else. And neither can you tell anyone else of any of this." She grimaced. "You meeting his mother will be … difficult."

"Yet it has to be done." He seemed to consider for a moment. "If I can get hold of the map, and we find this Mount Hope marked on it, what then?"

Yes, what then? She walked across the kitchen to stand beside Erin, who silently watched her, fear clear in her tired blue eyes. A fear Jessica echoed. *What do I want to do? What can I do?* She faced the bookseller. "What do you suggest? You studied these Axes. You knew of their power. What can we do?"

Robert's look was pained. "What did I really know? My parents knew far more than me. Far, far more. They were the experts here."

"Are they still alive? Can they help us?"

"No," Robert said quietly. "They disappeared a long time ago."

Tricia gasped. "Like Jessica? Like Beth?"

Jessica spun around to face Tricia. *What is she saying?* Her eyes widened. She turned back to Robert. "Could that have happened? Could they have … travelled?"

Robert's face suddenly looked tired, drawn. "I don't know. I really don't know. It wasn't clear what these artefacts did … But after this …" He sighed. "It's possible."

Other travellers to the Land of the Iyes? Naga mentioned nothing of this. Jessica forced a grip on her thoughts. *His parents disappeared. It could have been for any reason other than this.*

"You say you need this Staff?" Robert said, a weariness to his voice. "Then maybe you need to follow it."

"That may be the only option we have," she agreed. "But here's the problem. Lanky had an idea where it may have gone, but that was thirteen thousand years ago. Right now, it could be anywhere."

Robert searched her face. "You have seen and heard more than any of us. What does your heart tell you?"

My heart? "My heart—"

'*Tells you to go north,*' came a calm, ethereal voice in her mind.

Jessica froze.

'The Staff is there. Hurry. Help will be there. But you must be there to receive it.'

Despite the panic of the moment, she formed the question quickly. 'Who are you?'

Silence answered her, and she somehow knew the presence had gone as quickly as it had arrived.

Amid the confusion of her suddenly racing mind appeared a belief of unexpected certainty. The voice was no creation of a stressed mind. It was real. *And it knew about the Staff. It said help will be there.* But who or what was it? *Can – should – I believe it?*

Maybe. Maybe not. Right now, chasing answers to those questions was a distraction. *And I won't risk being betrayed.* She needed to drive this herself.

Girding herself, she turned to Robert. "If there's a mark on that map in the north, then that's where we go first. After that … Well, first, let's see what we find."

"Then I'll prepare the way." He climbed to his feet and picked up his keys. "And I plan to come with you," he said, fire in his eyes. "I also wish to see what lies in the north." He made for the door.

"Best we get ready," Tricia said as he left.

Erin shook her head. "No, Trish, you and I can't."

Tricia frowned. "We have to help them."

"We already have," Erin said softly. "But we can't leave town while the police continue their investigations. The officer, Fletcher, made that pretty clear."

"Aah!" Tricia exclaimed, hitting her fist on the table. "But we need to help!"

Jessica's gut twisted. She wished her friends could stay with her, but they couldn't. And not just for the reason Erin gave. "You've already helped, Trish. You brought Robert, who's the key to getting that map. But Erin's right. You have to stay because I don't want you two drawn into this any further."

"But—"

"No buts. There are things happening here way beyond our understanding. Dangerous things. Believe me, I've seen them." *I've seen people killed. I've seen the devil.*

Tricia glared at Jessica but said nothing more.

"Are you certain you have to go, Jess?" Erin said in a low voice.

"I'm sure. I have to get back to Beth."

'And you are needed,' said the calm, ethereal voice.

*

Robert had returned, and her friend was ready to leave. Tricia rubbed the back of her neck, her frustration growing. *Erin and I should be going with her. We should be by Jess's side.* But that couldn't be. They were stuck at the cottage, ordered by the police officer to stay. *There's nothing I can do. I have to watch her walk out of here into a terrifying unknown.*

She took a deep breath and stood taller. *Come on, Trish. She needs you to be strong.* Girding herself, she crossed over to the breakfast bar, where Jessica and River conversed in low voices. As she approached, she cast a final look over them. Jessica wore Beth's baseball cap over hastily cut hair, and Erin's broad-brimmed hat drew eyes away from River's exotic features. Both wore sunglasses, t-shirts, and jeans. Even so, she was nervous. "The trouble is, Jess, you've a physique that's hard to dampen down, but I guess there isn't much else we can do."

Jessica adjusted her cap. "This was your idea."

"Then I guess it was a good one," Tricia said, forcing a smile.

"Are your bags packed?" Erin asked, coming to stand beside them.

Jessica nodded. "By the door."

Tricia glanced over to the door. "Hey, I thought you were travelling light? What's with the big bag – you carrying a sword or something?"

"Or something," Jessica answered, her smile fading.

Tricia raised an eyebrow.

Jessica spoke a few quiet words with River, then faced them. "Think we're ready to go."

A wave of nausea twisted Tricia's stomach, and she felt her barriers weakening. *This is so hard.*

Jessica walked up to her and drew her into a heartfelt embrace. In that moment, nothing needed to be said.

Eventually, Tricia muttered, "You need to go."

Jessica nodded and stepped back. Erin immediately rushed forward, throwing her arms around the tall woman. "Take care, Jess," she whispered as they hugged. "And you have Tricia's phone. Call if you need us, okay?"

"I will."

I'm not sure she will, Tricia thought. *Even if she needs it. She wants us out of harm's way.*

Jessica stepped back from Erin, then turned to Robert. "Ready to go?"

Standing by the door and looking as unsettled as Tricia felt, Robert nodded. His face grim, he opened the door, then glanced at Tricia. "Thank you for coming to see me. You have given us all a new hope." He walked out of the cottage.

New hope? Tricia thought as she watched Jessica and River pick up their bags. *Is that what this is? Then why do I feel so miserable?*

She felt Erin come to her side.

At the door, Jessica turned to them. She smiled. "I will get them back. I will be back." Then she turned away and walked out the door, River following closely behind.

No! Don't go! Her legs shaking, Tricia somehow held herself from rushing after her friend.

Erin put her arm around her and spoke softly. "We've done what we can, Trish. We have to trust that Jess will find a way to do whatever it is she needs to do."

But what can she do? How could you know what to do in such a truly insane situation? "How has this happened?" she whispered.

"I don't know, Trish," Erin murmured, pulling her closer. "I really don't know."

Dull pain tainted Tricia's thoughts. *It just can't be happening. Not to Jess. Not to Beth. We lost Eshe, we can't lose—*

She slammed the horrific thought aside. *No!* she berated herself. *Don't go there. I'm not losing another friend.* The flash of anger forced back the cloying sense of pain. In its place sparked a burgeoning resolve. She drew back from Erin, banishing her dark thoughts. "We need to help her, Erin. Somehow, we must help her."

"How? We can't leave this place."

A face from the bookshop surged into Tricia's mind. *The police officer ...* "We have to talk to that sergeant. Somehow, we have to convince him to let us leave."

"And how do we do that?"

Tricia's face hardened. "That's just what we're going to figure out now. Let's talk."

CHAPTER TWENTY-TWO

Without the Kade in their time, the adherents of the Dark remained weak. This gave the Guardian the chance she needed.

Robert glanced in the car mirror. All was still clear. Nerves afire, he opened the door.

"Be as quick as you can," came Jessica's voice as he climbed out. "We're exposed just sitting in the car."

Robert's stomach churned. "I'll try, but I can't rush this. I'll see you as soon as I can." He closed the door and walked up the street, his unease growing. How would this play out? Could he act out this lie in front of Rebecca? *You've done it for years,* he thought with grim veracity.

After only a short walk, he passed a shoulder-height hedge on the left, forming the border of the tiny front garden of Lanky's house. At the end of the hedge, he passed through the half-opened gate, then climbed a few steps up to the front door. He took a deep breath, then reached up and rang the bell. Moments later, a chain rattled, and the door opened.

"Oh, hello, Robert," Rebecca said, the slightest hint of disappointment in her eyes. "I thought, maybe …" She smiled. "Come in, do come in."

You thought maybe the police were here with some news? Which type were you expecting? "Thanks, Rebecca," he said, stepping past his age-long friend into the hallway.

She closed the door behind him. "Go through to the kitchen, and I'll get the kettle on."

He kicked off his shoes, then walked down the hall. "Unfortunately, I can't stay long, Rebecca, I've an errand to run."

"Just a quick cup then," Rebecca said, following him into the kitchen. "Drop your coat on the chair, and I'll make the tea."

He smiled. "Okay, a quick one then." *Take the chance now.* "Do you mind if I use the bathroom while you do that?"

"Of course not. You know where it is."

"Sure do. Oh, and here are some biscuits. Chocolate." He pulled a packet out of his jacket pocket. "I'll leave them on the table."

"Wonderful. I ran out yesterday, and I haven't been shopping yet. Not since …" She glanced at him, her face suddenly creased with worry. "Have you heard anything?"

Only that your son's alive. And that I may have found a way to save my parents. He shook his head, hiding the terrible guilt swirling inside. *Nothing I can tell you.*

Rebecca nodded, her anguish undimmed. She turned back to the kettle. "I'm expecting to see Fletcher later, but there was nothing new yesterday."

Robert flinched. "Is he arriving soon?" he asked, fighting the urge to turn to see if Fletcher was already standing behind him.

"Could be here anytime." He caught a flash of regret in her eyes. "I must admit, when you rang, I thought that was him at the door."

"It would have been good to see him," Robert lied. "But as I said, I can't stay long today." *Yes, you need to get moving.* "Excuse me for a moment, Rebecca. I'll be back down in a minute."

"I'll open the biscuits."

Robert quickly headed out into the corridor. Turning into the stairwell, he climbed the stairs to the bathroom. *Be quick and be quiet.* His heart pounding, he reached the landing, then glanced across to Lanky's door, which was closed. *Nice and easy does it,* he thought as he padded softly across the landing. He opened the bedroom door, which swung silently, then entered. Scanning the room – it was much tidier than the last time he'd seen it – he immediately saw it lying across the desk.

The map!

He crossed to the desk and picked up the rolled map. But where was the logbook? He carefully opened the desk drawer, but a quick search revealed nothing. Closing the drawer, he moved quietly around the room, scanning each visible area, but to no avail.

No time. The map will have to do.

Carrying the map, he crept back out of the room, closing the door carefully behind him. *Now the hardest part. Getting it out of here!* It was impossible to hide on him, the roll being not much shorter than him. He racked his brain. *That will have to do,* he thought, grasping one idea. *But first, the bathroom.*

After completing the charade of using the bathroom, he readied himself at the top of the stairs. *Let a little luck be on my side.* He climbed down the stairs, but instead of returning to the kitchen, he turned down the corridor to the front door. Reaching the door, he called out: "Just left something in the car – will be just a moment!" Without waiting for a reply, he opened the door and stepped outside—

"What did you say?" came Rebecca's voice from down the corridor behind him.

Drat! He quickly stepped out of the house and down the steps, then placed the map on the pavement side of the hedge, concealing it from view from the door. As he stood up and glanced over the hedge, he saw Rebecca appear at the doorway.

"What did you say?" she said.

"Thought I'd left my keys in the car," he said, walking back around the hedge to the steps to the house, "but just remembered I left them in my jacket in the kitchen. I must be going mad." He laughed. "Maybe I do need that cup of tea more than I thought."

*

A short while later, Robert stood. "Well, Rebecca, I thank you for the tea, the biscuits, but above all, of course, for the company. And it's great to see you looking so well."

Rebecca smiled. "You've been a great support, Robert. You know you are welcome anytime."

"I do. And it is a pleasure." He picked up his coat, and they walked out of the kitchen and down the hall. At the front door, he turned to Rebecca with a gentle smile. "I guess Fletcher will be here any moment. I'm sure he'll have good news for us before long."

Renewed strength returned to her face. "Lanky will be back soon, I'm sure of it. I know it."

He reached out and clasped her hand. "We both know it."

With a final gentle squeeze of her hand, he made his way down the steps. "Make sure you come and visit me at the shop – and if you get bored listening to me, you could always buy a book."

He heard her gentle laugh as he walked out onto the pavement. He glanced down and breathed a sigh of relief as he saw the map still lying against the hedge, out of sight of the door. Walking towards the map, he glanced over the hedge to the doorway ...

Rebecca still stood there, waving.

He pushed down a rising panic. *She'll see me take the map.* Thinking quickly, he looked down, then sighed loudly. "Need to change these shoelaces, they're always coming undone." He knelt, then, out of sight behind the hedge, he reached out and grasped the map in one hand. After an appropriate pause, he stood, holding the map down low behind the hedge. He waved with his free hand. "All secure. Bye."

As Rebecca waved, he turned and strolled away. And as he reached the end of the hedge, he heard the door close. Relief came in a sickening rush. *That was too close. Far too close.* Feeling as if accusing eyes watched him, he hurried on down the road to his car.

"What took you so long?" Jessica demanded as he climbed in, drained and exhausted. "Do you know how many people have walked past?"

Ignoring her, Robert slumped in his seat and sucked in deep lungfuls of air. *That was hard.* And particularly so because he'd deceived a long-time friend.

Again.

But they had the map. It had been close – that hedge had saved him. Glancing in the car wing-mirror, he looked back to Lanky's house—

And saw Fletcher walking past the house towards the car.

"Don't move!" he hissed, pulling out his keys, forcing his shaking hand to steer the key into the ignition. "Trouble behind."

Fumbling, he managed to start the car and immediately nosed out into the road, pulling over to the far lane and driving slowly away. He blew a deep sigh of relief. *Lucky I was parked facing that way.* Looking in the mirror, he saw Fletcher watching the car – then the sergeant turned and strode purposefully back up to Rebecca's house.

Robert's hands gripped the steering wheel tightly. "I think we have a problem. Fletcher might have seen you."

"What!" Jessica exclaimed. He heard her muttering to herself, then she spoke, her voice agitated. "We need to leave. Now. Drive to the carpark, and we'll switch to my car. If they're onto us, we won't have long, but maybe long enough."

"And then?"

Jessica grimaced. "We'll travel north, then stop someplace to take a look at the map. And hope it shows us where we need to go."

*

"I'm grateful for your visit as usual, Fletcher," Mrs. Warhurst said. "I hope we hear some news soon."

"You will be the first to hear, Mrs. Warhurst," Fletcher said as he headed out of the door. "Now, take care, and see you tomorrow."

"Yes, thank you, Fletcher. Goodbye."

At the pavement, he heard the door close, and stopped to gather his thoughts. He'd known Mrs. Warhurst all his life, and it cut him up to see her hurting. Oh, she hid it well, but he knew her pain. And he had no answers to give.

Although maybe that was about to change. *But what did I see? Something strange, that's what.*

On his way to meet Lanky's mother, he'd just turned into the road at the top of the hill, when, in the distance, he'd seen Robert pick something up from the ground beside the garden hedge. He then waved to Mrs. Warhurst and walked off down the road to a car. Robert's own car. As Fletcher had walked on down the hill, he had been sure he'd seen movement in the back of the car, but Robert had started up and driven away before he could get closer. *But I'm sure someone else was in that car.* Not something that he would have given a second thought on any other day. *But today ...*

Fletcher let his thoughts settle. During his chat with Mrs. Warhurst, he'd subtly drawn out information he needed; Robert had visited – just Robert, no friends – and he'd brought nothing with him nor taken anything away. But it was what else he had noticed that had sent alarm bells ringing. On instinct, he'd asked to take another look at Lanky's room. Mrs. Warhurst agreed, but left him alone, still not wishing to face her son's empty room. But he'd seen the room. And the desk. He'd seen the map had gone.

A scowl crossed his face. *We should have taken it.* But the logbook had seemed the more urgent evidence to take. Too late now; it was gone.

So, had Robert taken it? Was that what he'd had in his hand? And if he had taken it, why? A keen focus entered his eyes as he pushed back these unknowns. He may have few answers, but after days of no progress in the investigation into the disappearance of Lanky and the two young women, events were now screaming at him for attention: the woman's demeanour at the bookshop; Robert agreeing to deliver books out of hours; Robert potentially taking the map from Lanky's house. Minor events that might usually be ignored but put together with the call-out to the women's cottage the other night, cried out for him to act. *Something's happening. Right now. And I need to find out what – and quickly.*

His phone rang.

Pulling it from his pocket, he glanced at the number. His eyes narrowed. *Erin Catran.* He accepted the call. "Hello, Ms. Catran. How can I help you?"

*

Erin glanced at her watch. "He'll be here soon."

"I'm ready," Tricia said, glancing down at her steaming mug.

Erin saw her own nervous tension reflected in her friend's face. The police officer was coming, and Tricia would try to shake him off their back with a simple story. *A simple lie.* Then they could chase after Jessica and figure out how to help her. She glanced at her phone on the table. On trips together like this, they kept each other as friends in an app. *We know where we all are.* And Jessica had Tricia's phone.

She fidgeted with her fingers under the table. But were they doing the right thing? Yes, they could find Jessica, but she had told them not to follow her. And how could they truly know what was right and what was wrong after what they'd heard? It was all beyond understanding, beyond belief.

Her chest tightened. *Beyond belief* ... The memory of that day walking with her friends on the ridge was suddenly stark. *I felt something that day. I knew something bad was going to happen.* She'd thought it had been the break-up with Paul, a momentary reaction to that terrible betrayal. *But now, after all that's happened, was it really more than that? Could I ...* She clamped a hold on her disturbing thoughts. How could she have known what was about to happen? *That makes no sense. I—*

"Let me do most of the talking," Tricia said, breaking into her dark introspection. "I'll keep to the story that my grandma is sick, and that you need to drive me home."

Erin forced herself back to the moment. She replayed Tricia's words. *Grandma?* "That might work, except your grandma's dead."

"That's why I need to do the talking. You wouldn't be able to hold the lie."

"Fine. Then I'll—" She gasped as a cold shiver ran down her spine.

Tricia frowned. "What is it?"

"Something's not right," Erin whispered, her head aching. "I don't know—"

Sudden pressure slammed into her mind. "Something's here," she whispered, her eyes widening. "There's—"

Tricia screamed, then pushed back her chair and leapt to her feet. "Who are you!" she cried. "Erin, get away from there!"

Erin spun around. And screamed as she saw the figure before her. She leapt off her chair and ran around the table to join Tricia.

"Who are you?" Tricia yelled. "How'd you get in here?"

A tall, gaunt-faced man with white hair streaked black stood before them. He carried a dark-wood staff, and his thin lips were curled into a smile. "My master sends you greetings. Where is the Guardian?"

Her mouth impossibly dry, Erin grabbed Tricia's arm. "We need to get out of here—" She cried out as an intense pain shot through her chest.

"Do not move," the terrifying man murmured, a harsh smile still playing on his lips. "Else you die." Tilting his head, he glanced around the room. "Where is the Guardian?"

"I don't know what you mean," Tricia said, her voice wavering. She glanced at Erin, terror in her eyes, and stammered, "You okay?"

Ignoring a throbbing pain in her chest, Erin forced herself to nod.

"I sense no one else here," the man said. His smile faded and his cruel regard returned to them. "Neither of you is the Guardian."

He took a step forward.

Erin immediately pulled Tricia away, shuffling towards the door.

"Don't you come any closer," Tricia stammered.

The man laughed. "I sense no danger from you." He raised his staff …

Tricia held her hands to her throat and fell to her knees, gasping.

"Trish!" Erin cried, dropping to her friend's side, her hands shaking uncontrollably. *She's choking! He's choking her!* "Stop!" she cried, staring wide-eyed at the man. "Whatever you're doing, stop!"

"Where is the Guardian?"

"I don't bloody know where the Guardian is! I don't know what you're talking about!"

Tricia made a gurgling sound and dropped to the floor.

"Please, stop," Erin pleaded. "We know nothing. We—"

A terrifying glint lit in the man's eyes. "You know something," he said, stepping closer. "Tell me what you know."

Erin cowered from him, yet something inside refused him. *I can't tell him. I can't tell him about Jessica. He would—*

The man leaned forward, his eyes boring into her. "Yes, Jessica. Where is she?"

He can read my mind!

She stared helplessly at the man, hearing the horrific sounds of Tricia choking beside her. "She's gone," she said, desperately seeking something to appease the man without betraying her friend. "She left. I don't know where." *Don't think of it. Do not think of it.*

A diabolical presence loomed at the edges of her mind.

'Keep him out,' came a calm yet firm voice. *'Hold him back.'*

The man scowled. "You know. Tell me where this Jessica is."

"I don't know!" Erin cried, fixing her eyes on the black streak in the man's hair, vainly trying to blank her mind of anything else. "Please believe me. I don't know!"

"You are worth nothing," the man spat. "You will d—"

Someone knocked on the door.

The man's eyes blazed with anger.

Then he vanished.

Beside her, Tricia gasped, hoarsely gulping in air.

Her head feeling as though released from a vice, Erin dropped to her friend's side. "Trish," she breathed, resting a shaking hand on her shoulder. "You okay?"

"Give me a second," Tricia wheezed, slowly pushing herself up. She sat, slumped forward, head in hands.

Dazed, Erin climbed to her feet. A terrifying sense of the attacker remained, seeming to foul her very soul. *He could read my mind. He did this to Tricia.* "Who was that?" she whispered. *And what was that voice I heard?*

Her breathing laboured, Tricia looked up. "Someone I don't want to meet again, that's for sure." Her hand went to her neck. "It was as though fingers of steel were squeezing the life out of me. Are we sure he's gone?"

"I think so," Erin whispered, noticing angry marks appearing on her friend's neck. "He ... he vanished."

"I heard him. He knew Jessica's name. He—"

Someone hammered at the door.

"Open up," came a voice from the letterbox. "It's the police. Open up."

"It's that sergeant!" Tricia wheezed. She climbed unsteadily to her feet, rubbing her neck.

Erin flicked a fearful glance at Tricia. "What do we do now? And that man. He wasn't normal. In no way was he normal. And he's after Jess."

"I know," Tricia said, staring at the place the man had been standing, "yet who would believe what just happened here?" Wincing, she turned to Erin. "We're in the same place we were. Even more so. We have to get to Jess and warn her." She glanced to the door. "We need to convince this officer to allow us to leave. I'll stick to the story we planned."

"But look at you. You're in no fit shape to talk to him. Neither of us are."

"We've no choice," Tricia said as a hard rap struck the door. "We can't just ignore him. We have to let him in."

*

Fletcher's cynical gaze flicked from one nervous woman to the other, his fingers tapping the table in tune to his distrust. "Try again, Ms. Williams. That story was baloney. You may have a gran, but if you do, I'd bet my house she's still hale and hearty. You don't have permission to leave town until this investigation is complete."

He saw her face fall and a deep pain enter her eyes.

And he saw the marks on her neck.

His sharp eyes locked onto hers. "Let me tell you what I think. I think you know Robert Martin. I think that your friends know Robert Martin. I believe one of your friends drove off from Lanky's mother's house today in Robert's car. And I believe someone tried to strangle you – recently. Maybe even just now." He shot a glance at Ms. Erin Catran – who quickly dropped her eyes. *Could she have done it?* But Ms. Williams looked a strong woman. It didn't seem likely. *Then who?*

He sat back in his chair, stroking his short goatee. "If you've nothing else to say here, I suggest we head down to the station and continue our discussion there."

"No!" Ms. Williams exclaimed, sitting upright. "No," she said more quietly, looking at her friend.

Fletcher's eyes sharpened.

"Look," Ms. Williams said, fidgeting with her fingers. "There are things happening here that you'd find very hard to believe. Extremely hard."

"I don't—"

"Yes, I'm sure you hear many people say that, Sergeant," Ms. Williams said, looking up. "But do you have people suddenly appear out of thin air and try to strangle you?" She held his eyes. "I mean, literally, *appear out of thin air.*"

Fletcher frowned, thrown by this new tack. "Look, just tell me the truth. Tell me—"

"My friend isn't lying," Ms. Catran said, her voice quiet yet firm. "I saw it too."

His frown deepened. "Describe him."

"No," Ms. Williams said. "We don't have time for that now."

He sat up straight. "Now hold on. We will—"

"We'll take you to Robert," Ms. Williams said quickly. "We'll take you to Jessica."

Ms. Catran sat up in her chair. "Trish! What are you doing?"

Her friend placed her hand on her arm. "We have to warn Jess. That man is looking for her. Hunting her. This is the only way now."

Ms. Catran stared at her friend for a moment, and then she slumped back. She nodded.

"Hold on," Fletcher said, his head spinning. "You know where your missing friend is?" The connection was swift. "That's who was in the car! That's it, isn't it? And Lanky? And your other friend?"

Ms. Williams hesitated. "Safe," she said, yet her voice was unsure. "I can help you find them. But only you."

He couldn't believe what he was hearing. He'd expected these two knew something, but this? What had they become involved in? And who was this man they claimed had been here? *The bruises on her neck ...* Things were slipping out of his control. It was time to take them in for questioning and figure out the truth of all of this.

He climbed to his feet and reached for his phone. "You two need to come with me. You—"

"No!" Ms. Williams exclaimed. "Only you. Else it will be too late."

He paused. "Why?"

She glanced at her friend, and then back to him. "There are things here you wouldn't believe," she said, tension in her voice. "Things others wouldn't believe. But to be very clear – if you make the wrong move here, people will die. We must get to Jess now." She leaned forward. "We can take you there. We can take you there now."

Studying her face, doubt swept in. Whatever was going on, he recognised the genuine plead for help. He saw it in her eyes, and the eyes never lied. *But that doesn't mean I should—*

"Give us this chance," she implored. "You can help us, and we can help you find Lanky and the others." The desperate need in her voice was raw and urgent. "We'll take you there. Now. Then see for yourself and decide what you have to do. But we must leave now."

He ran his hand through his short goatee, his mind racing. *Get them back to the station and question them there,* insisted the rationale part of him. *She says people could die,* countered another voice, quiet yet compelling. *She says we must move now.*

His gut knotted. *I can't let Lanky die. I can't let any of them die.* He needed to find out what they truly knew. He needed to do it now. And the quickest way to do that? "I give you one chance," he grated. "One only."

He saw tears form in the woman's eyes. "Thank you," she whispered. "Thank you so much."

I hope others will thank me after this, he thought, regret already taking hold. *But I've made my bed, now I need to lie in it.* He loosed a strained sigh. "Where do we go?"

CHAPTER TWENTY-THREE

The pact was well made. The Geddon remained hidden. But the pact did not halt the war. No, enmities ran far too deep for that.

Skirting the rugged, mist-shrouded peak, Stealth's stomach lurched as they plunged through wispy low cloud, descending with terrifying speed. The jagged ridges of the mountainside flashed past in a blur as Rakana angled towards a narrow ravine on their left. Stealth gasped as they arrowed through the entrance, the Ancient's backswept wings barely clearing the walls of the gorge. Before he could catch his breath, they shot out into a deep mountain valley where the dragon banked hard, skimming over the tree canopy of the far valley wall before plummeting down towards a sparkling emerald-green river wending its way along the verdant valley floor. Their speed increasing, he clung on as the dragon weaved her way along the river towards the valley head – his gut wrenched once more as the Ancient turned viciously, climbing rapidly up the steep, terraced face to a rocky platform high above, where finally they slowed, landing softly on the broad, rocky ledge.

Stealth's head slumped onto the dragon's shimmering scaled back, and he lay there, breathing hard.

'Descend. We cannot stay here long,' came Rakana's voice.

He sucked in several deep breaths, then wearily pushed himself upright and looked around. They had alighted on a wide, rocky ledge, which jutted out from high up the steep mountain cliff face, offering impressive views of the river valley below. At the back of the broad platform lay a shadowy opening into the mountainside, while to one end of the ledge, a well-worn trail ran away along a narrow terrace on the cliff face before dropping out of sight below them. *So, others frequent this place.* He forced his aching leg up and over the dragon's back, then carefully slid off to the ground—

He spun around as a menacing snarl sounded behind him. Four large black wolves stalked out of the cave, heads low, hackles raised as they walked purposefully towards him. Reaching for a blade, he took an involuntary step back.

'He has my protection,' Rakana said in his mind.

'And mine,' growled a commanding voice.

The black wolves halted a few paces from him.

Releasing the tension in his blade arm, Stealth caught movement within the shadowy depths of the cave entrance behind the wolves. Piercing topaz-yellow eyes gleamed in the darkness. Then the shadow moved. *Another wolf. A massive wolf.*

Rakana swung her imposing head to the shadowy presence within the cave. *'We must talk. The Warriors are growing in power.'*

'Agreed.'

Rakana's mighty frame loomed towards him. *'Stay here,'* the Ancient rumbled. *'And do not annoy the guards.'*

He quickly stepped back to allow Rakana to pass – the four wolves also parted for the dragon, but their unnerving gaze never left him. As the Ancient approached the cave entrance, he caught a brief flash of white as the massive wolf stepped out to greet the Ancient. *Who is—*

A black wolf loped towards him, snarling.

Stealth stepped away, cursing under his breath. As the wolf halted, he glanced back towards the dragon and the white wolf, intending to observe. A second wolf let out a low growl and padded forward. Stealth backed away once more. The second black wolf sat back on its haunches.

"Okay," Stealth muttered. "I get the message. I'm not to witness this meeting."

Shaking his head, he turned away, trying to ignore an unbidden image of a wolf springing at his undefended back. Walking to the lip of the platform, he sat, then, sighing, he looked out across the green valley to the mountains beyond.

They had arrived at a remote place, a place naturally hidden within the depths of a vast mountain range, with no evidence of human activity seen at any time during their flight. Not that he would have seen all, given the speed they'd been travelling. Their route in had been a complex, twisting path. *A most convoluted path. Ensuring we were not followed.* This was clearly a place the Ancient wished to remain undiscovered. But why? What lay here that was so important? And who was this great white wolf? He sighed. His master would tell him. Or not.

He relaxed and closed his eyes. A moment to rest ...

He awoke to the sharp crack of thunder behind him, accompanied by the howling of wolves. He leapt up to find two new arrivals standing before him.

"So, the dragon's servant accompanies her on this visit," said an older man with sharp silver eyes, his cloak a ragged patchwork of leathers, a Black Staff in his hand. Three wolves ambled back to their holding position in front of the cave, but the fourth padded up to the man, dropping to its haunches at his feet.

Stealth held the shaman's gaze. What fate had brought Shade of the Ka to this place at this time? "I find her company more pleasurable than most," he responded.

The Ensi's Shade smiled. "Pleasuring a dragon must be a most interesting encounter. But I'd be more interested in the reason for your visit. A visit made in such interesting times ..."

"Maybe you would care to answer the same. And maybe introduce your companion?"

"This is *my* home, remember," the Shade replied, still smiling. "What other reason may I hold than that? And my companion? I have nothing to hide from you. This is Cyrene, a mage of the Islanders."

Stealth stepped up to the tall woman, scanning her gaunt face, noting her long fair hair flowing to her shoulders. A mage. The Islanders' name for a shaman. He knew little of the Islanders, and even less of their mages – no one he'd met had ever seen one. *I doubted their very existence.* And yet, here a mage stood. "Stealth," he said simply, holding out his hand.

She ignored his hand and simply bowed her head a fraction. "I greet you, servant of the Ancient."

"You are a long way from home."

"Yes," Cyrene replied slowly. "A long way indeed."

Silence fell.

It seems all that will be said has been said.

"Well, it seems we have said what little needs to be said," the Shade murmured. "And it seems your master now wishes to leave."

Turning, Stealth saw Rakana's forbidding frame approaching. *I slept longer than I realised.*

"Rakana," the Shade said, half bowing. "The Ensi wishes me to thank you for your continued support to the Ka and their land, and bids me to assure you that the pact with you remains binding and ever strong. The Ensi—"

"Yes, I thank the Ensi for these inspiring words," the dragon rumbled dismissively into the crisp mountain air. Her fearsome head swung to the mage. "Why are you here?"

The mage bowed, far more deeply than to him, Stealth noted.

The mage straightened. "My people have the same interests, Ancient One." She glanced to the shadowy figure in the cave mouth. "We wish to ensure our alignment continues."

"And yet your people still worship Taran," the dragon rumbled.

"Taran has served us well," Cyrene said, her voice hardening. "That will not change."

The dragon's jaws opened slightly, and a putrid wave of heated air washed over them. "So long as all follow the same path." She angled her sculpted head, turning a fierce eye onto the mage. "You will continue to aid those who need it?"

"We will, Ancient One," Cyrene said, a strength to her voice. *"That* does not change."

So, what does change? Stealth thought. But he said nothing.

A rumble sounded deep within the dragon, and her head swung around to land a fiery eye on the Shade. "And you? You insist on following your path?"

"I hold my beliefs, Ancient One, and I will follow them. I aid as agreed within the pact, but my view of the enemy remains unchanged."

"You are a fool, Shade. Your Ensi is a fool. You humans are all fools."

The old man shrugged. "That may be so, but we do what we can. We do what *needs* to be done."

The dragon's burning eye raked the old man. "And the other?"

Stealth noticed the slightest twitch to the Shade's lips. "I hold control," the shaman said quietly.

He is uncertain of this. That is dangerous. His gaze shifted to the Black Staff the Shade carried. Kaos blessed and daemon-bound, this staff was a rarity amongst shamans – he knew of only one other, carried by a shaman of the Meso tribes. But while the Shade's skills were enhanced by this artefact of the Dark, the daemon's presence was worrying – it required a formidable mind to resist its deviant will.

"Maybe the time has come for you to remain here," Rakana rumbled.

"No," the Shade grunted. "There are things I must complete, and my time here is short."

And with that, he placed a hand on the mage's shoulder, and they walked together towards the cave entrance, where the massive wolf waited in the shadows. Then, they and their host melted into the darkness.

In the silence that followed, Stealth studied the gloom of the cave. *The Shade enters a place I know nothing of. Why is he allowed here?* He turned to Rakana. *Choose your questions wisely.* "What is this place?"

The Ancient held a fiery eye on the mouth of the cave. "This is a place that should not be visited." The dragon's deep voice echoed off the steep wall of the mountainside.

Which means do not ask more on this. But ... "And the mage. A shaman, I believe?"

"Not quite, but close enough."

"And they follow their own god, Taran? Is this god aligned with us?"

A rumble sounded deep in the belly of the dragon. "Have you learnt nothing, mortal?"

"Master?"

The Ancient swung her fiery eye to face him. "What have I taught you? Of gods? There are those with more knowledge and understanding than you, mortal, those with more wit. That I understand. But just because some keep themselves distant – hidden – this does not make them gods."

"But you said yourself these people worship Taran."

Anger flared within the Ancient's eye. "You humans worship those who appear to have power over nature. You know not how this can be, and from this is born fear. Fear that becomes appeasement, then service, then worship – you make them a god." Another rumble of thunder emanated from the dragon. "Ignorance does not create a god, but this, it seems, is a curse of your kind."

Stealth inwardly sighed. This was heading down a path he'd been down with the Ancient before – there would be no benefit in arguing. "Are these Islanders aligned with us?" he asked, changing the angle of his question.

"For now," Rakana said, swinging her head back to the cave. "But Taran? That remains to be seen."

"Who is—"

"No more questions," she growled. "We return home to our guests. The enemy is moving, and we must prepare. There are things to be set into motion. Tonight. Take your seat, my loyal friend, and I will explain what we shall do."

A short while later, they sped high above the mountain peaks, heading north. *The Land is stirring*, he thought wryly, holding tightly to the neck of the dragon as the cold wetness of a cloud streamed by. The

Ancient, the Shade, and a mage of the Islanders, all meeting at this hidden valley of the wolves. Which of the Ancient's false gods had twisted fate to conjure this unlikely convergence? Cold unease gripped him. *I don't know, but I know I don't want to revisit this place again.*

'If you ever return here,' came Rakana's voice, *'then hope you have found the Song.'*

'What song?'

But the Ancient remained silent.

They flew on, Stealth struggling to make sense of what he'd seen and heard.

He failed.

*

One weary eye half open, Shadow forced himself up into a sitting position. *That's far enough for today,* he thought, holding his heavy head in his hands, and yet again reminding himself to moderate his enjoyment of those delicious nectars. But how many times had he said this? *And last night did we not refer to it as backstabber?* Become too friendly with such a brew, and that was indeed its nature; he carried many a scar from prior engagements.

He sat for a while. And for a while more.

Eventually, he lifted his head. Ignoring the pounding in his temples, he glanced around. The pitiful remnant of a torch flickered in the corner of the chamber they'd slept in, but there was no sign of Sy. He had no recollection of returning here. No surprise there; he must have drunk half of the vat.

The torch sputtered and the light dimmed. He groaned. No matter how bad he felt, he didn't fancy wandering around in the dark. *Guess I should move and find out where Sy has gone.* He clambered to his feet, and after taking a moment for his stomach to settle, he reached for his water pouch. Licking his dry lips, he pulled out the stopper, then took a small sip.

Shadows danced in the chamber.

Turning to look for the new source of light, he heard footsteps approaching down the passageway outside. As he replaced the stopper and dropped the pouch onto his pack, the light in the tunnel grew.

Sy appeared at the entrance, holding a fresh torch. "You need fresh air," he signed with harsh flicks of his fingers.

"No," Shadow muttered. "I was heading out to find you. And now you're here, we can stay awhile until my head clears. Then we can eat."

Sy walked over to the dying torch, pulled it out of its wooden holder, then strode back out of the chamber and into the passageway, taking both torches with him.

"Hey!" Shadow shouted. "Come back!"

The echoes of Sy's footsteps receded down the tunnel, the light in the chamber fading fast.

"Kef!" Shadow cursed. "That's a dirty trick."

He quickly grabbed the warmest jacket he could see, then hurried after Sy, who was already a distant glow. Gaining on Sy, he threw several expletives at the man's back. Sy walked on.

After a meandering route through half-remembered tunnels, they arrived at the massive stone doors marking the main entrance to the Ancient's lair. The doors stood open.

"Well, some nice exercise, Sy, and I admit it's given me an inkling to take a little food, so how about we head back now?"

Sy walked over to the rough-hewn wall, placed the burnt-out torch on a vacant holder, then walked on up the glistening ice tunnel, his brightly burning torch in hand.

"Kef!" he grunted again. "What is it with him this morning?" He shivered. "It's cold out, you fool!" he shouted after Sy.

Sy walked on.

Muttering to himself, Shadow pulled on the fur jacket he'd grabbed. *That's a good fit,* he thought in passing as he fastened the front with the wooden toggles. *I need to talk with Stealth about this design.* Putting his hands in the pockets of the thick jacket, he trudged on up the tunnel after his friend, sparkles of light glinting off the icy walls from the torchlight ahead. As they climbed higher, daylight cut through the thinning ice above, casting a cool ocean-blue light around him. *Another day, I could see a beauty in this ... But today, all I feel is cold.* As he grew closer to the end of the ice tunnel, the light changed again as the blaze of daylight flooded the tunnel, a blinding intensity after the gloom of the caverns. *Not the best remedy for a sore head.*

Shielding his eyes, he walked out into the open, glancing around to find Sy. He could see little to his right, where the full sun hung bright in the sky, creating a dazzling glare bouncing off the snow on the ground before him. It seemed he had slept in longer than he'd thought, the sun having cleared the eastern sky. Putting the sun to his back, he waited while his eyes adjusted to the light, then saw Sy sitting on a boulder swept clear of snow. "That looks cold. Do you mind if I don't join you?"

Sy ignored him.

Squinting, Shadow glanced out on his wider surroundings. He stood on a slight rise above a small plateau, a wall of ice rising behind him. A track of sorts gently climbed its way up towards them from disturbed snow-laden ground below – *where we must have landed a few nights ago* – and beyond the plateau edge lay the white featureless expanse of the ice-filled valley plain. To the west and to the east, rugged valley walls emerged from the plain, their steep rocky faces painted with snow and ice, and scattered hardy shrubs. Jagged white peaks of the tallest buried mountains rose majestically to the sky.

He turned to the view behind him but was too close to the ice wall to see much beyond its crest, only a distant white summit, partly seen – the peak they had seen on their nighttime approach. He looked back out over the valley. Could they travel through this ice-locked land? It might be needed if they couldn't get away soon. *The Ancient may not understand urgency, but I do.* His Ensi needed him. He had to return to his homeland soon.

He walked over to Sy. "You fancy making a run for it?"

"Where to?" Sy signed.

"That way," Shadow replied, pointing south.

"It's a long way for just two people."

Shadow agreed. If they knew the lay of this land, they could steer a route away from the worst of the rugged terrain, lessening the challenge. "It wouldn't be easy, I agree, Sy. But if we make little progress with this dragon, we can do it. We will do it. We should test that valley floor later – if it's hard enough, it could make good walking ground."

"It's hard."

So Sy had already scouted the area. "You have the better of me today. Did you see Stealth before he left?"

Sy nodded. "Before he left with the dragon."

"Ah, so it was an errand with his master. Did you talk with the Ancient?"

"I don't think I'm so favoured."

"Favoured? That is a matter of opinion, my friend. Being in the thoughts of an Ancient is not to be envied."

His eyes now adjusted to the snow-enhanced glare, he scanned around, seeing the odd activity here and there. Mostly birds, both airborne and on the ground, but also the occasional distant movement that might hint at a larger animal. *Maybe—*

Something hit him in the side of the head, and a flurry of snow scattered over his shoulders. "Ow. I take it you want to say something?"

"What do you make of Stealth?" Sy signed. "And his story?"

Shadow frowned. What did he think? Being honest, in his stupefied overnight state, he wasn't sure he'd fully processed it yet. "An entertaining tale for his guests," he offered, flashing his fingers.

"Do you believe it?"

"No reason not to."

"And his claim to be from the Ka?"

Ah, so Sy had heard that too. So, there was the core issue. A fellow Ka. Or so he said. This was something the Ensi had not mentioned to them – but how much did the Ensi tell? He sighed. As much, or as little, as the Ensi wanted.

Stories within stories.

"It may well be true, Sy. In fact, if we stop to think about it, why would he lie about that? What benefit does it give him? And could that tribe he described have been our tribe from many sun-cycles ago? Very possibly. Everything he said was consistent with what we do and what we say today." He glanced around the icy wilderness and shook his head. "But leaving that to stay here? That's something I don't understand – why would a skilled man of ambition hide himself here on the edge of humanity? What did he say? He agreed to stay one sun-cycle? Well, that obviously didn't pan out."

"What did your council meetings tell you of this? Or the other Disciples?"

"You know I can't answer that, Sy," Shadow said, smiling. He paused, then shrugged. "They told of some aspects of the Ancient, yes. But of a Ka member serving her? No. Never."

"If this Stealth is indeed a Ka, why the need to keep us here to send a message south? Why can he not do this?"

"A fair question, my friend. One that my befuddled head can't answer right now. Hmm. Another meeting with our new friend seems in order."

"One where you keep your wits in hand, rather than your cup of wine?"

"Have no fear. Sore head aside, my hands are more than capable of sharing my wits with my wine."

Sy quickly signed: "Incoming."

Shading his eyes, Shadow squinted down the valley until he locked onto an object low in the sky. As they watched, the dragon flew into range, banking above the disturbed snow-covered ground of her landing site, sweeping wings seeming to exert little effort as she made her controlled descent. Powerful legs flexed as she took her weight, then the Ancient lowered her left flank.

A figure clambered down and walked towards them.

The dragon raised her wings and launched skywards, a quite unnatural act for such a colossal beast, but obviously effective, as she quickly gained height, swinging away into the sun to the west.

"I hope Stealth is bringing some food," Shadow said to Sy as the dragon's servant approached. "I'm really quite ravenous."

CHAPTER TWENTY-FOUR

*How deep compassion? What might
lie beneath, waiting to burst forth?*

Groaning, Spider coaxed his stiff, resisting body into movement, then, wincing, carefully levered himself up to a sitting position. Battered and bruised, but at least I'm alive. It had been a night of restless sleep, fighting stabbing pains from his damaged ribs and shoulder, and haunted by horrific images of the brutal battle. It was good to now be awake. Tired, yes, but leaving the night's struggles behind him.

He looked around for his pack and, seeing it to his left, reached over with his good arm and dragged it over. His ribs screamed in protest, but he ignored them; he needed to eat. Searching inside his pack, he pulled out a packet of dried meat. After fumbling with the binding, he unwrapped the layers of dried leaves, then pulled out a thin, dark strip. He quickly tore off a piece with his teeth.

"Hungry?" came Growl's voice behind him.

"Starving," Spider mumbled, savouring the rich flavour of the meat. The parcel wouldn't last long.

"Hunger is a good sign," Growl said as he came into view.

"The better sign this morning is we're still alive." He tore off another piece. As his enigmatic travelling companion approached, Spider glanced to the distant hills. "Any more trouble heading our way?"

"Nothing that is visible to us, friend of ours. But will it remain so? That we cannot say. If you are able, we suggest moving on as soon as we are ready."

Spider winced. "Might be a little slow this morning, but, yes, we should move on." He briskly rubbed his hands. "And there's a chill in the air. Another reason to get moving."

Growl reached down and checked the straps on his pack. "The winter will again arrive a little earlier this sun-cycle. Soon, we will need to move all day and every day to keep warm."

Spider gave a wry smile. "Or sit by a roaring fire all day."

"And when your little packet of meat is gone?"

"Then I would ask you to bring me some more."

"It seems the fly is feeling better this morning. It attempts humour. That seemed far away last night, yes it did."

Throbbing pain in his chest and shoulder, Spider grimaced. Nothing about this journey so far evoked humour, and yet what to do, except move on. He looked down at the remaining strips of meat in the parcel. *Save what's left. Who knows what else will bear down on us today?* He carefully closed the leaves around the remaining ration, retied the binding, then looked up at Growl, who was now kicking dirt over the dying embers of the meagre fire. The man – *the shaman* – and his wolf had once again proved valuable allies. For whether their attackers, those fighters of the Azgoth tribe, had targeted him or the old man and the wolf – or both – the fact was that Growl and his companion had helped save him. *I owe him my life.*

And yet, can I trust him? I respect him. But can I trust him?

The answer came quickly, arising from deep instinct. *I can't. Not fully. And yet I may need to keep him and his wolf by my side on this journey.*

The Azgoths were allied with the Ka, the big brute of a man had said – *the one I killed* – and the Ka's tentacles were spreading deep into these northern lands – lands he had to safely navigate to reach the Iyes's White Crags camp to tell of the Warriors' arrival. He glanced at Growl. *And to do that, this one's aid may prove invaluable.* Yes, maybe that was the best way. Travel with this shaman and his wolf, then let the tribe leaders decide his fate when they arrived.

Decision made, Spider glanced to the southern hills. Just how many more hunters of the Ka were abroad in these northern lands? *And how are they finding us?* He looked back to Growl. "What I still don't understand is how these hunters are targeting us. Could they be using animals? Birds? As you do with Streak, could the enemy be doing the same?"

Growl looked up but was slow to respond. "It is possible," he said eventually. "Some tribe shamans sense the energy of the Land, and a few may wield it in some small way." His sharp eyes fell on Spider. "You must have seen this?"

Spider hesitated, immediately thinking of Naga's far-seeking. But as far as he knew, she didn't converse with animals. "Maybe," he replied, unwilling to share knowledge of the Iyes. "But who knows what tricks these shamans use?"

Growl regarded him with an unfathomable gaze. "Yes, maybe some hide what they truly know."

Spider stood, unflinching. He added nothing.

Growl sighed. "But there are difficulties, yes, many difficulties, in using animals in the way you describe. There must be an intelligence, a very high intelligence in that animal. You cannot impose your own on such a beast. No, no, this would not work. Birds? No. Not the right sort of intelligence for this, they would not understand. Just confusion is all you would receive. Wolves? Yes, maybe, but few. They must hold a particular intelligence to understand what is happening, to understand what is being asked and how to respond."

Spider considered the man's words. "Yesterday, you claimed no evidence of scouts on the ground, and now you say nothing can do it from the skies. So how do they find us? Could someone be tracking us from afar?"

The furrows on Growl's brow deepened. "Distance – that is the problem, even for one who may prove to be a most powerful shaman. To track people from afar …" He shook his head. "No, people are difficult. Maybe if they carry a potent artefact, then, maybe, yes … Maybe possible to track these from a distance. But people alone, no, so difficult."

Well, that doesn't help us. But then what? He noticed Growl staring at him. "What?" Spider said, frowning.

"An artefact," Growl said, his face clouding with suspicion. "Do you carry something of power?"

"An artefact? Power? Are you crazy? I wouldn't know what one looked like."

As soon as the words left his mouth, an image flashed into his mind. A bone carving. The gift from River lying in his pocket.

"Are you sure? Nothing you found? Nothing given?"

Spider fought to hold his breathing steady. "Nothing," he replied, holding the man's keen gaze. For the first time, Spider noticed the faintest flashes of silver in the man's dark eyes.

Growl studied him for a moment longer, then shrugged. "This may have explained it," he muttered. "Something given. Something not what it seems. But if not, then it cannot be. And so, we know not how we are being found." He straightened. "We are best served by moving and reaching our destination quickly. Are you now ready to leave?"

"As ready as I can be."

"Good, good. Try your pack and see what you are able to carry. What we can carry, we will. The rest we should leave behind."

Wrapping a hold on his nerves, Spider walked across to his pack. *An artefact. That could be tracked? Surely it can't be.* He ran his fingers over the smooth, precious carving in his pocket. *A gift from someone close. Someone trusted.* He immediately quashed the insidious thoughts. No. This was River's. Special, yes, but not in the way Growl suggested.

He let it drop freely in his pocket. *Move on.*

*

Lanky pulled the nape of his jacket closer around his neck as the biting wind whipped around them. The day was colder than the one before, and his body was cooling after the exertion of the morning trek south. And aching. His wound was healing fast – abnormally fast – but his body felt drained. *But we must push on. We have to try to catch up with Spider.*

"It's definitely his," Amber said, the young healer examining the bloodied tunic in her hand. "Here's his mark – he's says it's the body of a spider." She held it up, showing the circular engraved mark to Naga. She half smiled. "Once he's made a tunic he likes, he won't let it go until it falls in pieces from his body."

Naga, standing beside him, nodded. "What else?"

"We've counted five bodies," Dune said, his long dark hair swaying in the wind, "and Spider isn't one of them, thank IY."

Freya stepped forward. "Spider's camp was here," the short woman said, gesturing to her right, "and the unknown man and wolf were still with him. The other five bodies tally with the five tracks we saw over the rise." She gestured to the southeast. "It seems those five travelled as a group, then split – likely when they saw Spider and the other man approaching from either side of the rise. My guess is that, somehow, Spider knew about their approach and made a wise tactical move to split the attacking group."

"Wise, I agree," Gravel said, his hard eyes scanning one of the dead men, "but would have failed if it were not for the wolf's strike on their attackers' flanks. These men look hard-bitten fighters – too strong for Spider to hold for long."

Freya glanced at Gravel. "The person with Spider is a fair fighter themselves, probably accounting for two of the attacker's deaths."

"Agreed. From what we've seen from the tracks, he, or she, doesn't seem much heavier than Spider, but, yes, a very capable fighter." Gravel's brow furrowed. "And a valuable ally of Spider's here."

Lanky watched and listened in awe. He'd already observed the excellent tracking skills of this group, but it was the forensic analysis of scattered, scant evidence that was the most impressive. They were dissecting this battle site with the same thoroughness as at the previous site, where Spider and this unknown other had dealt with two different assailants.

He turned to Amber. "Are Spider and this other moving faster than us?"

"Possible, but unlikely," Amber replied. "It's clear that Spider is injured. And what's been discarded suggests he can't carry his usual load. They'll be travelling at a slower pace today."

"So we may catch them." He frowned. "I wonder who this ally of Spider's is."

Gravel's lips curled in disgust. "One who can influence wolves, given the evidence here."

Lanky echoed the Shield's distaste. *I've taken a dislike to wolves. And I'm wary of anyone who actively seeks them out.*

"I don't like the smell of this," Gravel said. "We need to catch up with them as soon as we can."

"Have you still no sight of Spider, Mother?" Amber asked. "Your far-seeking …?"

Naga hesitated. "The tracks suggest they are not far ahead, maybe half a day. But I still do not sense him."

Lanky glanced at Naga. She wasn't admitting it, but he was sure she was more badly hurt than she had let on. "Why can't you sense him?" he probed. *Will she offer any more now?*

She considered for a moment, then: "I was granted an extraordinary gift from IY, but there are times when I am unable to see. I accept this and know to use it wisely when I am able." As Naga glanced to the south, he saw sorrow in her eyes. "But for now, it escapes me, and this was an unfortunate moment to lose it."

Carefully studying her, he believed all she'd said, all those carefully chosen words, and yet even so, she was hiding the full truth. He thought back to the unknown force that had attacked Beth while they lay injured. *Naga helped protect us, but I think, somehow, the Enemy damaged her shamanic power.* And he had an idea of why she remained silent. *She doesn't want me to fear facing this Enemy.* But it was too late for that. The fear was constant. *But what does her injury mean for us, for the tribe? What—*

"Do not worry about me, Warrior," she said, clearly reading his concern. "I have little role in what is to come." She held his eyes. "It is now for others to come to the fore."

The Warriors, you mean. He drew a deep breath, settling his own thoughts. "I think all will do what they must." *And I must give Beth time to find the Staff, time for us to figure out how to reunite with Jessica and get ourselves home.*

"Yes, all should do what they must," Naga said with sudden fierce intensity. "Else all we cherish will be lost. But in this moment, we face a more immediate concern."

Spider. Lanky glanced to the others. He tensed as he saw they were silently watching him. *What are their thoughts about what they've heard? And what do they see?* His gut twisted. *They hope for a saviour. But they got me.* He strove to hold back a rising panic. *Why? Why am I here? I am no saviour. I am —*

"Hold steady, Warrior," came Naga's low whisper beside him – a voice for his ears only. "You will find your way."

But where will it take me? Home?

'It will take you where you need to go,' came a calm, ethereal voice. 'Trust in yourself. Trust in your friends.'

Another voice. Not Dysam's. But one he had heard before. *It is the voice I heard back home. 'Who speaks?'*

No reply came.

His jaw clenched in frustration. What game was this unseen entity playing? Because this wasn't helping. And yet a part of what had just been said was true. *I am who I am, and I'll do what I think we need to do.*

Steeling his thoughts, he faced Naga. "We need to move on. We can't help Beth or Jessica here."

The faintest of smiles appeared on her lips. "Agreed." She turned to Gravel. "They will reach the camp tomorrow, after midday. I would like to meet this companion of Spider's before they arrive. Spider has a wise head and would not willingly compromise the camp's location. Even so …"

"Injuries can hamper the strongest of minds," Gravel growled.

Naga's face hardened. "We have gained what we needed here. Pull everybody back. We leave now."

*

For most of the day, they marched in relative silence across the expansive grassy plain, each lost in their own thoughts as they left the rugged hill range far behind, angling towards higher ground to the north. Beth could easily believe she travelled with her trusted army unit from back home. This group of Iyes was well trained and organised, maintaining a steady but relentless pace, carrying packs designed for the job and with a uniform fit for purpose. *These people know what they're doing. This is their land.*

And they'd made excellent progress as her strength continued to grow – today even better than the last. But now, following their fifth rest stop of the day, the strain of the long march was slowly wearing her down. Thankfully, Bear had said it would be their last stretch of the day, pointing away to a spot to the northwest, where they would rejoin the escarpment and make camp. It was also there that they would catch up with Scorpion and Shorty, who were further afield, hunting.

Reaching the end of a stand of taller grasses, Beth could see Svana crossing a boulder-strewn rise ahead. Bear, up front at point, was out of sight beyond the boulder field. Beth looked back along their travelled path but couldn't see Knuckles. He would occasionally drift off to the right or left of the group's path, following the allocated role of the rear guard to check for any threats from behind.

She turned back—

The hairs on the back of her neck rose, a surge of adrenaline kicking in. She quickly glanced around but saw nothing. *Calm down, girl, what's got you all jittery?*

But her body refused to calm one iota. *Something is tracking us.*

She didn't know how she knew it, but she was as sure as the sky was blue that something was on their tail. She immediately dropped to a crouch, slipped off her pack, then, grasping her Axe and spear, she slowly moved forward, scanning all around—

She saw a flicker of movement.

She froze, every muscle and tendon straining to keep herself stock-still. Only her eyes moved, snapping into focus …

Onto nothing.

Nothing? Had she just imagined it?

'No. It is there,' said a voice in her mind.

Remaining still, she forced her eyes to focus …

And saw glimpses of a sleek, pale-yellow body moving through grasses away to her left. *How did I not see that?* She gritted her teeth. *Don't worry about that – you see it now.*

Stilling her breathing, she sank lower. Masked by the lightly swaying grasses, the whole body of the creature wasn't fully visible, but it was clearly an enormous beast, maybe just under a metre tall and around two metres long. And it was clearly stalking their group. Not a classic, slow, furtive stalk, but a bold and threatening tracking. *It's targeting someone!*

And from the direction it was heading, it would intercept her!

She held her breath as the creature paused, lifting its nose to the air. It didn't seem to have a line of sight on her yet, and as the wind blew lightly into her left cheek, it hadn't locked onto her scent either. *Stay still, Beth. Very still.*

The creature lowered its head and passed into thicker grasses, moving out of sight. She immediately crept forward, keeping low, pushing to the right to parallel the path the beast had taken. Within seconds, she reached the outer edge of the stand of thick grasses, catching glimpses of the boulder field ahead. She inched forward until only a few taller grasses separated her and the open area …

And there was the lion. Not a lion she had ever seen before – leaner, shaggier hair, and very sharp featured – but definitely a lion.

And it was staring right at her!

Instinctively, she tightened her grip on the haft of her Axe, and a surge of energy coursed through her. She returned the lion's menacing gaze. The lion lowered its head, then stalked slowly and purposefully towards her.

An acute calmness descended. *No chance to run now. Engage!*

She stood tall, then strode a few paces closer and whistled loudly.

The lion paused.

Ahead, Svana stopped walking and spun around.

And Beth readied herself.

Letting out a loud cry, she launched herself towards the lion, intending to scare it away. Instead, it crouched, snarled, then leapt to meet her charge. She dived to the side, twisting herself around and thrusting sideways with the spear. A tremendous weight hit her shoulder, and with a flash of pain shooting through her body, she spun around in the air, landing heavily on the ground. Immediately, she moved to push herself upwards, but a bestial growl sounded in her ear – an explosion of pain ripped through her as razor-sharp teeth scraped the back of her head and closed over her shoulder.

'*We have you!*' a triumphant voice cried in her head.

Acting on impulse, she closed her eyes and focussed on the voice – and stood staring down at a cloaked figure, silvery-grey hair visible beneath his hood, a jet-black staff in his hand.

"Yes, we have you," the figure rasped, oblivious to her presence. "We—"

"You have nothing," Beth growled. She swung her Axe.

The figure half turned, a stunned look on his grey-bearded face—

Then he vanished, the Axe passing harmlessly through the darkness of the Glade.

Loud shouts and cries sounded from afar …

She blinked …

And the jaws of the lion released.

Breathing hard, Beth twisted away, and with blood streaming down her body, she scrambled up into a warrior's crouch, keen eyes scanning around. Knuckles stood to one side, shouting wildly while Svana pulled a javelin free from the lion's flank, using the rope attached to its end. A second spear dangled from the animal's chest, evidence of Beth's weak initial strike. Breathing heavily, and with the animal distracted, she rushed to recover her fallen Axe …

As she grasped the haft, the lion turned, snarling, to face her once more. Another javelin whistled in from the right, striking the lion a glancing blow to its neck. Roaring its defiance, the beast turned to find its assailant – as it did so, her spear dragged loose from its chest and fell to the ground. Facing Bear, who had joined Svana on the rocky higher ground, the lion emitted a series of low, fearsome snarls. Both Iyes readied themselves to face a charge from the enraged beast.

With little conscious thought, Beth took a step towards the lion – it swung its head towards her, its deep, guttural growls cutting a primeval fear through her stomach. But the lion was clearly hurt and uncertain of its next move. *That shaman controlled it, forced it to attack me.* She steadied herself, suddenly sure of the words she should speak. "You're free again, my friend. Leave now while you still have your life."

The lion let out a low growl, its piercing amber eyes locked onto hers.

Neither of them moved.

Then, almost imperceptibly, the lion slowly moved its head right and left, assessing its surroundings. *It's checking its exit route. Come on, take it!*

The lion looked back at her. It took a step forward, growling loudly. And then another step.

"Hold," she whispered to the others as the lion halted, its head swinging again, first to the left and then the right. "Do not move."

Keeping her eyes locked onto the lion, and a firm grip on her Axe, she took a single determined stride. "Don't make a foolish mistake," she hissed, staring into the lion's eyes. "These people are not for you."

Raising its head, the lion issued a sequence of sharp, angry growls.

"You have only this chance," Beth growled back. "Leave."

The lion snarled, its eyes fixed on hers …

And then, with a final snarl, it swung around and darted away, picking up pace as it disappeared into the grasses.

Beth instantly dropped to her knees, utter relief flooding through her.

She looked up as Knuckles arrived by her side, breathing hard. "You did well, Warrior," he panted. "But come, you're injured – we need to treat you quickly."

Her adrenaline plummeting, searing pain flared in her shoulder. She forced herself back to her feet and looked around.

"Thank you, Warrior," Svana said, striding up to her. "I didn't see it. You made a brave decision, and I thank you for it."

Beth glanced back to the thick grasses. "I think it was targeting me." She looked back to Svana and forced a smile. "But you're welcome."

"How could I have missed it?" Knuckles whispered, his face drawn.

"It was ... difficult to see," Beth said slowly. "I struggled to see it. I ... sensed it. It was being masked. By a shaman ..."

"We can discuss this later, Warrior," came Bear's calm voice as he approached. "But, if you are able, we should continue on. The northern escarpment is close, and it will be safer to camp on that higher ground."

"I'd prefer she doesn't bleed out before we get there," Svana said, a note of admonishment in her tone. "I'll treat her wounds and then we'll see. While I do that, you two can call in our hunters. Their big ears will have heard the commotion, and they'll want to know the gory details."

Bear briefly glanced at Beth, then he nodded. He gestured to Knuckles. "Let's retrieve our weapons, then we'll call in the others." The two walked away.

"I'll fetch my pack," Svana said to Beth, and she ran after Bear.

Beth saw the three Iyes quickly recover their discarded packs, then collect the weapons used in the skirmish. As Knuckles and Bear headed away to intercept the hunters, Svana ran back to her.

"Let's get these off," she said, gesturing to Beth's jacket and tunic, "then we can assess the damage."

With her last layer of clothing removed, Beth saw the deep gouges in her upper arm and shoulder. *I was lucky.*

She felt Svana's light touch on her shoulder. "The wounds are not as deep as I feared. We can clean and then bind them." She looked up at Beth. "And I've heard you heal well."

Beth managed a weak smile.

Svana reached for her pack. "You were lucky he only grazed your thick head and didn't gain a clean grip on your neck."

"He?" questioned Beth.

"He? Oh, it was a male. And how do I know? Because he made too many mistakes."

Despite the pain, Beth's smile widened. "How so?"

"The female would have evaded detection," Svana said, searching through her pack, "killed one of us, then slipped away unharmed. Like most men, this lion was lazy."

Beth smiled. "Well, I'm not sure of that, Svana. Knuckles and Bear can't be called lazy."

"I didn't say they don't have their uses, Warrior. Sometimes they make me happy. But their execution can often be wanting – don't you think? Now hold still. This will hurt."

*

"You'll waste our firewood doing that," Freya said, her eyes glinting as she watched Lanky poking a stick into the fire, sending a flurry of sparks dancing into the air. "Can't you leave it alone?"

Lanky glanced at the young woman, who lay to his right, enjoying her night off from guard duty. Looking at her now, relaxed and mischievous, he wouldn't recognise her as the deadly hunter he'd seen in action on their journey south. *Never judge a book by its cover.*

He turned back to the glowing fire. "I like fires. Some of my best memories are as a child, camping with my father. He let me build the fire and then tend it all evening. He—"

"He must have had plenty of wood, given the way you fuel our fire."

Lanky grinned and scraped his stick along a glowing splintered log, sending another fiery swarm into the evening air. "I could do this every night."

"Then all our trees would be gone." Her twinkling eyes studying him, Freya pushed her thick, curly hair back from her face. "You say that in your age you're from this part of the Land?"

He nodded. "I lived – or will live, I guess – back near where I first met you. In a village at the head of the lake."

She tilted her head. "This village was a large camp? Where did you go in the winter?"

"The village was a very large camp," he replied, picking his words carefully. "A camp of many, many families. It … our winter was not so cold as yours. We could stay there all year around."

"And the hunting was good?"

He hesitated, then: "We had many more animals to choose from – or at least different animals. Ones we could eat through all the seasons."

Freya sighed. "Your time seems to be a good time. I hope my life is still in your land."

He glanced up at her. "Your life?"

Beside him, Naga smiled. "She means her children's children's children – you see?"

As Naga's words drifted across the campsite, a tremendous sense of awe swept over him. *All life in my time is descended from those who live here now. These people could be ancestors of mine.* It was a truly stunning thought. He glanced at the young hunter. "Your life could easily be in my land, Freya. But you realise that if that is so, then you're already a very distant grandma?" He saw Freya's puzzled face. "Ah, well, let's see … You would already be a mother of this many children." He held up both hands, again, and again, and again.

A twinkle returned to Freya's eyes. "That would mean I should start soon."

He cast his eyes down under the heat of her gaze. "Ah yes …"

"Well," Amber laughed, "you might need to watch yourself, Warrior." She winked at Freya.

Lanky felt himself redden and was glad of the dim light.

Sheba leaned forward. "You colour, Warrior. Are you feeling the heat?"

"Leave him be, you three," Naga said with a faint smile.

Freya laughed. "You're well protected, Warrior." She tilted her head. "This night."

Lanky poked the fire a bit harder, and they laughed.

"I wonder how the group in the north is doing," Amber said as the group quietened.

Sudden tension soured the air. "I guess I've been wondering the same," Lanky murmured.

He felt Naga's sharp eyes on him. "Then you should contact her."

He shifted a smouldering log in the fire, triggering a swirling shower of sparks. "And how do I do that without being in one of your sacred sites? Or involving the warg?"

"You are a Warrior," she said simply. "And you have already used a Glade."

He glanced at her. "So it will work here?"

She held his gaze. "Try. The more you try, the better equipped you will become."

Her words triggered a tremor of unease. *And where does that lead me?* He regarded her for a few heartbeats longer, then blew a resigned sigh. He needed to speak with Beth. He set down the stick. "Okay, let me try."

"Ah, good," Freya murmured. "The fire should have some peace now."

"And I'll need a little quiet," he shot back.

Freya smiled – but remained silent.

*

Ignoring all whispering doubts, Lanky closed his eyes. *Okay, let's see. This is what I did last time.* Freeing his mind, he allowed it to drift, to float within the ether. *Find the right Cord,* came the thought, seeming to rise from the depth of instinct. He reached out, sensing the ether around him for the path to a Glade. *Or to a Gate if I choose another.* Sensing a particular vibration to his right, he locked onto the chosen Cord—

A rich vibrancy flooded his mind, and with a faint tingle, he entered a Glade.

Unnerved, he glanced around. He stood on another craggy summit, surrounded by a deep, impenetrable darkness. Rippling power surrounded him, and beyond, unseen, something unknown, something cold, and in his mind a faint ache. *I still can't believe this. How can I do this?*

Because you are a Warrior.

He grimaced. *I'm no saviour.*

He glanced around the bare, rocky plateau that was the Glade. *Yet I can't ignore this.* Warrior or not, it was inescapable that he – and Beth – had access to something truly remarkable, truly unbelievable. *No, not unbelievable. I see it. I feel it. It is real.* Cold tension stirred. *And I am engaging it with it. Because we need to get home.*

Drawing a slow breath, he settled himself. *I have to talk to Beth.* Glancing around the barren plateau, he suddenly recalled her disdain at his choice of scenery. *Maybe I shouldn't bring her to this mountain again …*

He stumbled slightly as the rocky summit disappeared, then, catching his balance, he steadied himself to stand proudly on a snow-covered beach beside a frozen lake. A faint smile crossed his lips. *This will do. I like winter.*

Closing his eyes, he formed the image of a young woman in his mind – a woman with a determined face, small scar on her cheek, dark hair, keen eyes … "Beth. Can you hear—"

He flinched as a voice cut through the ether. "Lanky? Lanky, was that you?"

He watched, astonished, as Beth's form materialised in the Glade.

Her eyes wide, she stared at him for a moment, then glanced around. "Impressive," she said, slowly relaxing her stance. "But I could have done with some sun."

"I can't believe it!"

"*You* can't believe it? You appear unannounced in my head and then say you can't believe it? You called me, remember?"

"Sorry, sorry," Lanky stammered, shaking his head. "Wow. That was easy."

"What did you do?"

He held up his hands. "Just thought of you and then spoke. In my mind."

"With *your* mind, it's a miracle you could think of anything."

"Ha ha." He walked up to her. "I wanted to find out how you're doing. Is everything okay? Where are you? What's been happening – ow!" he exclaimed as sharp stabbing pains ripped into his shoulder. "What the hell is that?"

Beth frowned. "You okay?"

He rubbed his shoulder. "Felt like something ripped its teeth into me. I—"

"Oh, that's interesting," Beth murmured.

Lanky scowled. "Why is something stabbing my body interesting?"

"You asked me if everything was okay – I instantly remembered the lion biting me in the shoulder, and—"

"What! A lion – ahh. Stop it, that really hurts."

"Ah, sorry," she said, not looking sorry in the least. "Seems it's not only words that are picked up in this Glade."

"Then stop whatever you're doing," he grunted. He glowered at her, then, finally convinced she wasn't going to project any more pain, he relaxed his stance. "A lion? What the hell happened?"

"Long story ..." A flash of concern crossed her face. "Have you heard anything more about Jessica?"

His expression darkened. "I can't get hold of Fen. How about Garrion?"

The flare of frustrated anger in the ether gave him his answer.

"I thought the warg was sulking, but if Garrion isn't responding either ..." He shook his head. "Not the most engaging allies."

"This shows we can't rely on them to be around. Even more reason for us to talk, to share what we know."

He sighed. "Then we keep doing what we're doing. Talking of sharing, you've still not told me what happened with this lion?"

He listened in shocked silence as Beth described the encounter with the lion and cloaked shaman, and then of her group's progress north, including the sight of the stranded Isle of Vannin.

"You were very lucky, Beth," he said as she finished. "This Enemy seems to have a long reach. Does Bear know who that shaman might have been?"

"He's unsure. Probably the shaman of the Ka, one called the Shade. But he's also heard rumours of a powerful shaman emerging from a tribe allied with the Ka. The Meso tribe, or something like that. But whoever this shaman was, it's someone who knew what they were doing."

And if these shamans could reach them like this ... *I must tell Naga. And it makes me even more nervous of this character with Spider.*

"What's wrong?" Beth asked, clearly sensing his disquiet.

"Wrong? How long do you have?"

"Give me the short version."

He relayed their progress over the last few days. "So, we should arrive at Rind's camp tomorrow afternoon – and it can't come soon enough."

"Not good. Not good at all. I hope Spider is okay. Why can't Naga see him – sense him?"

"She's saying it's one of the occasional lapses she suffers."

"But you don't believe that?"

"No. My guess is that she was injured in some way when she defended us from that shamanic attack."

"And she's worried that you knowing would make you even more wary of this power? Even more stubborn – if that's possible."

"Wary? No question," he said with force. "There's something very, very real here. An astonishing power. One we can access and use. But something we can fully trust? Well, now we tread more dangerous ground."

"Well, without it, I'd be dead from that poisoned blade, and you could have died from the wound you took. We—"

"I know," he said, holding up his hands. "I know that. But beyond that healing power? These daemons claim all is well if we fully embrace them, but here's my wary scepticism. Things don't come free. There's always a catch. And while some things are running deep, I'm not happy to step too far into that murky water." He grimaced. "And I don't trust the warg."

His disquiet deepened. Why didn't he trust the warg? Was it the daemon he feared? Or something else? *They say there are ancient Warriors within us. What if it's these Warriors who the Iyes truly call? Not me. Not Lanky. Someone else.* The fear swirled around a name. *I fear becoming Dysam.* Drawn by the chain of his disturbing thoughts came the now familiar surge of anger. *No. I'm no one else but Lanky. And that will forever be.*

Steadying his shaking hands, he refocussed. Beth was looking at him intently. "It's okay. Just reminding myself why I hate the warg."

Her eyes narrowed. "Well, I won't tell you what to do there, but I'm putting my trust in Garrion. In these battles, you have to grab whatever advantage you can and make it work for you."

He frowned. "Garrion seems to have more sense than the warg. Not that either deigns to speak to us right now."

"I'll repeat what I said before – even more sense for us to talk."

Lanky sighed, rubbing the growing stubble on his chin. "That I agree with. And today is a reminder to keep our guard up. And act wisely. You took a big risk facing off with that beast."

Beth held his gaze for a moment, then turned and stared out across the frozen lake. "That shaman controlled it," she said in a low voice. "Forced it into an action it hadn't wanted to take. When we stood face-to-face, and it was free – free from the shackles of that shaman – then I knew I couldn't take its life. I—"

"It had just attacked you, Beth. It's a dangerous animal."

She turned back to him and shook her head. "When I saw there may be a way out, an avoidance of killing … Well, what are we if we don't show compassion, show restraint?"

A shiver ran through Lanky. *Restraint.* A word triggering a remembered conversation with Jessica about their time as captives of the Ka, and of their rescue by Beth. And of how Jessica had stopped an ice-cold Beth taking a man's life, the life of their guard. How much was Beth in control back then? What restraint had she shown? *Maybe I should mention—*

"What's that?" Beth asked, looking around. "Is that singing?"

He realised the moment had passed. *Okay, not right now. Another time …*

He attuned to the surroundings, then couldn't help but smile as he heard the rich voice of the young hunter. "It's Freya," he said, the tension easing from his mind. "She has a wonderful voice. A bit like mine."

A flicker of humorous derision cut through the ether.

Sensing Beth listening to the drifting song, he brought the rich clarity of Freya's voice into focus. The range and subtle depth of her exotic voice wove mesmerising textures and flavours in his mind, easing his worries and delighting his soul. His fears, his frustrations, seemed to slip away, the cheerless shadows of his mind cast aside by a glorious light. Nothing else mattered, but that wondrous voice. Nothing else existed.

He listened in rapt delight, until finally he realised Freya had stopped singing – yet his mind sang on, still holding on to the joy and the hope she had gifted them.

"A good note to finish on, I think," Beth murmured, breaking his reverie. Her gaze drifted, momentarily elsewhere. "I should go. Need some rest before we head out at dawn."

Reluctantly, Lanky pulled away from the brief yet heartwarming respite from the cold reality beyond. He refocussed on Beth. "After what you've been through today, that sounds like a good plan." He paused, then: "Take care on your journey, Beth. That shaman you saw today shows this enemy of the Iyes has a long reach."

"I will. We all will. And I wish you a safe journey south," she added, genuine concern in her eyes. "I hope you find Spider, and all is well."

"So do I," he said, a whisper of unease running through him.

Beth's image began to fade. "Let's talk again in a day or two … And maybe then I choose the scenery. Bye for now …"

"Bye …"

She vanished.

He stood for a time, gazing along the snow-covered beach. Then he turned his gaze to the frozen lake. Ripples of the swirling energy of the Glade caressed him, an energy he knew he could reach for and draw within him, an energy he knew now he could wield. And that scared him. They were slowly being drawn further and further into the embrace of this land of a long-past age – *but we don't truly know what we're doing here.* He tensed, frustrated. If it was this unknown god of the Iyes who had wanted them here, then why didn't it speak to them? *Talk to us, IY, dammit. Talk to us!*

He drew a deep breath, then released it in a long sigh. *One step at a time. Give Beth the time she needs to find that Staff.* He needed to get south and somehow mobilise the Iyes's allies to engage the Ka. *Keep their eyes away from the north.*

Too late, came a voice from a part of his mind. *That unknown shaman knew where Beth was.*

Then all the more reason to distract them. *Get to this Iyes camp. Understand more, then act.* Because he was learning one thing. *Stand still and we'll die.*

He took one more look around the frozen landscape, then reached for the Cord—

He stood once more in the flickering glow of the camp's fire.

Unsettled, he glanced to the north, and prayed to any gods listening. *Keep her safe. Please.* Then he crept back to the fireside, where Freya had begun another song. He lay down to listen, ignoring the faint whispers of dread at the edges of his mind. *Keep safe, Beth. Stay vigilant.*

CHAPTER TWENTY-FIVE

The perils of seeing your own future ...
It is why only the Guardian should travel.

Sickened, lost, and utterly disorientated by a bewildering array of disturbing sights and sounds beyond her recognition and understanding, River feared the Land she had known had gone forever. Leaving Jessica's home, she'd seen the first glimpses of the alien landscape of this distant future of her people. First, a seamless rock surface sculpted by this land's makers to form a snakelike river running as far down the hill as she could see. Then, beyond this river's boundary lay an unnatural patchwork terrain of sparse vegetation framed by a vast web of rambling rock walls, their purpose unknown.

And then the beast. Yet another of the unimaginable creations of this land's makers, inconceivably crafted from the now familiar smooth materials she saw all around her, this beast sat on the river of stone. Jessica explained that Robert controlled the beast – the car, as she called it – and that once inside, it would take them where they needed to go. Her stomach churning, River had no option other than to follow Jessica inside. Where else would she go? What else could she do? She had to continue to trust Jessica.

But when the beast roared, she'd attempted to get out. A basic flight response – what was there to fight? Jessica had calmed her. "I know the sound is disturbing, but I promise it can't hurt you." River had sat back in the seat, uneasy and on edge, praying to IY that the nightmare would soon end.

With the car growling in anger, they'd moved on along the stone river – the road, Jessica called it – and soon encountered other incredible dwellings of this area's tribe, each fantastically constructed, but each varying colours, sizes, and shapes.

And then other growling beasts – other cars. All travelling the stone river. All with a human inside. Their controllers, their drivers.

And so many people. Walking along the side of the road, sometimes entering or leaving the looming stone houses, they were clothed in a myriad of styles and colours of a type and variety no artist of her time could create. As they had travelled past these people, she saw them talking to each other, or smiling, or gesturing; she saw them acting in the same way as those in the car with her. *They are also like me,* she had thought. *But they are also different.*

Beyond the road lay the stone houses, becoming wider, taller, and more connected. Soaring above them, these huge edifices formed sheer cliff faces and ledges for birds to perch on before they swooped down to the road to feed.

And beside all these staggering sights lay numerous other smooth, regular objects and materials of this land's makers, their angular and rounded designs creating a landscape beyond her comprehension – a landscape that did not seem real.

They'd eventually arrived at the dwelling of the mother of Lanky. Robert had left, leaving a tension in the air. On his agitated return, they'd quickly moved on, and soon, in a blur of confusion, they'd swapped cars in a place packed with other such cars, all sitting on the same stone surface. It seemed these cars needed the stone river to travel. In fact, to her eyes, these people had covered so much of the ground with stone, there was little vegetation remaining in this village of theirs.

Leaving the village behind, they travelled briefly through a land more recognisable to her, only occasional dwellings scattered throughout. But even here in this greener realm, the vegetation wasn't the same. Fewer trees, different trees, but also a fragmented landscape of unfamiliar shapes and patterns. Vegetation, yes, but somehow ordered and controlled. *I see the hand of these people even here.*

As they travelled on, the villages grew larger, innumerable dwellings sprawling together to obliterate all signs of fertile ground. The roads widened, the cars travelling faster than most animals could run. And ever onwards the stone river ran. How had the people built this? These people held tremendous power – a frightening power.

And now, after all they had encountered, they had entered the widest stone road yet, one spanning many, many spear lengths across. Huge beasts travelled with them – and against them – each moving at an incredible speed, supported by spinning objects, some as tall as her. How all these cars and more massive beasts moved, she had no idea. There was a power here beyond her imagining.

And this constant noise. Noise from their car. Noise from the cars outside. And noise from the wind. It was relentless.

She closed her eyes, hoping to find an escape from the nightmare. But flight seemed impossible. She calmed her breathing. *Remember Naga's teachings ...*

Her heartbeat slowing, the tension in her chest easing, she pulled her tormented mind away from the distressing assault on her senses. *Remember my Land. Remember my people.* She drew herself further and further from the bewildering realm outside and drifted into calmer waters ...

A vision of a laughing young woman appeared, eyes sparkling as she danced away from a playful lunge from a thoroughly drenched man.

"I'll get you back for that, Ravine!" her father called, chasing her mother down the riverbank.

The image flickered, and now showed her father drying by the fire as her still-dry mother watched him, smiling.

"You are too slow, Father," River said. "And your eyes are no good."

"I need eyes in the back of my head to look out for your mother's tricks." Her father laughed, turning his tunic around to dry the other side.

"You made a big splash," said her sister, Sheba. "Like a whale of the Great Sea."

Her father smiled. "I'm sure it was, but I think you could make a bigger splash for me tomorrow."

River jumped up and stood before him, hands on her hips. "If I can stand on your shoulders to jump, then I *can* make a bigger splash than you."

"Okay, it's a deal. I look forward to seeing an enormous wave sweep down the river ..." He winked. "But only if your mother tries to make a bigger splash after you."

"You will, won't you, Mother?" River said quickly.

Her mother had smiled at her. "You father may be slow, but he's quite sneaky. But yes, I will try – but I think you'll be difficult to beat."

"I will – can we do it now?"

"Yes, and I want to try," Sheba said, standing tall beside her sister.

Her mother had laughed. "No, it's too dark now. We wouldn't be able to see whose waves are bigger. And anyway, it's far too cosy here." She pulled the girls in close, cuddling them into her warm, soft body. "I love you," she whispered.

"And I love you, Mother," River replied.

Love. A simple word, but life's greatest gift. A precious treasure that spawned the rawest emotions and the most evocative, passionate memories. And this was one of her sharpest memories, a radiant reminder of the boundless love binding her family. One that had grown slowly yet relentlessly.

Only to shatter so completely.

The next morning, springing upward off her father's broad shoulders to begin her special dive, she heard her mother's shout of encouragement from the shore – or so she'd thought. She hit the water, creating – she was sure – one of the biggest splashes she'd ever made. Surfacing, she shook the water out of her hair, already turning to see mother's reaction …

But something was wrong! Her father grabbed her and called for Sheba to follow. He started towards the riverbank, forcing himself against the weight of the water. "Ravi! What's happened? Ravi?"

When they finally reached the bank, her father dropped her to the ground and ran towards her convulsing mother. She and Sheba made to follow—

"Stay back! River, run to the fire and get a blade! Now!"

A terrible dread ripping through her gut, River raced to the fire, grabbing the first pack she came to with shaking hands. Struggling to breathe, she fumbled around inside for a blade—

"The blade, River!"

Panicking, she emptied the pack. There was no blade. She grabbed the other pack and emptied that. She saw the sheen of a blade. Grasping it, she ran back towards her father, who was dragging her mother from the area she'd fallen. Sheba stood to the side, crying.

"Stay back," her father ordered, his voice shaking.

River froze as she saw two snakes slithering through the undergrowth away from them.

Her father dragged her mother a little further away, then gently lay her down. "The blade!" he called.

She ran to him and handed him the blade. He quickly made a small cut on her mother's lower leg, then leaned down, sucking blood from the fresh wound. River stood beside Sheba, shaking, not knowing what to do. Her father straightened. "No. Ah no," she heard him whisper under his breath.

And then River saw them – two further marks on the other leg – two separate pairs of incisions.

Her father turned to her, desperate fear in his eyes. "Go back to the main camp and get help. You remember where the camp is?"

She nodded, unable to speak.

"Good. Go now and go as fast as you can."

And how fast had she run? She had run faster than the wind. And help she had brought ...

But a help that was no longer needed.

And now an image that would never leave her. Her father, sitting hunched, rocking gently, her mother's head lying still in his lap. Tears streamed down his face, each drop falling softly onto her mother's still lips, lips that would never say her name again.

It had taken many sun-cycles to push this tragic image to a hidden place and replace it with the beautiful memories of her wonderful, joyous mother. A mother who looked over her from beyond the Horizon.

But now this place – Jessica's land – had pulled back the worst nightmare of her life.

'Be strong,' said a voice in her head, clear as the song of a nightingale.

'Mother?'

'No, River. I knew your mother, but sadly, I am not her.'

'What then? What enters my dreaming?'

'A friend. One who can help you.'

'How?'

'By you helping me. Jessica must keep hope. Remember hope—'

A hand grasped her shoulder.

Her eyes shot open. *What's happening?* Panicked, confused, and feeling trapped, she started for the door—

"Whoa! It's okay," came Jessica's voice. "Remember where you are. It's okay."

River froze, then turned, her eyes wide.

Jessica gently squeezed her shoulder. "It's okay, River, I'm still here. We've stopped for a break. We'll go outside for a short while. Okay?"

The panic slowly eased. She nodded.

As Jessica made her way out of the car, River slumped back into her seat, trying to clear her head. *Outside. Yes, outside would be better than in here.*

I hope.

*

"That was easier than taking you inside," Jessica said as the two women emerged from the dense undergrowth. "But it's a good thing it's quiet here."

They walked back to the empty bench, where Jessica sat on the far side, giving her a view over the carpark of the motorway services. River stayed standing, her body tensed, her face strained.

Jessica sat in silence, allowing River time to settle herself. *She's finding this hard. Very hard.*

After a while, River spoke, her voice uncertain. "Someone came to me again. She said she was a friend. A friend that would help us."

A friend? Or an enemy? "Do you trust her?"

"She said she knew my mother."

Jessica's eyes narrowed. "Is that enough?"

"No. I heard only a little before you woke me."

"Ah. I'm sorry."

River winced. "I had dreamed enough."

Jessica reached out and held River's hand.

"Do you like this land?" River murmured after a moment.

Jessica looked at her in surprise. "It's my land," she said slowly, "and it just is what it is, I guess. There are many things I like, and many things I don't. But I do like living – and I live in this land. So overall, yes, I like it."

"But why do your makers create such things?" River asked, gesturing to … everything. She pointed at the carpark surface. "Why do they cover the ground with this?"

Such a simple thing, but how to explain? "We have creative people, those who work to make our lives simpler. Like this," she said, gesturing to the asphalt. "It's so people like us can travel across the land far faster than we can just on foot. To carry food, clothes, medicines – lots of stuff – to where it's needed. We couldn't survive as we do without it."

"And these cars of yours. Noisy, smelly – how do you live with them?"

Jessica glanced at her old car. "We can improve them, I agree. But people, makers, are working on that too." *To stop us poisoning the very air we breathe.*

"The air here is bad," River said, screwing up her nose. "Sickening. It prickles my nose."

"Being this close to the motorway doesn't help. That many cars put out a lot of … smoke."

River stared at the passing traffic. "Where is everybody going?"

"Well," Jessica began, searching for a straightforward answer. "Think of any task, like going to see family, or going to do a job, or going out for food – anything – and there will be somebody out on that road, travelling for that reason."

"And their families, and the tasks they're doing, are all at the ends of this road?"

Jessica smiled. "They are. You can reach all the houses in the land travelling on those paths – without ever leaving this surface."

River turned to her. "How far?"

"To the very edges of the land. And even then, you can take your car onto a boat and travel across the water to the next land, and then continue your journey. How far? A long, long way."

"Do all peoples have these cars?"

"Most."

River fell silent for a moment, then: "Your makers are skilled beyond belief. How did this happen?"

Jessica realised, yet again, the utter impossibility of her understanding the depth of the chasm separating River – a fellow human from the same planet – from the world of this age. How could anyone truly understand? How could you possibly unlearn what you knew – to really and truly put yourself in an imagined position where these things did not exist? Humans were supreme adapters. Changing circumstance, changing technology, changing climate – humans dealt with all these issues as needed. But to attempt to unlearn, to remove all unconscious bias, all the memories, to attempt to imagine what River truly felt? No, this was not possible.

River and her people did not use metals; had not yet invented the wheel; did not farm, nor domesticate animals; had no paper or pens – the list could go on and on. But River's people were obviously advanced humans, as the complexities of their own thoughts and words clearly showed, a sophistication that would lead their children's children to develop the world as it was today.

This is their children's world.

But to pull River here and expect her to understand? No, this was like throwing Jessica into a space station and telling her to go outside and do a spacewalk. The gulf would be too great to cross.

And we have no time to try.

Glimpsing Robert at the far side of the carpark, she pulled herself back to River's question. "Very smart people from your land developed all this, River. Not in your own lifetime, but in the generations that followed. Your daughter's daughter's daughters did it. And all these people here today have a connection back to someone in your time. We are the same people."

She saw the doubt in River's eyes. *And there's nothing right now I can do about that.* She gestured to the carpark. "Robert returns."

River watched the man walk towards them. "What do we do now?"

"Now we finally see the map."

*

Robert laid the map on the table, then rolled it out, fully covering the table's surface.

"Wow, that's a map," Jessica said, moving in for a closer look. It appeared to be professionally drafted and printed, similar to an antique ordinance survey map; in fact, for all she knew, that might be its origin. It was covered in extensive markings of both pen and pencil; text and symbols lay scattered about both the map and its borders. "It's a map of the Ranges," she said, scanning around the map. "Or at least the majority of it."

Robert nodded. "The legend here is the one I originally created before I handed the map to Lanky."

"Wait, this was your map?"

"It was. It was part of the package of reports I handed over to Lanky." He leaned over, peering at the map. "Let's see now. The black stars are the original locations my parents surveyed. Those two marked in red were ones they were particularly interested in." He adjusted his glasses. "Lanky was sure these coordinates were shifted to disguise the actual location." He moved closer to the map. "I see he's tried various corrections. See here," he said, pointing at the legend, "the red star labelled S-1 by me now has five labels below it. The last is S-1e. Where's that located?"

Jessica leaned over and examined the map. "Well, this red star nearest me is S-1. Let's see; 1d, 1a, – ah, 1e is here, in this valley. So, let me get my bearings. Well, that's the village over there to the south, and this valley …" Her breath caught. She looked up at Robert. "That's the valley to Low Bridge, the place where I first met Lanky. Where he saw the writing and found the Staff. He must have marked this on the map that same day."

"And see here," Robert said, palpable excitement in his voice. "He has written 'fell, found writing' against that mark in the key."

"So, what about the other one there? S-2," she asked, pointing to the other red star.

Robert peered at the legend. "Again, five entries below the main red star. And S-2e has something against it." He looked more closely. "It's not so clear, but I think it says, 'fall correction'."

"What does that mean?"

"My guess is that it's the same adjustment he used for that first red star. Where's that 2e mark located?"

Jessica leaned further over the map. She gasped. "It's near Pike O' Dalr in the Long Valley."

"And the relevance of that?" Robert asked, peering at her over his glasses.

"It's the location of one of the safe caves of River's tribe," she said in a hushed voice. "The cave I was in when I was transported back here." She stared at the map, stunned. "To see it like this … On his map … It's incredible, truly incredible"

"Lanky found the key to the puzzle," Robert whispered.

"The key," Jessica murmured, grasping onto his words. *The key to find the Staff?* "The red star in the north. Where's that?"

Robert gestured to the far end of the map. "It's on the insert over there."

Walking to the end of the table, she examined the detailed insert map. She quickly saw a now familiar red star, and sure enough, offset from it were other pencil markings. "This says S-10. What happened to three to nine?"

"My parents' research generated many potential sites to study – in different parts of the world. I believe Lanky still has those maps." Robert looked back down at the map. "According to the key here, the most current location is—"

"Let me guess, S-10e?"

Robert smiled. "Correct."

"Well, this inset map is a detail of part of the northwest tip of the country. And that 10e location appears to be sitting on …" She leaned closer. "Mount Hope," she whispered. Her heart leapt. "It's as he said," she murmured to herself. *And as that voice said.*

Robert looked over at her, his eyes shining. "Is it possible? Is it possible the Staff is there?"

His words arrowed to her very soul. Was it too much to hope? That the ice dragon had taken it to this place. And that these millennia later they would find the Staff there? *And what chance we'll then find a way to return to that past age? Find a way back to Beth and Lanky.* A trickle of hope seeped into her thoughts. *That voice said the Staff will be there. Lanky's maps say there's something at this Mount Hope.* She looked across at Robert. "I don't know how it could be possible, but neither do I know how *any* of this is possible. But what other option do we have?"

"Then we travel on? We travel to this Mount Hope?"

"I know what I want to do, but I need to speak with River." She studied his face. "You don't have to go on. It may be better for you to return home."

Robert shook his head. "I invested much of my early life in this. You might even say I am responsible for all that has happened." He held her gaze. "I need to see what is at this journey's end."

Jessica grimaced. "My bookseller friend, something tells me it will most definitely not be the journey's end. But I welcome your company."

She turned to River.

*

River listened as Jessica spoke of their findings. She was familiar with the concept of a map, that you could sketch the directions and distances of points of interest, and that another could use it to help navigate their route, aided by known features on the ground or by the sun, moon, and the stars above. But nothing remotely like this – not in its style nor its complexity. And yet as she followed Jessica's description, recreating the landscape in her head, she immediately connected it to the patterns on the map. "Here," she said, pointing at the red star closest to Jessica, the site of the Warriors' arrival. "This is the location of the other refuge in this area."

"It is!" Jessica exclaimed. "I didn't know it was so close."

"Warrior Beth visited this site. Where I tried to kill her."

"What!"

"I was mistaken. And I missed."

"You can explain that one to me later," Jessica said, frowning. "Other than these two, are there any other such sites in this area?"

"No. As we spoke of with Naga and the others before we ... left, there are several refuges in the lands to the south, west, and east, but none here, or to the north."

"But now we have this," Jessica said, turning to the far end of the map. "A map of the area far to the north, beyond your snow and ice front. And here is another of these marks."

River glanced to the patterns at the far end of the map. These had no familiarity, made little sense. But if Jessica was right and they lay far into the frozen lands? She looked up. "In the past, several of our tribe made forays into these icy lands, but never far. And they found nothing that would draw them back. But our Story talks of the ice dragon as a creature of the north – its lair could be there." She frowned. "But if so, how would someone know of it?"

Brow furrowing, Jessica looked down at the map, scanning the three red stars. "I don't know, but here are three marked locations, two matching places known to you." She paused, pursing her mouth. "So what lies at this third?"

River looked to the inset map. "Do you know this place?"

"No, but this is a detailed map, so we know how to get there. The mark lies on the southern flank of the mountain called Mount Hope."

River froze, the remembered words of the unknown voice startlingly clear. *Remember hope ...* "Mount Hope?" she whispered.

Jessica looked up, her eyes narrowing. "What is it?"

River slowly shook her head. "I wasn't sure ... But now ..."

"Not sure about what?"

"The dream ... in the car ... the last thing I heard. The voice said 'remember hope'."

Jessica's eyes widened. "Are you certain?"

River nodded.

"But you don't know who speaks with you?"

"No." She glanced at the map. "But after this, maybe it is indeed a friend to us."

Jessica pursed her lips. "Maybe." But how to be sure? "When – if – this voice returns, tell me. Tell me all it says."

River nodded again.

Jessica looked down at the map, peering at it intently. "All that we see – and hear – points there." She looked back up, her face hardening. "And so that's where we'll go."

Jessica turned to Robert and spoke with him briefly.

Moments later, with the map rolled up, they returned to the car.

To the beast.

To the nightmare of this age.

*

"We're definitely close now," came Erin's tense voice from the back of the car. Fletcher glanced in his rearview mirror and saw her peering at her phone. "They've stopped again," she said. "Somewhere near the village ahead."

"Okay, then we'll drive through and try to get a better lock on them," Fletcher said, moving off from the traffic lights. "Once we reach the other side of town, we'll park up somewhere – maybe at the distillery."

As they drove on towards the hillside settlement, he felt a growing tension in the car. *Maybe this is it. Their final destination.* He drew a deep breath. *At last.*

They had been on the road for hours, slowly gaining on the car ahead, helped by the two breaks Robert had taken on the way. And now, if Erin's phone app was accurately tracking her friend, they were only a few minutes behind.

But behind what? He'd been told just enough by these two women to keep him with them, but he was sure so much more remained hidden. Was this a kidnapping ransom he was heading into? Was Robert involved? *Surely not, he's a close friend of the family.* Were these women here accomplices, willing or forced? *They were certainly scared. And those marks on Ms. Williams's neck, those were real enough.* He let out a low sigh. So many ideas, so many conjectures continually running through his mind, but each time he thought it through, he came to the same point. *I can't push too hard – I can't scare them away. I need them with me. I have to take this chance to find Lanky and the two women.*

And yet restless doubts remained. Had this been a wrong call, travelling alone with no backup? Yes, maybe, but Ms Williams – Tricia, as she'd insisted he call her – had been adamant this was the only way she would help.

So this was how it would be for now.

Behind him, Erin spoke. "They should be just up here on the right."

He saw a roadside cafe coming up. "Stay down," he ordered. He heard the women shifting position on the back seat.

With no traffic behind him, he slowed while maintaining a sensible speed as he approached the cafe. *Don't look suspicious.* As he cruised past, he scanned the small carpark – only three cars sat outside, none of them Robert's. He frowned as they drove past. "Are you sure the phone says they're here? Robert's car wasn't there."

"Certain," Erin said. "According to the phone, we've just passed them."

"Then your phone can't be working properly," he grated. "Robert's car wasn't there."

"Your eyes aren't working properly, more like," Tricia grunted. "Let me take a look. Hiding down here is hurting my neck."

Muttering under his breath, Fletcher continued for a few hundred yards and then turned into the muddy ground of a gated field entrance on the right. Reversing, he pulled back out onto the main road, then headed back to the cafe. "Okay, stay low, but watch on the left as we go past."

They soon approached the cafe. "See, Robert's car isn't—"

Fletcher jumped as Erin cried out. "There!" she cried. "That yellow car in the carpark. That's Jessica's! And there's Jessica!"

Glancing to his left, Fletcher caught a glimpse of a tall figure walking to a bright yellow car. "Jessica's car?" he exclaimed as they drove on past the cafe. "A bright yellow car? Why didn't you say that Jessica had a car with her? I thought we were following Robert's car!"

"Don't shout at us, Mr. Police Officer," Tricia said angrily. "You were the one who said they were in Robert's car. See, that's why you needed our help."

"Help?" Fletcher spluttered. "Withholding information like that isn't helping. What else—"

"Forget the car!" Erin exclaimed, looking out the rear window. "Go back! We need to speak with Jessica."

Fletcher glared at her in the car mirror. *I thought it was Robert's car they'd taken.* He silently cursed. What else had he missed?

"Go back!" Erin hissed.

Gripping the steering wheel tightly, he looked to the road ahead. "No," he said, trying to calm himself down. "Not yet. I want to see where they're going. When we arrive at wherever the hell they're going, then we'll speak to them for sure."

"That's not—"

"We're going to follow them to their destination," he snapped, glaring at Erin in the mirror. "That is not negotiable." *I want to see who else is involved. Then I call in the calvary.*

Erin made to say something, then fell silent.

Scowling, he looked back to the road. "Are they moving?"

"No. They're not ... Hold on! They are now!"

"Which way?"

She cursed. "I can't tell yet."

Driving on, he saw a poorly lit lay-by on the left, and slowing, he turned in and parked the car beneath the single dimly glowing streetlight. He glanced to the back of the car to see Erin still studying her phone. Her face was strained, fear in her eyes. As he watched her, waiting, his anger slipped away. *She's hurting. They both are hurting—*

At that moment, Erin glanced up. "They're moving north."

He nodded ... then forced a smile. "Sorry for shouting," he said quietly.

She gave a small smile back but added nothing more.

He held her gaze. "I can help you if you tell me more of what's happening."

Erin seemed to consider for a moment, then she shook her head gently. "You wouldn't believe our story, Sergeant. You—"

Tricia screamed and Erin cowered back into her seat, her eyes widening as she stared at something behind him.

Fletcher spun around, frantically scanning around him. "What is it?" he breathed, staring out into the gloom. "What—"

He jumped as a man stared in through the windscreen. A gaunt-faced man with long white hair, streaked black.

The man was smiling.

"It's him!" Erin cried. "The man who attacked Trish!"

Heart hammering in his chest, Fletcher reached down for his baton torch. He flicked it on, then, grasping it tightly, he flung open the door and leapt out of the car. "What do you think you're doing!" he yelled, rushing around to the front of the car. "What …"

The man had gone.

Vanished.

He swung the torch around the lay-by, seeing nothing but shadowy trees and scrubland beyond. No sign of the white-haired man. He stood for a moment, trying to steady his breathing. This was the man who'd been at the cottage? What was he doing here? *And who is he?*

Unsettled, he turned back to the car—

And stifled a cry as the man's smiling, gaunt face stared back at him.

Stumbling backwards, Fletcher tripped and fell. Throwing his hands out to catch his fall, he rolled, then scrambled back to his feet to face the stranger.

Still smiling, the man regarded him with an unwavering gaze. "Where is the Guardian?"

He clamped a hold on stripped nerves. "Sir, I am a police officer. Step back and—"

"You are searching for her," the white-haired man said, taking a step towards him and raising a dark-wood staff.

Fletcher's hand tightened around the heavy torch. "Sir, stop where you are and put that down. Now."

The man walked on, his eyes seeming to burn as black as the night.

An icy terror ran down Fletcher's spine.

"Tell me where the Guardian is. You—"

The man grunted as a figure flew into his side. He stumbled but held his feet, then turned and struck Tricia a glancing blow across the shoulder. She cried out and fell to the ground.

Fletcher leapt forward—

And the man disappeared.

"Get the bastard!" Tricia cried from behind him.

Fletcher stared, disbelieving, at the place the man had stood. *He just vanished. He was there and then …* "He just disappeared," he whispered.

He turned in a daze as Erin ran past him. "Trish! Are you okay?" she said, dropping to her friend's side. "What were you thinking of?"

Tricia sat herself up, rubbing her shoulder. "Not sure I was thinking. Just wanted my revenge."

"It *was* the same man," Erin whispered as she examined Tricia's arm. She sighed in relief. "He's done no lasting damage."

"Help me up," Tricia said. "It's cold down here."

Fletcher reached down and helped her to her feet. "So, this was the man that attacked you back at the cottage?" *The man she said appeared out of thin air. And who, just now, seemed to vanish into thin air.*

"The same," Tricia said, still rubbing her shoulder. "No question."

He looked back to the place the white-haired man had vanished from. *This is unreal. This doesn't make sense. I can't deal with this...* "I have to get backup," he said, stepping towards the car. "This man is dangerous. We need—"

"No!" Tricia said quickly, stepping in front of him. "We don't have time. We need to get to Jess. Now!"

Fletcher shook his head. "This is getting out of control. We will—"

"If you don't help us," Erin said quietly but firmly, "then I'll destroy this phone."

He turned to see Erin glaring at him, her phone in her hand.

"Yes," Tricia said quickly. "That's what she'll do. And I'll help," she added, standing tall. Her eyes locked onto him. "You said you'd help. You said you'd protect the lives of those who are missing." She took a step towards him. "Well, you can help by finding Jessica with us. Only then will you know what to do next."

What to do next? Against a vanishing man? Licking his dry lips, he looked around the empty lay-by. Where had the man gone? How had he escaped so quickly? *Without you seeing him.* How did he explain that to HQ? He put his hand to his chin and rubbed his goatee. *What the hell do I do about all this?*

"We are helping you," came Erin's soft voice. "We're taking you to Jessica."

"And helping Lanky and our friend Beth," Tricia added.

"So help us," Erin said. "And quickly. We have to warn Jess."

He studied them, his mind churning. *There's still a chance*, a part of him urged. *You can find out where they're headed, who else is involved. Don't lose this chance.*

But you could stuff up big time here, Fletch. Your job's on the line.

"They're still moving north," Erin murmured. "Please, we need to follow."

He saw the raw anguish in the young woman's eyes. *The answer is always in the eyes...*

He blew out a sharp breath. "One last chance. Then I make the call."

Relief flooded across their faces.

Uneasy, fearful he just made a terrible mistake, he regarded them with a stern gaze. "We'll keep going, but we keep our distance. If we intercept them, who knows what stories *they* will spin. No, I need to know their ultimate destination."

"But the man ..." Erin blurted. "We have to warn Jess now."

"We'll follow close. If this man appears again, I call backup."

Erin turned to Tricia, a strain returning to her face.

"We have no choice," Tricia said. "He has the car."

A few minutes later, they were on their way again. Resuming their shadowing of a bright yellow car.

CHAPTER TWENTY-SIX

*The Iyes understood little of the Ancient;
but the Ancient knew much about them.*

"And so, tell us again, oh great and cunning hunters, how you captured these juicy roots for our breakfast." Svana winked at Beth as she stirred the steaming contents of the birchbark bowl heating on its bed of embers by the dawn's fire.

"Just wasn't our day yesterday," Scorpion muttered, wrapped in several layers of clothing to keep the chilly morning air at bay.

"And it doesn't help us when you pick a fight with a lion," chipped in Shorty, the tall man's face obscured within the gloom of his hood. "Makes everything around jittery – gave us no chance of approaching anything unseen."

"And nothing should have approached us unseen," Bear said, a faint edge to his voice.

Everyone fell silent, accepting Bear's simple admonishment.

And yet a little harsh, Beth thought. It had been a clever cloaking of the animal by the unknown shaman, revealing the skill and reach of this distant enemy to the south. She glanced to her Axe. But she'd caught the shaman unawares and seen the flare of fear in his eyes. *Maybe he'll be wary of trying again soon – it may have bought us some time.*

She looked out through the scattered trees surrounding their campsite to the verdant plain beyond the escarpment. But how had the shaman managed to attack them here? Via a Glade, yes, but how precisely had he done it? Her eyes flared with a spark of anger. *If we are to survive here, we need to know our enemy.* She felt the warmth of her Axe in her hand. *And we need to know what we can do against them.*

She looked back to the fire. She needed to speak with Garrion to learn what she could do to defend herself against attacks such as this.

But the daemon had still not reappeared. Her thoughts darkened. What had happened to Garrion? Where was she? And if she didn't come back …? Beth gritted her teeth. *We must continue on. We must find the Staff. And I need to stay alert, watch for danger, and act as I can.*

Drawing her feet under her, she glanced at Knuckles, who remained unusually quiet. *Still hurting that he didn't detect the lion. And yet it wasn't his fault.* Around the camp, all save Svana, who tended the steaming bowl of stew, seemed too subdued and pensive. *And we've still a long way to go.* She lifted her head and forced a smile. "So has everyone else seen this impressive sight that Bear has in store for us today?"

Scorpion, his long hair bunched in the collar of his tunic, turned to her. "Not me. This is the furthest west I've been."

"He's usually too busy back in camp," Shorty said, "or on a source, showing off his skills with those tricky hands of his. Now you're seeing what you miss out on, Scorpion – you should ask Bear to let you out more."

Beth heard Svana mutter something under her breath.

"Source?" questioned Beth.

"Yes, a source," Shorty said, pushing back his hood, misty wisps of his breath swirling around him. "You know, of good material – the right stone or gems. If he finds a valuable source, you can't move him for days. Isn't that right, Scorpion? That's why he doesn't see all these wonderful things we do. That's why—"

"That's why our tribe has the best blades, tools, and jewellery of any tribe," jumped in Svana. "Pity you two don't know how to use them."

"Hmm – a person might think you're defending young Scorpion there," Shorty murmured, his eyes twinkling. "Anything we should know?"

"Pah. You have a single-track mind and a cloudy one at that. Maybe a clout around your ears will help you clear it."

Shorty laughed. "Before you do that, Svana, can I at least take a bowl of that wondrous-smelling broth before it gets spilled in a fight?"

Svana shook her head dismissively but leaned over, and using two stout sticks, lifted the bowl from the embers of the fire and placed it on the grass between them. "It's not much but will get us on our way." She rapped one of the sticks on Shorty's hand as he leaned in with a small wooden bowl. "Beth first. She needs it more than you."

Shorty looked pained. "I was only going to taste it."

"Your tasting is another's gorging," Svana admonished. She turned to Beth. "Move faster, Warrior, else you'll starve."

Beth smiled, leaned in, and scooped a bowlful of the steaming soup. Moments later, all were taking their fill of the warming soup, its heat driving away the chill in their bones. While bitter, the food was a welcome treat. *Not the worst I've tasted,* Beth thought, chewing on a potato-like tuber. *And maybe I'll be missing this further north.*

Within a short while, the last mouthful passed her lips. Almost immediately, Bear climbed to his feet. "Prepare to move out. We must make use of this good weather." He glanced at Beth. "And today, I hope to show you something quite wonderful."

Ignoring the dull ache still nagging her shoulder, Beth climbed slowly to her feet. "Well, you've caught my interest by this mystery of yours, Bear. I look forward to it."

Together with the others, she quickly gathered her belongings and repacked. Despite her aching shoulder, she insisted she carry her pack – but quickly had to admit defeat. Redistributing some of Beth's pack between them, Bear strapped the lightened pack to his front. *I'll take it back tomorrow ... Maybe.*

With the fire buried, they broke camp and set off to the northwest, heading away from the escarpment and pushing on through scattered woodland towards the drier open terrain beyond. Ignoring the fiery pain in her raked shoulder, she strode after Svana. *Tough it out, girl. We've a job to do.*

Yet as she walked on, a burgeoning strength – a growing vigour – rippled within her body and mind. She glanced to the brightening sky. She couldn't see it, but she was certain it was there in the ether. *There is a rich energy in this Land. This Land is helping me.* She felt that if she reached out, she could grasp it, mould it, use it as her own. *I have used it. I used it to reach the Glade.* She frowned. *But I don't know how I do it.*

She sucked in a breath through gritted teeth. *Where are you, Garrion? I know I can do more if you show me how.* But no matter how many times she called, the daemon didn't appear. Her frustration grew. Who aided them now? Who could help them find the Staff, find Jessica? *And who will aid us against those that seek us?*

Shaking her head, she pushed her frustrations to the shadows of her mind. "Focus on what's before you," she muttered to herself. "And stay alert." Steeling herself, she walked on.

As the sun crept above the eastern range, she felt a little of its warmth on her face, though a chill still hung in the air. The broad grassy depression they had traversed the day before now lay long behind them, and ahead, the view was opening up as the hills to their right arced away from them. In the distance, Bear and Svana were picking a route through the rougher terrain. Looking back along their trail, she saw Knuckles, Scorpion, and Shorty following, their eyes constantly scanning their surroundings.

But there was no sign, nor sense, of any potential threat.

Turning back, she noticed that Bear had veered off to the left and now stood beside a stand of trees on a low ridge. He waved them over. Beth walked on a short distance, then picked up an animal trail heading towards Bear.

As she drew closer, Bear walked on into the trees. Intrigued, Beth followed, stepping through the sparse undergrowth of the copse before emerging at the edge of a deep, wide canyon.

"That's pretty impressive," she murmured as she took a step closer to the edge.

The rocky ground fell away in front of her, dropping in stages to the canyon floor some two hundred metres below. Looking across the vast chasm, she saw the golden sunlit edge of the far canyon wall. *Must be eight, maybe ten kilometres away?* She tracked the rugged wall of the canyon far to the south, then turned and followed its path to her right, where the valley floor seemingly ran on forever to the north. At the canyon's base on the side closest to her flowed a wide, emerald-green river.

"So this is what you wanted to show us?"

"In part," Bear said, looking down to the canyon floor below.

As Beth scanned the stunning scene, her breath suddenly caught. *Now I see what this is.*

"Quite a sight," came Scorpion's voice behind her.

Beth gazed at the breathtaking sight in awe. "I think Bear was right, Scorpion. It's spectacular." *And in my time, the North Channel of the Sea of Eir.* She looked across to the far side of the canyon. *Which makes that the island of Eir.* But instead of a sea filling the canyon, only a river. *It's incredible. I could walk to the island.*

"Good hunting down there, I think," Knuckles said, coming to stand beside her.

"Is that where we're going?"

Bear turned to her. "Possibly. Once before, I travelled a little further along this coast, and the going is good as far as I went. If we run into difficulty later, then yes, we could head down and travel in the deeper valley."

Beth and the group stood admiring the view as the sun rose a little higher in the sky.

"Let's move on," Bear said eventually. "You'll see a good amount of the valley as we travel on, but this is a particularly good spot. And the trees help screen the surprise."

Beth smiled. "It was a magnificent surprise."

"It may not be over," Bear said, a curious smile on his lips.

Her brow furrowed. *So, what else does he have waiting?*

"So, you'll join the hunt a little more now, Scorpion?" Shorty said behind her.

"If all your trips are like this, then of course I'm in." Scorpion glanced at Bear. "If I show Shorty how to make good blades, we could switch jobs for a while."

Bear chuckled. "An excellent plan. I think the change would be good for you both." He started back towards the stand of trees. "Okay. Let's move on."

"Now hold on," Shorty said quickly as they followed Bear. "I think you misunderstood ..."

Following Svana, Beth grinned as she heard the banter continuing behind her. *No use arguing, Shorty. That's one up for Scorpion this morning.*

*

Following the best ground, they continued north, making good progress as the sun passed its zenith, travelling along its arc in the western sky. Their own path drifted sometimes further, sometimes closer to the canyon edge, and when close, provided glimpses down into the valley.

It took a while for Beth to grasp what was nagging her, but as she passed another viewpoint, she hurried to catch up to Svana. "Have you noticed the swirling currents down there? It's a pretty violent river for such a flat-lying valley floor."

Svana glanced into the valley. Her eyes widened. "It's what Bear was hoping to see!" she said, her voice rising with excitement. "Let's get to the next overhang up there, and if we're lucky, we'll see." She rushed ahead.

Confused, Beth hurried after her. They ran a few hundred yards, then climbed up onto a ledge overseeing the valley in both directions. "We're in time," Svana panted, gesturing to the north. "Look!"

Her heart racing, Beth scanned the valley. It took a moment, but then she saw it – a huge swell racing down the river from the north, overspilling the banks and inundating the land to either side.

"And there!"

Swinging around, Beth stared in wonder as a broad second swell swept in from the south. *A tidal surge,* she thought in amazement as she glanced first one way down the valley and then the other. The sea had retreated far, but clearly still gained entry into the canyon at the turn of the tide. From both sides. *And it's heading in now!*

She heard the men join them.

Knuckles came to her side. "Thank IY for allowing me to witness this."

Beth glanced down into the canyon. The previously roiling river had settled to a calmer state, yet to either side, the two great waves raced on.

The group watched, transfixed.

And then the immovable object met the irresistible force. Neither willing to give way, the tidal surges met in a violent maelstrom, spectacular spouts and sprays erupting into the air, great swirling waves crashing over the riverbanks, sweeping into the land beyond to erode a little more of a valley valiantly striving to hold the storm at bay.

The noise echoed down the canyon.

Beth watched, awestricken, as the great swells merged into one, rippling waves leaping up to the sky before crashing into a chaotic surge of white foam. Scattered flocks of birds took to the sky, and she caught sight of several animals – deer, she thought – bounding away from the flood sweeping across their grazing land. *A true force of nature*, she thought, mesmerised by the sight.

And then, almost as quickly as it had formed, the great swell collapsed back into two chaotic waves, which raced away to the north and south along the swollen river, swarms of eddies rippling across the now widened estuary, majestic in their own right, yet pitiful echoes of their so recent violent clash.

"And we want to go down there?" Beth breathed as the river waves dissipated.

"The waters have grown since I was last here," said Bear, who had walked back, unnoticed, to rejoin them.

"Grown?" *Sea level getter higher?* "Doesn't that mean it's getting warmer?"

He shook his head. "It is growing colder – and quickly – but during the warmth of these many past generations, the sea has eaten its way back into this valley. Though if we cannot halt the return of the ice, then the waters will once more retreat."

Beth watched the last remnants of the great wave ripple away. "That was an impressive sight, Bear," she said in a hushed voice. "If you plan on showing me more today, I may be very disappointed after this."

He laughed. "No, Warrior. That is all. Come, let's—"

"Yes, I know," she said, smiling. "Let's move."

She glanced down at the quietening river, then turned back to Bear. "How about I take a turn at the back for a while?"

"That okay, Shield?" Bear asked Knuckles.

"Hmm, towards the back, yes, but let Scorpion take the rear."

"Agreed. Then let's move." Bear made his way from the canyon edge, followed by Knuckles, Shorty, and Svana.

Beth knelt down to her pack. "I'll catch up, Scorpion."

"It's okay, I'll wait."

"No, you go on. Just need to relieve myself."

"Okay." Scorpion gestured towards Svana, who stood by a lone birch. "I'll wait for you over there."

A minute later, pressure relieved, Beth turned for one last look across the great canyon. *The island of Eir. And I can walk to it. Unbelievable.* She pushed a stray strand of wind-blown hair from her eyes as she scanned the vast chasm. *No, believable,* she told herself. The sea came in, the sea went out, daily, yearly, over millennia and epochs. Gentle ebbs with the daily tides and grand movements as the climate warmed and cooled. *But it never seems real. Never until you see it for yourself.*

She glanced to the north, where a flock of raucous birds had just taken to the sky, appearing as a distant swarm of bees against the clear blue horizon. Below the scattering birds, she caught a flicker of movement above the river. Casting her gaze to the river, she frowned. She saw nothing. *I swear I saw something there. I—*

She froze as an indistinct shape appeared, its shadowy wings arcing to the sky as it hurtled towards her …

Then it vanished.

A silent scream coiled within her chest, strangling her breath. *The dragon comes!* As she half turned to yell a warning to the others, her vision blurred and a crippling nausea twisted her stomach. Swaying, she fought against a sudden fog in her mind. *It's attacking me. It—*

"Beth! Run!" came Svana's desperate shout from a distance.

Wracked by a convulsive pain, Beth crouched, squinting through the thick, blurry haze blighting her vision.

"The dragon!" Svana screamed. "Run!"

I can't move, Beth thought, fear ripping through her as her limbs refused to act. *What has it done!* Blind, paralysed, she felt her world imploding. *How has this happened? How did we not see it?* Wrung with savage dread, she fought with every ounce of her strength to move … but she failed. *No! Not like this. Not—*

'Fight!' commanded a fierce voice from deep inside, and a surge of rippling energy coursed through her body.

The world snapped back into focus.

She leapt to her feet, reaching for her Axe—

An immense rush of air slammed into her chest, and a huge shadow darkened the sky as a massive beast swept up from the canyon below.

Staggering, she managed to grasp hold of the Axe.

The beast's talons raked out, knocking her to the ground. As her hand slipped from the Axe, the talons closed around her, and a voice hammered in her head. *'Fight me, and they die.'* A thunderous, crackling roar erupted in the air, and a tremendous heat blasted her face.

She heard screams.

No! What is it doing to them!

'Tell them now! Fight and they die!'

"Stop!" Beth screamed, terror coursing through her veins. "Stay away! I command it!"

There was silence for a heartbeat, then another thunderous roar and searing heat.

'They do not listen. Repeat.'

An horrific image flashed into her mind – of Knuckles, Shorty, and the others burning in a fiery inferno. "Stay away, damn you!" she screamed. "Stay away!"

Silence fell ... and then the dragon's claws clenched ever tighter.

She screamed.

'Fight, and you will die first.' The claws relaxed a fraction. *'Do you understand?'*

"Yes," she gasped, struggling to breathe.

'Fight, and they die next.' The claws relaxed a little more. *'Understand?'*

"Yes," she wheezed. "Dammit, I understand."

'We go.'

Hauled violently into the air, the ground racing away from her as they arrowed into the sky, she fought against the wild terror lashing through her. With the agonising pain of the crushing claws biting into her body, she forced herself to move. Straining, she reached over her shoulder and felt a surge of relief as her fingers brushed the Axe strapped to her back. *There is a chance.*

'That is no help to you now, Warrior,' came the dragon's voice. *'You are cut from the A'ven.'*

Ice-cold air rushed over her as they hurtled ever higher into the sky. *The A'ven. The energy of the Land. I know it, but not how I know.* She shivered as the bleak reality of the beast's words hammered home. *I no longer sense it around me – the beast has severed my final hope.*

Abject despair washed over her. *I have failed. I'm so sorry, Jess, but I've failed.* Faces of her friends and family flashed before her. *I've failed you all. I—*

'Enough!' hissed a strident voice in her mind, the voice of the one called Bethusa. *'We live. I live. And I have no wish to die.'*

'Who are *you*?' Beth managed as the vehement will of the other swept through her.

'One who should be fighting this war,' rasped the biting voice as the dragon streaked through the bone-chilling air. A ripple of granitelike ferocity surged through Beth. '*Survive this engagement, then look for the opportunity. We must survive!*'

Through the fog of intense fear swirling within, Bethusa's cry rang as a glimmer of light in the darkness. Beth grasped onto that flickering light – that forlorn hope.

Survive.

Retreating from the horror that had befallen her, she drew her life force deep inside. As they hurtled on through the icy-cold air, her body numbing, she allowed herself to drift to the edge of consciousness …

Yes, survive.

Survive to fight another day.

*

Impervious to the heat of the burning vegetation behind them, the distraught group stared in horror at the diminishing shape in the sky to the north.

"No! No! No!" Shorty cried, driving the butt of his spear repeatedly to the ground.

"Curse you!" Knuckles spat at the now distant beast.

"Why did I let her? Why!" Scorpion cried, turning to the group. "Why!" He slumped to his knees, his head bowed, his long hair dangling limply as if mirroring his heartfelt pain.

Svana said nothing, her devastation writ on her face.

I have failed, Bear thought, his shoulders slumped. *Failed my tribe, failed the Warrior, failed IY.* None of them had seen the danger approaching. They had been complacent, allowing the Warrior to stay behind. Alone. A moment only. A single moment to utterly destroy their mission. He stared to the north, dazed and bewildered. *She is gone. The one we needed most is gone.*

How long he stood there, staring blindly to the north, he didn't know. He was lost, devastated, unable to think.

"What are we going to do?" came Scorpion's wavering voice, breaking the silence.

Bear gave no answer. He had no answer.

"What are we going to do, Bear?" Scorpion said more sharply. He grabbed Bear's arm. "What are we going to do?"

"Scorpion," Svana growled. "Step away. Remember yourself."

Scorpion's wild eyes remained locked on Bear ... then the distraught man staggered away, head bowed.

"And Bear. Remember yourself also," Svana said, in a quieter voice. "This is not over. We need a decision. Now."

Bear flinched as her honest words lanced into him. *I am their leader – yet I do nothing.* He looked over at Svana, who was standing tall, wisps of smoke still trailing from the ragged scorch marks on her blackened tunic. Her fierce eyes studied him.

This is not over. Her words. The words of a very brave woman. A woman who he'd heard call out a sharp warning, then race alone towards the Warrior before he'd fully registered what was happening. He'd thought her finished when the gout of flame had rolled from the dragon, seemingly engulfing her – her screams had sliced through him like a blade – and yet, somehow, she had emerged out of the flames unharmed, rapidly closing the gap to the Warrior.

And then the Warrior had commanded them to stop. Bear had seen Svana slow ... *But she didn't stop.* Only on hearing the Warrior's second command had Svana halted and dropped to the ground.

And then, as suddenly as it had struck, the beast – and Beth – were gone.

"Bear?" Svana prompted him.

He looked out over the canyon, refocusing his thoughts. Self-pity and regret led them nowhere. *This is not over.* Simple words, but the right words for him to hear at the right time.

A determined set to his jaw, he turned to see four faces staring back at him: Svana, looking resolute and unyielding; Scorpion, head bowed, his face anguished and tormented; and Knuckles and Shorty, faces shocked and disbelieving at what they had witnessed.

"We have a choice," he began slowly. "We can turn back south to rejoin our tribe and the Warrior Lanky... There may be another path that he would now want us to take." He paused. "Or, holding to our plan, we continue north, maintaining the belief that the site Lanky identified is the home of the Ancient ... and where it is now taking Beth."

Scorpion lifted his head, fire in his eyes. "We must go on! How else can it be?" He glanced at the others. "Return? And say what? That we failed our Warrior? That we handed her to the Ancient? No, that can't be. We must go on."

Bear looked to Svana. "And you? What do you think?"

She considered for a moment, then her sharp eyes locked onto Scorpion. "I don't think the decision is that easy."

Scorpion glared at her. "Why?"

"First, Beth is the only one of us who has been to this mountain in the north, who had seen it in her time. How will we know this place? How—"

"Because we all heard the description, that's why," Scorpion said quickly. "It's the tallest peak in that most northwestern land. Visible from the sea."

"Yet it is difficult to judge the mountains from the sea. And do we truly know its shape? Beth knew, we don't. Oh, she described it, but that isn't the same as seeing. And do we know its position along the coast? Beth had the map Lanky drew – that's now gone." She turned to Bear. "And say we find this mountain. Then what? What are we looking for? Not even the Warriors knew this." She shook her head. "No, this decision isn't easy."

She straightened, standing taller, her face hardening. "But what of any of this is easy? We knew the challenges we faced, but we all believed the Warrior Beth would find a way to this mountain, a way to the Staff. And we believed we could aid her." She scanned their faces, her eyes burning brightly. "And now? What is it we can do now?" She looked at them in turn – at Scorpion, Knuckles, and Shorty – as though daring them to challenge her. "What we can do is this," she said, her voice rising. "We can stand up and stand proud, and remember we are Iyes! We can stride out of our misery and follow that beast who just took our Warrior! That is what we can do!"

"Yes!" Scorpion shouted, clenching his fist.

Svana stepped closer to them. "Do we ever abandon those of our tribe?"

"No!" Scorpion and Shorty shouted together.

"Can we find our Warrior? Will we find our Warrior?"

"Yes!" came the defiant cry from the three, their voices carrying out into the valley beyond.

She turned to Bear, passionate hunger on her face. "That is what I think."

Bear regarded the energised faces before him, and his heart leapt. "You have spoken well, Svana. And you are right – this is not over."

He turned to the north, his mind clear, their path now set before him. *We are coming, Warrior, and we will not rest until we find you – no matter how long that takes.*

CHAPTER TWENTY-SEVEN

Iolaire was a most long-lived daemon. She proved a good pairing for River, but even I – or IY – didn't see just how valuable she would be.

Spider was hurting. And the fever was growing. But not far, now. Not far. He undid the straps of his pack, allowing it to drop to the ground with a groan of relief. Should have ditched it a long time ago. Relieved of the weight, the pressure and pain easing from his shoulders, he pushed on, knowing now they were closing in on the hidden camp of the Iyes.

Not far. Keep moving.

He gritted his teeth and strode on, dropping first into a gentle valley before slowly ascending a lightly wooded hill. As they passed out of the trees, he finally saw the dense, thicker forest in the distance.

His destination. *White Crags.*

As he stopped, his legs wavered. He steadied himself. *So close now. Stay strong.* He took his water skin and drank heavily.

"Can you continue?" Growl asked beside him.

Spider nodded, unsure whether that was really true.

But how to continue? That was now the question.

He glanced at the old man, who was watching his wolf prowling in the distance. He was a shaman of sorts, no doubt there. *And one who saved me, of that there's also no doubt.*

But could he trust him?

He helped me. I'm alive because of him.

But still, I don't know him. And still, I can't bring myself to trust him.

He drew a quiet breath. But this was now for others to decide. *I need to take him to Rind. To the leaders. Better we keep this man in sight and find out what he wants. Let them listen to him and decide his fate.*

He glanced to the fearsome wolf. *But not this wolf. This wolf sees too much.*

Girding himself, he turned to Growl. "I'll take you to the Iyes, but you must leave the wolf here."

"Ah, so we are close. Interesting. How close, we wonder? Well hidden, we say. Streak has sensed nothing. No, nothing."

"It is a distance yet. Even so, there will be eyes upon us."

Growl's dark eyes locked onto Spider's. "Streak is not easily stopped from moving where he will. Those watching eyes will not see him."

"Then you'll need to work hard to stop him, else we don't move."

Growl smiled. "Maybe Streak is already moving where he will."

"That would not be wise. That may make you seem … my enemy."

"And that would not be the intention, no, not at all." Growl's laughter was tinged with amusement. "But if those eyes are on us, why not seek their attention now? Your people can come to help you here."

They wait to see what I'll do. And I don't want the wolf to see them. "Call the wolf in," he said simply.

"No need."

Frowning, Spider glanced around. The wolf sat on his haunches behind him. Shaking his head, he set off for the distant forest. He heard Growl follow.

As they walked on, he glanced back. There the wolf remained. Watching them. His uneasy gaze returned to the forest ahead. *I hope Rind can figure this one out.*

He journeyed on in silence, treading heavy step after heavy step, until sometime later, to his utter relief, he approached the fringe of the forest. His energy spent, his vision blurred, he almost fell as he reached the first of the great trees. Steadying himself, he stumbled on into the gloom of the forest. *Almost there,* he told himself again. *You can make it.* He forced himself on, feet crunching through the leafy debris on the forest's floor. He glanced around. *Come on, where are you?* Almost immediately, he saw movement to his right, and then to his left, and within a couple of heartbeats, armed men and women flanked them.

"Spider," a woman said, stepping forward. "Welcome home."

"Hello, Arash. This is my guest."

And then he fainted.

*

"No sign," Freya said, breathing heavily as she approached the group.

Gravel frowned. "Okay. Rest a moment and then stay close." He turned to Naga. "It is pointless to continue to send scouts to seek him.

Spider is where he is now, and we'll be at the camp before the shadows begin to lengthen. We should continue to push on."

True, Naga thought, but her body was not what it had once been, and it creaked with every step of the journey. Wasn't it only recently that she had been able to run all day, relenting only when her body finally demanded food? Days when she would spring out of bed, ready for the day's new adventure? *No. That was a time long past.* Her mind was still willing, but her body refused to play. "It is time that you pushed on, Gravel. Take Dune, Amber, and Sheba with you. And the Warrior."

"With respect, Mother, I suggest we stay together. True, we're only a half day from White Crags now, but an enemy is abroad, and we can't be sure where. We should continue as we are."

"Clear and true advice as always, Gravel," Naga said with a smile. Her smile faded as she looked to the hills ahead. "But I am worried and impelled to reach the camp as soon as we can. And for me, that is just not possible – I need time to rest. Let us hope it is just the weariness of an old woman that causes my disquiet. But if not …"

"I don't agree, Mother. I say again, we must stay together."

Naga's voice brooked no challenge. "No, Gravel. You go on. And now."

Gravel glared at her.

"And your attempts to unsettle me, to plant seeds of doubt in my mind, have not worked for many sun-cycles. You have my final command, Gravel. I will see the Warrior before you leave."

Gravel continued his display of defiance … then his shoulders imperceptibly dropped. He nodded. "I will speak with the others."

Naga watched him walk away. A good man. An indomitable man. One who had served the tribe well. She would miss him. She sighed. *Strange, I have lost my power, but I sense my journey's end. What game do our gods play?*

Yet she knew that question was unanswerable. What did she know of gods? Her knowledge was of the Spirits and of IY – of the Land. She looked up to the sky. *Something lies beyond here, I am sure of it. But I cannot see it. Cannot see them. Or understand their game.* She glanced over at Sheba. *What I know is that this one must be protected, concealed from the Dark and those who seek to destroy the future of the Iyes – concealed from the evil that is coming for me.*

A sense of urgency overwhelmed her. *Please, River, you must return. You are needed soon. You are needed now.*

*

Humming to himself as he sat on the decaying trunk of a fallen tree, Lanky watched the exchange between Naga and Gravel. It was clear that the Shield disapproved of what he was being told. As their conversation ended, Gravel made his way to Dune, who was binding his long hair behind his neck. As Naga walked towards him, Lanky stretched out his weary legs. He was fit, fitter than most back home, years of his youth scrambling around the hills of his home countryside toughening up his body. *But I'm no match for these people.*

He had been so very close to them for several days now – embarrassingly close at times – and with the natural nosiness of most people, he'd been unable to ignore what was on display: patches of dyed artwork on some, large scars on others; thicker limbs, smaller limbs; a usual variety of shapes and sizes. But generally? Lean bodies, sculpted and defined. His was – what was the word – softer. *Yes, softer.* And now his soft body was paying the price.

Letting the last softly hummed words of his tune drift on the cool breeze, he climbed to his feet. "What's the plan?" he asked as Naga approached.

"I wish Gravel to travel quickly on to White Crags camp. We don't know what state Spider will be in when he arrives, and I need one of us there to explain what has been happening – both with Spider and events in the north."

"You still don't trust this stranger?"

"I still don't know who this stranger is," she said. "Trust? That is not really an option."

"So, Gravel will travel alone?"

"No. Dune, Amber, and Sheba will travel with him. And I'd like you to also join them."

"That's fine by me. What was Gravel's objection?"

Naga smiled. "You were watching."

He smiled back. "I'm nosy by nature."

She glanced to where Gravel stood talking with Dune. "He is worried about leaving such a small group to continue by themselves."

Lanky's smile faded. "I can understand that. This isn't a safe land." He inwardly winced, remembering the spear in his side. *I've seen it. I've felt it.*

Fidgeting with her bracelet, Naga turned back to him. "There are risks in everything we do, Warrior. We just need to find a path through them. And sometimes the path becomes very clear."

He caught a look in her eye – of one who'd made a hard decision. *But one she is sure of.*

"You and the others must push on and travel quickly," Naga continued. "I am afraid my body will not allow that – the curse of the passing sun-cycles."

He studied her face. *There is more here unsaid.* "You're certain about this?"

"I am. And if you are rested, I would like you to leave now."

He grunted a laugh. "If I could, I'd take a full day's rest to stop my body complaining." He saw her fingers caressing her bracelet. "What aren't you telling me, Naga?"

He caught a fleeting fear in her eyes, then it was gone. "Some things must remain with me, Warrior. That is my burden."

He sensed the hidden pain. He nodded.

"But whatever I do, know that all I do is for my tribe. And as my tribe needs the Warriors, all I do is for you."

Lanky smiled. "That sounds like a title for a song." She tilted her head, and he shrugged. "I like music."

Naga's gaze lingered on him, then she looked up as if peering to a distant place. "I once met an old shaman, who said the Land could be saved by a Song."

He heard a particular tone in her voice, a resonance to her final utterance. *A Song.* "And why did this shaman say that?"

She hesitated. "That shaman I met had heard it from his grandfather. He said it was a belief of a tribe from the most southerly valleys known in the Land. Rich valleys, verdant valleys, ones said to be the birth of all peoples. He said there was one from that place who held a Song that could be sung at the end of time. A Song to call a Redeemer, one who would save all life of a condemned Land."

He saw a flicker of uncertainty in the old woman's eyes. "And did you believe him?"

Her gaze drifted once more, then she released a slow sigh. "Nothing is told of this in our Story. Nothing has been told by the Spirits." A half smile crossed her lips. "As you like your songs, so do most peoples of these lands. The shaman spoke of a hope for his own people's future, that is all." Her smile widened, deep, craggy wrinkles animating her face. "But I would have liked to hear his Song."

Lanky studied her deep-lined face for a moment, then glanced to the sky, seeing thick clouds drifting in from the north. *A song to save the world.* In this twisted land, anything could be possible. But he couldn't go chasing the half-remembered dreams of some unknown people. *Focus on what's before you.* He looked back to Naga. "I can leave now, if that's what you wish."

"Good. Then it is agreed." Her smile fading, she tilted her head a fraction. "Have you spoken with Beth today?"

He shook his head. "No, why?"

"I wished to know if she had spoken with the daemons."

He bit back his irritation. "I doubt it. They seem to have disappeared."

"It is unexpected," Naga said, her brow furrowing. "Maybe it will be possible at a Sacred Site. Another reason for you to travel ahead."

"And when I get there," Lanky muttered, "I'll have some words to say to the devious warg. Maybe you should be there when I do."

She reached out and placed her hand on his shoulder. "There is little for me to advise you now, Warrior. You alone must forge the path ahead." She smiled. "You have a good heart, Lanky. Always trust your heart and follow where it leads. That way lies salvation for us all." She gently squeezed his shoulder. "It is time to leave. My heart goes with you. Always."

As Naga stepped back, a warmth in her eyes, a sudden rush of emotion surprised him. He steadied himself and held her gaze. "It's not been the easiest of introductions," he said with a wry smile. "As you said, trust isn't always an option." He saw her deep-set eyes studying him. "I still don't understand what's truly happening here, but it's clear you've striven to help us as you can. And for that, I'm grateful."

Naga smiled, inclining her head a fraction.

He absently rubbed his chin. "And I hear what you say. That you believe this is a Land – a people – under threat, and that we're here to aid you." His hesitation was barely noticeable. "And if I *am* someone who can help, then I will help … somehow, I *will* help. But I need to know what I'm doing – I won't be forced there."

Naga nodded. "That is all I needed to know, Warrior. It is what I hoped to hear." She looked past his shoulder. "I see Gravel waits impatiently for us. I suggest you join him before he collapses." She looked back at him, brightness in her eyes. "Good luck, Warrior. Travel well, Lanky."

He drew a deep breath. "I will," he said, reaching for his pack. He smiled. "And we'll see you later tonight – we'll have the fire ready."

As he turned to say goodbye to the others, he didn't quite catch her reply.

Within a short while, he, Sheba, and Dune were standing beside the impatient Gravel. Amber and Eagle hugged one last time, and then the healer made her way over to them. Gravel immediately strode off, followed by a grinning Dune.

Amber waved again at her intended, Eagle, then faced Lanky and Sheba. "Shall we follow our Shield? We wouldn't want him to become impatient, would we?"

*

Naga watched the group leave, and then joined Eagle and Freya by the fire they had lit. Lanky had not heard her parting words. *No matter, they were not important for him.*

She turned to Eagle. "If you would take this watch, I will rest my weary legs, and my even wearier eyes. Wake me once that wood is burnt, and we will make our final push."

And with that, she eased onto her side and closed her eyes. And dreamed of River.

<--->

River could only lessen the onslaught of the nightmare by closing her eyes and shutting off the torrent of blurred images flashing past on either side of her. The relentless cacophony of sound continued, but not the stream of disturbing, alien sights. *What have people been doing to this land?* The worst had been travelling through landscapes devoid of vegetation – *dead stone deserts made entirely of these dwellings, these roads, these ...* She knew not how to describe those places, unable to assimilate all she was seeing. How many people had it taken to change the land in this way? How long had it taken? It was difficult to believe that people alone could do this.

And why?

As they'd travelled on, a greener, more familiar landscape returned, but the respite had been brief – it was repeatedly broken by these areas of devastation ... of desolation. *How did people live in these deserts? How did they survive? Where was the food?*

Where was her Land?

Finding it impossible to talk to Jessica above the relentless roar within the car, she withdrew as far from her surroundings as possible.

And dreamed.

She was flying, soaring high in a clear blue sky, her wings flexing as the warm air from a thermal streamed past. She looked down on a mountainous landscape of verdant valleys, deep blue lakes, and imposing, towering peaks, a landscape untouched by the hands of these people, a land she might have called her own. Joy filled her heart, and flexing her wings slightly, she veered to the right, heading to the tallest peak.

'Mount Hope,' a voice said in her head as an eagle, more than twice her size, appeared at her side.

Startled, she veered away from the newcomer, but surprisingly, held no fear. 'Who are you?' she asked.

'I am known as Iolaire,' came the reply.

'You have visited me twice before. Why?'

'I think you know why.'

Calmness enveloped River. And a feeling of familiarity. But also, a confusion. 'Who are you?'

'I am here to help you … Revri.'

A sudden surge of energy coursed through her veins, and sensing a great danger below, she banked sharply and began to dive towards the distant mountain beneath her.

'Pull back,' Iolaire said firmly. 'You must wait.'

River continued to dive, the air streaming past her sleek body and diamond-folded wings.

'Pull back!' Iolaire commanded. 'Now!'

The grand eagle swept repeatedly across her path, forcing River to slow her descent.

'Patience,' Iolaire murmured by her side as she pulled out of her dive and levelled off. 'The time to reveal yourself is not yet here. But your time will come.'

Blinking, River felt her tiny heart beating fast. 'What do I need to do?'

'Aid the Guardian, the one known to you as Jessica.'

'The Guardian?'

'The one who travels the Continuum.'

'How do I aid her?'

'I will help you. When you return, listen for me. And do not tell of me to the other who seeks the Staff. A danger lurks here that cannot know who we are. Yet.'

'The other? The bookseller? Why—'

She became aware of someone nudging her and saying her name. "River, wake up, we're here."

'Listen for me, Revri. I will guide you.'

She felt the sharp nudge in her arm and opened her eyes.

*

"Good, you're awake," Jessica said. "We've arrived." She watched as River awoke from her deep sleep. "You okay?"

River grimaced. "I was dreaming. My head feels like a swamp."

"Well, that will soon shift – we've some walking ahead of us. Come on, we have to figure out where we go now. Robert is already out there."

As Jessica made to move out of the car, River grabbed her arm. "Wait!" she hissed. "The voice. I know who it is."

Jessica froze. "Who?"

River glanced outside, then turned back to Jessica. "A friend," she whispered. "One named Iolaire. She will help us. Guide us. But she doesn't wish her presence to be shared with this man."

Jessica's eyes narrowed. "Do you know why?"

"She said there was a danger here. She said another seeks the Staff."

"Robert?" Jessica breathed.

"That wasn't clear." River held Jessica's gaze. "But I trust her. I heard a truth in her words."

But the words of whom? "Iolaire is a daemon?"

River hesitated. "I believe so," she whispered. "Taking the form of an eagle."

She speaks with a daemon ... Jessica stifled a gasp at a stunning thought. *Could it be? Could River be the fourth Warrior?* But she had no Axe. Didn't she need an Axe?

"We must be ready," River said, glancing outside. "The danger has not yet revealed itself."

And the fourth Warrior is not yet revealed. Jessica's jaw tightened. Maybe it was River, maybe not. *Stay in the moment. Deal with what's before you.*

She glanced out the car window. Robert had rolled out the map on the car bonnet and was studying it intently. Deep trepidation stirred at the echoes of River's words. *Another seeks the Staff.* This bookseller had sought ancient artefacts long before Lanky. Did he know of the Staff? Did he search for this Staff? Or did this Iolaire warn of another?

She saw Robert look up and gesture for them to join him. Unease continued to gnaw at her thoughts. *It seems we've arrived in the right place, but I hope this Iolaire is indeed a friend, else what might be awaiting us?* But they had to keep moving. "Okay," she whispered. "We'll continue as planned but stay close to me. If your friend speaks with you, or helps in any way, then guide me."

River nodded.

Shortly, gathered around the car bonnet, Jessica studied the map, tinged pink from the onset of the gathering sunset. "Well," she said, holding her voice steady. "What do you think?"

Robert glanced down at the map. "I've never studied this area, but Lanky has given us a place to start our search." He pointed to the pencil mark beside the red symbol on the map. "See there, at the edge of that small plateau? These contours mark a steep-sided embayment. And it's, what, less than one kilometre over there? We can follow the lower trail, then cut across to the right."

Jessica examined the map closely. The marking was quite clear. She glanced at the steep grassy slope they'd need to traverse. Even in the fading light, the flattened vegetation marking the start of the trail was clear. Despite the creeping unease in her stomach, she felt a growing urgency to get moving. *Because what other choice do we have?* "Let's do it. The light will be fading fast. You said you brought torches?"

Robert nodded. "I'll grab the GPS too."

Jessica followed him to the back of her car, where he opened the trunk. She waited until he'd grabbed what he needed, then she reached in and pulled out the canvas bag from the dark recess of the trunk. She paused. Was this the right thing to do? *I don't know, but I can't leave it.* She unzipped the bag, then lifted out the Axe and hefted it in her hand. *What part will you play in this?* She closed the trunk and joined Robert and River.

Robert's eyes immediately fell on the Axe. "Can I look at it?" he asked in an almost reverent manner.

"Best later. We should get going."

He hesitated, as if about to ask again, then walked away towards the trail. But not before she'd caught the briefest flash of annoyance in his eyes. She watched him for a moment. He'd searched for these Axes for decades, so his desire to examine one was understandable – but there had been something more in his face. *An eager anticipation …*

Her unease deepened. *What does he hope for here? What is it he desires?*

She turned as River tapped her arm. "I take that as a sign," River whispered, pointing upwards.

Jessica looked up. An enormous bird soared above them, its long, broad wings silhouetted against the deep violet sky, dwarfing the mob of harrying birds looking to chase it away. As it banked, she saw the V-shape of its raised wings – a golden eagle.

She looked back at River. "Okay," she said quietly. "Make sure you keep us on the right track."

They walked on after Robert.

*

"I think we've lost mobile coverage," Erin said from the back of the car.

Fletcher glanced at his own phone. There was no signal. He looked back at the road. "Well, there's only this one road through this valley. When it reaches the coast, we'll pick up the signal again."

They drove on in silence, the road winding through the eastern side of the old glacial valley with the peak of Mount Hope ahead to their right – the last peak before the northern sea.

"That's a car ahead," Tricia said, pointing. "Is that them?"

Feeling a rush of anxious anticipation, Fletcher slowed the car, peering into gloom. Was this it? Was this where Robert and the others had come to? *Then don't give yourself away.* "Difficult to tell from here. I'm going to drive past, so get yourself down – and quickly."

As they approached, the headlights lit up Jessica's yellow car, which was parked in a small lay-by.

"That's it!" he exclaimed as they passed. "But there's no one in the car."

Steering the car onto the grassy verge ahead, they came to a stop.

"Wait here, I'm going to take a look."

He got out of the car, grabbed his jacket and torch from the boot, then started walking to the yellow car. He stopped and turned as he heard footsteps behind him. "What are you two doing?" he hissed to Erin and Tricia, who were following him.

"Going with you," Tricia whispered.

"Oh no, you're not. Get back in the car. We don't know where they are or what they will do. And we don't know if that madman with the staff is around."

"Exactly, and so we're not staying in the car by ourselves."

Fletcher glared at her, then shook his head and headed on down the road.

Within a minute, he had finished scanning the car. "Car locked. No one inside. What are they doing? Where have—"

"There!" Erin whispered. "A light!"

Fletcher looked up to the hillside and saw the torchlight in the twilight gloom. Or rather several lights. He looked back to the road, checking up and down the lane. Nothing. No other cars – just this one. What were they doing? *And is that madman here?*

He turned to the others. "I'm going to follow them. I'll give you the keys to the car, and you can drive on to the end of the valley. When you reach the main road, you should have a signal and you can call my office. You have the number of …" He stopped as he saw Tricia glaring at him. "What?"

"No," she said simply, shaking her head.

"What do you mean no?" He frowned. "You're *not* heading up there with me. Who knows what's happening here?"

"I told you hours ago – we need to see Jessica. We're coming with you."

"You don't have a torch," he said, exasperated. "You won't be able—"

He stopped as Erin held up a torch in her hand. "It was in the back of your car."

After another few rounds, he threw in the towel. "Okay," he growled. "But you better keep up – I'll be moving fast."

"Come on, Trish," Erin said, switching on the torch. Then they charged on ahead of him, heading up the trail towards the dancing lights on the hillside.

Swearing under his breath, Fletcher raced after them, glancing nervously into the shadows. *What the hell am I doing?* His bitter laugh was mocking. *You made this bed, Fletch. Now you get to see what lies in it.*

CHAPTER TWENTY-EIGHT

How much did Naga see of what would happen? Only a fraction, I believe, only shattered fragments from some lost turning of the Continuum. But at the end, she served us well. She hid what needed to remain hidden from the eyes of Krull.

Lanky tensed as a stocky young man stepped out from the forest's shadows, but quickly relaxed as he heard the man's warm greeting to Gravel. The introductions were brief. The stocky man's name was Darius, and he held guard duty for the day. He was pleased to see Gravel, but even more keen to take them on to camp, where Rind was waiting. Gravel grunted for them to follow the guard. Lanky saw Darius's gaze linger on him briefly before the guard walked away. It starts now, he thought grimly. I am to meet them as a Warrior.

They followed Darius deep into the dense woodland, picking their way through the thick undergrowth, following no obvious trail. Yet Darius walked confidently on, holding a steady bearing. At least it appeared so to Lanky. But in this tangled confusion of bowed, gnarled tree trunks, who could be sure of their path? *And yet, I sense we hold our way.*

Whether their path lay straight or not, it wasn't long before the gloom of the forest gave way to a suffusing lightness, and within a few strides more, they broke out into the sunlight. They stood within a broad clearing, through which ran a rippling stream. To either side of the clearing lay the dense woodland, but directly ahead, the sparkling waters of the stream wound their way through the widening clearing towards a broad sunlit gorge, flanked by tree-topped white crags. *Hence the camp's name,* Lanky thought. A camp cleverly concealed within the depths of the forest.

Following the stream to the camp, his nervous tension grew. They had finally arrived at their destination, and now he was expected to rally the allies of the Iyes to fight in a war he'd known nothing of such a short time ago. *And how do I do that? Me, a mechanic.* And yet here he was, walking into the camp of an ancient people to declare himself a Warrior. *This is madness. Truly insane.* He felt the Axe firmly strapped against his back. The Axe of a Warrior. He drew a deep breath. *I do what is needed to give Beth time. We must find the Staff. We must find Jessica. Then we will see.*

Nervously humming to himself, he continued on towards the gorge, where two men detached from the shadows of a thick-canopied tree. After a brief discussion with Darius, the two ran on ahead. Lanky's group slowly followed their path, the stream gurgling happily to their right. Drawing closer to the camp, Lanky caught his first glimpses of large hide-covered huts, all pitched on the sunlit northern side of the gorge. A well-ordered, established camp. *A home for these people.*

Walking on, he saw several people heading their way. They were led by a slightly shorter individual wearing bands of beads around her arms, neck, and legs. Stone beads, wooden beads, beads of bone … *She likes beads,* was Lanky's first, not particularly earth-shattering, observation.

"Rind," Gravel acknowledged as the two groups closed.

The young bead-wearing woman, a familiarity about her, smiled. "Eloquent and effusive as always, Gravel. And good to see you too. And Amber, and Sheba," she said, turning to the women standing beside him, "a welcome return to you."

"And good to be here again," Amber said, rather more formally than Lanky had expected.

Still smiling, Rind turned to Lanky. She inclined her head a fraction. "And?"

"Ah," Gravel responded. "So, Spider has not yet told his tale?"

"Spider has been sleeping since he returned," Rind answered, her eyes not leaving Lanky's.

Why does she look familiar? he thought, scanning her slightly rounded face, which was framed by an unruly riot of short-cut curls.

Rind held Lanky's gaze. "No, Spider has not yet deemed it fit to wake and educate us on why he returns as the sole representative of this group – nor why, Gravel, you bring with you an interesting companion."

Gravel cleared his throat. "Then—"

"Then it seems we need an introduction," Lanky said, stepping forward, trying to clamp a hold on his nerves. "I'm Lanky. Somehow, I've become a temporary visitor to your Land – and now to your camp. Pleased to meet you, Rind."

Rind nodded, her deep brown eyes studying his face. "A Warrior, no less," she said in a relaxed voice. "It is a pleasure and an honour to meet you." She held out her hand. "Welcome to White Crags."

Hearing the genuine warmth in the welcome, Lanky reached out, grasping her arm above the wrist. "A pleasure to meet you too, Rind," he said as she firmly gripped his arm in return. He thought he noticed the faintest flash of green in her eyes. "And this is a pleasant surprise," he said, withdrawing his hand.

"Meeting me?" she said, raising an eyebrow. "Why is that?"

"No … I don't … I mean this camp here," he said, confused by her misunderstanding. "You wouldn't realise it was here. It's quite a surprise when you come down out of the woods."

She smiled. "It's one of our best-kept secrets, Warrior. And long may it remain so. You'll have a chance to look around and meet the others later. But first" – her smile faded – "I need to learn of what has happened. Spider is keeping strange company, one that makes me nervous."

*

As the evening twilight fell, Lanky, led by Rind, ambled through the sprawling camp. Warmly, yet self-consciously, he greeted those who approached him, mostly younger children, curious about this strange newcomer in their midst. And what a difference the presence of the children made, transforming the sparse travelling camps of the last few days into the warmer, welcoming atmosphere of this small community nestled inside its secret gorge.

It seemed a world away from that discussed at the meeting he'd just left.

A meeting still churning at the edges of his mind.

Together with Gravel and Amber, he had told of what they knew, condensing and summarising as effectively as they could. Rind, with three of her core trusted tribe members, had listened in charged silence until the story was told, then quizzed them carefully, yet with restless urgency. Once all had been told, questioned, and considered, they'd agreed to immediately reach out to their allies, and Lanky had stoically accepted the need to act as the catalyst for action, beginning with the Islanders to the west.

"Our staunchest allies," Rind had said. "They understand our Story. And they will understand you – a Warrior."

"But they're not part of the Iyes?" Lanky had questioned.

"They hold their own beliefs. Their own protector. Taran. The god of the Great Sea."

"And why do they support you?"

"Because they too are persecuted by the Ka," came Gravel's fierce response. "They too strive to protect their people, their legacy."

"But they are headstrong," Rind had added. "We need to be clear with them on what we want, on what we must do. We need to guide them. And for that, we must hear from our scouts, to better understand our own next moves."

As the meeting had moved on, they'd also agreed that Gravel would meet with the strange traveller who had arrived with Spider – an Iyes that Lanky had not yet met – to better understand who the unknown man was and what he wanted. From the evidence seen on their journey south, it seemed the traveller had greatly aided Spider, but the old man had been reluctant to talk with anyone other than leaders of the Iyes themselves.

Pulling himself back to the present, Lanky frowned. From the tracks they'd seen, the traveller kept a wolf as a companion. An unnaturally large wolf. Maybe after Gravel had spoken to him, he needed to pay this old man a visit himself. *I don't trust wolves.*

Lanky glanced around and saw they'd reached the furthest outskirts of the camp. To his right, two boys were trying to knock a lump of wood off a post with rocks. The smaller of the two hollered with delight as he sent the fragment of wood flying. Laughing, the taller boy sprinted off to reset the target. As they walked on, they passed a young toddler picking up ants with a stick before dropping them in her bowl and returning to show her mother, only to find that, somehow, they had disappeared. He stood and watched for a while as the girl walked back and forth, her bright face set in unwavering determination, until finally her mother clapped, congratulating her daughter on her success. The words were lost to him, but the joy on the girl's face was not.

He smiled. "This is love," he whispered to himself.

He felt eyes on him and turned to see Rind quietly studying him. A smile crossed her lips, lighting up her face, then she turned and walked on. He glanced back to see the beaming girl returning to the ant trail to find another wondrous prize for her mother.

Reluctantly turning away, he walked after Rind. These precious moments were a beguiling window into the regular lives of these ordinary people of the Iyes tribe, a people from a most distant age but with a passion and drive as strong as any of his own age. He sighed. This was a calm moment of observation he doubted would come again.

He caught up with Rind. "Your scouts ... Two days and they'll be back?"

She nodded. "And then we'll hear more of what happens in the south. But from what we know already, it's clear that the Ka are moving, mobilising many of the tribes of their so-called empire, and pushing north and east from their strongholds. It's also clear they expected your arrival here." She fidgeted with the stone beads on her wrist. "To have penetrated that far north, to have attacked you at the Arrival site ... They have prepared well."

He glanced at her. "But I guess you too have prepared?"

She hesitated. "I might say that we have ... But ..." She came to a stop and looked up at him. "But how can you truly be ready for this? This is as our childhood stories – heard, but not believed."

"You didn't believe the Iyes tribe Story? That seems odd in someone chosen to be a leader."

A wry smile crossed her lips. "Does it? Why? What do you think a leader to be?" She studied his face. "Whatever you think, it's better to ignore the definitions, the supposed traits – the oddities you refer to." She shook her head gently. "Just do. Just act. The people will either choose you or they won't. And no, I didn't believe." She tilted her head slightly. "And I can't believe you are a Warrior."

He laughed.

"What's so funny?" she said, smiling.

"Been there. Had this conversation. A Warrior? Hah. Even I don't believe it. And what is a Warrior supposed to be? To do? That, I still don't know."

"So why are you here?"

To find Jessica and try to get home. To see my mum, my friends. His immediate reactions didn't surprise him. But his next thought did. *And maybe to help these people.*

He glanced back to the camp, where he saw a child scampering past the nearest hut, a whittled stick in his hand. *Can I walk away from here? Can I leave them to their fate?* Naga's words came back to him. *Will I stand on that faraway mountain and watch an evil unfold while I do nothing?* That part of him that so desperately wished to return home was quick to respond. *It's not your battle.* Yet a deeper part of him, one urging him to listen, said that this *was* his battle; that he couldn't abandon these people. *I am a Warrior.*

He tensed. The more he battled against it, the harder it was to ignore those words. *I searched for all those years for lost artefacts of power ... yet never did I believe I might need to use them.*

"Warrior?" came Rind's soft voice.

He turned to her. "Why am I here?" He shrugged. "I need to understand more of what's happening to me – to the others – and maybe I can learn that here."

Rind's keen brown eyes held his. "And now you turn the tables, Warrior. What is it that I can give, one who did not believe my own people's Story?"

He sighed. "That I also don't know, Rind." He ran his head over his stubbly chin. "But maybe two nonbelievers can surprise people."

She studied him for a moment. "Maybe," she murmured. She turned and walked down to the babbling stream. Stopping by the water's edge, she looked back towards the camp. "Did you have news of a woman named Svana?" she asked in a quiet voice.

Ah. That was why she looked familiar. "She's your sister."

"Good observation, Warrior. Yes, she's my older sister. My big sister." She smiled. "If by only two sun-cycles."

"Well, I didn't really spend too much time with her. But, when I last spoke with Beth, it seemed the rest of the group was in good health and making fair progress. But, sorry, I don't know much more."

Tension eased from Rind's face. "That is enough, Warrior. That is good." She looked down at the glistening water and fell silent.

Suddenly, Lanky felt as though he was intruding on a private moment. "Think I'll return to the camp. My legs are starting to complain again."

"Of course. You must rest. We'll walk back together." She stepped back up the bank.

"Good. I think we should—" He gasped, then stumbled, as a searing pain ripped through his head.

"Warrior!" Rind exclaimed, dashing to his side and grasping his arm. "What's wrong?"

Holding his pounding head, a stringent metallic taste fouled his mouth. "Something's wrong," he grated, his skin crawling, his head feeling as if it would explode.

"What is it?" Rind hissed, her keen eyes scanning around them.

'Ready yourself, you fool,' came a harsh voice inside. A voice he knew well. A voice he feared.

Dysam.

'The shaman reveals himself,' Dysam rasped.

His head shot with stabs of pain, Lanky forced himself to move. He reached back and grasped the haft of his Axe—

A surge of energy ripped through him, shattering the pain, and flooding his body and mind with a rich, vibrant elation. He stood taller, strength coursing through him, a crystal-clear sharpness in his mind. *I am Lanky. I am a Warrior.* He drew a huge lungful of air. *And I must act!*

His eyes narrowing, he scanned the camp. As his gaze passed the southern wall of the gorge, he sensed intense ripples of energy streaming to the sky. He pointed to a shadowy cave entrance at the base of the steep white cliff face. "What lies there?" he rasped, his deep voice cutting through the crisp evening air.

Rind, her expression focussed and alert, followed his gaze. "The Sacred Chamber. We placed Spider there to aid his healing."

Staring towards the white cliff, Lanky sensed a deep, cloying presence within the cave, a deep and pervasive malevolence corrupting all around. *One of the Dark is there!* His eyes burning with an ice-cold fire, he hefted his Axe and drew more of the A'ven's potent energy. "Cover the exits to the gorge," he commanded, already striding down the bank of the stream. "And ready yourselves for battle."

*

"There it is!" Freya exclaimed, pointing to the distant woods. "The Crag's forest." Grinning, she turned to Naga. "We're almost home. And remember, you agreed that Amber and Eagle's ceremony could be held at this visit to the Crags." Her eyes sparkled. "Amber asked me to remind you."

Naga frowned … but smiled inside. "Are they both then ready for this? Are they sure they want to move so quickly?"

Freya's smile slipped. "Quickly? They've known each other for ages now. And they wouldn't have declared for each other unless they were ready. I don't think they moved quickly, Mother."

Naga's facade slipped and she smiled. "You are too easily deceived, Freya. I am just playing with you."

Freya grinned. "Then we can hold the ceremony?"

"If the circumstances allow, Freya, it will be held."

Freya's eyes lit up. "Thank you, Mother. Amber will be thrilled."

Amber and Eagle make a wonderful pairing, Naga thought as they walked on. *A great match.* She smiled. The ceremony would be a brief but welcome celebration for all during this time of stress. *It will—*

She froze, nerves suddenly afire. Looking back along their trail, tell-tale movements in a stand of tall grasses betrayed the imminent threat.

"Mother?" came Freya's concerned voice. "What is it?"

"Go!" Naga commanded, fear tearing through her. "Catch up with Eagle and get to camp."

"What? Why—"

"Do as I say, now!" Naga barked, glaring at Freya. "Your lives depend on it! Get to the camp as fast as you can!"

Freya, her anguished eyes wide with alarm, immediately sprinted away, racing ahead to catch the others.

Naga watched Freya and the others flee, wincing at their heartrending glances back her way. *At least they will be spared.* Her body cold with rising dread, she looked back along the path they had trodden. Without her far-seeking, she had not sensed the enemy's approach. *But I will never fail to sense the Dark's presence beside me.*

An enormous wolf stepped out from the tall grasses, followed by three figures racing towards her. Bitter regret filled her heart. It seemed this was her time to die. *And yet I had so hoped not like this.*

She fought to still her fear. She had done what was needed. Sheba and her baby were safe, and Lanky had been given the chance to judge Spider's companion. *I have done all that I could. I must hope it has been enough.*

Only one final task remained.

As the three figures approached, she reached for the last breath of energy remaining within her. *River. Please be ready.*

*

"So, it seems the beast was on the right track after all," said the tall, lithe woman standing before Naga, two wiry men standing behind her. "Not a creature I'd choose to trust, but who can gainsay your own tribe's shaman? And if our description is correct" – the woman took a step closer – "then before us stands the enemy's shaman, her only protection this lone boy."

What!

Naga turned and was chilled to the core to see Eagle racing towards her. "No!" she cried. "Eagle – go back!"

A cold blade pressed against her throat. "Too late," the woman rasped. "Drop your weapons," she commanded to Eagle, "else she dies."

"Don't listen, Eagle. Run!" The blade dug into her throat, drawing blood.

"Drop those weapons! Now!" the woman commanded.

Her body numb, Naga saw Eagle hesitate, clearly unsure what to do – and then he dropped his spear and bow.

"No," Naga whispered.

"Do what needs to be done," the woman said in a cold voice behind her. The two wiry men strode towards Eagle.

Horrified, Naga forced her frozen limbs to move – but cruel hands held her back. "Eagle, run!" she gasped, fighting to breathe. "They will not spare you!"

But as the woman had said, it was too late.

The two men reached Eagle. One grabbed the young Iyes by the arm, hauling him to the ground – the other thrust a spear into the back of the prone man's neck.

Eagle screamed.

Naga cried out with a despair as if her own soul had been ripped from her.

"I'd like to let you watch a while," the soft voice said behind her, "but I don't believe I have the time."

Searing pain exploded across her throat, then she was roughly pushed to the ground towards Eagle. She landed heavily on her side, her head bouncing off the hard ground – and then she came to rest, gurgling, her back to the mortally wounded Eagle.

"And here ends the line of the devil shaman," came the woman's silky voice. "Come. We must leave before those who fled raise the alarm and return – we should not intrude on their time of joy and celebration."

The harsh laughter drifted away, and soon all was silent, save her anguished, laboured gasps. She held her hand to her throat and felt the stream of blood seeping through her fingers. She coughed, and blood spurted out of her mouth.

No! It cannot end like this! How could it? After innumerable generations of continuity – of preparation – down the Iyes shamans' line, how could this be? To die here alone, unwitnessed, a mere speck of dust lost in the mists of time. All lost ... *Forever?*

And Eagle ...

Harnessing what pitiful life energy she had left, she somehow turned to face Eagle. *Move,* she commanded herself, and with a trail of blood in her wake, she dragged her trembling body towards the stricken man. His eyes lay open, his mouth opening and closing slowly, but no words were spoken. His spirit was leaving him. Naga pulled herself to his side, then reached over, placing her shaking hand on his head. Unable to speak, she simply stroked his hair and smiled.

"Amber," he whispered. "Tell her ..."

His words were lost in his final rattling breath – then he lay still.

Tears streamed down Naga's face. This was not what she had seen. *What have we done wrong?* A terrible sense of desolation overwhelmed her. *And River. How did we lose you too?* She struggled to breathe. *I have failed. I have failed you all.*

"You have failed, indeed, shaman," came a deep, rich voice from above.

Naga tried to turn her head, but her body wouldn't respond. A hand roughly grasped her chin and pulled it to the side. Through tear-filled eyes, she saw a powerfully built, shaven-headed man smiling down at her.

"A pity," the man said, holding her head in a vicelike grip. "Nefra was a little too efficient. But I still have time."

Time?

The man's eyes suddenly seemed to burn as the sun, and she cried out as a clawlike force tore into her. She stared in horror at the smiling face above. *He searches for something. He ...* Her terror grew. *He searches for the shamans' Story!* With all her remaining strength, she forced the Story deep within her soul. *You will not have it! You will not gain what must remain hidden.*

As the demoniacal claws raked her mind, her vision swam and her life force drained away. The man's face blurred.

She blinked.

The face of a scorched man loomed over her. *Who are you?*

"Today, I am Krull," the man said, as if hearing her. "But tomorrow, my destiny awaits."

Naga blinked ... and the face of the clean-shaved shaman returned. He was scowling. "Where is the Kade?" he hissed.

In the fog of her dying mind swirled a breath of confusion. *I know of no Kade.*

As the dread shaman raked through her mind, chaotic images flashed before her: of her laughing, crying, swimming, fighting; of pain and of happiness; of anger and of joy.

"Where is it!" the shaman roared.

The light faded and darkness encroached.

The shaman roared in anger, then a tremendous pain tore through her as the ghostly claw ripped out of her mind. Her head slammed into the ground as the shaman released her.

She felt no pain. Only confusion. She lay still, her breathing slowing.

The malevolent presence of the unknown shaman vanished.

It is so dark – when did I close my eyes?

*

Spider awoke, his blinking eyes slowly bringing into focus a dimly lit ceiling flickering in the light from unseen torches. He quickly sensed a familiar presence. *The Spirits are here.* He was in the Sacred Chamber. But tension lay in the air. Something was very wrong. *What—*

The light suddenly dimmed.

Then the clattering of falling rocks, scattering on the ground.

And then distress! *From the Spirits!*

He forced himself into a sitting position and turned ...

And there, wielding a Black Staff – a staff seemingly wrenched from the dark childhood tales told of the Iyes's Enemy – was the tall figure of the shaman. *Growl.* The shaman smote the Black Staff against a sacred painting on the wall—

There was an explosion of ... blackness, and a complete section of the wall collapsed.

"What are you doing?" Spider cried, breaking free from his numb horror. Attempting to stand, he stumbled and fell. As he scrambled to his knees, the Black Staff appeared before him. He looked up into the face of Growl, who looked down on him, sorrow written in the man's silvery eyes.

"I am sorry, Spider, I really am."

"Who are you?" Spider panted. "And what are you doing?"

"We play this game again?" Growl smiled. "This time, I really don't want to play. And it would take too long to truly answer."

"Well, try," Spider said, snarling. "I gave you my trust."

"But never really trusted me – isn't that the paradoxical truth?" Growl looked up. "I like you, Spider. In a different life, we could have been true friends. But—"

"I don't think so," Spider spat.

"But what you believe," Growl continued, slowly shaking his head, "and the company you keep, well, that is not compatible with the one I serve. *I* might be inclined to let you live, but" – his face contorted into a snarl, his black eyes afire – "*we* are not!"

Growl swung the staff, aiming at Spider's skull. Instinctively, Spider thrust his right hand up to protect his head—

As the staff struck his arm, there was an explosion of light, and Growl flew backwards through the air, crashing into the far wall before collapsing to the ground. Spider stared at his hand in disbelief. Light streamed through his fingers. *What happened? What ...*

Movement caught his eye, and he saw Growl picking himself up from the ground, his eyes ablaze. "Your trinket will not save you now, Iyes scum." Growl strode towards him—

A great roar boomed into the chamber, and a huge figure strode through the entrance. Spider gaped, stunned. *The injured Warrior? They healed him!* He watched, frozen, as the massive figure strode across the chamber.

"Time to die, my friend," echoed the Warrior's voice around the chamber as he launched himself forward, swinging his Axe in a vicious strike at Growl.

A tremendous crack of thunder rocked the chamber as the Axe collided with the Black Staff. Spider rolled away to the furthest wall, cowering as far from the terrifying combatants as he could. Shaking, he turned to see a sphere of sizzling energy growing out from the Warrior's Axe, and immediately opposing it, a cloud of intense blackness oozing from the shaman's staff. As the clashing energies collided, both adversaries took a step back, forced apart by the searing heat before steadying themselves, their faces twisted with savage intensity.

Both held firm.

The spheres of light and darkness grew, each fully enclosing a combatant within a crackling shield. The spheres continued to grow, but unable to expand beyond the other, they distorted, slowly forming a seething vertical barrier between the two adversaries. A strikingly pungent smell reached Spider. *As a lightning strike.* The barrier between the two combatants quivered and sparked—

A streak of black lightning hammered into the Warrior's white sphere. Then again. Spider watched, horrified, as with each devastating strike, the ominous dark sphere slowly advanced, devouring parts of the Warrior's shield as it encroached. The shaman's attack was relentless, bolts of sizzling black energy hammering into his opponent's diminishing shield, until, with a final blast, the white sphere vanished, leaving the Warrior standing defenceless.

"Is this the best that IY offers?" taunted Growl from inside his shield. "Her strongest Warrior? Pathetic. You disappoint us."

Lanky smiled.

Growl frowned.

"You may be disappointed, my friend," Lanky said, stepping forward. "But you are going to die." He strode through the boundary of the black sphere.

"What!" Growl cried from within. "No!"

The sounds of Growl's frantic struggles echoed around the chamber … then the dark sphere suddenly vanished. Lanky stood tall, grasping the gasping man by the neck.

"Look out!" Spider shouted as he saw the shaman lifting the Black Staff.

Lanky saw it too late, and the weapon struck him hard on the back of the head.

The Warrior staggered, his grip slipping from the shaman's neck.

Growl's face contorted with rage. "You think you are strong, but you know nothing. You—"

Loud cries erupted from the entrance, and Rind, followed by a stream of fighters, stormed into the chamber.

Growl held up his Black Staff – and vanished.

As Rind and others rushed to the Warrior's side, Spider pushed himself up and sat, hands shaking, staring at the now empty space where the shaman had stood. *I brought him here,* he thought, wretched guilt burning inside. *I brought the enemy into our midst.*

"Spider!" said a concerned voice above him.

He looked up to see Amber kneeling down beside him. "I'm okay," he said, somehow managing a smile.

"No, you're not. Your rib's still broken, you've a gash in your shoulder, and the redness still attacks your spirit." Her eyes softened. "But you're alive. Now let's get you out of here. You need to rest."

Spider took her proffered hand, and she helped him to his feet.

"Come with me." She guided him to the exit.

He pulled back, and glanced over to Rind, who talked in a low voice to the Warrior. "A moment, Amber. I have to speak with Rind and the Warrior."

Amber hesitated, then sighed. "A moment only, Spider."

He nodded, then slowly made his way over to Lanky and Rind.

"Ah, the Spider awakens," Rind said as he approached. "But seeing as you can only just stand, maybe you shouldn't be off your sickbed just yet?"

Spider forced another smile. "True. I've been better." He glanced at the Warrior and saw the face of a tired and confused young man. *Is this the same man who just entered here?* "But I'm better than you, the last time I saw you, Warrior." He saw the puzzled expression on the Warrior's face. "A story for later," he continued. "For now, I thank you for saving my life. I owe you."

Lanky smiled. "It appears you were doing fine by yourself. How did you stop that blow?"

"I've no idea. I thought that was your doing."

"Not me," Lanky replied. He glanced down. "But I sensed an energy in whatever you held within your hand."

It was now Spider's turn to look confused. He lifted his hand and opened it. Lying in his palm was the gift from River. The horse carving.

"You didn't want to be parted with it," Amber said by his side. "We tried several times to take it from you, as we didn't want you to drop it ..." Her smile was gentle. "But we finally realised there was no chance of that."

"Another story for later," Lanky murmured with a tired smile.

"It will be short tale," Spider said, still looking down at the bone carving. He turned it gently in his hand. "It was a gift. A great gift." He looked up and faced Rind. "I'm sorry," he said, his voice wavering. "So sorry ..."

He saw a flash of anger in Rind's eyes, then it was gone. "No lasting harm has come of it, Spider. But this is a lesson to us all. The Enemy is here. Trust only those we know."

Spider nodded, a terrible rent in his gut. What damage could the shaman have done here? He glanced at the despoiled artwork on the chamber's walls. What had Growl wanted to do? He looked back to Rind. "I—"

A panicked voice rang from the chamber's entrance. "Rind! Rind! Naga – she's under attack! They will kill her!"

CHAPTER TWENTY-NINE

The perils of drink. Or an opportunity?

Stealth excused himself soon after his return with the Ancient, claiming important chores to complete. He did, however, leave freshly caught hare together with tubers and berries from his store, which Sy cooked up into a tasty and satisfying meal. Later, fully replete and far more amenable to Sy's wish for fresh air, Shadow returned with his friend to the ice tunnel entrance, where they found Stealth tending a small fire, whose light was beginning to out-compete the late afternoon sun.

"Join me," Stealth said, glancing up, strands of his lank grey hair brushing his shoulders. "As you can see, some space remains around my fire."

"We'd be most pleased," Shadow said warmly. He glanced at the modest fire, then at a neat stack of split wood to the side. "I hope you don't mind, my friend," he said, stepping over to the wood cache and selecting a couple of logs, "but I wish to remain warm tonight." He walked back to the fire, carefully placed the logs into the glowing embers, then sat down on the rock closest to the heat.

Shaking his head, Sy settled himself on the rounded rock he'd found earlier.

"Ah," Shadow exclaimed, the fire's heat nicely toasting him. "My head has finally rejoined the land." He looked out into the ice-clad valley. "A very dramatic and peaceful place. I can see why you might sit out here to relax after your day's exertions – although I'd want a bigger fire."

Stealth's eyes glinted in the firelight. "That, I can see."

"And I hope we're not intruding too far into your peaceful solitude," Shadow continued. "Last night was enjoyable, but for you, there may be such a thing as too much company."

"If so, I haven't yet reached that place." Stealth smiled. "You're welcome to share my fire" – the dragon's servant looked down at the newly placed logs – "and make it your own."

Shadow laughed. "I'm gladdened by your continued hospitality." *Which I hope will stand my questioning.* He cleared his throat. "I hope you won't think your guest is prying too much if he asks why a fellow Ka left his thriving tribe behind and chose to stay here for such a time. Did you not agree to only one sun-cycle?"

Stealth was slow to respond. "This, I could answer, but you won't like my words."

"Difficult to believe, my friend. Even so, my interest remains – but to answer is your choice."

They sat in silence, broken only by the crackling fire and the distant calls of birds returning to their roosts, then: "I'd been on an evening mission with my master," Stealth said, his low voice carrying easily across the fire. "The route home had taken us close to my home camp, and my master asked if I wished to visit. Being only six turns of the moon since I left, I was unsure. Did I want to remind myself of what I was missing? Could it weaken my resolve to complete this assignment? I set those doubts aside, the pull of the tribe too great.

"She dropped me in secret a short distance from the camp – to the south in open ground, close to the camp's boats at the river – and I was given until the moon dropped to return. As my master left, I walked in the moonlight on the clear trail north. It was only a few moments later when I heard voices. Not wishing to trigger any undue or hasty reaction to my sudden appearance in the darkness, I backtracked towards the boats, peeling off into low bushes to wait until they passed."

Stealth gazed into the fire as if seeing again the events of that night. Shadow wondered again what missions the Ancient was undertaking. A question he needed to get to … with care.

"After a short while," Stealth continued, "I could see by the moonlight a group approaching down the track, their voices carrying clearly to me. 'They're just down here,' I heard a familiar voice say. It was one of the Temple Guard. I'd no idea what they were doing there at that time of night. Soon, a group of four passed, two carrying a bundle between them. 'Here,' the guard said as they approached the boats, 'you can pitch your tent over there. At first light, take that boat there.'"

Stealth drew a quiet breath. "Another man thanked him, one I recognised well: Harl, a skilled maker, brought in from another tribe." Stealth glanced over at Shadow. "He became a good friend of mine and was close to being accepted as a Ka. Harl thanked the guard for their help and apologised for choosing to leave the tribe."

"Ah. Two leavers. Always a disappointment to see people leave the tribe – but it's their loss."

"Indeed," echoed Stealth. "It was their loss." He paused. "The guard indicated they should set up their tent, offering to help. But as the brothers bent to pick up the tent, the guard and his companion struck. I didn't see the killing blows, just two screams. There was a brief struggle, and then silence."

Shadow stared unbelieving at Stealth, whose grim face flickered in the light of the fire. "Within a few moments, the bodies were thrown into the river. The guards recovered the tent – if indeed that's what it was – then moved back along the trail. 'More scum cleansed from the land,' the first guard said. As the harsh laughter faded, I heard nothing more. I remained hidden, chilled to the bone, until I heard my master appear. I rejoined her, and we left."

A chill seeping through him, Shadow glanced at Sy, who gazed calmly ahead as though he hadn't heard the tale. *Or ... or what?* He shook that thought from his mind and looked back at Stealth. This couldn't be. The Temple Guard protected the leader of the Ka. *And our leader protects our people.* "How sure are you that this was the work of temple guards?"

"I know the men. I travelled with them on several missions. They *were* temple guards."

Shadow shifted his weight, trying to unravel what he was hearing. But the story made no sense. Why kill two leavers? People who couldn't cope with the rigours of the Ka home tribe, or couldn't accept the tribe's beliefs, were free to leave and return to their vassal tribe. "These men, these two brothers, must have been guilty of some crime." Although as soon as it was said, it sounded hollow.

"Guilty?" Stealth said angrily. "This was not the treatment of guilty men. You know this. These men were tricked and led to their deaths – no, to their executions."

"No," Shadow said, fighting his own doubts, "it can't be true. You're mistaken in what you saw."

"I know what I saw then," Stealth said in a voice as hard as granite. "And I know what I saw later ..." His eyes narrowing, he climbed to his feet, looking to the western sky.

Sy also stood, gesturing to the west.

Shadow's eyes lingered on Stealth, then he turned and followed their gazes. Searching the distant horizon, he saw a dark speck drifting slowly below the broken clouds. As he watched, the shape grew in size as it flew towards them.

The dragon was returning.

Sy flicked his fingers. "The beast carries something."

"You have better eyes than me," Shadow said, squinting. But as the Ancient grew closer, he saw an indistinct shape held in her talons. *What catch today? One for their meal, or for her own?*

Suddenly, Stealth swore, then rushed away. "Follow me now! And ready any arms you have." The dragon's servant ran off into the gloom.

Shadow stared after the man in confusion. "What's going on? And I don't have any weapons on me." Climbing slowly to his feet, he saw Sy already racing after Stealth. "How about a few more explanations around here?" Shaking his head, he hurried off in pursuit.

Muttering to himself, Shadow reached the landing site just as the dragon flew in. Rather than landing directly as it had earlier, the Ancient circled around the back of the site, approaching them from the east before slowing, then hovering a short distance in front of them. He could now see a figure dangling from her front left talons.

"To me!" Stealth commanded, stepping off the hard, frozen ground onto a patch of softer snow. As Shadow and Sy followed, Stealth called to them, "Get ready to neutralise any threat – but do not kill."

Shadow tensed. *What are we dealing with here?*

As the downdraught of the dragon's wings drove wild, snow-filled eddies around him, he hurried after Stealth, taking a position immediately below the dragon. *Not a place I'd readily choose to stand—*

The Ancient dropped the body.

As the body hit the ground, Stealth immediately sprang forward, grabbing something from the prone figure's back. Shadow crouched, waiting for an attack from this nameless threat.

"Stand down," Stealth said, a relief in his voice as the dragon rose into the sky before wheeling away towards the landing site.

Relaxing his fighter's stance, Shadow slowly approached the still body. *What do we have here?* Pushing the ice-covered figure over with his foot, he knelt down, brushing snow and ice from the lifeless face. "Well, well," he gasped in surprise, the memory of his encounter with the fierce fighter – *no, Warrior* – still raw.

"You have met this mercenary?"

"Indeed, I have. And thought I'd left her to die." He tilted his head a fraction. "It seems she can die twice."

His brow furrowed. Yet when the Ancient had been attacked, revealing the axewoman as a Warrior, he'd had his doubts. *I warned the Ancient that the poison might not work. I said we should return to finish her.* His own answering thoughts mocked him. *That was only needed because you failed to defeat her in a fair fight.* Pulling away from the uncomfortable truth, he sighed. No matter. The task was done.

His attention shifted to Stealth's bounty. "Her axe," he murmured. "A great prize. It seems this day belongs to Kaos."

"It would seem that way," Stealth answered. "Help me bring the body inside. There may be something I can learn from it."

"You're welcome to it. The dead make me squeamish."

Stealth raised an eyebrow.

Shadow leaned down and grasped the Warrior's stiff legs. "A pity this one was not born on our side. She was a smart fighter." *And yes, a hard one to kill. Another lesson, Shadow. Do not be complacent again.*

As they lifted the body, he glanced at Stealth. "A dead Warrior. I believe this calls for a celebration. And it just so happens I believe my head has cleared from last night. Maybe a cup or two of your wine?"

Stealth smiled. "A celebration indeed. Let's make it a night to remember – or maybe if the night goes well, it will be a night we won't remember."

Shadow laughed as they moved away with the body. "I doubt I could forget this day, nor would I wish to. My leader must hear my name in this story."

But as they hauled the body inside, his smile slowly faded as Stealth's bleak tale crept back into his mind. *Those leavers ...* He banished the thought before it could form. *That was not my tribe. That's not who we are.* His sigh was troubled. *I think I'll take more than a drink or two tonight. There are some things I don't want to remember.*

*

Groaning, Stealth hauled the icy body along the narrow, torchlit tunnel, one of several smaller passageways leading from the dragon's main chamber. He'd left Shadow and Sy to head to his quarters, where he would meet them later. This task, one commanded by the Ancient, was now for his eyes only. *Later? Well, that was later.*

Seeing a faint reflected sparkle on the wall, he stopped, laid the body on the ground beside a trough of water, then turned.

The portal lay before him.

He drew a slow breath. Since he'd first seen one of these strange, alien structures, they had fascinated him. Clean-cut, using a technique beyond anything he could imagine, they were adorned with immaculately carved blue and white crystals, which sparkled in the light of a flame. And from the smooth translucent floor of the alcove, they effused a very faint glow. The first sign of their massive latent power.

That first-seen alcove had for such a long time remained a mystery. Until he had finally seen the figures within. Until he understood who those figures were.

Warriors!

Glancing down to the still body, he sighed. Dealing with this one would be different. The others had walked in.

He manoeuvred the body into a sitting position, and then, dropping to one knee, he hauled the woman up and over his right shoulder. Grunting, he levered himself up, then shuffled into the alcove and positioned her against the back wall, holding her in place with his weight. His hands now free, he grabbed the ends of the two leather straps secured to wooden stakes hammered in the wall and tied them tightly under the woman's arms and around her waist. *Good*, he thought, breathing heavily. As he stepped slowly away, the woman slumped – the leather strapping stretched slightly before holding tight. Now able to work more quickly, he drew in the straps, raising the body more tightly to the wall. Then, reaching for other straps bound to the wall, he secured her legs and feet.

He stood back and examined his work. *That should do it.*

Grunting in satisfaction, he began the next phase of his task. It took many trips – back and forth between the main chamber and the alcove – but finally, he'd built up sufficient gold around the feet of the Warrior. He nodded to himself. *That should suffice.*

Wiping his brow, he retrieved the torch from the wall, then extinguished it in the trough of water.

He waited.

Moments only, then a faint golden glow lit up his face as the portal activated.

He smiled. *Yes, that should suffice.*

He turned away and walked on through the passageway towards the main chamber.

A familiar question drifted through his mind. What was the task of this Warrior? But as with each before, he knew not. And maybe he never would. The Ancient thought over a timescale that was impossible for him to imagine, and the Warriors fought their battles over ages far beyond his reckoning. *I'll be long dead before many leave.*

He sighed as he walked on. Two tasks successfully completed. *They think the Warrior dead. And the Staff is secure.* One task remained. *And it starts with a drink with my good friend Shadow.*

CHAPTER THIRTY

It was one of the hardest choices to make. To incarcerate an innocent is terrible enough – but for thirteen millennia? No, this was not an easy decision. But they are Warriors.

Climbing up between two tall rocky bluffs, they entered the gloom of a steep-sided reentrant, cut deeply into the twilight-lit lower reaches of Mount Hope. Reaching the centre of the embayment, Jessica halted. A shiver of anticipation – and fear – ran through her. They had reached the place in the north marked by Lanky on his map. She looked along the long, tight curve of the reentrant's back wall, which lay in shaded darkness, then scanned upwards, following the steep ridge as it flattened out, merging into the grassy slopes above. *But is there anything here?*

She glanced across to Robert, who stood a short distance away, looking up to the peak of Mount Hope, just visible beyond the mountain's lower reaches. He had remained silent as they'd traversed the lower slopes, yet she'd seen the growing anticipation on his face and a suppressed fervour in his eyes. A part of her understood. He'd searched for such artefacts for so long, why wouldn't he be excited, tense? But a greater part recalled River's words; Iolaire didn't trust him.

Harsh realisation gripped her. *And neither do I. He expects to find something here.* The Staff? Or something more? Her hand clenched tightly around the haft of the Axe. *I don't know what he wants, but if the Staff is here, it's mine. It's my way to Beth ... and to Lanky.*

Her disquiet growing, she turned to River. "What should we look for?" she asked, keeping her voice low.

River gestured to the shadows of the steep rock wall. "Iolaire says an ancient site once lay here. She believes it will still be here, somewhere along this rock face. Its entrance will be marked."

"What kind of mark?"

River hesitated. "Most likely a carving, but Iolaire didn't know for sure." Her eyes darkened. "She also warns of an approaching servant of Kaos. We must hurry."

Dread twisted in Jessica's gut. A servant of Kaos? The burnt man? "Do you know what approaches?" she whispered.

Her expression grim, River glanced to the rocky bluffs at the entrance. "A daemon of the Dark. And a shaman. Iolaire said that if they arrive, we will know what to do."

Despite her fear, Jessica scowled as a spark of anger ignited inside. "We know nothing," she rasped in a low voice. "Nothing."

"Then search quickly. Time is against us."

She glared at River, then glanced away. *This isn't River's fault. And she's right. We must—*

"What is she saying?" Robert said, his torchlight flicking into her eyes.

Holding back a sharp retort, Jessica drew a deep breath. *Stay calm. We need everyone's help right now.* The torchlight flicked away, and she saw Robert walking towards her. "We're searching for a carving on the rock wall," she said in an even voice. "We—"

"Hold it right there!" came a cry from behind as a bright torch beam flashed across them. "Police."

Cursing, Jessica turned to see a figure standing by one of the stone bluffs.

"It's Fletcher," Robert said in a strained voice as he came to her side. "The village sergeant. How did he find us?"

Jessica stared at the new arrival. *The police officer who came on the motorbike when we rescued Lanky from his fall.* Her jaws set, muscles tensing. *We didn't need this.* "Don't come any closer," she shouted, trying to buy time. "It's not safe here."

"Whatever's been happening here," Fletcher said, "it's over." She saw him take a step towards them. "Who else is here?"

I need him out of here. "Stay back," she snapped. "Else people will be hurt. You—"

"Jess!"

Jessica watched in disbelief as the shadowy outlines of two familiar figures clambered up to stand beside Fletcher. She shone her torch at the three figures now standing by the stone bluff. "Trish? Is that you?"

Two figures detached from the shadows and ran towards her.

"No! Stay here!" Fletcher shouted, striding after them. "This is difficult enough already."

"Jess!" Tricia shouted, sprinting across the embayment, Erin by her side.

"What are you doing!" Jessica hissed. "I told you to stay away. I—"

"Someone is after you!" Tricia spluttered, trying to catch her breath as she stopped in front of Jessica.

"It's true," Erin panted. "He tried to kill Trish, he—"

"He what!" Jessica exclaimed.

"I need to warn you now, Ms. Owens," said the sergeant as he approached. "I'm going to arrest you. You do not have to say anything, but it may harm your defence if you do not mention when questioned …"

"Leave it, Sergeant," Tricia said sharply. "This is not—"

"Hold on," Jessica rasped, holding up her hands in frustrated anger. "You all need to back off." She glowered at her friends. *I don't need them here. Not now.* But Erin's words had shaken her. *Someone tried to kill Trish? What—*

"Jessica!" River called out. "Danger!"

Jessica spun around. *What now?* She scoured the gloom of the darkening twilight, but saw nothing. "What did you see, River? Where—"

She gasped as a sudden crawling sensation ran up her back. Fingers caressed her neck, and an oily metallic taste oozed into her mouth. A desperate desire to run swept over her. "What is it?" she whispered.

"An Enemy daemon!" River rasped. "It approaches!" She turned to Jessica, her eyes burning brightly. "Give me my Axe."

Jessica stared at her, stunned. "Your Axe?" she stammered.

Ignoring her confusion, River reached over and hauled the Axe out of her hand. Jessica watched in utter amazement as the girl hefted the Axe, then strode away, seeming to grow in stature with each determined step, her presence looming over all around.

Jessica's sense of dread slipped away.

River halted in the centre of the embayment, feet set apart, glaring towards the two stone pillars at the entrance. Watching. Waiting for what was to come with a steely confidence, a calm surety of purpose.

In that moment, Jessica saw the incredible truth. *She is a Warrior! She is revealed.*

Yet in the midst of the stunning revelation, another thought hammered into her mind. *If River took the Axe, then what am I? What—*

"This madness must stop," Fletcher demanded. "You're just making things worse for yourself. Put that axe down."

She turned to see Fletcher staring out into the gloom at River. "You don't understand," she hissed. "You understand nothing." She heard the biting irony in her own words. *You say he understands nothing – yet neither do you.*

"Then tell me what you're doing here." He gestured to River. "And what she's doing."

"They grow closer," came River's calm voice. "Search quickly, else the chance will be gone."

Gone? "Get out of here," she hissed to Fletcher. Her wilful gaze levelled on her friends. "And you too. Now!"

They didn't move. "We want to help, Jess," Erin whispered, her face drawn.

"We need to help," Tricia said, wiping her brow.

Jessica glared at them. *I don't have time for this.* She turned to Robert, who stood, eyes flicking between her and River. "Look for a mark on the rock wall, a carving, anything out of the ordinary. You find anything, you shout. Okay?" The bookseller nodded, then hurried off into the shadows cast by the steep cliff wall. There was a brutal urgency to her words to Tricia and Erin: "You have to go. Now. This place isn't safe."

Tricia's eyes flicked to the darkness beyond. "No, Jess. We're not going back out there."

Erin held Jessica's fierce gaze. "You need help, Jess. What are you looking for?"

Jessica fought back a howl of frustration. Didn't they understand? She didn't want them hurt. And yet her exasperation couldn't deny the stark reality. *I'm not going to get rid of them. And I do need help.* Biting back the guilt, she did what was needed. She gestured to Robert by the rock wall. "Help him. Look for anything unusual – writing, carving … anything. Shout if you find something."

Tricia nodded, gritty determination masking her fear. "Come on, Erin. Let's see what we can find." They ran off to join Robert.

Jessica turned to the sergeant, now a confused and worried-looking young man. "You really should leave."

Fletcher straightened. "That's not going to happen. Where's Lanky? Where's the other girl?"

"They're safe. But they need help. Help to get back here."

"Get back here? Where are—" His eyes suddenly widened, and he spun around, staring out into the darkness.

Jessica's own fear surged as an eerie, fell shadow shrouded her mind. "It's too late," she breathed.

"What's happening?" Fletcher whispered, his voice wavering.

Her hands shaking, she stepped to his side. "The servants of Kaos come."

"Kaos? What—"

A triumphant voice cried out from beyond the entrance. "Guardian! We have found you!"

Guardian! A name that evoked ravening terror. A name from her nightmares. *The burnt man comes for me!*

As a shadowy figure strode between the rocky bluffs, a terrible stench, a malevolent hatred, engulfed her. Swinging her torch onto the figure, she saw a tall, gaunt-faced man stride through the entrance pillars and into the light. His long white hair, streaked with black, was swept back over his shoulders. In his right hand, he carried a staff.

A gasp of perverse relief escaped her. *It's not the burnt man. Thank God, it's not him.* But it was a shaman, of that, she was sure. *I sense his aura. I sense his ghostly breath of power.* Hairs on the nape of her neck suddenly stiffened as the bitter tang of the man triggered a shadowy, foreboding memory. *I've met this man before. Somewhere, sometime, I've crossed his path.*

"Keep searching," came River's commanding voice as she faced the approaching figure. "Another is coming. I must deal with this one first." She walked forward, a faint glow surrounding her.

A bitter taste lingering, Jessica watched, transfixed, as River approached the shaman. *I can't leave her alone.* Stepping towards the Iyes girl, she felt a rich vibrancy in the air around her. With no conscious thought, she reached for its power.

"Stay back, Guardian," River growled, her eyes fixed on the shaman. "This is not your fight."

Jessica halted. *Guardian? She uses the name spoken by my enemy.*

And River's voice … *That was not her.* "River?"

"Not River, Revri. Stand back and continue your search. Be quick."

Revri? Who was Revri? Uncertain now on how to act, she watched as River halted before the shaman.

The gaunt-faced shaman smiled. "So, a Warrior comes to play. But alone? Unwise, I think, on a night such as this." His smile broadened. "Prepare to die."

Jessica froze as the shaman's words sliced through her soul.

Prepare to die.

She stared at the man in growing horror. The mocking tone, the murderous lust of his aura. *It's him! It's the one who killed Eshe!*

"Neither you, nor the daemon, will pass," River growled.

Jessica staggered, then fell to her knees, a bone-chilling realisation tearing through her. *It's the one who slaughtered my sister. It's the one who destroyed my life.*

"You cannot stand against us, Warrior," the white-haired shaman rasped. "Alkazar is here."

Jessica gasped as a crawling sensation erupted across her body, as if a thousand spiders had hatched out on her skin. Sickening despair ripped through her stomach. She bent over and retched.

"Find what we need, Guardian," River growled. "The daemon comes."

Her whole body trembling, Jessica forced herself to move. She wiped her mouth and looked up. The shaman stood with a mocking smile, holding River's hostile gaze. *He killed my sister. He killed the one I loved.* Rage erupted with her. *He killed her. He took her from me …*

She climbed to her feet—

An explosion of light flooded the clearing.

Someone screamed.

Formless dread descended upon her, quelling her burgeoning rage. Shielding her eyes from the intense glare, she cried out as a cold, clammy finger caressed her cheek.

We come for you, Guardian, hissed a harsh voice in her ear.

Shaking, she glanced around but saw nothing beside her. As the blaze of light faded to a daylight glow, she looked to the pillared entrance … and saw River standing, her arm aloft, light streaming from her Axe towards a shimmering wall of sparking energy streaming across the entrance. *Revri's shield,* came an unbidden thought. She saw nothing beyond this wall, but sensed an alien presence beyond, dark tendrils of its fearsome mind striving to reach her.

River spoke, her voice suddenly hard and bold, solid and unwavering: "Find what must be found. I cannot hold against this daemon for long."

Jessica, stood, trembling, struggling to breathe. *The one who killed my sister is out there. He killed Eshe.* She took a step forward.

"Turn back," River rasped. "You cannot fight this battle."

"He killed Eshe," Jessica whispered, taking another step. "That man slaughtered my sister."

There was the briefest hesitation from River, then: "I will do what I can to avenge your loss, Guardian, but I say again, you cannot engage here. You must—"

An ear-shattering crack of thunder rent the air, its echoes reverberating around the reentrant.

"Please," came River's wavering voice. "Do your part, else all is lost."

Jessica stared out towards the rocky bluffs, seeing the coruscating wall of energy blazing between her and her sister's killer. Fraught anguish twisted her gut. *I can't reach him.* Her vision blurred. *I've failed again.*

"Guardian. Please. You must act, else we fail."

Fail … Jessica blinked, a tear rolling down her cheek. *Yes, I must act.*

Her gaze lingered on the shimmering wall of energy, beyond which stood the murderous shaman. "Destroy him, River," she whispered in a glacial voice. "Wipe him from this earth." Her glistening eyes hardened. "And this I swear, if you escape her, devil, I will find you. Somewhere, sometime, I will find you." Wiping her eyes, she forced herself to turn away. *But I will not forget you, devil. Be very sure of that.*

"What's happening?" came Fletcher's wavering voice by her side.

"Stay here," she hissed. "Do nothing. And pray."

Her mind shattered, her body shaking, she stumbled across to those frantically searching the rock wall, now illuminated by the Axe's radiant light. "Have you found anything?"

"Nothing," came Robert's stammering reply. "I'm going to try over there."

She saw him head further away to the right. "Trish? Erin?"

"Nothing," Tricia answered, voice shaking, scarcely her own. "The scrawl of some tourist vandal. What do we do now? What's happening back there?"

A great evil has come. And a devil who killed my sister. "Keep looking," she called, forcing the pain away. "It must be here."

But staring at the rock face, doubt ripped through her. Were they mistaken? Was there nothing here at this place Lanky had marked on his map? But no, there had to be. That voice had told River there *were* carvings here. *But what sort of carvings? How big? How …*

The words of Tricia lashed through the chaos of her thoughts. *The scrawl of some tourist …*

A desperate hope lit. "Trish!"

"What!"

"Those markings you saw – a tourist, you said – where?"

"They were back over there."

"Show me!"

"Okay, okay," Tricia stammered. She ran back along the rock face, quickly followed by Jessica. "Here … No, here … Aah! Where were they?"

"Trish, we don't have time for this. Where are they?"

"You'll only get me stressed, Jess," Tricia hissed. "They're around here somewhere ... Here! They're here! Look!"

"Let me see!" In the light of Tricia's torch, she saw a scrawled name, scribbled in red ink on a smooth section of rock.

Her hopes shattered in an instant.

Tricia glanced at her, fear etched on her face. "This can't be what we're looking for ... Is it?"

Jessica stared blindly at the graffiti, knowing their last chance had gone. "No," she whispered. "It's not." She looked up and scanned along the length of the long shadowy rock face. "We just don't have time."

Tricia glanced back towards the pillared entrance. "It's bad, isn't it?" she whispered.

Jessica's gut twisted. *We could die – and that devil could escape.* She saw the terror etched in her friend's face. "Not if River – Revri – can hold it back," she said, fighting to hold her voice steady. *But what use is that?* she thought, despairing. *We find nothing except the work of vandals.* She brushed her hand angrily against the graffiti ...

And her fingers caught on a sharp indentation in the rock.

Frowning, she ran her fingers back over the graffiti until they caught once more on a narrow indentation. She peered closer, angling her torchlight onto the vandalised surface. The stone beneath her fingers was smooth – *unnaturally so* – with a deep vertical groove carved into its surface. She ran her fingers along the sharp edge of the furrow, and then up into a small circular depression above it ...

A visceral shiver ran through her, a remembered tale from Lanky suddenly vivid and raw. *Could it be?* Wild, desperate hope surged. "Erin! Robert! Search over here!" She turned to Tricia. "Look for any indentations like this. We—"

The light dimmed and shard-like fingers of hate caressed her mind.

We come for you, Guardian, whispered a silky voice. *This one cannot hold us.*

"I cannot hold much longer," River cried, voice strained. "You have little time."

Fighting an overwhelming urge to flee, Jessica glanced towards the rock-pillared entrance.

River stood tall, rippling streams of crackling energy flowing from her Axe to feed her shield. But now the shimmering white shield was tainted by ragged stains of intense black, their edges sizzling with frightening intensity. Crackling and sparking, the blackness was slowly devouring the white energy of the shield, steadily yet inexorably destroying the defence.

Then, to her horror, the ragged black stains rippled and bulged, violently surging outwards towards River to form grotesque, misshapen faces, their deep, hollow eyes glaring out at the Warrior with bestial hatred. The twisted faces raged at River, vacant maws screaming unheard threats, morphing from one horrific visage to another.

River grunted and took a step back.

And another.

"What *is* this?" came the faltering voice of the sergeant by her side.

"It's the unbelievable courage of a young woman," she whispered.

"Jess!" Tricia cried. "Here!" Jessica instantly turned to see her friend pointing to something much lower down on the rock wall. "It's another mark in the stone."

Jessica quickly stepped to the wall, then leaned in, using her angled torchlight to better highlight the carving. She ran her fingers over the marking. "A letter 'y'," she whispered, her heart racing. She glanced up to the mark she'd already found. "And an 'i'." Hands trembling, renewed hope coursed through her. *The Staff ... Lanky found these letters when he discovered the Staff.* "This is it!" she cried out. "We've found—"

"We are out of time," River grated, her strained voice now half broken.

"No! This is it!" *And I know what he did!*

Thrusting her left hand up, she pressed her fingers firmly against the letter 'i', then brought her right hand down towards the letter 'y' ...

Her fingers almost touched it—

But the light faded—

And the Dark stormed in.

She froze as her mind was assailed with visions from hell, and all around her, heartrending screams of unbearable pain and suffering erupted: the cries of tortured minds, the chilling sounds of death.

A feeling of utter failure, of devastating loss, flooded over her.

They had failed. *I have failed.*

'You thought you could escape death,' came a pitiless voice. 'But you couldn't even save your own sister as she lay dying before you. You may as well have driven home the dagger yourself. You killed her. You failed her.'

As the brutal truth stormed through her, Jessica collapsed to the ground. *I couldn't save her. I killed my sister.*

'And look at these people around you. The friends you have destroyed. Their lives wasted. Lost. A vacant mirage. All because of your miserable existence. Who did you think you were? You are nothing. Nothing!'

A ferocious onslaught of anguish and despair battered Jessica, a litany of her abject failings and wasted life.

'You seek love, one to stand by your side, but there is no one who loves you. Who could ever love one such as you? You would taint their spirit for an eternity with your twisted soul. You are nothing.'

Jessica cowered beneath the onslaught, all defences stripped away until there was only a shell of herself remaining, a tiny wisp of her spirit that the slightest breath would blow away. Through tear-filled eyes, she saw her wonderful friend, Tricia, collapse to the ground. She saw Erin and Fletcher, their barely recognisable faces twisted in rage, grasping each other's throats with manic fury ...

Yet she remained bound, unmoving, crippled by a sense of utter loss. *My sister died. My friends are dying. I don't deserve to live. I must ...*

Something stirred deep within her dying soul.

I am nothing. I will ...

She felt the faintest brush of her loving sister's hand.

I will ...

She saw the minutest flame flickering in the deepest darkness of her being.

Jalu?

Guided as if by an unknown hand, Jessica reached for the flame ...

She gasped.

For in this minutest of flames – in this single spark of humanity – lay a spirit with a strength beyond her imagining. A spirit with a defiance so deep and so strong that no man, no woman – no daemon – could lay it asunder.

And out from this deepest well of her being swept a primeval will to survive.

Battered by the relentless savagery assailing her, she allowed this wondrous gift of life to suffuse her and forced her gaze to the shadowy wall before her. *I will not submit. They will not defeat me.*

Forcing her arm to move, she reached for the carving—

The onslaught on her mind and body became a fervid frenzy, a savage defilement of her soul. Blood oozed from her skin, scorched strips of flesh peeled from her body, and her hair was stripped from her head. Her mind was torn and sliced as though razor claws ripped through her skull.

And yet through the merciless assault on her very being, she forced herself on. *You will not defeat me!*

Closer and closer she drew to the carving ...

Until her fingers touched the 'y'—

The immense blast hurled her backwards through the air, sending her crashing violently to the ground.

She lay, dazed, a chaotic, crashing avalanche of rocks rumbling behind her.

As the clattering faded into silence, she lay for a moment, drawing ragged breaths, echoes of the foul assault polluting her mind. *And yet it didn't defeat me ...*

She forced herself to move.

Her head pounding, she wearily pushed herself up. Quickly assessing herself, she felt only throbbing bruises from her fall. No torn skin, no bloodied face – no physical trauma from the brutal attack.

Sudden panic cut through her befouled mind. *Where are my friends?* She scrambled to her feet and looked around—

A clawing, malevolent presence engulfed her.

The daemon is still here!

'Come, Guardian,' came an oily voice. 'It is time for you to die.'

She cried out as a taloned hand seemed to thrust deep inside her, icy claws caressing her soul.

'I, Alkazar, claim you, Guardian,' the daemon rasped. 'You are mine. You—'

"No!" a voice thundered. "You are mine!"

As a dazzling white light streamed into the skies above, a primeval roar of pent frustration rent the air – the clawing hand instantly vanished, and the phantom-like mass of the daemon swept out of the clearing.

Hearing a clatter of rocks behind her, Jessica spun around ...

And she watched in disbelief as Beth, with a face of murderous thunder, strode out of a glowing cavern in the mountainside, immense, fiery sparks crackling around her, lighting up the sky and pushing back the darkness as a wave would treat a single grain of sand.

"I," Beth growled in a slow and deadly voice as she strode down the scree slope of shattered rocks. "Have," she continued, striding out onto flat ground of the clearing. "Survived!"

Beth hefted her Axe, then hammered it down to the ground.

A huge shock wave blasted out through the pillared entrance through which the daemon had fled, sparking violent explosions out in the valley beyond.

"And I," she spat, running forward, "am now finally free!"

A blaze of light erupted from her Axe, then a bolt of jagged lightning lanced out into the valley, triggering another massive explosion.

Dumbstruck, Jessica watched as Beth disappeared from view, flashes of jagged lightning and violent crashes of thunder following in her wake.

As the raging storm rolled down the mountainside, others came to her side.

"What was that?" Erin whispered.

"That," Tricia said breathlessly, her eyes wide, "looked like one mightily pissed-off lady."

CHAPTER THIRTY-ONE

To first experience the unknowable, the untouchable, cannot be easy. I suppose there was a time this happened to me. But I cannot remember.

Resting her head on the cold ground, Jessica closed her eyes, desperately trying to push the horrific images from her mind. But the image of her sister's killer was hard to dispel. *And he may have escaped* – she grimaced – *as he did after slaughtering my sister.* The police had searched, appealed for witnesses, but no one had ever been found. The killer had vanished. *But this shaman was that killer. I know the smell of him. And that voice.* "Prepare to die …" Long-buried anger flared, white-hot and cut with venom. "If you can hear me, devil, prepare to die."

Visions of a revenge delivered with an unforgiving hand assuaged her terrible hurt for a time, but as her anger ebbed, echoes of the evening's terror returned. The horror that had descended upon them had been more than the devil shaman. The foul wraith of Kaos – for surely sent by the nemesis of the Iyes it had been – had fought with insidious malevolence to break her spirit. And it had come so close.

But it failed.

Savage relief swept through her. It had failed because she'd resisted the daemon's vile lies. It seemed there was a part of her that could not easily be broken. *And that part I need to build up and build stronger.* Her next thought arrived with a terrifying certainty. *I'll need all the strength I can muster for what is to come. This is not the end.*

Of that, she was deadly sure, but what lay ahead?

A spark of anger flared. *We continually step into the unknown. We need help. I need help.*

A name flashed into her mind.

Jalu.

At her lowest point – at her darkest moment – why had she thought of this name? The name the daemons called her. *Who is Jalu?*

'Someone close to you,' came a calm, ethereal voice.

Jessica started and snapped open her eyes. *'Who are you?'* she quickly pushed into the ether.

She listened for an answer from the whispering voice – a calm voice she had heard before – but she heard nothing save the thunder reverberating in the distant valley. She sensed, once again, that this presence had vanished as quickly as it had arrived. It seemed to refuse to engage fully.

Her thoughts raced. Who, or what, was this voice, this presence? *Does it fear detection? Does it fear me? Or is it a deception?* It seemed it had been proved right in its guidance on the Staff's location, and right that someone would aid her; Beth's arrival had been as deadly as it had been dramatic. But again, who was it? Could she trust it?

Trust nothing, came her immediate answer.

And yet what if it could aid her?

As her thoughts spun, spiralled around, Tricia's face appeared, a forced smile on her lips, fear in her eyes. "You okay?" her friend said, her voice shaking as she knelt, placing a hand on Jessica's shoulder.

Jessica inwardly sighed. The unknown voice would have to wait. "I'm okay," she said, forcing her own smile. "Just resting."

"You can do that when you're dead." Tricia cast her eyes nervously around. "Right now, you need to figure out what we do now." She glanced to the valley. "Beth is back," she murmured, a glimmer of hope in her eyes. "Maybe we can just leave now?"

Leave? Yes, you, Erin, and the others are leaving. She glanced out into the darkness. *But Beth and I ...* "Help me up."

Grasping Tricia's proffered hand, Jessica climbed to her feet. She glanced to the collapsed rock wall where a faint glow emanated from the gaping hole above the shattered rubble. *I saw Beth emerge from there. What the hell happened?* "Is everyone okay? Where did ..." She froze, her stomach twisting. "River! Where is she?"

"Relax," Tricia said softly. "She looks surprisingly good for someone who was doing" – Tricia's brow furrowed – "whatever she was doing." She gestured to the shadows of the pillared entrance. "She's over there, watching the light show. Here, take this."

Allowing the moment of panic to settle, Jessica took the torch Tricia offered, then made her way to the shadowy gloom of the rock pillars. As she approached, she saw River sitting cross-legged, looking out into the valley, the Axe resting in her lap. She looked tired, scorched, but whole – and with a head of spiky, frazzled hair.

"Nice hair," Jessica said. "You look like you stuck your fingers in a plug."

River turned, her brow furrowing.

Jessica half smiled. "Never mind." Seating herself next the girl, she studied River's face. "How are you?"

"Exhausted, confused, but very happy to see Warrior Beth arrive. Very happy."

She saw the weariness in the girl's eyes. *River's eyes – and River's soul. This is River, not Revri.*

And Revri …?

That question would be asked …. *But first …* Her stomach twisted. "Did you destroy the shaman?"

River grimaced. "The daemon was too strong. I could not pass. I am sorry."

She reached out and placed her hand on River's arm. "You did more than enough tonight. You saved us."

River held Jessica's gaze. "The shaman escaped tonight, but one day, your revenge will come."

Jessica heard the utter conviction in the girl's words. She drew a silent breath. *And in this, I agree. It* will *happen.*

She looked out into the darkness of the plain beyond, seeing flashes of jagged lightning as Beth continued to battle the daemon. The air was pungent with a sharp, acrid smell, and swirls of spent energy swept past in the ether. As another crack of thunder rent the air, she shook her head in astonished wonder. "How does she do this? And how did she get here?"

"She is a Warrior," River said simply. "And get here?" She hesitated. "I spoke with Iolaire. It seems the Warrior has been here for some time."

"What!" Jessica exclaimed, turning to face River.

"She was protecting the Staff, awaiting our arrival."

Jessica stared at River, her thoughts suddenly twisting and tumbling. *Then the Staff is here. Inside the mountain. But Beth …* "How long has she been here?"

"Since you left my Land."

Jessica gasped. "She's been in there since … since I left? For thirteen thousand years?"

"Iolaire believes this is so."

Jessica's aghast gaze fell blindly on River. *Thirteen thousand years … It can't be …*

As the chilling revelation settled like a poison, numbness crept over her. Beth had been here through all the ages since they'd parted? Through year after year, century after century? *For millennia ...* Her mind recoiled, refusing to believe. How was it possible? How could Beth have survived? *How could her mind have survived?* "It just can't be true," she said in a whisper.

"I only tell of what Iolaire believes." River's expression darkened. "And it seems the Warrior may have had little choice."

"She was imprisoned?" Jessica breathed.

"It may be. Iolaire is uncertain. It seems this secret has been deeply buried."

Imprisoned within the mountain ... for thirteen millennia ...

Heartrending sorrow filled her. *Beth ... what happened? What did they do to you?*

Sudden anger burned through the numbness enveloping her soul. "You say this has been hidden, held as a secret, yet someone knows what happened. Someone locked her in there for millennia. Alone!"

"It is hard to accept," River said quietly.

"Hard to accept? No, it's vile, it's sickening. Nothing anyone could say would justify this." Jessica looked out at the continuing storm. Imprisoned. For an eternity. What would that do to a person? *What has it done to Beth?* "Who would do such a thing?"

"One who knew better than us that we would need her here."

Jessica spun back to face River. "Nothing can justify locking my friend in this place for millennia. Nothing!"

River's expression was unflinching. "Yet I say again, we needed her."

Jessica made to say something more ... but despite her anger, the echoes of River's words silenced her. For deep beneath her simmering rage, her own thoughts answered. *River is right. We needed Beth. She saved us.*

River tightened her grip on her Axe. "We must repay a small piece of the debt we owe this Warrior. We must complete our mission. We must find the Staff and return home."

The Staff ... Repay the debt ... Despite the anger of the moment, Jessica knew this was also true. And those other words of River? *'One who knew better than us ...'* Who knew? The voice she had heard? The daemons? *What game is being played here?*

As her anger ebbed, cold certainty took its place. Whatever the game being played, it was one she needed to better understand. One she would better understand. *I will repay the debt owed Beth – and I will find out who did this to her.*

A series of lightning flashes tore across the sky.

"She has not been outside for … a while," River murmured. "I doubt she wishes to return – but knows she must."

Jessica grimaced. *What does Beth truly know in this moment? What does she feel?*

She is a Warrior, came the cool response from deep inside.

And there again was a terrifying reality of this unfolding nightmare. *We cannot yet walk away. This Land is drawing us in, leading us … somewhere.*

"We must enter the mountain," River said.

Enter the mountain and recover the Staff. Return and find Lanky.

And then?

She dragged her fingers through her unkempt hair. *No use standing here worrying. Act.*

The shock of Beth's incarceration raw and lingering, Jessica pulled her unsettled gaze from the valley and fixed it on River. *Here lies another mystery.* "You hold an Axe …"

A flicker of unease crossed the girl's face. "Yes, I become a Warrior, it seems." River looked down at the Axe in her lap. "I remember the battle clearly – yet I did not feel in control."

"You named yourself Revri."

River took a moment to answer. "Maybe I did, but who is Revri?" She glanced at Jessica, the fierce intensity in her eyes dulled by a shadow of fear. "I held so much power in my hands. Iolaire aided me, but Revri controlled me." Her eyes glinted in the torch's light. "I believe she was once a Warrior, an ancient Warrior long before my time."

Jessica frowned. Revri, Jalu, these names of others unknown. *What are—*

"And they call you the Guardian," River said in a quiet voice. "The Staff Holder."

Jessica's breath caught. The Guardian. The name the daemon, Alkazar, had used. The name Revri had used. *The name the burnt man of my nightmare used …* "You used this name. What does it mean?"

"I don't know. I'm struggling to understand what *I* am, *who* I am – and what I have become."

What I have become …

Jessica cast a suddenly fearful glance to the glowing entrance in the rock wall. *The Guardian. The Staff Holder. And the Staff lies within this mountain …* What awaited her here? Familiar frustration welled. They'd been thrown into the fight, blindfolded and unprepared, by entities unseen. And now, too much was happening with too little time to understand.

Her steely brown eyes turned back to River, the faintest flash of green flaring before dying as an ember spiralling from a fire. "You said Beth must be repaid," she grated. "You're right. But someone else needs to pay – and I will find out who." She climbed to her feet, then faced the glowing entrance. "We should go. It's time to see what awaits us."

"And them?" River said, nodding to the group silently watching them.

Jessica frowned. "Yes, this mess. A moment only, then we leave."

*

Fletcher was still shaking. It was far beyond him to understand the horrific sights, sounds, and feelings of this horrendous night – way beyond him – but he knew he never wished to experience them ever again. He glanced briefly at Erin, who sat quietly in the light of an upturned torch on the ground.

She avoided his eyes.

He winced. How they had ended up at each other's throats, each attempting to strangle the other, he didn't know. Rage and disgust had appeared from nowhere. At her incompetence; at her sly looks; at her nasty comments; a litany of her evil slights against him. Before he knew what was happening, they had attacked each other, each maniacally trying to kill the other. How long they fought, he didn't know, but suddenly, accompanied by crackling bursts of lightning and thunder, the rage had vanished, leaving them both holding the other by the throat, staring at one another as though each was mad. He was still fighting to make sense of it, but as yet hadn't had the courage to speak to Erin.

He looked up as the once missing Jessica walked over with the girl with the Axe – the one who had bravely fought against the terrors that had descended upon them. Who was she? He glanced at Jessica. And who was this woman, the one who seemed to sit in the midst of the impenetrable web surrounding their disappearance?

Jessica placed her torch on the ground, adding to the light around them, then stood, gazing down at them. "We've little time. Each of you know some of what is happening here. Admittedly, some less than others." She glanced at Fletcher, then looked back around the group. "Our goal from the start has been to get Beth and Lanky back, and—"

"Well, we got Beth back," Tricia interjected.

"... and to get River back to her time," Jessica continued. She turned to Fletcher. "This has been a distressing way to learn more of what's been happening, and I know I give you so little time, but I have to ask you, what do you intend to do now?"

Do? What can I possibly do after this? "Right now, I don't know," he mumbled, struggling to accept – to believe – what he'd seen and felt this dread night. And what he'd done. "I attempted to kill your friend tonight. I don't think I'm best placed to make calls on what next, do you?"

Jessica saw his genuine pain. "Don't blame yourself for whatever thoughts raged within you tonight," she said softly. "Or for whatever you did. This entity River battled was the stuff of nightmares, a visitation from hell."

"But you didn't succumb," he whispered.

She seemed about to respond ... but remained silent.

"So, you're going to go in there?" Erin said, glancing to the rock-strewn cave entrance. "You're going to go back to ... to that other place?"

"I must. I owe it to Lanky."

Fletcher heard the faintest edge of fear in her voice.

"And Beth?" Erin asked as a crack of thunder rolled in from the continuing battle in the valley below.

"She will return with us," said the girl with the Axe.

Fletcher noticed Jessica turn in surprise. The axe lady smiled a thin smile and held up the Axe. "I understand all you say."

Jessica studied her for a moment, then nodded.

"I can't go in there," came Erin's whispered voice. "I can't go with you. I just can't."

Jessica's face softened. "I'm not asking you to, Erin. And even if you wanted to, I wouldn't let you come. There are things happening here that I can't draw you into."

A look of immense relief crossed Erin's face – yet a sadness burnt in her eyes.

Jessica's attention shifted back to Fletcher. "I ask again. What is your intent?"

He tried to settle his scattered thoughts. *I understand nothing of what I've seen. What the hell do I do now? What do I report back?* He took a deep breath and climbed to his feet. *Focus on the here and now.* "My goal from the start has been to find Lanky, you, and your friend. So far, I've found you." He hesitated, girding himself for what he was about to do. "You believe you can find the others? You can bring them home?"

"I do," Jessica said, holding his gaze.

He searched her face, seeing nothing but a surety of purpose. He glanced back at the girl with the axe, a girl who had done things he didn't understand but who had clearly protected them from demonic forces that had sought to destroy them – entities beyond his means to engage. He looked back at Jessica, his decision made. "I'm trusting that you can bring Lanky home. And bring your friend home. The rest … It won't be easy, but I'll find a way to deal with this. To explain it." He turned to Erin. "But I'll need help."

Erin looked up and met his eyes. She gave a brief nod, then held up her hand. "Help me up." He helped her to her feet, then she stood, studying his face. "You've seen what we've seen. I think we can help each other. And I'm sorry for … hurting you."

He grimaced. "It should be I who apologises. I—"

"Save the apologies until later," Jessica said sharply. "It's time you left."

"Are you sure of this, Jess?" Tricia said, her eyes flicking to the glowing opening in the cliff face.

"I'm sure. I have to bring Beth and Lanky back."

"Then I'm coming with you."

"No," Jessica said firmly. "You're not. You're going to head back with the others. I can't …" She frowned, then spun around, eyes fixed on the pillared entrance to the clearing.

A furious pressure erupted in Fletcher's head, and he watched in astonishment as a powerful figure strode into view between the rocky bluffs.

"Come, Guardian!" the fierce woman commanded. "There is work to be done!"

Spellbound, he watched as the young woman known as Beth, tendrils of smoke streaming from her body, strode past them and on up the scree slope to the glowing cave. Halfway up the slope, the steely-faced woman stopped and turned. "Where is the traitor?" she asked in an ominous voice, her ruthless eyes looking around the clearing. Then her head snapped to the glowing opening. "You fools! Pray that we are not too late!"

Fletcher watched in bewilderment as she strode up the slope, then on into the cave entrance, disappearing from view. "What traitor?" he said, turning to the others.

"Robert!" Tricia exclaimed. "Where's Robert?"

Robert … In the aftermath of the brutal attack, he'd forgotten about him. "Why does she call Robert a traitor? Why—"

"He's not here," the axe lady said, walking up to Jessica. "We must follow Beth."

Jessica stared at the glowing cave entrance. "He's going after the Staff. But why?" Her expression hardening, her gaze sought out Fletcher. "You seem a good man, Sergeant. I trust you. Look after my friends and do what you need to do to help them. To protect them."

That won't be easy. "I will," he said simply.

Jessica faced Erin and Tricia. "No time for long goodbyes," she said softly. "I will be back." Ignoring Tricia's pleas to join her, she stepped forward and hugged each of them in turn. "Get back to your car and get ready to go. If Robert doesn't return soon, then leave. That's in your hands now." Her gaze lingered on them, then she strode off with River by her side.

Fletcher stepped to Erin and Tricia's side and watched Jessica and River climb up the scree slope towards the cave. As they disappeared from view, his thoughts darkened. *I've let them walk away. I've let them step into the unknown.* He shivered. *An unknown to me, but to them …?*

He stood in silence for a while, then loosed a fraught sigh. "We better get going. Who knows what else may arrive here?" He reached down to pick up a torch—

"Trish, no!" Erin cried out behind him. "Come back!"

Fletcher spun around and saw Tricia running up the scree slope towards the entrance. As Erin made to follow, he grabbed her arm, pulling her back. "No! It's too dangerous."

"But she's going after them!"

"You heard your friend. They'll send her back."

Erin stared wide-eyed after her friend. "Trish! What are you doing?" she shouted as Tricia disappeared into the entrance. Then she turned to him, tears glistening in her eyes. "What do we do?" she whispered.

Fletcher glanced back to the entrance. "Jessica was clear. We can't go in." *I can't risk another life.* "So, we wait. Jessica will send her back out."

But as his words drifted away into the darkness, ominous doubts rose. Maybe the horrors of this night were not yet complete.

CHAPTER THIRTY-TWO

She remembered this adjustment. But others ...?

His lungs straining as he pushed onwards towards his prize, Robert ran down the wide tunnel, plagued by the horror that had assaulted him outside: a malevolent, hateful presence that had driven its baleful claws deep into his soul, forcing him to almost fatal despair. Only when the fearsome woman had appeared from the bowels of the mountain had the deadly pressure released from his mind, allowing him to slip away in the confusion.

Slip away to find the Staff.

I must gain the Staff!

Yet a gnawing unease had settled on him. What was that evil that had tainted his thoughts? And had not the friend of Jessica saved them? *I'm betraying them. I'm ...*

No!

No, he couldn't falter now, allowing these weak thoughts and emotions to detract from his goal. A goal set many years ago by the great god that had spoken with him, promising he would free them – free those most dear to him.

I must save them.

And now this mighty god had spoken again, telling him the Staff was his, telling him where it lay. He had to reach it before the others.

Robert rushed on towards his target. *So close now.*

A distant light appeared in the tunnel, and racing on, he soon entered a huge well-lit chamber, the polished white stone of its gleaming walls and ceiling dancing with yellow and red light. In the centre of the chamber stood a raised platform.

His heart thundered in his chest. *This is the place my god described.*

His eyes locked onto the platform. But where was the Staff? He stepped forward, frantically scanning the chamber. *Where is it?*

"Looking for this?" came a relaxed voice from his right.

Robert gasped as a tall figure strolled out from behind a stone pillar, the Staff held casually in one hand. "Who ... who are you?" he stammered. *No one should be here! Only the Staff.*

"One who is preventing you from condemning us all."

Dazed, a terrible dread rising, Robert forced himself to step towards the calm-faced stranger.

"Don't even think about it," the man said evenly. "You couldn't fight a mouse and win, and I won't hesitate to kill you." The man tilted his head. "Is that what you want?"

Robert stared at the stranger, despair flooding through him. *I can't fight him.* He glanced to the most precious object in the man's hand. *But the Staff ... I need the Staff.* Trembling, he tried to move – but the heartrending truth held his feet frozen in place. *I can't take it from him. He would kill me.*

His world crumbled around him. Everything he had worked towards for most of his life was vanishing in front of him. "Please, you must let me have it," he pleaded. "They will kill them if I don't. Please!" He realised he was on his knees, tears streaming down his face. "Please—"

"No!" The icy voice rent the air, menacing echoes reverberating around the chamber.

As Robert spun around, he saw the fearsome woman striding towards him, death written on her face. A part of his tortured mind knew who this was. *Beth. The friend Jessica spoke of. One who the Iyes call a Warrior.*

And she is about to kill me.

The stranger with the Staff quickly stepped between him and the Warrior. "You can't do this, Bethusa."

"Try stopping me," the woman snarled, continuing to stride towards him.

"I *will* try," the young man replied in a calm voice, "and in doing so, I may die – but I will try."

The fearsome Warrior slowed – then halted. "Move!" she commanded, quivering with rage. "He must die for what he has done."

The man stood calmly resolute. "It is not his time."

The Warrior snorted her disgust – yet her face grew uncertain.

"You have done what was needed," the unknown man said.

The Warrior glared at the man, but her rage seemed to be wavering.

Then she shook her head and blinked. The aura of destruction around the Warrior vanished, and in a metamorphosis so unexpected that Robert scarcely believed his own eyes, a tired young woman now stood before him.

"Welcome back," the young man said, the faintest sense of relief in his voice.

"He needs to pay for what he has done," Beth said, her eyes locked onto Robert.

"Agreed. But now I'm confident he will get a fair hearing." He looked slowly around the chamber before resting his gaze back on Beth. "Was it so long ago we came here? Were forced here, I should say." His eyes brightened. "Yet what a time together. We've grown here together, we've fought here together, we've protected this Continuum from those of the Dark who seek to enter. We are Warriors, lovers, friends. We are one." He smiled. "I've grown used to this place, and even to the cursed Gate." His face suddenly seemed tired, drawn with hidden sorrow. "But we knew this time would come. We knew we must part."

A tear rolled down Beth's cheek. "You can still come with us."

The man stepped to her, and reaching out, he caught the falling drop. "You know that's not possible. My final task is here, and then I must return." He hesitated. "But not as I am. Nor you as you are."

"I don't understand," Beth said, her voice breaking. "Why must this be? After all we've endured at the Gate? We've earned this time. Please … it's not fair."

The young man's sigh was heartfelt. "You know that can't be. If we stay now …" He paused, looking over at the passageway. "They're coming," he whispered. "I must hide – they'll misunderstand if they see me now."

"Don't do it!" Beth cried, tears now streaming down her face. "We've given enough. Let others do what's needed now."

The man leaned close. "We have loved," he said with a gentle kiss. "But unless we do what is needed, we may never have loved at all."

Beth reached out and pulled him into a fierce embrace. "I will find you," she said, her voice steadying. "I will find a way," she continued with passion.

The stranger broke the embrace but held on to her hand and looked into her eyes. "And when you do, I look forward to seeing that beautiful smile."

She looked at him, tears still streaming down her face – and smiled.

"See. Who can resist that?"

The echo of footsteps grew closer.

"Stay strong," whispered the man, squeezing her hand. "And remember me."

He pulled his hand away, slipping the Staff into her open palm. Beth closed her hand around it.

The unknown man turned away, walking towards a tunnel to the rear of the chamber, where a faint golden light pulsed. Pausing, he glanced back and smiled. "And remember, the wine tastes sweetest on the harshest trails we tread." He held his hand up to his heart, then turned, and was gone.

Robert, drained and utterly defeated, watched Beth hold her hand to her heart, then drop to her knees, staring blindly towards the golden light.

And behind her, two women rushed into the chamber.

"What have you done?" Jessica hissed, glaring at him.

*

Jessica rushed into the massive chamber and came to a halt, staring at the scene before her: Beth squatting on the ground, head in her hands, slowly rocking to and fro with the Staff by her side; Robert standing, shoulders slumped, his face drawn, his eyes distraught. "What have you done?"

Robert flinched but said nothing.

Jessica gestured to River. "Watch him," she said, then strode over to Beth. Wretched anguish sliced through her as she saw the deep distress on her friend's face. *Locked in here for millennia.* How much had she suffered? And what terrible hurt now? As River stood beside Robert, forcing him to kneel, Jessica dropped to the ground beside her friend. "Beth," she whispered. "Are you okay?"

Beth continued to rock back and forth. She gave no answer.

Jessica's heart wrenched. What had they done to her? What unknown horrors had she endured? She placed a gentle hand on her friend's shoulder. "I'm here for you now, Beth," she whispered. "I will help you." *In whatever way we can, we'll help you.*

Beth said nothing.

As the stunning vision of Beth storming out of the mountain to fight the daemon flashed through her mind, a shocking thought forced its way to the fore. *Is this still Beth?*

She forced the thought away. *This is my friend. She needs me.* "Take your time," she said, gently squeezing her friend's shoulder. "I'm here. I'm not going anywhere without you."

Beth continued rocking, her eyes downcast.

Tormented by her own anguish, Jessica climbed to her feet and turned to River. Her anger flared as her gaze fell on the bookseller. "Get him up," she demanded, striding over to them.

River hauled the limp man to his feet.

Jessica glared at him. "What happened here? And I've no time for lies."

Robert, shoulders slumped, his cheeks streaked with tears, stood shaking, not meeting her eyes. "I lost," he whispered. "And now I have lost them."

"Lost who?"

"My parents ... I failed them."

What! "What have your parents got to do with this?"

The bookseller finally looked up at her, his tear-streaked face wrought with pain. "I thought they were dead," he whispered. "But then *he* spoke to me, told me they were captive in a land, far, far away. He could save them, he said, but needed the artefact – he needed the Staff. All I needed to do was ..." He glanced over towards Beth. "But I failed – and now they will die."

He wants the Staff? To free his parents? "Who told you this? Who asked you to do this?"

"One who can help you," Robert said, a sudden savage desire on his face. "He *will* help you." Hope burned in his glistening eyes. "What do you need? We can talk with him, and he will understand."

Jessica glared at him. "Who? Who can help us?"

"A god," he answered in a hushed voice. "An ancient god. One with great power."

An ancient god ... Her chest tightened with the brutal certainty of who this would be. "And did this god tell you his name?"

"I can't tell. He said never to tell."

Jessica loomed over the pitiful man. "Tell me his name. Else I'll ask this Warrior to talk with you alone."

River hefted her Axe.

Robert's eyes flicked to her. He licked his lips. "Kaos," he whispered. "His name is Kaos."

River gasped.

Disbelieving, Jessica stared down at the bookseller, a cold chill settling over her. Kaos. The one who was rising against the Iyes. The one who sought to destroy that peoples' land. *The one who stands behind the burnt man.*

Robert's eyes locked onto hers. "This god can help us. See around you now, see what he foretold. He knew the Staff of Power lay hidden in my land. He knew I could find it. He knew—"

"Knew *you* could find it? It was Lanky who found the Staff."

"Yes, but who was his inspiration for this? Who gave him all he needed to find it?" Robert's face filled with pain. "I tried, but I failed. I needed someone who could see the things I couldn't. Lanky proved an invaluable asset."

"An asset? Is that all he was to you?"

Robert's eyes flashed. "No!" he said fiercely. "No, he was always more than that. Much, much more."

The acute passion in the man's words was visceral. *He was always much more ...* Sudden realisation struck. She looked again at Robert's face, seeing the lines of his mouth, the shape of his nose ... *Could it be?*

Robert held her gaze. "There is an evil in the land," he said in a quieter voice. "Surely you can see this. Look at the violence and destruction around us. We are destroying ourselves. We are destroying the world. With the aid of the Staff, he can help prevent this – he *will* prevent it."

Jessica fought to contain a surge of anger. Anger that this man could endanger the life of one she now believed was his son, and anger that he endangered the lives of her friends. "You are a fool," she hissed. "You've been misled. You follow the wrong god. You—"

"You believe you follow the right path," Robert said, shaking his head. "I understand. It is not your fault. But look at the violence you saw tonight, see what evils you felt. You don't see that you are part of this. You don't—"

"We fought that evil, you fool!" Jessica shouted, glaring at the traitor.

"I know you truly believe what you do is right, but you are caught in something you don't understand. Join me. Let us take the Staff to his people – you will see the truth of his words."

"And who are these people?"

"A proud and great people, the Ka. They aid the god's efforts to remove the evil from the world. Please," he said, holding out his hands. "Join us, and we can help them with their fight." His eyes shone with fervid desperation. "And you can help me save my parents."

An imperious voice echoed around the chamber. "They will already be dead, you fool."

Jessica glanced across to see Beth slowly climbing to her feet.

"No!" Robert cried, his eyes wide. "You lie! The Staff – all I need to do is give them the Staff." He turned to Jessica, desperate need shining in his eyes. "You must help me. It is the only way."

She ignored him, her eyes studying Beth as she slowly walked towards them. A hard smile played on her friend's lips, and her eyes blazed with wrathful fury. Jessica suppressed a cold knot of fear. Was this still her friend?

Beth stopped a short distance from them. "As this planet has journeyed around its sun, I have been locked in this place, fighting at the Gate, millennia spent defending this world from the savage hordes of the Dark." She took a step forward, baring her teeth. "And for thirteen thousand years, I have sensed the grand changes in this land around me: the growth and decay of the ice; the vast journeys of animals and people across the planet; the futile wars – the futile loves – of those same animals and people." She glared at Robert. "And for servants of the Dark, my patience has worn thin – I have no patience." She hefted her Axe, moving her hand back for the throw.

Jessica froze as she realised what was about to happen. "No!"

Beth released the weapon. It flew straight and true, striking Robert cleanly in the head. His head cleaved, he fell like a stone. And lay still.

Silence.

Jessica stood stock-still in horror as the blood streamed from the fatal wound. *She killed him. She executed him.*

"We need to go," Beth growled, holding out the Staff to Jessica. "Others of the Dark may soon arrive."

Her hands trembling, Jessica stared at her friend, waves of revulsion sweeping over her. How could she have done this? How could she have mercilessly killed the bookseller in cold blood? She saw her friend's ice-cold eyes staring back at her. *No, this is not my friend, this is not Beth. This is another.* "Why?" she stammered, an overwhelming sense of despair swamping the chamber. "Why did you kill him?"

Beth cast her contemptuous eyes over the dead man's body. "He served the Dark. He chose the wrong side in this battle." She looked back up at Jessica, a glacial rage in her eyes. "I sacrificed all to aid you, and this feeble scum almost destroyed all that had been done." She bared her teeth. "He condemned himself by his actions."

A traitor, yes, but to be executed like this? She caught movement by the entranceway, and turned to see Tricia on her knees, her hands over her face. *Trish! No! What are you doing here? You didn't need to see this.* She turned back to Beth. *No one needed to see this.* "You didn't need to kill him," she whispered.

Beth glared at her. "Do not waste your breath on this one, Guardian. Your battles lie elsewhere." She turned to walk away. "We waste time. We must go."

Jessica grabbed her arm, burgeoning anger sweeping through her. Drawing a hissed breath, she squared up to Beth. "I say again," she said through gritted teeth. "You didn't need to kill him."

Beth faced her, her face cold, unrepentant. "He was of the Dark. He served Kaos."

Jessica glared at Beth. "Misled by Kaos, yes. Served Kaos, maybe not. And even if he worked for the Dark, who gave you the right to do that!" she hissed, gesturing to Robert's prone body with one hand and pushing Beth's shoulder with the other. "Who gave you the prerogative – the authority – to pass judgement on that man! To pass sentence on that man!" Pushing her face into Beth's, she demanded, "Who!"

Beth smiled at Jessica, her eyes suddenly burning like fire. "I have learnt the judgement of man from thirteen thousand years of listening." She pushed back. "Of listening to the cries of the innocents as they are slaughtered in their mother's arms, or as they cower, quivering in fear before their executioner, not understanding their crime." She pushed Jessica backwards again, her smile hardening. "I have learnt from the screams of those who lay dying in fields of blood, dying for a cause not understood. And I have learnt from those who suffer in silence, unheard, unwitnessed by the world around them." She cocked her head. "Silent? No, they are not silent at home with the one they loved – they scream like the others when broken and beaten. But unheard. Yes, unheard."

Beth glared at Jessica. "And all this suffering because of men like this," she spat. "Men with spines of water. Clever men – oh yes, clever, devious men – but men willing to sacrifice innocent, unsuspecting lives to chase their own worthless goals. And what did this achieve?" she asked in an icy voice. "These millennia spent destroying others. Torturing others. Nothing! NOTHING!"

Jessica faced the woman's cold fury, unblinking, but quivering with her own rage. "That may be so, but you've just become one of them."

"You know nothing," Beth spat. She strode across to the fallen bookseller, grasped the bloodied Axe in her free hand, then paced to the stone platform. Pulling herself up onto the dais, she stood tall, then held out the Staff. "We leave now!" she commanded. "I have had enough of this place."

Jessica stared at her, shaking, a flood of tumultuous emotions fouling her mind: rage, horror, and utter disbelief that Robert was dead. Nausea twisted her stomach. *He never deserved this. Whatever he did, he never deserved to die like this.*

"Iolaire calls her Bethusa," River whispered by her side. Jessica turned to see the Iyes girl staring at Beth, a deep tiredness etched on her face. "As with Revri, I believe her to be an ancient Warrior."

Bethusa. The swirling mists obscuring shapeless memories briefly parted. *I have heard this name before. I know this name.* And that was chilling. *How can that be?*

River looked to Jessica. "I don't know what really happened here and am truly sorry for this man's death. But we cannot stay. We must return. I must return."

At River's words, cold numbness descended over her. And a stark reality. *I came here for the Staff. I came here to get Beth and Lanky back.* Whatever horrific madness gripped Beth, Lanky remained trapped in another time. *I have no choice; I must attempt to travel back to the time of the Iyes.*

She glanced at River. "Give me a moment."

River nodded. She crossed over to the dais and climbed up next to Beth.

Feeling sick to the core, Jessica walked past the bloodied body of Robert, then knelt down by Tricia's side.

"I've made a terrible mistake, Jess," Tricia said in a whisper. "I shouldn't have come. I wish I'd never seen …" She glanced over at the dead man, then looked away, raw anguish in her eyes.

Jessica felt cold. *I wish none of this had happened. I wish I'd never met Lanky. I wish I'd never seen this Staff. I wish …* She hardened herself to the heart-wrenching regret. She wished many things, but none of it changed anything. She was here. Robert was dead. Lanky was trapped in another time. *I must act.* She placed a shaking hand on Tricia's shoulder. "I know," she whispered. "This is hell. But I have to keep moving. I have to find a way back to Lanky." *The Staff … I must somehow use the Staff …*

Tricia looked up at Jessica, her face distraught. "I can't leave you alone with this, Jess. If you're going, then I'm coming with you." She looked over to Robert's dead body. "I don't know how I can help, but I know I can help more than that."

Jessica studied Tricia, suddenly uncertain what to do. If she could find a way to travel back to the time of the Iyes, there was no way that Tricia should go with her … *And yet Bear tells of four Warriors. Lanky, Beth, River … If I am the Guardian, then am I also the fourth Warrior? Or does that Axe belong to another yet unrevealed?*

Like Tricia?

"We must leave," came Beth's insistent voice. "Now!"

Tricia grasped Jessica's arm. "I can't stay here, Jess. Not while you and Beth need help."

Jessica wavered. *But you can't help us.*

She can if she is the fourth Warrior, she answered herself.

That doesn't matter. We just need to find Lanky, and get home.
Home? But I'm the Guardian.
So what! What the hell is the Guardian!
'One who is needed,' came the ethereal voice.

Jessica felt as if her mind was tearing itself apart.

"Please, Jess," Tricia whispered. "You need friends by your side. I can help. Somehow, I can help you."

Jessica fought to calm her fractious thoughts. *Ignore all else – focus on what's before you now.* She held Tricia's gaze, selfish hope rising in her heart. *Another friend by my side …* "Are you certain of this?" she whispered. "We may not … we may not get back."

The fear in Tricia's eyes deepened. "No, I'm not certain at all. But I am coming with you."

"Now, Guardian!" Beth commanded.

Tricia glanced to the stone platform. "And that isn't Beth. I don't know who it is, but it isn't Beth."

Jessica looked up at the intimidating – *terrifying even* – woman glaring down at them. The most frightening thought was that they were both wrong. That it *was* Beth. She pushed the dread thought away. This was Beth in body only. *It must be.*

She looked back at Tricia. *She may be a Warrior. You may need her help.* Gritting her teeth, she forced herself to her feet. "Stay close and follow me."

Tricia quickly stood, then glanced over at Robert's body. "What about …?"

Jessica followed her gaze. *Yes, how could she leave the bookseller like this?*

A thought sprang unbidden. *The Warrior, Bethusa, was right; Robert made a deal with the devil. He deserved …*

She slammed a hold on the contemptible thought, sickened that she'd allowed it to come to the fore.

'And yet, therein lies some truth,' said the ethereal voice.

Jessica's eyes flicked around her. "Who are you?" she whispered.

No answer came.

Jessica clenched her fist. Someone was playing games. But who?

With a sharp release of breath, she glanced back at Robert's bloodied body. The sudden sense of guilt was raw. *I should go to the sergeant, Fletcher. I should tell him all.* Her sense of guilt deepened. *But I can't. I must keep moving.* "I feel sick, Trish, but there's nothing we can do here. We have to leave the officer to deal with this." *Somehow, he needs to deal with what we've left.*

Her face drawn, Tricia said nothing.

Jessica took her hand. "We need to go."

Tricia gave a faint nod.

Her gut twisting, Jessica walked with Tricia to the platform, where they clambered up to stand beside River.

Jessica faced Beth. "What do we do?" she said in a cold voice.

"Take us back," Beth said, a drip of blood falling from the Axe held loosely in one hand. Lifting her other hand, she held out the Staff. "You need this."

Jessica frowned. "I don't know—"

"You are the Guardian," Beth rasped. "The Staff Holder. Take the Staff."

Scowling, Jessica grabbed it from her hand. "Fine. What do I need to do?"

"You are the Guardian."

Her eyes blazing, Jessica took a step towards Beth. "Stop saying that, damn you! I don't know what that means."

A gentle hand rested on her shoulder. "Jessica," River said softly.

Jessica continued to glare at Beth.

"Jessica," River pressed. "Iolaire says you must make use of the Staff now, before it's too late."

She turned to River, frustration boiling. "But how? I don't know how."

"Iolaire says this knowledge lies within you. Of how to travel. Of how to navigate the timelines of the Continuum."

Jessica snorted a bitter laugh. "Then she's wrong. I know nothing of this Continuum." She glared down at the Staff. "I know nothing of how to use this cursed thing."

"Believe in Iolaire's words. Believe, then focus on what you want to do. The Staff will aid you. It will allow us to travel."

Travel ... River's words pushed through her anger. *This is why I'm here. To return to Lanky. To help him get home.* "But how?" she whispered.

"Focus your mind on what you want. Focus all your energy on that."

I know what I want. I want ... She gasped at a sudden flurry of startling visions. Discordant visions, fragmented visions. Of unknown people, of unfamiliar places. Of a vast, midnight-black vista scattered with a myriad of swirling galaxies. Of two lifeforms appearing as pillars of intense white light. Of a roiling sun looming beyond. Of ...

She forced the bewildering scenes from her mind. What was happening to her? She looked blindly around. *What am I?*

'Please,' came River's voice. *'Use the Staff now before others come. Focus on what you want to do.'*

Focus on what you want ... River's words echoed, insistent. *But what does that mean?*

Despairing, she looked out from the dais ...

And she saw the broken body of the bookseller on the ground.

Realisation struck with a sharp intake of breath. *Focus on what you want.*

As she stared at the bloodied body, at the one who had been so senselessly slaughtered, her hand clenched tightly around the Staff. *I know what I want.*

Standing tall, she set herself as though to face an oncoming storm. Then, ignoring everything but the Staff in her hands, she poured her heart and soul into her wish. *This is what I wish.*

'And so, I will aid you,' came a woman's voice; calm, yet steeled with an unbending will.

She cried out as a granite-like force gripped her soul. Pain exploded, then a sickening wrench seemed to tear her apart.

Darkness. Hellish creatures screaming in frenzied rage as they strove to reach her. Tremendous pressures assailing her mind, her soul. Yet she lived. Somehow, she survived.

Then a tremendous crack and the darkness vanished.

Waves of pain fast receding, she staggered. Steadying herself, she looked up in dazed confusion – she stood before Robert, the Staff warm in *her* hand.

Drawing deep, shuddering lungfuls of air, she heard a voice.

Robert was talking.

"A proud and great people, the Ka. They aid the god's efforts to remove the evil from the world. Please, join us, and we can help them with their fight. And you can help me save my parents."

A terrible ache in her head, Jessica stared at the bookseller. *I ... I've heard this already.*

Haven't I?

An imperious voice echoed around the chamber. "They will already be dead, you fool."

She glanced around to see Beth slowly climbing to her feet. A shiver ran down her spine. *I have seen this. I know this.*

"No!" Robert cried. "You lie! The Staff – all I need to do is give them the Staff." He turned to Jessica. "You must help me. It is the only way."

Jessica watched as Beth slowly walked towards them, a hard smile on her lips, her eyes blazing with wrathful fury. Fighting to clear the fog from her mind, Jessica watched Beth stop a short distance from them. "As this planet has journeyed around its sun, I have been locked in this place, fighting at the Gate, millennia spent defending this world from the savage hordes of the Dark."

Jessica grasped at a nagging thought, one hovering at the fringes of her consciousness. *I did something just now. I changed something.*

But what? And why?

Beth took a step forward, baring her teeth. "And for thirteen thousand years, I have sensed the grand changes in this land around me: the growth and decay of the ice; the vast journeys of animals and people across the planet; the futile wars – the futile loves – of those same animals and people …"

The truth suddenly lanced into Jessica's mind. *She killed him! This happened before, and she killed him!*

Beth glared at Robert. "And for servants of the Dark, my patience has worn thin – I have no patience." Beth hefted her Axe, moving her hand back for the throw—

Jessica leapt forward and struck the side of Beth's head with the Staff.

Beth dropped like a stone.

"Jessica!" River cried. "What are you doing?"

Pivoting, Jessica found River facing her, Axe primed.

Her breathing ragged, Jessica held up her hands. "Hold! There's a reason for this." Fragments of shattered memories lay scattered, distant, yet hauntingly familiar. *She killed Robert. I'm sure of it. I have … corrected it.* She held River's eyes. "Trust me."

River's sharp eyes scanned Jessica's face, searching, evaluating … then the tension eased from the Iyes, and she dropped the Axe to her side.

Jessica immediately rushed to Beth's side and breathed a sigh of relief as she saw the gentle rise and fall of her friend's chest. She ran her fingers over her scalp, grimacing as she felt the huge swelling above the ear. *It will hurt, but nothing worse. No one died here tonight …*

Hearing a movement by the entranceway, she turned to see Tricia watching them, eyes wide. She climbed to her feet. "It's okay, Trish. You can come over."

Tricia hesitated, then slowly walked towards her. "Is she okay?" she whispered, looking down at Beth's prone form.

"She has a thick head. She'll be fine." Jessica saw the distress in Tricia's eyes. "Believe me, this had to be done." *I'm sure of it.*

Shaking, Tricia said nothing.

Jessica glanced across at Robert, who lay cowering on the ground, his fearful eyes flicking between her and River. A gruesome vision seared into her mind – him lying on the ground, blood streaming from a vicious wound in his head. Beth had killed him, she was sure. *But I took us back. Somehow, I prevented it from happening.*

But how?

'You are the Guardian,' came the ethereal voice that haunted her. *'You walk the timelines of the Continuum.'*

"Who are you?" she whispered.

Again, no answer came.

A game continued. But who played the game?

And who am I?

She shivered. *I am the Guardian.*

As ghostly images continued to flicker in the deepest shadows of her mind, she clenched the Staff tightly. She needed to return to Lanky ... *And I need to understand what's happening to us.* Because one brutal reality was clear. Devils of the Dark were here. In her world. In her time.

And one of them killed my sister.

"Jess?"

Steadying her shaking hand, she turned to Tricia.

"I know you told me to leave," Tricia whispered, her voice wavering. "And maybe I should have left. But I can't. You need friends by your side. I can help. Somehow, I can help you."

And somehow, I knew you would say that. Jessica placed her hand on her friend's shoulder. "If you're truly certain, I would like that very much."

Tricia nodded.

Jessica squeezed her shoulder, then turned to River, her expression hardening. "You and Trish get Beth up there. Move quickly – I don't want her waking up here."

Her attention shifted to the cowering man on the ground. "You!" she said, a bite to her voice. "You don't know how lucky you've been. You don't get to die tonight."

Robert looked at her blankly.

"They have deceived you," she continued, steel in her voice. "Someone used false promises to draw you to their sickly flame. You say your task was to deliver this Staff to them? That has failed. And one person will be very glad you failed. Lanky." She glared at the bookseller, taking a step towards him. "But how devastated will he be to hear your part in all this? You now get to walk out of here with your life. I suggest you use the rest of it more wisely." She raised her Staff. "And if I see you again ..."

She held up her hand as he tried to speak. "There's nothing more I want to hear from you. Go! You have ten seconds to clear this chamber. One … two …"

Robert scrambled to his feet.

"Three …"

The bookseller bowed his head, and with slumped shoulders he scurried to the tunnel entrance, a broken man – no, a treacherous coward who had betrayed the one who had trusted him.

As Robert disappeared from view, she made her way to the stone platform where the others were now waiting. She climbed up beside them, then glanced at River. A ghostly shard of a memory glistened. "Focus on what you want …" River's voice, words once spoken.

Fighting a sudden moment of doubt, she felt the surety of the Staff in her hand. *No doubts. Act.* Closing her eyes, and settling her thoughts, she formed the image of a time and a place in her mind – and the image of a young man with tousled hair.

'The energy you need is all around you,' said the ethereal voice.

Feeling the sudden warmth of the Staff in her hand, Jessica gasped as swirling rivers of diaphanous, shimmering light glowed in the ether around her. *The A'ven,* she thought, absently, mesmerised by the pulsating, restless aurora sweeping around her. *Energy of the Land. An energy I can use.*

'I will aid you, Guardian,' came the voice. *'And Jalu will aid you. But you must also aid us.'*

The Staff tingled in her hand, and the sense of another drew close. A formidable presence, one redolent of antiquity, one unyielding in their belief.

She blinked, and a sublime calm fell over her.

The Guardian instinctively knew what she must do.

Opening her mind, she reached for the A'ven … and smiled as a rich, vibrant energy swept into her, coursing through her veins with a pulsating, latent power. Without hesitation, she quickly scanned the ether for the Cord she needed, one whose silent vibrations hid it from all but the most powerful minds. Sensing the particular energy she needed, she locked onto the Cord—

A blistering surge of pent energy ripped through the ether, and the chamber vanished.

Moments later, together with a dazed River and Tricia carrying Beth, she guided them through the warded Threshold of a Gate.

Into the Void.

Agony seared her mind as the ravening creatures of the Dark descended in a rabid frenzy. She slammed up a shield, hearing the soul-chilling cries of fury from the seething horde denied their prize. Turning to the glowing wonder of the vast Continuum below her, she quickly scanned for the time she needed.

The age of the Iyes …

*

Sensing the disturbance in the ether as the Guardian travelled to a Gate, the young man stepped out from the shadows and walked back into the empty chamber. The pain was raw, his heart sundered. Yet still he believed. "We'll find a way, Beth. Somehow, we will find a way to be reunited."

'It may be possible,' came a familiar, soft-lilted voice in his mind.

The young man raised an eyebrow. *'Possible? I'd have thought you of all people, IY, would know that all things are possible. I'd have preferred you to have said "It will be so."'*

'That is not … possible.'

The man laughed. *Laugh, else I'll cry.*

'You need to return now,' IY murmured. *'You will not remember.'*

'I'm prepared.' I think. He looked around the chamber. *'How do I leave here?'*

'The Guardian. She will return.' There was a heartbeat's pause. *'If she understands.'*

The young man forced a smile. *'Then I will try not to kill her when I return to my people.'*

'That is possible.'

The man's breath caught. "I could truly kill the Guardian?"

No answer came. Then he sensed IY leave.

The man stood for a moment, a shadow of unease whispering inside. What devious game was being played? *I know a part. But which part?* Understanding the futility of the question, he sighed, then glanced around the chamber. His keen eyes landed on the stone dais. Did the Ancient still live in this time? What was she to the people of this age? He sighed again. Yet more questions that would remain unanswered for him. He knew what he knew, and all else lay with the vagaries of the gods.

He glanced further to his right to the dark shadows behind the two great stone pillars, beyond which lay the portals. *My home and Beth's for millennia.* A remembered acrid taste fouled his mouth. *We fought while we waited. We protected the Gate against the Dark's incursion into the Continuum.* The pang of grief was raw. Yes, he and Beth had protected the Staff, aiding the Guardian – but they had lost each other. Drawing a long, slow breath, he shook his head. "I hope this is all worth it."

And now, just one more task remained.

A short while later, he stood in the darkness of the entrance tunnel, studying the myriad of stars visible in the night sky through the opening ahead. *I could just walk out of here and explore this unknown new world of my future. I could learn. I could adapt. I could …* He hesitated. *I would then surely lose Beth … and Bethusa.*

Sighing, he steadied himself, then drew from the A'ven. Releasing a sizzling bolt of intense white energy, the roof of the tunnel ahead shattered, collapsing with a deep roar of crashing, splintering rocks.

He turned and strode away, a storm of dust and debris engulfing him.

Returning to the flickering light of the main chamber, he brushed himself down, then stood for a moment in silence.

In utter silence.

He held his breath and listened.

He heard nothing.

And after millennia exposed to the relentless fury of the Dark at the Gate, this was a true and exceptional wonder.

Except I lost her.

He took a slow breath. "And there is the irony," he said to the empty chamber. "What is the joy of silence without the voices of those you love?"

"Are you ready?" came a purposeful voice from the shadows.

He turned in surprise. "So, you understood quickly."

"*I* understood," the Guardian said simply. "I, Jalu."

The man tilted his head slightly, studying the tall young woman with the striking brown eyes he'd seen leave with Beth and the others. *It is the same woman, but …* "So, you've taken control? You take a great risk."

"For this moment only. You can't die here."

"Well, I thank you for that. And the other?"

"Until this task is done, she lies deep. We must leave. We don't have much time."

He forced a smile. "I thought you had all the time in the world."

The Guardian's determined eyes held his. "Yet what if that world ceased to exist?"

To that, he had no answer.

A short while later, he stood on the dais, holding her hand. "So, I won't remember." He cocked his head. "Will Beth?"

The woman's face was grim. "As with many, not until it is time."

A harsh smile played on his lips. "This cursed game—"

The force that struck him was immense, with a will as cold as ice. An explosion of pain erupted in his body and mind, and he felt himself torn from the chamber and thrust to a Gate – and then beyond the Threshold of the Gate into the Void. An onslaught of terrifying, distorted images flashed before him as the Guardian fought her way towards the time she sought. Bestial claws raked out at him, glinting razor-sharp as they sought to tear at his mind. Searing strikes of energy of the Dark thundered into them, rocking his soul to the core.

And yet the Guardian held the terrors at bay.

The assault around them became a swirling inferno of ferocious savagery.

And yet still the Guardian held firm.

He felt his mind beginning to fracture as the Void buckled and twisted under the immense cataclysm around them. *I'm dying. I—*

An immense crack of thunder ripped through him as they exited the Void and reentered the Continuum. In his time, his Land. With thunder reverberating around his skull, he staggered, gasping, staring blindly at the chamber around him—

Subtle pressure touched his mind. Darkness descended and he collapsed to the ground, his thirteen-thousand-year mission forgotten.

The Warrior now lay buried in the deepest, furthest reaches of his consciousness.

The man who remained groaned as he awakened from an uneasy and fitful sleep, one disturbed by hellish nightmares not suffered since he'd been a child. *Maybe one too many.* He inwardly cursed his foolishness – a fruitless curse uttered countless times before – then curled up, holding his thumping head, girding himself for the misery to be endured before he could engage once more with his wonderful, exhilarating life.

*

"Look! She's coming!" Erin cried, seeing a shadowy figure staggering out of the tunnel.

"That's not her," Fletcher said, frowning. "It's Robert!"

The figure caught sight of them. Then ran.

"Wait!" Fletcher shouted, moving towards the fleeing figure.

Erin grabbed his arm. "No, don't! We have to wait for Trish!"

Fletcher watched in confusion as the shadowy figure disappeared into the gloom. "What's he been doing in there?" His brow crinkled with indecision. "I should go after him, but after what's happened here, I can't leave you alone."

Erin held on to his arm. "And I don't want you to go." Cold with growing dread, she looked back to the glowing entrance. "Please, Trish," she whispered. "Get out of there."

They waited. And waited.

But it was not to be.

She screamed as an explosive crack shattered the silence, then cowered as the cliff face collapsed in a crashing rumble, thick clouds of dust billowing into the air.

When the air cleared, the entrance was gone.

"No!" Erin cried, staring in horror at the shattered cliff face. "No!"

"What in God's name happened?" Fletcher whispered.

Erin began to shake. "She's gone," she stammered, tears welling. "They've all gone!"

Feeling Fletcher's arm around her, she collapsed against him, sobbing.

"May whatever god be listening help them," Fletcher whispered.

Torn into grief, Erin fought to breathe. *This can't be happening. I can't have lost them. They must—*

She gasped as an ethereal voice sounded in her mind – a familiar voice, one that had spoken to her once before in what seemed like another age. *'Their path is not clear, but I will help as I can. As will you.'*

Fletcher pulled back, his eyes flitting around them. "What is it? What did you see?"

She looked up, her tear-filled eyes staring blindly around her. "Someone spoke to me," she stammered. "One I've heard before."

Fletcher's eyes widened. "Trust nothing here. This place isn't safe. We need to go."

'He is right. Your friends live. Leave here now. Your time will come soon.'

Through the bleak anguish, sudden hope rose. "The voice says my friends live," she whispered.

"Don't listen, Erin," Fletcher said, taking her arm. "We need to leave, before anything else arrives."

Erin pulled away. Wiping her eyes and sniffing gently, she turned to the jumbled chaos of the landslip, no evidence remaining of the cave entrance her friends had entered. "I don't know who or what this voice is, but I have to believe what it says." *That my friends are safe. That I will see them again.* Sniffing again, she stared at the shattered cliff face. "The voice said their path isn't clear." She turned to him, clinging to a desperate hope. "So, they are on *a* path. They are alive."

Fletcher grunted a weary sigh. "I don't know, Erin. I know nothing except we can't stay here."

She wiped her eyes, then straightened, a fierce resolve coursing through her. "I believe they are safe." Images of River and Beth flashed into her mind. Two women who had fought against the evil that had come against them. Two women who had fought to protect them. "They're strong," she avowed. "They will keep Jessica and the lad safe. I *will* see my friends again."

She saw the doubt on Fletcher's face before he quickly hid it. "I'm sure you're right," he said quietly. He straightened. "Let's go. I'll have to tell of what happened here." He winced. "Tell *something* of what happened."

Erin glanced back to the collapsed cliff face. Tell what? Nothing would be found here, she was sure of it. *Yet they still live.*

She turned back to Fletcher. "And Robert?"

Fletcher swung his torchlight to the trail. "We'll wait awhile at the car. He either shows, or he doesn't." She heard the irritation in his voice. "He chose his own path."

She hesitated, but deep down she knew it was true. The bookseller had clearly come here for some reason of his own. She drew a quiet breath, hoping he would find them at the car. Because they needed to speak with him. What did he know that could help them understand what had happened here?

And the voice? What of that? "Your time will come soon," it had said. She grasped onto the hope that the voice offered. *I have to believe someone will aid us, will aid my friends.* She would wait to see if the voice returned.

Cold and exhausted, she took a final look at the collapsed cliff face, then nodded to Fletcher. "Okay, let's go."

After a time, they'd made their way back down the mountain.

Where they waited for Robert.

*

On a moonlit mountain, a mouse watched a tall creature trudge up the rugged trail.

She watched, and followed, hoping the creature would drop a morsel of food as she had seen others do before. But the creature walked away from the trail, heading to the steep cliff. *No trails there,* thought the mouse, *not even for me.*

She watched as the creature stood at the cliff edge, swaying in the slight breeze. *Is it looking for food? Can it fly?*

The creature made a move to jump. Or so she thought. It collapsed on the ground, emitting strange noises. *Maybe it is a large mouse,* she thought.

As she came closer, the creature moved and climbed to its two legs. Then it turned away from the edge and walked back to the trail, soon disappearing into the night.

Unfortunately for the mouse, the creature left no food, only a marking of its territory. *Maybe it will come back,* thought the mouse, then it too scurried off into the night.

CHAPTER THIRTY-THREE

She was strong, but it was too early.
Oh, how hindsight is such a curse.

A wild, crackling storm had exploded around River, then all had disappeared into a chaotic darkness as she was swallowed into the maw of the Void. And now, she saw nothing but sensed an immense power of the Dark striving to reach them – to destroy them.

And she felt the Guardian. Around them. Protecting them.

From annihilation!

What terrors roam this Void?

The terrifying pressure around them grew as the ferocity of the unseen attackers intensified. She heard someone screaming. *Me or another? Who—*

A tremendous pulse of energy slammed into her, and a searing pain ripped through her mind. *We can't survive this! We—*

A collision of colossal powers, then a wrench of her mind and soul … and the malevolent pressure vanished.

Stumbling, River caught her balance. Head pounding, nerves afire, she drew deep lungfuls of air and quickly glanced around. She stood on the stone platform in the chamber beneath the mountain, flickers of yellow and red light playing on the walls.

We escaped with our lives …

But we're still here!

She turned to see Jessica and Tricia standing beside her, Beth at their feet.

Jessica looked dazed, uncertain, sweat dripping from her brow. "Did I succeed?" she whispered.

Nauseous waves in her stomach, River frowned. "I don't know. This looks to be the same place."

Jessica pushed damp hair from her brow. "And yet I remember travelling through hell …"

"You protected us in that hell."

"Me … or another?" Jessica murmured as if to herself. She glanced around, then looked up, as if gazing to something beyond the chamber. "This is the same place. This is the mountain. But this is your time."

At River's feet, the Warrior Beth groaned …

Then a faint yet insistent tone cut through her mind.

A calling from afar.

A calling from one she knew.

A deeply buried, untouched part of her consciousness reacted in an instant, reaching out and travelling – far-seeking.

She snapped to Naga's mind. *'Mother! I am here!'*

*

It is so dark – when did I close my eyes? It—

Suddenly, a part of Naga's mind lit up with lucid clarity! *'River?'*

'Mother! What has happened. You're hurt! How do I get help—'

'River, we don't have time. I am dying. Will you accept me?'

'What! No! Mother, you can't be—'

'River, please! It is growing dark, so very dark. Will you accept me?'

'Yes. Yes, I accept!'

With all her remaining energy, Naga released herself to the connection.

She released the Story.

'It is done,' she breathed, wondrous joy flooding her dying mind. *'May IY travel with you. Mother.'*

But as her spirit fled, a terrible memory shattered that briefest of joys. *The burnt man!*

'Beware, River … Beware the future … Beware the …'

A darkness descended …

The physical being of Naga lay next to Eagle, her hand lying limp on his forehead – and a look of horror on her face.

*

River collapsed.

Tricia dropped to her side. "Great, two down now," she muttered.

"Hold on to both of them," Jessica said, grabbing River with one hand and the Staff with the other. *We must get to Lanky. I want to get to Lanky.*

Pain lanced through her forehead—

The chamber disappeared.

*

"Rind! Rind! Naga – she's under attack! They will kill her!"

The cry drove like a blade through Spider's heart. Rind and Lanky immediately peeled away and rushed outside, others quickly following. Spider turned, meaning to follow.

"Hold!" Amber cried, stepping in front of him. "You're not going anywhere. We'll find out more soon enough."

Spider's agitated eyes remained fixed on the chamber's entrance. "What do they mean? Who do they mean? We have to find out what's happening." He made to pass her again.

Amber blocked his path. "Spider, listen to me," she hissed. "You can't do anything useful as you are. The most useful thing you can do is stay here, out of the way. Let them find out what has happened. We'll know soon enough. You need to rest—"

A crack of thunder, then Spider's eardrums popped as he was hit by a concussive blast.

He fell, struck his head …

His awareness faded.

*

Following Rind, who was streaking ahead of him, Lanky was crossing the stream when a sharp crack rent the air. He spun around to see a stream of dust pouring out of the cave he'd just left. *What attacks us now?* He turned to Rind, who had stopped, her eyes wide.

"You go on," he signalled, then sprinted away towards the cave.

Axe clenched in one hand, he charged into the chamber, ready to tackle the next invader … and came to a halt as he saw the bodies lying scattered on the floor in front of him. He scanned around for his adversary, but as the dust settled, he saw and sensed no one. Immediately suspicious, and suspecting a trap, he stood stock-still, keeping each of the bodies in sight.

One of the bodies groaned.

He cautiously stepped forward, scanning the ground as he edged towards the moaning body. As he approached, the moans ceased, and the figure pulled itself upright, their hand held to their head.

He gasped as he recognised the young woman's striking features. "Jessica?"

Rubbing her head, Jessica muttered as if to herself, "There must be a better way to do this." Then she looked up. "Hi, Lanky."

"You're back," he managed, unable to believe what he was seeing.

She offered him a weak smile. "Quite how, I don't know, but yes, I'm back." She raised her hand. "And see what I've brought."

Lanky stared at the Staff in outright disbelief. Then he looked back at Jessica's strained face. "I can't believe it," he whispered. "What happened?"

Jessica looked around at the other, now groaning bodies around her. "That will take some telling." Her gaze fell on Beth, who lay on her side, holding her head. "And some things may prove difficult to tell."

CHAPTER THIRTY-FOUR

IY. Or I?

The silent procession made its solemn way through the shadows of the trees towards the clearing, where a ring of tall torches burned brightly in the cool evening breeze, their richly coloured flames dancing against the backdrop of a bloodred sky. As each mourner passed into the ring, they paused at its centre. Choosing to kneel or remain standing, each spoke a few quiet words, their heartfelt messages reaching only the one lying before them.

Some reached out with their hand, wanting – maybe needing – to make a final contact. Others left a small personal token, placing it with care in a position thought proper before walking sombrely away, acknowledging River as they left, then assembling in a growing crowd between and beneath the tall flickering torches.

Finally, Lanky, Jessica, and Beth entered the ring together. Without speaking, and with no prior discussion, they split; Lanky walked to the left of the bier, Beth to the right, and Jessica to the head. River approached and stood beside Jessica. They all gazed down, some with tears in their eyes, at the body of Naga.

The once Mother of the Iyes lay on a soft bed of grasses, bedecked with colourful flowers, and adorned with the gifts of the tribe. Multihued stone beads and gems lay scattered beside assorted shells from the shore of the Great Sea. Delicate carvings of bone, stone, and wood lay on her chest as testament to the love of her people. And beside her feet lay a polished green axehead. Jessica looked back at Naga's face. *She looks so peaceful.* A woman lying as though enjoying just another few minutes of pleasant dreaming before waking to stretch and climb out of bed.

But that was not to be. This life was complete. And she had been prepared for the next.

Jessica had watched Amber earlier in her reverent preparation of both Naga and Eagle, and although both were to be honoured separately, they were both treated in a similar way, with their skin carefully covered with a rich ochre paste followed by a sprinkling of red powder. Treated equally maybe, Jessica thought, but Amber had added adornments to Eagle's body, potent symbols of her love for the Iyes scout: a lock of her hair, blood from her veins, and soft words spoken to be heard by his spirit. She, and the tribe, would honour Eagle tomorrow.

But this night, Naga's now bloodred body glistened in the light of the flames, ready and waiting for her transition to the realm of her Ancestors. Jessica looked up and glanced at Beth, who kept her head down, eyes averted. Her friend was back – back in the land of the Iyes, and back as Beth, the friend she had known for so many years. *Not that brutal other who came to the fore. The one called Bethusa.* She studied her friend's face, seeing the strain and suppressed pain. She had heard Beth's tale of being captured by the ice dragon, but her friend had no memory of what had happened thereafter. Neither did she recall what she'd done in that chamber under the mountain. *I remember fragments of what she did – what I undid – but I won't tell her. I won't tell anyone. I can't. Not yet. She needs time to recover.*

As did they all …

The sharp, brutal memory was suddenly strong. A gaunt-faced shaman, his long white hair streaked black. *The killer of my sister. The killer who fled yet again.* An ice-cold rage returned. *One day, I will find you, devil.*

"Warriors," came River's quiet voice. "Do any of you wish to speak?"

Jessica slammed her thoughts away. They were for another time. Drawing a quiet breath, she glanced at Lanky – he met her eyes, and she nodded.

Lanky shifted slightly, then gazed down on Naga's face. "We've only known you, Naga, for a very short time," he said, his gentle words carrying to the outer ring of mourners, "and in a time of stress and conflict, both for you and your tribe – and for us travellers.

"In this short time, we can't see nor understand but a fraction of your feelings, of your intentions … of your dreams. But what can't be hidden is the feelings of others, the love of others. And that love is clear in the friends, the family, and the tribe around you."

He glanced at Jessica. She smiled and nodded her approval.

He gave the slightest flicker of acknowledgement, then bowed his head to Naga once more. "What we can't deny is that you readied this tribe to receive us. To receive and attempt to educate us."

That's true, Jessica thought, glancing at Naga. *You carried your beliefs, your Story.* And how many others before her? Over millennia. *But it was you who needed to act. And you were ready.*

"It's clear that without you," Lanky continued, "without your tribe, we wouldn't have survived here."

Also true, Jessica thought, remembering the horrific first few hours of their arrival.

"And so, on behalf of the three of us who first arrived, I'd like to thank you, Naga, and hope that your ancestors greet you warmly as you travel beyond the Horizon." He then leaned in and kissed Naga's cheek.

With tears in her eyes, Jessica did the same.

Beth remained standing, her head still bowed.

Uncertain of what to do next, Jessica glanced at River.

"Please stand behind me," River whispered.

Jessica nudged Lanky and mouthed, *Follow me.*

As Jessica and Lanky stepped away to stand behind River, Beth raised her head and gazed down at Naga. "I didn't trust you," she whispered. "I still don't trust you."

Her breath catching, Jessica stared at Beth, fearing what she was about to say.

"But I can't deny," Beth continued, her tired eyes studying Naga's face, "that you did what you thought right. And maybe what you did was needed for me to become what I've become." She paused briefly, then: "You were a remarkable woman, Naga, and I accept that, in these times, you had to make tough decisions. But even so, I ..."

Jessica held her breath.

With gentle tenderness, Beth laid her hand on Naga's cheek. "I think you understand." Then she turned away and walked to Jessica's side, giving her a weak smile.

Jessica released her breath in a low sigh. *Panic over.* She reached down and held Beth's hand, giving it a gentle squeeze. Her heart settling, she looked back at River, who was now standing with her arms stretched aloft.

"Spirits of the Land," River called out, "hear our pleas. Ancestors of old, listen well to your children. Friends assembled here, gather your thoughts, and speak your mind."

A multitude of voices sounded out at once. Shouting, whispering, singing – a heartfelt outpouring that left Jessica breathless. Fragments made themselves heard and then were swept away in the torrent.

"Mother!"

"… as a child—"

"… the rock of this people—"

"… I pray for your son—"

"… I thank you for—"

"… light her way—"

Jessica closed her eyes and let the raw emotions wash around her.

'She was an extraordinary woman,' came a voice in her head.

'It appears so,' Jessica replied.

The world shimmered and the people, the torches, all disappeared. Jessica stood in a Glade.

Opposite stood a woman. Of no great height, of no great age, she wore a dark green chiton tied off at the waist with a black sash, and sandals on her feet. Simple attire, and one offset with a head of short, spiky hair. "Do you know who I am?" the woman said, a slight lilt to her voice.

Jessica studied her, suddenly on edge with a simmering frustration – resentment even – at this elusive god of the Iyes. "Yes, IY, I think I do."

"We have been lucky, Guardian. It seems we all have much to learn."

Guardian. Always the Guardian. "Why are you here?"

"The power gathered in this moment is immense," IY said as a faint image of the mourners appeared around them. "The Enemy cannot intrude. I needed to be sure you understood who I am."

"Ha!" Jessica muttered. "I think we'd need to spend my lifetime for you to explain yourself – I presume we don't have that time."

A faint smile played on IY's lips. "No – but we have *some* time."

"Good," Jessica said, glowering at her. "Then first, what is the Guardian?"

"The one who walks beside the Warriors as they protect the Land from the hordes of Kaos," IY answered without hesitation. "The one who can travel the timelines of the Continuum, guarding Warrior companions journeying by her side."

Jessica frowned. "I know nothing of the Continuum."

"And yet you have travelled its pathways."

And yet I don't know how. "What am I supposed to do?"

"You are the Guardian, not I."

"Will you help me understand?"

The spiky-haired woman tilted her head. "I stand before you now."

Jessica glared at her. "Then tell me what I am supposed to do."

IY held Jessica's fierce gaze. "Defeat Kaos and prevent the release of the Geddon."

Jessica strove to hold back a rush of fear. "I know nothing of Kaos. I know nothing of this Geddon."

"Then you know you have much to learn." IY glanced to the blurred image of the mourners. "And here we have little time." She turned back. "Maybe you have other questions for this precious moment?"

Jessica bit back a curse. *The questions I have are unending.* "Who locked Beth away in that mountain? Who almost destroyed my friend!"

IY tilted her head a fraction. "Have you not asked her these questions?"

Jessica scowled. "Why should I do that! You know she remembers nothing! Knows none of what happened after her capture by the dragon. Don't play a game with me."

"Which game, Guardian? There are many."

Jessica took an aggressive step forward. "Now I believe you. But I'm talking about my friend. What happened?"

The spiky-haired woman's smile faded. "Some things cannot yet be told."

Jessica's anger flared. "*Nothing* has yet been told! Answer!"

She staggered under a wave of immense power rolling off the woman. She forced herself steady, holding the biting gaze of IY. *Stay calm. Understand.*

"You do not yet know enough," IY rasped. "You have much to learn."

"Well, teach me!" Jessica grated. "Tell me what I need to know." She girded herself and took a step closer. "And tell me what happened to my friend!"

IY glared at Jessica ... and then smiled, the anger in her eyes slipping away as though never unveiled. "You were well chosen. All of you." She turned away and walked up to the faint image of Naga shimmering in the Glade's boundary. "She was an extraordinary Mother, and a fine leader of her tribe. But there was no powerful shaman within – she needed the artefact to aid her. But this one" – IY's gaze turned to the image of River – "she is strong. Yet I sense something more ..." She fell silent.

"You haven't answered my question," Jessica said, a coldness to her voice. "Don't waste my time."

"Time," IY said, turning to her, a peculiar intensity to her gaze. "What did it feel like? To have that power, to travel afar?"

I felt scared as hell. I felt lost. I ... "Stop wasting time," Jessica repeated. "Or I leave."

IY studied her for a moment, then nodded. "But know this, Guardian, what I say here cannot be repeated. You understand?"

"I make no promises."

A faint scowl appeared on IY's face. "You and Lanky are quite alike, you know? What makes you such suspicious people?"

"I'm leaving," Jessica said, detaching from the Glade.

"There is a traitor amongst us," IY murmured.

Jessica froze. "Who?"

"The one suspected is being watched. Most carefully."

"And you won't tell me who?"

IY walked up to Jessica, her face hardening. "You fled this Land because the Enemy reached you, allowed into the Sacred Chamber by the traitor. This cannot be allowed to happen again. We must capture the traitor, and to do this, for now, only I and one other shall know of my plan."

The memory of the meeting with the daemons flashed into Jessica's mind. And of the arrival of the burnt man. *I fled, but ...* "I didn't hold the Staff. How did I travel?"

"*You* control your moves within the Continuum, Guardian. It was *you* who chose to flee to your own time." IY shook her head slowly. "That was unwise."

Continuum? A distorted memory of their hellish journey back from her time flashed into her mind. *I travelled beyond the Continuum. I travelled in the Void.* She suppressed a sidling fear. *But I don't know how I did it. I don't—*

"Somehow you found the energy you needed. Or someone provided it for you."

"Why would ..." Jessica drew a sharp breath. "Someone wanted me gone."

"That part is certain. The Enemy wants you dead or gone from this Land before you understand – before you accept – who you are." Her face thoughtful, IY sauntered away. "Is it possible?" she said as though to herself. "If she sought to escape, had a destination in mind ... Yes, he could have provided the energy needed."

"The energy?"

IY turned to her. "You – and the Warriors – access the A'ven. The Land's energy, as the shamans call it. The energy of the Dark, as others name it. It's what you feed from. And to travel as you did, you needed a vast source of energy. And knowledge. Knowledge you did not have."

Jessica grunted a harsh laugh. "Because we are told nothing."

"But to get back here from your own land," IY continued as if she'd not spoken, "you held the Staff. It provided ... assistance."

Memories returned ... of an ethereal voice ... and of another presence, an indomitable presence of antiquity. "Who aids me?"

"In this moment, that cannot be told."

Jessica bristled, her anger overflowing. "You wish my aid in your fight against this Enemy but give me nothing in return. No answer on my friend. And the dragon? What of that? The beast stole the Staff and took it to that mountain. Was that its lair? How did the Staff survive there? How did it survive through the ages to my time? And the remaining Axe – is that mine?"

"You do not hold an Axe," IY said calmly. "You are the Guardian, the Staff Holder."

Jessica frowned. "Then the fourth Warrior is—"

"The fourth Warrior is not yet revealed. For that, we all must wait."

"Then what of my friend, what of the dragon, what of—"

"Some things have remained hidden for millennia, Guardian, and I will not risk those being discovered now, just as the Enemy rises. Know that the Enemy had to be distracted, the Continuum disrupted. The Staff had to be made safe." She held Jessica's eyes. "To protect that which needed protection required ... sacrifices."

Jessica's eyes widened. "Beth?"

IY nodded imperceptibly. "She helped protect the Staff through the ages."

"But she was imprisoned for an eternity. She—"

"Eternity? You – as the Guardian – would know that not to be true. It was a mere drop in the ocean against the span of the Continuum."

"Not for my friend!" Jessica said fiercely. "She was locked up for millennia. She—"

"She is a Warrior," IY said, her bright eyes locked onto Jessica's.

She is a Warrior— The realisation struck with sudden brutal clarity. "She was fighting the Dark. She was defending a Gate."

IY remained silent.

She is a Warrior. She was doing what a Warrior does. The hairs on her nape rose. *How do I know this?* "Who am I?" she breathed, turning away, staring out into the darkness.

"You are the Guardian."

But who am I?

She was suddenly drowning under a relentless tide of writhing emotions, tangled thoughts. "I can't do this," she whispered, her back to IY. "Beth can't do this."

"For now, the Warrior has a reprieve," came IY's calm, lilting voice behind her. "Because some things must remain hidden – both from the traitor and from Kaos. Beth will not remember, and you will ensure it remains this way. That which has been concealed must remain concealed. Do not talk of this with any other."

With a desperate groan, she fought to calm the maelstrom of her mind. She had no choice. *I can't abandon my friends.* She faced IY. "It almost destroyed her," she whispered, remembering the Beth she had seen. "It *had* destroyed her. The Beth I knew would never kill in cold blood."

"Kill who?" IY said, her eyes narrowing.

"The bookseller," Jessica said, indistinct images returning of that horrific night. Seeing IY's confusion, she frowned. "You didn't see?"

A momentary look of pain crossed IY's face. "You travel, but that wonder is not one I share. But that is for another time. What happened?"

The dark waters in which Jessica floundered seemed to grow murkier. *This is a god?* Didn't gods know everything?

"Guardian – we have little time."

Jessica searched IY's face. If this woman lied about being tied to this age, she couldn't see it. *But how much else is hidden from me?* Doubts lingering, she relayed the events of that night in the chamber beneath Mount Hope.

IY's eyes widened. "You are sure you did that?"

"I'm sure. It's hazy, unclear, but I'm certain I did it."

"How?"

Jessica stared at IY, stunned. "You're asking *me* that? I thought you were the one with all the answers. What's going on here?"

Frowning, IY ran her hand through her spiky hair. "How did that happen? Jalu has not yet …" Her words trailed away, her gaze locking on to Jessica. "You did more than travel the timelines of the Continuum – you forced a part of it to reset, to erase what had been." Fear burned within the woman's eyes. "Never again attempt this. You may destroy yourself, others, even whole worlds."

Her words defied sane reasoning. *Too much, too fast.*

IY walked up to Jessica. "There is one who comes who will aid you. Until then, never again attempt what you did. You hold a power in your hands that could wreak irreparable damage."

Emotions surged: alarm, frustration, anger. *I don't know what I did. I know nothing.* But to do nothing? To promise not to use a power that may aid them. *After all Beth suffered ...* "No, I can't promise anything. If I believe it will save lives, I will—"

"No! You must not," IY hissed, her face hardening. "Wait for the one who comes, else you may lose all we have gained."

In the silence that followed, Jessica was suddenly struck by the absurdity of what was happening. What mad world had she entered, where she argued with a god? A laugh, a sound edged with hysteria, escaped her.

"You are the Guardian," IY said, eyes locked onto hers. "Yet you have much to learn. Do not let ignorance destroy us."

Jessica drew a steadying breath. The Guardian? Maybe. Maybe not. How could she know what she truly was? *All I know right now is that I'm blind.* Blind to the truth of the power in the Land. Blind to what she was supposed to do. She glanced at the spiky-haired woman. And blind to whom to trust.

The image of a tousle-haired lad formed in her mind. *Except one.* "What I'll promise is that I'll speak with Lanky. Then we shall see."

"Good," IY breathed. "That is good."

As Jessica saw the tension ease from the woman's shoulders, her own fear grew. *A god is afraid of what I might do.* And that thought was terrifying. *I need help. I need ...* She remembered IY's words. "You said someone comes to aid me. Who?"

IY studied Jessica, then glanced up and around. "The lamentations are finishing, and the field is weakening. I must leave. But know that the one who comes is Jalu. Keep the Staff by your side, and she will come to you."

The name echoed in Jessica's mind. *Jalu.* The name that had come to her in her bleakest moment, when her mind had been savaged by the daemon, Alkazar. "Who is Jalu?" she said in a quiet voice.

A hard glint flashed in the spiky-haired woman's eyes. "That is for another time. I must leave, else the Dark will find me." An urgent edge crept into her voice. "This settlement is not safe. The tribe must move. The tribe leaders must gather their allies and prepare for the coming battles. But fighters on the battlefield will not win this war. No, stealth and guile are needed. And the capture of the Kade."

Jessica sank further beneath the murky waters. "The Kade? What's that?"

"It is a source of Kaos's power in this world. For now, it is enough to know that you must find and capture it." Her eyes darkened. "If not, the work of the Dark here – and the destruction in your time – will continue."

"Wait, what destruction in my time? There is no ice age in my time. There is no Kaos, no …" Horrific memories swept to the fore. The daemon Alkazar. The devil shaman … *The one who killed my sister.* The truth sidled up to her. "This god of the Dark attacks my world …" *Killed my sister?*

"Ice, desert, there is no difference to Kaos. He has a far greater game at play." IY's intense gaze locked onto Jessica's. "And Kaos in your time? Do you not see the growing stresses on your land? On your people?" Her lips set into a sardonic smile. "Could you believe this Enemy has the power to influence your people? Powerful people, ones with no interest in the longevity of your world?"

Her words carried a chill to Jessica's heart. Were the people of her time susceptible to influence? Were the leaders in her time ignorant of the planet's distress? The answer to that was clear. But the influence of a god? "This Kaos is at work in my time?"

"Kaos is active across many fronts, and to his delight, humanity is working for him, whether knowingly or not. Warming the planet, poisoning the air and water, destroying life's very environment needed to survive. An attack not seen for over sixty million years."

The K-T extinction. Three-quarters of all the planet's species wiped out in a geological blink of an eye. "This is the work of Kaos?" Jessica breathed.

"The Dark is a potent force, Guardian. You have seen but a glimpse of their power."

A glimpse … Then what hell lay beyond their sight? What hell awaited their planet?

Prickling unease filtered through the grim foreboding. Her eyes narrowed as she identified its source. "You said you can't travel the timelines … How do you know about my world, your future?"

IY held Jessica's gaze. "That is also for another time, Guardian."

Jessica bristled. "You reveal little of what you know, yet you wish for my help. That doesn't work."

"I tell you what I can, when I can," IY said, her eyes flaring. "And I tell you that Kaos is a force far more terrible than you can imagine. He seeks this planet's destruction. He seeks to release the Geddon."

"The Geddon?" Jessica breathed, a nameless dread rising.

"A destroyer of worlds, an unstoppable force of the Dark that if released, we would not defeat. This world's – your world's – Armageddon."

The words were as talons thrusting deep, violently raking her soul. "Naga said nothing of this," she whispered.

"The Iyes, as all tribes in this Land, hold their tragic tales, ones told amongst so many others by the fire at night. Tales told to entertain and shock, but tales not truly believed. This was such a one. I needed her to know nothing more. This truth was not for her people."

But it is for me, Jessica thought, fighting a sudden panic.

"Kaos fights on many fronts: within the Land, at the Gates, and by striving to release the Geddon. He seeks the annihilation of all life – of Life itself."

Jessica heard the subtle change of tone. *Of Life ... She speaks of it as precious. She speaks of it as much greater than life ...*

"To him, Life is his antithesis," IY continued, "an abhorrent disease to be eradicated at all costs. But Life is resilient. And we of the Light are resilient. We resist him and his agents of the Dark – you and the Warriors resist him. But always the threat of the Geddon looms over us all. If Kaos releases the Geddon, all is lost." IY placed her hand on Jessica's shoulder. "Find the Kade. Find the source of Kaos's power and bring it to me."

Jessica's fear drove hungry roots deeper within her. Armageddon? The destruction of all life? It couldn't be. Her gaze narrowed on the spiky-haired woman before her. "Who are you? What are you? How do you know these things?"

The hint of a smile crossed the woman's lips. "I serve the Light," she said simply.

Jessica searched her face. What game was she playing? *And why do I play it?*

Frustration flared. *Enough,* she hissed to herself. *I've sunk deep enough into these murky waters.*

And yet she knew that wasn't so. She would need to wade deeper and deeper because answers lay far beneath swirling waves of deception. "You say we must find this Kade," she said, a bitter edge to her voice. "Where? What is it? What does it look like?"

"I sense it in the Ka homeland. But it is well masked. It ..." IY glanced up. "The lamentation has finished. We will be separated now. We will talk again."

"No," Jessica snapped. "Answer my questions!"

"You can sense the Kade," came IY's distant voice as the flickering light of the torches swept into the Glade. "The one who comes, Jalu, will aid you."

The Glade vanished, and Jessica found herself standing beside River.

"Please move out of the ring," River said quietly. "I wish time here alone."

Fighting a sudden dizziness, Jessica nodded. Confused, angry, she walked unsteadily away, passing through the ring of tall torches before halting, head bowed, struggling to make sense of what she'd heard. The Kade? The Geddon? Jalu? And could she trust IY? *Maybe. Probably.* But she needed to tread carefully. And she needed space to think, to talk with the others about what she'd heard.

"Are you alright, Warrior?" came a concerned voice to her side.

Nerves scraped raw, she looked up to see Dune standing beside her, his long flowing hair appearing as licks of flames in the warm light of the torches. *No. Your god speaks in riddles.* "Yes," she managed. "I'll be okay in a moment."

Dune nodded gently, misunderstanding her emotions. "It is a tough time for us all."

Through the remnants of her anger, she heard the pain in his voice. *Yes*, she thought, thinking of Dune's twin brother, Scorpion, his fate still unknown along with the others of Bear's party. *This is a terrifying time for us all.*

Dune stepped to her side and reached for her hand.

Feeling the warmth of his hand, she clasped it in hers. She felt Dune's eyes on her, then he looked back to the mourning circle.

Her battered mind raced on. Yes, she must tread carefully, but what path to take? She immediately grasped one option. She held the Staff. She could take them home. But that spark of hope instantly died. Because, whether by chance or design, a sheltered part of her consciousness knew they were trapped on a path towards a different fate. *We are Warriors. They call me the Guardian. And Armageddon comes.*

And yet another scattered thought. *Warriors ... Beth held an Axe, Lanky and River held Axes. But IY told me that the remaining Axe was not mine ... So, who is the fourth Warrior?* She stood in silence, feeling uncertain and alone, as the unanswered question joined the multitude of others clouding her world, her sense of what should be done. Of what needed to be done.

Her troubled gaze caught the funeral circle. Her sigh was heartfelt but unheard. *I must leave these fears for another day.* For despite the horrors swirling beyond her sight, in this moment, she had to honour Naga; she had to pay her final respects to the woman who had tried to help them.

Comforted by Dune's gentle hand, she studied the ring of silent Iyes mourners gathered around the torchlit ring, their faces sad, yet resolute; their heads bowed, yet a strength in their frames. *They genuinely loved and respected her.* She looked back to the now sanctified body of Naga. *Yes, she tried to aid us, but maybe she was as lost as the rest of us.* She grimaced. *And it seems her god didn't share all she knew.*

As the flickering flames of the torches played across their faces, Jessica and Dune held their own silent vigil, each providing much-needed comfort to the other.

And disturbing, foreboding questions continued to harry Jessica's mind.

*

At some unseen signal, Jessica heard a quiet murmur pick up around the ring of torches. It seemed the ceremony had been completed. She glanced into the ring. River remained standing at the head of Naga's body, her hands held before her, palms facing forward as she continued her own private lament. Jessica noticed River now wore Naga's bracelet on her left wrist. A Warrior. The new Mother. And a shaman.

Another unknown.

"Hello," whispered a familiar voice at her side.

"Hi, Trish," Jessica said in a low voice. "You okay?"

"A rabbit in the headlights right now – or is that torchlight? Either way, a scared rabbit." She sighed, then gestured to the funeral ring. "This was a beautiful and moving ceremony. What happens now?"

Jessica turned to Dune. "What *does* happen now? To Naga?"

Torchlight dancing on his sculpted face, he said, "River will finish the ceremony here" – he adjusted the string of beads around his neck – "and then Naga will be taken for internment within the caves – to a protected place. Only River and Rind may see that final resting site. The bearers will be blindfolded."

"I understand Eagle will be buried at a woodland site near here – so they inter only shamans within the caves?"

"They inter those closest to the Spirits within. This protects them from those that recognise their power and would seek it even after death. The energy of those interned adds to the power of the Sacred Site. It is as it should be." He paused. "And now, if you'd allow me, I'll leave to speak with Amber. She …" He left it unsaid.

Jessica placed her hand on the young Iyes's shoulder. "Of course. You don't need my permission, Dune."

Dune smiled, then walked away into the shadows beyond the torches.

Jessica sighed, then relayed Dune's answers to Tricia. As she finished, she glanced around at the groups around them. An unexpected warmth suddenly rose. "I haven't spent much time with any of these people ... in fact, I've spent most of my time wanting to get us away from this place. But now? Now I know these people."

Tricia glanced at Jessica, raising an eyebrow. "I can understand that," she said slowly. "I see these are a very close people, a family – but please don't tell me you want to stay? I've things to do, people to see." She ran her hand through her tight curly hair. "I've a hair appointment in two weeks' time." Jessica allowed herself a small smile. Tricia tilted her head. "But seriously, I wanted to help you get to Beth and this lad, Lanky. And they're here. Don't we just go back now?"

Jessica's smile faded. "I don't want to stay, but neither can I leave." *I am the Guardian,* came the unbidden thought. "There are things happening here I need to understand, things that may impact the world in our time." She looked back to River, who remained standing at the head of Naga's body. "I believe I need to help." *I must help.*

"We seem to have made a slight jump from 'let's find Beth and Lanky and get home as quickly as we can', to 'let's save the world'. And how is it we do that exactly?"

"We?"

Tricia smiled. "The world always revolves around a pair of heroes."

Jessica studied the determined face of her friend. *Heroes? Then are you the fourth Warrior?* She suppressed a spasm of fear. *Could you – could I – bear that burden?*

She hardened her heart. That was something to be faced another day. "Before *we* do anything," she said, keeping her voice light, "we've a lot of catching up to do. Come on, I need to find the others."

"I hope it's a little quicker than last time."

*

Lanky had suggested that they find a quiet spot, and Beth had silently acquiesced. She had followed him and the faint light of his flickering torch a short distance down the gorge and then up the winding trail to the lookout point on the ridge. Now, with the torch planted in the ground behind them, they sat in silence, the last vestiges of the dying sun visible in the western sky to their right and the glow of the still valley below them. Only the occasional hoot of an owl or the howl of a wolf broke the stillness of the moment.

Lanky looked up to the sky. *Another incredible display.* At that very moment, a shooting star streaked brightly across the sky.

"Naga believed we are all made of stars," Beth breathed, her strained face tilted to the sky. "And that all would return there someday."

"That could well have been her then," he said softly.

"I think I'll believe that to be true," she whispered, still looking upwards.

Lanky glanced to the far horizon where the moon was rising and already casting a faint shadow from the birch tree to their left. *A moonlight shadow.*

"I had a dream last night," Beth murmured. "That I watched the vastness of the night sky complete a thirteen-thousand-year journey in but a few moments, Vega completing its duty as the North Star to be relieved by Alpha Draconis and then by Polaris. I held the entire map of this sky in my head – all the stars, the planets, and comets. And the entire map moved so fluidly, as though I were watching a movie."

Lanky said nothing. He needed to tread carefully.

We don't know how deep the wounds cut.

Jessica had related to him the fantastical account of their arrival at Mount Hope, including Beth's sudden – no, miraculous – appearance out of the mountain, where she had fought off a great evil to protect Jessica and the others. And Beth had told the tribe of the failed journey north, and of her capture by the ice dragon. *But she doesn't know how she escaped and found her way to Jessica in another age.* What happened during that forgotten time? What other trauma? He suspected Jessica knew more than she'd told him.

But that's okay. For now.

For Jessica had become the person he trusted here the most. If there was something to hold back, then she had good reason. But in this moment, he felt an immense pressure. He didn't want to mess up with Beth by inadvertently treading in the wrong space.

Beth spoke again in a low voice. "And do you know I can tell you names of ancient chieftains who resisted their enemy's push into these lands?"

Lanky shook his head.

"And that I have a pit in my stomach as though a family member has been ripped from my heart?"

What!

Beth continued to look up at the sky. "I don't know what, but something bad has happened, Lanky. Why do I suddenly know these things I shouldn't – and why do I grieve so?"

She turned to him, an emptiness in her eyes. "What has happened?"

He fought a rising panic. How did you answer questions like this? What if he gave the wrong answers? What if—

'Are you a wolf or a mouse?' a voice growled.

He silently cursed at the now familiar jarring presence within him – the one they called Dysam. *'Get out of my head!'*

'You're not strong enough. Let me free.'

"Go away!" he shouted, forcing the belligerent presence down deep inside.

"What?"

"No, no, not you, Beth – it's this damn …" He sucked in a sharp breath. *She doesn't need to hear my problems.* He waited a moment to be sure the voice had gone. All remained silent. But the worry remained. The abrasive presence was growing stronger. He needed to strengthen his defences, lock it away.

Beth was studying him, brow furrowed. Then she looked back out across the valley. He saw a deep pain in her eyes.

Come on, Lanky. She needs your help.

He placed his hand on hers. "Beth, I know you don't remember how you escaped from the dragon and found your way to Jessica, but from what she told me, you showed incredible bravery protecting them from that daemon at Mount Hope. Staggering bravery." He shook his head. "I've no idea what happened, but the fact is that you *did* escape. You *did* find Jessica. And that tells us one thing – whatever happened, it didn't defeat you; you were still ready to fight for your friends."

He saw her watching him. Listening.

"But whatever you did will have taken a huge toll on you, way beyond my imagining. Heck, you've every right to feel as sick and tired and drained as anyone ever could. You've been through hell." He squeezed her hand. "But you know the most important thing? You have people here that really, really care for you. You have the love of the friends you came on holiday with. Okay, not the nicest holiday ever, I grant you that …"

A faint smile touched her lips.

"And that hint of a smile is the nicest thing I've seen in days. Another one of those and you get to carry the torch on the way back. There! You've got the torch."

She clasped his hand more tightly.

Lanky smiled, a great worry easing. *She will pull through. In time, and with help from us all, she will understand what happened …*

His smile slipped as he thought back to her words. *I had a dream last night …* "The other things you mention …" He grimaced. "I'm sorry, Beth, I really don't know why or how you know these things, or feel these emotions, but I'm sure, in time, we'll figure this out." He squeezed her hand again. "But for now, it's really important you keep talking about it. Just keep telling us what you're thinking, what you're worried about. Anything at all, just talk. Please."

He saw tears at the corner of her eyes.

"And it's okay to cry."

As she collapsed onto his shoulder, he wrapped an arm around her, protecting her private place of grief.

A short while later, Beth lifted her head, then sat back up as Lanky withdrew his arm.

"Thank you," she said, wiping her eyes. "You've reminded me I do have great friends here. And I promise I will talk. And I'll remind you that you encouraged me," she said with a faint smile.

He grinned.

"But …" Her smile faded. "It has also reminded me that someone did this to me. And that has changed my view on our involvement here. I think it can be called revenge." She fell silent and looked down into the gorge below.

With a sudden worm of unease squirming in his stomach, Lanky's own smile faded. Beth's hurt and confusion had morphed into a growing anger. Had he said the right things here? *I guess we wait and see.*

He glanced up to the night sky. *And me? What do I feel?* A peculiar angst settled on him. *I know what I want. I want to see my mum again. I want to see my friends. I want to get home.*

And yet … And yet he felt a growing pull on him, a drawing of his soul into this Land, a relentless pressure to drop his defences and engage.

Engage with what?

With the power of the Land. With the Axe. With the warg. With Dysam.

With the Enemy.

I am a Warrior! The time for fear is over. There is work to be done!

Suddenly recognising the burgeoning energy surging inside, he instinctively smothered it, dampening it down, chasing eddies to the further reaches of his mind. A bitter taste in his mouth and dying echoes of a potent power ringing in his head, his expression hardened. *Whatever comes will be on my terms. I am in control. No one else.*

He felt eyes on him and turned. Beth was staring at him. Smiling. Her eyes afire.

Beth?

"You're right," she growled. "There's work to be done."

EPILOGUE

"I believe I had one too many last night, Sy," Shadow said, approaching the Ancient's chamber, carrying the hangover of all hangovers. "But that celebration was needed."

Sy ignored him and walked on.

"You're just sorry you left early," Shadow muttered, entering the dragon's lair.

His body was screaming in complaint of its pickling, but it wasn't every day you could drink to the fall of a Warrior. A Warrior that had taken two attempts to kill.

A tremor of doubt rippled through his addled mind.

No, this time, she's a dead Warrior. He wouldn't let his stewed mind dampen the joy of last night.

Although those dreams had tried their damnedest.

He had no idea what time they'd finished drinking, only that this entire day had passed him by – a day lost to the fractured dreaming of a pickled brain. And his mind had taken him places he never wanted to go again. A quite evil backstabber indeed.

Although ...

Although what?

Why did he feel something was missing?

His head pounding, he and Sy made their way across the chamber, led by Stealth, who looked as sprightly as ever. Did the man not suffer the same stab in the back? *Maybe he's immune to his own wine?*

"Good evening, friend," boomed the Ancient's voice, accompanied by the scraping of her talons across the stone floor.

His startled heart raced as Shadow saw the dragon climb up onto the pedestal, then gaze down at them with a fiery eye. "Good times," proclaimed the Ancient. "Momentous times."

He nodded – and then instantly regretted it as waves of nausea ran through his stomach. He waited for it to pass, then turned to Stealth. "You won't hit me again if I speak to the Ancient, will you?"

Stealth smiled, and a rumble of laughter sounded from the dragon. "Speak. I allow it."

"Good," Shadow said, turning slowly back to face Rakana. *Now concentrate. I need to be a good representative of the Ka here.*

By not throwing up?

Get on with it.

"It is an honour to be here at such a great time, and I thank you on behalf of the Ensi for your destruction of this Warrior. May I ask, where did you find her?"

Didn't Stealth tell you this last night?

I can't remember, curse it.

"About fifteen days south of here," rumbled the dragon. "Making her way north."

"With others?"

"They were of no consequence. This was the prize."

"But it shows these Warriors are now moving. Do you know where the other Warriors are located?"

"One is moving south. The other travelled far. But today they are of no threat. Tomorrow? We will deal with that when it comes."

"Well, I suppose that is true. But what can we do against these Warriors? And when can I return? I must bring this news to the Ensi."

"I agree. Stealth."

"Yes, Master."

"Is the communication ready?"

"It is ready, Master."

"Good." The Ancient swung away from them and climbed down from the platform. "We leave now."

Shadow gaped at the retreating figure, then glanced at Stealth, who shrugged. "I suggest you grab your things and follow the Ancient. Now means now."

Shadow turned to Sy – but the impatient one was already moving. He shook his head. "Now this is just undue haste. I don't do haste – unless someone is trying to kill me."

"Well," Stealth drawled, "I suggest that unless you quickly grab some warm clothes, that could happen on your flight home."

Cursing, Shadow hurried away, striding after Sy as fast as he dared.

*

Fully laden with his pack and extra clothing, and breathing hard after the long walk up the tunnel and down the moonlit track to the landing strip, Shadow came to a halt beside Sy and Stealth. "Thanks for waiting for me down there, Sy," he panted, feeling like emptying his stomach – again.

"No problem," Sy signed.

"Did you get everything?" Stealth asked.

"Everything that I could sensibly bring, given I have to carry this extra layer of clothing. I leave the rest as a gift to you. You may—"

The dragon's sharp command echoed in his head. *'We go now. I have little time.'*

"Here," Stealth said, handing Shadow an object.

"What's this?"

"It's the message for your leader."

Shadow turned it over in his hands. "It feels like a roll of bark."

"Well done," Stealth said. "I can see you're alert today." Shadow scowled. "This is for your leader's eyes only," Stealth continued. "I presume we can trust you …"

"You know I wouldn't be here otherwise." Shadow slipped the roll inside the collar of his jacket and retightened the cords.

Stealth stepped to each of them and clasped their wrists. "Good luck, my friends. I enjoyed your company over these past days and hope I didn't bore you with my tales."

"Not at all," Shadow replied, already feeling the icy bite of the wind. "And while it seems a poor idea at the moment, I know I'll need to talk with our winemakers – it seems they're not quite the masters of the art they claim to be. I wish I'd been clearheaded enough to get your recipe and method. It would—"

'I go now, even if you don't,' boomed the thunderous voice of the Ancient.

"Okay, okay," Shadow muttered.

With Stealth's help, the two men clambered up to their positions at the base of the dragon's neck, and before they were fully settled, giant wings unfurled, and the beast rose quickly into the air.

"We'll have some beautiful wine waiting for you," Shadow shouted through the blizzard thrown up by the beat of the dragon's wings. "Visit soon!"

Stealth's answer was lost, blown away in the wind.

As they picked up height and speed, Shadow looked back to see the lone figure walking back up towards the fading glow of the ice tunnel entrance. Soon, as Stealth extinguished each torch he passed, the ice tunnel faded into the darkness, lost amongst the myriad of the night's shrouded secrets. He shivered. What would drive someone to do this, to live and serve this beast abandoned here on the edge of humanity? The vision of two brothers murdered in the night appeared unbidden. *This? No, this alone wouldn't account for it.* There were things later, Stealth had said. But what things? And Sy? His reaction had been strange. Hadn't it? *What if...*

He forced a hold on his thoughts, dragging himself back from their dark embrace. *That wine messed up my head for the day, that's for sure. Don't get distracted by one man's tales – you've your own job to do and that is challenge enough.*

Despite the throbbing pain in his skull, he smiled. And the most important thing? *I'm good at what I do.* He adjusted his grip on Sy as they were rocked by turbulent air. *Sy and I, we are both good at what we do.* Capture and deliver the Staff to the Ancient – that had been their mission. *Accomplished.* Kill Warriors if they could. *One killed.* Okay, not by his hand, but certainly the Warrior had been weakened by his intervention. And, beyond this, he'd gleaned intelligence on the Ancient, her site, her servant – all good information for the Ensi and for the Ka. *Not bad. Not bad at all.*

That there was still much to do, he recognised. But that was for another day, and, he was sure, would have its own tales to tell. *For now, I'll take a breath and consider this a mission executed well.* He tucked his head more comfortably into the fur of Sy's tunic, settling himself for the long journey home. *And while I consider my wonderful work, I need to make sure I don't fall off this fell beast.* As quiet cackling emanated from the dragon, he gripped tightly onto Sy. *This might be a long, long flight home.*

This ends the First Part of
the Warriors of the Continuum Trilogy

GLOSSARY

The A'ven: an energy of the Land recognised by, and accessible to, very few.
The Continuum: a concept of the Iyes, a continuum of ages constantly in flux, yet all aligned, compatible, all changes adjusted unseen, no paradoxes allowed.
Cords: energy strands allowing those with the power and skill to transfer mind (and body if possible) to Glades, Gates, or particular places within the Land.
The Iyes daemons: allies of the Iyes Spirits, appearing in the form of venerated life of the age.
The Dark: a hidden threat, a presence deemed to be linked to the god of the Ka, Kaos.
The Enemy: Iyes name for their collective enemy of the Ka, Kaos, and agents of the Dark.
A Gate: a gateway between the Continuum and the Void.
The Horizon: the transition between the Land and the Spirit realm.
The Land: the Iyes tribe's known world, a world they strive to protect.
The Light: an unseen force/presence deemed to be linked to the god of the Iyes, IY.
Sacred Chamber: a warded place for the Iyes to connect with their Spirits
The Spirits: the Iyes's collective name for their ancestors and other sentient life who aid them as they can from beyond the Horizon.
The Story: the Iyes's ancestral story held by the tribe's Mother.
The Void: a memory of a place beyond a Gate.

BY ROGER P. HEATH

The Warriors of the Continuum Trilogy

ARRIVAL

Coming soon

DECEPTION
LIFE

www.ingramcontent.com/pod-product-compliance
Ingram Content Group UK Ltd.
Pitfield, Milton Keynes, MK11 3LW, UK
UKHW040952270425
457920UK00003B/163